APOLLONIA

A novel by
Christopher Leppek

swanhorse

APOLLONIA

A SwanHorse Press Book
Monte Ceceri Publishers, LLC

Copyright © 2016, 2023 by Christopher Leppek

Cover design: Roland Leppek
Book design: Lisa Leppek

First edition by Palaver 2016

For additional information, bulk or educational purchases, and other resources, please contact Monte Ceceri Publishers.

Publisher's Cataloguing-In-Publication Data:
Leppek, Christopher, 1954– author
Apollonia: A novel / Christopher Leppek
978-1-949512-08-3 (cloth)
978-1-949512-09-0 (paperback)
978-1-949512-10-6 (eBook)
1. United States—History—Civil War, 1861–1865—Fiction. 2. Fantasy fiction, American. 3. Love stories, American. 4. Time travel. 5. Ethics, Modern—19th century—Fiction. 6. Ethical problems—United States—Fiction. 7. Slavery—United States—History—Fiction. 8. Moral development—Fiction. 9. United States—Fiction. I. Title

MONTE CECERI PUBLISHERS
P.O. Box 60623
Savannah, GA 31420
www.montececeri.com

*This book is dedicated to
all those individuals, living and dead,
whose faces, stories, lives, and souls
became the essence of the characters
who dwell within these pages.*

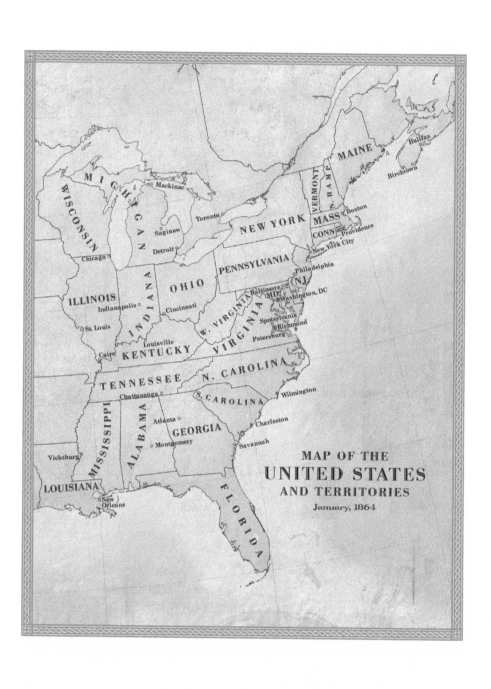

MAP OF THE
UNITED STATES
AND TERRITORIES
January, 1864

PRELUDE

I

Not a soul, to this day, knows precisely what it was that befell Jonathan Chase when he set out on what he believed to be, and what actually may have been, his homeward journey.

It was and would always remain impossible to say how it all happened, but as his sojourn lengthened and deepened far beyond what he ever would or could have imagined, the why was always the easiest question of all.

Apollonia was the why.

That fact was more than clear throughout the course of his journey, but it was not obvious from the beginning. It did not strike him, like a divine inspiration, when he first glimpsed her face—a glimpse that was, strangely enough, not of life but of its reflection. He felt a great deal at that moment—perhaps even the first disorienting pincers of love—yet he had no idea what would shortly ensue, no knowledge of the where or, immeasurably more important, the when. That knowledge would be made manifest in its own good time.

All of these things happened later, after the beginning, which unfolded, as beginnings often do, at a time of tumultuous change. He would eventually come to realize that what occurred on the stormy breast of a great and terrible mountain was his threshold, his twilight, his dawn, his crossroads—whichever numinous symbol best fit.

That day, when change and magic flew silently and unseen on an alpine wind, arm in arm with terror, an awful chasm loomed below, and he came under the uncertain shadow of his own equinox, fearful and marvelous at once. When he grew aware of it, he would wonder whether its essence was vernal or autumnal, whether it heralded life or betokened death.

In fact, it spoke of both.

There came in the life of Jonathan Chase, when he was still a relatively young man, a time of great upheaval. It was an era seemingly composed of loss and sorrow, but because he was a dreamer, and also because he was a realist (at least so he believed), he came through his ordeals intact.

It surprised him that what he felt, as the gun blue silhouette of the Rocky Mountains grew ever smaller in his rearview mirror, was not grief but freedom. The sensation was precious, since he had been imprisoned for a very long time and the bars of his prison had been many and strong. He had forgotten what free will felt like.

It seemed a selfish, even a cruel, thing to admit, but he could not avoid the steely truth of it. His separation from Rachel had unchained him, not so much from her as from himself. Somehow, the emotion of emancipation did not feel appropriate. It felt as if the sky at this moment, this point of his departure, should be brooding gray or troubled by towering thunderstorms, but it was neither. It was clear and calm, as was he.

In some remote and romantic corner of his soul, Jonathan vaguely wished that their parting had been more melodramatic, more poetically resonant, than it really was. He had concocted a little fantasy and, for a while, had played it over and again in his mind, reenvisioning their last day together in exquisite, painful detail. In it, the terminus had been death, instead of divorce, and he watched helplessly as the golden August sun illuminated Rachel's rich chestnut hair, sending a fiery glint through the solitary tear that ran down her delicate cheek. He imagined that she had wanted desperately to survive and had fought death fiercely to the end, all the while knowing that her defeat was preordained. How her courage had awed and humbled him, and she had forgiven him his trespasses—his erratic moods, his slow but inexorable withdrawal from the world—bidding him to try to love again one day.

In the stark, ungilded glare of reality, there was no such verse, only pragmatic prose.

Rachel still lived—back in Denver, already invisible in his rearview mirror—and, in all probability, was not terribly worried whether Jonathan ever loved again or not, so consumed with her own existential struggles and ponderings. Nor had he ever glimpsed an ardent tear on that fine, porcelain cheek, even though he sensed that somewhere deep inside her, in a place even she was no longer able to reach, she loved him still.

None of which was to say that their parting had nothing of the dramatic about it. It had, in addition to drama, plenty of suspense and danger, not to mention the bizarre. And death, or at least the threat of it, had most definitely played a starring role.

It began in August—that much was true—though the setting was not a deathbed but a mountaintop.

It was the middle of the month, and the forecasts were reassuring. While the heat blazed in Denver, the weather over the mountains was expected to be cool and storm-free. The summer was certain to have melted virtually all the snow from the summit of Longs Peak, and Jonathan and Rachel knew that any new snowfall—even at more than fourteen thousand feet—was likely to be two weeks away at least. It seemed the perfect time to make the trek.

In their five years together, the two had climbed any number of the towering mountains whose shadows fell upon the city they called home. Like the Rockies themselves, Jonathan and Rachel were strong and fit and loved the outdoors with an innocent passion. They were not, however, "outdoor enthusiasts," a term they used to mockingly refer to another class of climber entirely, those who boasted loudly of their exclusive courage and endurance and covered their ostentatiously athletic physiques in specialized clothing purchased in pricey stores. Jonathan and

Rachel compared such stereotypical elites to yuppies, another term they never used without a sneer.

On the other hand, they were, in their own words, "mountaineers." They wore jeans, T-shirts, and clunky but practical hiking boots and carried simple, straightforward packs. In their youthful confidence and arrogance, they took pride in considering themselves alpine troopers, disdaining the ropes, straps, and pitons of the technical climber in favor of the steady pace and hard patience of the long way to the top.

They could hike for hours on end and loved nothing more than spending their days in the piney air and supercharged sunlight of the high country. They savored the brisk nights when they eagerly allowed their bodies to intertwine in the soft warmth of a sleeping bag, breathing in each other's clean, hard-earned sweat.

That's what both of them had envisioned for the Longs Peak hike that fateful August day. They would begin, as Longs's summiteers always did, well before sunrise. They would slog the steep, occasionally perilous eight miles to the lofty summit, eat a quick snack as they fancied themselves on top of the globe, and descend back to tree line. There, tired and exhilarated with their achievement, flush with the elation that only such a journey can provide, they would make love beneath a canopy of crystal stars.

A year later, as Jonathan stared at the long ribbon of even highway before him, he wondered how things might have been had it turned out that way.

He shook the notion away, dismissing it as useless speculation. Rachel was gone from him, now and forever. She had disappeared from his sight, having fallen into whatever spiritual realm or void her physical experience on the mountain had forced upon her. It was unthinkable, unfair, unreal, and nonetheless as intractable and undeniable as a rock wall. Even if he would never truly be free of the pain it had caused him, he had finally accepted it.

In truth, he had accepted much more than that.

Even before the waves of loss and confusion had begun to recede, he had responded to Rachel's departure with a strangely deliberate process of erasure, a far more absolute method than closure. He visualized the transition even as it was under way. He pictured himself as a snake in shedding season or an old piece of furniture about to be refinished. The methodical stripping away of his external identity felt to him like a powerful solvent might feel to a chair, coated with layers of long-discolored paint. He felt a certain pain as these outer coatings were stripped away—they had, after all, been there for a very long time—but he had to admit that the procedure was also refreshing in ways he would never have imagined.

He had watched as a sequence of outer selves quickly dissolved—layers of himself vanishing like suddenly unwelcome ghosts, followed at last by their host and creator, the smiling straw man of deeply protected illusions Jonathan now knew he had once been. The man who had been familiar to the eyes and minds of his family, his colleagues, even poor Rachel, had been nothing more than a mirage.

Only very recently had he come to realize that the colors of his exterior had never really been painted with his own hand. That, in fact, had been the grand apex of all his many illusions. It had taken him precious years and a personal cataclysm to come to this knowledge of sheer simplicity. He felt like an utter fool that he had only now accepted these truths, but also like a man spared the gallows for having done so at all.

As to the people who had once surrounded his life, all of them—and all they had come to represent—were now pieces of ponderous baggage he'd just tossed from his back and left by the side of this endless and lonely road.

That life was over. That man was dead.

Dawn approached like an angel. The air was crisp and windless, the sky free of even a wisp of cloud. Jonathan and Rachel began their ascent nearly two hours before sunrise, and their progress was steady.

When the sun finally broke over the eastern horizon, they were approaching timberline. By nine o'clock they were traversing alpine tundra, tasting the thinning air in their lungs, marveling at the rainbows of wildflowers, which seemed to fill every available space between the rocks and boulders that lay scattered in increasing profusion.

Despite the steadily gaining rise, they kept their pace as they made their way through the mountain's geological phases, each of them fondly christened by climbers who had gone before—the chaotic tumble of the vast Boulder Field, the dizzying panorama visible from the Keyhole, the lung-straining ascent through the Trough beneath the towering and daunting Keyboard of the Winds.

There were few others on the mountain that day, and those who had opted to brave Longs were apparently of the endurance variety. They were well ahead of Jonathan and Rachel, despite the couple's own unbroken progress, and even before clearing the Keyhole they met a dozen hikers already making their descent from the summit.

The final phase was the toughest and most dangerous. From a lofty perch known as the Notch, they edged their way with careful sideways steps over a stretch appropriately named the Narrows. Their path had become nothing more than a ledge jutting across the imposing wall of the mountain. It was no more than two feet across at the widest spots, considerably smaller at the narrowest. Above them was several hundred feet of solid granite, the stony face of the summit itself. Below was a considerably greater distance of emptiness. Jonathan could only guess how many hundreds of feet yawned beneath them, poised on this thin sliver of stone. From where they stood, the details of the landscape at the bottom—high mountain lakes, stands of conifers, white ribbons that might have been roads or trails—looked like the terrestrial scenery from an airplane's window.

Jonathan never would have admitted it to Rachel, but their tenuous tread across the Narrows frightened him. He embraced the sheer wall of granite before his face and kept his eyes firmly fixed on its rough surface, fearing to look down into the chasm below, knowing that he would likely grow dizzy and begin to wonder how long a falling human body would take to reach solid ground and at what speed it might arrive.

Rachel, a few steps behind him, adopted a similar stance as she made her way on the ledge. She seemed strong and resolute. If she feared the path, Jonathan saw no sign of it.

Slowly and with great care, they inched their way across, probably in much less time than it felt like, and together breathed a sigh of relief and exhaustion when their feet finally found more substantial ground.

There was not much left. The final segment of the route was the Home Stretch, a sharply inclined surface of solid rock. It was a grinding climb, especially as the air painfully thinned, but not terribly dangerous, so long as they were careful with their steps and postures.

They reached the summit at one o'clock and immediately felt every sensation they had eagerly anticipated and for which they had worked so long. Utterly alone on the wide, flat plain, they stood on the rocky mountaintop and took in the vista surrounding them, every inch of it dramatically lower in altitude than where they now were. They smiled and embraced, silently congratulating each other.

It would always be a crystalline moment in Jonathan's mind. Even now, whenever he thought of Rachel, it was at this moment, with the surreal blue of the sky above them, the warmth of the high-altitude sun on their faces, the soft wind blowing and mingling their hair as they kissed.

They considered making love on the summit and talked about how marvelous and racy a secret that would be, just between them, but they quickly dismissed the thought with a laugh. How could they be sure no other climbers would arrive behind them?

Instead, they sat down sensibly and ate their snack, as originally planned. They stretched out beside each other on a reasonably smooth rock and closed their eyes to the warm sun and gentle zephyrs that coursed the summit.

Fatigued and content, they fell into a deep sleep in each other's arms.

They awoke, more than an hour later, to a different world.

Gone were the benign sun and gentle zephyrs. Instead, leaden clouds raced across the sky not far above their heads, along with a howling wind that Jonathan somehow knew would soon be roaring. The almost balmy air of an hour ago had grown chilly and was moving steadily toward cold. It smelled of wet rock and cold ozone. He felt little flecks of ice strike his face.

The invading storm intensified with the same malevolent speed at which it must have crept up on the mountain. As they stood up to put on their parkas, Jonathan felt the hair rise on the back of his neck. He roughly forced Rachel and then himself back down onto the rocks, just as a bolt of lightning struck a spot less than twenty yards from where they had been standing.

Now he saw fear in Rachel's face. That was what that pale, bewildered look could only be, he thought, realizing his own face must have looked much the same.

There was no need to talk. They knew they had to get off the summit and fast. If they could get down the Home Stretch, traverse the Narrows, and cross over to the other side at the Notch, Jonathan was fairly certain they could find relative shelter and safety until the storm subsided.

He also knew it would be a challenge to get there.

Holding their upper bodies low, painfully aware of how tempting a target they made for the next lightning strike, they dashed back toward the high end of the Home Stretch. Paying no mind to the cold wetness of the rock, they slid downward on their bottoms, using their feet before them as brakes. It was not easy going, since the ice flecks had quickly evolved into a drizzly sleet and the mountain's surface was rapidly growing slippery.

Before they reached the spot where they would have to enter the Narrows, the storm unleashed its full fury, announcing its arrival with deafening thunder that drowned out even the winds. Lightning snapped in electric blue spiderwebs over their heads, and the sleet fell so densely that they could see only a few yards in front of them.

How quickly the moods of the mountain change, Jonathan thought in a daze as they continued their awkward slide. An hour prior, they were sitting happily in the middle of a sunny postcard. Now they found themselves under nature's siege, pathetic little creatures in the vast hall of the mountain kingdom, the Gothic domain of the merciless storm king himself.

Only the Narrows remained.

The long shelf stretched before Jonathan as he took his first step on the slick rock. The worsening sleet obscured the far end of the ledge, but he knew it was only forty, maybe fifty, yards ahead of them. He remained confident that if they could make it that far, they would be fine. On the far side of the summit, they could huddle against the back wall, gaining at least a little shelter from the icy rain and making themselves a much harder target for the lightning. They would wait out the worst of the storm and finish the descent when conditions improved.

Jonathan insisted on going first. He edged out onto the ledge and made slow, sideways sliding motions with his feet. Like the ascent, he looked straight ahead and put his fingertips on the wet rock an inch or two in front of his face, more as a guide than a security grip—the stone was much too slippery for that. When he was three feet ahead of her, Rachel followed, imitating his motions as she made her own way.

He did not know how long it took to reach what he figured was the halfway point of the Narrows—afterward, his memory of the event was distorted and dreamlike—but it seemed like a long while. Their progress was necessarily slow; the considerable distractions of sleet, wind, and lightning discouraged any sort of speed.

He looked to his left, desperate to see how close they were to their destination. He was relieved when he spied the Notch through the icy haze, no more than twenty or thirty feet away. He decided at that moment that they were going to make it, turned his face back toward Rachel, and said the words "almost there," knowing it would encourage her.

Rachel never heard those words.

What happened next would forever dwell in Jonathan's memory more as a nightmare than an actual occurrence. The physical environment in which it occurred was itself surreal. The sky above them and to their backs was of a strange and sinister hue: blue steel, autumn twilight, the midnight of the soul. The depths below were invisible, filled with dense fog—steam hovering inside a witch's cauldron, concealing the contents within. Every molecule of air seemed in chaotic motion with the turbulent winds, and all of it was laced with crackling lightning that snaked and twisted with such frequency that one bolt seemed to entangle itself with another.

It was the lightning that brought it about.

The thunderbolt did not strike Rachel directly, nor did it even strike close enough to send a dangerous charge into her body. But it was near enough to startle and terrify her, and that was all the mountain needed to have its way.

The lightning struck home somewhere on the cliff's surface above them. They heard the electric snap of the strike and, almost at the same instant, a bellow of basso thunder so loud that they felt it in their bones.

She screamed, just once, and reacted with a start. It was a tiny motion, in reality, just a little jump backward, no more than two or three inches. But on that ledge, covered as it was with the icy rain, and before that solid rock wall, fatally smooth and impossibly slippery, it was enough.

Rachel's left foot came down on the lip of the Narrows, not firmly enough to find purchase. The toe of her hiking boot slipped off, and her body went down with it, her right foot catching the ledge only by the merest of margins. Her hands scrabbled at the cliff surface—Jonathan heard the horrible sound of her nails scratching fruitlessly at the unyielding granite—and then gravity took over. Her right foot could no longer hold its grip, and it too went over the side.

Jonathan remembered these details in agonizing slowness, but they happened in an instant, so very, very fast.

⁂

There was nothing more than Rachel's ten fingers keeping her from disappearing into the murky void beneath her. And these, already numb with cold and bleeding from their violent slide down the rock, almost immediately began to slip.

Jonathan could not run to her. He could only slide sideways, back the way he came, at a virtual snail's pace. If he were to try to move quicker, he would surely go over himself. So he edged his way to where she hung from the ledge, her ten slender, slipping fingers supporting, for the moment, her entire weight.

He never gave a thought as to how he would go about it—he just went through the motions and did it, drawing his inspiration, no doubt, from some mysterious, adrenaline-drenched closet of his primal subconscious.

Both of them remained perfectly silent as he began. Carefully, with agonizing slowness, he lowered himself onto the ledge, gradually moving his legs behind him so that he eventually positioned himself in a full prone position, stomach down, upon its icy surface. Squeezing himself as close to the cliff wall as he could, he brought his hands to where hers still managed to cling to the edge.

He didn't have to tell her that she would have no choice but to let go with one hand in order to grasp his or that this would be the most likely moment for the plan to go terribly wrong. Both of them knew it.

Later, Jonathan would envision that failure a thousand times. He imagined feeling her cold, wet hand slip through his, seeing that last terrified expression on her face, hearing that final scream, quickly swallowed up by the fog and wind and thunder.

This was not how it happened. Rachel did let go of the ledge with one hand, but it immediately found his and did not slip away. And then her other hand did the same.

But it was only the beginning of their struggle. At once, Jonathan felt Rachel's weight begin to pull him toward the edge, and he knew there was nothing for him to hold onto. There was only one way for this to work.

Jonathan had never been more than average when it came to physical strength, but for a precious few seconds he suddenly grew very strong. He resisted gravity's pull toward the abyss and then, groaning against the effort, began to fight it. Not only did he stop Rachel's slow descent away from him, he was actually reversing it. His prone position on the Narrows was tenuous at best, not at all conducive to the task of pulling a human body up from what was almost a ninety-degree angle, but he pulled nonetheless. He pulled against the odds, against his own limitations, against the deadly designs of the mountain, against the seeming will of God.

He felt the muscles and tendons in his arms and back strain, and then scream in pain with the effort, but still he pulled. Eventually, the task grew even harder, as Rachel's head, and then her chest, grew level with the ledge, until Jonathan's arms were raised above his own position and rapidly reaching their full extension.

And still he pulled.

She made her own move at the perfect moment. Looking directly into Jonathan's eyes, Rachel heaved one leg back onto the ledge and used it to scramble for purchase on the narrow surface. She made a sound like crying as she inched herself back up, with Jonathan still holding her hands. Finally, with one last groan of effort, her center of gravity shifted. Rachel brought her left leg up beside the other, and she—like Jonathan—lay fully prone on the stone shelf.

Even then, when the worst was over, they said nothing. Laying head to head, their bodies stretched out in full exposure to the weather, they gasped the desperate breaths, and already began to feel the exclusive pain, of survivors.

They stayed on the Narrows for nearly an hour, soaking wet, freezing cold, bruised, and bleeding—but both alive.

At that post-climactic moment, Jonathan might have said that, except for their cuts and scratches and rapidly beating hearts, they were completely fine. And he would have been wrong.

When the worst of the storm had passed, Jonathan instructed Rachel what to do next. She obeyed his directions without protest or argument, in fact without any verbal response at all. Their journey across the scant remainder of the ledge was neither graceful nor dignified, but in their physical condition and recently terrified state it suited them well. They remained in their prone positions, still head to head, as Jonathan slowly began to shove himself backward. Rachel followed, scooting herself forward. In less than two minutes, they reached the blessed end of the Narrows and found themselves sitting on the Notch, a precipitous perch to be sure, but infinitely safer than where they had just been.

They embraced, and Rachel wept, long and deeply, her sobs wracking her own body and shaking Jonathan's. They looked into each other's eyes, and Jonathan saw—although he did not yet understand—the shade of terror that lingered in hers.

"My God, Jon," Rachel managed to say through her weeping, her first words to him since they had set their feet upon the ledge that nearly killed them. "Oh, my God."

He tried to calm her, tried even to laugh at the sheer audacity of their escape, but Rachel did not return his feigned lightheartedness or respond to the expression of reassurance that Jonathan tried to put on his face. For a long time, she merely cried, the plume of her breath in the cold air marking her gasps like exclamation points.

Eventually, they began the descent. Their progress was slow, because the steep pathway remained wet and slick and they trembled in the cold. But they advanced regardless, breathing air that grew more substantial and steadily warmer as they went, feeling the treacherous sleet beneath their boots gradually become nothing more than damp earth.

It was late evening and nearly dark when they reached the trailhead, thoroughly sore and exhausted. Jonathan cleaned Rachel's wounds, and then his own, with the first-aid kit he had carelessly left in the trunk of their car. He helped her into the vehicle and began the long, dark drive back to Denver.

Rachel fell asleep almost immediately, and Jonathan drove in solitary silence. Their brush with death—their millimeter-close, face-to-face confrontation with it—already felt surreal to him.

Only the moans that Rachel began to make in the midst of her fitful slumber—pitiful sounds with an unmistakable thread of animal terror at their core—served to remind him how terribly real it had been.

Jonathan and Rachel survived the mountain—"defeated" it, he would say to himself more than once afterward, picturing the peak as some sort of conscious, anthropomorphic foe—but the mountain exacted its own terrible price.

The irony of their breaking apart was somehow the most striking feature of the whole episode to him, more lasting, more damning somehow, than the surprise, the shock, the sheer pain of its course, the numbing depression of its aftermath. It still amazed and puzzled him that Rachel could be so courageous, so strong and determined, yet so shattered by the trauma of the experience. It still astonished him that his reward for saving her life would be her rejection of him.

Somewhere deep inside, he knew even before they finished their ignominious crawl across the rest of the Narrows that she had been irrevocably changed by the experience. Something profound and intrinsic within her—her heart, her soul, maybe her DNA—had been permanently damaged in those eternal seconds during which she hung with cold and bleeding fingers from that ledge. The way she walked by his side down the remainder of that wicked and vengeful mountain—her silence, her unblinking stare at the rocks beneath her booted feet, her emptiness—provided him with a deadly accurate hint.

Rachel had stared death in the face, looked it directly in the eye. She had glimpsed the abyss, hung suspended in its maw, breathed in its stormy breath, and, at some point in the course of that awful process, become someone else.

She never stopped loving him. She told him that over and over again, even as she begged for him to leave their bed, and then their house, and finally her life. She would always love him, she said. And he believed her.

None of that was the point, of course.

Jonathan still wasn't entirely sure what the point was. Nor could Rachel ever fully articulate it. It was too deep, too personal, to put into such banal expression as words. Nor, he realized now, could she ever have explained something it might take her a lifetime to understand herself.

But he saw in her eyes—those mystical, playful, knowing eyes that were the first reason he fell in love with her—that she was telling him the truth. She was no longer the woman who had fallen in love with him, married him, made love to him on so many sweet and intimate nights. That woman had become an echo, a page in a dusty scrapbook. She was no longer the same; therefore, they could no longer be the same.

The pleading, the arguments, the weeping had lasted for weeks. When Jonathan finally surrendered to the iron will of her resistance, he did so more out of exhaustion than any sense of understanding or empathy. He could slam his head against a brick wall only so many times.

They parted for the last time on the shaded porch of the now empty structure they had once called home. They expressed their love for one another with the same innocent passion they had always felt. They cried, and laughed a little, and held each other's hands.

And then he walked away.

In some ways, he thought, it was a cinematic farewell scene, but there was no carefree exit from the theater, no "reality" to return to. The movie of Jonathan's life came to an abrupt end at that moment, its celluloid tail flapping wildly in the glaring white light, disconnected and erratic.

It was then that his self-reinvention began in earnest. He became a solitary leaf, newly fallen from its tree, cast by the wind into the current of a swiftly moving stream.

II

Virtually everything that comprised the material fortune of Jonathan Chase—in lighter moments, he liked to think of it as his "estate"—accompanied him in the ancient car he was piloting over the tawny grasslands of the high plains.

In the spacious trunk of the 1949 Chevrolet Fleetliner were a suitcase of clothes, a battered but still tuneful Guild guitar, and two modest boxes of miscellaneous possessions. In the front seat with him, illuminated by the brilliance of the morning sun, were a Texaco road map and a handful of necessary day-to-day objects. These, a slim roll of twenty-dollar bills, and the Chevy itself now constituted his entire wealth. If he were to die today, they would be the only physical legacy Jonathan would leave behind.

Everything else to which he might once have laid claim—an oversized and thirsty SUV; a professionally landscaped, spacious, and expensive home in one of the Denver's more prestigious suburbs, along with the considerable material bounty within it; a handsome accumulation of 401(k), money market, and savings funds, stock certificates, and insurance policies that, taken collectively, were worth far more than any figure Jonathan would once ever have imagined owning—he had freely given to Rachel. To her vaguely dazed amazement, Jonathan hadn't put up a fight for any of it, nor had he uttered a single cross word during the entire legal transfer.

Nor, for that matter, in the nine months since his self-willed impoverishment, had Jonathan felt even a single twinge of regret.

In fact, the lightness he felt in his newfound poverty—and in his recent release from a life he now regarded as an imprisonment—was almost intoxicating. His outer paints had all been stripped away, and what was left was the original and natural wood, a surface Jonathan had not known since his childhood. He liked the feel of the cool air upon its naked surface, and he remembered how fond he had once been of his own grain.

Through what was left of Colorado and nearly all of Nebraska, Jonathan marveled at how little pain he was feeling and wondered at the state of clear serenity in which he found himself. His senses were keyed to expectation and impendence. The feeling of vulnerable openness fostered by his situation exposed him to infinite possibilities. Something was waiting to happen, specifically to him, yet he knew absolutely nothing about the nature of that something.

The mystery and anticipation thrilled him and brought his senses and emotions into acute sharpness. It was somehow akin to falling in love, although he still had no idea of the source of these feelings.

Denver, his starting place, was becoming a distant memory, its lights having already faded into the chilly, rose sunset. Open prairies surrounded him, harvested fields stretching toward far horizons, roads guarded by infinite phalanxes of telephone poles. His being harmonized with the timeworn icons of this land—the skeletal windmills, their wheels spinning lazily in the twilight breeze; the dry, forgotten ruins of old prairie houses and barns; the omnipresent grain elevators and water towers, looming beacons to distant towns.

As he traveled eastward and evening stole the skies, he watched the flat ground gradually give way to gentle hills, and in their sere beauty he sensed a tender and timeless music. It was played with a long descending chord on a wailing steel guitar, rising and falling and curving with the terrain itself, supported by a soothing highway rhythm. It was hauntingly beautiful, mysteriously old, and essentially American, just like the land it was hailing and the season that was falling.

To Jonathan, it was a signal from the future, even as it was an echo of the past. He didn't understand this strange music but somehow knew that only he could hear it.

The dauntless Chevy pressed on through the night, dependably if not very quickly. The greater part of the Great Plains had surrendered to Jonathan's restless sojourn by dawn.

Iowa stretched before him now, an endless undulation of land slowly revealing itself in the half-light. From his position on the road, his car making its way over the contours and bends of the countryside, his progress felt almost sensual. Here, the scenery was more verdant, although it too was steadily giving ground to autumn, and it rolled constantly. He imagined one of Grant Wood's paintings, with land such as this, rising and falling and swelling with a woman's soft curves. He allowed himself the pleasure of knowing the yield of her flesh beneath his caress. He felt himself melting into her warmth, evanescing into her sweet landscape.

In his own way, he supposed, he was doing what men do when they make love: returning to the womb from which he himself came. He was completing a profound and natural circle. He was going home.

The word "retreat" did not occur to Jonathan. Discarding the raiment of his old life did not seem like surrender. He had not lost the battle; he had won it and was now returning home a victor, he told himself. The arduousness of his long conflict had taken a toll, that much was true, but in leaving behind his life with Rachel—in separating himself from the people with whom he had once been close—there was also release.

There were, of course, prices to be paid for this liberation, troubling implications to his present homeward journey. It meant facing time, for one thing. His hometown would not be the same place it was long years ago, and Jonathan most certainly was not the same person. The children with whom he had once played were adults now, settled and established, with houses and cars and jobs and worries. Some had surely achieved success and fulfillment; others, no doubt, were ruined; still others already dead. He, on the other hand, was returning to their midst as poor and free and unencumbered as the child who had left on a cool dawn in what seemed like, and was, another era.

Somewhere deep inside, this disturbed him, but he successfully dismissed the doubt as lingering echoes of his former existence. He was beyond all that now and would allow nothing to obscure the intoxicating pleasure of his freedom, his still unfocused love.

The sun surfaced from beneath the horizon almost timidly and then grew into a blazing golden-scarlet disk. It lifted itself from the earth entirely and, finding partial cover behind an isolated cloud, sent towering rays of yellow-gold beaming across the sky.

Jonathan saw the sunrise a welcoming beacon and a good omen on this, the second day of his eastward journey. The rising sun was pulling him in the direction he wanted to go, and like other aspects of his existence, he was acutely aware of that direction, knowing that in American terms to go back has always meant to go eastward. Americans invariably go "out" West and "back" East, as if the drift of the nation's seminal exodus were forever imprinted on its collective memory.

To the East, then, in return. Back to the womb. Back into himself.

He left the interstate in Council Bluffs and coursed through southern Iowa on an assortment of county and state roads, selected at random save for their general eastward tack. It quickly became clear that whatever pagan gods might rule the harvest—some ancient Earth Mother or corn king, Jonathan mused—were now in full ascendancy in this agrarian land.

Some of the farmers had arranged harvest displays near their houses, strange little tableaus of autumnal icons—pumpkins and squash, pointy-hatted witches, smiling scarecrows. These things seemed marvelously sinister to Jonathan, with their gourd heads and stick arms enveloped in tattered, wind-tossed cloth.

By afternoon, he found himself in Amish country, where corn was still put up in neat rows of shocks and leaves were still burned near roadsides, sending sharp essences into the air. The Amish farmers were a living reflection of olden times. He saw one of them following a large horse patiently pulling a plow through the stubble of a modest cornfield, another throwing hay into a wagon with a pitchfork.

These people did not strike him as quaint and nostalgic oddities, as they must appear to the many summertime tourists who come to gape at them. Instead, Jonathan saw them as genuine, strangely immune to the pervasive and artificial trappings of modernization. The harmony of their straightforward simplicity fascinated him.

As the road swept past their farms into the coral dusk, Jonathan rolled up the Chevy's windows. The air was brisk, nearly cold, with the earthy tang of autumn on the breeze.

It was already well into September. The cornstalks that were still standing had taken on the brittle amber tint of the season; the trees were putting on their paint box shades. Jonathan contemplated their other cycles as well. He imagined their youth, their blushing green promise in spring, their rich scent on balmy summer nights.

Now, he heard their impatient rustling and paid heed to the whispered wish of the autumn: to return to the dark earth from which they sprang. To go home.

Nightfall found Jonathan in a weathered red brick town on the big river. He nourished himself on Coca-Cola and oranges from a grocery as worn and old as the town itself. He rented a room on the upper floor of a downtown hotel that hadn't been fashionable since long before his birth. It was still and seedy, with transoms, steam radiators, and bathrooms down the hall. Its dowdy crookedness appealed to his sense of the aesthetic—his appreciation for the faded glories of the past.

Before retiring, he walked for blocks, seeking to expel the relentless rhythms of the road from his tired body. He attracted some notice from passersby apparently unaccustomed to seeing strangers in their midst—just as the incongruous Colorado plates on his chrome-and-black anachronism of a car invited stares—but his actual appearance was not extraordinary. He stood just shy of tall, moderately muscular, although his frame looked somewhat leaner than it should, and his pale, angular face bore a countenance that a poetically-minded observer might have called grave. In his worn jeans, tucked-in dark T-shirt, oversized pea jacket, and dark hair worn well over the current fashion for length, he projected a mildly tatterdemalion appearance. Vaguely, he had the look of that which he was—a wanderer, a man with nothing to lose, a lost soul.

As midnight approached, the storm clouds that had been trailing Jonathan for most of the day finally caught up. They were potent and violent. He reached the tiled floor of the hotel lobby just as the torrents came, and he spent the next hour watching the rain and lightning through the lurid glow of the old neon perched outside his window. Eventually, he slept.

Much later, he awoke in his unfamiliar bed in this unknown room, in the knowledge that he was no longer alone.

Jonathan did not know for certain whether that which followed was merely a vivid dream, a ghostly visitation, or a remarkably sensory instance of somnambulism. What he did know was that it felt as real as any experience he had ever lived.

He looked all about him in the momentary fear and confusion of sudden awakening, yet all was obscure. He held his breath so as to listen, yet all was still.

The window was open, its sheer curtains waving gently into the room, casting dancing shadows on the floor. Cool air, spiced with rain and fallen leaves, chilled his bare chest.

After he convinced himself that the sensation of presence had been false, he lay back against his pillow with a weary sigh but found sleep difficult to regain.

The feeling of being watched, or merely seen, of being with somebody or something with a purpose directed at him, refused to leave.

He saw her just as he was drifting back into the embrace of slumber.

It was only a silhouette, really, only a shadow in relief against deeper shadows in a corner of the room, but there could be no mistake that what he saw was the figure of a woman. She appeared young and slender, with full hair falling to her shoulders. She may have been wearing a long dress, narrow at the waist and wider at her feet. He thought he could distinguish a lighter shade where her face must have been, but no features were discernible in the gloom.

He rose from the pillow, drawing nearer to the figure, and detected her scent— lemon verbena, he thought, and the fragrance of soft hair recently dampened by the rain.

"Who are you?" he asked, startled by the surprisingly loud tenor of his own voice. "What do you want?"

She shook her head and withdrew, holding out a hand as if to defend herself from him.

"Who are you?" he repeated, beginning to rise from the bed.

"No!" she warned, her voice a desperate, windy whisper. "No!"

He started for her, the bedclothes falling from his body as he reached out to the shadowy corner. As he drew near, he felt her frightened breath in one sudden gasp. But his hands clasped nothing, and with the surprise of that discovery, he realized in an instant that her visual presence also was gone.

He stood there in the dark, feeling the night dance across the length of his exposed body. He shook his head, realizing as he did so how foolish he must have looked. But he was alone. There was nobody to witness his folly.

An hour later, after water and cigarettes and much restive pacing, Jonathan's slumber finally returned. When it did, he fell into a dream and once more glimpsed his elusive caller, in the same uncertain form in which he had glimpsed her before, and in this vision he knew who she was. But by morning, his mind had efficiently filed away the entire episode as an ordinary dream, leaving behind only the barest tatter of memory.

With gypsy restlessness, Jonathan left the river town and its crooked hotel early in the morning. The rain had stopped sometime during the night but pulled in its wake a sudden change. Jonathan felt it on the bridge over the river—the smell of cooling earth, the scent of summer dying. After a brief flirtation with crisp and golden days, the dark edge of autumn arrived, announcing itself with a leaden overcast that loomed beyond the horizon.

The clouds cast the little towns along the road into an almost nocturnal gloom. The windows of houses and stores glowed saffron, and people walked briskly through the mist, clutching long-unused coats tightly about their bodies.

The countryside was dim and dusky. Except for occasional glimpses of brilliantly orange pumpkins that alone seemed defiant to the shadow, the environment appeared to have lost all color.

"Eleanor Rigby" drifted through the Chevy's radio, its forlorn voices and strings seeming to rise from the landscape itself. It was a song Jonathan remembered from his childhood, and it sent him into the same feeling of pensive reflection it used to inspire.

Yesterday's exhilaration was gone. He knew this and accepted it, as yet another price to be paid for his newfound freedom, but he felt his solitude—the knowledge that he had joined "all the lonely people"—like the keen blade of prolonged hunger. Rachel's wake had been considerable, and Jonathan was far from adjusted to her absence. He was beginning to think that the only way for him to move on might be to allow her memory to grow faint. Part of him was reluctant to do this, dreading the idea that she would eventually become more illusory than real.

Yet he also sensed he could no longer afford to cling to his own past. If he allowed himself to think too much about her, he still longed for Rachel so badly that the pain became crippling.

Better to keep his eyes on the road ahead, he thought.

But almost as soon as he conceived the tough gunslinger's phrase, he questioned it. Was his direction really ahead, or was he just deceiving himself? Was he trying to escape and, if so, from what?

Certainly, there was Rachel's decision, in all its shocking, heartbreaking, humiliating certainty. He held no illusions about his desire, indeed his need, to escape from that. But what about everything else? Had it been necessary to throw everything else away?

I don't know, his rational voice replied.

But then came another voice, one from somewhere deeper inside him, one he had only barely heard before and the existence of which he was only dimly aware.

This voice said: *Yes!*

There was no denying that Jonathan had been very thorough, very methodical and deliberate, in the sudden absoluteness of his severance from the man he had once been—the man of whom the scarecrows with their vapid smiles now reminded him. He had shocked everyone, himself included, with that process.

In topsy-turvy fashion, his inner voices continued their debate, sometimes agreeing with one another, more often not. Resolution was replaced with doubt and vice versa.

He had fought the separation from Rachel fiercely. He had gone through disbelief, sensitive discussion, heated argument, and finally pleading, all of it in vain. She had remained resolute and unbending, and in the end, Jonathan had given up.

No, not given up, that buried voice murmured. *Accepted the reality of it. Saw the precious opportunity in it.*

He realized now that somewhere in the midst of their raw separation, a line had been crossed and that, once it was, everything was suddenly different. It was then his severance had begun, and once started, it would not be stopped.

She had expected him to at least negotiate over their material possessions, not merely forfeit virtually everything. Surprised and apparently disturbed, she had asked him why and only looked more troubled when his only answer was an enigmatic smile as he signed the necessary papers.

Nor had his father and employer—for they were the same man—seen it coming. Jonathan had, by virtue of the rights of corporate nepotism, a comfortable and secure corner office in the family firm, an established Denver company that dealt in parts, at one time for radios, then televisions, and now computers. He had done his job as inventory manager—essentially a keeper of lists and a tracker of codes and numbers—competently and, to all appearances, happily for years. His father and older brothers, who also worked there, were proud of him and regularly bragged about the quality of his work to their clients.

Naturally, then, when he announced his decision to resign his position, each of them in their turn asked him why. In reply, he gave his blood relatives nothing more than the same enigmatic smile he'd offered his ex-wife.

Jonathan suspected that his refusal to answer these quite logical questions stemmed from a simple fact: He did not know the answer himself.

For the last few months, his life had felt like a long row of carefully positioned dominoes. When the first one—Rachel's departure—fell, it struck the next, which struck the next, until the entire elaborate row had collapsed. Her leaving had toppled the first tile holding the pattern together.

That was no explanation, he knew. It was merely an attempt to describe a sequence of events that by themselves made no obvious sense. He believed that he had loved Rachel—he believed he loved her still. He had liked, if not loved, his professional career and cared deeply for his family. He had felt comfortable and at home in Denver.

So how could all of that suddenly become so meaningless, so easy to leave behind?

That quiet, persistent voice deep inside answered his own question.

Because it was all false, it said. *Because it was the wrong path. These were not the things you were supposed to be doing. Those people and those places were not your destiny.*

His logical mind engaged the debate. *Then what is my destiny?*

It lies before you, the voice said. *At the end of this road.*

Through the length of that ashen day and the duration of its night, Jonathan followed a meandering course over narrow back roads of Illinois and Indiana. He passed through towns and cities with hardly a glance away from the road, longing to return to the open country where he could sense the growing age of the trees and breathe the lonely autumn on the air.

Old roadside signs marked the way at junctions and where the road approached towns. In their archaic script and long-faded paint, they urged travelers to purchase Coca-Cola, Lucky Strikes, Pepsi-Cola, Kendall Oil, Burma Shave, and Grapette. Jonathan wondered whether Grapette even existed anymore, whether this sign had reached the acme of obsolescence—to proclaim something that itself had passed into extinction. He felt an undeniable sense of kinship with the rusty old signs. He appreciated how they had been forgotten, like he felt forgotten, and how they were now nothing more than relics, shabby reminders of other times and other lives, just as he was himself a walking vestige of another life—a scarecrow left behind in a field harvested long ago.

At some point during the night, Jonathan's car negotiated a northward turn and crossed the line into Michigan. His journey was nearly complete, and he knew that once he arrived there would be much work to do, an entirely new life to build from scratch. In spite of the turmoil and uncertainty of his recent life, he still recognized the existence, and felt the necessity, of a future.

The foundation of that future had been seen to, with characteristic efficiency and formidable will, by Tess, his cousin, one of the few people he remembered from his early childhood. They were close in age, children of parents who were fond of each other. They had spent countless hours in one another's company and, in the innocent way of children, had convinced themselves and each other that they were bound together for life.

That was not destined to happen. Unlike Jonathan's family, Tess's had stayed in Michigan. She herself had remained in Saginaw after coming of age and had, to all appearances, thrived there. She was now the mother of two healthy and intelligent children, and the wife of a man who had apparently found the process of accumulating money to be an easy challenge. Jonathan had never met Dave but liked him well enough on the telephone. He felt obliged to like him, in any case. How could he not like a man who, sight unseen, had offered Jonathan a chance to rebuild his life?

The opportunity would not restore Jonathan to his former level of material fortune—it would, in fact, provide for little more than his basic sustenance, at least at first—but this did not bother him. It would require hard physical work, for which he longed, and offer long hours of quiet and solitude, for which he was desperate. He looked forward to working for Dave, in fact, and felt confident that he would prove successful at what his cousin's husband liked to call "my little West Side venture."

That would be tomorrow's task. Tonight, the woods and roads of Michigan greeted Jonathan like a mother's arms. He felt a primal comfort just being back on the great peninsula, feeling its pervasive moisture on his skin, for here the haze of the surrounding Great Lakes was part of the air itself. The scent of that air was unique and intimately familiar. He breathed it in like incense, sensing its subtle changes as he headed northeast—the gradual addition of pine and spruce to the tang of harvest apples and dry corn. He could not resist the sweetness of the night.

Dawn was breaking over the eastern horizon as the slipstream profile of the Chevrolet rounded the last bend into Saginaw. Jonathan's arrival in this tired but still graceful old city—the place of his birth—was anticlimactic. There was no great promontory from which to view it, for the valley here was perfectly and relentlessly flat. One entered Saginaw neither by descent nor ascent, but almost by a gradual horizontal osmosis.

The city was still asleep, with no one but milkmen making their rounds. The deep indigo of the dawn twilight was clear, illuminated by a huge crescent moon that hung like an ornament just above the tops of the trees. Behind and above it glowed a bright morning star, perhaps Venus.

The juxtaposition of the two forms reminded Jonathan of Islam and caused him to fancy himself as a weary pilgrim who has finally reached his Mecca.

III

So much had changed.

Most of what Jonathan saw at the edge of the city was entirely new and remarkably similar to other places. He might just as well have been driving into Peoria or Terre Haute or Muncie—all of which he had recently passed through—or any other Midwestern city of similar size and age. He cursed the era's voracious appetite for uniformity.

Still, somewhere beneath it all, he sensed that a unique essence, some vague but quintessential subterranean stream of the city of his youth, still existed. He felt it amid a cool, clear dawn, traversing empty streets whose names he recognized but whose destinations he had forgotten.

On the outskirts were fast-food stands, commercial strips, and sleek office buildings where he vaguely recalled crops or livestock once occupying the land. But as he traveled closer, toward the heart of the city, into areas he actually remembered, he felt strong sensations of familiarity.

These deepened when he turned into a suburban expanse that had been so new when he was a boy that lawns had yet to be planted. The nearby woods where he had once played countless games of war and adventure were nowhere to be seen, but he spied at once the two-story dwelling where Larky—the first girl he had ever kissed—once lived. They were only five years old, but memories of the afternoons Jonathan spent with her still jolted him like a pleasant electrical shock.

He turned again, this time onto a road that had lost virtually all of the rural quality he remembered—the place of his nativity.

He identified the exact spot where his first home had stood. It had been a plain frame dwelling of Civil War vintage, a onetime farmhouse with a long porch and simple triangular gables. His mother had always detested the place, saying it was cold and drafty and filled with mice, but for Jonathan it was the setting of mystery and limitless wonder. Its scale, so cramped as described by his mother, seemed vast to Jonathan with its overgrown foliage and ancient fences. Its utilitarian plainness struck his young eye as grand and imposing.

He sighed as he allowed the mental picture to fade. He already knew that the house had been gone for at least twenty years. In its place stood a bland church, a plastic sign near the road announcing the Sunday service schedule.

Less than two hundred yards away, however, there still stood a cozy, white bungalow, graced with a long, gently inclining lawn, where his grandparents had once lived. He had spent countless days and nights exploring the house's nooks and crannies or braving the dense woods that embraced the backyard. He wondered if there were still fabulous sand dunes out beyond those woods—once the scene of supercharged hunts for relics of old battles between the Chippewa and

U.S. Cavalry, battles that never happened in reality but which Jonathan still recalled from his elaborate fantasies. He looked toward the back of the house and saw that the edge of the property was met, just beyond the familiar profile of a crooked old cedar, by the lawn of a much newer and more affluent dwelling. He doubted whether any dunes remained.

Half a mile down the road, he came to a little building he knew as Lawndale Market, where, on muggy summer days, he had purchased bottles of tart lemon-lime or spicy ginger ale.

He stopped in front of the old store—remarkably still in business under the same name—and took in the long, even stretch of the road. He saw a line of comfortable, upscale suburban houses, warming beneath the just-risen sun. It looked neater, less rustic, more settled than what he remembered.

He recalled with uncanny clarity the old road as it once appeared from this very spot. In his mind's eye, he saw an abandoned farm where, on August nights, the most succulent pears could be taken by anyone willing to brave barbed wire and whatever spirits might haunt forsaken orchards. He saw lilac bushes crowding the lane, so huge they seemed like trees, and inhaled their ambrosial scent on April mornings. He remembered riding on the tail of old Betsy, his big brother at the handlebars of the ungainly yet swift balloon-tire bicycle, and how deep and dark the ditchwater once seemed to him.

Traces of those days remained. Some of the trees were obviously very old, the ditches still ran, although not so dark and deep, and here and there a towering roadside bush might have been a lilac. Yet all of the spaces between these landmarks had been filled with things that had played no part in Jonathan's past. He felt challenged by their presence, their intrusive insistence on marring a picturesque scene that had been engraved, in color and fine detail, into his mind.

He grew troubled, haunted by images and faces he did not want to glimpse. He thought of his grandparents who had long lain in their graves, of distant family members and Larky and other childhood friends. He questioned what madness had driven him to abandon everything that mattered in Denver. He pictured the look in Rachel's eyes on their last day together. He wondered whether she was happy, whether she was beginning to understand whatever it was she had glimpsed on the mountain. He wondered whether she was missing him. In spite of himself, he began to think of star-crossed lovers, of loves destined to die, of loves that could never be.

At last, his emotions, drawn from some mysterious sorrowful well, crept up without warning. He tried to be strong and fought to suppress the sobs crawling from his middle into his throat. He manfully kept them at bay, but the tears had their way despite him. As if in defiance, first one, and then another, and finally a steady stream coursed down his cheek onto his chin.

Outwardly, it seemed a quiet and gentle storm, but internally Jonathan felt every atom of its intensity. It shook him to the core, and when it had run its course, he felt light and calm, refreshed as if he had just taken a long drink after a prolonged thirst.

Noon found Jonathan, after a comfortable nap in the car, sipping coffee with his cousin, Tess, and her husband, Dave, in their tasteful living room of a sprawling ranch home in one of the more esteemed, if not quite exclusive, new neighborhoods. Tess was still as lovely as he remembered her, although middle age was leaving subtle lines of worry and stress on her well-defined face. Dave, on first impression, was slim and athletic-looking, dressed in a comfortable cardigan and slacks. He had the articulate enthusiasm—coupled with a skill for persuasion that was as effective as it was undetectable—of the experienced and successful salesman he was.

"It used to be a neighborhood market, Jon," he said in a familiar tone. "The kind they had in the older parts of town, before the 7-Elevens and Circle Ks and God knows what else came in and dominated the small grocery business. It's been empty for a good fifteen years, but it's not in terrible shape—most of the renovations are already done—and the house is right next door, so you won't have to worry about commuting."

Dave leaned closer, warming to his subject. "It's a nice old West Side neighborhood," he said quietly, as if revealing an important secret. "I'm sure it's going to be a really hot area pretty soon. And I'm not talking about yuppies but hip people, you know, bohemians, artists, musicians. Saginaw is just dying for that kind of scene, and this is the perfect place for it. They're going to want dark bars, coffee shops with musicians at night, art galleries, and"—he paused for effect—"used bookstores."

He handed Jonathan a folded computer printout. "Here's the inventory. Five thousand titles, all hardback, all in good condition or better. I got everything at a couple of auctions. You wouldn't believe the price, but this is all good stuff, Jon. I know it's going to sell."

Jonathan glanced at the titles: a mix of classics, popular current editions, some of the better-known biographies, and an impressive selection of history, mainly local and regional. There were several sets of authors' collected works. Here and there was an eccentric item, an obscure mystery, or a cult horror novel. He didn't yet know a great deal about books, but it seemed like a reasonable inventory for the used bookstore he would soon be managing.

"I'll leave the pricing and acquisitions totally up to you," Dave continued, apparently delivering a well-prepared presentation. "There's a computer in the house that's already online, so you can keep up to date on the trade via the Net. Plus, I'd be glad to give you some tips on appraising and purchasing, even though, as you know, books aren't exactly my line. For example, there's—"

Tess interrupted him. "Why don't we save that for later, Dave?" she said as diplomatically as possible.

"Jon," she said, turning to her cousin, "the house is already furnished, except for a few odds and ends. All you'll need are some groceries to start with. It's very comfortable. You could stay there tonight, if you want to."

She paused and smiled. "We really want you to do this, Jon," she said. "It will mean a lot to us if you're running the store. You're family, you know."

Jonathan looked at Tess and Dave, moved by their generosity and trust and affected by Tess's kind words, the first that had been addressed directly to him in many months. He felt their warming effect, but he also sensed an edge in her voice. He could tell that Tess had already anticipated what he would be thinking, and it was making her uncomfortable—that he might take their confidence as an act of charity, and a particularly brave one at that, considering his recent behavior had been erratic at best.

He cleared his throat and put his coffee cup on the table. "I'm honored," he said quietly, "and I'm touched. You don't how much it means to me that you've made me this offer. That you have faith in me."

He smiled at his hosts. "Look, it's pretty obvious that I'm down right now. Things have been rough, I can't deny it, and I probably haven't handled it all with perfect maturity or . . ."

Tess started to speak, but Jonathan hushed her with his hand.

"What I'm trying to say is that you needn't worry. I'm at a crossroads, a pretty big one, but I want you to know I'm as sharp as I ever was, maybe even sharper. I'll do a good job for you at the store. I'll work hard, and I'll really try to make it successful. And I think it will be."

His words seemed to lift some of the tension that Jonathan had correctly sensed. Tess and Dave were obviously relieved that the uncomfortable subject had been broached, which gave Dave additional time to discuss his favorite subject: business.

"Okay, Jon," he said. "Here's the setup. You run the shop for forty hours a week, maintain it, handle its accounts and inventory, both online and actual. For that, you'll get eight hundred dollars a month. That doesn't seem like much, but the house will be yours, rent free with utilities paid, so I think it all rounds out to a fair sum. When the business starts turning a profit, you'll pick up twenty-five percent of the till. How's that sound to you?"

Jonathan smiled at Dave's rapidity and directness. No wonder the guy was hauling it in.

"It's fine, Dave. In fact, it's great. What's next?"

"The wood and braces for the shelves are in the shop. They need to be installed and finished. The floor needs refinishing, and we'll have to replace the overhead fluorescents with something softer, more bookish—maybe indirect lighting and lamps. After that, it's only a matter of stocking the shelves. Everything is in the cellar, marked and sorted in cartons."

"I'll get to work tomorrow," Jonathan replied, rising to leave.

Dave handed Jonathan the keys, saying he would help with some of the heavy work, and assured him that there was no need for them to sign any papers. "If family can't do business on a handshake, who can?"

In precisely that spirit, Jonathan offered his hand for a firm acceptance of the deal. Tess gave him a soft hug. It seemed an auspicious beginning.

Jonathan found the store and house after only one or two wrong turns. It amazed him how some hidden internal compass, apparently relying upon a long-dormant memory file, seemed to activate, guiding him to his destination.

His objective was in one of the oldest parts of town, the West Side, only seven blocks from the Saginaw River, the city's great geographical, class, and racial dividing line. It was a dense and leafy vicinity with dwellings of Victorian and Edwardian vintage, ranging from ostentatious manses to modest family homes.

The bookstore was the last in a string of other storefronts occupying almost half a block. Among them were a coffee and tea shop, a small art gallery, and "Samantha's Tarot Grove," which proudly displayed a large Egyptian ankh in its window.

Like its neighbors, the bookstore was a plain, one-story brick rectangle. It bore midsized display windows in the fashion of its original function—a turn-of-the-century neighborhood market. Across the top ran a battered tin sign that boasted in Spencerian script that this had once been the "Throop Street Market." Jonathan had learned from Dave that "Throop," in the long-established vernacular of the city, was always pronounced "Troop."

The entrance was covered by an old screen door that had once been gilded in the bright colors of the Rainbo Bread emblem and the words "Is Good Bread!" painted across the mesh. Jonathan thought it a nice touch and decided to ask Dave to keep it for the bookstore.

Immediately adjacent, and connected to the store by a narrow passageway, was the house that was, as of today, Jonathan's new home. It was a painfully thin dwelling, but quite tall—three stories high, having apparently been built in its tortured shape for reasons of an equally narrow lot. It was bordered by a spiked wrought iron gate and short fence and fronted by an ornate porch. An eccentric, eclectic place, it was clear that its designer had been very fond of Victorian trimmings. The odd *engrelure* of its spinsterly form boasted scalloped shingles, arched windows, geometric brick patterns, a flamboyant bay window, and tiny peaked dormers with leaded panes.

Jonathan loved the house immediately, feeling a welcoming presence in its baroque peculiarity and savoring the strong sense of the past that it exuded, like musty perfume, onto shady Throop Street. He opened the gate—it creaked agreeably—and ascended the four stairs to the small porch. The address had been painted in fancy gold numerals on the transom above the heavy front door. It opened easily to Jonathan's key, and the scent of old wallpaper and wood sighed from the interior.

Tess had done a marvelous job furnishing and decorating the house. She had made sure that every room had at least one framed print on the wall—quaint old landscapes, hunting scenes, and pleasant rural vistas. The furniture was of many styles and kinds, but most of it in reasonable shape. The age of the pieces roughly matched that of the house itself, which Dave had mentioned was 1875.

Basic supplies and equipages had been carefully seen to. Everything electrical, mechanical, or digital seemed to work fine. After a quick survey of the shadowy kitchen and pantry, the lofty old parlor that would serve as his living room, the heavy balustrade on the narrow staircase, his second-floor bedroom with its ornate fireplace, and the unused third story, Jonathan brought in his meager luggage. He placed his guitar next to the Queen Anne chair in the parlor and sat down.

He smiled to himself. He could not deny the ease of his arrival here, the warmth and trust of Tess and Dave, his good fortune in having so many of his immediate needs taken care of. The house was perfect and already felt like home. He felt similar confidence regarding the prospects for the bookstore, once it was up and running.

Yet somehow the place was more than comfortable. As he took in his new-old surroundings, Jonathan somehow sensed that it would be in this setting that he would meet whatever it was that awaited him and that it would not be long in coming.

He was still unsure whether he should welcome, or dread, that prospect.

Work became the dominant theme of Jonathan's life for the next ten days. He spent these days alone, or in Dave's company, turning the old mercantile into an acceptable bookshop. There were floors to sand and finish, walls to spackle and paint, lights to take down, and lamps to put up. Long shelves of redolent pine were assembled and finished to a satin sheen. Carton after carton of books were hauled from the basement and arranged by type and author on the shiny new shelves.

After removing the old market sign and painting the exterior façade, he and Dave hung a sign above the door, an old-fashioned wooden swinger in the style of colonial artisans. It bore the figure of a raven, painted brilliant scarlet instead of black, in reference to the bookstore's emblazoned name: "The Red Raven." Jonathan had persuaded Dave that his original moniker—"*Le Corbeau Rouge*"— was too pretentious for Saginaw at this early stage of its bohemianization.

The grand opening swiftly followed, and the day was perfect. Cobalt skies provided the perfect backdrop for October foliage so brilliant it taxed the eyes. A brisk sixty degrees put everyone in an energetic, expansive mood. Tess and Dave had advertised the opening effectively, and for eight hours a steady stream of customers filed through the door, partaking of coffee and cookies, all of them greeting Jonathan warmly. They were a varied assortment of genders, ages, and ethnicities, some dressed in denim and flannel and others decked out as if for a night at the philharmonic. They seemed educated and well-read and, just as the indefatigable Dave had predicted, reasonably hip.

By the time the last customer departed after seven o'clock, the charter clientele had purchased an amazing two thousand dollars' worth of books, a figure that sent Dave into a state of entrepreneurial ecstasy. Although Jonathan tried to remind him that this was an opening, a onetime event, and that the pace would surely slow almost immediately, Dave would not be denied.

Jonathan's forecast was prescient. The next day saw a dozen customers, only three of whom walked away with a purchase. Subsequent days would see more, especially Saturdays, but he soon learned that traffic and trade would be modest until the store settled in and became more of a neighborhood fixture. As it was, The Red Raven—whose revenues went mainly to Jonathan's attached salary and expenses—was losing money, but not a great deal of it. Dave remained optimistic and expressed full confidence in his manager.

Jonathan quickly settled into the peaceful gait of his new existence. He sometimes spent hours alone in the store but seldom found himself bored. There were books to rearrange and dust, floors to sweep, accounts to be maintained, and when all these were seen to, no shortage of good stories to read.

To gain fluency in his new vocation, he scoured "books on books" and internet sites to comparison shop and chart trends in the esoteric, ever-shifting realm of book collecting. He learned even more from his customers themselves, a surprising number of whom were happy to spend half an hour or more expounding on titles they knew. They reminded him of fishermen, always eager to weave sagas of treasures found or lost and the thrill of the hunt. He liked their yarns and learned from them. Although far from an expert, he soon found his own sea legs.

After two weeks, he began to recognize repeat customers—the corpulent man from the First Ward who had a taste for French romances and a passion for anything involving femmes fatales; the plain housewife who seemed to purchase at least two novels a week, usually in the five-dollar range, mostly bestsellers, for what appeared to be a voracious reading jones; the ponytailed literature professor from Saginaw Valley College who was forever on the lookout for new and unusual material to consider for his students.

Jonathan also began to acquire "scouts" and learned how valuable these energetic souls could be to a used bookshop. They hunted books in their spare time, using keen eyes to spot popular authors, first editions, and, occasionally, truly rare volumes. Jonathan was able to pay them little more than modest sums for their finds, but they seemed less interested in profit than the chase itself.

Phil, for one, was passionate about it and loved to tell tales of the estate sales and barn sales where most of his searching was done. An avid reader himself, his knowledge of authors and titles far surpassed the little expertise Jonathan had been able to amass. He was openly and proudly gay and immediately announced his attraction to Jonathan, who declined the opportunity for romance with a strikingly handsome young man, although he tried to do so sensitively.

Diana was another avid hunter, a specialist in church sales and secondhand shops, and demonstrated a talent for spotting the unusual. Raven-haired with an ivory complexion, she dressed all in black—beret, turtleneck, long skirt, and funky, button-up shoes—and was never seen without dark shades over her eyes. She spoke with an elegant accent that Jonathan surmised might be Polish or Romanian but which Diana herself would refer to only as "Old Country."

She had a charming touch for bizarre but strangely perfect phrasing, some of it plainly foreign, much of it borrowed and tortured American slang. When something surprised her, she said she was "stupidified." When something struck her as strange, she called it "berserk." She referred to people who acted foolishly as "doodahs," to those overweight as "shmentuzahs," to gay men (especially her competitor Phil) as "queer bait," and to things or people she liked as "sweeeet."

With her malapropisms, her air of mystery, and her sleek black profile, Jonathan wondered if Diana was some exotic, twenty-first century witch. He had to admit that he felt an undeniable attraction to this strange woman but also knew that he was not seriously considering a relationship. It was far too early for that.

His entire social life, in fact, lay in a state of accepted stasis. He seldom ventured far, except for his own treks to scout books and weekly dinners with Tess and Dave that, at least for Dave, were little more than excuses for business updates.

Along with his cousin and his benefactor, Jonathan also was grateful for the one living creature he had so far allowed into his life. Pluto was an ebony black cat with enormous citrine eyes. The feline had first haunted the old house and then the shop, as if seeking out Jonathan in particular. He was lean from hunger and, with the first morsel of food offered by Jonathan, became as loyal and affectionate a friend as if he had lived there since kittenhood. In less than a week, he had become an aesthetically perfect fixture at The Red Raven and clearly enjoyed the attention paid him by customers.

After an obligatory hour or two of alley roaming, Pluto would spend his nights at his new master's side, next to the chair when he read, at the foot of the bed when he slept. The presence of the cat felt elemental and warm for a man who was beginning to feel the approach of winter's cold.

October passed like spiced wine—bright, deep, and aromatic. The lengthening shadows, earlier sunsets, and gaining chill of the season energized Jonathan and fueled a gradual sense of anticipation. He slept only a few hours each night and began to take modest walks throughout the city, which soon turned into long rambles that often lasted two or three hours.

Occasionally, he encountered glimpses of things that jogged his memory—particular buildings or signs, the angle of certain trees on street corners—that might have been echoes of his own childhood. He had plentiful memories of his upbringing here—accompanying his father downtown as he shopped during a snowy Christmas season, an old barbershop that smelled of aftershave and cigars, a drugstore with an ancient soda fountain—but never found an actual object that corresponded to them.

While his recollections of Saginaw were of a bustling place, much of the city now bore a tired appearance. Many houses on the East Side stood in a state of virtual ruin. Most of the once thriving downtown businesses had closed, and no successors had been attracted to their quarters. The West Side fared somewhat better, gamely striving to preserve and utilize vestiges of the city's more prosperous past, but even here the oppressive spirit prevailed.

Saginaw was a place whose best days were obviously well behind it, of which its current citizens seemed painfully aware. Everywhere was evidence of apathy and surrender.

Jonathan grew weary of this cruel present and developed a preference for thinking about the past, or at least whatever picture of it his imagination was able to conjure. This was especially true when he wandered into the East Side. There he studied the old First Ward avidly, attracted to the faded glory of what had once been the city's most prosperous district. Most of the massive and once elaborate houses were pale echoes of their past selves, many were dilapidated beyond repair, but Jonathan found himself increasingly capable of ignoring the less glamorous here and now.

He imagined the well-to-do men who had built these homes on wealth amassed during Saginaw's brief but frenzied golden era, when it was America's leading producer of lumber. Much of the physical infrastructure of the American West had been constructed with wood from Saginaw's prolific mills. On the giving end, most of Michigan's seemingly endless virgin forests had been efficiently and greedily cleared.

In the course of that historical plunder, the men who had lived here well over a century ago had become, like the gold and silver barons of Colorado, fabulously rich. The ruins of their affluence on these dark streets told Jonathan that their empire, however glorious it had once been, had fallen in the way of all empires.

In spite of its decline, however, Saginaw still fascinated him with an elusive lure that drew him close and made him feel welcome. Perhaps it was this same essence, he thought, that had drawn Longfellow, whose Evangeline stopped here on her mournful journey from old Acadia only to find "the hunter's lodge deserted and fallen to ruin"; de Tocqueville, who braved the hazardous forests in the very early days to view this outpost of civilization in the wilderness; and Paul Simon, who composed a dream of hitchhiking from Saginaw in an American song that captured the spirit of a restless generation.

All had described Saginaw as a place passed through, but not forgotten, by travelers. It had been depicted by artists as a lonely way station, a place for searching wayfarers. Sometimes during his own restless walks, Jonathan fancied himself such a wayfarer and, much like the voyagers of earlier eras who had passed this way, he had no idea where his destination might lie.

His walks left him sufficiently exhausted to face solitary nights, save for Pluto's vigilant presence. Each twilight was quiet and governed by strict routine. Jonathan would seldom retire before the wee hours of the morning, when the street was still as a grave, and frequently, during his brief slumbers, he would dream.

The dreams were amorphous, of mist and fog, consisting mainly of feelings—curiosity or anticipation, sometimes unfocused fear. There was invariably a presence, an intelligent, human sentience, lurking somewhere in the fluidic substance of the dream itself, but always lurking in the background, sensed but never visible.

In ways his waking mind couldn't begin to understand, he was drawn to this presence and desired to grow closer to it. He vaguely recalled that he had actually seen that presence, in a hotel room five hundred miles behind him. Now, he was starting to remember these feelings upon awakening and holding them close through the succeeding days. He was more alone than he had ever been in his life, yet felt not alone at all.

All Hallows' Eve came as sinister as its reputation. The skies shifted between streams of ragged clouds, seemingly hell-bent on reaching Lake Huron, and breaks of clear sun, wan gold in the morning, smoky amber in the afternoon. What leaves remained on the trees were dry and rustled noisily in a brisk southwesterly wind. One by one, they were wrested from their perches, joining hordes of their fallen brothers to dance whirling dervishes in streets and alleys.

The day had been busy. Customers sensed the approach of Michigan's late autumn, a time usually spent safely indoors where good books quickly became prized assets. The scouts were busy, too. Phil came by with three boxes filled with a complete set of the works of Ambrose Bierce, a reasonably intact edition of Poe, and an immaculate 1937 set of *Compton's Encyclopedia*. He walked away with two crisp one-hundred-dollar bills.

Diana stopped in during the late afternoon, proudly placing two large shopping bags onto the counter.

"Happy Halloweeeen!" she intoned in her remarkable accent. "I have books for you, Jonathan. Come take a look."

Her most recent finds had been acquired at a farm sale near Hemlock. They included a number of Victorian "lady's novels," books with titles like *Beneath the Old Home Arbor* and *The Violets of Summer*. They were painfully outdated and obscure, but beautifully bound, and Jonathan already knew that a surprising number of buyers purchased such books for no more reason than their attractive appearance on shelves. Diana's bags also contained a few common reference books, two or three battered children's primers from the late nineteenth century, and what appeared to be an old photograph album. She was happy for the forty dollars that Jonathan offered and waved the bills as she departed—more witchlike than ever—into the gloaming of the wild October night.

Jonathan closed down the shop and prepared for a quiet evening. He ate a simple supper, entertained himself and Pluto for most of an hour on the guitar, and finally took a look at the books he had purchased earlier. He had dusted and priced most of them when he took out the old photo album.

It was bound in dark leather grown brittle and faded, with an elaborate script forming the words "Family Album" in gold leaf on the embossed cover. He flipped through the heavy pages, each containing a daguerreotype, tintype, or ambrotype of somebody's relative, their names written beautifully in pencil beneath each one. They were mostly studio posed, and virtually all of the subjects, even the children, looked uncomfortable. From the prints, the hairstyles, and the clothing, Jonathan guessed that the album was roughly of 1860s vintage.

He gazed at the solemn visages of the past—Ada Lou Hopkins, a mildly corpulent woman, hair done up in a bun so tight it must have caused considerable pain; Timothy Foley, a middle-aged man with an amazing growth of curly beard and a somber, infinite quality to his stare; Phineas Creede Foley, a hungry-looking, top-hatted fellow whose eyes stared eerily in opposing directions.

He wondered about their circumstances and occupations, about where they had lived. He saw the awareness in their eyes and found it easy to imagine the sound of their voices and subtleties of their expressions. They had all once been vital, thinking, loving, hating, hoping, dreaming—living—beings, yet there was probably little more than these slabs of fading paper to testify to their lives. Was there a single soul still living who had ever seen these people in life? Did anyone pause by their overgrown graves to consider the life that was once attached to the name inscribed beneath a plaintive epitaph or the words "Rest in Peace"?

It gave him a chill to think that he could throw each of these photographs into the fire and thereby erase the last surviving legacies of entire lives. And that nobody would ever care, or even know, and that the same could one day be said of virtually all human beings in their turn. What an awesome, terrible power time reveals itself to be.

He turned the page and saw her for the first time.

The effect was immediate and startling. Jonathan drew in his breath sharply when the pale clarity of her eyes gazed out from her sepia-toned prison. Unlike the others, she looked neither annoyed nor uncomfortable. Instead, her image projected a dreamy wistfulness, which, although perfectly childlike, was somehow knowing and womanly.

Her beauty had been very powerful. It still was.

Her face was delicate and oval, eyes large but narrowed a little for the portrait. The nose, slightly turned, formed the perfect crown for full lips that curved somewhat downward at the corners, casting a melancholy shade over her expression. The hair, either light brown or dark blonde, was done up in braids on the top of her head, with more braids descending over her neck. Jonathan imagined that if undone, her hair would be full and luxurious, reaching perhaps all the way down her back. He imagined her brushing that golden hair on a long-gone night before her mirror, a flickering candle providing faint illumination. He imagined her regarding her own wistful image in the looking glass, admiring the reflection in her dreamy, woman-child way. He was seeing her from the back, dressed in something light, crinoline perhaps, and saw her turn her head and smile slightly as he softly approached.

He swept the image from his mind, realizing in amazement that it had physically stirred him. But there was already something profoundly and disturbingly deeper to what he felt. He was lightheaded and dizzy. He had no choice but to make renewed contact with those eyes.

He had never seen her before—of course he had not—but there was a powerful familiarity about her, a maddening trace of something, which her face—like the melody of a long-unheard song or the whiff of a faint scent—drew from somewhere deep inside. Jonathan sensed a closeness with the image and believed, if only for a moment, that a subtle trace of communication had successfully made the connection between his mind and hers.

He shook his head and forced a laugh. He must be thinking of someone he had once known—a girl in school or somebody at the office—somebody whose face bore a remarkable likeness to this one. Shortly, he would recall her name and whatever memories he had of her. Either that or conclude that his unlikely reaction to the old daguerreotype was nothing more than the aftermath of some emotional exhaustion.

But the photograph made him uneasy. He had never before experienced such an immediate and intense reaction to a real woman, let alone a portrait. It seemed unnatural.

Before closing the album, however, he could not resist looking at the pencil-scripted name beneath her faded image.

"Apollonia Foley," he read out loud.

Jonathan placed the album on the table. "Never heard of her," he said to nobody but himself.

Jonathan skipped through the musty volume of Poe that Phil had brought, trying to indulge himself in the macabre bleakness of the opening of "The Fall of the House of Usher," only to abandon the story once its setting was established. He allowed his mind to adapt to the metronomic rhythm of "The Bells" and then followed "The Raven" through its infinitely sad entirety.

But he was too distracted to really appreciate the words on the pages, too anxious to surrender his mind to the lure and manipulation of any writer. With the last "Nevermore," Jonathan shut the book and leaned back in his chair, closing his eyes against the soft light of the lamp, closing his ears to the barely perceptible ticks and settlings of the old house. Despite the hour and his fatigue, he didn't sleep but fell into a deep and troubled reverie.

The face of Apollonia Foley would not quit his mind. He wondered who she was, where she lived, whether she really looked like her portrait. The enigmatic expression on her face fascinated and troubled him, the downward curve of the lips, the slightly sharpened arch of one eyebrow. He wondered how she looked when smiling, when laughing on a brilliant morning, the sun sending streaks of mellow gold through her hair.

And then, with an almost physical pain in his stomach, he found himself grimacing at the absolute knowledge that she was long dead—that her life had, in ways unknown, most definitely ended and that the end had surely occurred long before his own existence had even begun.

Despite this certainty, some stubborn emotional sliver of his mind refused the knowledge.

An inner voice told him how foolish and futile these ruminations were. It was nothing more than an ancient photograph that had survived the years by sheer happenstance. Dumb luck happened to drop said photograph into his hand. End of story. And she—well, she was nothing. Wherever her forgotten dust and bones now reposed, it mattered nothing to Jonathan. Why in the world should it?

But as soon as this voice paused, another pushed it aside. This one asked questions—speculated, fantasized, wondered—all about her.

At some point during the night, these reflections, seeming to alternate in random sequences, must have surrendered to the powers of sleep or at least something like it. It was a troubled state, a twilight phase between waking and sleeping.

Deep in this limbo, something demanded his immediate attention. Some instinct, of which he was barely aware, was trying to warn him of something. Though no sound awakened him, he started, and the tales of Poe clattered from his lap onto the rug. He opened his eyes to see that the house was as quiet before, but something lay beneath the innocuous stillness. A familiar sense of presence, elusive and intangible, was in the air.

Jonathan realized that the sensation was identical to his earlier vision in the hotel room in Iowa. It possessed the same contradictory but coexisting qualities of surreal dreaming and physical reality.

Pluto had already wakened, his back slightly arched, the hair on his tail starting to rise. A low moan emanated from somewhere deep in his chest.

Jonathan rose slowly from the chair and began a careful search of the first floor, peering into the dining room and the dimly lit kitchen, silent save for the drip from a leaky faucet, and paused at last at the foot of the two-flight staircase. He looked directly upward. And froze.

The figure at the top of the stairs was cast in shadow, but a random beam of lamplight illuminated the lower hem of her long dress. It was a heavy satin of deep crimson, a color once called claret. The garment deceptively dimmed to black at her shoulders. He saw the silhouette of her head, narrow and delicate, the outline of her hand on the banister. She appeared to be descending but then, as if she had suddenly seen Jonathan standing below, paused and quickly withdrew. She turned into the upper hallway, and as she did he caught a glimpse of her side profile in the full light of his bedroom. The hair was honey blonde, the eyes gray or blue, the complexion smooth and fair.

The face was that of Apollonia.

His fascination extinguishing any lingering fear, Jonathan bounded up the stairs. He knew, however, even before he reached the top, that he would not find her. That she would no longer be there. That, in any sort of physical form, she had never been there at all. He took a cursory look through all the upper-story rooms, made sure the windows had not been opened, but knew that the effort was wasted.

The late-night visitant in that Midwest hotel—forgotten until this moment—returned in a sudden surge of clarity, as did the powerful but unfocused feelings he had felt on the lonely highways heading east. These memories blended with the image he had just glimpsed on the stairs, the nebulous dreams, and the old photograph in the album to form a perfect nexus. He understood at once that they were all one—one image, one sensation, one overriding desire.

He did not understand the import of this epiphany—nor did he know its nature—but he no longer believed it to be the mere stuff of dreams. He had confidence in his ability to distinguish between hallucination and physical fact, and he had little use for the traditional concept of ghosts.

Neither dream nor mirage nor apparition, she was somehow very real—all of this was painfully and strangely real—although Jonathan had absolutely no idea from which plane she came.

But already he feared, against all logic and defiant of intractable reality, that he might be falling in love with her.

His fall into the past had already begun.

If truth be told, Jonathan had always been a child of yesterday. For as long as he could remember, he had favored old-fashioned art, architecture, literature, aesthetics in general. He had always seen the past as purer, nobler, more genuinely romantic and dramatic—more elementally real—than the present. Comfortable with the antique and naturally suspicious of the modern, he had driven cars since his youth but never felt at ease with the speed and motion of the automotive machine. It even still amazed him that television images were not only possible but commonplace, and for him the internet remained nothing more than a convenient mystery. In writing or in person, his formal manners had earned him chiding from the casual denizens of an informal age, and his very bearing caused some to say that Jonathan had somehow been born in the wrong century.

All that, however, had been mere admiration. What was happening now was quickly growing into obsession.

A part of him worried about this and sought to analyze the phenomenon: He was at war with the present, with *his* present specifically, and was distancing himself from a lonely and uncomfortable "now" by retreating into a halcyon "then" of his own imaginative making.

Yet it all seemed so natural. He felt comfortable in this eccentric old house, at peace among the published words of long-dead authors, content here in an archaic corner of a forgotten city.

He sensed that Apollonia was the likely source of these feelings, but this, too, felt perfectly natural, even as he recognized how strange it would seem to someone else. He suspected neither poetic romanticism nor morbid fascination in his feelings for this echo that had once been a woman.

He accepted these feelings without seriously challenging them, and as he did, a sort of metamorphosis slowly overtook him.

He began to remember long-forgotten things from his own youth, here in Saginaw, and even—it seemed to him—to remember things from a time that preceded his own existence. One such memory—actually, a mysterious mixture of memories—became a symbol for all of his thoughts and feelings.

This icon existed on a corporeal and an emotional plane. He had experienced both dimensions as a child, on certain mornings, when the early light would sneak through his curtains in a peculiar way, promising days in which there would be no obligations, no schedules, no limitations. It was a vaguely ecstatic sensation, innocent yet knowing—an exquisite state of essential clarity.

It hadn't happened often, perhaps no more than four or five times in all, but the memories remained vivid. With no warning, and triggered by no stimulus of which he was ever aware, a wave of happiness would sweep over him, filling him with a calm and peaceful contentment. It was soothing, like warmth.

The feeling would always subside after a few enchanted moments, but as it ebbed, Jonathan would gaze from his bedroom window. And in the indeterminate distance, at the opposite end of an open field, he would glimpse a structure that came to mark the Saginaw of his youth. The boy had named it simply the Gray House, for it was painted the grayest of grays, as chromatically neutral as the steely November skies that lingered over the semirural vicinity enveloping his boyhood home.

In stark reality, the Gray House was nothing more than an old farmhouse that had somehow avoided demolition to stand alone and forlorn, well away from anything else made by human hands.

Yet it stood before his wondering gaze, silent and static, and filled him with a strange marvel. The house held something within its gray walls, in its inconspicuous and passive way. It tempted him with a mystery it concealed within itself, hinting of memories long forgotten but with an imprint that remained. Or, strangely, of memories somehow never known—an inexplicable conundrum of memories yet to take place, of a past that lay somehow locked within the future.

For the briefest of moments, the lonely old house would then appear to him with the sharpest, preternatural focus. Jonathan could see plainly every shadow on its surface, every texture of its weathered clapboard and warped glass; he could almost taste the rusty water from its well, smell the accumulated essence of fruit and spice in an ancient pantry he couldn't see but knew must be there.

And then the aspect of the Gray House would revert to its natural state, appearing once more to be faraway and drab and old and ordinary, and the boy would look away, realizing even at his tender age that the moment had passed.

Jonathan had left Saginaw well before he had either the courage or the opportunity to physically set out for the place and to face its mysteries from up close. He left it just as he was growing to love it, but the Gray House never left him. It never ceased its pull, and it never let him forget.

On the first Saturday of November, Jonathan drove out to his old environs to seek the house, hoping perhaps to find within it some clue to his present state. He traversed all the roads that had been there in his childhood, roads that might have conceivably passed by the site of the house. He carefully studied the surroundings and walked the most likely routes.

He found no trace of it. The perspectives and visual relationships had all been altered by years of building and landscaping. After two hours of fruitless searching, he paused in defeat, wondering whether there had ever existed such a house at all or whether it was merely a childish chimera.

He was unsure why the house had once more become so important to him but knew that it held some significance. In the midst of the cold day, hands tucked into his jacket pockets, collar turned up against the wind, he looked again in vain confusion at the arrays of modern dwellings and manicured lawns. Nothing was familiar, but he sensed the house was there somewhere—at least an echo of it— and in his mind it appeared with a clarity he had never before seen.

Though the Gray House eluded him, Jonathan soon decided to pursue his other obsession, and by now, at least to himself, he was being utterly honest about the fact that this was exactly what it was.

The Red Raven was doing a modest but steady trade. The weather had turned dark and moody, with low clouds and cold rain that chilled the city in fitful starts and pauses. It should have been a quiet and relaxing time, but Jonathan found himself pursuing far more challenging ambitions than merely curling up with a good book and a lively fire.

He resolved to track down whatever traces Apollonia might have left behind.

He began with a minute examination of her photograph, carefully removing it from its sleeve in the album and reading the elaborate script emblem on the reverse. "J. Wingfield Photographers," it read, and in smaller letters, an address on Genesee Street in "East Saginaw." Jonathan recognized this as the original name for today's East Side, before its merger with "Saginaw City," today's West Side.

This was, of course, a significant discovery. It established that Apollonia had indeed hailed from this region or at least spent time here. That would make the search much easier.

Along the oval border of her portrait, he found tiny words embossed in the once white paper. With a magnifying glass, he was able to detect a tiny imprint, reading: "February, 1864."

Another eureka. He had already established her name, her location, and the date.

He checked the other photographs in the album as well, finding that most of them had been taken in Saginaw or Bay City, its sister city closer to Saginaw Bay, and that they all dated between the years 1861 and 1877. There were a number of individuals named Foley, including Apollonia, and in some of the faces Jonathan detected a subtle resemblance to her.

The album's last photograph proved an extra bonus. It was a shot of three people, taken outdoors, the only non-studio view. The trio stood before what appeared to be the brick wall of a large house. One corner of the photo revealed the edge of a window. On the other border could be seen an iron trellis nailed to the house itself. A few dry shoots of a climbing plant twined their way through the lattice's prongs.

The group included two men and a woman who stood between them. Jonathan was almost certain that the woman was Apollonia. She wore her hair in much the same fashion as her other picture, but the wind had pulled loose a few strands and they waved across her face. Her dress was plain and dark colored, much more somber and modest than the elaborate satin ensemble she had worn for her formal portrait. She squinted against a bright sun, causing her to effect an expression that was almost a smile. It was as glorious as Jonathan had anticipated. The sight of it brought a powerful sensation to his chest, and he could not help smiling back at her.

He studied the two men who flanked her. One of them, rather short, stood stiff and straight. He wore a rakishly angled derby and held the stump of a cigar in his mouth. His youthful expression was defiant, pugnacious. He reminded Jonathan of a scrappy boxer. A brother, perhaps?

The other, somewhat taller, had apparently moved his head during the slow time exposure of the old camera. His face was a solid blur, although Jonathan was able to discern dark hair beneath a low-crowned hat. He was of medium build.

The date embossed on this photograph was "March 7, 1864." Written beneath it, in the former owner's customary pencil, was a single word: "Riverdale."

Armed with these clues, Jonathan made himself into a detective of the past. He began with Diana, who had sold him the album. She readily supplied the name of the farmer who'd held the barn sale and gave Jonathan directions to his place near Hemlock, a few miles to the west.

Jonathan drove the distance in a hopeful mood, passing through the little town itself and past flat farmland bordered by stands of bare trees, whose skeletal outlines against the wintry sky looked strangely human.

The farmer's plain white house stood well back from the gravel road beneath tall trees that, in a warmer season, would have bathed it in shade. Jonathan parked and knocked on the wooden door.

A young woman answered. Her expression revealed fatigue and, at the sight of this stranger at her threshold, more than a hint of suspicion.

Jonathan told her his name and a brief summary of his business: He was the new owner of an old family album—he held it up to show her—and was convinced that there might be some historical significance to the photographs. He had come in search of information that would help him begin his investigation.

"I think that was Jerry's," she said flatly. "He's in the barn. The door should be open. Tell him what you're after."

Jonathan thanked her and walked back to a weathered, paintless barn so tilted and sagging that it looked as if the next snowstorm would be the last it would ever endure. The husband was sitting before the door, the long barrel of a hunting rifle propped on his lap. He was running a cloth along the barrel and looked up in curiosity at the stranger's approach.

He stood briefly, took Jonathan's hand in a firm grip, introduced himself, and quickly sat down again. "Excuse me if I keep working," he said in the curious Michigan accent, whose rounded vowels often sounded Scandinavian to those from other regions. "Elk season is on in three days, and I have a lot to do." He squinted at the wintry sky and scratched his chin through his bushy beard. "Feels like it's gonna be a good season."

Jonathan produced the tattered album. The man took the book and glanced cursorily at a few of the old portraits.

"I thought I sold this last weekend," he said.

"You did," Jonathan rejoined. "That's how it came to me. I'm running a used bookshop in Saginaw. I bought it from the woman who picked it up at your sale. I'm curious about some of the photographs."

"Yeah, well, I'm afraid I can't tell you a whole lot about it. I think it came to me from my grandmother when she died, oh, ten, fifteen years ago already. She told me that it came from her mother. It's pretty old stuff."

"I would guess from the time of the Civil War," Jonathan said. "Do you think there's anyone still living who might know anything about the photos or the people in them?"

The man momentarily stopped stroking the gun. "Maybe. Aunt Violet is still alive. At least, I think she is. She had a pretty good head for the old family stuff."

"Aunt Violet?"

"Violet Hunter. My grandmother's little sister. Seems pretty strange to call her a 'little sister.' I mean, she's over a hundred years old. Last I heard, she was living in the city in a home for old folks. You can ask my wife if she still has the address in her book."

Assured that there was little chance of any other living soul having knowledge of these ghosts from the past, Jonathan thanked the hunter. The wife copied the address from her book, a little reluctantly, for this insistent stranger.

Saginaw was in its most somber November mode when Jonathan set out for the nursing home on the East Side the next day. He decided to walk, the distance not being great, and found himself on this still Sunday morning enveloped in a dense blanket of river fog. All sounds were muffled and soft, even the horn of the great freighter beneath his feet as he crossed the Holland Street Bridge, pulling into the river en route to some distant destination up or down the lakes. The streetlamps remained lit in the gloom, and the infrequent cars rolled through the chilly mist like glowing bubbles.

As he walked, he glanced at the sidewalks running parallel to the streets, some of them laid in elaborate brick patterns, some in large flagstones, others in cracked and heaved slabs of concrete. On many of them were dates—1910, 1905, 1897, 1888, 1875—placed alongside the emblems of long-dead masons. The closer he came to the center of the city, the older the dates grew; as he moved away, they became progressively newer. It was like walking along a time line.

The home was just east of downtown. Its residents were safely ensconced in an old gingerbread house, rambling and fancy, that wore a mansard roof atop its single tower like an old-fashioned hat. It immediately seemed an appropriate place for a woman more than a century old.

Jonathan knocked and soon saw the face of a middle-aged woman, apparently the caretaker, peering out at him through a narrow window in the door. She was overtly suspicious. He explained his reason for coming, saying that he was doing historical research on the Foley family of Saginaw and wanted to ask Mrs. Hunter a few questions about a photograph album he had. The caretaker indicated that she would ask on his behalf and disappeared for a full five minutes. When she returned, she nodded through her little window and finally unlocked the heavy door.

"I'm sorry about the wait," she said in a genuine tone. "This neighborhood can get a little dangerous, you know, and I'm..."

"Don't mention it," Jonathan reassured her. "I understand. I didn't have the telephone number, or I would have called first. I promise not to take long."

"Violet is one hundred and five years old, you know," the caretaker cautioned. "She has agreed to help you with your photographs, but it wouldn't do to upset her or even to get her excited, if you know what I mean. At that age, they're like dried flowers. One little puff of wind and...," she made a whooshing noise with her mouth.

Jonathan nodded as warmly as he could and followed the woman down a long hallway. They opened a door at the end and entered a spacious room dominated by a handsome diamond dust mirror and an elegant sofa.

At first glance, he didn't notice Mrs. Hunter at all. She was a tiny figure, so lean that it appeared it might be difficult for her frame to hold her head in an upright position. She had perfectly white hair, done up in a tight bun that reminded him of some of the photographs in the album he was carrying. She wore thin gold spectacles on a face that was an endless map of deep wrinkles. One eye peered largely through the glass lens, pale blue in color, and reminded Jonathan uncomfortably of a story of Poe's. She wore a simple print dress and sat in a wheelchair, whose automatic controls, upon his entry, she navigated with unexpected expertise to within a foot of him.

"You're Mr. Chase, then?" she inquired in a frail, birdlike voice. "Come and sit down on the sofa, young man, and show me what you have in your hand there." She turned to the caretaker. "Now, Charlene, dear, if you would be so kind as to bring us a little pot of tea. It isn't every day, after all, that a handsome young man comes to pay old Violet a visit."

The caretaker smiled nervously and quietly left the room.

"I've brought an old photograph album...," Jonathan began.

"Whoa, there!" she rejoined in her bird's voice. "Can't hear a word you're saying. Here, let's try that again."

She held up a long metal horn to her ear, a conical device he had seen in old children's book illustrations but never in real life. The archaic hearing aid resembled a miniature horn for a windup Victrola.

He repeated his statement, explaining how he had come into possession of the old photographs and offering a reason why he wanted to learn more about them. He mentioned that he believed it had once belonged to Mrs. Hunter's older sister.

She nodded, this time in understanding, and peered at the first image in the album. "Yes, that's right. I can tell already. This was Rosetta's album. It came from our mother when she died, and she got it from my grandmother. I remember looking at this when I was young. Later on, you see, Rosetta was so picky about it. Hardly ever let anyone touch the thing."

Now free to handle it without restriction, Mrs. Hunter touched the album lovingly, stroking the weathered leather binding. She sighed and focused her enlarged eye directly into Jonathan's.

"Rosetta was a sweet girl, though," she said softly. "Loved her children so much. Took such good care of them. Even little Virginia, who wasn't, you know, quite right up here." She pointed to her temple. "Elevator never quite made it to the top floor. Pretty girl, though, talented in some ways, hardly able in others."

Jonathan let her ramble, then gently guided her back to the album, opened to the photograph of the bearded man with the faraway look in his eyes. She recognized the face at once.

"That was Timothy Foley. See, it's written right here." She directed a shaky and bony finger at the inscription, as if that would tell him everything he needed to know.

"He was my great-grandfather, the first Foley to settle in the Saginaw Valley. I never knew him, of course. He died maybe thirty years before I was born. He came from England originally, Coventry, I think, and began with a small farm down to the Tittabawassee. Then he discovered how much money could be made with the lumber trade that was just starting up at the time—this is, oh, the 1850s, I should think."

"Did he do well at the lumber trade?"

"Oh, he did marvelously, yes. He set up a big sawmill down to the river. They used to float the logs down the Tittabawassee from up North, you see, so he was in the perfect spot. He made a fabulous fortune, so I understand. Built himself a big, fine house, and cleared hundreds and hundreds of acres to expand his farm. Yes, old Timothy Foley did quite well by himself."

The next photograph proved to be Timothy's wife, Alexandra, about whom Mrs. Hunter seemed to possess an impressive number of stories. Alexandra, it turned out, had been almost legendary in her time. In her later years, she was known in Saginaw as the elegant and dignified matron of the highly respected and influential Foley family. Few remembered that in her youth she had been a fiery frontierswoman, capable of helping to clear vast expanses of trees, stumps, and brush, trading regularly with displaced Chippewa and Huron, and, one time, shooting to death a timber wolf with her husband's heavy old musket, an act that, as Mrs. Hunter put it, "surely saved the old man's life."

Next came the photo of the top-hatted young man whose eyes veered in opposite directions.

"Phineas Creede Foley," Mrs. Hunter said confidently and then chuckled merrily. "He was Timothy's son, my great-uncle. I remember him from when I was a little girl. Of course, he was an old man by then. We used to call him 'Cross-eyed Phin.' Never to his face, of course. He had the funniest walk, like a duck, which wasn't at all his fault, but was funny to us nonetheless. He was a nice enough fellow, I suppose. But never very talkative. Always a private sort of man. Never did find a woman to marry him." She sighed.

The next page revealed a strikingly attractive young woman. She had what appeared to be jet black hair, wound in a long and elegant braid around her neck and falling back onto her breast. Her eyes were large and dark. Her expression exuded gentleness.

"Emily Foley," Mrs. Hunter intoned warmly. "Timothy's daughter and my grandmother. The sweetest, kindest soul our Lord ever saw fit to place upon this earth. It's from her that I learned all these stories. Grandma knew so many interesting things. She lived to be ninety-five, you know. Lived in the valley all her life, most of it in her father's house. How I loved spending afternoons with her in that old place. We'd have tea on the cold afternoons, and while she was knitting, we'd talk and talk, usually about the old days. Sometimes, when she told a sad story from the old days, she would cry. Sometimes, if the story was funny, she would laugh so prettily. She sounded just like—"

They were interrupted by the caretaker, who carefully set a small tea service before them. The caretaker poured tea for Mrs. Hunter and indicated for Jonathan to help himself. She didn't speak otherwise, but he detected an inquiring expression directed at the old woman. Apparently satisfied that the discussion wasn't proving too taxing for Mrs. Hunter, she quietly retreated.

There followed a sequence of photographs that Mrs. Hunter didn't quite recognize. She theorized here and there about a cousin or an uncle and mentioned that this or that one might have been mere friends or "Joshua's people," apparently indicating in-laws.

At last, their perusal brought them to the one photograph that interested Jonathan. Like him, Mrs. Hunter gasped when she first saw the image. She took the album in her trembling hands and brought it close to her luminous and watery eye.

"Goodness me," she said softly. "I haven't seen this since I was a little girl. Oh my, yes."

Mrs. Hunter regarded the portrait with an expression that puzzled him. She seemed to be studying the face, as if she was trying to learn something from those pale eyes and that wistful visage.

"Aunt Appy," she said.

Jonathan finally took in a small breath and tried to sound casual. "What do you know about her, Mrs. Hunter? Did your grandmother ever tell you stories about Apollonia Foley?"

The old woman smiled ironically and returned the album to its new owner.

"Oh yes, young man, she certainly did, but only rarely, always in hushed tones, and never when there was anyone else about. Aunt Appy, you see, was quite the notorious one, quite the rogue, so I understand. Every family must have its black sheep, I suppose. Still, it was so very sad what happened to her."

So heedless of time had he grown in listening to Mrs. Hunter that Jonathan hadn't noticed it was already afternoon. The sun managed to break through the pervasive fog for a few minutes, sending welcome rays of light into the room. The beams passed through a collection of antique bottles Mrs. Hunter had placed on a window for decoration, and their time-tinted shades—rose, cobalt, lavender, deep amber, and ice blue—sent colorful bands across her wrinkled face.

Jonathan also glimpsed the glint of a tear in her normal eye. She realized that he'd noticed.

"Silly girl!" she admonished herself, daubing the tear with her hand. "Pay me no mind, young man. You see, I'm not crying for Apollonia. I mean, I never knew her. She was dead long before my birth, I'm sure. It's just that grandmother never once spoke about her without crying herself. Aunt Appy was one of those sad stories she used to tell."

Jonathan said he understood. Mrs. Hunter sipped shakily at her tea and continued.

"She was Grandmother Emily's cousin, Appy was. She was not from around here. She was a Southerner, from Georgia, I believe. Her father was Zachariah Foley, Timothy's brother, who headed south while his brother headed north just after they arrived from England. Zachariah had a big plantation down there. Had dozens of slaves, so I understand. The brothers had been close, Zachariah and Timothy, and sent each other letters. My grandmother used to have them. I wish I knew where those letters were now. I'll just bet you'd find them fascinating, young man."

Jonathan nodded. He knew that he would find them fascinating indeed.

"Anyway, it was sometime during the war—the Civil War, that is—when Appy suddenly came north to stay at her Uncle Tim's place here in Saginaw. Grandma was never sure why it was that she came. She suspected that there must have been some trouble at home, maybe even a scandal. But come she did, with her own personal slave in tow, no less. My great-grandfather was quite an abolitionist, and Grandma remembered that there was some trouble when Appy arrived with a black man to carry her bags and drive her carriage. But I guess they must have worked it out somehow.

"She was at Riverdale—that was Timothy Foley's estate here on the Tittabawassee—for a few months, maybe half a year. Grandma told me that she became fast friends with her cousin. They talked endlessly and spent many hours exploring the old woods that used to be all around, even though it was dangerous and they had been warned not to stray far from the house. Wild animals, you see. There were still plenty of them in those days.

"But it was because Aunt Appy and Emily became such good friends that my grandmother was always so sad about her. You see, something had been going on at Riverdale. Aunt Appy was involved in something that was, oh, let's call it 'untoward.' Grandma thought it might have had something to do with something secret, something bad, but she never knew for sure. She overheard quiet whisperings at night and more than once glimpsed strange men who lurked around the house, out in the woods, staying just out of sight. She believed there had been meetings in the woods and that Aunt Appy might have been in on them. That she would skulk out late at night, Grandma used to say. She knew because they shared a bedroom in the old house. Some nights, Appy would be gone for hours.

"But in the end, all anybody knew is that one day, in the early springtime, the household awoke to find her missing from her bed. Her slave was gone, too. Without a word, mind you. All without a word. They simply vanished into the night. The sad part is...," Mrs. Hunter paused and wiped another tear from her eye. "The sad part is, young man, that Apollonia Foley was never heard from again. She never returned to Riverdale. Nor did she ever go home to her mother and father in Georgia. Not a soul ever received so much as a letter from her. Not even a rumor. Something terrible must have happened, but nobody ever knew what it was."

She glanced again at Apollonia's image. "And here she is, the poor thing, looking so young in this old picture, preserved in the amber of memory. She was such a pretty woman, don't you think? A face like an angel. It's so mysterious, so sad."

Jonathan tried to hide the emotions Mrs. Hunter's very old news conjured. The thought of Apollonia disappearing had not occurred to him. He had often contemplated her grave and imagined visiting it—indeed, hoped to actually do so—to be at least that close to her. He had often contemplated, with an utterly illogical jolt of anguish, the circumstances under which she had died. Now he knew that there was no grave, at least not one that anyone would ever know. For whatever family had remained, her death had been a mystery. Nobody in her own time had ever discovered what happened to her. How could he, a century and a half later, ever hope to know more?

Mrs. Hunter lowered the horn from her ear and looked Jonathan in the eye.

"That's all there is to know, young man," she said. "It's one of those stories with no ending. And it will never have an ending."

Jonathan was not yet ready to relent.

"Do you know anyone else who might know something about her?" he asked.

"Oh, my gracious, I don't think so. Why, even when I was just a little girl, there were very few who knew anything about her. Uncle Phin surely knew something, but he was not the sort of man one discussed old stories with. My grandmother was the only person who ever told me anything, who even knew who she was."

"What about relatives in Georgia? Were there any descendants?"

"Apollonia never married, so far as anybody ever knew. And she was an only child. When she disappeared, the line of the Southern Foleys disappeared with her."

Jonathan showed Mrs. Hunter the last photograph in the album. She was able to identify Apollonia but had no idea about the two other men in the picture.

She did, however, have one more clue to offer.

"I think this was taken at Riverdale," Mrs. Hunter added. "It seems familiar to me. It's such a tragedy what they've done with the place, don't you think?"

Jonathan started. "What do you mean?"

"Well, the old place is still there, don't you know? But just barely. It hasn't been lived in for nearly thirty years, since my cousin Bea passed away. The family just fights over it, cousins fighting cousins and nieces fighting uncles, all of them my relatives. They've wanted me to take sides, but I've refused. I find the whole thing terribly disgraceful. In the meantime, of course, Riverdale just sits there with the weeds taking over."

"Where is the house?" Jonathan asked, trying to sound casual.

"It's off State Street, just where it goes across the Tittabawassee. Most of the old grounds are gone, of course—they were sold off, piece by piece, until there was hardly any land left, and the traffic is just horrible there now. It won't be long before it's all gone."

Mrs. Hunter smiled faintly at Jonathan. "Just as all of those dear people in that album of yours are long gone, young man. Just as all of us will soon be gone, myself included. Myself especially. You must know how old I am."

He assured her that he knew.

Mrs. Hunter glanced out the window. The sun had once more retreated behind the fog, and the lines of light cast by the colored glass were no longer evident on her face. Jonathan looked at the wizened and peaceful visage, so ancient and worn, yet with eyes that had seen life more than a century ago. Eyes that still held the fire of consciousness and curiosity, even the shadow of youth.

"If you should live to be as old as I am, then you will understand what I mean," she said quietly, extending a shaky hand. "I feel like one of those old, old trees in California. There's nobody around who remembers the things that I do, nobody for me to share my memories with. It's terribly lonely to be where I am."

Jonathan held her skeletal hand, feeling fragile bones beneath gossamer skin.

"You have been very kind to me, Mrs. Hunter," he said. "I've enjoyed speaking with you more than you can know. I'm in your debt."

She smiled faintly. "I'll call that debt by asking you to visit me once in a while. How about that? I do enjoy telling the old stories to someone who cares."

He promised that he would return and meant it.

"My final words of advice, young man, are for you to be careful."

"Why?"

She regarded him with unmistakable wisdom and experience. "You're such a young man, with a long and wonderful life ahead of you. You should be out there living it, instead of spending your time talking to an old lady like me, instead of poring over dusty old photographs. The past is dead and gone. Take advantage of the moment."

He rose to leave, merely smiling at her very sensible advice. As he left the room, he watched as she expertly guided her wheelchair closer to the foggy window. She craned her thin neck to gaze into its gray opacity. In her tiny, birdlike voice he heard her say, softly and to herself, "Evening is coming on, the night owls are coming out, and Momma is calling her children home. Calling all her little children home..."

She said it in a lilting, sing-song cadence, almost like a lullaby, as if she had recited it many times. He closed the door gently behind him.

Jonathan walked directly home after his visit with Violet Hunter but didn't even bother to enter the house. Instead, he warmed up the Chevy and drove, as if drawn by a magnet, to the location she had described as the onetime estate of Timothy Foley and the temporary home of his wayward and mysterious niece, Apollonia.

The fog thickened in the waning afternoon, virtually emptying the streets of traffic. He cruised the milky path of Court Street, headed west on the usually busy State Street, and soon approached the bridge spanning the Tittabawassee River.

There was almost no traffic as he pulled off the road just before the bridge and gazed at the fog-enshrouded environs. In a sizable island formed by the intersecting streets, Jonathan spotted what appeared to be an undeveloped piece of land. It looked perhaps half the width of an ordinary city block and was totally overgrown. A long-neglected stand of maples, oaks, and birches fairly filled the small plot, and a tangle of bushes and vines closed the gaps between the trees. All of them were bereft of leaves. Jumbled together, with the silvery patina of dormant winter flora, they posed a forbidding obstacle.

He switched off the engine and walked across the deserted street to the lot. An ancient wrought iron fence encircled the land—ornamental and stylish once upon a time, rusty and twisted now. An equally decayed "No Trespassing" sign hung loosely from a sagging gate. The gate had long been locked and the chain appeared solid, but Jonathan was undeterred. With a careful look in all directions, he cautiously climbed over it, trying not to shake the ramshackle fence. With equal care he descended the other side, landing amid sharp branches. He quietly made his way through the foliage, his footfalls falling silently on a thick bed of damp leaves.

The house, which had once been so distinctive it had its own name, stood about fifty yards back from State Street, so closely surrounded by foliage that it was invisible from the roadway. This had perhaps saved it from the worst assaults of vandals but had not spared it the ravages of the elements.

It wore its decades of abandonment plainly. It had once been painted white, but the dull red of its bricks now peered through, everywhere except for the old mortar lines. Not a single window appeared intact, and various pieces of the old house—an iron balcony here, a shutter there—either hung loosely from the structure or had fallen unheeded onto the ground. Gaping holes appeared in its roof.

For all its decay, the glory of the old place was still possible to envision. It was a large house of two stories, shaped evenly square. Its roof sloped gently in four directions, except for a small cupola that still protruded from the center, appearing to Jonathan to be almost a lookout or viewing platform. Its windows were narrow and arched and looked like staring eyes.

He walked around the edifice, fighting brush all the way, and found a window through which he could enter. He struggled through, his panting echoing off the walls of the empty interior. The floor in this area, apparently a large dining room, had once been beautiful hardwood, inlaid in intricate patterns. It was now gray and cracked, with open holes in many places. The floor was littered with broken glass, bird droppings, and dust so thick it appeared to have been years since a human foot had trod here. The plaster walls were water-stained and crumbling, with long shreds of brittle wallpaper still clinging here and there. It smelled dank and musty.

A once ornate staircase led from the big room to the upper floors, but several steps were missing and the balustrade was obviously clinging by nothing more than a rusty nail or two. Jonathan decided not to attempt the ascent. He had a cursory look at the other rooms on the ground floor, all as decrepit as the first one, and finally exited through the same window.

The place had an air of eldritch brooding about it, sad and sinister all at once. If ever there existed a perfect candidate for a haunted house, Jonathan thought, this would be it.

He stood outside and surveyed the crumbling, old estate, knowing that Apollonia herself had once lived here, imagining that she had once laughed, and perhaps cried, within feet of where he was now standing. He imagined her as she passed her months here, through rain and shine, the days and the nights. It was from this house, he thought, that she had disappeared on her mysterious and final errand. And it was to this house that she never returned.

He spotted the remains of the iron trellis that had once supported a vine and, on a long-gone afternoon, had supplied the background for a photograph of three people, one of whom was Apollonia. There could be no mistaking its unusual design, but the metal was now so corroded that a piece of it crumbled into rusty dust in Jonathan's hand. He tried to position himself in what he felt would have been the exact spot as Apollonia, almost as if to absorb some latent trace of her life force by standing on ground upon which she had stood.

But he felt no such force, and the absurdity of the effort darkened his already sagging spirits. He had, until this moment, nothing more than her photograph and his dreamy visions by which to feel any connection with her. In those images, her youth and beauty remained evident, but the dilapidated condition of Riverdale provided a rude awakening. Its decline reminded him mercilessly of the relentless march of time that had proceeded between her era and his. It forced him to recognize the idiotic futility of his feelings for her—feelings that, by now, he had no choice but to recognize as nascent love.

What a travesty, he thought. The sensation caused by his dissolving illusions was desolate and frightening. He wanted to be away from this funereal ghost of a house. He rushed through the weeds and brush toward the gate but tripped on the tendril of a vine, falling onto the moist humus below. He began to rise, resting his hand upon something solid. He lifted it from its long-concealed grave beneath the leaves.

It was a sizable piece of marble, almost too big for Jonathan to hold. It had once been the head of a statue, cracked and yellowed now but still revealing the quality of its workmanship. The face was childlike, with long curly locks and full cheeks—perhaps that of a cherub or angel. Like Hamlet with his skull, Jonathan held the head before him and looked into its eyes.

He thought of how Apollonia had probably once gazed into that very face, but it was then bright and new, still attached to a body that had form and substance, just as she herself had been vital and alive and whole. Now the angelic head was nothing more than a useless piece of refuse, just as Apollonia was nothing more than dust.

Jonathan cursed loudly in God's name and hurled the relic through one of the gaping windows of Riverdale's skeleton. Even before it landed inside and clattered across the floor, he knew that the curse was meant for himself.

Winter arrived in the last week of November, casting its shadow on the city. The snow was light but steady, the cold painfully penetrating.

Jonathan did his work at the shop diligently, if somewhat absentmindedly. He went out seldom, although he had Thanksgiving dinner with Dave and Tess and their two children, eating his first full meal in days, watching the Detroit Lions narrowly defeat the Green Bay Packers, and believing that he had successfully concealed from them the strange nature of what he was feeling.

Part of him longed to use the word love to describe his connection to the ghostly Apollonia. He had experienced love before and knew only too well what it was like. That voice rejected as inadequate such words as "infatuation" and "obsession." What else could this be but love?

Another voice within him mocked the very idea. That part of him knew that the other was desperate for validation, and it strove to crush the effort. What could be more invalid, this voice demanded, than infatuation, obsession—love, for God's sake!—for someone who was no more than a faded memory?

His visit to Riverdale had convinced him of what he already sensed but had refused to admit—that his feelings for Apollonia amounted to an impossible and aberrant anomaly, caused, no doubt, by the intense changes he had recently undergone. He understood that her image had become a bizarre icon for some deep inner need.

It was undeniable that he was lonely, that Rachel's rejection had left him bereft and empty. He longed for closeness, specifically for the closeness of a lover. He also considered that his attraction for her image might be connected to his growing sense of distance from his own time. He was realizing more than ever that he loathed the violence, the restlessness, the vulgarity of this time and yearned for the sense of purpose, the honor, and the grace of times gone by.

Was it not logical, he asked himself for the hundredth time, that his loneliness and alienation might be causing him to seek refuge in the supposed utopia of a distant era, a bucolic but imaginary retreat from his real existence? He tried to convince himself that Apollonia had become the symbol for that emotional shelter.

Still, one driving force resisted every attempt of his logic to put these thoughts into perspective—he could not free himself of his feelings for her.

He existed in a twilight state, trapped between day and night, between the cold rationality of logic and the warm succor of emotion. By the hard light of the sun, he realized what a fool he was; by the soft glow of the moon, he gloried in that very foolishness. The opening notes of a certain song would allow his affection for her to wash over him. The song's coda would bring the dull agony that his passion was—and would always remain—the ultimate form of unrequited love.

As these struggles waged war, one side slowly but surely began to prevail. Apollonia's photograph had been carefully removed from its album and placed in a pretty gold frame that now sat on a small table in Jonathan's parlor. He would gaze at it while he strummed his guitar—serenading her, if the intent of his heart were told—and imagined that her fair eyes followed him as he moved about the room.

Tess noticed the portrait one Saturday afternoon, when she came to deliver some papers for her husband and sat down with her cousin for an hour of coffee and conversation.

"Who is she?"

Jonathan hesitated in his reply and tried, at first, to downplay its significance. He passed it off as something he'd found in the store inventory, an antique portrait that enhanced the Victorian decor of the house.

Intuitive as a cat, Tess knew better. She pressed him.

Reluctant at first, he eventually surrendered to her queries, desperate as he was for someone with whom to share his secret. He poured his story out to her, omitting no detail, no matter how strange, softening no dimension of his feelings. He said that he had no idea why any of it was happening to him and that he had questioned his own sanity more than once.

Tess regarded him intently with her intelligent green eyes. "Don't say that," she said. "You're no crazier than I am. If you were, I'd know it. This is happening to you for a reason."

Her response caught him by surprise.

"I have no idea what the reason might be," she continued, "and I can't even imagine what it is, but I wouldn't dismiss it as nerves or depression. It seems more tangible. There are things we don't understand but which happen to us anyway, to some of us at least. Maybe you're one of those people. It could be a projection of something that's deep inside you, something that needs to get out, or it could be something that's happening independent of you—some kind of communication maybe. There are such things, Jon, as synchronicity, reincarnation, clairvoyance. I've seen them before."

"Come on, Tess. I'm not denying that those things might be possible, but happening to me? I've never had anything paranormal happen to me, never had anything close to what some people call a spiritual experience. I'm deaf, dumb, and blind to all of that."

"None of which means that something is not happening to you," she counter-thrust. "All I'm saying is not to be afraid of it. Try to look at it as a challenge—find out what's behind it. Once you understand it, I'm sure it won't trouble you nearly as much."

She was so casually confident with her version of things that Jonathan was unable to argue. When she was ready to leave, he gave her a long hug and thanked her.

Defiant of its futility, Jonathan went on with his search.

Hovering somewhere between excitement and self-contempt, he spent many spare hours walking through the snow to the library, the newspaper archives, and the historical society in pursuit of information—any little detail—that might shed light on her life. He found plentiful references to her uncle, his farm, and his lumber mill. Among other places, Timothy Foley merited a glowing biography in an old book on Saginaw history, where his portrait joined those of other "Pioneer Builders of the City." The man was regarded as one of the city's most prominent and prosperous founders, but in no account of his life did Jonathan uncover one sentence, even one word, relating to the youthful niece who had spent a small portion of her own life in his eminent house.

He called every Foley in the telephone book and discovered that none of them descended from Timothy. Not surprisingly, none had ever heard of anyone named Apollonia.

It appeared that Violet Hunter had been right. She was the only living soul who even knew of Apollonia's existence.

As November faded into December, the snow finally ceased. The cold remained, however, and the clouds left their lofty posts only on rare occasions. The deep, dark Michigan winter had set in, feeding on the icy breath of the northern lakes, and seemed quite content to stay.

This suited Jonathan. Despite the cold, he still took his solitary walks through unseen alleys and byways of the city. As he did, he found himself picturing the streets as they might have appeared a century ago or more. He could have sworn that on one or two occasions, when fog was obscuring the outlines, he had actually seen vestiges of the past. As he passed certain houses—unusual ones or those perched on corners—he could almost see these places in other times. He saw long-skirted mothers calling out to playful children on darkening summer evenings. He saw men in derbies and vests walking back home after long days at work, cigars clenched in their teeth, a beer or two deposited under their belts. Only at first did he dismiss these images as hallucinations.

He seldom went for several minutes without thinking of Apollonia. He pictured her in a thousand scenes, conversed intimately with her on a thousand subjects. He envisioned her with the golden light of autumn illuminating her equally golden hair, watched spring breezes ruffle her dresses. He imagined the pitch of her voice, the sensation of her breath on his face, the softness of her lips.

Thus deepened an already deep and dark December, as went the words to an old song that Jonathan had grown to like. Yuletide arrived amid an electric rainbow of lights that graced the old houses on Throop Street and wound around the conical forms of conifers. No tree graced the parlor of Jonathan's house, however, and only on Christmas Eve itself did a carol drift through its air.

He plucked the strings of his guitar in an approximate rendition of "Coventry Carol," its soothing, haunting melody a powerful echo of the past. He didn't know the words to the song, so he merely hummed, gazing at Apollonia's portrait all the while. He chose that song because Coventry was believed to be the English city from which Apollonia's father and uncle originally hailed. It was the only gift he could conceive of giving her.

The carol finished and the hour growing late, he put away the instrument, gave Pluto one last stroke, and picked up the portrait.

For the briefest of moments, he saw clearly. He had just serenaded a ghost—no, less than a ghost, because there was not even an ethereal dimension to Apollonia. She was an utter nonentity. For that moment, Jonathan believed that he might be going mad, but he managed to push the thought away, knowing that one look into those mystical eyes would cure him of any unwelcome illusions of reality.

"Merry Christmas," he said to her softly and took the picture upstairs.

Outside, the snow drifted. Winds howled against the narrow house like the restless souls of sailors lost in the gales of Lake Huron. Jonathan parted the curtains for a look at the street below. A single car braved the slippery street, its headlights illuminating a cascade of falling snowflakes.

He placed her portrait on the pillow next to him, kissed her through its glass, and turned out the light. Not bothering to remove his sweatshirt and jeans, he pulled the heavy quilt over his body. Weary from a long day of selling books and thinking about Apollonia, Jonathan fell quickly into a deep sleep.

At some point during the night, he began to dream.

He dreamed he was walking down a rutted dirt road, surrounded by dense foliage on both sides. The air was damp and pleasantly cool, like springtime. He sensed that he had been walking for a very long time and was growing tired. In the distance, he glimpsed something near the side of the road. As he drew closer, he realized that it was an old-fashioned coach or stage. It had left the road violently and lay on its side, one spoked wheel squeaking as it continued its futile spinning.

Jonathan began to run, fearing that someone might be hurt. When he came upon the coach, its door opened shakily, and a young man emerged into the light.

He wore an antique military uniform, deep blue in color, two vertical rows of brass buttons on the front of his officer's tunic, yellow stripes along the sides of the legs. There was a deep red stain on the man's chest, another on his leg.

He stood and straightened his rumpled uniform. He acted as if he were unhurt.

"Are you . . . ," Jonathan began.

The man turned to him, as if just now made aware of the dreamer's presence. It was like looking into a mirror. The uniformed stranger was, undeniably, Jonathan himself. The mutual and instant awareness of this fact stopped both men in their tracks.

There were subtle differences. His double had longer hair, cut in a fashion that Jonathan himself had never affected. His face featured a mustache and beard, which seemed to have only recently been allowed to grow, and was smeared with what looked like blood. He wore an expression of pride and hurt and an elusive trace of desperation—an expression Jonathan knew his own face had never borne.

Still, it was impossible to deny that the two men were the same.

His doppelgänger took a step closer to Jonathan and looked directly into his eyes. Jonathan, in turn, took his own step closer.

They did not speak. They regarded each other with mirrored faces of controlled surprise and open recognition. There might have been a trace of suppressed hostility in their gazes, but not to the degree that either acted upon it.

Jonathan's dream double at last took a step back. He turned to where the dirt track stretched away behind him but brought his gaze back to Jonathan. He still didn't speak but raised an eyebrow in a way that instantly communicated a question and expressed the expectation of an answer. Jonathan understood the question at once and replied in the same silent yet expressive manner the other had evinced.

Then it was gone. The dream dissolved, swept into the oblivious currents of his slumber.

With no waking awareness, Jonathan's hand reached to where Apollonia's portrait lay. He brought it close to his chest beneath the blanket and seemed to regain his restful sleep. Pluto snuggled closer to his master for warmth. Outside, the heedless snow continued its swirling, the lost sailors their sorrowful wailing.

INTERLUDE

January

A year, a number, a piece of time,

A distance in living, a state of mind,

Begins as a woman awaiting her lover,

Glowing and empty, foreseeing the cover

Of nightfallen white and crystalline hush

And wind-driven angels who come in a rush.

To begin, a confession: I am no poet.

I know this all too well, yet I insist upon writing poetry, or at least lines of lyrics which, in more adept and inspired hands, might have been poetry. It has not always been thus. If truth be told, although such lyrics have danced and bounced around in my head since my youth—not an amazing feat, considering how empty my poor head has always been!—I have not, until today, actually taken them to pen. Why I do so now I am not entirely sure, but I have always been given to trust impulse and instinct (as perhaps we shall see as this journal continues), and these are the forces which compel me. Put your poetry into words, these voices insist, and not only this, but begin a diary as well. I have always considered both arts rather quaint and prosaic—schoolgirl fancies, if you will—and I suppose they still are, and yet I am persuaded, indeed ordered, to practice them myself, and so here we find ourselves.

I caution you, however—whomever "you" might someday happen to be, even if only myself as an old and sentimental woman—that I am far from a prolific scribe. I shall compose these passages when I can, and thereby be done with them, much as we are done and finished with time itself once it has passed us by. (Or at least we so assume!)

I write these words upon the fifth day of the first month of the Year of Our Lord, 1864. It shall be, I am quite sure, an eventful, if not immemorial, year, and

I do not assert this without trepidation. There will surely be "trouble aplenty," as dear Jeremiah might be given to say, and yet I hope there will be something other than trouble as the year marches forward. I am young—my stars, not yet twenty-four!—and hope still springs strong and forcefully from the fountain of my heart. The trials which await me are great indeed, and quite impossible to forecast, but I shall face them and, with God's help, survive them. That is more than enough to hope for, I expect, yet I confess to being a greedy young woman. I yearn for more than survival.

My dreams hold out this greater promise to me in a way that is both taunting and intriguing. For in these dreams I have beheld a man from very far away, and he has beckoned to me. There is a great deal more to these visions of mine, these dreams of a beckoning fair stranger, yet I shall hold them close to my breast for the present. Is not a lady entitled to her own few secrets, even within the pages of her diary?

Of my past, I shall say very little, for there is very little to say. I have been privileged and pampered, and dearly loved, by parents who are as precious to me as the stars above. I have been well schooled in preparation for a womanhood that is expected to be as privileged and pampered, and as full of grace, as my girlhood has been. I am fluent not only in the science of managing a household and its staff but in proper form and all manner of social niceties. I am said to be uncommonly conversant in fine literature, as graceful as a swan at the waltz, and remarkably adroit at music. If you think me arrogant in this autobiography, I forgive you, as perhaps you shall forgive me if I confess that there runs through it more than a tiny stream of satire, and perhaps more than a little bitterness.

Enough of the past. Of my present, I have more to say, but alas, most of it is not the stuff of happy poetry.

I am, and have been for several months, far from my home. This breaks my heart and is wearing away at my spirit.

If truth be told, I am but a spoiled and delicate hothouse flower, a Southern exotic rudely transplanted into the harsh soil of an alien and hostile place, a Northern place, where winter rules with a bitter wrath. My life has not prepared me for such a season. A life spent in the temperate balm of Savannah provides no defense against the frozen wastes of this place known, curiously, as "the Saginaws." This winter shocks me in its ferocity and offends me with its stubborn persistence. These Northern skies are not skies of light, but of perpetual gloom, forever gray and melancholy, foreboding and threatening. The countless trees, bereft of their leaves, stand stark and bare against such skies, and the wicked sight of them fills me with a dread chill and shadows of death.

There is little grace here, and no elegance or beauty. Saginaw City is little more than a camp, boisterous and filthy. East Saginaw aspires to grander heights, but it, too, is crude and raw, a rude aspirant to a truly cosmopolitan locale. Most of the people I see are transient, not at all settled. They seldom smile as they scuttle about in the sawdust and snow. Their ranks are filled with money-grubbers and immigrants, hypocrites and ne'er-do-wells, opportunists and exploiters.

As I have written, it is a Northern place, the very image of a Northern place which I pictured in my mind when I was still in my beloved South. I could never be happy in such a place as this, although I confess to feeling like a villain for writing such words. My Uncle Timothy and Aunt Alexandra have done their best to make my "stay" a warm and loving one. Phineas is an eccentric but dear man, and Cousin Emily is precious. She tries so hard to be kind. There is such sweetness in her soul—such goodness that I can never know myself. I smile to them and strive to be gracious in their presence, all the while knowing the lies that have placed me in their lonely house by the forlorn river.

They fully believe everything I have told them, that I left Savannah last summer simply because my parents are apprehensive for my safety and welfare, fearful that the army of the Union would soon be descending into Georgia to plunder its crown jewel of Savannah, fair city of my birth.

I do not know whether that calamity will come to pass, but I do know my kin must continue to believe in my lies, for falsehood is integral to the task I am compelled to undertake. It is a necessity, for if my aunt and uncle knew the true reasons for making my perilous northward journey, that dreadful journey during which we had to cross the lines of hostile armies and maneuver around the places they had chosen to fight, they would throw me into the frozen snow this very minute and leave me there to die. Afterward, they would groan at my memory and refuse to speak my name.

Nor would I blame them for doing so.

Not long ago, I dared hope to be spared my task. I received news, and although the person who was the subject of that news would undoubtedly call it bad, to me it was the opposite. It was the first ray of hope I had been permitted to see in many weeks, yet it was soon dashed. Scarcely had I heard this news, new information was forthcoming concerning plans to resume that which had been interrupted. How easily the lamp of hope is lit, and how easily put out again.

I am so alone in this frozen land. I am so empty in my frozen heart. I do not wish to be here. I do not wish to do what I have to do.

Still, I must be honest with myself, if with nobody else. Sometimes I fear my despondency has naught to do with Michigan in the wintertime, nor the horrible, never-ending war, nor even with my solemn and cursed promise. I fear it is simply this: My life has not prepared me for happiness in this world.

JANUARY

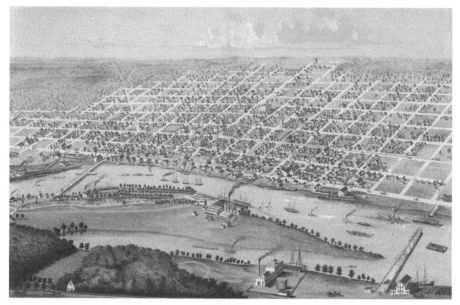

SAGINAW CITY

HE AWOKE TO THE CHIME OF A BELL, distant but clear. He felt something gently brush his cheek and, in the strange middling state between sleep and waking, half-dreamed that the caresses were the soft fingertips of Apollonia.

It was the cold that pulled Jonathan into full wakefulness. It was not mildly uncomfortable, as if a window had been left open, but penetrating, bone-chilling cold. When he opened his eyes, he felt the sting of the temperature on their surface. His breath extended in a long, vaporous plume.

He jerked to a sitting position and beheld the strangest scene of his life.

The caresses on his face had not been the hands of his phantom lover, but snowflakes. He was not in his comfortable bed on Throop Street, but outdoors, in a wide field of new snow, more of which was falling listlessly from a sky that resembled a white cotton canopy. The primal essence of winter—the fresh tang of the snow, the chill that made him pull his arms tightly around his chest, still clad in last night's sweatshirt—enveloped him. It was so real, so absolute, that Jonathan at first did not wonder about how he had gotten here.

He wondered soon enough. He found himself in an open expanse, bordered at a distance of about fifty yards by coniferous trees, tall and narrow, greenish-gray in their snowy coats. He didn't see another person nor hear a sound except for the bell.

His mind methodically considered the rational options.

Was he dreaming? No, the intensity of the cold, the bite of the snow on his underside, the taste of snowflakes on his tongue were not the flimsy fabric of dreams, but tactile, tangible realities. There was no need for him to pinch himself. The winter was taking care of that.

Had he gone mad? Had his obsession with Apollonia finally exacted its price and sent him plummeting into this extremely realistic mental break? No, he knew he wasn't hallucinating, nor was he even thinking irrationally. He had never been more sure of anything in his life.

Had he wandered in his sleep? Had he somehow risen during the night and walked far enough from the city to reach this unknown place? Considering that he was in open country, that would have to be at least fifteen or twenty miles, he estimated, a formidable hike in the best of conditions, let alone in a somnambulistic trance on a freezing night. It seemed impossible, but it was the only conclusion that the rational side of his mind would allow. The other choices were impossible, so sleepwalking it would have to be.

He understood, moreover, that the fact of his presence in this frozen field— clad only in light indoor clothing—necessitated something more immediately important than determining how he had put himself in this position. He would have to find shelter before he froze to death. He could tell by the state of his hands—no visible signs of frostbite and only faint numbness—that he could not have been lying here for very long. Either he had just recently completed his trance-driven stroll or . . . ultimately, he had no alternative explanation.

Putting aside his questions for later, he rose stiffly from the ground, brushed considerable snow from his clothes, and began walking in the foot-high drifts. He saw nothing but woods on all sides.

As he walked, he startled a snowshoe rabbit, barely distinguishable from the surrounding whiteness, which bounded with graceful leaps into the woods. Another sound of the bell, the same call to which he'd awakened, came from his left. It hailed from a considerable distance, but impossible for him to determine in the snow-filled air.

Before him, not visible until he was nearly there, the meadow dipped gently downward. A long slope stretched away from where he stood, the ground interrupted frequently with what appeared to be hundreds of tree stumps. He shambled downhill until the grade slowly rose to a gentle incline.

The rise revealed a sight that took Jonathan's breath away.

There was a city there, or a town, at a distance he estimated to be a mile. It was a place he did not recognize. He knew he had never seen this place, but something—the general lay of the land or perhaps the course of the river in the distance—was vaguely familiar.

From what he could see, the town was perhaps two miles long from left to right. He guessed that perhaps one hundred or a hundred and fifty buildings were in sight. There were many small log structures and some ordinary-looking houses with peaked roofs and wooden walls. A few larger buildings were clustered together in a central area. Few of them had more than four or five stories. From virtually every one a tall column of white smoke rose, either from brick chimneys or peaked metal smokestacks.

Even at this distance, Jonathan could see that there were horses—quite a few of them—scattered throughout the settlement, some of them pulling equipment, others tied before buildings.

No audible sound emanated from the place, but there was a scent that had managed to drift to where he stood. It was sweet and pungent alike, a blend of smoke from wood and coal, animals, and something that bore the essence of fresh pine resin.

He began walking toward the town, then stopped. He sat down in the snow with a dizzy feeling in his head, momentarily oblivious to the cold. He stared at the profile of the town, a brownish smudge against an opaque white landscape.

Already, Jonathan knew.

His senses and logic reeled against the knowledge—tried to force a thousand rational explanations into his mind, tried to reconcile, to justify, the irrational—but he knew. He could taste it in the air.

He did not yet accept that truth, but he would no longer try to deny it. He decided he would face it, vaguely aware that he really had no choice in the matter. He regained his feet and resumed his clumsy stride, now heading in the direction of the little city.

As he reached level ground, trees blocked his view of the place, but his inner compass told him where to go. Before long, he saw the profile of a narrow road and was soon upon it. The unbroken blanket of white told him that no one had traveled here since the snow started to fall.

Once on the road, it took him less than an hour to reach the outskirts.

The first building he came to was a log cabin, its crude roof adorned with a cross fashioned from two pieces of rough wood. Before the building stood a brass bell atop a wooden pole—perhaps the one that had wakened him. Smoke rose from its tiny chimney, and a man was standing by the door. He was tall and thin, mostly bald, and had a long, narrow nose. He was dressed in a black coat that came below his knees and was hugging himself against the cold.

He smiled at Jonathan as he approached and then beckoned him forward with a wave. Jonathan came closer and nodded at the man. The man, in turn, looked his visitor up and down, a little too closely for Jonathan's comfort, then spoke in a deep, soft voice.

"Welcome, friend. I see you come in a hurry. It must be the cold. It's warm inside. Go, find a chair." He held open the crude door.

Jonathan wanted to ask the man where he was, wanted to tell him that he had somehow lost himself, that he had awakened in a strange winter clearing, but the little building was indeed warm—blessedly warm, Jonathan thought—and he didn't pause to speak. He passed through the doorway and soon felt the heat radiate its way through the stiffened contours of his body.

It was coming from a tiny iron stove that sat squarely in the middle of an unadorned rectangular room. The room smelled strongly of burning wood, as well as the fresher scent of the pine logs of which the structure was made. A dozen simple chairs had been arranged in two rows, and a crude pulpit stood atop a small wooden stage. The only lighting came from two small glass windows.

Four of the chairs were occupied. On one of them sat a youngish man, thin and pale, with ragged clothing and a tattered overcoat. On another was an enormous brute of a man, bearded and thick-necked, wearing a heavy woolen shirt of red-and-black plaid. On the third chair, a woman, hawk-faced and rapier thin, her hair pulled back into a glossy bun. On the last sat an adolescent boy, squirming and impatient, perhaps the son of the angular woman.

As Jonathan entered, they stared at him, with gazes ranging from challenging to apprehensive and vaguely hostile. They scrutinized his running shoes, his blue jeans, his plain sweatshirt, and his wet, tousled air with something more than curiosity. Jonathan pretended to pay them no heed, taking an isolated chair near the stove and holding his hands toward it. In a few minutes, his fellow worshippers seemed to have forgotten him altogether.

The man Jonathan assumed to be the preacher came in at last, closing the door against the snow. He appraised his tiny congregation, sighed deeply as if disappointed at the poor turnout, and apparently decided that five was better than nothing. He began with a lengthy reading from Luke and passed gracefully into a short but fascinating sermon.

"Brothers and sister," he said, "in this time of strife and conflict, in these days of challenge, we stand in need of constant guidance. Let us pray to the Almighty for that guidance and for the strength all of us will need in the days ahead."

The worshippers, Jonathan included, bowed their heads in response to this invocation.

The preacher began again. "The Lord knows our winters are fierce out here in the Northwest, our food can be scarce, our labor plenty hard, but our lot is a blessed one when compared to that of our brave young men in Virginia and Tennessee. Try to imagine the winter they are having, brothers and sister, try to contemplate the perils they face daily, and when you do I know you'll want to join me in praying for their welfare and safety."

With every word the preacher spoke, Jonathan's suspicions as to time and place were being confirmed.

The congregation prayed in unison with their leader, reciting verses that sounded only vaguely familiar to Jonathan. The prayer completed, the preacher thanked his listeners and held out his hat. Each of them dropped a coin or two. He thanked them personally as they left—Fred, Josh, Lillian, and her apparent son, whose name was not spoken—and, standing in the open doorway, turned back to Jonathan.

Jonathan realized with a start that he had nothing in his pockets—no coins, no wallet, and no keys.

He shrugged his shoulders in a sign of helplessness, and the preacher smiled weakly in return.

"You're new around here, aren't you, son? I'm Reverend George Haxtun. Pleased to make your acquaintance." The reverend offered his hand in greeting.

"Jonathan Chase," he replied, shaking the hand firmly. "The pleasure is mine."

Jonathan didn't say more in terms of who he was or what his business entailed in whatever strange place this happened to be.

Reverend Haxtun stepped in on his own. "Where you from, Mr. Chase?"

Jonathan started again. The answer did not occur to him immediately.

He cleared his throat and made a considerable assumption. "I'm from here, you know...from Saginaw."

"No," the reverend smiled. "I mean, where'd you come *from*. Land's sake, hardly anybody actually *comes* from here."

"Oh," Jonathan replied. "Well, from out West. Denver."

"Ah yes," Haxtun said, smiling vaguely now. "I do believe I've heard of the place. Somewhere out in Kansas, isn't it?"

Jonathan was amazed at the man's obvious deficit in geography, but opted for politeness.

"That general direction."

"So you new in town?"

He felt guilty about it, but lied, realizing that the truth would hardly fit the situation.

"Been here a few months now."

"Yes, well, just about everybody's new in town, to one degree or the next. Where you staying, East Side or West?"

"On the West Side. Throop Street."

"Ah," the reverend said, looking vaguely curious again and perhaps a little uncomfortable. He suddenly clapped his hands against the cold and stepped back into the church. The wintry air had apparently exhausted his curiosity.

"Well, Mr. Chase, do remember that St. Agnes in the Wilderness is always open, whenever you might happen to need a helping hand, a warm cup of broth, or just a kind word. And I do look forward to seeing you on Sunday. In the meantime, I would wish you a very happy New Year, sir."

"And a happy New Year to you, Reverend..." He had already forgotten the man's name.

"Haxtun. George Haxtun. Nice to meet you."

The door of the little church closed softly, and Jonathan once more found himself alone in the snow. Despite the cold, he stayed by the church, pondering not so much his present situation but a rapidly growing sense of unease—perhaps even dread. The reverend had referred to "our boys in Virginia and Tennessee" and seemed to have barely heard of Denver. He had looked at Jonathan's sweat-shirt and jeans with raised eyebrows, as if the attire was utterly alien to him.

The worshippers in the rustic little chapel were just as perplexing. There was something odd about them. Their expressions seemed muted and somehow un-natural, as if their faces were slightly askew. There was a hardness in their eyes, a way of squinting that suggested deprivation and toil. And Jonathan had the uneasy feeling that he had appeared just as bizarre to them.

And the church—St. Agnes of the *Wilderness*?

Again, he applied what logic he could to the situation. The preacher seemed to have acknowledged that they were indeed in Saginaw, which provided him with at least one concrete fact.

In the next few minutes, as Jonathan resumed the road and headed toward town, he would encounter more facts, and all of them, in the direct language of lawyers, were incontrovertible.

As he walked, it felt as if he were in a somnambulistic trance. There was a dreamy surrealistic quality to the scene, but he experienced its sharp crystalline reality at the same time. He strode on pathways that were no more than frozen mud tracks, past snug-looking little houses—at first sparsely situated but growing steadily denser. He attracted the stares of men dressed in shapeless, long woolen coats over rough trousers and women in identical coverings under which appeared to be calico or gingham dresses. He saw, through tiny windows, glowing kerosene lamps and flickering candles.

Still, he wasn't sure—he didn't really believe—until he reached what ap-peared to be a main thoroughfare. The street was paved with worn wooden blocks, recently cleared of snow, and was closely bordered by neat rows of red brick or clapboard buildings and sidewalks made of wooden planks. Some of the buildings had evergreen wreaths tacked to their doors.

A handful of people, dressed like those he'd already seen, moved carefully along the slippery sidewalks. A dozen or so horses also were visible, some attached to wagons, others tied to hitching posts. For all its activity, the street was amaz-ingly quiet.

Without allowing himself time to hesitate, Jonathan opened the door to one of the buildings—the word "Emporium" was painted in circus letters across its façade—and stepped inside. The air was warm and smelled of coal smoke. The walls were lined with shelves reaching to the top of the tall ceiling. Each shelf was filled with items packaged in paper or tin.

A small man in an apron stood behind a counter and quickly turned to Jonathan. He had a large mustache and straight black hair, glossy with tonic, parted severely down the middle. He wore tiny gold spectacles at the tip of his nose.

"Help you, sir?" he inquired.

Jonathan could think of nothing to say to the man, but held up a finger, as if to signal that he was considering his purchase.

He stared at the labels of the items on the shelves. He recognized none of the brand names but did know some of the products—tobacco, corn starch, balsam, indigo dye, coffee, tea. Others, with names like tincture, liniment, plug, and horehound, were only vaguely familiar.

He also noticed a calendar behind the clerk, a large paper display illustrated with a romantic print of an attractive woman. Beneath her ample but graceful figure, the informational portion was turned to January.

On both sides of the month, in decorative and undeniable script, were numbers denoting the year: 1864.

After staring at the numerals for what seemed a long time, Jonathan reacted to the solid fact with a strange sort of calm. He did not gasp or tremble, nor jump to the conclusion that he was hallucinating.

At the same time, he was not yet entirely ready to accept it. At that moment, he made a very deliberate decision not to try to explain what was happening, nor to rationalize it in any way. He decided to approach it with as much logic and clear thinking as he could muster. He would start that process by observing this strange new world—or old world—he had somehow fallen into.

He left the store without saying a word to the befuddled clerk. For several hours—as the snow slackened and then quit, eventually allowing even a little muted sunlight to seep in between the clouds—he simply walked the streets. He felt the sting of the cold through his thin clothing, and on his fingers and ears, but paid it little heed. There was a growing hunger in his belly, which he likewise managed to ignore. He also disregarded the stares of the infrequent pedestrians he encountered.

What he saw along the street, whose name he soon learned was Michigan Avenue, and along several of its parallels was shocking for only a few minutes. The inexplicable impact and intractable strangeness of this place soon gave way to a numb fascination. Although his emotions remained deliberately and subconsciously muted, he was enjoying what he was seeing.

The world in which he had gone to sleep the night before had utterly vanished.

In its stead was a world Jonathan once believed to be entirely lost, a fading image from a forgotten time. For the most part, it was composed of small stores and shops and even smaller houses; of clattering wagons and steaming horses; of slushy streets and oaken barrels; of weak kerosene lamps inside buildings and flickering gaslights on iron posts outside; of people poised and dressed as in a Currier and Ives print.

Any number of signs and clues told him that he was in the same geographical place. The name "Saginaw City" was emblazoned on several buildings and what appeared to be a produce wagon. It was undeniable that he was still in Saginaw, on its West Side, to be specific, remembering that this part of town had once gone by that name. When his wanderings brought him close to the frozen river, he confirmed his relative position.

It was, to his stranger's eyes, an alien landscape. While it bore many of the physical trappings reflected in the twenty-first century's beliefs and clichés about the nineteenth, it also was exotic and enticing.

Like most people, Jonathan had viewed the past as old and dead, as flat and static as a faded photograph, which rendered it unreal. What he saw here, was experiencing with each step, was the opposite. This place—this time—was new, dynamic, real. It was living and breathing, rough and spontaneous, fragrant and malodorous, alternately still and noisy.

It was absolutely alive.

But Jonathan was freezing. The gradually failing light told him that the afternoon was growing long. The temperature steadily plummeted. His fascination notwithstanding, the practical needs of survival soon asserted themselves in Jonathan's mind. He began to seek shelter, acting in the sober, methodical manner he had planned. He surveyed several streets and buildings before he found a squat shed tucked away in what looked to be an alley.

It was a stable, its large wooden door secured by a mere metal hook, and he entered it quietly, wrinkling his nose at the strong smell within. The animals inside—five or six horses and two cows—stirred only momentarily at his arrival. One of them, a well-fed Holstein, was lying on her side in the deep straw and didn't seem to mind when this unfamiliar human nestled alongside her back. Jonathan covered himself with a blanket he found abandoned in the straw. It was smelly and filthy, but soon began drawing the animal's heat.

Sleep did not come immediately. Instead of surrendering to his fatigue, Jonathan relinquished his self-imposed ban on seeking an explanation. He tried to process as much of the hard data of his bizarre day as he could but invariably found himself thinking in circles.

First of all was the rock-solid fact of his physical presence in 1864. His mind reasoned that there must be a logical explanation—perhaps even a scientific explanation—for his slippage through well more than a century's worth of time, but he didn't have the tools to exploit that conclusion. He was far from a scientist or even a clever student of science. He knew little more than the barest terminology of physics and relativity. He'd heard time referred to as a separate dimension and had foggy memories of something the science fiction writers liked to call a space-time continuum. He had once read a theory that time did not move in a linear fashion, as most human beings perceive it, but was in fact a nonspatial dimension, which, under certain circumstances, could actually be traversed. In other words, the past, present, and future—and each of their infinite moments—were happening simultaneously, not sequentially or chronologically as was commonly understood.

The ramifications boggled Jonathan's mind, but he understood that none of his speculations was of any use and none of his dime-store scientific theories struck him as very credible.

He toyed with the nebulous notion that he might have somehow triggered the transition himself, through his steadily growing obsession with the past and his gradual but decisive disassociation with the present he had known. Already he supposed that his slippage—or whatever it was—might have been caused by something much more profound than molecules or speed or light or dimensions.

He wondered whether it had something to do with spirit. He considered the possibility that he had come here simply because he had wanted to, subconsciously willing himself out of his own time into another. Without a clue how, even without any conscious effort, he had somehow managed to cross a line that had always been considered absolute and inviolate.

But as the weak winter light faded, casting the stable in deeper shadow, Jonathan found himself doubting these theories as well. Such thinking amounted to mysticism, something he had always distrusted, even as he sensed that science had never had, and probably would never have, all the answers to existence.

His thinking had completed yet another circle.

His only resolution was to continue on his practical course. He could not hope to explain his presence in 1864, a time that existed more than a century before his own birth, but he was utterly powerless to deny it. He was definitely here, in living, breathing, physical form, and since he could not find a reason for his arrival, he had no idea how to plan for his return.

And even then, before he had finished his first day in his new-old time, Jonathan wasn't sure that he wanted to return.

His circular thoughts took their inevitable toll. Eventually, he slept. At some point during the night, he dreamed of a face he had seen in his visions before, but this time the features were sharper, the colors more vibrant and penetrating. He dreamed that he heard a voice, just above a whisper, calling to him.

If any fragment of that dream survived at his waking moment, it was instantly dissolved by something very cold, and very painful, at his neck.

Jonathan awoke with a start, the filthy blanket still covering him but the warmth-radiating cow no longer there. It took him only a moment to realize that the unpleasant sensation at his neck was coming from the tines of a pitchfork and one moment longer to discover that its long wooden handle was being wielded by a man.

As his vision cleared, he saw the figure through his own breath in the icy air—short, thin, dressed in what appeared to be worn overalls and a moth-eaten coat of some indeterminate cloth. The face, beneath a shapeless felt hat, was pale and gaunt, partially covered by a sparse beard. The eyes were filled with fear.

The figure managed, however, to find his tongue.

"What's your business here, mister?" he said, his voice high and tremulous.

"I...," Jonathan began.

"You're in my stable, mister, with no clear reason to be. Tell me your business." The pressure from the deadly points of the pitchfork increased slightly.

"I slept here so I wouldn't freeze to death," Jonathan replied. "That's my only business. I don't mean any harm..."

"That's called trespassing," the man said, a trace of confidence, perhaps of relief, entering his voice.

Jonathan was beginning to dislike the feeling of the prongs on his neck and of lying on his back in the straw, facing this man in a position of submission. He toyed with the idea of making a move for the pitchfork but decided against it. A man as nervous as this one was likely to be quick with his hands.

"I understand, sir," he said, trying to keep all tones of defiance out of his voice. "I happen to be without money and without a place to stay. It was awful cold last night. I came in here to stay warm. That's all there is to it."

The man looked to be at a loss for words, but he didn't lower the tool. He flinched when a voice came from behind him—a woman's voice—shrill and authoritative.

"Take the damn fork away from his neck, Jacob," the woman said in a tone that brooked no debate. "And take a look at the stranger. He's as skinny as a broomstick. You can see he ain't no threat."

The man obeyed at once, withdrawing the pitchfork but keeping it in an aggressive position. Jonathan immediately breathed easier. The woman appeared from behind the man's shoulder—she had apparently been listening at a safer distance—and stepped further into the stable. The first word that occurred to Jonathan when he saw her was "solid." She was big—a good six inches taller than the man—but not obese; merely solid. Her face was austere and largely expressionless, much like her hair, twisted into the painfully neat and compact bun that seemed so popular here. Hands on her ample hips, she stood over Jonathan and appraised him.

"Well," she said at last, "I 'spect you're getting weary of lying on your back like an ailing 'possum, stranger, so why don't you stand up and give us a decent prospect."

Jonathan rose slowly, his limbs sore from his makeshift bed and the merciless cold. He shook straw from his dirty clothing when he stood straight. The man took a step or two back, but kept his weapon at the ready.

"My, but you're a sight," the woman said, looking him up and down. Jonathan was suddenly aware of his appearance. He knew that his hair must be sticking out in lunatic angles and that his stubble had already gotten a good start.

"Where on earth did you come by such ungodly attire?" she asked.

Jonathan almost instinctively began thinking of a proper response, realizing that the only believable story under these circumstances would be a creative lie. He didn't know it at the moment, but this was soon to become a very frequent habit.

"I'm a sailor, ma'am," he said, unconsciously beginning to deepen his formalized manner of speaking that friends from his own time had regarded as archaic. "I've come in off a schooner on the bay, and I'm afraid I've had a stretch of bad luck of late."

"A schooner?" she repeated and then laughed a booming, mirth-filled guffaw. "Why, it's the heart of winter, stranger. The only way a schooner could come in off'n the bay at this time of year would be on a mighty big sled!"

Jonathan smiled in spite of the situation and tried to keep up the deception. "Yes, ma'am. You're right. My ship came to town in October. I've been here since then, did okay for a time, but I lost everything the past couple of weeks with gambling."

The woman grinned a little, displaying a new face that was far less daunting.

"Paying the devil's wages, eh?" she said and chuckled. "What's your name, stranger?"

"Chase, ma'am. Jonathan Chase." It was the first truth he had spoken.

"Well, Mr. Chase, I'm Marybelle Duncan. This here's my husband, Jacob." She looked at the thin man, still holding his pitchfork like a ceremonial spear.

"Jacob," she said with forced patience. "Put down that damn fork." He obeyed immediately, and she returned her gaze to Jonathan.

"I consider myself a good judge of character, Mr. Chase, and my impression of you is that you're more or less an honest man, fairly peaceful by nature, though perhaps not the smartest lion in the pride. Would you say that's a fair shot?"

He smiled again. "I'd say that's about right, ma'am."

She returned the smile. "Well, then, come on inside the house. I'll have breakfast on the table in no time at all."

The coffee she served was bitter and cloudy, and flecked with grounds, but it was very hot and tasted like heaven to Jonathan, who sat at a simple wooden table in Mr. and Mrs. Duncan's tiny, but warm, kitchen. Her eggs and bacon were even better.

Mr. Duncan had precious little to say in the course of the meal, his suspicions obviously not yet put to rest regarding the disheveled stranger who had appeared unannounced in his stable. Mrs. Duncan, on the other hand, was as curious as she was commanding and put Jonathan's practical dishonesties to an immediate and challenging test.

"How long you been a laker?" was her first question, uttered between bites of breakfast. It took Jonathan a few moments to grasp what she was talking about.

"Just one season," he began. "I'm not exactly an old salt."

"I'll say you're not," she boomed with yet another laugh, "since the lakes are all freshwater! Where's your home port?"

"We started in Duluth in August, hauling copper," he lied and, beginning to feel confident, made a stab at elaboration. "Put into Thunder Bay before we made the Soo, stopped at Mackinaw and Alpena, rounded Tawas Point, and then came into Bay City."

He was grateful for his lifelong fascination with maps; his ability to name ports on Lakes Superior and Huron was impressive even to himself.

"You did pretty good time," Mrs. Duncan replied. "So what's your hometown, Mr. Chase? I mean, before you signed on in Duluth."

He made an immediate decision to continue handling this inevitable question with half-truths, hoping that his memories of fifth-grade Colorado history hadn't all faded away.

"Colorado Territory," he replied. "Denver City."

She whistled long and low. "Glory be, now that's something, ain't it? I've never met a soul from Colorado. How about you, Jacob?"

Her husband looked up from his steaming tin cup. "Hell, Marybelle, I've never even heard of Colorado."

She waved him off with her hand. "It's a brand-new territory, way out West. Big tall mountains. Am I right, Mr. Chase?"

"That's right," he said. "President Lincoln made it a territory just three years ago."

"Gold rush country, as I understand it. 'Pikes Peak or Bust' and all that jingo."

"Yes, indeed."

Mrs. Duncan, obviously a woman who kept up with the news of the day, gave him a piercing stare. "So why is a young man like yourself wasting away out here in the woods of Michigan, when you could be making millions out in them goldfields?"

He smiled and poured himself another cup of coffee from a blue spatterware pot on top of an iron woodstove.

"It's not as easy as the newspapers would have you believe," he said. "A man needs considerable luck to find the right spot to dig, and if he wants to make the most of it, he'll have to find capital in order to make the mine productive. Most of the prospectors leave the fields poorer than when they came. Besides that, from what I've heard, most of the good strikes are already over."

He had no idea how much of what he was saying was true, but it sounded credible enough and Mrs. Duncan seemed satisfied with the answer. She immediately headed into practical territory.

"It occurs to me, Mr. Chase," she said, spooning more scrambled eggs from a skillet onto his plate, "that you're a man in a bad way at the moment, that is to say, you look like you could use a little silver in your pocket. It so happens we are in need of a hand. It's not a great deal of work—maybe three or four days—but if it's worth five dollars to you, we'd be much obliged. I've got a bunk in the scullery just there. You wouldn't have to spend your evenings with the livestock. What do you think, Jacob?"

Mr. Duncan put down his cup and took another long look at Jonathan. His eyes seemed to have lost some of their mistrust. He even made a feeble attempt at something other than a frown.

"That's a good notion, Marybelle," he said with the faintest hint of amity.

The deal was struck with no input whatsoever from Jonathan, who didn't mind at all.

Mrs. Duncan's three or four days of labor turned into twenty. The promised five dollars in wages turned into twenty-five—a fairly substantial sum in 1864, Jonathan was soon to learn. And he earned every penny of it. The work was hard and steady and of a sort he had never done.

The Duncans made their living with their modest stable, renting out their horses by the day or week to anyone in the vicinity who happened to need a mount or draft animal. Two of their geldings were big Clydesdales, perfect for hauling heavily laden wagons. They were frequently in demand, even in winter, when customers often used them to pull sleighs—a common mode of transport in this deep-frozen valley. The others, intended for light hauling or riding, saw less regular use. The two Holsteins were there for sustenance alone. Mrs. Duncan milked both daily, and her cheese and butter were the richest, most delicious food Jonathan had ever consumed.

He needed the calories. He and Jacob spent at least ten hours a day in the frigid stable, sawing wood for new stalls, shoveling out amazing quantities of accumulated dung, hauling hay from a nearby stack into the loft. They also repaired the Duncans' solitary wagon, a claptrap affair used for hauling supplies. Jonathan lifted one detached wheel, while Jacob clumsily worked to repair the iron rim, and learned in the process how astonishingly heavy hickory could be.

Jacob wasn't much of a talker, but on occasion he would open up to Jonathan, who was eager to learn about this strange new environment. Apparently, "the Saginaws," as the two cities were collectively called, were growing quickly, much too quickly for Jacob's tastes. The lumber trade was booming, with new sawmills seemingly opening up by the week.

The lumberjacks came in droves during the warm season, spending most of the summer in town, Jacob said, where they worked in the mills, shipyards, or cooperages, where barrels were made.

In the cold season, they headed up North by the thousands—"like the Hebrews of yore on exodus," as Jacob phrased it—bound for the woods. They would cut through the winter, when the snowpack made it easy to pull logs down to the "rollways," steep hills adjacent to rivers. In spring, when the rivers thawed, the logs were rolled down the hills, then floated by the millions into the Saginaws. The greatest daredevils of all the shanty boys in the winter camps were the "river hogs," men who physically rode on logs, using long pikes to clear jams and keep the precious lumber moving down the river. Near town, the massive logs would be gathered in booming grounds, where they were separated by brands denoting their owners—remarkably similar to cattle out West—tethered to rafts, and floated farther downstream. Once they reached their owners' sawmills, the logs were pulled from the water and set out to dry, and by early summer the lumber would be ready for finishing.

The winters in the Saginaw Valley were usually comparatively quiet for this reason, Jacob explained, but the jacks would all be back by spring, with plenty of money in their pockets, which meant plenty of drinking, whoring, gambling, and brawling.

"When the mills are going strong in the summertime," Jacob said one morning, "the sawdust is so thick in the air you can hardly take a breath. And come Saturday nights, East Saginaw is fit to be tied. You'd think the town was filled with howling banshees the way those jacks and shanty boys carry on. Speaking strictly for myself, I always look forward to fall when the jackasses head back to the woods."

On the other hand, the Duncans also harbored resentment toward a relatively new class of people they sneeringly referred to as "the gentry." As West Siders, they invariably associated these folk with "the other side," or East Saginaw, which most Saginaw City residents saw as an elitist, pompous place, worthy of the fiercest detestation. The gentry, Jonathan learned, were the owners of sawmills, shipping lines, or shipbuilding concerns—the well-capitalized profiteers of the burgeoning lumber industry and its spin-offs. They were still a small faction but obviously growing.

"They wear silk and satin," Mrs. Duncan sniffed over a splendid dinner of ham and potatoes. "They stay at the hoity-toity Bancroft on the other side, then build their own fine houses. They look down their noses at working folk like ourselves. One would think they'd melt like beeswax if they had to get their fine shoes muddy."

The city seemed to have little interest in anything beyond lumber, and Jonathan was amazed at how little attention was being paid to the war. The local newspapers carried occasional dispatches from the front, but the news seemed scant and distant. He read that Union and Confederate forces were in winter camp and that most engagements were limited skirmishes, but he also detected that Saginaw County was still a relative frontier in this time. It was busy with the never-ending streams of lumber that floated down the rivers from the north and obsessed with the prospect of quick profits. Places like Virginia and Tennessee seemed a very long way away. Most of the locals he met considered issues like union and slavery other people's problems.

That didn't exempt them, of course. The Saginaws, like every Northern city, had been compelled to do their part. Jonathan learned that Saginaw City and East Saginaw had already organized several of their own contingents, including the Twenty-Third Michigan Infantry, which had been in battle for two years, and the Twenty-Ninth Michigan Infantry, which was just getting organized now.

Mrs. Duncan was characteristically outspoken and opinionated on the subject.

"Damn fool thing, this whole war anyway," she told Jonathan one evening. "Think of all the fine boys who've been killed. Why, Sophie Jenkins, the laundry-woman from just down the road, lost her son last summer, in a place called Gettysburg. I knew him. He was a gangly, skinny, freckle-faced whelp, but a fine boy for all that. He didn't deserve to die in some godforsaken cornfield in Pennsylvania, that's for certain. I think of all those young men whose killing is yet to come. And for what? To free the darkies? Well, any fool knows that the South would have had to give up slavery sooner or later in any case. The world is a-changing fast, and Dixie ain't no different."

She sighed as she expertly navigated a paring knife through apples. "It's all just so sad, Mr. Chase," she said, and Jonathan saw a look on her face he'd never seen before.

He was grateful that she didn't ask him why he wasn't in the army himself. He hadn't yet devised a lie to explain that.

He saw his first soldiers on a Saturday morning, when he accompanied Jacob to East Saginaw. They walked across the frozen river in a light snow, with Jacob explaining that had it been summer they would have taken a rope ferry. Next summer, though, would be different. He pointed to a series of timber pilings that extended about a third of the distance across the river. It was hoped that the Genesee Street Bridge—the first to span the river—would be complete by July.

Near the riverbank, perhaps a dozen soldiers were throwing snowballs at each other in front of a saloon. They were dressed in spotless deep blue uniforms, kepi caps with crossed rifle insignias, and powder blue overcoats with little capes on the back. They laughed and cursed as they dodged each other's missiles and nodded pleasantly to Jacob and Jonathan as they walked past. They were hardly more than boys.

"Fresh fish, biding their time, waiting to be shipped out," Jacob said knowingly. "I doubt they'll be laughing once they join up with Grant."

Jacob had unspecified tasks in East Saginaw. He implied that there were provisions he needed to purchase, but Jonathan suspected that these were alcoholic in nature. They separated on Genesee Street, and Jonathan took his first good look at the East Side.

In his own time, this district had been downtrodden and tired looking—clearly the more desperate side of town. Now it was the opposite. While Saginaw City, although considerably older, still looked the part of a fledgling lumber camp, East Saginaw had its eye on becoming a Victorian metropolis. The downtown buildings were considerably taller and more often made of brick than wood. Through some of the windows, Jonathan glimpsed such luxury items as crystal glassware and jewelry and clothing made for socializing, not working. Graceful wrought iron lampposts were placed at regular intervals on the neatly shoveled sidewalks. The streets were paved with the same wooden blocks as the business district on the West Side, but these thoroughfares were wider and considerably busier. Delivery wagons and solitary riders jostled alongside elegant carriages, some driven by well-dressed liverymen. The sidewalks bustled with an odd assortment of men and women in fashionable topcoats—apparently members of "the gentry"—and tough-looking bearded men in rough woolen clothes and stocking caps, apparently idle lumberjacks or millhands. Jonathan, concealing his twenty-first century attire beneath one of Jacob's ratty old coats, definitely seemed more a part of the latter group.

He walked through several of the streets, marveling at the huge, elaborate new houses that had been built on the periphery of downtown and admiring the understated luxury of the Bancroft Hotel.

He rested on a bench on busy Lapeer Avenue and took in the sights. He realized how easily he had acclimated to 1864 and how familiar—how right—it had almost immediately felt to him. He had hardly given a single thought to his own time. It struck him that he hadn't felt this good, this at home, in a very long while.

A clamor around the corner arrested his thoughts. He heard the robust cheer of men, followed by the strangely muted sound of gloved hands applauding. Rising to his feet, he turned down a nearby street and saw a small crowd in front of a towering flatiron building.

The building was crowned with a clock tower, extending well above its three stories, topped by a cupola that vaguely resembled an onion. At the apex was a bronze statue of a man, head held high, hand tucked into his coat in classic Napoleonic fashion. Just under the roofline was the massive clock, beneath which, in one of the tower's windows, the figure of a live man appeared. When his top hat and head emerged into the chilly air, another cheer went through the crowd.

"Good morning, gentlemen!" the man shouted in what sounded like a German accent. "Who would care for a vest today?"

As the crowd roared, Jonathan nudged the tall man next to him. "Who is that?"

The man looked at Jonathan with surprise. "Why, that's Little Jake Seligman, of course. He runs the store inside."

"What does he mean about the vest?"

The man impatiently grimaced. "Little Jake is fixing to throw out a few vests. Any man who catches one, and manages to bring it inside the store, will get himself a new suit of clothes—free of charge. Now let me be. He's getting ready to throw."

Little Jake proceeded to toss three black vests into the air. As they fluttered downward, the men jostled one another in an attempt to predict the garments' landing points. The tall man next to Jonathan elbowed him hard in the ribs, then shoved him rudely to the side. On the slippery wooden cobbles, Jonathan sprawled hard onto the street. When he tried to rise, he felt another man's knee in his back, forcing him once more to the ground. He managed to get up on his third try.

A few yards away, a throng of several men wrestled in a heap that reminded Jonathan of a rugby match. Somewhere amid their grunting and cursing, he heard the sound of fabric tearing.

"Another one! There!" came a shout to his right, and several men pointed to the last vest, drifting slowly to the ground. They positioned themselves beneath it, arms raised to the sky, when a gentle change in the wind sent the vest veering away from their grasping reach. The garment flew in the direction of Jonathan, now standing relatively alone. It dropped directly into his hands.

The group of men turned, eyes hungry with greed and sport, and headed for him.

Jonathan had never been an outstanding athlete, but two seasons of high school football had taught him a few things. He'd been a second-string defensive back, and his favorite challenge was anticipating the moves of a receiver or running back. He wasn't the best tackler, but he was very seldom juked by an offensive player. He used the same technique now, dodging first one, then two, then three of the scrambling men, their feet unsure on the slick pavers. He maneuvered himself through their hands to the ground-floor entrance of Little Jake's store and, then, with a motion a matador might admire, slipped through the door into the warmth of the building. The vest in his hands hadn't been touched.

Little Jake himself had arrived on the first floor by then, panting from a rapid descent down the tower stairs. He indeed was little—perhaps no more than five feet tall—but a striking figure nonetheless. He wore an immaculate pinstripe suit, girdled by a heavy gold watch chain. His full hair was snowy white, as was the large, perfectly combed mustache on his lip.

Three men stood before Jake—two bedraggled shanty boys, with the tattered remnants of vests in their hands, and Jonathan, whose vest was intact. Jake slapped each on the shoulder in turn.

He told a clerk to measure the two other men for their suits and then gave Jonathan a firm handshake. "You have your vest in one piece!" he exclaimed. "I've seen only one or two fellows do it. You must be as nimble as a rabbit. I think I'll give you something a little special, Mr...."

"Chase," he replied. "Jonathan Chase."

"Yes, indeed. A nice black three-piece would suit you just fine, I think. Of course, Mr. Chase, all I request in return is that when people ask about your fine new clothes, you tell them you received them from Little Jake's, the finest clothier in the whole peninsula, yes?"

"Yes, of course," Jonathan said with a smile. "I'll tell them just that. This sort of thing is good for business, I take it?"

Little Jake winked and spoke quietly, as a tailor unrolled his tape and began measuring Jonathan. He addressed him as if he realized that he was somehow different from the average lumberjack he resembled, as if he sensed a kindred spirit.

"This is a wild and wooly town, my friend, full of wild and wooly men," he said just above a whisper, his *w*'s coming out as sharp *v*'s. "When a businessman wishes to advertise his wares in such a place, he must do it in a spectacular way, in a way that is understood by the clientele. Otherwise, he'll be ignored."

Jonathan nodded, gave Little Jake his sincere thanks, and submitted to the tailor. He considered the day's good fortune a positive omen for his next task at hand.

Jonathan had been back in this time for nearly a month—if time, for him, could still be measured by such conventional means. He had quickly overcome whatever shock had occurred with his slip into the past and had adjusted to his new reality with remarkable speed and minimal psychic trauma. His policy of blindly accepting the undeniable, even without explanation, coupled with his sheer fascination at living in the past, had made the transition remarkably smooth.

In the midst of that, and in spite of the physical demands of the labor he had agreed to perform, Jonathan hadn't forgotten her.

Apollonia had been on his mind, even before his first encounter with 1864 humanity in the rustic St. Agnes of the Wilderness, and had seldom left it since.

He had worked to put the facts together. He knew from the date of the photograph he had owned in his former, future life that she had been in Saginaw in February of 1864—or, more accurately, was about to be. The photograph had been taken—was soon to be taken—at Wingfield's, an East Saginaw studio on Genesee Street. Jonathan had seen that studio just a week ago. His heart had nearly leaped into his mouth at the sight of the gilt-painted name on the window. The second photograph—the one with two unidentified men flanking Apollonia—had been taken at Riverdale on March 7, 1864.

February was just a few days away, he knew, and March 7 was only a few weeks after that. It was likely that Apollonia was already here, living at Riverdale, only a few miles to the west of his own humble abode with the Duncans.

The thought of his presence in this very time and place—the thought of her sheer proximity—was maddening. In his own time, she had been nothing more than a ghostly image on an ancient tintype. She had been real only in his dreams, an all-encompassing vision but ultimately futile and unattainable.

Now, whenever he walked on a street, he glanced at the women passing him by, wondering whether he'd see her as a living being.

His fascination for Apollonia had only grown more intense and obsessive. But now, with the thought of her so near, Jonathan's feelings were tempered by what he could not deny was a deep and troubling dread.

Now she was real—alive, breathing, physically within reach. What if he were to discover that she was attached to another man, someone whom nobody in Jonathan's own time knew anything about? What if she were to meet Jonathan and think nothing of him? What if, in real life, he were to see her and realize that his fantastical obsession wasn't strong enough to withstand her flesh-and-blood reality? And what was the dark and frightening secret to which Violet Hunter, granddaughter of Apollonia's cousin Emily, had alluded?

These thoughts troubled him as he labored alongside Jacob Duncan, but Jonathan knew that they would not be nearly enough to deter him from his course. During his entire stay with the Duncans, he had been planning for his encounter with her.

He'd asked several lumberjacks in town what they knew of Timothy Foley who lived at Riverdale. They all knew the name and uniformly spoke of him with respect. He was well known to them because of his sizable sawmill operation and banking grounds on the Tittabawassee. Several had worked for him and found him to be a fair employer and a "plain dealer," apparently a high compliment.

None of them, however, knew anything about a niece from Georgia who had come to stay with the prominent Timothy Foley. They knew about his daughter, Emily—one of the jacks called her a "fetching lass, by jimmy"—but nothing about his mysterious niece.

None of this swayed Jonathan. He intended to make Apollonia's acquaintance soon.

He was very pleased with the suit that Little Jake had made for him. As soon as the tailor was finished, Jonathan went to the East Side to pick it up and spent the princely sum of ten dollars purchasing accessories worthy of the attire. The finished ensemble—striped charcoal and black trousers, a vest and long frockcoat in midnight black, black felt top hat with a low crown, white shirt, scarlet cravat, overcoat, and plain gold pocket watch—made him into a new man.

When he walked back to the Duncans in his new apparel, the people on the street regarded him as a gentleman, men tipping their hats in his direction, women smiling and quickly looking modestly downward. The jacks and millhands stepped aside as he passed them on the slushy sidewalks.

Marybelle Duncan whistled long and low when he entered the house, openly admiring the man who had left a few hours earlier as a laborer in scarecrow's clothes and returned a fashionable dandy.

"Could it be that Mr. Chase has got a touch of courting on his mind?" she asked, adding her signature guffaw. Jonathan merely smiled in response.

With Apollonia never far from his mind, he made his move late one afternoon when there was no work to do at the stables. Wearing not his fine new suit but a strange combination of nineteenth- and twenty-first-century clothes, he borrowed one of the Duncans' horses, taking advantage of the sporadic riding lessons Jacob had been giving him.

It was the first sunny day Saginaw had seen in weeks, with bottle blue skies and glistening white snow blanketing the landscape, the snow crystals and frost shining like diamonds in the sun. The air was sharp and chilly but not freezing, and the streets in town had lost much of their ice.

He took his roan gelding out on State Road—the very same thoroughfare that in his own time was called State Street—and headed west, just as the huge orange sun was settling into the milky horizon. He rode for half an hour, through country that grew ever more isolated, before he came to the place he was seeking. He reined in his horse just outside the decorative wrought iron fence that surrounded Riverdale.

He drank in the sight of the estate he had visited not so long ago, when it was a sagging, derelict ruin. Before him now, Riverdale was resplendent, its arched windows and intricate carpenter's trim standing out in the sharp relief of the lengthening shadows. The house itself, its spotless white paint glowing coral in the sunset, seemed vast, much larger than the heap he had seen before. A brick drive led from the gate to the front of the house, where it swept past the front porch in a wide arc. A tall statue of an angel stood in the little circle formed by the drive, her soaring wings held high behind her robed back.

When he looked at the angel's childlike face, Jonathan realized that, in another time, he'd once held her marble head in his hand and, in rage and frustration, thrown it through one of the house's windows.

Sitting atop his mount here and now, with the angel in her full glory, Jonathan discovered that his rage and frustration no longer existed, nor had any reason to.

A piercing, lonely wail came from the thick woods on the far bank of the Tittabawassee, just west of Riverdale's grounds. Jonathan recognized it as the howl of a timber wolf—which, like panthers, had yet to be totally driven from the valley—and it was soon answered by two or three others. With the sun now below the horizon, they were gathering for their nocturnal hunt.

Their howls gave him a chill, and the wolves' unseen presence, even more than the humans and their habitations, reminded Jonathan of the strange place in time he occupied.

Nobody was visible on the grounds or in the house as he watched. But just before directing the gelding back onto the road, he saw movement in one of the second-story windows. A lace curtain stirred. Inside the window, on the sill, he glimpsed a brass chamber stick. It was removed by an unseen hand and then replaced on the sill, its flame now lit, a frail beacon against the winter twilight.

As the burning candle was placed in the window, Jonathan glimpsed the hand that put it there. It was long and delicate—the hand of a woman.

February

Descending through ever deepening days,
Of ice on the winds and fog on the bays,
Gray blankets drape trees standing lonely and bare,
With hungry black arms vainly hailing the air.
The depth of a darkness when life is away,
And hope is awaiting another day.

A bleak lyric, I admit, but a true reflection of where I find myself, and where my soul dwells, on this dark winter's day. There is a deathly stillness in the house, for Uncle Timothy is down at his office, still burdened with the unexpected departure of one of his most important clerks. Phineas has gone to town on some errand or another. Emily is at school, and Aunt Alexandra is working with the maid in the pantry.

I sit alone in the silence of my room, where the only sound is the scratching of my pen against this paper, occasionally joined by the writer's sigh. Outside my window, I see an everlasting pall of wintry gray. The trees are as bereft as I have striven to describe them, and the plain tombstones in the little cemetery across the road only add to the somber prospect. Such have been virtually all of the days since Christmas.

But do not grow impatient with me! I am laboring under the weight of melancholia, it is true—a case of the "bona fide blue devils," as Jeremiah would call them—but I am not without means of escape.

I have my dreams, for one thing, and these have never failed to captivate me. Many of them are of home, of course, but not long ago I dreamt that I was walking through a dense fog, searching for somebody whose name I was calling. I spoke the name many times, yet when I awoke I could not, for the life of me, remember whose name it was. It was frustrating, to be sure, but there was a hopeful, almost encouraging, quality to the dream, and it has stayed with me since.

I also have my memories, and these need not be of melancholy occasions. I choose, rather, to make them pleasant ones, sunny and warm, which, with their rich and comforting fabric, will suitably protect me from this lonely northern chill.

At this moment, I am remembering a spring afternoon long ago. I am but seven years old. The air is deliciously hot and damp, and there are distant clouds on the western horizon, heralds of a storm that is yet some hours away. I am alone, save for Rebecca, my gentle yet very agile mare, and we are traveling in a lazy and meandering way on the road that heads to town. Papa's indigo is coming in full, its foliage a vivid chartreuse green, still without signs of the beautiful little purple flowers.

Rebecca and I have nowhere particular to go, and there is not a soul about to see us. The slaves are all busy back at the house, and the overseer is nowhere to be seen. I take advantage of the luxury of privacy and ride Rebecca full astride, like Joan of Arc.

And why should I not, since there is no one to scold me that such a posture is most unladylike? I want so badly to tell them that nothing in the world looks quite so ridiculous and awkward as a woman riding sidesaddle, just as there is nothing quite so foolish as worrying over which fork to use for the salad and which for the entrée. My world is as stiff and formal as the starched shirts Papa wears to church on Sunday, filled as it is with manners and etiquette and rituals and silly proprieties. There are times, especially at dinner, when I simply want to scream and pull my hair and do something mad, perhaps throw a potato across the room. What marvelous fun it would be to see the expressions on Mother's and Papa's faces, not to mention how funny Sally would look when those big white eyes grew even bigger and she said something like, "Why, Miss Appy! Whatever on earth are you thinkin', throwing that there tater across the room like that?"

But today—thank God!—I am alone, far from the linen and silver, and dinner is already over and done with. There is only me, Rebecca, and the sweet nectar of the Georgian springtime. We travel, gently at first, past the rows of young indigo, and then, as we pass by the long stand of pines just beyond the property, we ride like the wind itself, for I can sense that Rebecca is simply itching to run at full gallop. She responds to my heels like a champion, and I can feel the sting of her long hairs on my face as she streaks onward. I raise my right hand, imagining the fearful sword that Joan of Arc wielded against her foes, and can almost feel the mighty thunder of her army behind me, their banners flying and horns blowing, their eyes shining with the certainty of righteous victory.

It is almost as if Rebecca and I are one, a Pegasus of speed and spirit, and it feels as if we can fly off together—just like that, lift from the ground and sail into those blue, blue skies. Beneath us, the plantation will grow smaller and smaller, and then Savannah itself, and then the whole state. We will be flying at last in a dome of stars, free from all the strife and hypocrisy and foolishness and evil of the world below, heading toward somewhere unknown, somewhere far, far away, yet good beyond our sweetest dreams.

Ah, but what a day, and what a daydream, that was! How sad it was that it had to end and that brave Rebecca and I never really lifted off the ground. Yet such is life. For every such daydream comes a nightmare, and for every such bucolic day as that comes such a bleak day as this.

And so I accompany the sound of my pen with yet another sigh, for you see that I have come back to the present time and place, once again in my room at Riverdale with the afternoon growing ever darker. I part the curtain and look outside—the river remains frozen and unmoving, the road desolate.

A week ago, I glimpsed a strange rider out on that road, and it was not a daydream. At first I thought it might be Archer's man, that wretched cretin with a heart of flint, but that was unlikely. He would never dare to show himself here at that time of day.

I thought also perchance he is a highwayman, furtive and dangerous, and then laughed at myself for thinking it. My stars! This is the most remote corner of the old Northwest Territory, not England of two hundred years ago.

But who could it be? It was growing dark, and I had only a moment to study him. The stranger wore a long coat and a low hat and had dark hair. He paused at the front of the drive and regarded the house. He stayed for but a minute or two and then reversed his direction, heading his mount back toward town.

He may simply have been deterred in his travel by the river, but I do not truly believe so. I believe he came here to look at the house; that in some unknown way, the sight of Riverdale was important to him. And more than this—there was something familiar about the stranger. Not familiar in the sense that I have actually seen him before, mind you, but in another sense, a sense that still eludes and distracts me, but not—I confess with a blush—in any unpleasant way.

FEBRUARY

EAST SAGINAW

RIVERDALE SAT UTTERLY ALONE, an isolated human outpost thrust amid pines and maples, between the ice-choked river and the now frozen fields. Beneath the silhouettes of a dozen towering trees, spared the ax only to grace the grounds, the domicile nestled itself against nature's pervasive breast like an orphan child might cling to an adopted mother. It occupied its shady corner of the primeval woods almost defiantly, seemingly oblivious to the fact that not another house stood for several miles in any direction to serve as its neighbor.

The house itself, its spacious grounds, and the surrounding acreage that Foley had laboriously cleared of trees and stumps in order to work the soil resembled precisely that which it was—a salient of human order in the midst of the perfect chaos of the wilderness. Riverdale was an incursion of civilization into a natural enclave that had survived for eons without any appreciable changes at man's hand. The Ojibwa, the Ottawa, and assorted other tribes who had so recently resided here, and whose hunting and migratory trails were still visible in some of the surviving stands of wood, had carved no more lasting mark upon this terrain than had the hare or the wildcat. Until the arrival of white men like Foley in the last few decades, the only force willing or able to alter the face of this land had been that of God, through floods, snows, and lightning.

One unfamiliar with the spirit and tenor of these times, as was Jonathan, might have found the very sight of Riverdale laughable, so glaring was its visual incongruity, so ostentatious its arrogance. Foley had cleared a full two acres for his lot, the majority of which had been neatly leveled and trimmed into a vast and lush lawn of emerald grass that flourished, at least during the warm months, beneath the shade of those venerable trees Foley had had the foresight to preserve.

Cutting through the expanse of the lawn were unnaturally straight sidewalks of neat, rectangular bricks. One stretched from the house's back porch all the way to the distant rear of the property, where a sizable stable and long red building, topped with a cupola that ran its entire length, had been built. Another skirted the periphery of the house itself, enclosing now dormant beds of ivy, lilac, and juniper that had been carefully planted close to the dwelling.

Yet another line originated at the ornately trimmed porch at the front of the house; it encircled a tall marble statue of a winged angel and then continued, arrow straight, to the front gate that opened on the earthen track of a course known as State Road. The gate, in turn, served as the visual apogee of a tall fence of heavy wrought iron, imposing with spikes yet delicate with artful swirls and bends, that girdled the entire lot.

The fence, which Jonathan would learn had been imported at great cost from Pennsylvania, managed to give the appearance of protecting the homestead's man-made serenity from the daunting wilderness that lay immediately beyond.

It resembled a fairy-tale palace, at least to Jonathan, now standing before Riverdale's gate on a cold and sunny Sunday morning. The house and grounds themselves were grand. The knowledge of who was living within turned it into something considerably greater than that.

He was dressed in his fine new suit, polished shoes, gold watch chain, and top hat. His overcoat wasn't nearly enough to protect him from the deadly February breeze that blew in from the north—and the attire might have been a bit too formal for the occasion—but Jonathan was out to make an impression.

He had seen the notice in a tiny office on Washington Street, an office that served as the East Saginaw agency for Timothy Foley. Foley based some of his clerks there, who, among other things, took care of his workforce—paying, hiring, and discharging jacks, pond workers, and shanty boys as circumstance, and the seasons, required. The posted notice was to the point: "Temporary bookkeeper needed for lumber firm, millpond & booming grounds operator, sawmill proprietor. Inquire within. T. Foley, Sag. Twshp."

Jonathan had hesitated before submitting his name. His work in his family's firm in Denver had certainly dealt with numbers, including occasional tallying of revenue and debt, as had his time at The Red Raven, but Jonathan wasn't sure he could actually tackle the job Foley was advertising, especially in this era when even the most basic adding machine was still distant decades in the future.

But he realized that he could not afford to miss the opportunity. He had spoken briefly to the businesslike agent, set an appointment for the coming Sunday, and went on his way.

And now Sunday had arrived.

He pulled the rope attached to a brass bell at the gate, sending a loud clang toward the house. In a few moments, the front door opened, and Jonathan was not surprised to see that Timothy Foley, Esq., had not personally come out to greet him. In his place came a tall, middle-aged woman, dressed in black-and-white maid's livery. She unfastened the gate, nodded when Jonathan announced his name and business, and bade him follow her into the house. He tied the Duncans' mare to a stone hitching post behind the angel statue.

When he crossed the threshold, Jonathan's heart suspended itself. With a sensation in his chest of fear and excitement, as well as something less immediately obvious, he walked into a spacious foyer, its walls covered in patterned red satin. He gave the maid his hat and coat and followed her into a large study, just to the right of the foyer, passing nobody else on the way. The walls of the study were lined with books, most of them leather-bound with gilt lettering on their spines, positioned on bookshelves that towered at least nine feet toward the tall ceilings. A maritime portrait of a large schooner, sails billowing in a vigorous wind, dominated the space above a massive mahogany desk.

Behind that desk, in a commodious leather chair, sat Timothy Foley with the authority and self-confidence of a king upon his throne. He was tall and thin, dressed in a somber gray suit. His hair was gray, turning to white, worn long and wispy past the neck. A long and narrow beard provided a precise point to his already sharp chin.

When he rose to shake Jonathan's hand in a firm, masculine grip, Jonathan realized who Timothy Foley was—a strong, independent, probably stubborn man whose accumulated power and wealth were the inevitable results of those traits. Despite a certain patient sadness in his eyes—a subtle characteristic Jonathan had seen in the old tintype—Foley came across as straightforward and no-nonsense, and despite the fact that Jonathan's mind kept drifting toward a young woman who was probably somewhere within this very house, the lumber baron made a strong impression.

"Well, Mr. Chase," Foley said in an authoritative baritone, "tell me something of your qualifications for the posting." He motioned Jonathan into an empty chair and resumed his position in his own.

Jonathan provided a brief litany of semi-truths, including his coming from Colorado. In professional terms, he told Foley that he had handled the ship's books during his season aboard the fictitious lake freighter and in earlier years had kept accounts for an equally fictitious clothing store in Detroit.

"One of my more important bookkeepers left me in the fall," Foley replied, "in the apparent belief that he could make a better living during the cold season if he took up a saw and started taking down trees. I'm not altogether sure he isn't right, but the fact is that this man's work hasn't been touched since October. He handled accounts receivable and payable for my booming grounds. I presume you are familiar with the term, Mr. Chase?"

Foley raised a questioning eyebrow.

Jonathan had done enough of his lumber homework to field the query. "Yes, sir, the place where you sort out the logs by brand for the different lumbermen, yours included."

Foley nodded, apparently satisfied. "I would need you to bring those books up to date, to ensure that all bills are paid and that all money due us is duly and smartly received. What I mean by that, Mr. Chase, is that I would expect you to make personal inquiries in instances where such payments might prove difficult to collect."

"I understand completely, sir."

Foley rubbed his hands together, his mind apparently made up. "I would like everything neatly tied up before the rivers thaw. I expect the assignment will last three months. If it takes any longer than that, I will expect you to explain why that is. I will pay you two dollars a day and provide room and board. I have a bunkhouse out at the back of the property. My male domestic staff and indispensable winter office workers live there, as will you. My cooks prepare three meals per day for every man in my employ. Your office will be down by the river, in my main administrative building at the booming grounds. It's less than half a mile from the house."

With matters of business concluded in his usual methodical manner, Foley leaned back in his chair and gave Jonathan a look of finality.

"Does that mean I have the job?" Jonathan asked directly.

"Yes, it does," Foley replied with equal directness. "Can you be moved in and ready to work in two days?"

Jonathan assured him that he could.

The Duncans said they were sorry to see Jonathan go. He believed them but also knew that his work for them was virtually done and suspected that his salary and board were probably straining their already meager income. It was, in any case, an amicable parting. Marybelle provided a delicious going-away breakfast and a motherly hug. Jacob drove him to Riverdale in his wagon and gave him a handshake before heading back into town.

Now, as he unpacked his scant belongings into a small dresser adjacent to a simple metal-framed bed, Jonathan realized how rapidly he was integrating into this world.

He had been in 1864 for several weeks and found with the passage of each day that he thought less and less of the century from which he had come. Entire days came and went in which he concentrated solely on whatever tasks lay before him—and on Apollonia—and didn't think even once about his own time or the still unexplained manner in which he had been removed from it. He felt increasingly as if he had belonged here from the beginning, as if his slippage in time had actually been a correction, some mysterious means by which the scales of chronology had been set aright. His near acceptance of that notion—and his own adaptability—amazed him.

Not that he was entirely happy. His longing for Apollonia, and the unsettling lurking unease he felt at her proximity, made him profoundly anxious. She seldom left his thoughts for long. He sensed that his first encounter with her was near, and the imminence of that probability was the focus of his obsession.

He stood in a long, narrow room filled with at least a dozen plain beds identical to the one that had been assigned to him, each of which had a small pine dresser of three drawers to the side. The room was barracks-like, with plank floors and a bare timber ceiling. Two woodstoves provided heat. A space at one end of the building was used as a dining room, where meals would be brought thrice daily by the house staff. On the other end of the building was a small washroom with a pump. Behind the bunkhouse was an outhouse where other necessities were seen to.

The military atmosphere was enhanced by its orderliness and cleanliness and the gray woolen blankets that covered each neatly made bed. It was, Jonathan concluded, a spartan, largely cheerless place, but the long row of windows along the building's front—which provided a clear view of the main house perhaps fifty yards away—reminded him of why he had chosen to come here.

Dressed in his suit and overcoat, he walked to his office on his first morning at Riverdale, following a well-beaten trail through the snow. It was not a difficult walk despite a hovering cold mist. The office, on the upper floor of a makeshift wooden building hard by the edge of the frozen river, was manned by only two other workers—Hagenauer and Simmons—both about Jonathan's age. They greeted him with what sounded more like relief than cheer and immediately put him to work, piling onto his high clerical desk a formidable stack of ledgers, receipts, and correspondence.

Hagenauer gave Jonathan basic instructions on the firm's method of doing things and soon returned to his own stool and high desk, covered with its own accumulation of paper.

Jonathan lit a candle in the copper holder issued him and began trying to decipher the intricate, often elaborate handwriting he found on the receipts, bills of lading, letters, and bank drafts. He soon realized that the penmanship would be the most challenging aspect of the work. The accounts themselves would not prove terribly difficult, although the quantity of overdue work was considerable.

But the more the better, Jonathan thought to himself as he busily scratched his fountain pen across a bill. The more work he had here, the longer he could stay.

At noon, he accompanied Hagenauer and Simmons back to the bunkhouse for lunch, and there he met the men with whom he would be sharing quarters. In addition to his two fellow clerks, there was a sallow, balding, humorless-looking fellow in formal attire named Jarvis, who shook Jonathan's hand limply and announced himself as Riverdale's butler; a grizzled, toothless old man by the name of Hicks, the groundskeeper; a quiet, blue-eyed, bearded man of indeterminate age who went by the name of Rankin and apparently worked as a hunter.

"That venison stew you're eating there," Rankin said to Jonathan, pointing to his bowl, "is because of me. I keep the Foleys in meat come the wintertime."

Finally, there was Jeremiah.

He sat apart from the rest, at a far corner of the large, rough-hewn table in the dining room. He remained quiet, eating his stew slowly, as if savoring it. His face—of a deep, even brown—seemed almost youthful, but the tightly curled hair on his head was a snowy white.

Jonathan approached him as he had the rest, extending his hand, saying his name, and introducing himself as Foley's new bookkeeper. When he did so, the other men stopped eating and stared. Jeremiah himself looked up at Jonathan with wide, surprised eyes and took his hand for only a moment. He seemed very uncomfortable.

"I'm Jeremiah, Massa Chase," he said in a thick patois that spoke of someplace, and something, very distant. He nodded, as if there were nothing more to say.

On his way back to the office with the clerks, Hagenauer broke into laughter.

"Holy Jesse himself," he said, "I thought that old nigger was fixing to croak and fall over when you shook his hand like that, Chase."

Jonathan turned to the lanky clerk, genuinely confused. "What did I do?"

Hagenauer laughed again. "Lordy, you really are from the boondocks, aren't you? Don't you know that nigger's a slave? He isn't accustomed to white folks coming up and introducing themselves like that."

"A slave? In Michigan?" Jonathan asked, still honestly confused. He had forgotten something he had been told in another time.

"Why, yes, even here in Michigan," Hagenauer replied. "He could be free anytime he wanted to, I suppose, since slavery has never been accepted here. I hear tell there's some of those underground railroad folks still down in Battle Creek or thereabouts, and what with Lincoln's proclamation, I'm sure they'd be overjoyed to help him out. But old Jeremiah? No, sir. He's as loyal as an old hound dog to Miss Foley. He wouldn't leave her side if you put a gun to his head."

The light bulb finally went off in Jonathan's mind.

"You mean Mr. Foley's niece—the one from Georgia?"

"That's the one. She's some Southern belle, all right. Came all the way up here from Savannah, bringing her nigger in tow the whole way, like she was the

Queen of Prussia. Like she didn't know there was a war going on all around her. Must have been quite a sight to see."

When they returned to their office at the booming grounds, Hagenauer took Jonathan aside for a little advice. It might be better for everybody, he suggested, if Jonathan didn't get too friendly with the black man. It would likely make the other fellows uncomfortable.

Jonathan only nodded in response.

That night, however, back in the bunkhouse, he made a conscious choice to ignore the counsel. While Hagenauer, Simmons, and Rankin played poker at the table—using pine cones as tender—Jonathan dragged a chair next to Jeremiah's bunk, tucked tightly against a far wall, well away from the others. The slave, still dressed in his worn overalls over a patched red union suit, pulled himself up to a sitting position.

Speaking quietly and ignoring the stares he felt coming from the others, Jonathan addressed him directly. "I didn't mean to make you uncomfortable to-day," he said. "I've been told that it's not customary for a white man to introduce himself to..."

"A slave?" Jeremiah asked in his low, raspy voice. "No, Massa Chase, I reckon it's not custom, sure enough. But that's all right. You mean well, I can see that, so never you mind."

"Do you think it's okay if I speak to you now—I mean, if I speak to you on a regular basis? If you want to speak, that is..."

Jonathan realized how clumsy he sounded. He had never spoken to a man bound to servitude. The very idea repelled him, clashing with every notion of civil rights to which he had ever been exposed, but he could not deny the hard fact of Jeremiah's existence before him. He found himself fascinated to be talking with an actual slave, but he didn't quite know what to say. Nor could he deny his own selfish motives. He hadn't forgotten whose slave Jeremiah was.

Jeremiah smiled widely at his discomfort. "It don't bother me none if'n you speak to me, Massa Chase, so long as you ain't bothered by what the other white folks think."

He paused and gave Jonathan an appraising look.

"I hears tell you don't come from round here, that you come from out West," he said, even quieter than before. "Hope you don't mind me askin', Massa Chase, but just how far west is that?"

Jonathan laughed in spite of his efforts to be quiet. "Way out there, Jeremiah," he said. "Farther than you can even imagine."

His friendship with Jeremiah did not cause Jonathan any serious problems with his bunkmates and daytime colleagues, but he definitely sensed their result-ing coolness toward him. For several days, he was addressed only curtly in the office and not invited to join their evening card games, at which the men refreshed themselves with occasional shots of whiskey.

That was fine with Jonathan. He cultivated his friendship with the slave as far as circumstances permitted. At first, Jeremiah said very little about his own background—or that of the family he worked for—but as days passed, he took Jonathan increasingly into his confidence.

Jonathan learned that Jeremiah had belonged to the Southern Foley family since birth, "many, many years ago," he said, apparently uninterested in his own age. He had worked as a "house nigger" until he reached manhood, then spent a good many years in the fields, and more recently had been brought back into the house—"settin' up the fires, cleanin' up the pots and the pans, such work as that."

The Foleys' treatment of the black men, women, and children in Georgia, Jeremiah explained, rather evasively, was "better than some folks, not so good as others."

Jonathan also learned that Zachariah Foley—Apollonia's father—owned more than two hundred acres of fertile bottomland just west of Savannah. He had nearly one hundred slaves to his name and worked most of them on a vast plantation of indigo, a crop used to manufacture blue dye. The family lived in a massive house aptly named Bluefield—"a glorious palace," Jeremiah called it—and were counted among the region's most prominent and prosperous.

"At least things was that way before the war," Jeremiah qualified one snowy evening in the bunkhouse. "Now the slaves is getting restless. The white folks, too. They knows that the Northern men are comin' down there, getting a little bit closer ever' day. And they knows when that happens..."

He lowered his voice to a whisper and glanced at the other men in the room, each of them reading silently by candlelight in their beds.

"They knows when that happens that things gonna be changing fast, Massa Chase. Things gonna turn mighty tricky for the white folks who keep slaves, once those Northern men get down there."

"And you'll be a free man," Jonathan added.

"Yes, sir, I suppose I will," he said with a serious nod. "And what will I do with myself, then?"

"You'd be *free*," Jonathan rejoined. "Free to do whatever you'd like. In fact, Jeremiah, you could do that now. Lincoln says you should be free, and you're way up North, hundreds of miles from the nearest slave state. You could just walk away, and nobody would ever be able to find you. You'd just have to wait till the war is over."

Jeremiah smiled, but his expression was worried. "Yes, Massa Chase, I suppose I could do just that. But I'm nothin' more than an old nigger, you see, who can't read a word, can't hardly count numbers, who ain't ever done anything more than pick crops and clean house. Who's gonna want such a man as that?"

He paused, the worried look fixed on his face. "Besides that, I've got a duty to Miss Appy. I gotta be there to help her out, you see. I've known that girl since she was in the crib. Was my own sister who nursed her when she was just a tiny thing. I couldn't just go off and leave her here all alone, so far away from home."

Jonathan was touched by the old man's affection for his charge, but the mention of Apollonia's name sharpened his inquisitive instincts. He seized the chance.

"Why is she up here, Jeremiah?"

The slave's eyes narrowed at this, regarding Jonathan with a look that betrayed his protectiveness.

"Massa Foley don't share such secrets with me, Massa Chase. I'm just doin' what I was told to do and that's to stay by Miss Appy's side no matter what happens, no matter where she goes to. But if'n you was to ask me, he sent her up here because he knows the end is comin' soon—this here war's gonna come marching right down Abercorn Street in Savannah soon enough—and he don't want his precious little girl to be around when that particular judgment day comes down. And the way I see it, he's a smart man."

After this conversation, Jonathan put his curiosity aside when talking with Jeremiah, fearful of making him suspicious. They found other things to talk about and occasional things to do; Jonathan even discovered that Jeremiah kept a guitar beneath his bunk and that he was quite a skillful picker. He played a quiet, melancholy sort of music on the instrument, strumming simple progressions with eerie echoes of the modern blues with which Jonathan was familiar. He hummed melodies above, below, and in between the chords, but never sang lyrics.

He let Jonathan try his hand on the guitar one afternoon when the sun made a rare winter appearance and it was almost warm. They sat near the back of the big house as Jonathan familiarized himself with the instrument's compact body and catgut strings.

The song that came to him was "Eleanor Rigby." Jonathan sang the lyrics as his hands found sure purchase on the strings. The plaintive melody sounded beautiful and haunting, almost baroque, on the archaic instrument.

"I've never heard such music, Massa Chase," a clearly pleased Jeremiah told him. "It sure is pretty the way you play it, but my Lord, it does make one sad to hear such a tune."

In the house behind them, where they couldn't see, a slender white hand quietly lowered a window sash and gently closed lace curtains.

It was Jarvis, the Foley's butler, who, on a dark, late Saturday afternoon, gave Jonathan the news he had been hoping for.

"Mr. Foley has instructed me to inform you," he said in a vague accent that always sounded to Jonathan like a deliberate affectation of sophistication, "that he has been pleased with your work in the booming grounds office."

The butler, attired in his usual black-and-white livery, raised an eyebrow at Jonathan, who lay atop his gray-blanketed bed.

"And he requests your presence at the family's table for dinner tonight."

Jonathan caught his breath, which seemed to have been abruptly halted, but managed somehow to speak. "He wants *me* to come to dinner?"

Jarvis gave a quick glance at the timbered ceiling of the bunkhouse, an imperious gesture.

"Yes, you, Mr. Chase. He occasionally asks members of the staff and crew to dine with the family. It's one of his customs. Dinner will be served precisely at seven and," he glanced at Jonathan's casual off-duty attire, "do dress properly for the occasion."

As Jarvis headed back to the house, Jonathan felt his pulse quicken and a nervous, queasy feeling enter his stomach. He was actually going to meet her. The sheer magnitude of that fact hadn't yet fully registered in his mind, but he was already reacting to it.

In his two weeks at Riverdale, he had not caught so much as a glimpse of Apollonia. His life in the quiet winter gloom by the river had already fashioned itself into a dull and predictable routine. He spent his daylight hours going over Foley's business papers and his evenings reading or having an occasional conversation with Jeremiah or Hagenauer. Apollonia had seldom left his thoughts during these methodical days, but she was safely ensconced inside the big house—a place where Jonathan had no proper business to be.

He began to dress, trying hard not to think of the imminent encounter. He had first seen her photograph in an ancient discarded family album, had grown obsessed with her based on something he saw, or sensed, in that picture, and now—in another circumstance, in another time—he was about to meet her face-to-face. The keen rhapsody this inspired in him was matched only by his terror of the prospect.

At seven o'clock, dressed in his one and only suit, Jonathan approached Riverdale's front entrance and rapped the heavy brass knocker. Jarvis opened the door, greeted him with only a nod, and showed him into the foyer. He bade him follow through Foley's study, past a spacious parlor, and into a large, exquisitely appointed dining room. The table was set in beautiful blue-and-white porcelain, silver, and linen. Candles in tall holders illuminated the table.

Timothy Foley, dressed in simple black, nodded as Jonathan entered the room, then rose to shake his hand. In his baritone, he introduced each of those assembled.

As he did so, Jonathan noticed with a start that Apollonia was not among the four persons seated at the table.

"My wife, Alexandra."

A slight but dignified, gray-haired woman, clad in crimson silk—still bearing clear traces of what must have once been considerable beauty—gently extended her hand for him to shake.

"My son, Phineas."

A dark-haired man of about thirty, clean-shaven and dressed in an ill-fitting gray tweed suit, rose from his chair and shook Jonathan's hand vigorously. Jonathan saw that his eyes were somewhat crossed and immediately remembered a nick-name—"Cross-eyed Phin"—that Violet Hunter had once mentioned.

"Pleased to make your acquaintance," Phineas said in a friendly, high-pitched voice.

"And my daughter, Emily," Foley said in a conclusive tone.

Emily, like her mother, held out a hand to Jonathan, who grasped it softly. She was extremely pretty, with large brown eyes and black hair tied into a long braid. As she gave Jonathan a shy, possibly coquettish glance, he realized that he had just shaken the hand of Violet Hunter's grandmother—the woman who had passed on the few surviving tales of Apollonia.

Foley, still standing, then announced his guest.

"This is Jonathan Chase. He is bringing our long-neglected accounts at the booming grounds up to date and, if I may take advantage of the occasion to say so, is doing a mighty fine job of it so far. He comes from Colorado Territory. Am I right, Mr. Chase?"

"Yes, sir," Jonathan replied. "Denver City."

"Well, then, let us commence," Foley said. As he and Jonathan took their seats, the door to the kitchen opened on cue, and a maid walked in with a tureen of steaming soup. She set the dish on a sideboard and paused beside it at attention.

Jonathan hoped he succeeded in hiding his disappointment at Apollonia's absence. He wanted desperately to ask where she was, why she wasn't at the table, but knew that the question would have been highly inappropriate.

In any case, his answer came quickly enough. Emily gave Jonathan a warm smile and began to speak, but Foley silenced her with a raised hand.

"Excuse me," he said to his family and guest and then directed a shout at the staircase that terminated in the large hall next to the dining room.

"Appy!" he boomed. "The meal is set!" He looked at his family with a slightly bemused grin on his usually sad features.

Jonathan's first glimpse of her in life came upon that staircase.

It seemed to him a frozen moment, in which the standard ticking of the clock had been replaced by an infinitely slower cadence. He felt dizzy, as if standing on the precipitous edge of someplace high and narrow, beautiful and treacherous all at once.

He heard her footfall at the top of the stairs and then saw the narrow outline of her shoe, a severe, high-laced affair of black leather, followed by the long hem of her dress. It's blue, he thought—midnight blue, so dark and somber and grave it might as well have been widow's black. The dress, like Emily's, was remarkably wide and full at its hem and painfully narrow at the waist.

As her figure descended, robed in a sea of indanthrone, he held his breath. He'd seen that very vision before, of course—the ghostly figure of Apollonia drifting dreamily down a staircase—in his dreams and in those vague but disturbing visions in lonely moments at the bookstore. The thought began to dawn on him that they must have been precognitive glimpses of a moment he was destined, only now, to witness. Either that or he was experiencing an event that had already taken place. The concept gave him a brief shudder.

In stark reality, Apollonia's entrance could not have lasted more than a few seconds, but to Jonathan the scene seemed to unfold with extravagant leisure, a living form of slow motion. He indulged in the sensation, paying no heed to whether he was staring impolitely.

She was glancing down at her shoes, demurely, with each step, an expression that momentarily concealed the eyes that had so captivated him in the photograph. But her face, her complexion, her lips, the gentle nape of her neck, swept enticingly by a few stray strands of golden hair—all this he saw, in vivid color and unmistakably in life, and all much more beautiful, far more striking, than his mere imagination or his troubling dreams had ever enabled him to envision.

He saw in profile the features of her face, so delicate, so finely wrought—so classical—that they seemed to have been etched with masterly skill in translucent shell, like the old cameos his grandmother used to keep hidden in a box. The nose was of an aristocratic length and form, turned up just slightly at the tip. The lips, untouched by any cosmetic, were childlike and full. Her skin was as smooth as lustrous marble, and nearly as pale, yet from beneath it emanated a soft glow, a subtle radiance that hinted at something—at health, perhaps, or youth or some untold secret. Her hair, tied up plainly atop her head, was the gentle color of honey, darker than blonde yet lighter than brown, like summer wheat.

He forced his eyes away from the image, casting his gaze down toward the blue willow china and glinting silver on the table. She cannot be that beautiful, he thought. It is impossible for anyone to be that beautiful.

He tried to focus on any imperfections he may have glimpsed. Surely something about her was less than splendid, and he imagined a single tooth out of place, a fullness to the cheek, an imperfect line to the eyebrow.

He pushed against the overwhelming effect her presence was having on him and cast aside the romantic notions and poetic imagery to which he had always been prey and now seemed more vulnerable than ever before. But he knew he was seeking to convince himself of a lie. He knew all too well how vain it would be to try to deny this woman's allure, her already powerful hold over him.

He kept his eyes lowered, hearing the rustle of her skirts as she approached the table and took her place behind the chair. When he looked up at last to behold the object of his dreams, he found her staring at him.

Apollonia's expression was formal, yet not arrogant. Her eyes spoke volumes as they gazed unblinking into his. They were the most beautiful eyes he'd ever seen. They were pretty in the conventional sense, but that described only a fraction of their power. They were blue, of a luminous medium shade that immediately brought to mind the fragile sparkle of blue topaz. There was intelligence within that crystalline blue, intelligence and quiet compassion, but there was also fire, a spark that contrasted with, yet seemed a part of, the inherent cool aloofness they projected. The cold fire, the brittle strength, of those eyes perplexed him.

"Miss Appy," Foley announced, his voice shattering Jonathan's thoughts. "I'd like to introduce you to our new bookkeeper, Mr. Chase. He's recently arrived from Colorado and is working on the accounts for the booming grounds. Mr. Chase, this is Miss Apollonia Foley, my niece, who comes from Georgia."

Unsure of himself, and equally unsure of the era's appropriate etiquette in such encounters, Jonathan rose from his seat and nodded his head and shoulders lightly, a subtle bow. He extended his hand and received hers in turn—its softness sending electric currents into his arm. He gazed into her riveting eyes for only a moment and then, with effort, focused on a necklace of transparent amber beads that glowed warmly against the deep blue of her dress.

"I'm pleased to make your acquaintance, Miss Foley," he said as formally as he could manage.

"Pleased, I'm sure," she immediately returned, sliding her words in an elegant Southern drawl, her voice as soft and languid as molasses on a summer's day in Dixie.

Dinner, Jonathan soon learned, was a highly ritual affair at Riverdale. After grace, which was recited by the family patriarch, the courses followed one another with precision—hearty, heavy dishes in the fashion of the times but excellently prepared.

The men at the table dominated the conversation.

There were a few questions about Jonathan's work with the books and his recent trips to town in order to collect payments past due. Then the elder Foley spoke of his high expectations for the "winter harvest," as he called the flurry of tree cutting that was presently going on in places with names like Clare, Hale, and Roscommon. He spoke of a potential twenty percent increase in profits over last year's cutting and expressed satisfaction that two new sawmills in Saginaw City would be up and running by the spring thaw.

Jonathan noted to himself that the lumber baron made no mention of the fact that his crews of shanty boys and jacks up North would be replacing hundreds of square miles of majestic virgin forests with barren, stump-dotted prairies in their ambitious wake. He said nothing about it, of course, fully aware that such ecological concerns were a good century away from being taken seriously by more than a few.

Foley's son, Phineas, with his strangely tremulous voice and distracting eyes, spoke at length about the watch business he had just recently established on LaPorte Street in East Saginaw. In the past few months, he had discovered a steady and growing demand for timepieces, including a surprising number of high-quality specimens. He reported a strong trade in watch repair and was thinking of moving into clocks. Jonathan wondered how adept at such precise work Phineas could actually be, considering the apparently skewed perspective of his vision.

Jonathan himself spoke very little, answering a cursory question or two about Colorado Territory. He was relieved that the other men were so eager to dominate the conversation. He was growing weary of the memory recall and creativity his recurring lies demanded.

The three Foley women said virtually nothing, each of them merely nodding or smiling in appropriate gestures of response to the men. Jonathan glanced at Apollonia only occasionally, and then very quickly, but each time he did he found her serious eyes looking back at him.

With the completion of dinner, the party disbanded. Mr. and Mrs. Foley, pleading a busy morrow, excused themselves and disappeared up the stairs. Phineas, glancing at his handsome gold watch, said it was late, time to ride back to the city, and with a firm handshake to Jonathan bid good night.

The three who remained—Jonathan, Apollonia, and Emily—accepted Emily's suggestion that they have port in the parlor before retiring. Jonathan felt the strange combination of joy and terror return to his chest.

They sat before a blazing fireplace, sipping their sweet wine for several minutes without speaking. Emily, at Jonathan's left, and Apollonia, on his right, both seemed hesitant and shy as they stared hypnotically into the flames. At last, the silence became overbearing for him. He pushed away his nervousness.

"I find myself amazed at this place called Michigan," he said, cursing himself for sounding idiotic.

"Oh?" Emily immediately replied, edging closer in his direction. "In what way, Mr. Chase?"

"All this activity, this hustle and bustle. The way the forests are being turned into lumber, the way the city is growing so quickly."

Emily smiled sweetly. "It's an exciting place, isn't it? One sees progress everywhere."

Apollonia sighed and spoke at last, her quiet, elegant voice contrasting sharply with Emily's girlish pitch.

"One sees snow and sawdust everywhere, Emily. You know that. It's like living in Siberia."

She leaned forward, giving her cousin a pretty smile, as if to let her know that she wasn't being entirely serious. As she leaned back, she looked directly into Jonathan's face, holding her smile and raising one eyebrow.

He took the cue. "I take it you're not terribly fond of the Saginaws, Miss Foley," he said.

"I confess that I am not, Mr. Chase, although my relatives are the loveliest people on earth. My tastes are what they are, created and cultivated in a faraway place that's vastly different from this."

She forsook her smile and replaced it with a serious expression that bore traces of both deep intelligence and queenly privilege.

"But my preferences are a tiresome subject. We hardly know anything about you, Mr. Chase. Tell us what brings a man from the distant West to such a place as Michigan."

He strove to answer her questions with as much honesty as he could, which meant that he tried to say as little as possible.

"I'm a traveler," he replied. "That's all."

"Of course you are," Apollonia returned, apparently undisturbed by the brevity of his response. "Any fool can see just by looking at you that you are no more from these parts than I am. It is as plain as day."

"You're an observant woman."

"I am, Mr. Chase. I am indeed."

Emily quickly finished her port and rose. Despite her smile, her dark eyes bore the faintest trace of anger as she said good night. It seemed to Jonathan that she had sensed Apollonia subtly but firmly taking control of the conversation and that this was something she had previously experienced.

After gently kissing her cousin on the cheek, Apollonia sat back against the green velvet of her chair and tilted her head slightly, appraising Jonathan with the piercing blue of her eyes. He thought he saw cautious skepticism in the trace of a smile she bore.

"Well, then," she began, somehow narrowing the gap between them, "tell me something about Denver City. I have heard it called an absolutely beastly place."

He was relieved that she was steering the subject into a safer zone, yet vaguely unsettled by the thought that she was doing so intentionally—that she was merely deferring her true curiosities.

"I don't know that I would consider it beastly," he said, trying to sound slightly defensive, "although it can be a little rough. It's full of miners, of course, and such folk as mule skinners and cattle drivers. They tend not to be genteel, it's true, but one grows accustomed to their ways."

"Aren't they terrible drinkers and brawlers, those men, rather like the lumberjacks in these parts?"

"Some of them. It's best not to go into certain parts of town at certain times of night. One could be shot or stabbed for absolutely no good reason. But there are plenty of nice folk, too. Churchgoing, clean-living, honest people, if you catch my drift."

She raised her eyebrows in honest puzzlement. "Catch your drift, Mr. Chase? I beg your pardon."

Once again, he felt like an idiot. "An old sailor's expression," he said with a laugh that he hoped sounded casual. "It means, 'if you understand me.'"

"I see," she drawled, the cautious skepticism back in her eyes.

"And what of the war? I do not believe I have heard anything of the position that Colorado has taken."

Jonathan squirmed in his chair, again silently trying to recall his primary-school history lessons.

"Well, officially, Colorado's gone for the Union, of course," he half-guessed. "Not that it would mean a great deal to President Lincoln at this point."

Her eyes sharpened. "What do you mean?"

"The Rocky Mountains are an awfully long way from the fighting, Miss Foley. And I have serious doubts that most people out there would relish the notion of traveling back East to die in a fight that is of very little concern to them. It really isn't our fight, you know. What does slavery have to do with Colorado?"

"I suppose that's true," she said quietly, casting her gaze beyond the tall arched windows to the black night outside. "It is a very fortunate thing—a luxury, really—for you Westerners, not to have to concern yourselves with such matters. It is a terrible calamity, this war. An absolutely beastly thing."

"I couldn't agree with you more."

She rose from the chair and approached the window, parting the lace curtain to get a better look at the nocturnal winter landscape. "Where do you stand on the war, Mr. Chase? You are a Westerner. Is the whole thing of very little concern to you?"

"In fact, it concerns me very much, Miss Foley."

She returned her gaze to him, sharp interest back in her eyes. "Do tell," she pleaded.

He was getting slowly better at Victorian mannerisms, more adept at adopting the starchy, painfully polite ways of these people, and he tried to put this skill to use.

"Well, I beg your pardon, ma'am, because I realize you're a Southerner and all, but I have to say that I support the Union."

"Indeed?" She had retaken her chair. "Yet you do not serve in Mr. Lincoln's army."

It was the difficult question he had until now escaped being asked, and he realized that he had no answer for it.

"So far," he offered, "my circumstances have not been conducive to military service."

"I see," she said, again in straightforward acceptance of an evasive answer. "And is your support for this war grounded in your belief in preserving the union or in the abolition of slavery?"

He was distracted by her sheer beauty as she sat across from him. The powerful blend of wisdom and innocence in her eyes transfixed him as he struggled for words.

"Both," he said at last. "The union is very important, but I also believe in emancipation. To put it simply, I think that slavery is wrong—terribly wrong. It is an institution whose time has come."

"Indeed?" she said again. She lifted her chin slightly, sighed, and placed her hands primly in her lap. "Well, Mr. Chase, at least you are safely in the majority in these parts."

She leaned back and yawned, covering her mouth with a delicate motion of her hand. Jonathan presumed it was a polite signal and rose to leave.

Apollonia took his hand as he offered it, but this time her grip was considerably firmer and she didn't immediately let go.

"By the way, Mr. Chase, I heard you playing Jeremiah's guitar out back the other day. I must say you are adept at the instrument."

He blushed and thanked her.

"But the melody you were playing—I'm not familiar with it. A melancholy song."

"'Eleanor Rigby,'" he said, automatically improvising. "It's an old English sea chantey about loneliness."

She laughed freely, a sensual, womanly sound, and offered no explanation for her mirth.

"A sea chantey, you say. Well, my stars."

She smiled faintly and ironically as she released his hand, and he felt the warmth—and pain—of that smile in his very soul.

The metronomic drudgery of Jonathan's routine resumed after that one encounter with Apollonia, keeping pace with the uniformly gray, unfailingly deep-chilled surroundings. He longed for a chance to see her again, to hear the knowing depth of her laughter, to bathe in the mysterious light of her eyes, but opportunities did not present themselves. His days were spent poring over the steadily dwindling pile of paperwork at the booming grounds office; his nights spent reading or listening to Jeremiah's humming and strumming and inevitably retiring early in his narrow, solitary bed.

One day it snowed from dawn to dusk, dropping a thick powder on the already deep layer of snow on the ground. The sky cleared after dark, allowing a brilliant full moon to illuminate a magical winter landscape of frost-sparkled trees and glittering banks of undisturbed snow. Near midnight, unable to sleep, the moonlight drew Jonathan out of his bunk. Quietly, he wrapped himself in his overcoat, filled his newly acquired corncob pipe with tobacco—the occasional pipe had replaced his occasional habit of cigarettes that, he supposed, hadn't yet been invented—and stepped out into the night.

Through plumes of his own breath, he stared at the warm glow emanating from the rear windows of the big house and wondered what she might be doing at this hour—reading, he guessed, or running a brush through that honey hair, which must be amazingly long once released from the elaborate high style in which she kept it. No, he concluded. It was almost midnight. She was almost surely asleep.

His reverie was cut short by the sound of the bunkhouse's far door, which opened on the side of the building, and then the soft sound of legs cutting through the knee-deep snow. Instinctively—without really considering why he was doing it—Jonathan stepped a little closer to the wall, into a deep shadow.

It was Jeremiah. He was dressed in his woolen coat, a stocking cap, and heavy boots. Looking furtively right and left, but apparently not seeing Jonathan, he traversed the portion of the lawn between the bunkhouse and the stables. Quietly, he unbolted the big door and walked inside. Jonathan could hear the faint stirring of the horses within. A moment later, Jeremiah reemerged, holding one of Foley's stronger and faster mares by the reins. He led the horse to the side of the lot, where the tall wrought iron fence was interrupted by a seldom-used gate.

And then she appeared.

Distracted by Jeremiah, Jonathan hadn't heard her open the back door of the house and hadn't seen her moving wraithlike toward Jeremiah. She was dressed in a long, dark cloak, her head covered by a hood, hands protected in leather gloves. Although she glanced in Jonathan's direction—and in the moonlight he confirmed that the figure was indeed that of Apollonia—she did not see him in the shadow.

When she reached Jeremiah, the two spoke for a moment. Jeremiah seemed to be pleading with her intensely, although in a low whisper that Jonathan could not hear, and Apollonia repeatedly shook her head. Finally, Jeremiah, appearing resigned, nodded. He plodded back to the bunkhouse, following his own trail of footprints through the snow, and quietly closed the door behind him.

Apollonia did not hesitate. As soon as Jeremiah was gone, she placed a foot into the stirrup and with remarkable grace lifted herself into the saddle. Jonathan saw that she mounted the white mare the way a man does, with legs on either side of the horse's back, not in the traditional sidesaddle fashion of most women riders. He heard her quiet voice as she urged the mare through the gate, out into the unbroken whiteness of the field beyond.

Jonathan decided on the spot to follow her, not dwelling on his reasons for the sudden action nor giving himself time to talk himself out of it. He traced Jeremiah's path to the stable, released the door, and went inside. He chose a chestnut stallion, a horse that was aggressive to other riders but which, for reasons unknown, had taken to Jonathan on the occasional days when his work required him to ride into the city. He quickly saddled the animal and led him out the same gate through which Apollonia had disappeared just minutes before.

Her horse had left an obvious trail in the snow, even more sharply defined by the moonlight, and Jonathan hardly had to guide the stallion in the right direction. He rode slowly, deliberately not wanting to get so close that she might spot him. He crossed the road, already packed down by the wheels of carriages and wagons, and reentered unbroken snow on the other side. He rode up a gentle incline, soon coming to a lonely country cemetery surrounded by a short iron fence. The arches of the marble tombstones and the severe profiles of the crosses looked ghostly in the lunar glow, and Jonathan was glad when he left the graveyard behind.

The trail then wound through a dense pine wood, passing between trees so closely that Jonathan sometimes had to protect his face from the whipping boughs. Finally, he reached a clearing at the end of the wood.

There was a little settlement there, an assortment of wooden buildings, dominated by one long two-story frame structure with a waterwheel in the back, no doubt frozen in place since last fall. As he drew nearer, Jonathan made out the block letters painted on the front of the building: Shattuckville Mills. There was something vaguely familiar about the name. There seemed to be nobody about, and no lights were visible in any of the buildings.

Jonathan followed Apollonia's trail quietly, his horse's regular breathing revealed in the clouds that formed before his mouth in the frigid air.

From Shattuckville, she had set out eastward on what was clearly a road, a straight east-west track. It was only after a mile or so that Jonathan glimpsed a stone marker at a junction. It identified the thoroughfare as Shattuck Road. He remembered the name with a start. He had walked along this road in the not-too-distant past—and the very distant future. He remembered that his grandparents' house, in another century, would one day be built somewhere along its length. He had no way of telling where it would eventually be, since both sides of the path were heavily grown over with tall trees.

After riding for some twenty minutes, and as the trees once again grew sparse, he discovered where her trail had ended.

When he saw the house, set a little way back from the road, he recognized it immediately. He remembered its unadorned cracker-box shape, its ordinary peaked roof, its rectangular windows—remembered it in dreamy but photographic detail from his own childhood. He had glimpsed it from his bedroom window in the distance, wondered about it, grew fascinated with it, and later—as a man— had failed in his efforts to once more find it.

And here it was again—not yet a Gray House, but a perfectly white house that well matched the snow all around it. It stood just as Jonathan had remembered it, but all alone now, with not another house in sight.

Seeing the house gave him a chill. He felt a lump in his throat and moisture came to his eyes, forcing him to blink so it wouldn't freeze. He was remembering the house from his own past, which in turn was the distant future from his present perspective. He tried to grasp the meaning of this conundrum, tried to put into focus the reason for its importance to him. When he saw it as a child, did his fascination stem from the fact that he had been here before, long before the reach of his own memory at that moment, long before he could even have been aware of it? What message had he tried to send to himself through the veil of time?

What was so important that had happened here?

Or was about to happen?

The path of Apollonia's horse ended at the spot where the mare was now hitched to a post. Two other horses were tied alongside hers. There was light inside the house, although he could only see its yellow outlines on the borders of shades that had been drawn on all the windows.

He put aside his fears and dismounted the stallion, tying him to a bare oak some twenty yards from the others. He also put aside his conscience and whatever respect he might once have had for Apollonia's privacy. Her clandestine nocturnal ride to this forlorn spot gave him a sinister, dreadful feeling. He sensed that something was wrong, that she might be in need of help.

And so, stealing quietly through the snow, he made his way to a window at the side of the house and knelt down to peer within. Through the narrow opening at the edge of the shade, he gazed into a plainly furnished sitting room, illuminated solely by the flickering glow of a fire in the hearth. He saw Apollonia only partially, sitting on a cane-backed chair. She had removed her cloak and was attired in a simple, long black dress. She was rubbing her hands to warm them and speaking quietly to someone else in the room, a person he could not see.

He placed his ear against the frigid glass and was able to make out the faint sound of her voice and that of another person, clearly a man. He captured only broken pieces of what they were saying.

"The ice..."

"Has to be soon..."

"Cannot deviate..."

"You know there is no choice in the matter..."

Suddenly, Jonathan felt the press of cold metal against his temple.

He knew without looking that it was the barrel of a pistol, but he slowly turned his head regardless. As he did, the person holding the gun kept pace, dragging the barrel across his skin until it pressed directly against his forehead.

A tall man with long black hair was at the other end. He was dressed from head to toe in what appeared to be fringed buckskin. The subtle slant of his narrowed eyes and sharp angle of his cheekbones told Jonathan that the man was what people in 1864 called an Indian.

He spoke softly but deliberately.

"Very soon, stranger," he said, "you will regret that you have done this."

And then he cocked the trigger.

March

With blustery force and white ships at sail,

With wakening hope for darkness to fail,

Armies of time wage war in the skies

To crown light triumphant as winter dies.

A roar in the heavens gives voice to a fight

That rages on sky-seas of blue and white.

Change rides high on the winds today. I can feel its force and its pressure, just as the billowy clouds outside my window must feel the wind which pushes them to their unknown destinations and fates. Everything around me seems unsettled on such a day—the sky, the trees, my own life. I fear, naturally, that this impending change will be for the worse, but I am not yet so morose that I do not hope for betterment at the same time. I will be frank and admit that some of the changes which have ensued since I last took up this pen are hopeful ones.

In any case, there is a daring and restless side to my nature which welcomes change at any price, for I have never been fond of ennui, and this, for weeks on end, has been my lot. Life at Riverdale, at least for one who does not work or have a daily docket of tasks to perform, can be a monotonous and lonely prospect indeed.

My aunt and uncle are preoccupied with the considerable responsibilities of their lives, and I understand that they have little time for their spoiled niece. There are my cousins, of course, but I rarely see Phineas. He is a busy young man, ardent in his business ventures, and besides, when I do see him, it seems we have very little to talk about. He is a fine and decent person, but one, I fear, with whom I am forever destined to remain on strangers' terms.

Emily is a dear, of course, the brightest thing about my life here. I talk with her just about every night and take inspiration from the sheer energy of her spirit.

She is so young, so full of life and enthusiastic about all manner of things, but that is also to her detriment. For I am no longer as young as she. My stars, I am six years older! I am well beyond the coy intrigues and girlish coquetry that so prevail over her life, and I confess—cynical old maid that I am!—that I sometimes grow weary of all her gushing and blushing.

And whom do I know here besides these dear ones? There is Jeremiah, of course, and the mere fact of his stately presence brings strength to me, but I see very little of him these days. He lives apart from the house, as is proper, and there is precious little for him to do on my behalf.

Then there is only Jasper, the cretin, and the silent Indian who has lately become his shadow. He comes from somewhere around these parts, a member of the Chippewa tribe, I believe, and is named Aanakwad, which means "cloud." Jasper has taken to calling him, simply, Cloud, and I have followed suit for the sake of convenience.

I have the distinct displeasure of encountering these two individuals every fortnight or so, but the nature of the relationship is hardly one that could be termed friendship. Cloud hardly ever addresses me and looks through me as if I were as transparent as glass. The cretin does deign to speak in my direction, but only of "news," if any has arrived, and then only in the sneering and condescending tone at which he is so masterful. I know the tone well indeed and have heard it before. It is that of the poor and unschooled Southerner, placed by circumstance in a position of some superiority or authority over the aristocrat. I detest him for it.

There is, you might rightly surmise, a great deal more I could say of these two men and my association with them, but I beg your forgiveness if I am circumspect in this regard. Suffice to say that we are bound by sensitive matters, to put it mildly, and I cannot be sure that these pages will never be seen by eyes which are not supposed to glimpse them.

Be that as it may, I do have one new person to add to my scanty list of acquaintances, and what an unusual addition he is. He is Jonathan Chase, only recently arrived at Riverdale, having taken the vacant clerkship in my uncle's office. He is a wanderer, albeit a skilled one, and claims to have come from the distant West and to have recently labored as a seaman aboard one of the lake freighters.

I saw him before I met him. He was sitting in the yard with Jeremiah, with whom he has apparently, and very strangely, struck up a friendship, since they bunk in the same quarters. He was playing Jeremiah's guitar, singing softly and strumming the most enchanting melody. It was a plaintive song, haunting and lilting in a way that seemed very old and yet boldly new all at once. I could barely hear the lyrics he sang, but one was about "all the lonely people," and something about the way he sang it brought a chill to my spine and a flush to my face. He did not know I was listening from the window, but it seemed as if he were singing directly to me, as if he understood what was in my heart.

My fascination was only enhanced when I was finally fortunate enough to meet him directly. He was asked to the house for dinner a few weeks ago, and we were properly introduced. He is a striking man, tall with dark hair and the deepest green eyes. He tried to make a proper impression at the table but seemed awkward in his social skills—a trait which, of course, immediately prejudiced me in his favor. On the other hand, he stated plainly that he opposes slavery, which frankly did not surprise me and which I shall strive not to hold against him.

I confess—and not without a blush!—that the sight of his face and the sound of his voice made my heart race. All during dinner, I worried that I chose the wrong color to wear and, far worse, that my manner of speaking may have struck him as haughty and aloof. The Southern boys who have courted me all seem to regard haughtiness as among the most attractive of feminine features, yet Mr. Chase appears to be the sort of man who might feel very differently. It is strange. He seems, in some ways, as coarse and wild as these northern woods, almost a bumpkin, yet also refined and assured, but in a manner I have never seen and do not fully understand. He almost seems a foreigner, yet is so obviously an American.

He is a mystery in so many respects. I am positive that he was being dishonest in relating the details of his own background. He was not only withholding information but deliberately falsifying it, and I have never been one to be taken in by a lie (which, perchance, is why I am such a gifted liar myself!). Yet I saw such gentle compassion in those emerald eyes, and profound sadness as well, as if he has endured a greater grief than such a young man should ever know.

To this I confess: I am perplexed by this man Jonathan Chase.

You will think me a fool to admit it, but I am a very superstitious woman. I was raised in the woods of Georgia, close by the swamps and bayous where mysteries forever drift through the moss and the oaks. I believe in specters and in witches and in other things which it would shame me to say, and I must confess that I am already superstitious of Mr. Chase.

My superstitious nature forces me to wonder whether I have seen him before and whether I am somehow supposed to know him now. Was he the distant rider who stopped before the house? Was he the dark figure who approached me in that strange and unsettling dream? Why does my heart race when I think of him? Why do I wonder whether he is thinking of me?

Here is my most troubling question, based on what happened just three nights ago: Why was I overjoyed—when I should have been terribly frightened or horribly angry—when the mysterious Mr. Chase clumsily thrust himself into a place where he had no right to be?

Was it because I am beginning to dare hope that I may have found a friend at last, when I am in such desperate need of one? Or was it because his intrusion proves that he is indeed thinking of me after all?

MARCH

FORT MACKINAW

IT WAS ANOTHER MOMENT of seemingly infinite span, with Apollonia once more before him, but Jonathan felt no pleasure, and experienced no transcendent joy, in this encounter.

He stood in the opened doorway of the lonely frame house, the barrel of a stranger's gun pressed between his shoulder blades, and stared into the shocked eyes of the woman with whom he was falling in love. She sat in a simple cane chair in a plain black dress, obviously startled by the sudden intrusion, even more startled by whose face she saw now crossing the threshold.

Across the room from her, a man had risen from an identical chair. He had just pulled a long pistol from his belt and leveled it directly at Jonathan's chest. He was of short height, dressed in a long canvas coat, a brown derby perched on his head. The unlit stub of a cigar jutted between his teeth. He had the expression, the face, of a thug.

Jonathan recognized the sarcastic leer immediately. He was one of the two men standing beside Apollonia in the old photograph he'd found in the album. While the face of the other man had been blurred and rendered unidentifiable, this man's mien was unforgettable.

Nobody spoke at first. The man behind Jonathan prodded him with his gun. Jonathan stepped farther inside, followed by his captor, and heard the door close against the cold.

The short man in the long coat broke the silence. "Look what the Cloud dragged in," he said, emphasizing each word sinisterly and with a lilt that Jonathan pegged as rural Southern.

The Indian replied in a deep voice, with a faint accent suggesting that English wasn't his mother tongue. "He was listening at the window. He followed Miss Foley. I do not know this man."

The short man took a step closer to Jonathan. "Who in hell's name are you, mister?"

Jonathan remained silent. The surreal quality of the moment seemed to have seized his tongue.

"You had better start talking, mister, or I swear to God I'll blow a hole in you that a brewery wagon could drive through." The short man threw his cigar into the fireplace and raised his weapon to the height of Jonathan's head.

Apollonia rose from her chair. "Put down the gun, Jasper," she said in a shaky tone that held little of the cool assurance Jonathan remembered from their previous meeting.

"Like hell," the man replied, making no move to change his stance.

Apollonia's voice took on a stronger tone.

"I know him. He works for my uncle. I'm sure he means us no harm."

The man called Jasper practically spat out his response. "No disrespect intended, Miss Foley, but just how do you know that? If you ask me, this one looks like a spy, all right. You know as well as I do that everything depends on secrecy. One word from this Yankee son of a—"

She cut him off. "You put that down, Jasper! You listen to what I say, or I swear to you that nothing will happen the way Archer wants—nothing!—and you know I can do it. Do you want to try explaining that to Archer?"

Jasper listened this time. He lost his expression of fierce defiance and looked unsure of himself. He slowly lowered his firearm until it pointed at the floor, but he didn't put it away.

"You, too, Cloud," Apollonia said. "Take that pistol from his back."

Jonathan heard the man behind him comply. He moved beside Jonathan and finally appeared in full view. He was taller than Jonathan, broadly built, and dressed in fringed buckskin trousers and shirt. Moccasin boots of similar material covered his feet and reached nearly to his knees. His glossy black hair was long, tied back into a ponytail. His face, highlighted by eyes so dark they appeared black, was strong and impassive. It occurred to Jonathan that many women would find him striking.

Apollonia slowly returned to her seat. When she spoke, her voice was once more confident, smoothly in control.

"Now that we're not pointing guns at Mr. Chase, we can discourse like civilized people," she said, turning her eyes to align directly with Jonathan's. "And Mr. Chase, I'm quite sure, will be more than happy to tell us what he was doing outside our window after midnight on a very cold night."

Still, Jonathan hesitated.

"Now you see," Jasper said, beginning to raise his weapon again. "The silence of a guilty man."

"No," Jonathan said at last, his composure beginning to restore itself. "My name is Jonathan Chase, as Miss Foley said. I work as a clerk for her uncle, Mr. Foley, down at the booming grounds. I have no idea who you are, who this man beside me is, or what you are all doing here in the middle of the night."

Apollonia smiled slightly. Jasper shook his head, either because he didn't believe Jonathan or because the intrusion had caused an unexpected problem that held no clear solution. The Indian remained silent.

"I wasn't spying. I was outside the bunkhouse at Riverdale when I noticed Miss Foley walking to the stables. I saw her speaking to Jeremiah—perhaps arguing with him—and then watched her ride off into the woods. I thought something might be wrong, that Miss Foley," he set his gaze back on Apollonia, "that you might need some help. It's true that I followed you here, Miss Foley, but I swear that I wasn't spying. I was concerned, nothing more."

"But you were kneeling at the window," Cloud said, his implication as direct and clear as his voice.

"I needed to be sure that everything was all right," Jonathan replied.

Jasper reentered the conversation. "That's a tall tale if I ever heard one. If you were so concerned about Miss Foley, why didn't you call out to her along the way?"

"She had too big a lead on me. I had to follow her tracks."

Jasper whistled. "That's exactly what I'd expect you to say. How long did you say you've been working for Foley, mister?"

"I didn't say," Jonathan countered, his own tone now taking on a testy edge. "But the answer is about a month."

"A month? Not exactly an old-timer, are you? Looks to me like you hired on to Foley's operation in order to keep an eye on his niece and on us."

Jonathan didn't flinch in the face of this half-truth. "I already told you. I have no idea who you are or what you're doing here. And I'm not interested, just as long as Miss Foley tells me that she's all right."

Apollonia stood again, once more staring intently at Jonathan. Even in the dangerous absurdity of the moment, her look filled him with an unaccustomed warmth.

She smiled faintly. "I assure you that I am perfectly safe," she said quietly. "And I'm sure that you are telling us the absolute truth."

"Now how in the hell do you know—," Jasper began.

"You shut your mouth, Malcolm Jasper!" she shouted, her voice angry but still in perfect control. "I know because I know and that will have to be good enough for you."

She turned from Jonathan to face Jasper, arms akimbo on her hips. "Do you understand me?"

Meekly this time, Jasper nodded and shuffled a few feet back, away from her focused glare. She returned her eyes to Jonathan's, smiled once again, and spoke in a lower timbre.

"You have told us your story, and I believe it, Mr. Chase. I fear there is no escaping our own obligations in the same regard, but I hardly think this is a fitting time or place for such an involved discussion. We will have it later—soon—and, in the meanwhile, you will have to make a promise."

She raised an eyebrow, in direct query not coquettish pleading, and Jonathan nodded in agreement.

"You must promise me that you will say nothing of your ride through the township tonight, nothing of this house, nothing of your encounter with us, nothing of what was said here, nothing of Jasper or Cloud—not to a soul, Mr. Chase. If you can make that promise, then you can walk out that door, get back on your horse, ride back to Riverdale, and go back to your warm bed, just as if it were all a dream."

Jasper shifted his weight and muttered something beneath his breath, but he didn't make his protests heard. His gun remained pointing downward. Cloud merely looked at Jonathan with narrowed eyes.

"I promise," Jonathan said.

Apollonia nodded and opened the door, allowing the wintry air to invade the small sitting room. "Then we will speak later, Mr. Chase. Good night to you, sir."

He returned her farewell, tipped his hat, and allowed the icy embrace of the night to reclaim him.

The next morning, weary from the evening's events, Jonathan looked out the window of his rough-hewn office at the booming grounds. The Tittabawassee, lazy but strong in the summer, was now static, imprisoned in itself, in the last weeks of winter. But the slowly warming temperatures scarred its flat, immobile surface a little more each day, with crack lines blending evenly into the naked trees and slate gray sky.

He shuffled a new pile of papers into place, thinking little of the notations and equations he made in his log. His thoughts were exclusively on last night.

He had ridden home in the silent snowscape and returned to the bunkhouse with nobody seeing or hearing him. It was nearly three o'clock before he drifted off to an uneasy, restless sleep.

Now, with the sunrise invisible beneath the doldrums of the March sky, he realized that his surprise had only been momentary. He had already known. In another dimension, Violet Hunter had told him of Apollonia's strange comings and goings, her apparently furtive meetings with shadowy strangers in the vicinity of Riverdale.

Those stories, although they had traveled a century and a half before the old woman shared them with Jonathan, were true. They were happening right now.

Of more concern was what the venerable Violet had said about Apollonia's later fate—or, rather, the completely unknown nature of that fate. At some point in the story—possibly quite soon, Jonathan surmised—Apollonia would simply disappear, taking her slave and, in all probability, the shadowy strangers along with her. What had happened to her thereafter was an utter mystery.

Jonathan readjusted his perspective—a skill he was getting better at—by viewing the situation in the present tense. Of exclusive relevance in his circumstance was the question of what was going to happen to Apollonia after her departure, an event which had yet to take place.

How did it all fit in with the strange scene in the plain house of Jonathan's fascination? Perfectly, in his opinion. He had no firm theory as to what business was being conducted there, but it was being kept well hidden, and protected, and was therefore almost certainly illegal. The presence of the guns, and the apparent willingness of their owners to use them, only deepened this conviction.

The clues hovering over that obvious fact were themselves fairly clear. Considering Apollonia's Southern roots and apparent sympathies, and Jasper's unmistakably Southern accent, the activity most likely was related to the war. Jonathan had a vague idea of the work of the so-called Confederate Secret Service. At the very least he knew—and the realization was disturbing—that in the waning months of the war its operations had grown steadily more daring and desperate.

In the midst of all these anxious formulae and speculations, Jonathan felt something heartening. Apollonia had spoken on his behalf, protected him, quite possibly even saved his life last night. She had done it with courage and conviction and without really knowing what Jonathan was doing there. And she had looked into his eyes in a way she had not done before—deeply, it seemed to him, almost intimately. He realized that she did not seem at all a stranger to him when she did this, nor did she seem to regard Jonathan as one.

He felt as if they had crossed an unseen but important barrier together, as if a bond had formed. The feeling this gave him was hard to describe, but he knew that he liked it. He knew that it made the steely winter day seem much brighter and warmer and the prospect of dealing with furtive characters like Jasper and Cloud, spies or provocateurs or not, considerably less daunting.

He did not have long to wait for more substantial answers.

Apollonia's summons came to him two days after their encounter, in the form of a small piece of paper, secretly placed beneath his pillow in the bunkhouse, apparently while he was working. In elaborate, feminine script in violet ink, it read simply: "Knock quietly on the back door at ten o'clock tonight. There are matters to discuss." The note was not signed, nor did it need to be.

At eight o'clock, Jonathan heard a commotion in the yard as the Foleys' carriage was readied. He watched through the bunkhouse windows as Jarvis helped Mr. and Mrs. Foley and their daughter, Emily, into the rig. As its lanterns were lit, he heard Foley informing Jarvis that they would be returning before noon the following day—apparently an overnight stay in the city.

At ten o'clock, Jonathan quietly left the bunkhouse and its already sleeping tenants, knocked gently on the back door of the house, and entered as Apollonia—touching a finger to her lips—let him in.

A brass chamber stick in her hand, she led him silently through the pantry, kitchen, and dining room, into Foley's dark study, and, finally, into a small closet on one end of the room. Closing the door softly behind them, she led the way up a narrow spiral staircase made of iron. They ascended what seemed like many steps, which terminated in a trapdoor above their heads. With familiar ease, she raised the cover and pulled herself into a small room above. She reached for Jonathan's hand as he made the same move.

They stood in the cupola at the very apex of the house, in an unlit square room no more than ten feet by ten feet, surrounded on all sides by uncurtained arched windows. She had blown out her candle before entering, and the nocturnal view through the windows was stunning. The snowy landscape was visible for miles in some directions, where the land had been cleared, and obscured by woods in others. Under the silver light of the waning moon, the terrain looked beautiful and haunting.

Apollonia promptly sat crossed-legged on the plank floor, apparently not concerned with the plain calico dress she was wearing. Her hair was tied up as always, loosely this time, and she looked more beautiful than ever.

She spoke just above a whisper, in a low, even tone.

"Mr. Chase," she began and then hesitated. "I detest such formality. Might I call you Jonathan, at least in private?"

He smiled, mostly to himself. "Of course."

"Jonathan, then, first allow me to apologize for what happened the other night. It was dreadful to have those men pointing their weapons at you, I realize, and—,"

"Miss Foley," he interrupted and then hesitated himself. "Might I call you . . . ?"

"Yes," she said quietly, with her own smile. "Please do."

"Apollonia, please don't apologize to me. I'm the one who owes the apology. I stumbled into something that was none of my business. I acted like a stupid ox.

I interrupted something private and surprised everyone. It really wasn't my intention to do that, but I take full responsibility for everything. I just want to tell you that what I said about being concerned for you was the God's truth."

"I have already said that I believe you, and our apologies are already spoken," she said firmly, "but I am afraid that that will be the easy part of our conversation."

She leaned closer to him, giving him the faint but unmistakable scent of lemon verbena, and looked him directly in the eye. Her expression was serious, perhaps even a little frightened.

"Because of our unexpected meeting the other night, Jonathan, you are in great danger." She allowed that to sink in for a moment before going further.

"You might have surmised by now that my purpose in being in Michigan goes well beyond a niece's visit to her relations. I am here for a very important reason, Jonathan—I cannot yet tell you precisely what that is—but I implore you to believe me when I say that life and death hang in the balance of it, when I tell you that forces far beyond my own control are influencing events. Can you appreciate that?"

He nodded and gestured for her to continue.

"Jeremiah, of course, I trust like my own brother. I would not have dreamt of undertaking my task without him by my side.

"Cloud is a Chippewa. He has been in our employ for only a few weeks and, so far as I can gather, is purely a mercenary, a man of no particular loyalties beyond those to himself. In placing a gun to your head, Jonathan, he was doing only what he was told to do. I trust him as far as his responsibilities and duties go and do not fear him.

"Malcolm Jasper, on the other hand, is a man of both fierce loyalties and violent reactions. Unfortunately, his presence is absolutely necessary to the success of this mission, but he is under another's command, not mine. There are times when he will do my bidding, but my control over him is extremely limited."

She paused, keeping her deadly serious gaze on Jonathan's face.

"I do not necessarily trust him, and I do fear him. He feels that you have placed his mission—*our* mission, I should say—in grave jeopardy. He fears that you are a spy, Jonathan, and that even if you are completely innocent, your knowledge of our meeting puts everything in peril."

She took his hand in hers and leaned a little closer. Now she spoke in a whisper.

"I will state this plainly. He wants to kill you, Jonathan. So far, I have managed to keep him at bay, but I am not sure how much longer I can continue to do so."

Her words were dire, but Jonathan did not feel fear upon hearing them. Perhaps it was the touch of her hand or the glint of her eyes so close to his, but the prospect of Jasper's threat gave him no sense of dread.

"Are you warning me, then? Telling me to prepare to defend myself?"

She smiled softly. "Perhaps, but I am also prepared to make a proposal to you, Jonathan. I am asking you to join our mission."

He was not expecting this.

"You're asking me to go along with something I have no idea about, alongside a man who seems intent on killing me?"

His tone was incredulous and slightly sarcastic, and he saw the hurt expression on Apollonia's face.

"I'm sorry," he said. "I don't mean to make light of it, but I have to admit that your proposal comes as a bit of a surprise."

Her face and voice brightened a little. "Of course it does, but think about it, Jonathan. If you come along with us—if you become one of us—then Jasper will be able to keep an eye on you. His doubts will eventually be erased. And I can keep an eye on him—*we* can keep an eye on him. If you stay behind, I fear that he will do something—something dreadful—just to assure himself that you will not follow and that you will never say anything."

He let go of her hand and rose to look out the window at the still landscape.

"If I stay behind...," he repeated. "Which means that you're going somewhere."

"Yes," she replied, reverting to her low tone just above a whisper. "And quite soon."

"And you can't tell me anything about what you're doing? Where you'll be going?"

"Not yet, Jonathan. But in time you will learn everything."

He returned to the floor in front of her and, without thinking, took her hand back into his.

"A mysterious journey to places unknown, for purposes unknown. It sounds dangerous."

She briefly cast her eyes down. "I will not lie to you. There will be hardship and very likely danger."

"The danger of the gallows, perhaps?" he asked.

She regarded him with a momentary look of fright, as if she had not given sufficient thought to that possibility, but she quickly erased the expression. She did not reply to the question.

"And what about me, Apollonia? How do you know that Jasper isn't right—that I'm not a spy after all? Why are you so trusting?"

She drew nearer to him and held his hand tighter. A smile returned to her face. Her voice assumed a vulnerable tone he hadn't heard before.

"I just am, Jonathan. I sense something in you—something I have never seen before. It is true that I do not know you. I will go further than this. I find you just as mysterious as you must find me—you are so very different from others, you seem so strange, so open and yet so hidden—and yet I trust you. You must believe that I trust you deeply, and...," she paused, as if deciding to continue. "I need you."

"How in the world do you need me?"

"I confess that I am afraid," she said. "I fear my task. Even though I shall not shrink from it, I shall need an ally, a true friend, at my side."

They rose together, gazing once more through the windows of the cupola. Her voice regained its cool, confident tone.

"And, Jonathan, in honesty can you tell me that this," she spread her arms to encompass the grounds of Riverdale, "that this is so important to you? Can you honestly tell me that the sum of your hopes and dreams is to scribble in the ledgers of my uncle, here in this frozen land?"

He knew he couldn't tell that lie. He knew precisely what dreams had brought him here and were keeping him here.

"I cannot," he said.

She smiled. "So?"

"So you've just gained an ally."

She put her elegant hands on both of his cheeks and stood on her toes to plant a light kiss on his forehead. Her lips felt like the smoothest satin.

"We shall be great allies," she whispered.

Early the next morning, a Saturday, Jonathan received a vivid reminder of this commitment.

He interrupted his shaving to answer a knock at the door of the bunkhouse and was unpleasantly surprised to see Malcolm Jasper. Beside him stood what Jonathan took to be a camera—an unwieldy boxlike device perched atop the wooden legs of a tripod.

Jasper spoke quietly, so as not to be heard by the other workers within.

"Good morning, Chase," he said in an artificially pleasant tone. "I would be honored if you would do me the honor of stepping outside for a quick word or two."

Jonathan toweled off his face, put on his coat and hat, and followed Jasper into the yard. The short man carried his clumsy contraption with him. It was a bright, sunny morning with a steady breeze. The unfamiliar mildness of the temperature and the white fluffy clouds against the azure sky were early hints of spring.

"As far as the butler is concerned, I'm a photographer from the city," he said, gesturing toward the camera. "In fact, that's exactly what I've been doing for the past few months in East Saginaw, working for one of the studios on Genesee Street. At least that's been my daytime occupation. Quite an excellent ruse, I must say. Anyway, I told the butler that Foley hired me to capture a few views of the estate. That's a lie, of course, so I want to be quick, before the family gets back."

"You came here to talk to me?" Jonathan asked.

"That's right, Chase," Jasper said, putting his camera down near the side of the house and beginning to fidget with its levers. "Miss Foley has told me that she intends to ask you to come along with the rest of us. Is that so?"

He pulled a partially smoked cigar from his coat pocket, stuck it between his teeth, and lit it with a lucifer match he struck on his boot sole.

"Yes, it is. She asked me last night."

"And you agreed?"

"I did."

He held Jonathan's direct gaze without a blink. "Do you want to know what I said to Miss Foley when she made that suggestion to me?"

Jonathan nodded.

"I told her that she was a damned fool to even consider such a thing."

"That's not the sort of thing a gentleman should say to a lady."

Jasper laughed and spit at the ground.

"Well now, Chase, I won't deny that Miss Foley is a lady, but I make absolutely no claims to being a gentleman, so there's your explanation on that. But I didn't come out here to discuss my manners. I came here to tell you to disregard everything that Miss Foley said to you last night and to inform you that you will not be coming with us."

Jonathan kept his eyes fixed firmly on Jasper's. In them he saw the short man's determination and courage, his readiness and willingness to turn suddenly violent in order to get what he wanted. But he refused to avert his gaze.

"And you've wasted your time," he replied. "I gave my promise to Apollonia... to Miss Foley, and that's the end of it. I'm coming along."

Jasper's eyes narrowed. "You already know that I don't trust you, Chase. What you may not know is that I'm not a man to trifle with. There's plenty of men who once thought otherwise. They're all in graveyards now, feeding worms. It would be no trouble for me to do you the same."

Jonathan smiled. "Two can play at that game. You don't look immortal to me."

The short man made a move to reach beneath his coat but hesitated when he heard a sound from nearby the house.

Apollonia turned the corner. She was wearing a plain maroon dress and smiling widely.

"Why you must be the photographer from town!" she said loudly. "Uncle Timothy told me you were coming. You simply must take my picture standing here beside the house."

Jasper scowled but knew better than not to play along.

"Well now, I suppose I could do just that, ma'am," he said, his voice returning to its pleasant pitch. "Now, young lady, you stand right there, just before the trellis, and allow me a few moments to make the proper adjustments on the apparatus."

Apollonia took her position and grabbed Jonathan by the arm, drawing him closer.

"And Mr. Chase will be good enough to pose along with me, won't you, Mr. Chase?"

Jonathan nodded as Jasper tried to conceal his deepening scowl.

"And when you are ready," she said to the photographer in a quieter tone, "you'll come stand beside us. Put your camera on the timer so that you can be in the picture, too."

As Jasper fiddled with the device, she lowered her voice even further.

"I know why you have come here, Jasper. I know why you broke your promise never to enter these grounds. I have one thing to tell you. If you so much as harm one hair on Mr. Chase's head—if you even make one more threat to do so—I will tell Archer that you have put everything in danger, that you have forced me to make a decision which I do not wish to make, which *he* does not wish me to make. Please do not doubt me."

Jasper merely nodded—with hostile reluctance, it seemed to Jonathan—and announced that the camera was ready. He clicked the shutter with a long cable mechanism and then rushed to Apollonia's other side. He smiled just in time for the noisy, smoky flash that erupted. At that moment, Jonathan heard the wheels of a carriage on the road and turned toward the sound.

Apollonia lost her smile immediately. "That's my aunt and uncle!" she hissed to Jasper. "Take your camera and get yourself out of sight before they arrive, for God's sake!"

He wasted no time following her instructions, bundling the ungainly apparatus beneath his arm and heading for the other side of the house, away from the drive.

Apollonia turned to Jonathan. Her face was pale, the expression one of fatigue and worry. "I am so sorry, Jonathan...," she began.

"It's all right," he assured her. "Don't worry about me. I'll win him over in time."

She didn't look convinced.

"Just tell me one thing," he asked. "Who is this mysterious Archer you keep talking about?"

She sighed and brushed a strand of hair from her forehead. "You will see for yourself, Jonathan, soon enough," she said softly.

Jonathan's last night in Saginaw came in a week.

Apollonia had once again slipped a note beneath his pillow. Its message, characteristically direct, said: "We shall leave before dawn on Thursday. Jeremiah will tell you what to do. On the evening before, you will again be invited to dine with the family. I know that I can trust you, Jonathan, to say nothing to arouse their slightest suspicions or concerns."

The invitation was duly delivered by Jarvis early on Wednesday evening, shortly after Jonathan had finished his work for the day. He dressed in his suit and polished his shoes. Jeremiah, quietly strumming strange melodies in his corner bunk, nodded and offered him a knowing smile as he left.

The dinner was much like the last one, with Timothy Foley, his wife, son, and daughter in attendance. Foley spoke passionately of the warming weather and the approach of "the thaw," with its promise of endless streams of fresh logs flowing into the long-dormant maws of his mills and booming grounds.

Phineas, as cross-eyed and pleasant as ever, spoke of his hopes for a busy summer in his fledgling shop. With the Saginaws filled with lumberjacks, most of whom were loaded with winter pay, he hoped to "move many a fine timepiece."

Emily, blushing and alluring, was subtly flirtatious, and Mrs. Foley, in her knowing and dignified way, said very little amid the busy conversation.

Apollonia, once again, made her entrance in the dining room a bit later than the others. Dressed in forest green satin with a blood red ruby brooch at her throat, she was composed and demure, as befitted a pampered Southern belle, and gave no hint at her mysterious, potentially perilous plans for the coming dawn.

After the meal, she offered to play something on the harpsichord in the parlor. The family, with Jonathan in tow, were served their coffee and tea in the elaborately decorated room. They sat in a semicircle around the baroque instrument as Apollonia arranged her long dress on the bench.

She played beautifully, a melody vaguely familiar to Jonathan. It sounded like something from the Renaissance period, with a mysterious, forlorn air. As her long fingers ran over the keys, he found himself transported. He felt the echoes of a time, distant even from this one, and a place, equally far away. Between the minor key notes that she expertly maneuvered, he also felt a sense of beautiful sadness, of someone's heartache and resigned gloom. It seemed like she was telling the sad story of a ghost, someone whose life and loves were long ago forgotten, except in the heart and mind of this woman who was somehow able to conjure them with her music.

When she was done, the Foleys applauded enthusiastically, with Jonathan—startled out of his reverie by the coda—clapping louder than them all. "So beautiful, Appy," Emily said daintily. "But so very sad. Come, Cousin, play us something livelier, something to lighten the heart."

Apollonia smiled wanly at her cousin. "I am sorry, Em. I confess, I am not feeling very sprightly tonight. And I am so very tired." She rose from the bench and made the opening gesture of a curtsy. "Which is precisely why I must retire. I bid you all a very good night."

Before she left the room, she looked back at Jonathan. It was nothing more than a glance, but in that moment he saw the soft gentility of those carefully cultivated Southern manners dissolve, to be ever so briefly replaced by the steely glare of a very courageous, very determined—and possibly very desperate—woman.

By the time he got back to the bunkhouse, the lamps were extinguished, and the only sounds audible were those of the men sleeping. But just as Jonathan pulled his blanket over his body, he felt a gentle nudge at his arm.

It was Jeremiah, speaking in the lowest of whispers.

"You must have everything you want to take all ready, Massa Chase," he said. "I'll be a-wakin' you up long before the rooster does."

It was moderately cold and very dark in the old cemetery across the road from Riverdale. Jonathan and Jeremiah had gone to the far end of the graveyard, out of view of the house. They stood beside three horses that Jeremiah was holding by the reins—tall, fine-looking mounts that Jonathan did not recognize—and stayed mostly quiet.

Jonathan wondered what time it was. He glanced repeatedly at the eastern horizon but saw no hint of light, not even the illusory promise of false dawn.

He had spent the last five minutes whispering to Jeremiah, trying to glean from him some knowledge of their destination, some clue as to their purpose. But the slave had only shaken his head, over and over, and repeated, "That's only for Miss Foley to say, Massa."

He tried not to think of the date—March the fifteenth—and its historical significance as the Ides, but the thought of its ill omen, perhaps even its curse, hung over him like the blanket of the night sky.

At last, across the road, the pale oval of Apollonia's face loomed out of the darkness. She strode rapidly toward them in her long black cloak— hood over her head, woolen scarf across her mouth, long leather gloves on her hands and arms—appearing like a phantom. Behind her stood the grand house, dark and silent, and something told Jonathan that this was the last he'd ever see of it.

Apollonia, however, did not turn back to give Riverdale one last glance. When she drew near, she pulled the scarf away from her face.

"Everything is ready, Jeremiah?" she asked quietly, after smiling briefly at Jonathan. "The horses are fed, the packs well secured?"

"Yes'm," Jeremiah whispered back.

"Then we go."

They mounted their horses—a tawny mare for Jonathan, a dappled gelding for Jeremiah, and a black gelding for Apollonia. She rode hers in the confident, masculine style Jonathan had already seen, and their route closely traced the steps they had taken a week before, during his surreptitious pursuit.

When they reached the lonely white house, Jasper and Cloud were already astride their own horses, large canvas packs strapped behind their saddles. The two said nothing to the first three, silently falling into line on the road to the city.

Jonathan surveyed the house as they departed. Now, since most of the snow had melted in the slowly warming air, its pale simplicity stood out in stark contrast to the gloomy fields and woods surrounding it. Its windows blank and empty, its profile casting no visible shadows under the dark of the moon, it seemed lifeless and forlorn, but Jonathan sensed its significance nonetheless. He looked away from it reluctantly, almost as if it were the last familiar milestone he was destined to see on this strange journey.

They reached Saginaw City just as the first narrow bands of light were appearing in the dull sky. The city was stirring with its awakenings. In the windows of occasional houses, the light of a candle or lamp could be seen; from a few chimneys, a wisp of fragrant smoke. When they passed by the large, beautiful houses on Michigan Avenue, a clinking dairy wagon approached them, its well-bundled driver raising his cap in their direction.

Once they reached the river, the party turned north on the road that ran along the left bank. In just a few minutes, the buildings grew fewer, the trees and bushes thicker. A few more minutes and they had left the city entirely behind them.

Nobody had spoken a word the entire time, apparently eager to traverse the city with as little attention as possible. At an opening in the foliage, offering a clear view of the river, it was Cloud, surprisingly, who broke the silence. He halted his horse and pointed to the east.

In the still half-light, something was visible in the distance. Somewhere near the middle of the wide river, lights seemed to flit and dance, keeping constantly on the move. They had a bluish, opalescent quality.

"Spirits of the Saukee," Cloud said in his plaintive, deep voice.

"And who in hell are the Saukee?" Jasper responded, impatient and sarcastic.

"They were the people who lived here first, in the early times," the Indian replied evenly. "They were a peaceful nation, fishermen, not warriors. Until the Ojibwa, my people, came. They came by the lake and by the bay and formed war parties on both sides of the river. They struck the Saukee on the far bank and drove them to this one. Here they were struck by the Ojibwa on the near bank, until they fled to that island you see. But that night, the river froze, and the Ojibwa were able to cross over."

Cloud looked into the dim abyss, as if seeing reflections from the battle for the island.

"With their knives, the warriors of the Ojibwa killed all of the Saukee, the men, the women, the little ones, and left them there to rot and dry in the sun. This is how the Ojibwa came to live on the Saginaw. But the spirits of the Saukee live here, too. Tonight, they are restless. You can see them. They are searching for something."

Jasper pulled one of his narrow cigars from his coat and lit it, tossing the match into the river's gentle current.

"Road apples!" he said with a guffaw. "What you're seeing out there, Cloud, is nothing more than will-o'-the-wisps. Swamp gas. Nothing but rotting leaves. No Saukee spirits searching."

The Indian made no reply to this declaration. He gently pulled the reins and resumed the ride, the others falling in behind as a cloudy sunrise finally illuminated the countryside. The road grew steadily rougher and shrouded by tall trees, virgin timber—not yet fallen to the lumberman's ax—and it towered on a scale Jonathan had not thought possible. The woods featured occasional maples, oaks, and hickories, their winter limbs not yet revealing buds, but the conifers—pines, cedars, spruces, and hemlocks—were clearly the kings of this forest. They were looming and majestic, their deep green boughs contrasting with the gray sky in a way that struck Jonathan as dauntingly primeval and wildly northern. They were as still as stones in the dawn.

Their dark beauty shaded the travelers throughout the entire first day of their journey. They held to a northeasterly course, following Cloud, who appeared familiar with the narrow, frozen earth trails they traversed. Few words were spoken, even when they stopped to eat a hurried lunch of dried fish and apples. Everybody, including Jonathan, seemed intent on making good progress and putting Saginaw well behind them.

Their advance was determined. By early evening, when the gloom grew even darker, they had made more than forty miles. Jonathan wondered whether the horses or humans would last much longer, but through the tunnel of trees that lined the road, he saw a clearing ahead and, as they grew nearer, the vertical outline of a stone lighthouse, standing vigilant and alone. Beyond it was the massive, slate gray expanse of Lake Huron.

"Tawas Point," Cloud announced. "This will make a good camp. We will sleep near the tower."

They spoke briefly with the lighthouse keeper, a uniformed man with a huge, elaborate mustache who seemed more than eager for the company. When he asked them where they were going, Apollonia's straightforward yet evasive answer was "north." Undeterred, the friendly keeper offered a warm supper in exchange for company. As he prepared the meal, his guests went to work—Apollonia included—raising simple canvas tents on the stony ground. Apollonia would sleep in her own tent; Cloud and Jasper in another; Jeremiah and Jonathan in the last.

Before dinner, all five of them walked to the frozen shore, now buffeted by a chilly dusk breeze. The ice extended several hundred yards across the lake, but beyond it were tall whitecaps of water. They could hear the waves crash as the surf pushed against the floes.

"It is like I said," Cloud pronounced solemnly. "The melting is coming early this year." He looked intently toward the north. "We might be able to sail back."

For the next six days, they rode steadily, although their first day's remarkable headway was not to be repeated. The lake shore road north of Tawas—soon nothing more than a primeval Indian trail—grew even narrower and more choked with snow as they headed further into the wilderness. They kept their horses to a gentle gait, fearful of the holes and ice, and managed to make roughly twenty miles a day. It did not snow once during their journey, and the daytime air was cool, not cold. Although the drifts grew deeper as they trekked north, even here the snow was already beginning to slowly melt.

During the long days, Jonathan studied his mostly silent companions. Cloud was clearly the most accustomed to the wild surroundings. He seemed constantly alert, his eyes ever shifting as he surveyed the woods, the road, the icy shore. He sniffed the air frequently, snorting with a strange smile every time he picked up something he felt was significant, but never would he speak to his fellow travelers of what he had detected. He frequently leaped gracefully off his mount to examine tracks in the snow, some of which Jonathan could see were made by animals, some of which might have been human.

Jasper was sullen and withdrawn, obviously uncomfortable in the cold and unfamiliar with the terrain. He kept his collar up and his hat pulled low over his eyes, his hands wrapped in heavy leather gloves. When they made camp, he sat by himself, smoking cigars and sipping from a bottle hidden in his boot.

Jeremiah seemed nervous and apprehensive. He often peered into the black shadows of the woods, between the infinite trees, and shuddered. It seemed to Jonathan that Cloud's story about the unfortunate Sauks might have made an impression on him, awakening superstitions that may not have lain too far beneath the surface. Late at night, sharing a tent, Jonathan could feel Jeremiah tremble when the wolves broke the immeasurable silence.

They discussed his fears only once, after Jonathan had asked him about it. Jeremiah informed him that he might very well believe in ghosts, including those of Indians, but swore that he didn't fear them. "It's the living ones I'm afeard of," he said, adding darkly, "and that includes some of them out here with us." Although Jonathan pressed further, Jeremiah would not say another word on the subject.

Jonathan, although entirely inexperienced with the harsh demands of winter travel in this time and place, was fascinated by virtually everything. The bracing air and fragrant spice of pine and spruce were intoxicating, the gargantuan trees fantasy images from a Brothers Grimm fairy tale. He knew that predators lurked in that vast forest but did not fear them. Somehow he felt an instinctive kinship, out here so far away from civilization—so far from his own reality—and did not perceive them as foes.

He thought little of the journey's unknown destination and purpose. The whole surreal course of his life for the past two months seemed to have inured him to such speculations. He had arrived at the stage when expecting surprises had become the norm, when acceptance of the strange grew almost automatic.

That he was spending every day and night within a few feet of Apollonia did not dampen his spirits. Although she said little to Jonathan, or to anyone else, she glanced at him often, occasionally allowing a faint smile to cross her face. Draped in her long, dark cloak, its hood covering her head, she looked regal, a medieval princess on a perilous quest. Her eyes were fixed in a determination that was assured and commanding and that suggested that she was, at least in part, the leader of the wayfarers. Jonathan found it fascinating that, like some of the wolf packs who were sharing this forest with them, they too were led by an alpha female.

Although he could not yet consider his relationship with her to be a close one, he was falling steadily deeper under her spell. He was amazed how her confidence and courage were somehow kept in perfect harmony with her graceful femininity and how she seemed oblivious to the hardships of the expedition.

On the long ride, he always tried to position himself to catch glimpses of her profile, and with each one he captured, his sense of awe swelled. He was entranced by myriad details about her—the elegance of her accent or the way the color of her eyes was ever changing. When the sun was out, they were a dazzling azure; when clouds covered the sky, a leaden blue; by firelight, almost black in their depth.

In spite of his infatuation, Jonathan had not lost touch with his own good sense. He did not exist in a state of airy exaltation or intoxicated worship but felt more clearheaded than ever. The surreal strangeness of his existence in this alien time was challenging, but being with Apollonia served as an anchor. He knew that he was falling in love with her, though his feelings were no longer the fevered and obsessive fixation with which he'd once regarded her timeworn photograph. Now, having spent days in her physical presence, his feelings had grown much calmer, yet stronger and deeper. Although their discourse had so far been brief and sporadic, he sensed that this would soon change.

There were only occasional distractions from the daily ritual of rising early, riding steadily, carefully, and quietly, eating hurried meals, setting up camp, and sleeping in the starry, frosty nights, serenaded by wild creatures.

After seven days into their journey, they came to a tiny log cabin settlement called Harrisville. It was little more than a forward trading post for several lumber camps that had been set up in the area last summer, early thrusts of the ravenous industry that Jonathan knew would soon be consuming this region. It had three saloons, a blacksmith's shop, a general store, half a dozen houses, and a hotel, all made of the same newly cut and sawed virgin lumber.

At dusk, when they arrived, the town was already filling up with jacks who had just finished their hard days in the woods. To a man, they headed for the saloons, their shouting and howling soon echoing through the town's one and only street.

Several showed considerable interest in Apollonia, not surprising considering that there seemed to be precious few other females in residence. A couple of men smiled at her and clumsily lifted their woolen caps as she passed. She regarded them with the icy stare of a countess gazing at beggars.

The jacks made Jasper nervous, not because of their crude attentions toward Apollonia but by their very nature. "Goddamned Yankees," he hissed just beneath his breath. "Most of the bastards can't speak a word of English anyway."

The lumberjacks, in turn, didn't care much for Cloud. Although none was bold enough to confront the tall, obviously sturdy Chippewa, their eyes spoke nothing but contempt. It was clear that relations here between the Indians and loggers were far from cordial, and Jonathan wondered what species of bad blood had already flowed between them.

Sensing trouble, Jasper suggested that they waste little time getting off the rowdy thoroughfare. His companions, exhausted from the day's ride, were in no mood to disagree. They traded their rustic outdoor camp for rooms in the rough-hewn, but comparatively luxurious, hotel. For a dime each, they ate a meal of mulligan stew and fresh bread, and for five cents more apiece, all had a hot bath, with the exception of Cloud, who scoffed at the idea. After midnight, when the saloon-fueled hollering gradually faded away, they slept in the rare extravagance of soft beds and warm quarters.

The next night, a little more than twenty miles farther north, the travelers encountered an encampment of Hurons along the southwestern shore of Thunder Bay, just outside the lumber town of Alpena. There were a dozen men, perhaps twice that many women, and an assortment of children huddled around a huge campfire, surrounded by makeshift tents made of skins.

As the riders approached, the men rose, hands on spears or tomahawks, one of them gripping a musket. The jet-black eyes of the women and children, watchful and anxious, reflected the firelight as they regarded the strangers.

Cloud spoke to them in a tongue that was apparently familiar to both tribes. One of the men, presumably the leader, answered, gesturing at the white faces and uttering harsh guttural words.

When Cloud replied, he used a term that Jonathan recognized. He said "Mackinac"—pronouncing it "Mackinaw"—and looked toward the northwest. As the Huron nodded in understanding, Jonathan suddenly realized their destination.

Whatever Cloud told him seemed to mollify the others. Cloud turned to Apollonia and explained that the Hurons were a hunting party, well out of their own territory, and were planning to stay for only a few days. They wouldn't mind if the travelers set up camp adjacent to theirs for the night.

It was a strange but pleasant evening, with the curious children creeping slowly closer to the strangers' fire, then darting away when they were seen or their mothers called after them. At length—Jonathan guessed it must have been close to ten o'clock—the mothers summoned their children for the last time. They all retreated to the makeshift tents, men, women, and children alike, except for one man who took a lookout's post near the trail.

Seeing his silhouette against the murky moon, a long spear held firmly in his hands, Jonathan wondered what he was watching for.

On the ninth day, a strong and vaguely temperate wind began blowing from the west, allowing them to remove the heaviest of their garments. Rivulets of melted snow flowed over the path, which grew muddier and more precarious.

The thundering breakers of the great lake now sounded considerably closer to the shore, and the shelf of ice that protruded into the water looked weak and unstable.

Despite the roads, they made adequate progress. After a hard day's riding, the sun was still above the horizon, and the chinook still blowing, when they reached the place called Mackinac.

It stood on the very tip of Michigan's Lower Peninsula, looking out over the long straits where Lake Huron and Lake Michigan come together, their mighty heads blending in what always struck Jonathan as a kiss. He remembered being in this very place in his childhood—the distant future—and seeing the monumental bridge that spanned between Mackinac City and St. Ignace, the town on the far end, the southern tip of the Upper Peninsula.

There was no bridge here now, just five miles of cerulean water, looking very cold and very deep. The straits were virtually free of ice, with only small floes drifting here and there, and the open water seemed to run a steady course through the center channels of both lakes. A few small boats—fishermen's craft and ferries, mostly—freely plied the waters.

The town itself was more than Jonathan expected, certainly more substantial and established than anything they'd seen since Saginaw. There were several parallel streets of plain gabled houses and businesses with false fronts—most of them built with shingles and finished clapboard instead of the crude materials they had seen to the south. Dozens of busy-looking people were walking or riding about, seeing to late afternoon errands.

Jonathan knew something of the history of this place, how the French, and later the British, had ensconced themselves in a fort here, during their respective eras of colonial dominion. He knew that the Straits of Mackinac was a spot of obvious strategic importance, especially during times of military tension between the colonial powers and, later, the British and the fledgling Americans. Michilimackinac, the old fort that once stood on this shore, had been won and lost in battle several times, its control changing hands between the French, the British, the Chippewa, and the Sac.

Even in 1864 that fort and its battles were long gone. During the Revolutionary War, the British eventually moved their fortress to Mackinac Island, some ten miles out into the strait on the Huron side. This newer fort, itself the object of repeated military engagement between the British and the Americans, still existed and might still be manned, so far as Jonathan knew. Sensing its potential significance to the mission of his companions, he looked to the northeast but could not see even the island itself in the mist that was slowly rising from the surface of the lake.

They rode, virtually unnoticed, into the town center, drawing up their horses before a hotel, housed in a structure that looked amazingly impressive after another week in the woods. Once again, the travelers enjoyed the luxury of rooms, this time in an inn that was considerably more comfortable than the one in Harrisville.

Having secured their accommodations, Apollonia led the group to a quiet corner of the lobby, directing them to sit on chairs that encircled a blazing fireplace.

She spoke quietly, in a near whisper but the manner of an officer.

"We will need to take care of the dispatch tonight. We will all need to go."

Jasper and Cloud nodded their understanding.

"Are Jonathan's things ready?"

Jasper nodded once more.

Jonathan joined in, thoroughly weary of the ignorance their silence imposed on him.

"What things?" he asked, his tone deliberately blunt and direct.

Apollonia gave him a soft look.

"We are very near to accomplishing our goal, Jonathan," she said. "I realize there is much I have not told you. Soon, after we complete one very important task, I will tell you everything. You must know, after all, because your help will be required."

She turned again to Jasper.

"Do you have the spot selected?"

"Yes, ma'am," he drawled. "Not more than a hundred yards from the edge of town, but nicely shaded beneath a giant cedar. Nobody will see us."

They parted, agreeing to reunite at midnight, not in the hotel lobby but by the stable just behind it.

Jonathan spent the evening alone, dining on whitefish in a pleasant restaurant near the shore and briefly walking through the town. He returned to the hotel, bathed, and tried to sleep but found himself wide awake despite his fatigue.

He realized that their mission was on the brink of its culmination. He could feel the increased tension and sense of silent concentration in the others, especially Apollonia, who had grown quieter and more withdrawn. The fact that he still had no idea what he was about to do was no longer so easy for him to dismiss. Its secrecy, and her earlier warnings, gave him the first pangs of uneasiness.

But as he lay on the bed, watching the shifting light from his candle play on the ceiling, Jonathan realized that he was far from unhappy, in spite of everything. In fact, being with Apollonia was bringing him very close to a state that could only be called happiness. He had not felt this way in a very long time—perhaps he had never felt quite this way—and the gladness that filled his heart left very little room for fear.

They met at the stroke of twelve, as planned, behind the hotel. Around them, all was quiet, and the group walked slowly, following Jasper's lead.

They didn't have far to go. On the east side of town, in a dark spot concealed by trees just a few dozen yards from the shore, Jasper stopped at a telegraph pole. He inspected the shaft and its connections above, was apparently pleased with what he saw, and gestured to Cloud.

"This will do just fine," he said. "Go up there and grab me a wire."

Rubbing his hands together and blowing them warm, Cloud removed his moccasins and began climbing the eight-foot pole. He was graceful and steady, grasping above him with both hands and using his feet on the bare wood to move himself up. When he reached the top, he freed his right hand and gently lifted one of the telegraph wires away from its insulator, gave it a gentle tug, then, clutching the wire, quietly jumped to the ground.

"What's he doing?" Jonathan whispered to Apollonia.

"Tell Jonathan what we are doing, Jasper," she said quietly.

Taking the wire from Cloud, Jasper worked as he replied.

"We're fixing to send a message to the United States Army," he said in a low voice, removing a small mechanical object from his pocket. "This is my pocket relay. What I'm going to do is tap into this line, convince the receiving operator that I'm a Union telegrapher from the army depot in Detroit, and then proceed to send a message."

Jasper cut insulation away from the wire and began affixing it to his relay, using a penknife for both operations. He worked with the sure and practiced hand of experience. Jonathan was beginning to understand why Jasper had been included in this mission.

"Who are you sending to?" Jonathan asked.

Apollonia took the conversation for herself.

"Do you know where Fort Mackinac is?"

He turned to her and pointed into the straits. "It's just out there, on Mackinac Island. How are you going to get a message out there?"

"We're not going to," Jasper joined in. "There's no line going to the island. What we're going to do is send the message to the fort by way of the Western Union station, right here in Mackinac City. This message will travel less than a mile from where we're standing, and tomorrow morning, when the mail packet heads out to the island, the message will go along with it."

Jasper finished attaching his device to the line. Jonathan saw its miniaturized components—a brass arch and horizontal bands of metal and a small key, the instrument's respective receiver and sender.

"This is the tricky part," Jasper said, connecting a tiny wire from the sounder to the main wire. "Line goes dead for a few seconds when I do that. I've got to hope that the Western Union man wasn't listening. But, otherwise, we're all set to go."

He placed an index finger over the black button. "Now comes the second tricky part. I'm hoping that I remember the headers for the Detroit depot perfectly, and I'm hoping that my fist sounds something like the real operator. Odds are, the fellow here in Mackinac gets a lot of messages from Detroit. He'll be familiar with the way the sender works."

Jasper clicked Morse code for a few moments, reciting his words as he tapped them out.

"For Mackinac City: Detroit Army Depot with urgent message for commanding officer, Fort Mackinac."

He waited for a moment, then smiled widely when his little sounder began pattering a reply, which he also recited out loud, including punctuation marks and the word "stop" between sentences.

"Western Union, Mackinac, receiving yours. Is this Jones?"

Jasper turned to his companions and frowned. "See what I mean? He's asking questions. He already knows it's somebody else."

He clicked back. "No. Jones is off the wire tonight. This is Major Callahan. Are you ready to receive?"

The reply reflected a more formal tone. "Yes, Major. Please give Jones my best. Go ahead."

Jasper turned to Apollonia, nodded at the relayed wire in his hand, and said, "Your turn, Miss Foley."

She dictated the message to him in clipped, precise tones, as if she'd rehearsed it.

"Classified secret: for the colonel only. From Major Callahan, Detroit. As regards the prisoner Archer Blaine, subject of our last communication, I have finalized arrangements here and in Washington. We are ready to take him off your hands. Our party, Captain Jensen and Lieutenant Frank, are expected at Mackinac in two days, the first of April. I trust the prisoner will be made ready for transfer. Most important, Colonel: As before, make no reply to this message. Security here at Detroit may still be compromised. We must receive no messages on this matter. Your assistance and cooperation are most appreciated."

In a few moments, the other end of the line replied in turn: "Message received in full. It should be in the colonel's hands before noon."

Jasper rejoined: "Thank you, Mackinac. A reminder that this is army business—no discussion of message under any circumstances."

The Western Union man acknowledged the warning, no doubt accustomed to procedures of military secrecy. Both sides went through the rubrics of signing off, and Jasper began quickly removing his relay from the wire. With that completed, he went to work reconnecting the main line.

"Do you think the fort will honor our instructions not to reply?" Apollonia asked him.

Jasper worked as he answered. "Hard to say. We still don't know if they replied to the messages we sent them from Saginaw. Maybe the colonel wanted to confirm his orders. If that's what happened, then when me and Chase go out there in two days, we're going to be in for a very unpleasant little greeting."

He gave Apollonia a direct look as he handed the wire to Cloud, who began climbing the pole to restore the line to its proper place. "We've already discussed it, Miss Foley. There's no other way. We have to take that risk."

The mention of his name immediately snatched Jonathan's attention away from Jasper's fascinating display of nineteenth-century technological trickery.

"When *we* go out there?" he asked.

Apollonia gently took his hand. "I am sorry, Jonathan. We have left you utterly in the dark. Tomorrow, I promise, you will know it all."

The next day consisted of waiting. With whatever action the group had planned for the following day, the travelers rested their ride-wearied bodies in the comforts of the hotel.

At eleven o'clock, the proprietor knocked quietly on Jonathan's door and informed him that a Miss Foley was awaiting him in the lobby. He joined her there a few moments later.

She rose as he approached and held out her hand with a wan smile. "It is not very cold. We should walk along the shore."

Under a cloudy sky that looked much more threatening than the cool breeze felt, they strolled along the stony beach from one end of town to the other. Every now and then, Apollonia would nudge aside a stray piece of driftwood with her shoe. The breeze lifted strands of her hair and sent them flying across her face.

They stopped at a place where the shore reached its farthest apex into the waters of the straits. They sat on a wrought iron bench that had been placed at the picturesque vantage point.

She wasted no time broaching the subject at hand. Her tone was businesslike but soft.

"We are here to free an imprisoned man, Jonathan," she began, squeezing his hand gently and looking him directly in the eye. "I am sure you already know as much."

"He is from the South?"

"Yes."

"Then you and your friends are..."

She sighed heavily. "We are all working for him. His name is Archer Blaine, and he is associated with a Confederate agency known as the Secret Service. I suspect you know that too by now, do you not?"

"It hasn't been hard to figure out."

"And you know that I have trusted you. I asked you to come with us, all the way here, because I trust you. I know that you are going to help me, even though you stand against slavery, even though you favor the Northern cause."

She drew her face closer to his. "I was right to trust you, was I not, Jonathan?" He felt her breath on his face as she spoke.

"Yes."

Even as he answered, he pondered the response. Was he willing to do whatever this woman asked of him? Amid all the values and principles he held and honored, was Apollonia the only value that mattered to him now?

She smiled and drew nearer yet. She allowed the faintest trace of her lips to brush against his before she drew back again. The sudden intimacy did not shock him. Her closeness felt natural, almost inevitable. It was, it seemed to him, exactly as it was supposed to be.

"We will go over the details tonight, Jonathan, but the essence is this: Tomorrow afternoon, you will dress in a Union captain's uniform that we have brought with us. We will all board the late packet here in Mackinac City for the island. When we arrive, Cloud, Jeremiah, and I will go off by ourselves. You and Jasper, who will act as your lieutenant, will proceed to the fort and identify yourselves as officers from the army depot in Detroit. You will sign the necessary papers and take, into your ostensible custody, Colonel Archer Blaine of the Confederate States Army. We will all reconnoiter elsewhere on the island at twilight, at a location Jasper knows."

She looked out into the calm, gray water of Lake Huron, toward Mackinac Island, and continued. "Colonel Blaine is one of several Confederate officers being held as prisoners of war on the island," she said. "He has been in Union custody for nearly four months.

"He must remain so no longer. He has important tasks to perform," she paused and kept her gaze on the water, away from Jonathan, as if taking great care to choose her words. "Tasks with which I will be obliged to assist him."

She then turned to Jonathan directly, her expression no longer commanding but pleading. "And I beg of you, Jonathan, not to ask me—not yet, at any rate—about the nature of those tasks or about how I have come to be associated with them. It is far beyond my rights or abilities to say anything about these matters, even to you."

Jonathan nodded, at least outwardly accepting her need for secrecy. He steered the conversation back toward what he knew was a safe subject to share.

"I take it that the telegraph message Jasper sent last night was meant to be accepted by the fort as orders for the prisoner's transfer."

"Yes, exactly that."

He regarded her with admiration, realizing, with a newfound sense of respect, that Apollonia was undeniably a very formidable woman.

"It's very bold and clever," he said. "You've been working on it for quite a while, haven't you?"

She regarded him steadily. "I am doing only what I have been instructed to do, Jonathan, but, yes, the plans have taken a great deal of work to prepare. It is why I came to Michigan in the first place. My aunt and uncle were told that my parents desired to send me to the North for fears that Savannah might soon become a battleground. I fear that may indeed become the case before long, but the explanation was merely a pretext, of course, and warm souls that my aunt and uncle are, they were only too happy to welcome me into their home—into their country—for safe haven. They had no idea of my real purpose."

"What about Jasper and Cloud? How did you explain them to your aunt and uncle?"

"They have no idea of their existence. Jasper, who has long worked by Archer's side, accompanied me here from Georgia. Cloud is from somewhere in Michigan, and when Jasper heard of his skills as a guide and tracker in Saginaw, he took it upon himself to hire him. Since our arrival here last fall, Jasper has stayed well away from Riverdale, taking on a little work as a photographer so as not to attract suspicion. Along with Cloud, he stayed in that lonely little house in the township and kept mostly to himself, waiting for instructions. Every so often, late at night, I would meet with them to discuss the state of our plans, as you yourself discovered."

Jonathan already knew the answer to his next question, but asked it anyway, curious to see what she would say.

"What did you tell your aunt and uncle of your trip here to Mackinac?"

She frowned. "I told them nothing, Jonathan. It is very cruel, I admit it, especially after all their kindness to me, but there was no other way—no plausible reason I could give them for why I should leave of a sudden. They know nothing beyond the fact of my disappearance. No doubt the police have been searching, and not only for me, Jonathan, but for you as well. You disappeared at the same time, after all. Surely they must think the two are connected."

"Doesn't this endanger the plot?"

"They have no notion of any plot, no idea of where we might go. I believe they must be thinking something awful, that perhaps you and I were..." She looked down at her hands in discomfort and blushed.

"Be that as it may, it takes their suspicion away from the real situation, from that which we are here to do. In time, I hope, my aunt and uncle will learn the truth, and perhaps not detest me for it, but for now there is no choice but to do this cruel thing—to leave them anxious and worried and without answers."

She drew nearer once again. "Jonathan, you must know how grateful I am, how much comfort it is to have you with me."

He smiled as a response.

"Still, I must say it. Tomorrow, when you go to that fort, you will cross a line from which you can never retreat. You will become one of us—a spy deep in the enemy's territory, Jonathan, with all the peril and woe that might bring upon you. You understand that, do you not?"

He smiled again and gently stroked the back of her hand with his thumb.

"You amaze me more than I can say. You appear a gentle Southern lady, sweet and lovely—a cultured belle of the privileged class—but here you are, a daring spy, braving raw wilderness and uncouth companions alike, sending false messages by night, preparing to free a captured comrade from the enemy's very clutches. You're quite a cloak-and-dagger mystery."

She put her arms around his neck and brought her mouth to his ear.

"Perhaps I am, Mr. Chase," she whispered, "and there is still a great deal more you do not know about me."

April

A violet blush falls over the fields,

As lilacs come tumbling in bountiful yields.

On breezes that whisper like lovers at dawn

Come messages sweet and young as a fawn.

The heavens are misty with gossamer rain,

The world is awakened and growing again.

I sing of the springtime, as you can see, but mine are words of hope and longing, not of the present moment's experience, for where I find myself there is no springtime, at least not yet. It remains cold and wintry here, and I am merely retrieving my memories of home, where the advent of April comes as sweetly and softly as an angel's sigh.

As for me, I am far too busy, too worried, and too preoccupied to sigh. I was right to forecast change, for it has come to me in force. My life is a whirlwind such as I have never known, and I find myself both terrified and smitten by the many new things taking place.

I am no longer at Riverdale, to begin with, and I confess to relief at that fact. I think I should have gone mad had I been forced to remain within those walls for another day, yet the circumstances of my leaving are themselves hardly comforting.

We had mere days to prepare our departure after Jasper's receipt of the long-awaited command from Archer, which is to say his notification that the time was ripe for action. And action it has been! As I write these words, just after midnight on the first day of the month, I can hear the sound of the waves from the Straits of Mackinac, just a few yards away from this godforsaken hotel. I would never have imagined, in all my wildest dreams, ever spending a night in such a place as this.

And what a journey to arrive here! For an entire week, we have struggled through woods so vast it seems they would never end, with trees so tall it makes one dizzy to gaze toward their tops, and snow so deep one fears to stray from the path for dread of sinking and never being found.

I have seen woods before, the sweet and bucolic woods of my own home, but until this journey I have never seen a true wilderness. My stars, there have been wild Indians along our trail, who hunt in these fearsome forests, and have heard the close howling of wolves almost every night. And all through this arduous voyage, never far from our sight, has loomed that mighty and sinister sea, deep and gray, which seems to silently watch us as we travel, in the artful and malevolent manner of some primeval enchantress of the North. Her formal name is Lake Huron, but Cloud calls it something like "Karegnondi," and I have taken to calling her (only to myself) "Visigoth Huronic," for she seems such an eldritch, pagan goddess. You will forgive me, I hope, if I revert to my superstitious nature, but such wildness inspires it in my civilized soul.

My companions on this journey have been those whom I have already introduced—Jeremiah, Jasper, and Cloud—along with one very important addition, and his presence is perhaps the most important change of all.

I am speaking, of course, of Jonathan Chase. I no longer call him Mr. Chase, but simply Jonathan, and he in turn feels free, with my blessing, to call me by my Christian name alone. If this is suggestive to you of a certain intimacy between us, then you are an observant reader indeed, and I shall not, at least in the pages of this diary, be so timid and prim as to deny it.

Jonathan is here because I pleaded shamelessly with him to accompany us, and I made that plea because of the profound trust I place in him. During our journey, Jonathan has proven, and I am sure he will continue to prove, to be the ally which I have so desperately sought. I have told him very little of our plans and intentions—indeed, I dread the prospect of his ever discovering their true nature!—and yet he agreed to come, to knowingly put himself in hardship and peril, and has stayed by my side the whole way.

Dare I hope that he places the same trust in me as I place in him?

Dare I hope for more? Do I hope that he feels a longing in his breast which reflects that in mine?

Yes, I confess it, at this moment, with this pen on this page: I am becoming quite enamored of this cryptic man from the West, this man from a place I now think of as Somewhere Else. I thrill at the sound of his voice and even here, in this frozen land, grow warm at the sight of his face. There are times when my feelings are like a strong and spirited horse straining at the reins, threatening to break into an open run at any moment. My stars, I came within a millimeter of kissing him yesterday and without the slightest invitation! I have never behaved in so forward a manner. Jonathan seems such a dignified man, so deep and quiet, and I fear I might shock him and scare him away. I must take greater care in how I approach him.

Yet I refuse to be so genteel as to ignore my own question. I do hope for more, and if you consider me wrong to entertain such a hope, then you shall have to be satisfied with your condemnation, for be assured you shall not have my obedience.

That Jonathan will be with me today—that, indeed, he has agreed to take a leader's role in this most important task—gives me great comfort. Somehow I know that he will succeed and that this stage of our perilous and dreadful mission shall be over at last.

If only it were its conclusion!

APRIL

GEORGIAN BAY

THE MAIL PACKET, a small and ungainly sloop, pulled away from the Mackinac City pier at precisely eleven in the morning, as scheduled, and began plying its way methodically toward the island in gentle swells under a misty sky.

Jonathan and Jasper stood at the bow, apart from Cloud, who sat by himself on one of the deck benches, and from Apollonia and Jeremiah, who remained quietly and as unobtrusively as possible in the small passenger cabin behind the wheelhouse.

The two men looked authoritative and striking in their deep blue army uniforms with brass buttons and gold braid epaulets on the shoulders. Jonathan wore a wide-brimmed slouch hat, its front and back brims bent low, with the crossed saber emblem of the cavalry on the crown; Jasper wore a gold-bordered kepi, bearing no corps insignia.

Jonathan felt ridiculous in the uniform. He could not expel the idea of a costume party, no matter how hard he tried to pretend this was his normal attire. It seemed so absurdly *period* to him, yet he could not help but notice the glances of respect and admiration it drew from other passengers. It was clear that they took the finery of the United States Army seriously indeed.

One inquired as to the officers' purpose, saying that it was uncommon to see soldiers of higher rank than corporal on the vessel. Jonathan smiled and told him simply that they had "military business" at the fort, and the man politely left it at that.

Jonathan had spent the previous night being painstakingly instructed on what, and what not, to say to the authorities once they arrived. Jasper was his tutor, displaying an obvious in-depth knowledge of Union military procedure and intelligence. It was the most civil exchange the two had had: Whenever Jasper worked on something related directly to his clandestine responsibilities, as he had been for the past few days, his sullen, insolent air was replaced with a hard professionalism and steely confidence. He was clearly an experienced spy, and apparently a good one, but his underlying air of malice remained intact. Jonathan sensed that the man would kill him, or anyone else, in an instant, so long as he deemed the act professionally judicious.

They had gone over numerous details the night before, but after much hushed conversation at the hotel, it seemed to Jonathan that the core of Jasper's lessons was fairly straightforward: Betray no nervousness and say no more than you absolutely must.

Two hours after leaving the mainland, the packet tied up at the narrow pier on the rocky, tree-covered island. The snow there was almost gone, with only occasional patches visible in shady spots. The air was no worse than cool, and some of the trees were already budding, some of the bushes in early flower.

The small cluster of houses and stores near the shore reminded Jonathan of a New England fishing village. The settlement seemed sleepy and isolated, but the white stone fort, visible on a high promontory, was imposing and fierce with its iron cannons pointed in strategic directions out into the straits.

Cloud disembarked without a word to the others, as if he were a total stranger, and Apollonia and Jeremiah did the same. There were stares at the sight of a black man and white woman walking together—surely a rare sight in America's distant North—but they appeared to be stares of curiosity, not hostility.

Jonathan and Jasper walked up a narrow lane in the direction of the fort, their boots resounding on the paving stones.

It was not a long walk, and before long they found themselves standing before the tall wooden gates of Fort Mackinac. Two sentries with muskets perched on their shoulders saluted the visitors, and one of them, a corporal, inquired curtly as to their business. Observing protocol, Jonathan responded to the challenge.

"Captain Jensen and Lieutenant Frank from Detroit, to see the commanding officer."

The corporal had apparently already been briefed. Without another word, he directed his comrade to open the gates. The soldier informed them where to go, and the pretenders strode slowly and confidently through the quadrangle toward the colonel's office. The grounds of the fort were immaculate and pleasant, and every soldier they encountered was neat and respectful, each offering a smart salute.

"A day or two of this," Jonathan whispered to Jasper, "and I could start enjoying being a captain."

Jasper's only response was a muted command to hush.

They knocked on the proper door and were admitted by a thin lieutenant into the spartan office of the fort's commander, Colonel Thaddeus Dixon, bald on the top of his head and heavily whiskered in its lower regions with brilliant red muttonchops. Jonathan followed Jasper's lead, removing his hat upon entering the building and remembering not to salute while indoors.

"Gentlemen!" Dixon boomed, shaking their hands firmly and telling them to sit in wooden chairs placed directly before the orderly expanse of his desk.

"I received your wire yesterday," he said, taking his own chair. "How are things in Detroit, Captain?"

It was Jonathan's cue. "Things are fine, sir, thank you," he said. "Quiet, as usual." He detected a slight stiffening in Jasper and remembered what he'd been told about not improvising.

"Quiet, you say!" the colonel replied with a muffled laugh. "Why, if it's genuine quiet you want, I suggest you request a transfer up here. There's probably not a quieter fort in the entire Union."

The captain and the lieutenant merely smiled and nodded.

Sensing his visitors' reticence, the colonel abandoned his small talk. "So you've come for Blaine. He must be an important fellow if Washington is asking for him."

"That is my assumption, sir," Jonathan replied.

Dixon leveled a hard stare into Jonathan's eyes. "Assumption, you say? Which means either that you honestly don't know or you've been ordered to tell me nothing about it."

Jonathan merely smiled, this time remembering Jasper's dictum.

"Well, I can't say I'm surprised that old Dixon is being left out once again," the colonel said in an injured tone. "After all, I'm the fellow they sent all the way out here, halfway to Hudson Bay. Why the hell should they tell me why they want Blaine set free? I'm just his damn prison keeper."

In the face of the colonel's anger and pathos, Jonathan felt a sudden surge of confidence. "To be honest, Colonel, they haven't told us any more than they've told you. If you're just the keeper, then we're just the escorts. And permit me, sir, to set something straight: Blaine isn't being set free. He's being transferred."

Dixon looked sad and belittled—the expression, Jonathan thought, of a man who foolishly feels that something important, such as the war, was passing him by. He stared briefly at the ceiling, crossed his fingers across his considerable stomach, and apparently decided that he'd complained enough.

"As to that transfer, Captain," he said, his voice now businesslike, "I'd like you to sign this release." He slid a document across the desk and offered a pen. "How will you be taking him?"

Jonathan scratched his false name across the paper and didn't look up when he answered. "We've leased berths aboard a southbound freighter," remembering the pre-calculated lies he and Jasper had rehearsed. "We'll be taking him aboard this afternoon. Quickest and safest way back to Detroit, and a far sight easier than getting here."

"You might have a little trouble with the ice," Dixon rejoined. "Are you sure it's clear all the way down?"

Jasper, at last, entered the conversation.

"The navy says we'll be fine, sir," he said, his customary Dixie accent expertly replaced with an authentic Boston patois. "Unless we get another hard freeze, it's open all the way down."

Dixon retrieved the release paper from Jonathan and rose from his desk.

"Lieutenant!" he barked. The thin man was at the door in a moment. "Bring Blaine here at once. Have him in irons and tell him to bring his belongings."

He turned to his guests. "In all fairness, gentlemen, I'm glad to be shut of that one. I've never trusted him. Something about him never felt right. A little too cultivated for my tastes, too smooth, a little shifty in the eyes. I'll give him to you with cuffs on his hands. I suggest you keep them on until you've got him squared away."

"Thank you, Colonel," Jonathan said, shaking his hand. "I appreciate everything."

As they waited for the prisoner, the three grew silent. Dixon, apparently sharing their discomfort, asked what they knew of the progress of the war.

Jasper again stepped in, to Jonathan's relief. "Nothing more than you know, sir, I'm sure," he replied with deference. "From what we hear, Grant is preparing to cross the Rapidan, working to get an angle on Richmond. Nobody seems to know what Lee is up to. The talk is that we're in for serious fighting in the next few weeks."

Dixon sighed, as if lamenting the glory he would never earn in battles he would never see.

"We're a long way from the end, I'm afraid. A good deal of killing left, don't you think?"

Before they could reply, the door opened, admitting a tall man, hands cuffed behind his back. The lieutenant followed, a pistol pointed squarely at the Rebel Jonathan only knew of by name.

"Ah, Blaine!" Dixon said. "I have some news for you today. You're leaving Mackinac, bound for points unknown!"

Colonel Archer Blaine, Confederate States Army, was nothing short of impressive. He was a prisoner of war, immobilized in chains, an enemy's pistol up against his spine, yet somehow he gained command of the room just by entering.

He was towering and muscular and walked with erect deliberation. His dark hair was short and painstakingly combed, as was the narrow mustache that drooped almost to the end of his chin. His eyes, a pale sea green, stood out in stark contrast to his well-tanned face, dominated by a strong jaw and cheekbones.

Instead of a uniform, he wore ordinary civilian clothing—a short brown coat, plain white shirt, and baggy blue trousers—but his presence projected aristocracy and authority.

Blaine regarded the two Union officers who stood beside Dixon, the ghost of a smile on his face. If he recognized Jasper, he gave no sign of it. Jasper, in turn, observed Blaine with a convincingly hostile stare and removed his own pistol from his belt in an unmistakable display of dominance.

"You needn't worry about any of that, Lieutenant," Blaine said, his voice deep and resonant, his accent an elegant and refined drawl. "I will not be giving you gentlemen any trouble."

He turned to Dixon. "Did I hear you correctly, Colonel? Did you say I am to be moved?"

Dixon eyed the prisoner with scorn. "That's correct, Blaine. These officers have been given authority to oversee your transfer."

Blaine turned his gaze to Jonathan. "Might I inquire as to my destination, Captain?" His glance was sharply inquisitive, not as to the question he actually asked but who this blue-clad impostor really was. Jonathan thought he detected more than curiosity in that stare—he saw a personal challenge.

"You will be made aware of that information when it is fitting for you to know," Jonathan said coldly. "Until that time, I must warn you that you remain a prisoner of war. If you should make any attempt at escape, know that we will not hesitate to kill you."

Blaine's subtle smile returned, as if the uncompromising answer pleased him. "I would expect nothing less, Captain. When do we leave this fair fortress?"

"We leave now," Jonathan replied, turning to Dixon. "With the colonel's leave, of course."

"You have it, Captain. I'm happy to offer you a ride to the dock."

"That won't be necessary, sir, thank you. It's a small island. We'll take Colonel Blaine for a short walk and bide our time until the vessel is ready. We hope to sail before sunset."

Dixon managed a thin smile. "Well, then, it's been a pleasure, Captain, Lieutenant." He presented Jonathan with an iron key and then addressed Blaine. "I don't suppose that farewells would be appropriate for us, would they?"

"Oh now, Colonel, don't be so hard," the Confederate replied, grinning widely. "You've been a fine captor, to my way of thinking. After these weeks as your guest, I freely confess that I'll miss you and your command."

The glib remark did not amuse Dixon. With no further ceremony, he directed his lieutenant to stand down and see them out. The lieutenant marched Blaine out of the office, Jonathan and Jasper trailing behind, the latter's pistol still raised.

They made a strange procession as they walked through the grounds of the fort. Two or three Union soldiers offered Blaine warm goodbyes, their air of friendliness surprising to Jonathan. At the gates, the lieutenant ordered the sentries to let them pass, and with no more ceremony than that, Archer Blaine found himself a free man.

The unusual company—two soldiers with pistols at the ready, following a shackled man—attracted considerable attention as they crossed the little village into open meadowland, bordered at irregular intervals by tall stands of trees. The cool, humid air was fair with the faint scent of lilacs, blooming in thickets all around them, and the piquant spice of pine and spruce. The prisoner breathed in deeply, as if he detected his own freedom in the fragrance.

At a considerable distance from the last dwelling, when the dirt path took a bend behind a gentle rise, they stopped.

For a moment, nobody spoke. There was no greeting, no expression of congratulation, between Blaine and the two men who had just freed him.

Jasper broke the silence. "Give me the key, Chase," he said. "I want to take these irons off."

Blaine, however, shook his head. "No, Jasper. Not yet. We're too close to the fort—this whole damn island is too close to the fort. Somebody might see. I'll keep them on until we board. How long will it be?"

Jasper pulled out his watch. "Two hours, off the eastern shore. About a mile from here"

"Good. Where are the others?" Blaine asked.

"Just up the road a bit."

The colonel nodded, then finally took a good look at Jonathan. He briefly flashed a confident smile.

"I've not had the pleasure of your acquaintance, sir," he said. "Forgive me if my present posture prevents me from shaking hands. I am Archer Blaine. I am pleased to meet you and indebted as well. That was an excellent performance back there."

Jonathan returned his nod. "Jonathan Chase. And thank you."

Blaine raised his chin as he surveyed Jonathan, his eyes narrowing. It felt like a close personal appraisal.

"Your accent is Northern, Mr. Chase," he said. "Are you a Northern man?"

Jonathan held Blaine's eyes as he responded. "A Western man. Colorado Territory."

The confident smile returned, as Blaine steered the conversation—deftly, it seemed to Jonathan—away from his line of questioning. "The Rocky Mountains! I would love to see them. Haven't had the chance as of yet. Are they as splendid as the writers make them out to be?"

"Even more than that," Jonathan said.

It was plain from his expression that Blaine had more questions for the unanticipated newcomer—how he had come to join their party, why he was risking his own life to help him, what his sympathies were regarding the war—but he asked nothing. It seemed a careful move, the calculation of a man accustomed to taking considerable caution.

Instead he resumed walking down the path, the others following his lead. Blaine turned to Jasper as they strode.

"You have taken care of the horses?" Blaine asked.

"Sold on the mainland."

"Excellent. That was nice work at the fort, Jasper."

Jasper allowed his usually pinched face to loosen into a grin. "My pleasure, Archer. You know, it wasn't nearly as hard as I expected. The telegraph worked like a charm, and if Dixon isn't the most gullible fool in the whole damn Yankee army, then I'm Abe Lincoln's nanny."

They laughed together at his colloquialism, obviously old acquaintances, if not old friends, Jonathan thought. They spoke as men with a long, possibly turbulent history between them, friendly but without the warmth of friendship.

They walked a little farther, deeper into a wood, and were briefly startled when three figures emerged from a shadow—Apollonia, then Jeremiah and Cloud. The two parties came together slowly and silently.

Blaine did not so much as glance at the men. His eyes fell on Apollonia at once and stayed there. Jonathan immediately sensed something between them, an intense current of energy. He could not determine its nature, whether positive or negative, but he felt an unpleasant pang in his own belly.

"Appy," Blaine said softly, standing close to her and looking deeply into her eyes. "It is the realization of a dream to see you at last."

She smiled slightly and held his eyes but briefly, casting a rapid sidelong glance that captured Jonathan's eyes for a lightning moment, then looked demurely downward.

Blaine maintained his intense stare. "You have been a busy girl," he said. "Not only did you travel all this great distance to set me free—and did it beautifully, I must say—you have hired your own men. Jasper and I are old comrades, of course, but now I see this Indian behind you," he nodded quickly at Cloud, "and this Western gentleman here, Mr. Chase, who just did a fine job in hoodwinking Colonel Dixon at the fort. But I know neither of these men, nor have I ever heard of their existence."

Apollonia looked back up at Blaine, almost apologetically it seemed.

"We found it necessary to improvise, Archer," she said. "Jasper and I both felt we might need more help."

Blaine sighed deeply and cast his gaze at the gray sky, as if deliberately suppressing a sudden surge of anger. When he turned back to Apollonia, his face was harder, its refined expression replaced with the tough glare of a soldier. In that expression, Jonathan could see that the group had found its true leader, that Apollonia and Jasper had only been interim commanders. It was clear who was in charge now.

But if Blaine had intended to scold or reprimand Apollonia, he had mastered the urge. His face remained stern but his voice was satin smooth. "Well, improvisation is the first trait of a good soldier, Appy, especially in our corps. You have done your job well."

She nodded and smiled weakly. Jonathan saw something in her face he had never seen before. She appeared meek and submissive in Blaine's presence. The firm sense of control she had always projected seemed to have disappeared.

Jasper exhaled a long plume of cigar smoke and brought the conversation back to the present. "Folks, we have about a mile to walk and a little less than an hour to walk it. I suggest we be on our way."

All alone in the woods, they resumed the path. Blaine and Jasper took the lead, Cloud and Jeremiah fell in behind them. Jonathan was glad when Apollonia tarried a little and joined him at the rear.

They crossed a long open field, laced with early wildflowers, just as the sun made a brief incision through the mist. Almost in reaction to the sudden light, Cloud sensed something. He hesitated, raised his head, and once again sniffed at the air. An awareness crossed his face, as if he were seeing the invisible.

"This is war ground," he said quietly. "Many men died in this place."

Up ahead, Jasper laughed aloud, the mockery obvious in his voice. "Smelling spooks again, Cloud?"

"I see them," Cloud replied, searching the emptiness with his eyes, ignoring Jasper's scorn. "Men in red and men in blue—white-faced men, all of them—marching like toy soldiers, dying like men."

Jasper snorted and said to Blaine, "Damn redskin's been smelling spooks since we left Saginaw. We'd be in fine shape if we could get him to smell Yankees half as well."

The two Confederates laughed at the idea.

Apollonia gave Jonathan's elbow a little nudge and whispered near his ear as they resumed the walk. "But Cloud is right, Jonathan. I have read an account of it. This meadow was once a battlefield, during the War of 1812. The Americans were trying to retake the fort, landing by stealth at night, but the British knew of the plans. They engaged them here and defeated them soundly. A young major, in command of the Americans, was among the first to fall."

He looked at her in surprise, and she smiled back with a flash of blue eyes. She was proud, it seemed, of the impromptu history lesson she had just given, and eager, it also seemed, to let him know that she had not forgotten him amid all the activity.

For his part, Jonathan was simply relieved to see that Apollonia's spark had only been dimmed, not extinguished.

They waited on the northeastern shore of the island as the afternoon shadows grew longer. Blaine and Jasper stood apart from the others, talking quietly among themselves—secretive men, Jonathan thought, discussing secret plans.

Apollonia, Jonathan, and Jeremiah—who had been staying especially silent since Blaine joined the group—sat beneath the arching boughs of a mammoth hemlock.

Cloud squatted near the shoreline, picking pebbles from the water then tossing them back into the lake. The Chippewa seemed impatient, as if he was waiting for something. Eventually Jasper unceremoniously approached Cloud, placed several coins in his hand, and made a casual gesture of parting. With a nod, the Indian rose and walked to where the other three were sitting. His handsome face betraying no emotion, he announced that he was leaving.

"I have no business where you are going," he said to them. "I have other work to do. A fair journey to you."

Apollonia—who, it seemed to Jonathan, never liked or trusted the Indian—gave only a faint smile as a reply. Jeremiah rose to his feet and heartily shook the Indian's powerful hand. "I'll surely be missing you, red man," he said quietly. Cloud whispered something in Jeremiah's ear, slapped him on the shoulder, and turned to Jonathan.

Jonathan rose to his feet and grasped Cloud's hand, putting aside his memories of the pistol Cloud once pointed at his back. In the busy weeks since their first meeting, while Jonathan had not exactly come to grow fond of the Chippewa, he had found him far preferable than Jasper. The Indian's general silence and apparent thoughtfulness fascinated him, as did his obvious knack for mystical insight. In a way, he realized, he would actually miss him.

As Cloud took Jonathan's hand, he gently pulled him a few feet away from the others. Once again, Jonathan was amazed by the man's physical strength.

He spoke in a whisper and looked directly into Jonathan's eyes. "You are a strange sort of man, Jonathan Chase," he said. "I know that you have traveled far to come here—much farther than you say. I am curious about you."

When Jonathan said nothing in response, he continued. "It is your business why you are here, but I sense that you are a good man, and so I will trust you and give you a warning." He looked at Apollonia. "Protect this woman."

He then turned his face, for just a glance, to where Blaine and Jasper were conversing. "And beware of them."

He did not wait for a reply but released Jonathan's hand and walked directly into the inland woods. With his long raven hair and buckskin clothing, he seemed an integral part of the forest—as wild and ancient as the trees and animals themselves and just as much a part of the land. Jonathan knew that he would never see him again.

Jasper's harsh drawl broke the silence. "Ship ahoy!" he cried, pointing out into the lake.

The schooner, a lean, swift-looking vessel of perhaps fifty feet, had already rounded the northeastern shore. It was coming in close enough for Jonathan to see its remarkable spread of canvas and smart black hull, led by the colorful wooden figure of a flag-draped woman gracing the prow. Its sails looked full, and the ship appeared to be making good headway.

They watched in anticipation as the schooner dropped anchor a few hundred yards offshore and crewmen began preparing a small tender. Jasper, ever at the ready, flashed a mirror toward the vessel and received a bright flash in return. He produced his key and relieved Blaine of his hand shackles at last.

In twenty minutes, the boat reached shore. Three crewmen, dressed in dark sweaters and stocking caps, helped the passengers aboard and loaded the few canvas bags that now constituted their meager belongings. The sailors said nothing to their guests as they rowed back to the ship, and the passengers themselves remained quiet.

The brief trip was tense, with an air of danger hanging over the party. All of them looked back occasionally to the receding shoreline, as if expecting a company of troops—recently alerted to Blaine's clever escape—to gather and begin shooting.

But nobody showed up on the shore, and the travelers reached the ship without incident. They all climbed a rope ladder to the main deck, even Apollonia, who gathered her long dress around her ankles with one hand and, with surprising agility, raised herself up with the other.

Jonathan looked toward the canopy of canvas above him, rigged to masts that seemed as high as the ship was long. He had always been fascinated with old sailing ships; a painting of one had graced his bedroom wall as a boy. Now, to have actually boarded one, and to feel the swell of waves under its hull, felt almost intoxicating.

On deck, each of the guests was greeted in turn by the captain, including Jeremiah. He was slightly rotund and going gray at the temples and the tips of his well-trimmed beard. A dark blue seaman's cap, adorned with crossed anchors, crowned his head.

"Captain Tripp at your service," he said in a vaguely British-sounding accent. "Welcome aboard the *Huron Sprite*."

When he had acknowledged them all, he shouted a command to his boatswain. "Weigh anchor, Mr. Simpson!" he boomed. "We're under way at once."

Jonathan thought it interesting that the captain asked his passengers not a single question, despite their obvious strangeness—two men in U.S. military uniforms, one white man and one black man in ordinary civilian clothing, and a silent, melancholy woman in a plain gray velvet dress. Nor did he inquire why they had requested to meet his ship off this part of the island, instead of in the harbor on the other side. Jonathan surmised that the mariner was not American and that his curiosity had likely been suppressed when the trip was first arranged, probably by Jasper and almost surely with gold. It also occurred to Jonathan that the captain might be a professional smuggler, well accustomed to such secretive goings-on.

Captain Tripp was, in any event, a practical master. He turned to his guests for a brief talk, informing them where their cabins were located, when meals would be served, and that they could expect to disembark at Detroit—their apparent destination—during the evening of the following day. He also told them that "it has been a gorgeous springtime, by God, and the ice has all but melted away to give us a wide, smooth channel all the way down."

But before heading to the bridge, he looked into the darkening cloud-flecked sky. "But I do suspect...," he began, searching the early evening. "I do suspect that we will have a storm this night, so you had better prepare for a lively go."

He noticed the apprehensive looks on several of their faces and laughed reassuringly. "But do not be frightened, my friends. You have Tripp as your captain, who happens to be not only the best navigator but the luckiest sailor on the whole Great Lakes. Why just last fall, I was all booked to serve as first mate on the SS *Water Witch* out of Chicago. Don't you know it, but I missed her departure, made it to the docks half an hour late. She sailed without me, right on schedule! But it was late in the season, my friends—November, you know—and she ran into a storm out here on Huron. Tried to make port in Saginaw Bay but couldn't pull the whole way. She went down with all hands."

The captain sadly shook his head at his own story and then smiled, as if confident that he had somehow reassured his fellow travelers. But as they felt the ship pull free of its anchor and begin to head southward into open water, none of them, including Jonathan, felt particularly emboldened by the tragic tale.

All of them, except Jonathan, went below decks to their quarters. Jonathan stayed topside for a while, watching the busy sailors at their work as the sun—molten copper in a peach-colored sky—sank below the conical tops of Mackinac Island's ancient trees.

He did not know what lay ahead of him, nor even where this strange medley of war-tossed desperadoes was destined, but he did know that he was now one of their number and that, for better or worse, he would likely share their fate.

As night fell on Lake Huron, the crew of the *Sprite* began their nocturnal duties, lighting lanterns on the main deck, standing watch, and staying ready in case the captain ordered them to work sail. The eventide was calm, and the ship was driven by a cold northern breeze that sent luminescent clouds scudding across the bluish-yellow glow of a full moon—the seductive *clair de lune* of April. It cast a beautiful beam of moonlight across the waves and, for a little while, illuminated the outline of the mainland shore. As the ship headed farther out into the lake, the shoreline disappeared altogether.

As he watched it fade, Jonathan wondered when, if ever, he would set foot on that wild peninsula again and, if so, in what century it might be. It was a melancholy thought, akin to, but not quite the same as, homesickness.

Later, in his tiny cabin below deck, he ate a simple meal of fish and boiled potatoes, assuming that the others were doing the same in their own claustrophobic quarters. With considerable relief, he replaced his uniform with his own clothing.

He was restless. The swell of the lake was not so severe as to tempt sickness but enough to prevent him from falling into an easy sleep. Its effect was enhanced by the myriad unanswered questions that faced him.

He knew that the party was heading south, apparently to Detroit, but where from there? It was obvious that the group was on some sort of mission, with Blaine's escape from confinement only a necessary early stage. Blaine was needed for something, and it felt like something important. Both Apollonia and Jasper had projected a tangible air of anxiety, at times even desperation, during the journey to Mackinac and now back again, which forced Jonathan to believe that time was an important factor in what they were doing.

Nobody had said a word to him about their intentions in the wake of Blaine's escape from the fort, including Apollonia. He recognized that he was not yet trusted—and felt that he might, in fact, never be trusted—and had to admit that he found this understandable. Only he knew his real reason for coming along on this trip. His companions, perhaps excepting Apollonia herself, must have found his presence puzzling, if not threatening. Jasper had been suspicious from the beginning, and Jonathan sensed that Blaine was already leaning in that direction.

He agonized over the nature of Blaine's relationship to Apollonia, the strange energy he had felt between them. They had obviously met before, perhaps even knew each other well, but in what way and under what circumstances Jonathan had no way of knowing. The feeling this conjured in his heart was obvious and inescapable—simply raw jealousy. He wondered whether Blaine in turn might be having the same emotion and hoped, in some dark, possessive corner of his own heart, that he was.

At last he had enough of these relentless circles of speculation. He needed sleep and turned onto his side, relaxing his weary body into a more comfortable position. But in the long course of his ponderings, he had barely noticed that the motion of the ship had grown steadily more pronounced, its wooden creaking louder and more frequent. He pulled himself from bed, donned his coat, and returned to the main deck, grasping rails all the way.

Things were changing on the lake.

The waves, no more than lively a few hours ago, now looked angry, frothing with white crowns. The ship tossed in swells at least ten feet high. Its sails alternately billowed in strong wind or snapped back in the sudden lack of it. Several sailors manned the lines, their muscles tensed against obvious strain.

No trace was visible of the once charming moon. Rolling clouds covered the skies and hung so low they seemed only a few hundred feet above the surface. The air was cold and heavy with the scent of rain, and the wind whistled a sinister howl.

Jonathan heard Tripp's voice from somewhere aft and, clutching the rail carefully, made his way back to the bridge where the helmsman grappled with the huge spoked wheel. Behind him stood the captain, his head covered in a broad-brimmed sou'wester of oilskin, his body in a slicker of the same shiny material.

"Go careful there, lad!" he heard the captain call out to him. "Come up if you like, but watch your step!"

He climbed the stairs and found himself standing beside Tripp, looking out over the helmsman's shoulder into rising walls of foam-flecked water.

"Did I not tell you we were in for a bruising roll in the hay with the old lady?" Tripp shouted. He seemed to be enjoying himself.

The captain tapped his helmsman on the arm. "Keep her tail to the wind, Mr. Morris! Don't lag on the rudder like that! And favor it a little to starboard on the upswells! There you go, lad!"

He turned to Jonathan, speaking loudly into his ear. "Feels like we're doing an easy twenty-five or thirty knots, Mr. Chase. If it stayed like this, we could manage all right, riding her all the way down. We'd probably make Detroit in eight or nine hours."

The captain beamed, not a trace of fear on his face. "But it feels to me like the gale is on the uptake, just getting started..."

He nudged the helmsman again. "A little harder to larboard now. Hold her there just a bit longer before you let her back down."

Tripp nodded at Jonathan. "On the uptake, as I say, Mr. Chase! If it picks up much more, we'll have trouble keeping her in line. And these seas are as choppy as the devil. We could break deep."

Jonathan had no idea what Tripp was talking about, but both options sounded dire.

"What then?" he shouted back to the captain.

"Well, then, old Tripp will just have to think of something, won't he?" the smiling captain replied.

The rain began to fall, spotty at first, then steadily, and finally in torrents that varied between vertical and horizontal, depending on the mood of the wind. It stung Jonathan's unprotected face and made it hard for him to see. He told Tripp that he was heading back below.

"Good idea!" the captain answered. "And be so kind, will you, Mr. Chase, to tell the others that it would be wise for them not to venture up on deck. At least until things settle down."

Things seemed even worse below. At least when he was topside, Jonathan could see the water and feel the wind. It gave him some perspective on the gale and the ship's position within it. Down in the cramped passenger quarters, lit only by murky oil lamps, the storm manifested itself only in the ever-gaining, up-and-down—and sometimes side-to-side—motion. Jonathan was amazed that he was not yet seasick. He had never spent significant time at sea, and he wondered how he'd gained his sea legs in such short order.

He knocked quietly on the compartment where Blaine and Jasper were staying and then entered. Both were laying in their hammocks, apparently sound asleep despite the heavy swaying of their nautical beds.

Jeremiah, not surprisingly, was bunked in what appeared to be a closet with nothing more than a hanging blanket for a door. When Jonathan pulled the blanket aside, he found the slave seated on the deck, his arms encircling his knees. His eyes were wide, and despite the cold air that permeated the ship, his forehead glistened with beads of sweat.

"My ole grandpappy used to tell me stories about the sea, Massa Chase," he said over the gale's howling. "He's the one come over on the slave ship from Africa, you see, when he was just a little boy, no taller than a rhubarb plant, he used to say. My, but those stories were fit to conjure nightmares in a young boy such as I. Such storms they suffered, he'd say, such storms and such heat as only hell can cook up, iron chains on arms and legs and no room to stand up in, hardly room to sit without hitting your head on the wood up above."

He looked nervously at the planks above his own head. "Must've been something like this, don't you think, Massa Chase? Must've been a nightmare just like this one."

Jonathan did his best to reassure Jeremiah but felt dishonest in doing so, since he was beginning to have his own doubts as to whether the *Huron Sprite* was a fit enough vessel to withstand the forces of nature now gathering against her. He knew that there was no need to warn Jeremiah to stay put.

He came to Apollonia's cabin at last, tapped gently on the door, and heard her low voice bid him enter. He found her sitting on her tidy bunk, still wearing the velvet dress in which she had left the island. Her hair was loose and undone—Jonathan was amazed at its fullness—and she was slowly running a silver comb through its golden lengths.

Her face brightened when she saw that it was him. "Jonathan!" she said with a smile.

He smiled back. "I'm delivering a message from the captain not to go up on deck. The storm is growing worse."

She grinned ironically, without losing her good humor. "The captain apparently thinks his passengers are fools. I hardly think this is the night for a leisurely stroll along the rail."

Then her smile faded completely. "How bad *is* the storm, Jonathan? You should know. You were a sailor, were you not?"

He had practically forgotten that lie. "It's pretty serious, Apollonia. It looks like it has a lot of strength. It might last awhile."

"Could we sink?" Her face looked worried now.

"I doubt it. Tripp strikes me as an excellent seaman. He'll get us through all right."

She brightened once more, and her hand resumed its languid stroking of her tresses. "I'm not afraid, mind you. I have seen worse than this. Not in a ship at sea, of course, but worse nonetheless."

He raised his eyebrows, silently inquiring for details.

She offered none, deftly steering their talk in a new direction. Her tone was confidential. "I keep telling you, Jonathan, that I will explain everything in time. I so desperately want to, but there are promises...there are *vows*, which I am obliged to keep, and if I do not...well, never mind that now. But I do want to apologize for my silence and at the same time plead for your understanding."

"I do understand," he replied. "And I trust you. We're allies, remember?"

She nodded and gestured for him to sit beside her on the narrow bunk. He did, instantly feeling both the excitement he'd felt before and a certain modest discomfort, perhaps a new trait he was absorbing amid all this Victorian formality.

Apollonia took his left hand into hers and gently rubbed her thumb across his palm, putting him at ease immediately. She stroked in rhythm with the steep climb and fall of the ship itself. The feeling was warm and sensuous.

"You must think you are in the company of lunatics," she said. "All of this must seem very strange to you."

"I admit that it does."

"It feels much the same to me, Jonathan. These things we have been doing— this tramping through the wilderness, this lurking about like thieves, these lies and deceptions, this constant worry and danger, even this wicked lake—you must know these are things I have never done before. This is not the way I am. Until a few months ago, Jonathan, I was a spoiled little rich girl whose closest brush with danger was when I spurred my mare into a gallop. The farthest I had ever ventured into the wilderness was when I accompanied my father to the end of our indigo fields—barely two miles from the house. Please do not think of me as a tomboy, Jonathan. Do not think of me as unladylike or coarse."

He squeezed her hand gently. "I've already told you that I think of you as a total mystery, Apollonia. A wonderful mystery."

Suddenly, he felt bolder, in control of the moment and in pressing need of expressing something that had long been pent up inside him.

"May I speak directly?"

She nodded, a faint smile on her lips.

"I find you fascinating, Apollonia, ladylike and unladylike, strange and wonderful, dark as night and bright as day, soft as satin and hard as steel, all at once. And I'm finding it harder and harder not to think of you."

Her faint smile disappeared. Her eyes widened, almost, it seemed, in surprise. A trace of moisture was visible in their corners.

"You speak to me like a poet, Jonathan," she said quietly, searching his eyes with hers. "Nobody has ever said such words to me."

"I mean them."

"I have hoped...," she began but then hesitated. She ceased her stroking of his palm, and her hand gripped his tightly. "I must take care in what I say in response to such words. I must gather my thoughts. I..."

He put a finger to her lips, hushing her, and then, with a certainty only the heart can inspire, put his lips to hers. She did not withdraw but met his kiss and returned it. They seemed almost to fall into each other, in relief at their surrender, their spirits rising above the creaking ship and the angry lake, rising above a thousand fears and worries they had once believed in and that, in an instant, no longer seemed to matter. He knew that the softness and sweetness of that kiss, held defiantly against the violent swaying of the vessel, would remain with him for the rest of his life.

When their lips parted at last and their arms uncurled from each other, neither Apollonia nor Jonathan had any words to say. Nor did they need them.

The door of the cabin jerked open abruptly. The profile of Blaine, blurry with sleep, appeared in the gloom. He took in the sight of them, sitting side by side, very closely, on the bunk, and a scowl crossed his face. He bit his lip, as if suppressing anger or blocking cross words, but finally found his tongue.

"Here you are, Chase!" he shouted, his loud voice shattering whatever traces were left of the moment. "You had better come up with me. The captain says the ship is in trouble."

Jonathan, Blaine, and Jasper struggled up the ladders, across the pitching deck, and onto each perilous step to the bridge where Tripp was now manning the helm himself, soaking wet, his rain gear slapping wildly in the wind.

The lake had gone insane.

No longer did it merely roll and boom; it towered and roared. Frenzied bolts of lightning crisscrossed the sky, an electric lace curtain that illuminated turbulent clouds. At times, the bow of the ship seemed poised to plunge headlong into a solid wall of rising water, but the *Huron Sprite* was proving herself much stouter than Jonathan had given her credit for. She faced every furious wave the lake threw at them, perilously climbed their heights, crested, then began a long descent into the depths of the next swell.

And Tripp was proving himself worthy of his ship. All of her canvas was down, which even Jonathan could see was a very good thing. Tripp had apparently dismissed his helmsman, trusting only his own skills. He struggled with the wheel, trying to brace his feet on the slippery deck, grunting with the effort of ever-shifting exertion. The captain had even lashed himself with a strong rope to the spanker mast.

He shouted at his three visitors but kept his eyes on the roiling waves.

"This gale is proving nasty! I'm not taking her any farther south!"

Blaine shouted back at him. Even in the storm's din, Jonathan could hear the rage in his voice.

"What the hell are you talking about, Tripp? We have a deal!"

"We do not have a deal to die, now do we, Mr. Blaine? I am telling you that we'll not last another hour out here the way it is. I'm taking her into Georgian Bay!"

Blaine shook his head in the pouring rain.

"I can't afford to go there, Tripp! We have to make Detroit, and we have to make it tomorrow!"

Tripp finally took his eyes away from the lake and directed his gaze into Blaine's hostile stare.

"Not a chance in hell!" the captain barked.

"Then you leave me no choice, Captain," Blaine replied, as both he and Jasper reached into their shirts and produced long-barreled pistols. They pointed them with clear intention.

Tripp merely smiled. "Pull those triggers and it will be your last deed on earth!" he yelled. "Look behind you, you fools!"

Blaine and Jasper turned at the same moment Jonathan did. They saw that three of Tripp's sailors were standing behind them, aiming their own heavy muskets. The grim-faced seamen looked surprisingly sure on their feet, despite the bucking deck.

"Now put those peashooters down!" Tripp ordered, his eyes back on the lake. Blaine and Jasper, instantly recognizing their disadvantage, slowly placed their revolvers on the deck.

Tripp's next words were orders to his crew. "Put these wharf rats back into their cabins and lock the doors. If any one of them makes the least effort to get out, shoot him dead. The same for the lady and the darkie. Now go about it, lads!"

But before the mutinous passengers could be taken below decks, a crewman shouted out from somewhere far above them. "Light off the port bow!"

All of them turned to the left. Faintly visible in the distance, and disappearing again as huge waves blocked their vision of it, was a thin yellow beam that was somehow managing to pierce the storm.

The light—a beautiful beacon in the night—was the warmest and friendliest thing Jonathan had ever seen.

"Cove Island Light, by the grace of God!" the captain roared, good humor back in his voice. "We'll make it yet!" He looked to his passengers-turned-prisoners. "I'll have you lubbers on shore by dawn. If you behave yourselves, you just might live to see it."

The travelers rode out the storm in the enforced confinement of their quarters, no doubt grasping their bunks, or whatever else provided a semblance of stability, as the lake raged against the ship.

Even with his decision to change course, it took Captain Tripp more than two hours to steer the *Sprite* into comparatively safe waters. The mouth of Georgian Bay, a narrow stretch of water between Cove and George islands, was southeast of their position in the middle of the lake. Tripp had to force the vessel not only against the seas but also a stiff northern wind that fought to press the ship due southward and threatened to dash her against the rocks off Cape Hurd.

Jonathan was aware of none of these things while he stayed within his violently swaying cabin. They were explained to him later, by the captain himself, who sent a crewman to his quarters. The sailor instructed Jonathan to join Tripp on the bridge.

As the ship slipped into the bay, the gale's fury quickly weakened. The seas were still heavy and a steady rain was falling, but it appeared that the worst danger had passed. The crew had put some of the ship's canvas back up, and the *Sprite* was clipping along smartly on the brisk breeze. The narrow beam that Jonathan had glimpsed two hours before was now a brilliant blaze of light just off starboard, near enough that he could see the slender profile of the lighthouse tower that supported it and the rocky spit of land on which it was anchored.

"Heading into the bay," Tripp said as Jonathan arrived. The regular helmsman had relieved the captain at the wheel. "Much calmer already."

The captain produced two long cigars from somewhere beneath his raincoat and offered one to Jonathan, who declined. He somehow lit his own despite the wind and inhaled deeply.

"I let you come up, Mr. Chase," he began, "because my instincts tell me that you're not really one with those dogs below. I'm right about that, am I not?"

Jonathan nodded, pulling the big lapels of his coat closer against the remnants of the storm.

"I do not know, of course, what brings you together with them, and I will acknowledge that it's none of my business. Still, I am a stubborn old man, not much concerned with etiquette of any sort. What the devil are these people up to?"

Jonathan cleared his throat. "How much did they tell you when they hired you for the trip?"

"Jasper told me next to nothing. Only that he wanted passage from Mackinac to Detroit. They're Southerners, that much is clear. Their business must be the war."

Jonathan did not reply to this accurate conclusion, and the captain took note of his reticence.

"Hell, what business is your foolish American war to a salty Canadian such as myself?" Tripp resumed. "I'll tell you openly that it doesn't matter a whit to me whether the North or the South comes out on top or whether you keep the slaves or send them back to Africa, but something about those two fellows strikes me sour. I smell villainy and deceit on them, maybe even worse. I'll wager you feel the same."

Jonathan knew he was in a delicate position. He agreed with every word the captain was saying, but, as a member of Blaine's cadre—no matter how tenuous his position nor how uninformed he was kept—he felt a certain commitment, if not loyalty, to their mission. After all, Apollonia was definitely a part of the thing. Betraying them might mean betraying her.

"I am along to protect the lady," he said to the captain, minimizing the information he offered. "Of the mission itself, I'm as ignorant as you."

Tripp issued a curt command to his helmsman to watch for rocks, then gave Jonathan a hard stare in the eye.

"I believe you, son, and I will not ask you what in God's name a lady is doing in such company, but you're along for what appears to be a hell of a ride. I advise you to keep your eyes well open." He exhaled a long plume of smoke. "And I'd get myself a gun, if I were you."

They crossed into the waters of the bay just as the pitch night was transforming into a numb, gray dawn. The wind steadily decreased, and the lake once more settled into relative sanity. The dark outline of a pine-edged shore slowly appeared to their starboard as the captain steered the ship along the bay's western coast.

Jonathan asked that Apollonia be allowed out of her quarters, offering Tripp his personal guarantee that she would cause no trouble. The captain agreed, and she soon joined them in the fresh and calm air of the dawn.

Apollonia gave Jonathan a long look as he helped her onto the bridge. There was a trace of silent recognition of their intimacy of the night before, but her expression was hard to read. Her face was pale, laced with loose strands of hair that she had not fastened into their customary position. She looked shaken and tired.

She nonetheless made an effort at a smile and thanked the captain for her freedom. She also offered an apology for the "unfortunate confrontation" that Blaine and Jasper had caused. The captain acknowledged her words with a shrug of his shoulders.

After just a few minutes on the bridge, she said that she was going back to her cabin, pleading exhaustion, and left Jonathan without exchanging a single word.

"You had better take to your own in a few minutes," Tripp advised Jonathan. "I suspect it would be better if your companions didn't know you were up here talking to me. I'm taking you down to Hangcliff Point—not far away. It should be smooth enough to take you ashore in a launch."

"Blaine won't like that. This looks like remote country."

Tripp laughed. "It is quite remote country indeed, and Blaine can go to blazes for all I care. My original plan was just to sit tight here in the bay for a few hours, then resume the trip down to Detroit. It would only have delayed you a day or so. But I do not take kindly to passengers who point pistols in my direction, Mr. Chase, nor do I allow them to stay aboard my ship. I wish you good fortune and a safe journey."

Jonathan was right. Blaine very much did not like the idea of being put ashore, and he protested loudly, but there was very little he or anyone else could do about it, considering the squad of armed sailors who patiently watched the passengers climb into the launch and then accompanied them on the short ride. The usually talkative captain said nothing as his unwanted guests were escorted from his vessel.

They disembarked on a sandy strip of beach, bordered by a dense coniferous forest. No other signs of life were visible in any direction.

"What are we supposed to do here?" Blaine called out to the unsympathetic sailors, already rowing back to their ship. "We're a hundred miles from anywhere!"

He stamped the sand when they didn't respond. "Son of a bitch!" he cried out to the equally unresponsive trees. His companions stood quietly and stared at the desolate beach, bedraggled, their bags piled beside them. They looked like marooned pirates.

Blaine and Jasper might well have been the blackguards the captain portrayed them to be, but Jonathan was amazed at their resolute resourcefulness. Within an hour of being stranded on the Ontario peninsula, they had located a rustic but passable path that led in a generally southward direction and, with military authority, had marshaled their scant troops—Jeremiah, Jonathan, and Apollonia—into an orderly line.

For the first day, Jonathan was strongly reminded of their recent trek through Michigan, although their direction was now southward and Cloud had been replaced by Blaine. The country was utterly wild, heavily wooded and obviously not well traveled. Little was said by any of them as they trudged patiently, if not happily, through the bush, bags in hand.

As the afternoon waned, they met their first human being while making way for a noisy wagon that pulled up behind them, led by a weathered-looking mare of huge proportions and driven by a man with a wooly, matted beard and tattered buckskin clothing spoke of a life spent in the wilderness. His large wagon was filled with hundreds of fur pelts—beaver, it seemed to Jonathan—and a frightful stench rose from the tied bundles. He reined in his mare as he drew up.

"Now here is a sight I don't see every day," he called out in an accent remarkably similar to Captain Tripp's. "I hate to tell you folks, but you've a mighty long walk ahead of you."

"We are aware of that, sir," said Blaine, his smooth, good-natured tone instantly brought forth. "We were forced to make shore last night due to the storm and find ourselves in a most uncomfortable position."

"I should say so," the bearded man replied. "Most uncomfortable, considering the wolves and bears who roam these woods and the Hurons, too, some of them just as unneighborly as the varmints."

Jonathan could already tell that the driver was negotiating a price. Blaine was obviously aware of it as well.

"I have silver, if you're interested in taking passengers," he called to the driver, tossing a dollar coin at him.

The driver caught it, glanced at its liberty face, and smiled. "American, no less! Always quality money, eh?"

But he threw the coin back to Blaine. "It'll take more than silver to get your party down to London, which is where I'm headed." He waited for a response.

Blaine sighed, pulled a gold eagle from his pocket, and tossed it up.

The trapper seized the ten-dollar piece, let it glint in the afternoon sun, and smiled again. "That'll do just fine, good sir. I welcome each and every one of you to my humble abode on wheels."

They struggled into the wagon with considerable difficulty and shoved aside stinking stacks of furs to make room to sit. In a moment, the wagon was rumbling again down the path, jostling passengers and furs alike.

Apollonia caught Jonathan's eye after a few minutes, and a grin crossed her face. Something in her quietly ironic expression triggered a quiet laugh from him, which quickly became loud and heedless. In seconds, the entire party had joined him. The driver glanced back at his strange cargo, muttered something beneath his breath, and shook his head.

They spent most of the next week in the trapper's wagon, making little more than thirty miles a day on the slowly improving roads. They gradually grew accustomed to the smell and to the bruises that came with the constant jostling. More challenging was the mind-numbing boredom of the long and uneventful days, broken only by the trapper's enthusiastic tales of the fine season he had just completed and his expectations for excellent rewards once they reached the market in London.

Their nights were spent sleeping in the same wagon, with the driver's own body diminishing their already limited space. One night was particularly miserable, as a persistent drizzle fell for hours, soaking the thin blankets they used for protection.

The driver was generous in sharing his food, apparently considering their board a part of his fee. It consisted almost entirely of dried meats, heavily salted and tough as leather. On their first such repast, Jasper asked him what they were eating. "Hard to say," the trapper replied, chewing happily. "Might be 'possum, might be muskrat, might be squirrel—I got some of each, and they all taste pretty much the same to me." No one asked about the food again.

They fared through sheer wilderness at first, a dense expanse of birches and pines with few signs of human habitation, and then into country that was partially given over to agrarian pursuits. As they drew southward, beyond the wilds of the Bruce Peninsula, sleepy little towns began to appear, bearing English-sounding names like Williamsford, Durham, Cheltenham, and Ingersoll.

The travelers said very little to each other in the course of the trip, but it was obvious to Jonathan that Blaine and Jasper were uncomfortable in Jeremiah's company—that they found the idea of sharing a conveyance with a black man, let alone sleeping in the same place, an abomination. Jeremiah was equally uncomfortable in their presence, painfully aware of the utterly unorthodox arrangement.

The Confederates weren't overtly hostile to Jonathan, but their cold demeanor strongly suggested that they still distrusted him. It seemed that they wanted to discuss their plans, forced into revision by their ill-conceived actions on the *Sprite*, but felt it unwise to converse about such business before Jonathan and, perhaps, before Apollonia.

She remained glum and withdrawn, often eating only the barest minimum and always looking thoroughly unhappy. She made determined efforts to keep her dress clean and her hair groomed but ended up looking as dingy and run-down as the rest.

All the same, Jonathan stole glances at her—taking in the tangled hair, the smudged cheek, the rips and stains on the once elegant dress—and found her more beautiful than ever.

They made London at last, finding it not a glorious seat of power like the ancient city for which it was named but a businesslike agricultural town. It was unadorned and practical, much like the fertile plains surrounding it, but to the travelers, sore and sullen after a week in the reeking wagon, even its outskirts were a blessed sight.

Blaine immediately secured hotel accommodations, paying for their rooms with what appeared to be an inexhaustible supply of money. It did not escape Jonathan's notice that the quarters he purchased for Jeremiah were not in the hotel itself but in a hay-strewn loft in a stable behind the establishment. No one except Jonathan seemed to give the arrangement a second thought, including

Jeremiah himself. The travelers parted each other's company, happily it seemed. They washed and slept the deep sleep of the bone-weary.

The next morning, accustomed to rising with the sun, a refreshed Jonathan awoke early, dressed, and decided to take a walk before breakfast. As he was leaving the lobby and stepping onto the sidewalk, he felt a strong hand on his shoulder. He turned to see Blaine, impeccably groomed in a well-tailored, tan suit, with a natty flat-brimmed hat on his head and smelling strongly of bay rum.

"Chase!" he said. "Just the man I want to see. Are you walking?"

Jonathan nodded, and Blaine joined him. They strolled down the early morning street, gazing into the windows of still closed shops and stores. The leafy trees were fragrant with blossoms and newly thawed earth. The soft lavender of lilac and bold white of guelder rose stood in striking contrast to a background of pure green.

A block away from the hotel, Blaine lit a cigar and stroked his newly waxed mustache.

"We have been in each other's company for nearly a week, Chase, and we've barely said a word to each other," he said quietly. "I imagine you are a curious man right about now, and I confess to a touch of curiosity myself."

Jonathan smiled at Blaine. "Why don't you satisfy your curiosity first?"

Blaine stopped and gave Jonathan a direct look that was frank in its suspiciousness.

"All right, then. Let's begin with the most important thing. Why are you here?"

Jonathan had been waiting for this interrogation and was prepared with his responses. He had fashioned them, both true and false, with only one goal—to remain with Blaine's party, hence with Apollonia.

"Miss Foley asked me to join the party," he replied.

"And just how have you come to know her, Chase?"

He described his presence at Riverdale, his discovery of Apollonia's meetings in the little white house, and her plea that he join their party to Mackinac, without providing him with any reason for the journey. The answer was precise and honest, based on Jonathan's conviction that Blaine had already interrogated Jasper and Apollonia on the subject and was now looking for discrepancies in their stories.

Blaine seemed satisfied with what he heard. "Did Appy explain to you why she wanted you to go along? Was she afraid of something?"

"She had apprehensions. She felt she needed someone on her side."

"Why? She had Jasper and the Indian. What in the world might she be afraid of?"

"She didn't tell me that."

Blaine nodded. "And so you just went along. But I suspect there must have been something beyond your desire to help a woman who is essentially a stranger to you. What was it, Chase? Money? Adventure?"

"None of those. I had grown tired of Saginaw, tired of working in Foley's office. It seemed a worthwhile pursuit."

Blaine once more gave Jonathan his hard-eyed stare. Jonathan was sure, as if he had clairvoyant powers, that he could sense Blaine's driving desire to ask him whether his feelings for Apollonia went beyond a sense of chivalry. Blaine clearly suspected that there were such feelings—and was troubled by it—but seemed to find it difficult to pose the question directly.

Instead, he pulled back from the subject, resuming the walk, along with his casual, nearly friendly tone.

"You are a Westerner, Chase, which I find very interesting. What brought you to the East?"

Jonathan repeated his false story about being an unattached wanderer, a sailor, and finally an accomplice on Blaine's mission. He couldn't tell whether Blaine believed him.

"I am sure you know that Colorado is a Union territory," Blaine noted.

"Yes."

"Its cavalry is said to be top-notch for a frontier outfit. They gave the Texans a mighty licking out in New Mexico, and I've heard tell they gave hell to Billy Quantrill's boys down in Missouri."

"I've heard of those battles."

"You realize why I mention such things, of course?"

Jonathan returned his hard stare. "I know that you suspect my loyalties, Blaine, and I don't really blame you. All I can tell you is this: I have no personal or political sympathies with either the Union or the Confederacy. I realize who you're working for. Your cause seems just as good to me as the other. I have no problem working alongside you, if that's what's worrying you."

"That is precisely what is worrying me, Chase. I appreciate your directness in addressing the issue, but how do I know you are speaking truthfully? What assurance can you give me that you're not a spy? You must realize that Jasper is quite convinced of it."

"I can give you no assurance, Blaine, and very little evidence, other than the fact that I helped spring you from Mackinac. That ought to count for something."

Blaine's glare finally melted into something resembling a smile.

"It does count for something, Chase. It counts for a great deal, in fact, and once more permit me to thank you for that fine service. You are telling me that I must take you at your word, and so I will, for the present, but I am returning your directness with my own. I shall be watching you every step of the way."

"I would expect you to."

Blaine dragged deeply on his cigar, exhaling its heavy aroma into the flowery air.

"And now it is your turn to have your questions answered. I shall do my best, Chase, but I must be honest: In my line of work, information is given, even to comrades-in-arms, on a very limited and careful basis. I inform my colleagues only of what they need to know at a given moment, revealing more as time goes on. My reasons should be obvious. Should any of you be taken by Federals—as I myself have already been taken—there is only so much you could tell them. Such a capture might force me to alter my plans, but, with luck, it might not force me to abandon the entire mission. Do you understand?"

"Yes, and I respect your reasons. Why don't you tell me what you can."

"Very well. We'll be taking a train to Detroit tomorrow—finally arriving where we should have been a week ago, had it not been for that damned Tripp. From there we'll head south as best we can. We must go to Richmond, all of us, which is likely to be rather difficult, considering the position of the armies and their clear intention to collide sooner rather than later. We have to make it none-theless, no matter the obstacles. Once there, we shall be ready for the main thing. If you are still game by then and still alive," he chuckled at this, "then we will discuss things further."

Jonathan replied that he was perfectly happy with the plan.

Blaine, in turn, seemed relieved and satisfied that difficult subjects had been successfully discussed, potential problems resolved. He threw his cigar into the gutter and took in a deep breath of the redolent air.

"What a lovely spring it is, Chase! To smell those flowers is almost to forget that a war is raging a few hundred miles away. To feel that gentle breeze takes me back to old Dixie and the springtime of my youth."

Jonathan did not see Apollonia until the next day, when they boarded the train at the London depot. Somehow she had managed to restore herself to her customary state of careful elegance, draped in a fancy dress of deep red satin, a lit-tle hat of the same color atop her carefully arranged curls. She nodded and smiled at his good morning but kept quiet in the enclosed compartment in which four of them rode, Jeremiah having been relegated to an unknown spot somewhere else on the train.

An hour into the trip, the train was forced to stop, apparently to await repairs to a bridge somewhere ahead. The day was warm, and the compartment soon grew uncomfortable. Blaine and Jasper announced their intention to visit the club car for refreshments, and Jonathan politely declined their offer to join them.

He finally found himself alone with Apollonia.

"We should talk," he said.

She deferred a direct reply. "Do you not find it terribly warm in here, Jonathan?" she said casually, waving a delicate Oriental fan toward her face, once more expertly conjuring the persona of the spoiled Southern belle. She flashed a slight smile in the same vein. "Join me for a walk while we await the clear track, won't you?"

She took his hand as he helped her onto the platform and then locked her arm in his as they walked past the hissing engine into the streets of a village that called itself Wardsville, but which the railway depot identified as Glencoe.

They strode the meager length of the main street without speaking and then found themselves in a small fairgrounds where children were playing on a field. They sat on an iron bench beneath the shadow of a tall wooden bell tower that strangely resembled the lighthouse that had recently saved them on the lake.

"We do have things to discuss," she said, finally acknowledging his comment of twenty minutes ago. "But it is so hard to talk with..." She deliberately left the sentence unfinished.

"I've been thinking of you every minute since the storm," Jonathan began, immediately regretting the urgency of his tone yet not wishing to withdraw a statement so true. "It's been torture, being so close to you yet unable to say anything but the most meaningless things."

"I have thought of you, too," she said quietly, looking down at their feet on the grass. It seemed she wanted to say more but was deliberately avoiding it.

He sensed her hesitation. "Something is troubling you."

She sighed deeply. "Many things are troubling me, Jonathan, I confess. One of them is being here, on this bizarre journey, with these..." Again she left her sentence unfinished.

"And you are holding a great deal back from me, Apollonia."

She started and focused her gaze directly into his eyes. She took his hand and held it firmly, almost frantically, Jonathan thought.

"You think ill of me. My stars, I cannot blame you for that, considering the circumstances of our lives these past weeks. I know it has been mad, with everything so secretive and hardly staying two nights in the same place and seldom being able to talk, but I beg you, Jonathan, do not doubt my heart."

She gave a little gasp, as if she hadn't intended to include those last five words in her sentence, but she—like Jonathan—refused to retract them.

Jonathan stroked the back of her hand. "Then tell me something of your heart."

She blushed, a rare phenomenon for Apollonia, and smiled shyly.

"That is an impossible question."

"Not impossible, Apollonia, only difficult. Some things beg to be said, they struggle and rage and fit until they are said, and so I'm going to say them and let the consequences be damned. I have had feelings for you since the first time I saw you. And these feelings have only grown, day by day, until I can think of nothing else. I am in love with you, Apollonia, madly and blindly in love with you. When we kissed on the ship, I think it was the happiest moment of my life."

He felt her hand tighten in his.

"So I will put my question this way, and, if you wish, I'll say no more about it. Am I alone in such feelings?"

She brought her eyes back to his. He watched their pupils, bottomless black wells encircled by auras of icy blue, search the depths of his own. He was certain that he saw doubt in those eyes and perhaps a fear that he didn't yet understand, but he thought he saw something else, too.

"No, you are not alone," she whispered, softly touching his forehead with hers and drawing her lips close to his. He gave the kiss freely, this time without hesitation, and they fell once more into each other's depths, holding their embrace as long as their breath would allow.

When they drew apart, it was reluctantly. Jonathan opened his eyes just in time to see Apollonia opening hers. At that moment they wanted nothing more than to be close.

"And yet," she said softly, "there is so much you do not know about me."

He wanted to press her. He wanted desperately to ask her how she had gotten herself mixed up in matters of military espionage, how she had come to know Archer Blaine, and what might have once transpired between them. But somehow he knew that her statement was not intended as an invitation to pry. It was a request for discretion and respect for privacy. He chose to honor that unspoken request.

"You will tell me in time," he said. "I respect your silence. And I trust you, remember?"

She caressed the back of his neck with a finger. "And there is so much I do not know about you, Jonathan."

"There isn't very much to know."

She drew softly away from him, smoothing the ruffles of her dress. "I doubt that very much. I think, Mr. Chase, that I am not the only one guilty of holding things back, of keeping secrets. I sense that you have interesting stories, that you have been to interesting places." There was a playful, painfully feminine look on her face.

He felt his old defenses slowly kicking in, hating himself for preparing to lie to her. But he believed there was no choice. If he were to tell her the truth—to reveal his unexplained and utterly inexplicable journey through time—it would ruin everything between them. She would be convinced of his madness—what else could she think?—and he would lose her forever. He said nothing.

"I feel as if I have known you before," she continued. "I have strange, misty memories of you, but I cannot grasp them. The French have a phrase—déjà vu—that describes a certain feeling, a strong sense of memory joined with the utter inability to trace the memory. This is how I feel about you."

He brushed away a stray curl from her forehead but could think of nothing to say.

"When I heard you playing Jeremiah's guitar, there was something familiar in that sad, lonely melody, Jonathan. And I believe I saw you once, not so long ago, in some sort of dream or perhaps in a daydream. It was cold, and it was raining. It was dark, in a strange room I had never seen before. Everything was vague about it, except for your face. I remember the expression on your face—shock and surprise and pleasure, all at once. I was drawn to you but frightened at the same time. And then you faded away, like a ghost."

Jonathan was brought back to a lonely night in a Midwestern motel in his other life, while he was rambling eastward, returning to Saginaw. He clearly remembered the vision—could it have been his first glimpse of her?—in his otherwise desolate room and the scent of rain and lemon verbena that rose from her shadowy form. A chill traversed his spine as if someone had laid a cold blade against his back.

"It must have been a dream," he suggested, trying to keep his composure. "Perhaps a prophetic one."

"Perhaps," she agreed doubtfully. "And perhaps you keep your secrets close to your breast, as I do."

He kissed her hand. "Perhaps, my love."

The harsh whistle of the locomotive rang through the small town, alerting its passengers that its journey was about to resume.

"On our way once more, Jonathan," she said, rising from the bench. "But to where and to what?"

"It doesn't matter to me," he said, taking her arm as they walked back to the depot, "so long as we're together."

There followed a seemingly endless succession of days, one like the next yet each one distinct, the universal character of hard and determined travel. Each of them grew weary and silent in the repetitive sameness of railway cars, depots, and commercial hotels.

Detroit flashed by in less than a day, giving Jonathan only a brief awareness that he had, after all, returned once more to Michigan. Ohio was a patchwork quilt of farmland, rolling, then flat, then rolling again, with straw-hatted farmers busy behind beast-driven plows, making the most of mild weather for their spring planting. The countryside was awakening, the woods and fields viridescent in a pastel sort of way. In one hilly meadow, Jonathan glimpsed raintrees shedding their glistening blossoms, like falling stars, and the beautiful sight somehow made him feel sad.

Only occasionally did towns interrupt the countryside—drab places, mostly, with brick buildings and wooden sidewalks, the bigger ones with cobbled streets. The few actual cities through which they passed reminded Jonathan of Saginaw. They were urban progeny of the same time and culture, cast in remarkably similar molds to one another, much like the cities he knew from his own time.

The names of the places went by in a surreal blur, fleeting signposts on the roofs of railway depots—Defiance, Ashland, Columbiana, Steubenville,

Zanesville—as their zigzag journey reflected the wartime stress along the railways. Sometimes entire routes were closed to regular traffic, surrendering the right-of-way exclusively to military trains. Sometimes they would wait in a town, or just a forlorn junction, for hours on end, as seemingly infinite trains filled with military supplies or troops commandeered the rails. As a result, their route was haphazard and frequently defied directional logic. In order to go farther south, they would have to travel farther east than they needed to go or farther west.

Blaine, however, possessed an unfailing inner compass. No matter what delays or diversions were thrown in his way, he would quickly determine an alternate path, tracing the way along maps and timetables, and managed to keep the journey more or less on course.

One warm and sunny afternoon, they crossed the mighty Ohio and found themselves in that part of Virginia that had opted not to join the rebellion. Their train approached, labored hard to ascend, and then quickly descended steep mountains. They began to follow a southeasterly track, and Jonathan noticed that mounted patrols could occasionally be seen along the railway—armed protection, the conductor told him, against Rebel raiders.

Their last ride was on the Baltimore and Ohio Railroad. It stopped—with a tangible sense of finality—at a sleepy town called Petersburg, a lonely Union outpost on the disputed frontier.

"End of the line!" the blue-suited conductor cried to the few passengers who had stuck it out. As he walked down the platform, he pointed to the east. "Thataway's Rebel country! Enter at your own risk!"

Blaine, with his seemingly bottomless purse and clever resourcefulness, was unfazed. Within an hour of disembarking, he had purchased a light carriage and a rather tired-looking mare from a man who ran a rickety hotel in the town. Within another hour, the travelers were again on their way. As they traversed the last few miles that were left of Union territory, they passed through a tiny junction called Lost City, a name that struck Jonathan as ironically appropriate.

When they reached Virginia proper, they waited until after dusk to cross the unguarded border into the Old Dominion, with Blaine evidently wanting to minimize the chances that they might be stopped and questioned while crossing the line.

And as they embarked on their slow but steady course toward Richmond, their proximity to war was becoming plain. Although the fair Valley of Shenandoah was virtually illuminated with bursting greenery and blossoms, its glory was muted by a sullen overcast that had crept across the sky and by the recent leavings of great armies.

At first such evidence was scarce—here and there a stray military wagon missing a wheel or an abandoned cask stenciled "US" or "CSA"—but it became increasingly common as they continued. By their second day over the rutted Virginia roads, they were seeing broken and burnt artillery pieces, the fetid corpses of dead horses, and an assortment of military debris—canteens, shoes, canvas tents—littering the roadsides. A heavy smell that might have been gunpowder occasionally lingered in low-lying and swampy areas.

The places on their journey began to grow chillingly familiar to Jonathan. Rappahannock and Culpeper had once been, at least for him, mere names in a history book—where the North and South had done bloody work long ago and were doing it now. As he passed by the forlorn, forsaken towns, he began to feel the first pangs of dread.

The landscape steadily grew lonelier. Small towns seemed virtually deserted, and the fields began to look neglected. The only regular sightings of other humans were the frequent squadrons of Union cavalry that came riding, often very quickly, in a southward direction. Blaine had a keen ear and sensed their approach each time. He would have the wagon driven off the road, preferably to be hidden by vegetation, while the soldiers passed. It was obvious that they had already entered a region where traveling civilians might well be regarded as spies, and treated as such, but so far no patrols had stopped to question them.

When he saw his first unit of cavalry, it all began to grow real for Jonathan. The company roared past them, raising a great cloud of dust, offering only glimpses of the tired and hardened faces of the Union men. Their uniforms were sun-faded to a dull indigo, and steel sabers rattled at their sides as their foam-covered mounts galloped toward the front.

Jonathan watched Blaine and Jasper as the cavalry rode by and saw the unmistakable hatred on their faces, although they were not so foolish as to say or shout anything to their enemies, so perilously close.

Somewhere south of the Culpeper Court House, the travelers made a crude camp in a copse of chestnut and sycamore. They prepared a suitable supper of cornbread and bacon, fried over an open fire, and prepared to retire, the men taking blankets for a night under the stars, with Apollonia allowed to sleep in the covered carriage.

As she passed Jonathan in the dark, she touched his fingertips with her own. "Did you know that tonight is Walpurgis?" she whispered. "The night when witches dance and spirits rise from their graves?"

Her tone suggested that she was being humorous.

"I know it now," he whispered back to her. "Are you worried about them?"

"Not about witches," she replied, "but about what lies ahead of us, Jonathan." Her tone suddenly lost its lightness. "I fear that harm will befall us before we reach Richmond."

He took her hand, squeezed it, and brought it to his lips. "We'll be all right, I promise you."

He heard a soft laugh come from her and then a whispered "good night," before she disappeared into the carriage.

It was growing cool, and Jonathan wrapped his coat around him. He lay awake in the dark, contemplating his brave words—and wondering whether he believed them—as he listened to distant thunder and watched the glow of sporadic lightning to the south. He thought that the sullen weather was about to break with a thunderstorm, but then he heard Jasper and Blaine whispering to each other nearby.

"What do you think? Ten-pounders?" Jasper asked.

"Yes, and likely even bigger," Blaine replied. "From the sound of it, they're having a wild night down by the river."

Only then did Jonathan realize that the thunder and lightning were the discordant and deathly opera of war, near enough now to be seen and heard.

May

Life opens and blossoms and shines like a rose,
It lies in the sun as a soft wind blows.
The ground is all flowers and velvety green,
The air is cool showers and fragrantly clean.
The world at this time is a blessed place,
And all are in love with its youthful face.

Here is another confession from your faithful diarist: Yes, I speak of love. There is no use denying it, nor do I disallow that my muse comes from more than the angelic aspect of the world at this glorious season.

I find myself once more on Southern soil. It is the height of Spring, and I am in love—my stars, what more could a mortal woman want from this world? Ordinarily, of course, I would say that nothing more could be desired, that all was heavenly and perfect, but my life (as you well know by now, dear reader) is far from ordinary. For all of the blessings that have befallen me in the last month, the curses remain and the dread that follows them like constant shadows.

But I shall speak no more of shadows now, for the air is balmy and sweet with blossoms, the sky is blue, the fields are green, and Richmond lies only a few miles before us. More than all this, my love is by my side, and he is as happy as I.

There is no use in prolonging the tale. I speak, once again, of dear Jonathan. It has all happened so fast. It was while we were in the midst of a dreadful storm on that wicked lake, as our fragile ship tossed like a bottle on the waves, that he brought his lips to mine. I grew faint when we kissed.

Just a few days later, in a little park in a lonely Canadian town, he declared his love for me, so boldly and so beautifully. I struggled to find my breath, so pleasantly was I taken aback, but at last I opened my own heart to him.

Thus was the border between us crossed, and now nothing is the same.

A few weeks ago, I would have blushed to make such an admission, yet I feel no shame or reluctance now. If I could, I would shout it to the world. I would seek out the largest newspaper I could find and put the news on the front page in the most ostentatious type. I would paint it on the side of every barn on the long road to Savannah.

At last—at long last!—I know what the poets have been crowing about, what made the great composers write their symphonies, what inspired the artists and sculptors and authors to create their works of beauty. It is love, sweet, pure love, and there is nothing complicated or elusive or mysterious about it. My stars, it is the simplest, most natural thing in all the world.

Yet, for all its simplicity, it is a truth that had always eluded me, for until the arrival of Jonathan, I had never loved.

I do believe there was one man sufficiently sure of himself to have loved me. He was, as my father said so many times, a perfectly suitable candidate for my hand—refined, educated, wealthy, powerful, a landed and titled Englishman, no less!—yet I knew I could never return his feelings. I did not mind terribly that he was a goodly number of years my senior, but I could never have tolerated his aristocratic airs, his gentility, the very refinement that my parents found so alluring. Had I accepted his proposal, I would have been a liar and a hypocrite, and tell me what honorable man desires such a wife as that?

I was surely fancied, at least, by other men. I had suitors when I was younger. I attended a great many balls in Savannah and had my fair share of eager young bachelors asking for turns at the waltz. I did dance with them, flirted with some, even encouraged one or two. They were comely to look upon and often quite delightful in their comportment, but they seemed mere boys to me, inexperienced in the ways of the world and in knowing themselves.

I often think of them now, most, if not all, fighting for the cause; some, it grieves me to say, already perished on the battlefields. Of those who remain, I worry about their welfare and pray for their safe return, for they are my friends and I have affection for each and every one, but my heart pines for none among them.

Here is the difference: Were Jonathan to perish—God forbid even the thought!—I fear I would jump into the nearest river or throw myself from the nearest cliff, for going through the rest of my life without him would be an unbearable misery. I should lose my own will to live, and my very purpose for living, and would be astonished if the sun were to continue to rise.

Please do not misunderstand. The love I feel is not based on such dreadful fears. I mention them only to show the depth of my feeling. The love of which I speak, and which I have never before known, is something of the spirit. It rises high above such considerations as place and time and circumstance. It is of a bond between two people which is preordained, destined, fated to be.

I may gush like a fool—I apologize for it!—but I am not foolish. I have no illusions about Jonathan. He is a wanderer, almost penniless from the looks of him, sometimes awkward to the point of embarrassment, and he still conceals a great deal from me, even to the degree that he is not always heedful of the truth. I have only known him these few weeks, and I have but the vaguest idea from where he comes and why he happened so suddenly to appear at Riverdale.

None of this matters. We are in love—it is meant to be, *we* are meant to be—and I will defy every dubious and suspicious notion that tries to force its way into my mind. When I am with him, I can taste the sky itself, hear the music in every bird's song, see a rainbow on the dreariest day—I am blessed to feel the wonder and beauty of all creation.

All of this has given me courage such as I have never known, and this is a precious gift indeed, for courage shall surely be called for in the coming days. Despite love's intervention, my formidable troubles remain. I have yet to devise a means of escaping them and so, for the present, am compelled to comply with forces that are far stronger than I.

Much has been accomplished, all of which brings the dreaded moment of truth closer to its realization. With clever deception, we have freed Archer from his shackles, and he is now among our party. He is, in truth, our commander now, firm as steel in his relentless quest, anxious and impatient because of the imprisonment which has delayed him. He is a determined force that sweeps all of us along in his wake.

We have journeyed far, from the distant reaches of the frigid North, across raging seas, past forests, farms, fields, and towns too numerous to remember, over the mountains, and back into my own country, where the signs and sounds of war grow nearer by the day.

All along this trying course, I have brooded over my troubles and sought to extricate myself from them, all to no avail. Yet I find that I am no longer afraid. I know that I am no longer alone, that my ally shall not abandon me, that our love is too great to succumb to the evil forces that besiege. I shall fear no evil in the valley of the shadow, for Jonathan is with me.

MAY

THE BLOODY ANGLE

JONATHAN FOUND IT DIFFICULT to fall asleep that night, almost as if the witches of Walpurgis were indeed coursing through the Virginia countryside, perhaps as furtive heralds of the man-made storm that rumbled ominously in the distance.

He lay awake, looking into the cloudy sky above him, and thought troubled thoughts. He thought of Rachel, of whom he had not thought in a long time. He thought of his parting from her and the desolate freedom that separation had forced upon him.

He contemplated the strange ways in which he had reacted to that freedom—how he had grown dark and mordant, reclusive, perhaps even morbid in his obsession with the past. How—incredibly and impossibly—he had grown so obsessed with the past that he had somehow fallen into it and had gone so far as to will himself out of his natural existence into a state that could only be called unnatural, a state in which he had to conceal his true identity, his true place, as if he were a frightening freak or the carrier of some dreadful disease.

And yet—his sleepless mind persisted, arguing with itself—the oddity that Jonathan had become was not without purpose. He had not only willed himself out of his present, he had woven himself into the warp of history. He had conquered time itself, not just because he wished to escape his own but because he wanted, needed—was, perhaps, destined—to join his soul with that of another.

Was Apollonia not that other, and was not time merely the route by which he achieved this aspiration?

The insomniac battle in his brain raged like the military opera not far away, even as the eventual tides of sleep began to wash against the shore of his consciousness, casting shadows over his thoughts.

He asked himself how such a thing could happen. How could a man pass from one time into another? The dreadful notion entered his mind that Apollonia had not been, after all, real—that perhaps his growing love for her, and hers for him, and the whole strange journey by which he had reached her were nothing more than the hallucination of a man driven to madness by loss and loneliness.

As this thought slowly devolved into something resembling a dream, Jonathan found himself back in his silent house in Saginaw, although still somehow aware of Apollonia's presence nearby. He entered every room in search of her, climbed staircases from the basement to the attic, but found no trace. He called out her name and received no response. He grew still and listened for her footsteps or voice but heard nothing.

She is not here, his dreaming voice whispered. She has never been here.

He cried out when he reached this conclusion, and the cry he made fractured the thin membrane between dreaming and wakefulness and pulled him violently back into the stark reality of the world.

As he awoke, he felt a nudge, a gentle application of pressure to his ribs as if a curious fox had touched its nose to his body, and just off to the side of his line of sight thought he saw something moving in the inky blackness—a dark shape against an even greater darkness.

Jonathan started, rising from his crude bed in the grass. He peered into the night, but the darkness was almost absolute. The air was damp and scented with vegetation, the song of crickets echoed in the nearby woods. At last he was able to distinguish the blanketed forms of Blaine and Jasper, that of Jeremiah a little farther away, and the carriage in which Apollonia slept farther yet.

She had not been a hallucination, he thought to himself with profound relief. He really was here, and was *now*, and as if to remind him of this, the horizon winked with a murky orange light and the distant boom of artillery followed a few seconds later.

It was late—he could tell by the nocturnal sounds and smells—and a chill crept into the air. The fire glowed faintly with a few last embers, and a thin wisp of smoke rose from it. An owl screeched somewhere in the distance. He lay back on his blanket, placing his coat over his body.

This time, reassured of Apollonia's presence—safe in the knowledge of her physical reality—he slept deeply and well.

When he awoke, he was alone.

The screech of a bird broke his slumber, and he stirred to find himself in the midst of a dank fog that seemed to cover the world. Despite that, he saw immediately that the others had gone.

They left nothing behind, save for Jonathan's own knapsack, the repository of all his worldly possessions, which had lain beside him as he slept, and his blanket and coat that had served as a bed. Everything and everybody else had vanished. Last night's fire was cold and no longer even smoldered.

He rose with a cry, turning a full circle as if he might have missed something, but he remained utterly alone in the grove in which they had made camp. There was a moment of fear, a shot of childlike panic almost primal in its intensity. The shock and sheer strangeness of this sudden solitude were overwhelming, almost as jolting as the snowy morning when he had first awakened to find himself in Apollonia's time.

How could she do it? How could she leave him like this, without a word, without even the slightest hint?

These were his first thoughts and then, as the hurt of her absence began to sink in, finding an uncomfortable home in the pit of his stomach, this: Where had they gone? Why had they left him?

And then a return to her. He replayed their last moment of conversation the night before, her talk of witches and his comment about being allies—"Allies!" he almost said aloud—and their ordinary biddings good night. Had she been playing him, stringing him along until the opportunity to slip away presented itself? Had she been playing him from the beginning?

No, he argued. The night before, just before she had gone to the carriage, Apollonia had also said something about fear—her fear of something bad befalling them before reaching Richmond. Had she known something was going to happen or simply felt it? Was it possible that she had no idea that Blaine and Jasper had planned to leave Jonathan behind once dawn arrived, or had she been their faithful accomplice all along?

Or this, infinitely worse: Had something bad happened to her? He knew that she felt somehow endangered by Jasper and Blaine and that she feared, if not them, then their goal. When that prospect crossed his mind, like a keen knife opening his skin, a cold chill traveled from his spine to the top of his head.

These new questions were enough to fill his mind for the moment, which, in a way, was a mercy. He was temporarily numbed from the pain of what might be her desertion of him—let alone her simple absence—though he knew, as he sat back down on the ground, shaking his head, that this shock would subside and, when it did, the wound would do much more than hurt.

He had no answers to anything, but for more than an hour he looked into the silent fog and tried to find them. At last, when he was finally certain that his companions would not be returning from some unannounced early morning excursion, he began to think in logical terms.

They had been going to Richmond—both Blaine and Apollonia had said so more than once—but was it true? He had no way of knowing, of course, but their arduous journey from Ontario had been unerringly fixed on a stubborn, if erratic, vector for the Confederate capital. Why endure such a journey only to change their destination at the last moment? He knew that he was now reasonably close to the city, although he was unsure of the actual distance.

He did not rationalize why he should pursue them—no rationalization was necessary. Apollonia might be going to Richmond, and regardless of what she had done, or might have done, whether she was going of her own free will or by force, he would follow her. He didn't even debate the choice.

Even then, however, he knew that it would not be easy. For the past few days, it was clear to the travelers that great armies were on the move, and last night, not too far away, they had actually clashed. The direction in which the fight was waged was southeast, the same general direction of Richmond. Would it be wise to pursue such a course?

"The hell with it," Jonathan said to the fog-shrouded trees. He put on his wrinkled coat, gathered up his blanket, hung the knapsack from his shoulder with its strap, and put his dusty hat on his head. With no money in his pocket and not a crumb of food to his name, his shoes were soon making tracks on the unpaved road into the heart of the Confederacy.

He headed southeast for hours, feeling neither hunger nor thirst. The fog cleared by mid-morning and the day grew warm, but he barely noticed the outrageously green farms with their stone walls, the gentle woods at the edges of the patchwork, the brilliant cardinals and blue jays that darted among the trees, the picturesque grain mills with their huge wheels.

At first, anger was his sole companion. Somehow, it crowded out his fears for Apollonia's safety and his bewilderment at the sudden change in his fortunes. In their place emerged a fury, irrational and deep. He seemed unable to consider any options other than deliberate betrayal, and he felt that betrayal like the sting of a rapier. He did not care about the men, both of whom he knew had always and openly distrusted him, but Apollonia's disappearance—her abandonment of him—was a dagger thrust. How could she do this? How could she have kissed him, told him that she shared his feelings, when all the while she knew that she and her party of spies would soon be discarding him like yesterday's newspaper? His mind conjured words he seldom spoke or even thought, and he fantasized how absolute and righteous his rage would be when, and if, he saw her again.

But his body had concerns of its own. At noon, his thirst finally announced itself. He approached a cracker-box farmhouse and asked the bedraggled farmer for something to drink. The thin man, with long strands of gray hair vainly covering a balding head, obliged. He drew water from a pump and gave it to Jonathan in a tin cup. Without prodding, he then went into the house and came back with a few pieces of corn bread. Only when Jonathan ate them did he realize his hunger.

It was clear that the farmer was wary of this stranger with city clothes and a Northern accent, but he did not voice these suspicions. His hospitality was automatic and offered without resentment—a courtesy Jonathan knew would be very hard, if not impossible, to find in his own time.

He thanked the farmer as he returned to the road, and the man finally gave in to his curiosity.

"So where you bound, stranger?" he asked.

"Richmond."

The man grimaced. "Not a good time to be heading to Richmond. Don't you know the Yanks have crossed the Rapidan and are fixing to take on Lee down Chancellorsville way?"

"I heard them fighting last night," Jonathan replied.

"You might consider setting still for a spell before trying to get yourself down there. Either that or head due south, get down to Charlottesville, and then take the railroad in from there. If you're walking right fast, it might only cost you a few extra days."

"I have to go directly," Jonathan told him, shouldering his pack. He had no idea what Blaine and company might be up to in Richmond, or how long a stay was planned there, so time seemed of sincere essence.

"Suit yourself," the farmer said with a shrug. "If you stay on this road, you'll reach Germanna Ford down to the river in an hour or two. You just might get across down there, but I reckon the river'll be lousy with Yanks."

Jonathan closed the wooden gate at the road. "I'm much obliged for your help."

The farmer nodded. "Good luck to you, stranger."

He walked on. The food and water gave him renewed strength, but it also dulled his anger. In its place welled the pain he had earlier feared. Not only did he feel like a fool for allowing himself to be deserted so easily, he felt a fool of the heart. He had been used by the woman he loved, manipulated like a starry-eyed marionette on a stage. He had been led to believe that she shared his feelings—he had allowed himself to bathe in the joy this belief brought to him, a joy like nothing he had ever felt—and he had been a fool all along.

He still loved her, and he realized that it would take much more than this to quell that love and feared that nothing could. And as the afternoon grew warm and birdsong became the clamorous music of the woods, he began to discover, with a deep and constant aching, how much he already missed her. He could only imagine what that would feel like tomorrow or the day after that.

And underlying it all—his anger, sense of foolishness, longing, and confusion— was a persistent note of urgency. She might be in danger, in desperate need of his help, and even though that possibility seemed slim to him at the moment, he would not ignore it.

Fatigue slowed his progress as the day wore on, but his advance was fated to be halted in any case. As the shadows began to grow long, the quiet road that he had so recently had all to himself suddenly became an army's highway.

Jonathan retreated into the shade when the first Union soldiers came. The procession began with cavalry heading south, at first a few small patrols and squadrons racing by, then long columns of horsemen, jangling spurs and sabers as they moved deliberately onward. They were followed by a seemingly endless line of artillery, hundreds of field pieces on caissons, their barrels pointing to the rear as they were pulled by teams of stout horses.

Then the infantry: thousands of silent young men, muskets or repeater rifles perched on their shoulders, eyes shielded by the brims of their kepis, officers loudly exhorting them to "Keep up the pace, boys!"

Not one of them seemed to notice the man lurking in the woods off the side of the road. They kept their eyes fixed on the backs of the men in rank before them, and none of them smiled. They looked tired and resigned, but their youthful faces, most of them adorned with scant beards or mustaches, also appeared hardened and determined. These were clearly veterans of battles come and gone, preparing to face yet another, and they did not seem afraid of what lay ahead.

When the infantry had passed, still later stages of the complex military organism took their place—wagon after wagon loaded with supplies, along with ambulances and vehicles whose purposes Jonathan could only speculate.

They marched on through the amber sunset, the cobalt twilight, and into the pitch night itself, and as they passed, their restless clamor ceased to be audible to the tired man on a mission of his own. He fell asleep as he watched them, his back leaning against the trunk of a tree, his hands on his knees. And even as he sank into a dreamless sleep, they trudged into the night, a long blue serpent moving through the woods, preparing to raise its terrible fangs against an unseen foe.

Jonathan awoke as the dawn was breaking, a jagged scarlet gash against an eastern sky of violet blue. At first he was disoriented as to where he was and what he was doing there, startled by the racket of the military conveyances that were still rumbling southward, although their number seemed to be dwindling. There were now gaps of as much as five minutes between groupings of them. These seemed to be supply wagons, mostly, and one of them caught Jonathan's eye. It was a long, narrow conveyance, uncovered and piled high with what appeared in the half-light to be dozens of plain rectangular wooden boxes, just about the length and breadth of a man.

He was hungry and thirsty, sore from sleeping against the gnarly trunk, and realized that he faced a considerable dilemma. He began to think that he should have taken the farmer's advice yesterday and found a roundabout route to

Richmond. He had acted foolishly, out of anger and hurt, and he would pay for it now. The only way to Richmond from his present position was on the road he was traveling, yet that road had seemingly been commandeered for military purposes. And the traffic was considerable. In the hours he had spent beneath the tree's concealment, Jonathan figured that multiple thousands of soldiers had passed within yards of him and several hundred wagons and field pieces. He stood out glaringly in his civilian attire. Were he to try to simply walk the road to the river crossing, he had little doubt that he would be stopped and questioned. And what in the world would he tell them?

The idea struck him with the sudden clarity of thoughts that form in the first few moments after waking. He reached into his knapsack and fumbled among its few contents—remnants of yesterday's corn bread, courtesy of the farmer, his pipe, an envelope with a few surviving flakes of tobacco, a wrinkled handkerchief. At the very bottom, he found it. He pulled out of the bag the army issue captain's uniform he had worn at Mackinac. He spread out the tunic, trousers, and hat—all wrinkled and misshapen from their long journey but little worse, he thought, than what most of these road-weary soldiers were themselves wearing.

He retreated behind the shelter of the tree and hurriedly dressed in the uniform, gulping pieces of dry corn bread as he did so. He stood and tried to smooth out the worst creases, shaped the slouch hat into a semblance of its former self, and tucked the ends of the trousers into the tops of his boots. They were too short to be mistaken for regulation footwear, but Jonathan had noticed that a great many soldiers, apparently pressed by a lack of supplies, mixed pieces of civilian clothing with their uniforms.

Jonathan left most of his civilian clothing in a pile behind the tree, figuring he'd likely have little use for it in the near future. He saved only his coat from Little Jake in Saginaw, which he rolled up tightly and placed in his knapsack. The knapsack was as nonregulation as the boots but was roughly similar to those used by many of the regular soldiers.

He decided that he looked acceptable, waited for a break in the traffic, and then joined the road. He walked only briefly before he was overtaken by an ox-driven wagon laden with barrels. As he stepped off the road, he heard the wagoner call out to him.

"Looks like you're needing a ride there, Captain!"

Jonathan looked up to the bearded and bespectacled corporal in the driver's seat and shouted back. "Lost track of my unit! Trying to catch up!"

The driver waved him aboard. Jonathan climbed up to sit beside the soldier and returned his salute. "Much obliged, Corporal," he said.

"More than welcome, sir. What unit would you be heading back to?"

The question was so obvious that Jonathan hadn't given it any mind. "Fifth U.S. Cavalry," he announced, hoping that he had given the name of an actual unit.

"Ah," the corporal returned, with a puzzled look and a shrug. He adjusted his glasses and cleared his throat. "Would you be minding if I were to ask a question or two, Captain?"

"Ask, by all means."

"What do you conjecture they got stewing up for us, once we get across the river?"

"Hard to say. I haven't been briefed, but it feels like something big."

"Seems that way to me, too. I reckon General Grant will be going after old Lee pretty hard this summer. Think he's gonna be pushing that Rebel just about as hard as he can push."

"I believe you're right," Jonathan replied, hoping that he sounded like he knew what he was talking about.

Their conversation dwindled after that, and they rode in relative silence. Jonathan managed to put his remaining tobacco into his pipe and allowed himself a smoke, and a rare period of leisure, as the wagon rumbled on.

By mid-morning, they reached a traffic jam. As they approached the Rapidan River, the wagons and caissons drew close to each other, slowed to a crawl, and then stopped altogether.

"Pontoon," the wagoner said. "They're having us cross one at a time. We might be sitting for a spell."

The spell turned out to be several hours. It was the middle of a warm afternoon before Jonathan's wagon was waved onto the perilous-looking floating platform. The river itself, banked by gracefully arched trees, was not in itself very wide at this crossing, and the actual trip across lasted no more than five minutes.

On the southern bank, an officer awaited them. Jonathan had been watching him, amazed at his spotless dress uniform, complete with shiny gold epaulets on the shoulders and a slouch hat with its left brim rakishly pinned to the crown. The officer—he appeared to be a colonel—was asking questions of each driver and appeared to be directing them where to go.

As his own wagon approached, Jonathan saw the man up close. He had a narrow, hawklike face, adorned with an elaborately curled and heavily waxed mustache balanced on a long, pointy goatee beneath.

"What are you hauling?" he asked the driver abruptly.

"Hardtack and salt pork," the driver replied.

"You'll go to the main staging area, half a mile that way. Ask the commissary officer where to go once you get there."

The corporal saluted and prepared to crack his reins, but the colonel held up a hand to halt him. He took a step closer to the wagon and peered at Jonathan with contracted, piercing eyes.

"What's your command, Captain?" he asked, glancing at the cavalry insignia on Jonathan's hat.

"Fifth Cavalry, sir," he replied, repeating the lie.

"Fifth Cavalry, you say?" the colonel rejoined. "That's Fifth U.S. Cavalry?"

"Yes, sir."

The colonel cleared his throat. "Step down for a moment, would you, Captain?"

Jonathan dismounted the wagon and faced the natty colonel.

"What exactly is your position with the Fifth?" he asked.

Jonathan began to feel nervous. "In command of C Company," he improvised.

"Is that so? And tell me something about the Fifth, would you, Captain?"

"What would you like to know, sir?"

"Oh, I don't know," he said, twirling his mustache and tilting the scale. "Tell me what's different about it."

Jonathan's anxiety was growing. "I'm not sure what you mean, sir. It's just another regiment."

The colonel nodded, as if expecting just such an answer. He turned to two armed infantrymen who were standing to the side and beckoned them to draw near.

"Captain, for your information, the Fifth U.S. Cavalry is a colored regiment. Its officers are white men, of course, but if you were one of them, I would expect you to know that it's a black command."

He stroked his mustache again. "And besides that, the Fifth is not even part of this campaign. Far as I know, they're still organizing out in Kentucky somewhere. Perhaps you might want to explain why you're lying to a superior officer and why, as a captain of cavalry, you are dismounted, carrying neither sidearm nor saber."

Jonathan was caught cold and knew it. He had walked straight into something about which he knew next to nothing and for which he had done absolutely no preparation. He decided that further lies would only deepen the hole into which he had already fallen.

"I think, Colonel, that under the circumstances, it might be a better idea for me to keep my mouth shut."

The officer flashed a cruel smile. "You just might be right there, but I know other men who will have you talking soon enough. I swear to God, the Rebs must be getting mighty desperate when they try to place such poorly informed spies into our lines. I'll take it as a sign that victory is near."

He turned to his guards. "Put this man into the stockade."

He returned his raptor gaze to his new prisoner. "It's fortunate for you that we are expecting a big engagement in the next few hours. That might postpone your interrogation for a little while, and that's a boon for you. Most of the spies we capture in this army are hanged before the next sun rises."

After a mile's march from the river, Jonathan was forcibly shoved into the place that would become his home for the next week—a virtual cage, roughly but securely constructed out of newly cut trees, connected by long horizontal beams of crude lumber. It stood maybe forty feet by forty feet and was ten feet high, with one gate that was guarded twenty-four hours a day by four Union sentries armed with repeating rifles.

At first there were only two or three others within the enclosure, all of them uniformed enlisted men. They were silent and kept to themselves, taking particular pains to avoid Jonathan in the obvious belief that he was an officer—something essentially alien to them. By the second day, more soldiers were added as well as a couple of men in civilian clothing. Jonathan overheard that most of the soldiers were what the army called "stragglers," troops who wandered away from their units on the eve of a big battle. The stragglers would try to make their way to the rear, away from the real fighting, and then attempt to regain their units after the engagement was over, hoping their absence had gone undetected. He had no idea why the civilians had been arrested.

By the third day, all of the men in the stockade realized that they had been quartered on the doorstep to hell.

Jonathan heard prisoners muttering the word "wilderness," triggering vague memories of history lessons he had once taken, and from these he finally realized where he was. Less than a mile to the south of their position, the Northern and Southern armies were coming to death grips in a battle that would long be remembered in infamy.

None of those in the stockade could see anything. The narrow gaps between the posts allowed only glimpses of impenetrable woods. But they could hear it clearly enough. After the shooting began, the sounds of thousands of rifles, muskets, and pistols grew from a crackle to a collective roar, finally blossoming into a mad, communal shriek that numbed the ears. The sound of it seemed infinite. After a few hours, it took on a surreal, undulating quality, like the combined drone of millions of insects on a hot summer night. Jonathan found it difficult to imagine that this deadly cacophony was made up of individual men pulling individual triggers somewhere out in the dense foliage that constituted the field of battle. He found it harder still to contemplate how many of those reports signified a man's injury or death.

The imprisoned could smell the battle. The reek of gunpowder was only the first fragrance to reach them. Its blue haze soon grew thicker with the acrid scent of wood smoke, as the fighting triggered fires in the underbrush. Jonathan suspected that he was imagining it, but he kept thinking that somewhere beneath these odors he could detect the coppery scent of blood.

The armies fought steadily until the smoky dusk of the first day, but long after the fall of darkness the prisoners were roused by angry outbreaks of firing. As the night deepened, moans and cries, and occasional lone shots, rang out. Jonathan overheard one prisoner mutter that the more seriously wounded probably were taking their own lives, rather than face death by burning alive in the brush fires.

"Poor bastards!" the man said, looking directly at Jonathan.

As the battle raged into its second day, the population in the compound grew. With each additional soldier, the available space narrowed, and the men were forced into closer quarters. Tempers sometimes flared, and brief fistfights interrupted the static boredom.

These newcomers, Jonathan quickly discovered, were deserters—men who had fled from the actual lines of battle, only to be captured by their own cavalry once they reached the rear. From the way the guards violently threw them into the stockade, it was clear that the army considered deserters a more detestable breed than stragglers, perhaps even worse than spies.

One of them, a tall and thin foot soldier, was the only prisoner to befriend Jonathan. He introduced himself, with a respectful salute, as Private Zachariah Sullivan of Erie, Pennsylvania: "Eighteen years old, Captain, and already seen the elephant a dozen times."

Seeing the elephant, Jonathan learned, was military jargon for spending time under fire.

"Saw action at Antietam, Gettysburg, the second Bull Run, and Chancellorsville," Private Sullivan announced with a trace of pride. "And now, of course, here, wherever in hell this is."

The soldier whistled long and low. "Mighty bad out there, Captain, mighty bad. Why, there was one stretch where my whole battalion was obliged to lay down on the ground for more than two hours, for if you was to try standing up, you were sure to take a bullet lickety-split. Nothing could live out there that was over three feet tall, and God Almighty strike me down if I'm lying, you couldn't even see the sons of bitches who was shooting at you. They were hid as good as rabbits out in those goddamned woods. Might as well been invisible."

Jonathan quietly asked him why he had been confined in the stockade.

The youth's friendly face clouded. "Well, sir, it all just got to be a little too much for Zachariah Sullivan. By God, I've faced some of the worst in my day— hardly know how I got out of some of those scrapes alive—but this one..." A large tear emerged from the private's eye and snaked its way across his soot-stained cheek. "Well, Captain, this one just got to be too much. Cold as rain, I got scared, so I turned tail. I skedaddled, sure enough. And here I am."

The private sighed deeply. "I suppose it will be the firing squad for me. U. S. Grant is a great general and all, but he is not known for abiding deserters."

Jonathan clasped the private's arm, called him a brave man, and left him alone to his bleak musings. He walked to the perimeter of the stockade and peered between two posts. It was dusk, just light enough for him to see that the arteries of battle were still in full flow. Southward, the road was crowded with incoming wagons carrying more supplies and fresh troops. Northward, jostling for space with the incoming traffic on the rutted track, came wagon after wagon filled with wounded men. As night fell and their moans could be more clearly heard, the sound was so persistent that it became background noise, ultimately insufficient to keep the prisoners from falling asleep.

After three days, the dwindling sounds in the nearby forest signaled to those confined that the battle was coming to an end or moving farther south to another stage. The manic roar of weapons fire lowered to an intermittent crackle and finally diminished into irregular eruptions, almost as if the battle itself were going through its death throes.

During all that time, the stockade continued to fill with men who had tried to escape the fighting. They stopped coming only when the fighting ceased, but by then there was barely enough room for an individual to lay down full length. The prisoners subsisted on a meager diet of stale bread and foul-smelling water, rudely provided by the sentries three times a day.

For four more days, nothing happened. No one called for any soldiers by name, including Jonathan, who wasn't unhappy that he was being so long ignored, even while his anxiety grew about Apollonia's—and now increasingly his own— fate. The suspense of waiting to be questioned by intelligence officers, and the realization that he could neither tell them the truth nor convincingly lie to them, was driving him beyond distraction. He envisioned his pathetic performance in any such interrogation and repeatedly imagined what it might feel like to have a rope placed around his neck, knowing that he would momentarily take the fall. He wondered if the ultimate moment, when his neck snapped against gravity, would bring a surge of great pain or instant oblivion.

So preoccupied was he that he only thought of Apollonia occasionally and only then in a strangely abstract way. He came to the realization that he could no longer conjure an exact image of her face. He remembered her golden hair, her blue eyes, the gentle song of her accent, but the totality of her—the sensory reality of her presence—somehow seemed to be fading away. His confinement was colored by a deep and stubborn aching whose only relief, and that briefly temporary, was his one unshakable conviction: to regain her presence and at any cost.

On the seventh day, the army finally seemed to take notice of the forgotten prisoners. Early in the morning, an officer came to the gate and called for all men who had been assigned to the Fifth Corps to come forward. Some two dozen rose from the dusty ground and shuffled out the gate, toward whatever fate awaited them. The performance was repeated in the afternoon, with an order for men who had been assigned to yet another division of the army.

Perhaps thirty men stood and formed a single file. This time, Jonathan decided to join them. He removed his hat and took his place in line. He found himself behind the melancholy Private Sullivan, with whom he had held occasional conversations over the past week.

The phalanx moved slowly. Once outside the gates, they gathered in a disorganized group with no call to form ranks. There were only three or four laconic guards assigned to watch the shabby mob, and they seemed bored with their duty.

It was precisely what Jonathan was hoping for. As an officer began speaking to the group, delivering some sort of instructions, Jonathan looked at every guard's eyes. None of the guards was looking in his direction. He took a few slow steps backward, put his hat on his head, and soon found himself standing well apart from all of them. Even the prisoners themselves seemed not to notice his evaporation out of their midst. He appeared to be nothing more than an officer casually watching the proceedings.

He could scarcely believe his luck but couldn't trust it to hold for very long. He began to slowly walk away, down the same southeasterly road on which he had been captured a week ago, but he took one last look at his former fellow prisoners. He saw the dejected face of Private Sullivan and contemplated the sentence the army might have in store for him. He knew how foolish a move it was, but he did it anyway. He walked up to one of the sentries and tapped him on the shoulder.

"Corporal," he said in as authoritative a voice as he could project, "I want you to bring me that man there." He pointed to Sullivan. "I'll be taking responsibility for him."

The guard glanced at the officer who was still busy mouthing instructions to the prisoners and looked momentarily skeptical. A nervous glance at the insignia on Jonathan's shoulder seemed to remove his doubts. He asked neither for the captain's name nor for any authorization for his order. With a curt "Yes, sir," he took Sullivan by the arm and led him out of the group.

Before the dumbfounded private could say anything, Jonathan addressed him.

"I will deal with you myself, Private," he said in his firmest voice, "and by the time I am finished, you might wish I had not found you."

He turned back to the guard. "Carry on, Corporal," he said and was both amazed and relieved that the guard simply saluted and then followed the group of prisoners as they were led away.

Jonathan was left standing in a little clearing with Sullivan, who looked as if he were in shock. The sentries at the gate of the stockade were busy in conversation and paid no attention to them, nor did any of the handful of other soldiers who were milling about. The two of them simply walked down the road until they were out of sight.

"What in the hell just happened, sir?" the shaky Sullivan asked when they found themselves alone.

"We just became free men," Jonathan told him. "And I'd like it to stay that way. We must separate, in case they notice we're missing. I don't have any advice for you. Rejoin your unit, wherever it might be, and give them a good story. Or desert, try to make it back home—it's your choice. I wish you well either way."

The private's eyes once again welled with tears. "How can I thank you, Captain?"

"Don't worry about that. Just go. And take care of yourself."

The private stifled a sob, made a sad attempt at a salute, and took off down the road at a full run.

Jonathan walked at a slower pace, allowing distance to form between them. For the moment, the road was clear—no horses, wagons, or troops—and the solitude was soothing. That, and the last look he saw on the private's face, inspired his first smile in what seemed like a very long time.

He walked relentlessly southward, holding the direction like a migratory bird in autumn. As he dodged wagons and horses heading in both directions, he neither thought about what might lie between him and his destination nor cared. His stay in the stockade, surrounded by the horrible sounds of war, seemed to have numbed him to such higher contemplations. He was filthy from the stockade, thin from eating little food, sprouting the nascent growth of a dark beard, and seemed as driven as a ship before a gale.

Not that this deprived him of basic cleverness. He encountered other soldiers along the way and learned from them that he was traveling on the Brock Road. Through them he also learned that the main body of the Union force was not far ahead, perhaps no farther than five miles, and that if he moved quickly he could catch up with them by nightfall. He knew where the army was heading and what it was likely to endure before it got there, but he felt he no longer had any choice but to follow it.

Along the way, he passed through the very hell he had spent the last week listening to.

The road was a virtual tunnel through the thick foliage of the trees. The sharp tang of woodsmoke still permeated the air, and the stench of death hung over the woods like a foul blanket. Both sides of the road were littered with the dead, laid out in semi-regular rows, awaiting removal. There were many horses but even more human beings, wearing the uniforms of both armies. There were hundreds of each, it seemed, and Jonathan could hear crews of soldiers working in the depths of the woods to bring even more of them out.

He saw the horrors of their injuries—missing limbs, gaping bloody holes covered with flies, burnt flesh, decapitations. He saw the horrible expressions on some of the corpses' faces and, somehow even worse, the blank expressions on others.

He came face-to-face with the walking wounded, most of whom looked more dead than alive despite the fact that they were somehow able to stay on their feet. They came shuffling out of the dusk like zombies, bedraggled and bloody, staring vacantly, a few of them moaning quietly. They had been to the front, these survivors, they had indeed seen the elephant, and they looked it.

One of them, a short muscular man with a bushy brown beard, broke the ragged ranks and grasped Jonathan firmly by the arm. Beneath his cap, Jonathan could see a filthy rag that had been tied around the man's head as a bandage. It was virtually soaked in blood that still looked fresh. The man's blue eyes, striking against his tanned and dirty face, stared directly into Jonathan's as he barked out hoarsely: "Hughes! By God, it's you!" Jonathan tried to remove the man's iron grasp from his sleeve. "I'm not Hughes," he said quietly. "You're mistaken."

"Hughes!" the soldier persisted. "It's me! Simpson! By God, we were at Shiloh together, and here we are again, buddy!"

He continued staring and smiling at Jonathan, but finally, as if a veil had been lifted from his wounded brain, he seemed to realize his mistake. His grip slowly loosened, and his eyes shifted downward. Without another word, he let go and stumbled back into the pathetic column of zombies heading north.

And, somehow, all this horrific detritus, this grisly human aftermath of battle, was unable to penetrate Jonathan's emotional numbness. He looked at the wounded and the dead without shrinking, took in their smell with the air he breathed, walked in the face of long columns of weary and dejected Confederate prisoners being marched to the rear—all this he saw and thought only of his destination.

Rain began to fall, cooling the warm air. Jonathan raised his face into it and felt the grime wash away, stretching out his arms to catch even more of it. He felt a bit of his strength restored under its cleansing power.

He walked in the rain through the long night, so fatigued that he hardly noticed that at some point he had melded into a column of infantry heading in the same direction. The soldiers were as shabby and tired as he, but they had a grim determination on their faces and a purpose to their steady tread that perfectly matched his.

Very late in the night, as the rain pelted them, the column was called to a halt. Jonathan stopped as if he were one of their number. Word was passed down through the ranks that an advance on the enemy was imminent and that the troops were to go forward as quietly as possible, with no talking and with efforts to minimize all other noise. Surprise was important.

Jonathan passed the word on to the man behind him, not really thinking about what he was doing here or why. He was oblivious to details and kept his mind focused on the simple and solid: He had something to do and a place to go, and if a battle lay between him and what he sought, he would endure it.

In fact, the whole thing was becoming surreal, as if he were dreaming it all. He felt his physical and mental fatigue, knew that his stomach was trying to tell him that he was hungry, felt the hair growing on his face—all these sensory details were clear and unmistakable, but the broader context of his presence in this fatal time and place seemed ultimately unreal.

Try as he might, he could not place his own identity—Jonathan Chase, twentieth- and twenty-first-century man, former husband of Rachel, former employee in his father's firm, onetime fan of the Beatles, U2, and the Pretenders—into the shoes he was wearing at this moment. How had this man come to be here, marching with these hard-pressed soldiers into this battle? These soldiers were clearly not phantoms, and yet that's exactly what they were.

Or was *he* the phantom?

He tasted the rain on his tongue, smelled the sweat of the men before and behind him, felt the give of the mud beneath his shoes—all undeniable evidence of his presence—yet he felt more a voyeur, gaping at these men's struggles, tragedies, and deaths, than a participant.

It was true that he could feel little passion for their causes. Slavery, union, states' rights, even honor as these men understood the concept—all were lessons from schoolbooks, not the stuff of which his own heart had been composed. He was marching in support of none of these ideas, nor in opposition to them. They were yesterday's causes to Jonathan, resolved and settled a long time ago, despite the perversion of his presence here.

So why did he not abandon these ranks, disappear into the woods, leave these men to their own bloody causes and their own bloody times?

He wasn't sure, but he knew it was about her.

Everything had to do with her. She was why he had crossed the line of time in the first place and why he was now walking into an inferno, and whatever happened to him while inside that inferno, that would be about her, too. He was mere flotsam tossed on violent seas, a tiny piece of debris within a tornado's vortex of raging causes and bitter hatreds. He was an absolute stranger here, a lost soul without compass or place, but he had one last truth left to him, and that truth was Apollonia.

An infantry captain tapped him on the shoulder, bringing him back to full awareness of the moment.

"You're cavalry," the man said, a surprised tone in his voice. "What the hell are you doing here?"

Jonathan remembered his earlier mistake. "Sixth Cavalry," he replied, having learned that this particular regiment was indeed in the area. "Lost my mount and my regiment back in the woods."

The infantry officer laughed. "You lost 'em, sure enough. The Sixth just headed out with Sheridan, along with all the rest of the cavalry, going after Jeb Stuart out to the east. Lost your weapons, too, it looks like. Are you figuring on going in with us?"

"Looks that way to me."

"Well, I guess you're in the infantry now, so here, take this. We have plenty."

He handed Jonathan a long musket with a bayonet fixed to its barrel and a small leather bag of considerable weight. "You'll be needing these before dawn, I reckon."

Jonathan took the heavy weapon and thanked him.

The captain took a good look at Jonathan, shook his head, and smiled.

"Do you know where we're going?" he asked.

"Richmond, as far as I know."

The infantryman slapped his thigh and laughed again. "Sure enough, we're headed for Richmond, Captain! Eventually, that is. In the meantime, our worthy adversary, General Robert E. Lee, has decided that we must make a detour along the way. Little out-of-the-way place called Spotsylvania Court House."

In his former life and in his own time, Jonathan had given thought to that long-ago event known as the American Civil War. His knowledge of the conflict was shallow, formed in part by six or seven pages in his high school American history text and to a greater degree by a collage of collected images—Audie Murphy in *The Red Badge of Courage*, the angelic voice of Joan Baez recalling "The Night They Drove Old Dixie Down," the valiant black regiment in *Glory*, a half-forgotten macabre tale by Ambrose Bierce, the plaintive notes of "Ashokan Farewell."

There were varying degrees of realism in these attempts to depict the war. Some even attained graphic authenticity, but they all fostered illusions nonetheless. Partly because of such images, Jonathan had always seen the war as a glorious struggle of grand and dramatic people—men on steeds flashing sabers, tattered flags waving amid the smoke of battle, winsome damsels waiting for Johnny to come marching home. He had viewed it through the same rose-colored lenses with which he perceived the legions of Augustus or Napoleon—as something essentially more noble, more meritorious than the titanic global struggles, insane genocides, and prolonged terrorism of his own era—and in the process he had sanitized it. He had wrapped it in colorful bunting and lamenting ballads that were nothing more than the quaint propaganda of a romantic time.

He knew with dead certainty, as he slogged through the rain under a steely dawn, that these scales were about to fall from his eyes. If his glimpses of the ravaged Wilderness were not enough to make them drop, what lay ahead of him surely would.

Jonathan deduced this just by the din that emerged only a few hundred yards away from the regiment that he had joined. It was not the sound of glory. It seemed not even human, both because of its hideous mechanical strength and its animalistic fury. It was, in fact, a deathly farrago of many thousands, perhaps even millions, of smaller sounds—of untold numbers of rifles, muskets, and pistols firing; of artillery roaring; of feet stomping and bodies falling onto muddy ground; of shouts and curses and wails and screams.

It was beyond deafening and beyond madness. Hell, Jonathan thought, must sound very much like this.

The regiment was called to a halt when it came upon the one before it, which also had stopped. As yet another moved in from behind, the body of men compressed until they were shoulder-to-shoulder.

"Don't worry, boys!" he heard an officer shout over the noise. "You'll get your chance soon enough!"

He glanced at the men crowded around him, hands on bayoneted muskets raised to the gray sky. They seemed like boys, most of them, their youth obvious despite their beards, despite the hard look in their eyes. Yet they did not seem like frightened children. Nor did they seem particularly fierce or eager to fight. They evinced a steady calm and patience—soldiers doing their duty, warriors going to war—that seemed strangely but perfectly harmonious with where they were.

And, in looking at them, Jonathan realized that he felt no fear himself. A thousand moments in his life had caused him fear, but this most terrible moment—perhaps because of its sheer immensity—did not scare him. Instead, he resigned himself to it, willingly threw his fate to the winds of war, and immediately understood that this is what made his comrades-in-arms appear calm and patient.

Their wait did not last long. The column began inching forward, step by step, following the one before it—steers on the ramp leading to the killing floor, Jonathan thought—and the noise grew even louder with each foot's advance. Gradually, through the haze of rain and gunpowder smoke, Jonathan could see the orange flashes of muzzle fire and the silhouettes of men physically engaged mano a mano.

"Battalion!" the officer's booming but muted voice at last sounded. "Charge!"

Their turn had come.

As they surged forward, Jonathan thought he heard a bugle call. He definitely heard the roar of the men—a deep, ancient growl, loud enough to penetrate the bruit of battle itself.

The battalion moved in a long line, perhaps fifty yards wide, one to three men deep. In the distance, through the driving rain, Jonathan saw similar advances far to his left and right. A great wall of infantry was attacking at nearly right angles, from the west and the north, converging at what appeared to be a large salient point of the enemy, ensconced behind imposing earthworks that rose at least to a man's height. In some places, the Federal infantry had already overrun the works and were driving the Confederates back; in others, stacks of blue-clad bodies bore witness to more resolute resistance.

The goal of Jonathan's battalion, a frenzied nucleus of hand-to-hand fighting on both sides of the works, was less than fifty yards away. At first, the advance was graceful, almost symmetrical, but it quickly grew erratic as the soldiers began stumbling and slipping in the mud. Jonathan lost his footing and nearly fell himself, realizing with a dull sensation that it had been a human body that blocked his path.

Many of his comrades never made it any closer than this. They caught bullets that were coming relentlessly from the Confederate lines, the rounds' presence revealed only by daggerlike flashes from muzzles and an insectile hissing in the air. One man, immediately next to Jonathan, was struck in the midst of a fierce war cry that ended very suddenly, with a puzzled gurgle, before he fell like a stone.

It was an oddly monochromatic scene, the only colors on the drab field provided by the Stars and Stripes of the Federals and the Southern Cross of the Confederates waving here and there. Some of the banners were already trampled into the mud. He saw the enemy in action just ahead, the Rebels' brownish-gray uniforms were even more tattered than the faded blue of the Union, their hair and beards were longer, and their boots and shoes revealed rips and holes visible even in this limited light.

Those outside the earthworks were busy in direct combat with Northerners, an ugly, clumsy business of men struggling in random, jerky motions. Those still on the earthworks were either prone or kneeling, either loading their muskets or firing them into the advancing infantry. It appeared that still others behind them were fighting with Northerners who had managed to scale the earthworks and clamber onto the other side. There seemed to be a great many Confederates.

Jonathan imitated his fellow soldiers as they advanced, his musket held roughly parallel with the ground, bayonet protruding from its tip, moving in an instinctive crouching posture, as if to minimize the target his body provided. He held this stance until he reached the fighting, just a few yards shy of the earthworks, on ground cluttered with dead or injured men amid a tangle of branches and wooden spikes that had once served as a defensive barrier. It was hardly an organized or regimented engagement. There was no longer any evidence of rank-and-file or precise firing orders. It was a chaotic melee, a jostling mob of men and weapons that seemed intent on no objective beyond mutual annihilation.

His cognizant thinking stopped at this point, as pure instinct—of a kind he had never before experienced or even contemplated—took command of his being.

A lanky Confederate had just plunged his bayonet into the body of a Union soldier on the ground. He extracted the weapon from the man's torso, gave a loud yell of triumph, and turned to face Jonathan, who—without thinking, without even taking a good look at the man's face—pulled the trigger on his musket. The weapon discharged with a mighty kick, thrusting Jonathan backward, but its aim was true. The Rebel took the ball to the stomach, looked at the small red hole in his shirt, gazed for a moment at Jonathan with a startled expression, and fell to his knees, still conscious. Jonathan took a step closer, gripped his musket tighter, and thrust his bayonet into the man's chest. It felt like a kitchen knife slicing into a watermelon. The Rebel screamed at the death blow, grasped the barrel of the rifle, and looked straight into the sky, his cap falling from his head. He died in that position, raindrops collecting on his beard, and fell only when Jonathan, with effort, pulled the bayonet away from the firm grasp of the corpse and out of his chest.

As Jonathan rose from the kill, he turned to see another enemy approach, his bayonet aimed for Jonathan's middle. He was a short, clean-shaven youth with round cheeks and blond hair, an expression of innocence on his face. In an instant, he lost that expression, and everything else, as a bullet from somewhere slammed into the left side of his skull, sending a stream of blood and bone and gray cloth into the air. The boy fell to the ground in an awkward pile.

Jonathan turned again, this time only to see the wooden stock of a musket an inch or two from his face. The swung blow caught him squarely, smashing into his nose and sending him flat onto his back in the mud. The pain was immediate and severe, and he saw only stars as he waited for the sharp pain of a bayonet's intrusion—but it didn't come. When his vision cleared, whoever had struck him had vanished or had already died. Jonathan rose to his knees, dripping mud and streaming blood from his nose, and groped for his musket. He found it atop another man's body and regained his feet.

The fighting had moved closer to the earthworks but had lost none of its savage intensity. He wiped the blood from his face with his sleeve and looked for another opportunity.

He was not really thinking of what he was doing but instead acting out of some deep cellar of his subconscious, a forgotten but suddenly vital instinct to fight, a primal echo of days when men routinely fought to survive. He did not fully realize it at the moment, but he felt exhilarated and energized in the midst of this battle and, at some level still unknown to him, pleased with his survival and proud of his triumphs—proud even of the killing he had done.

He saw a Confederate rifleman fall from the top of the works, apparently struck from behind, and approached him. He took aim at the head of his enemy, a tousle-haired man who only then seemed to realize what was happening. The unarmed Rebel struggled vainly for a moment in the mud and then understood his hopeless position. He closed his eyes and made a rapid sign of the cross as Jonathan pulled the trigger—only to hear the hammer click impotently. He had forgotten that it was a single shot musket and that he'd already fired once. He had no idea how to reload it and realized that he would have to use the bayonet.

But he hesitated. Something in him stirred. Something in the sallow, fear-crossed face of this tatterdemalion Confederate, lying in the mud, having just made his peace with God, made him pause. The Rebel reopened his eyes and was staring directly at Jonathan. He said nothing but his gaze pleaded for mercy, and with no more thought than he'd given to his killing of another man, Jonathan granted it.

And this act, he discovered, was no less exhilarating in the awesome power it conferred.

Jonathan turned for the earthworks, which now appeared to have been abandoned by the Rebels. He scaled the awkward ascent and saw that there was still close fighting on the Southern side, although the Union forces seemed to be gradually driving the Confederates back from their lines.

He saw a Union officer on the ground, open-eyed and dead, and recognized him as the captain who only a half hour ago—an infinity ago—had laughed when Jonathan spoke of going to Richmond. He took the dead man's Colt pistol from his hand and hoped that he hadn't fired all of the rounds. He walked slowly and deliberately forward to where the infantry were still fighting and raised his pistol, looking for a target.

Before him, a man in blue and a man in gray were struggling with each other. Neither seemed to have any weapon left but his hands, and these they were using fruitlessly. They had grasped each other's necks but seemed to lack the strength to tighten their grips. They grunted and strained, swaying in the mud in a ghastly dance, until they both lost footing and fell.

Behind them stood a Confederate officer. He had begun to turn away, toward the south, but turned back when he saw Jonathan out of the corner of his eye. He was handsome with a fair face and dark hair and eyes, attired in a trim double-breasted tunic that perfectly matched his wide-brimmed hat. With his elegant mustache and the brass-handled saber still in its scabbard, he appeared to Jonathan like a Renaissance cavalier.

He raised his pistol just as Jonathan raised his, and for the briefest of moments, the two soldiers regarded each other. No fear or hatred crossed their faces, no terrible expressions of ferocity or savagery—just the level expression of two strangers who might as well have encountered one another on a busy street.

The reports of their pistols seemed perfectly synchronous, as did the wounds that instantly ripped into their chests, as did their graceless falls onto the sacred and forsaken ground of Spotsylvania.

He would never know how much of the rest actually happened or how much was a dream. He knew only that he experienced every moment.

At first, Jonathan felt only the demonic fury of the pain coursing through every fiber of his body, heard only the din of shrieking chaos in his ears, saw only multicolored comets against a sky of deepest black.

These receded in time, although the actual duration of time seemed to have lost its meaning. At some point, the pain retreated into a deep but dull ache somewhere near his heart. The sound diminished into a soft and hauntingly comfortable hum. His vision began to return, transforming into a murky montage of slow-motion battle images with gray sky and green foliage providing a strangely peaceful backdrop.

When he realized that he could not move from where he lay, Jonathan vaguely began to remember what had happened to him. But this state of partially awakened consciousness did not last. In time, he began to realize that he himself was fading. The quiet was becoming silence, the murky images encircled by a halo of darkness, the pain itself steadily losing its edge.

This comforted rather than frightened him. He was certain that it meant death, but somehow death seemed proper. He surrendered himself to it willingly, even gladly, with no conscious awareness of irony or loss.

And then he felt his body rise, a gentle sensation of ascension, easy and tranquil. His vision returned and he witnessed the savagery of war unfold beneath him. He recognized the rain-soaked ground of the field and the clumps of soldiers who still had the strength to fight inside the now shattered salient, saw the bodies of men strewn everywhere.

He saw his own body lying face up on the grass—eyes closed, face bloodied and swollen, a deep claret stain spreading over the breast of his tunic, his right hand still gripping the blue steel of a pistol—and found the scene perfectly natural.

He floated over the battlefield, amazed at the sheer size of it, the awesome breadth of its destruction. He gazed with a kind of dreamy wonder at a peaceful little church that stood near the periphery of the field. It was a plain clapboard structure with a modest steeple and simple windows, ordinary in every way except for the blasphemous spatter of bullet holes that had gouged its walls and door.

Somewhere beyond the church, he descended back to earth. He came down gently on a lonely country road, blessedly quiet and still, on which a coach had been parked. It was shiny and black and had neither horses nor driver. Somehow, Jonathan knew that the coach was waiting for him and that it would never need a horse or driver to draw it. He opened the side door and climbed onto the cushioned seats within. The coach began moving of its own accord down the rutted road.

He was content with his journey at first and confident of its destination, but something began to trouble him. As the coach picked up speed, he felt that something was missing, something was undone. He could not isolate the thought, and it increasingly vexed him. It was not something, he realized at length, but some*body*. It was somebody, and that somebody was a woman. He could not find her name, could not even conjure a picture of her face in his mind, but she was missing: She was not done with him, and he was not done with her. He knew that this absence was important, what remained undone critical. He could not leave her behind.

"Stop!" he cried, surprised how clearly his voice sounded in this state, but the coach did not heed him.

"Stop!" he cried again, and this time the coach, whose speed had increased a great deal, left the road. It tumbled over once or twice and came to a sudden halt on its side. The crash seemed very violent, but Jonathan felt nothing in the tumult of its upending—no fear and no pain.

He emerged from the door, now above his head, and climbed from the broken coach, one of its wheels still spinning. He stepped onto the quiet road and looked around him. Someone was approaching. It was a man. He was running and had almost reached the overturned vehicle.

When he arrived, Jonathan saw that the stranger was not a stranger. He saw his own face in the other's. It was clean and bloodless, unlike his own, and wore a certain innocence, also unlike his own—but it was himself.

The stranger who wasn't a stranger looked afraid and confused when he saw Jonathan. He gazed with wonder into his double's eyes and with a trace of edgy suspicion.

"Are you...," he began in Jonathan's voice and then grew silent, as if he suddenly realized the answer.

Jonathan replied with his own question. It was simple, and he needed no words to express it.

"Shall I go on?" he asked silently, conveying his meaning through his eyes.

The response also was given wordlessly but with clear certainty.

"*We* shall go on," he said, and he disappeared into the morning mist of the lonely road.

Jonathan knew the way back to the battlefield, and he knew that this time there would be no coach to carry him.

June

The year is half gone and the sun rules on high,

Thrusting his beams through the azure sky,

Warming the land with his glorious heat,

Hiding his face as the cumulus meet,

Till black clouds and thunder and lightning make war,

And sunshine returns through a rainbow's door.

I cannot tell you how difficult it was to pen those lines—so full of hope, so dauntless in the face of storms—nor can I properly describe the hardship of once more taking up this diary, once more putting the thoughts of my mind and the currents of my heart into words.

For my mind is naught but swirling anarchy, and my heart, my poor heart, has been broken in two. How does a person put such things into words? How does one conjure the art of expression when pain surrounds and fear rules? Most of us know the feeling of grief—I know now!—but what words truly convey that feeling? I am at a loss, and so I ask for your faith. I ask you to believe me when I tell you of my grief and pain and fear, and I hope that these few words of mine will be sufficient for you to believe, if not for you to share, my feelings—and if you cannot share them, my loyal reader, you may consider yourself fortunate indeed.

For there is much news to tell, and all of it—every cursed scrap—is bad.

I begin with the worst. Jonathan is gone. He is left behind, abandoned on the edge of battle—and with no word of explanation, nor of apology, from me. All I had time for on that dreadful night was a moment's opportunity to furtively slip the tiniest of messages to him, in the desperate hope that he might know that it was not me who was responsible for his betrayal, nor was it me—God forbid!—who desired it. Yet now I fear that he might never find it, might not even live to find it (or, pray that I am wrong, might already be dead), or might misunderstand it, or think ill of me or feel betrayed by me. I cannot bear this thought. Tears fall from my eyes when I think it—perhaps, in some distant century, you will still see the stain of my tears on this page. To think of being hated by the man I love!

Yet, for all my pathos, I must face the grueling truth. It *is* my fault that Jonathan's abandonment came about, as well as other dreadful things that came later. For it is by my blessing and mine alone—never mind how it was forced—that this entire affair has come into being. I could have stopped it before it truly began; I could have stopped it before we left Jonathan behind in that lonely grove. Indeed, I know that I could stop it now, this very instant. I could end this entire madness, just so long as I am willing to pay the price, but it is a price I fear I will always be unable to pay.

I hesitate. I say too much and ask your forgiveness for beginning to embark upon a sojourn I cannot complete. I have already related how I must remain circumspect in my confessions, but sometimes I forget myself.

To resume: It was Archer's intention that Jonathan be left behind. I fought him over it, I cried like a fool, but Archer was adamant. When I would not quiet myself, he threatened to kill Jonathan—a threat I took very seriously. Faced with the choice of his death or his abandonment, I chose the latter. It was as simple and as cruel as that. I cannot force from my mind the sight of Jonathan awakening in that place, alone, bewildered, and hurt—yet what else was I to do?

By the time he awoke, we were already miles away. We were fortunate that our final passage to Richmond began when it did, for our very approach had already been chosen by the generals as a stage for war. We were just ahead of it. Several times we were forced to leave the road to hide from Federal patrols—the main army was still some miles behind us. We reached the city, therefore, in less than two days.

Upon reaching Confederate lines, however, we were obliged to wait. The sentries and their superiors were slow to believe that Archer was a Confederate officer and that he and his companions had pressing official business in the city. At last, a colonel from Richmond vouchsafed for Archer, claiming to know him, and thus we were allowed in. It was none too soon, for we could already hear the sounds of battle to the north.

I found it curious, however, that Archer gave a false name to our own soldiers and that the colonel from Richmond seemed to think nothing of his lie. It was made plain that there is a great deal more to Archer Blaine than is known to me.

We entered our capital at last, but there was no joy in my heart in returning here. I took no pleasure in the knowledge that we were once more safe under the flag of the South, huddled near to its very heart. If truth be told, I barely took note of it, so distraught was I over Jonathan.

Alas, my woes were not yet all gathered!

Just a few days after we were lodged near the center of the city, Archer made another decision for which the only adequate description is evil. He compelled me—under the same conditions that have compelled me from the beginning—to sell Jeremiah to a dealer in Richmond. This too has broken my heart more than I can say, but it has been too recent a deed, and the look upon poor Jeremiah's face far too disconsolate, for me to describe it here. These pages have already seen enough of my guilty tears.

Suffice to say that the heinous deed was done and that once more I played the wretched role of villainess in sending a beloved one away from me, leaving him—just as I left Jonathan—to face whatever cruelty fate might have in store.

Archer and his cretin, however, are merry with their doings. They felt it necessary to be rid of Jonathan, whom they considered a likely threat, and Jeremiah, whom they felt an unworthy burden, and now that these obstacles have been overcome, it is just the three of us. In truth, despite their presence and their everlasting vigilance over me, I am utterly alone. They have taken away from me the two who stood by my side.

Now, friendless and alone, utterly at their mercy, I merely wait as Archer gathers information crucial to our mission. I am told we will not be in Richmond for long. I sense that Archer feels vulnerable here. He acts in a furtive manner, as if somebody might be looking for him, and seems impatient to be done with his business and soon gone.

As I wait, I languish in this bleak hotel room in the stifling heat, trying to ignore everything around me. I think of Jeremiah in his slave pen and wonder whether it will be his fate to be purchased by a kind owner or a cruel one. I wonder what he thinks of his "Miss Appy" now, after she so callously and heartlessly discarded him.

I think of Jonathan and fear what dangers might already have befallen him so close to those dreadful battlefields.

I hope, against all reason, that he has not forsaken me, that the love he expressed so tenderly remains stronger than his anger and his hurt. I do not deserve such devotion from anyone, let alone such a fine man as Jonathan, yet I remain a stubborn and selfish woman. I shall hope that his love for me remains, whether I am worthy or not.

JUNE

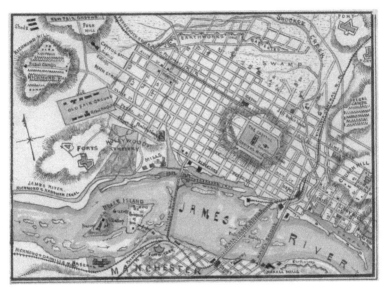

RICHMOND FORTIFICATIONS

HE WAS SWIMMING.

He swam instinctively, without deliberation or direction or memory—embryo-like, within a womb. He neither questioned his surroundings nor sought to define them. He was aware only that he belonged in this place without time or afference, and this awareness was limited to the moment-to-moment sentience that seemed all his brain was capable of.

Through this hazy gauze, he saw a nameless sea, first in an absolute void of pure black. This eventually morphed into lightening shades of gray that, in turn, became a milky white. The featureless borders of this curtain then slowly began to dissolve, holes appearing within its surface. Beyond these holes, he glimpsed images, in fleeting colors and shapes, of things he did not recognize.

As the openings grew larger and the images more visible, his consciousness began clumsily to respond, as if it were rewiring itself. He began to remember the names of some of the glimpses and sensations before him.

That is a man's arm was his first real thought. *And that arm is holding something shiny and sharp.*

Another: *That is a sharp smell—medicinal, like alcohol or iodine.*

Still another: *What are those people saying? They're not saying anything. They're moaning. They're crying.*

And finally, as if some critical turntable in his mind ceased to spin and found the right track with which to connect, the senses fell clumsily together.

He realized that he was lying on his back, apparently on some kind of cot, within a huge tent of beige canvas, supported by poles roughly hewn from raw timber. He could tell by sound that a lot of people were within this tent and that it was a busy place. He could tell by sight that a tall man in white clothing, grossly stained with red, was hovering over a man on another cot across an aisle. The first man was speaking to a woman in a long dress of blue pillow tick, a bonnet of similar material covering the back of her head.

A *hospital*, he thought.

Then: *A field hospital!*

"He's hemorrhaging again, Doctor," the woman said, her voice urgent.

"I was afraid of this," the man replied.

Neither was looking at Jonathan, who was straining now to keep up with the increasing speed of his reawakening synapses. *A field hospital*, he realized, *was a military hospital. He was in a military hospital, because he had done something military.*

"Scalpel," the man ordered the woman. Both of them were now leaning sharply over the prone figure, unaware of Jonathan's growing cognitions.

He had fought in a battle—a battle in a war—and he had been wounded.

"No, this side!" the man said to the woman, impatience in his tone.

He had been shot! He had been shot by another man—a man with a pistol and a hat. An enemy!

"That's good, now tighten it up a little," the man said, calm returning to his voice.

The battle was between the North and the South. It was fought under a rainy sky, on green land, close to a little out-of-the-way place by the name of . . . by the name of . . . Pennsylvania, Transylvania, something Sylvania.

"There, we have it, Maggie. Nicely done. This should improve things greatly."

The doctor and the nurse were no longer talking. They had placed their hands in a large metal basin and were vigorously washing them. The woman then turned to Jonathan—she was blonde and plump and pretty—and looked directly into his eyes. A wide smile crossed her face.

"Well, I'll be!" she cried. "Doctor, look at this! Our mystery captain has awakened."

The doctor's voice was deep and soothing. He had placed his hand on Jonathan's forehead and was staring intently at him. The pretty nurse was standing on the other side of his cot, still beaming like a proud mother.

"How do you feel?" the doctor asked.

"I don't know. Numb."

"That's good," the doctor rejoined. "Can you tell me where you are?"

"A hospital, I think."

"That's very good. And do you know where this hospital is?"

"Somewhere near...I can't remember the name...someplace near the battle?"

"That's right, Captain. We're about fifteen miles away from where the battle was. Spotsylvania. You remember the battle, then?"

"Sort of. I remember a man, a man with a hat..."

"Never mind. Can you tell me your name?"

Jonathan tried. He tried very hard, but the necessary connections were running into dead ends. He had only a vague sense of self and an utter blank on identity.

"How about your regiment? Can you remember that?"

Something stirred in a random strand somewhere deep within his head. "Cavalry. It was a cavalry regiment. I can't remember which one."

The doctor smiled. During his questioning, he had been probing Jonathan's body—peering into his eyes, checking his pulse, unwrapping bandages from a spot on his chest.

"Well, this is a very good start, Captain," he said. "For a while there, I was afraid you were determined never to come back to us. You've been in a coma for nearly two weeks."

"What happened to me?" Jonathan asked, now feeling dull rays of pain emanating from his chest.

"You took a bullet from a pistol. Missed your heart by less than an inch and then punctured your left lung. I'm amazed you survived long enough to be taken from the field."

"What field?"

"You were found well inside the Rebel salient—the Bloody Angle, they're calling it—right where the fighting was thickest. You were in with the Seventh Rhode Island Infantry, and those boys thought it was quite strange. Nobody out there knew who you were or why a cavalry officer was in their ranks. Any ideas on that?"

Jonathan tried again but could seize nothing. "I have no idea," he said. "My chest is starting to hurt."

The doctor nodded. "That's to be expected. You'll have to get used to it for a period. I'll have the nurse bring something for you. It will put you to sleep, but don't worry. That's exactly what you need right now, and I have every confidence that you won't leave us again."

Jonathan did sleep, although he had no idea for how long. When he came to, it was either sunrise or sunset—the light inside the great tent was reddish and angular. It was warm, and above the smell of medicine, he detected the rich summer scent of verdure in full bloom. It was quiet, save for the breathing of many men and the raspy song of some insect outside.

Although his chest throbbed with a deep and hungry pain, he remembered his conversation with the doctor. For a moment, he thought he had grasped his name, but it eluded him at the last second. He fought for it with a grim determination, but the precise combination of letters and sounds stayed maddeningly just out of reach.

He had vague impulses of past events. The man with the hat and the gun was still there, even clearer now. There were recollected shards of mud and blood and shouts of anguish. He could remember a long march with uniformed soldiers and an awful noise, but nothing before that.

It turned out to be morning after all, and Jonathan painfully propped himself higher on his slender pillow as the other patients began to stir. He soon wished they would fall back asleep, for they were clearly a miserable lot. Their moans began almost upon awakening, as did their demands for water and food. Soon, the still tent was bustling with a dozen nurses and several doctors.

One of them—apparently the doctor with whom he had spoken before—came to Jonathan's bed at last. He inquired as to how he was feeling and offered more sedative.

"Not just yet," Jonathan told him. "I want to remember. I want to have a clear head for a while."

The doctor nodded. "That may be a good idea, if you can take the pain. When it gets to be too much, tell a nurse."

He began to walk away but then stopped.

"Oh," he said. "I'd almost forgotten. We found this in your jacket after they first brought you in. I thought it might be useful."

He pulled something out of his pocket, handing Jonathan a delicate gold locket on a fine chain. It was smooth and simple in design, oval in shape. When he took it, he knew he had never seen it before.

As the doctor left to attend to other patients, Jonathan clicked the tiny latch and snapped it open.

When he gazed at the small picture within—a fair-haired woman with pale eyes and an enigmatic smile—he spoke aloud.

"Apollonia."

He recognized not only her name but her face. And in the instant it took for that information to reach his brain, the wall of his amnesia started to crumble. A series of images featuring the woman in the locket—a candlelit meeting in a small square room late at night, a glimpse of her atop a horse in heavy woods, the feel of her lips on his—flickered before his consciousness.

"Apollonia." He said it again, quietly but clearly.

The memories returned with the sudden violence of an avalanche. They forced their way into his mind, piling on top of each other, tumbling until they found places to rest. In a flash, he knew that he was Jonathan Chase, that he was in Virginia, that he had been searching for Apollonia, that he was lost in the past.

All the while, the face on the miniature portrait, painted with uncanny accuracy, seemed to stare at him from his hand. Even as his mind still scrambled with the cascade of restored knowledge, he felt a tug at his heart—strong enough to be detected amid the throb in his chest—as he looked into the tiny blue eyes.

But from where had the locket come? He had never seen it before, never glimpsed this portrait. He had no memory of that, but he did recall something. He remembered sleeping under the stars a few days before the battle—near Culpeper, he thought, amazed and relieved at the speed with which the name came. He remembered feeling a gentle nudging at his side late in the night. He thought it might have been the curiosity of an errant animal, but could it have been her? Could she have slipped the locket into the narrow and little-used pocket inside his coat?

He also remembered that it was the last time he had seen her. By the next morning, she had fled with the others. Why had she left the locket? Was it a fond farewell, an apology, a warning?

And then he saw a small piece of paper that had been neatly folded and tucked into the locket's golden cover. His heart began beating rapidly, amplifying his physical pain, as he carefully removed it and methodically flattened its tiny creases.

It was written in violet ink, and the script appeared feminine. The writing was distorted on the wrinkled paper, and cramped because of the minuscule surface, but the words were clear enough.

"Do not forsake me, my ally," it said.

Those six words did more to mend the broken man Jonathan had become than all the tinctures, ointments, and opiates of the medical staff in the field hospital. Upon reading them, he felt as if he had just been freed from the grasp of strong chains.

She had not deserted him, at least not of her own accord. That was the most important thing, the heaviest suspicion he had borne. She had not forgotten that he was her ally. She did not want him to forget her.

It remained possible, he allowed himself, that she really did love him.

Whether this knowledge saved his life, Jonathan would never know. He only knew that it made him once more want to live.

His physical injuries were only part of that. The psychic trauma of the battle was far greater than he would ever have imagined, and it lingered about him like a miasma. The plaints and moans of the other wounded soldiers in the long tent disturbed him greatly, not only because he understood their suffering but because they echoed the cries of the men ripped to shreds on the field.

One of those, he knew, was the man he had killed—a man he had shot point-blank before plunging a bayonet into his body to hasten his death. He remembered his shriek and the raindrops on his face and realized that this memory had already become a grisly icon, permanently emblazoned on his brain. He knew that the act had taken place in the heat of battle and tried to rationalize that, if he hadn't acted as quickly as he had, the Rebel would surely have killed him. Such is the price of war, he said to himself over and over, but there was no escaping that he felt much more than guilt for the killing—he saw himself as evil for the joy he had taken in the act. He could never again regard himself in the same light he had once enjoyed. He could never totally wash away that man's blood from his soul, just as he could never replace the life he had taken.

There would be no healing for that invisible scar, he knew, but the faint ray of hope that Apollonia's words brought to him was enough to allow hope for a healing of his body. His chest wound was a constant, unwelcome companion, its pain wavering in and out, seemingly in rhythm with the summer cicadas and katydids that droned in the nearby woods. The strong narcotic that was given to him twice a day—what he assumed was morphine—brought total but brief relief and always at the cost of mental clarity. He thirsted for the cessation of pain but dreaded the dreamy somnolence that always accompanied the drug.

At times, when the medicine's effects had weakened, his agony would grow so intense that he could do nothing but lie still, clench his teeth, and try to ride it out. Jonathan visualized the pain as a violent black stallion, bucking and leaping, trying to throw him off its back. So long as he held to the horse, he believed, he would eventually recover, he would somehow survive.

Compared to being shot, his other injuries seemed of little consequence. His nose had been broken by the rifle stock, and his knee had been grazed by a bullet or shred of shrapnel—probably while he lay wounded on the ground, the doctor speculated.

After several days, he asked the nurse to bring him a mirror and was shocked at what he saw. Although his face was no longer bruised, his nose now bore a crooked little hill at its upper end, indisputable evidence of its breaking. His whiskers had sprouted into a substantial brown beard, and his hair had grown wild and long, well over his collar. Much more striking than this, his face seemed to have narrowed and aged. It wasn't haggard or pinched, but drawn. It reflected suffering and sadness and reminded him of images of the dying Jesus that he had seen on crucifixes. In a strange way, his own face hauntingly reflected that of the Rebel he'd slain.

He looked like an entirely different man, Jonathan thought, and he realized that he had become exactly that.

He refused the nurse's offer to shave the beard. This was at least partially a calculated move, as Jonathan was beginning once more to contemplate his quest. He thought that his face now resembled the proverbial man of the times. It would be easier to blend into a crowd looking like this, and even certain people who knew him might not recognize him. That could prove valuable.

He had given the same careful consideration to his amnesia. Although it had disappeared quickly, he had deliberately not told the doctor or the nurse about his restored memory. He held to his story of utter forgetfulness, and they seemed to believe him. He knew that he could not possibly tell them the truth, and although he had no way of knowing how he would extract himself from his present predicament, he sensed that it would be much easier if nobody knew who he was.

Six days after waking from the coma, he began to walk. The first strolls, taken late at night and in direct disobedience of the doctor's orders, were painful and clumsy and lasted no more than two minutes, but he kept at it. Within another week, he was walking with the doctor's permission, able to course through the entire tent and back again, aided only by a cane. The first time he succeeded, he was cheered by a handful of bedridden soldiers who seemed to take heart from his progress. He bowed when they cheered and laughed along with them when he nearly fell on his face from the exertion of bending.

Before long, the doctor allowed him out onto the grounds. The warm summer air and brilliant sunshine strengthened him considerably, although the hospital environs were not a pleasant place. He found his massive tent to be only one of several, all gathered around a stately brick structure that Jonathan surmised had once been a plantation house. The lawn gracing the estate was now barren, its grass trampled into dirt, its trees pulled down. It was a bleak and dreary scene, with only a few ambulatory soldiers shuffling about and wagons coming and going to ferry wounded up to Washington, where, he learned, the big hospitals were located. Once, when he strayed near the border of the complex, he nearly stumbled into a ghastly legacy of the battle—a fly-shrouded heap of amputated arms and legs awaiting burial. The sight of it made him want to gag and weep at the same time.

As the days passed and his strength slowly returned, he spent more and more time beyond the hospital, taking in the balmy sun and enjoying the sanctuary of the woods that surrounded the grounds. There were sentries posted along the hospital's perimeter, but they were well aware of their distance from enemy lines and had little fear of guerrilla engagement. The guards came to recognize Jonathan in his mended trousers and open tunic, a large swath of gauze covering his chest. He became a familiar figure with his cane and crooked gait, and the sentries gave him no trouble over his increasingly long walks.

Late one afternoon, he strolled beneath a sky that clung to its radiance against threatening clouds in the west. He was already a mile from the grounds, well away from all of its terrible sounds, sights, and smells, when he came upon a narrow road. It was, more accurately, a dirt path, snaking almost stealthily into and out of shady groves of hardwoods, over and across summer fields with crops well along. The serpentine trail seemed almost a private course. There were no signs of recent use, and Jonathan encountered nobody as he walked along it. It passed through country that, despite its proximity, seemed to have totally evaded the destructive talons of war. The farmers who kept these fields, to judge by their handiwork, seemed to be going about their labors in full and blissful oblivion of the human apocalypse raging just a few miles from their houses and barns.

As the sun drew steadily toward the horizon, casting the leaves in brilliant relief of chartreuse light against lengthening shadow, Jonathan experienced his first moment of true peace in a very long while. He breathed in the fragrant air and listened to the birds, allowing the sun to caress his face and chest.

His mind wanted to return to its customary topics: Apollonia, her whereabouts and circumstances, the means by which he might regain her presence, how long it would take for his strength to be restored so he could actually do so.

But this time, unlike all the idle hours he had spent in the hospital, Jonathan resisted the impulse. He had already thought through all those thoughts, ad infinitum, and had come to realize that he was unable to forge a master plan with the little information he had at hand. He would have to take it day by day, as he had done before the battle, and rest his hopes on good luck and his sound, and hopefully improved, judgment. There was no use revisiting it all again.

Instead, as he savored his solitude and relished the moment's absence of physical pain, he tried to explore the strange fact of his existence in this alien time. Since he had made his passage through the portals of Chronos—how long ago was it? four months? five?—his life had been so harried, his waking thoughts so focused on one goal, that he had never seriously considered the astonishing fact that he was really, absolutely, undeniably here. Some of that, he realized, might have been a sort of sensory shutdown. His time travel was so improbable and so unexplained that the ever-practical mind simply stopped seeking explanations and turned instead to such mundane, but much more necessary, matters as staying alive. It seemed bizarre that he had already adapted to his new environment and reality, but his experiences of the past few months proved beyond a doubt that indeed he had.

He contemplated the sky and tried to reconcile that this was a sky from another time—from this time—and not his own. Its canopy of scudding, broken clouds and deep, grave colors felt as foreign, and yet as damningly familiar, as everything else around him.

As the western storm drew closer, the firmament grew moody and dramatic—a Gainsborough sky, like the one the artist painted behind *The Blue Boy* or Reynolds's portrait of the beautiful Perdita gazing mournfully at a brooding English countryside. It rolled and streamed with unsettled turbulence, casting random shadows across the land—a Romantic landscape of the Hudson River School—and its foreboding colors of rich gold, deep blue-gray, and blood crimson whispered of other times, forgotten lives, and long-lost realities. The trees that stood in silhouette against this background took on a soft, otherworldly cast as Jonathan watched their gaining motion in the wind. Like the sky itself, these towering oaks and ashes appeared painted in oil on old canvas and not a physical reality occupying the same space as his.

Could it really be, he thought, that everything really was different in this time, that the entire essence of reality, the whole temporal substance of the world itself, had changed so much in a century and a half?

The trees that surrounded him were old, some of them even ancient, perhaps survivors of the primeval forest that had covered this place before the white man's invasion. There was a queer but absolute absence of human noise, no trace of the ubiquitous background clamor in which it now seemed he had once spent his entire life. No whoosh of cars on some nearby freeway or road. No faint whine of jet engines in the cooling evening air. Absolutely no chance of picking up a stray radio signal or wind-borne scrap of stereo music. Not here. Not now. Such things lay in the distant future and—again the maddening paradox—in Jonathan's own increasingly distant past.

It was undeniably a different world that enveloped him now, and it exhibited this difference in very sensory ways: the unbroken quality of the land, the lack of mechanical sound, the purity of the air. One would logically expect such things to have changed in so many years, yet he sensed something else different about it all, and it was not merely the melodramatic sky that was now busily cloaking itself in ominous gray. Jonathan felt a difference in the atmosphere itself, maybe in the very molecules of which this air was composed, and he began to believe that this intangible difference, this elusive distinction, was starting to creep into the tiniest cells of his own body and the neurons of his very brain, bringing him invisibly but inevitably into tune with this arcane time, forever setting him apart from the one he had once known.

That is insane, he thought, taking a step upon the road that stretched lazily before him. He pushed the notions away. It was mad to think that such universal elements as the sky and the trees were somehow different in different times. Skies and trees and landscapes and people had not changed essentially in a mere century, or five centuries, for that matter. Perhaps the artists and photographers and poets of that time—of *this* time—expressed their visions differently than he would a century and a half later, but the basic things, the raw materials of the world, were basically the same. They had to be.

It was quite likely, he thought, that he could return to this bend in the road in his own time—assuming he ever did return—and he would see much the same scene that greeted him at this moment. This was a rural locale and had probably spent the succeeding decades relatively untouched by the hand of developing, ever-progressing humanity. The sky and the trees would remain unchanged.

And the people, in spite of the infinity of vicissitudes they had yet to witness, in spite of the histories they had yet to envision let alone experience, the people would be basically the same, too.

It was simply this: He had never really seen these things before. He realized with an almost physical sensation that, until this moment, he had never really seen the trees or the sky, or perhaps even most people, so distracted had he always been by the lights and the jets and the broadcast waves and the feverish, pointless frenzy of his time. Now, and here, free of these artificial distractions, he was projecting newfound clarity onto the never-changing, constant world. He was looking at everything in a new way with a much keener focus.

In the end, this was no panoramic painting come mystically to life, no charming woodcut of rural nineteenth-century Americana garbed romantically in quaint lore, even though this was indisputably that very place and time. He felt that the dreamy Romantics of this time had missed the point. The world had never needed embellishment or fancy to adorn its awesome glory or its awful perils. And the humorless rationalists of his own time had missed it, too. Their tireless efforts to streamline, to plasticize and digitize, and invariably to cheapen the world served only to obscure, not obliterate or even weaken, its glory and power.

He began the long walk back to the hospital under a cooling rain that was steady but light. There was utterly no fantasy about the moment he was experiencing, about the path on which he strode. This was life itself, nothing more or less, and he was most definitely living it now.

A month passed since the battle.

Jonathan's wound seemed to have progressed through the worst. It no longer bled or suppurated, and the pain, although present, had lost most of its edge. His knee remained weak and sore, however, and his general strength was limited. He found that his walks of more than a mile exhausted him and caused his left leg to stiffen and grow numb. He fashioned an improvement over his army issue cane, a crude walking stick of hickory from the woods, and with this he was able to extend the range of his daily hikes.

Enough of his vitality had returned, and the routine of the hospital sometimes grew so monotonous, that he volunteered to help out as a nurse's aide. Although the numbers of wounded steadily lessened—at least a dozen patients a day were sent north—there was still plenty to do. Most of the work was of the sort he would once have considered grotesque—cleaning wounds, emptying bedpans, changing and washing soiled linen—but it made him feel useful and, he was sure, contributed to his own recovery.

He was still officially known as the "mystery captain" and had been given by some the nickname "Mystery" for short, since he had yet to reveal that his memory had returned. It was partially for this reason—and, he believed, partially due to his labors in the hospital—that the doctor had not put him aboard one of the wagons bound for the Washington railroad.

This was a good thing, because he wanted to stay as close to Richmond as possible. He knew that the Confederate capital would be his next destination— it was the only clue he had as to Apollonia's location. He had no developed plans for what he would do once—and if—he managed to get there, but ideas were bouncing around in his mind, waiting for an inspiration to clarify and solidify them.

An early phase of that process was a very unusual soldier by the name of Miles O'Bannion.

He was about twenty-five years old, of average height, and handsome in a dark sort of way, with a long and thin drooping mustache that framed a perfectly trimmed goatee. He was proudly and obviously Irish and had lost his left arm in fighting quite close to where Jonathan had received his own injury.

He wore, with unconcealed pride, the most ridiculous uniform Jonathan had ever seen.

It was crowned with a cap that resembled a white beret or the flat hats worn by sailors of the U.S. Navy, and it had a large gold tassel that draped across the wearer's neck and brushed the shoulder. Next came a bright blue vest, with elaborate arabesque embroidery in scarlet and silken red buttons, that was worn unfastened to reveal a red satin sash around the waist. The trousers were baggy pantaloons, reaching the top of the ankles, like those of genies of Levantine lore. Spotless white spats and black shoes completed the bizarre ensemble.

Jonathan had heard of the gaudy uniforms of the soldiers who called themselves "Zouaves," but O'Bannion's was the first he'd yet seen. It looked to him like something that Sinbad might wear and, coupled with the corporal's accent, helped create a very striking, if eccentric, persona.

His personality matched perfectly. O'Bannion was as loud and flamboyant as his regalia, a shameless braggart.

"Corporal Miles O'Bannion, a child of County Donegal and, until the ides of May, a member of the Tenth New York Volunteer Infantry, specifically Company F, better known as the Morgan State Zouaves of Brooklyn, at your service!" were the first words he spoke to Jonathan, in a painfully thick brogue, when Jonathan had come to bathe the stump that remained of the Zouave's limb.

"I would give you my name in return," Jonathan replied, "if I knew it."

O'Bannion clucked his tongue. "Oh, that's all right, brother. I already know you to be the man with neither name nor memory. They call you Mystery, do they not? Now you can plainly see that I've gone and lost my arm, it's true, thanks to some nigger-whipping Johnny Reb—may his carcass be rotting now beneath the sun of old Virginny—and an arm is no small matter, but I pity any man who's lost his memory."

"The pity I can do without," Jonathan said, dipping O'Bannion's stump into a tin basin filled with warm water, "but your skills might come in handy."

"Might they now?" the Irishman replied, leaning forward from his cot, a mercenary gleam lighting up his eyes.

For it was well known in the hospital that O'Bannion, in addition to being an Irishman, a New Yorker, a Zouave, and an amputee, was also a passionate and resourceful businessman.

"What'll be your pleasure, then, my good Captain? Might you be wanting apple lady, bark juice, busthead—all fine liquors, to be sure, and all available through yours truly, although of varying quality and hence ranging in price—or might it be a touch of the poppy? Plenty of that to be had here in the tent, sure enough, and if the customer is a-buyin', then O'Bannion is a-sellin'.'"

"None of those," Jonathan answered. "And how in the world do you manage to get those sorts of things here?"

"Ah," O'Bannion rejoined, placing his finger knowingly to his nose. "I've got to keep my trade secrets, now don't I? Suffice it to say that the O'Bannion Mercantile is always open for business, whether you're preparing to open the ball against the Rebs or sitting here in a casualty tent. But never mind my ways and means. I'll wager that it's a fancy lady you'll be wanting. Been a while since you've had a merry toss in the loft, is it? Well, that'll cost a wee bit more, of course, but if you're up to a hike of three miles or so and are not terribly concerned about the relative, shall we say, pulchritude of the lady in question, well, then, I can meet your needs."

"I don't want a woman," Jonathan said, failing in his efforts not to smile.

O'Bannion's brown eyes widened, and a defeated look crossed his face. "You're a tough customer, brother, and that's a fact! I've just about run through the entire inventory. What in the world do you want of me, then?"

"I want to go to Richmond."

"Great Andy Jackson's ghost!" the Irishman exclaimed, pulling the remnant of his arm from the basin and splashing water all over. "You're not only an amnesiac, Mystery, you're a bloody lunatic!"

He spent several minutes staring intently into Jonathan's face, as if to read some hidden message there. When the salving of O'Bannion's wound was completed and the stump wrapped in fresh linen, the Irishman at last spoke again.

"First of all, before I even consider your request, I must know your reasons for wanting to go to Richmond."

"I'm not at liberty to say," Jonathan replied, helping O'Bannion out of his chair so that they could take a stroll in the relative privacy of the hospital grounds.

"Oh, you're not at liberty, are you?" O'Bannion rejoined, sarcasm laced throughout his brogue. He pointed a finger in Jonathan's face. "Well, here's a guarantee for you: There'll be no deal with me if your aim is to provide aid and comfort to the fewkin' Johnnies. I've already given my arm for the cause, and I've no desire to throw my neck into the bargain and all for a bloody spy!"

"Keep it quiet!" Jonathan whispered. They had found shelter from the hot afternoon sun behind one of the tents. He knew that those inside would have no trouble overhearing a loud conversation.

"I'm not a spy, O'Bannion. I swear to that. I have no intention of helping the Rebels."

The Irishman's defiant stance relaxed a little. "So why the hell are you wanting to go to Richmond, then? I hear the place is a bloody cesspool."

Jonathan paused before answering. He wasn't entirely sure that he could trust O'Bannion. He seemed honest enough, in his strange and mercenary way, and sincere about his loyalties. He was still a virtual stranger, but Jonathan finally decided that he had no choice but to be truthful. He was, after all, asking a great deal. He led O'Bannion away from the tent, toward the nearest grove of trees. They sat down in the shade.

"Okay, I'll summarize this because it's a long story. The first thing you need to know is that I am not a soldier." He ignored the Irishman's look of astonishment and continued. "I'm a civilian, from out West, although my beliefs are basically the same as yours—I'm a Union man. I was at Spotsylvania, remember? Not far from where you must have been, and the bullet they dug out of my chest ought to settle your mind on that.

"The second thing is that I have no amnesia. I know exactly who I am and what I'm doing here. My name is Jonathan Chase, and I ended up here because I was going to Richmond to start with. The battle happened to get in my way."

"Nice way of putting it, uh...oh hell, I guess I can call you Jonathan now, can't I?"

"That will be fine so long as we're alone. In the hospital, I have to remain anonymous."

"Fine by me, brother. You've started an interesting yarn here, I have to admit, but I'm still foggy on why you wanted to get to Richmond to begin with."

Jonathan took a deep breath. "I'm looking for somebody."

O'Bannion narrowed his eyes, an expression that gave him an air of focused expertise, not unlike a jeweler appraising a fine emerald.

"Ah," he said after a pause. "I'm beginning to smell a motive at long last. You're not a soldier, you're not a spy, you've lost neither your memory nor your mind—don't ask me why, but I happen to believe you on all those points—so why in God's green earth would a Northern man want to dive straight into the dyspeptic belly of the Southern beast? To my thinking, there's only one force strong enough to make a man try such a foolish thing. And that, my friend, non-Captain Jonathan Chase, would be love!"

The Irishman leaned back against the trunk of a tree, a wide smile across his face. "Am I right?"

Jonathan could not help but return the smile. "You're right, O'Bannion. You're as perceptive as you are clever."

O'Bannion laughed in triumph. "Well, she must be one hell of a lass."

"She is."

"All right, then. Miles O'Bannion needs hear no more. I consider myself no less a man of the heart, a firm believer that any man not willing to die for the sake of love is not fit to live at all."

The Irishman suddenly sat up from the tree, newly alert and intense. His mind was clearly marshalling its energies toward the challenge it had just been presented. When he spoke, he looked off into the distance in concentration, as if he were alone and talking to himself.

"It's roughly thirty miles due south of here, I should think. If you got past our own patrols, you'd have little problem the first half, maybe two-thirds, of the way, unless you ran into raiders. That's a possibility, but I'm guessin' they're a little skittish these days with Sheridan all over the countryside and Grant chasing Lee like Herod after Salome. I don't believe you would have to worry about Rebel lines per se, at least not on the north side, not with Grant threatening from Petersburg, but beyond fifteen or twenty miles, the Johnnies would likely have pickets or videttes, perhaps cavalry patrols. And the roads are no good. Every damn one of them is manned, or at least watched, and probably by some Tennessee sharpshooter who can put out a squirrel's eye at a league."

He turned his eyes at last to Jonathan, as if just now aware of his presence.

"Going cross-country would be quite the arduous and hazardous chore," he said. "With you walking no faster than my grandpappy and leaning on that stick, I'd say your chances of hoofing it into Richmond are nigh to nil."

He saw the dejected look on Jonathan's face.

"But don't despair, lad! I just need a while to think. As we Americans like to say, there's more than one way to skin the cat. Let me sleep on it."

"Thank you," Jonathan said. "But there's one more thing."

The Irishman's eyes rose in expectation.

"I don't have a cent to my name."

O'Bannion laughed and slapped his leg with his good arm. "Oh, that! Well, I've already figured this one'll have to be on the house. After all, since you're no soldier, I'm sure you're drawing no soldier's pay. And besides..."

He held up his freshly bandaged stump.

"I do appreciate what you've been doing for old lefty here. We'll consider it services in trade."

Languid summer days passed in the hospital as the patient population dwindled. All of the most severely wounded had been evacuated to the Washington hospitals or sent home. Those with moderate wounds had been either mended to varying degrees and returned to their units or assigned to the Veteran Reserve Corps, where their limited services might be put to use on various auxiliary and support tasks.

Three of the field hospital's four original tents, now emptied of their charges and their canvas and stakes taken down, were shipped somewhere else, no doubt closer to the fighting. Those left tending to patients heard from various messengers and freight-haulers that the main combat was now taking place south of

Richmond, as Grant relentlessly tried to punch through the city's defenses from Petersburg. That was a considerable distance from this spot, and the army surely needed new hospitals for the steady stream of casualties the war was producing.

Despite the growing tranquility of the place, Jonathan spent the period in a state of restless anxiety. He feared that with each passing day his chances of finding Apollonia in Richmond diminished. He felt bridled by the restrictions caused by his physical limitations and the challenges posed by the perilous countryside.

More than once, he gave serious consideration to merely setting out by himself, risking everything in a direct attempt to simply walk into the city, come what may. He stopped himself each time the thought occurred to him, however, remembering how such recklessness had brought him to his present state. Nor could he deny O'Bannion's knowledge of the military situation. The Irishman was a walking allegory of braggadocio and greed, but his knowledge of Union and Confederate positions, security procedures, and reconnaissance was too keen, and too consistently accurate, to ignore.

He concluded that he had no choice but to wait and resigned himself to walking the country in restless rumination and helping out the doctors when called upon.

O'Bannion finally broached the subject one warm morning, as Jonathan carefully wrapped linen bandages around his slowly healing stump.

"Still interested in that daft Richmond notion of yours?" he asked quietly.

Jonathan felt his pulse quicken. "Definitely," he replied.

"All right, then. I believe I've got something cooking in the stewpot that might just do the trick for you. Depending on how you feel about, shall we say, certain things."

"What certain things would those be, O'Bannion?"

"Well, to begin with, you'd have to become a fewkin' Johnny."

Jonathan paused in his task, trying not to look shocked.

"And, secondly, you'd have to become a prisoner—at least for a little while."

Jonathan resumed the bandaging. "Go on."

O'Bannion grew alert, sensing that Jonathan had not automatically rejected the idea. He sat up and spoke in a close whisper.

"You see, brother, the two armies still follow this quaint practice they call prisoner exchanges. From what I hear, there's many in the North who are saying the practice ought to be stopped, for it helps the Johnnies far more than it does us, which is probably true, but that's hardly our problem, now is it? The important thing is they're still doing it, once a month or so. It's a pretty simple procedure, you see. Each side brings each other's captives to an agreed-upon spot. It currently happens to be south of Richmond, a place called City Point, where Grant's headquarters are located at the moment. They call a flag of truce for a period, and then they simply let the prisoners walk back to their own sides. Presto! They're not prisoners anymore."

"Go on," Jonathan urged.

"You're with me so far?"

"It sounds very interesting."

O'Bannion beamed to hear the approval. "Well now, that's exactly how I've been viewing it! In fact, it strikes me as brilliant, if I may say so myself. So what we would do is this: Two days from now, there will be a gathering of Johnny prisoners on the Telegraph Road, about ten miles north of the city. Most of them got nabbed around here, right about the time we took our bullets. They'll be marched around the east side of town, toward the south, all the way down to City Point. Once there, they'll be paroled—made to sign a pledge that they'll never again take up arms against the United States—and then exchanged for Union boys. It's all as neat as a pin, I tell you, and if you're willing, I plan to have you marching right along with them as they go. Straight into Richmond itself and, who knows, perhaps whistling Dixie along with all the other rubes."

"But aren't there any records? Won't they know they've got an extra man?"

"Ah," O'Bannion said, tapping his nose. "You're a sharp one, and that's a fact. Yes, they do keep records of a sort, although I doubt they're particularly careful about who's who and what's what. After all, it's wartime—how bloody careful can they be? Still, it's wise to be prudent, I'm thinking, which is why you'll be taking the place of one, let me see"—he reached with his good arm into his pillowcase and pulled out a small piece of paper—"taking the place of one Caleb Petrie, a private who served with the Thirteenth Alabama Infantry, until he was captured by our fellows at Spotsylvania, that is."

"And what will Caleb Petrie be doing in the meantime?"

"The good Mr. Petrie will, thanks to you and your maniacal obsession with following a beautiful femme fatale into Richmond, become a free man, you see. He's not a simpleton, from what I'm told, and realizes that the great Southern cause is not very long for this world. He apparently doesn't want to needlessly croak along with it—an understandable sentiment, I'm sure both you and I will agree—and so, after he trades his papers for your hide, he'll simply fade away into the countryside. I imagine he'll keep his head low until things settle down."

"But how will we make the switch?" Jonathan persisted. "These men are in custody."

O'Bannion frowned like a teacher with a slow student. "Are you forgettin' who you're talking to? This is Miles O'Bannion, maker and closer of deals beyond compare! I've spent the last few days reconnoitering the situation, as is my custom when establishing new business relationships. My messengers have already made contact with a lieutenant at the prison camp down around the Chesterfield Bridge. He's turned out to be a reasonable man, willing to parley with someone—namely, yours truly—who has something he dearly wants, and never mind the object of his desire. And he will, shall we say, facilitate the exchange."

The Irishman leaned back in his chair, admiring the crisp white linen that Jonathan had neatly wrapped around what was left of his arm.

"And as for your sudden departure from this pleasant little retreat in the countryside, well, I see no problem there. They'll have to assume that you deserted, but since they've no idea who you are or where you come from, it'll be quite the chore to track you down, now won't it? Or perhaps they'll figure that old Mystery, being an amnesiac and all, simply wandered off into some unknown oblivion."

O'Bannion casually began rolling a cigarette with one hand, a complex and delicate task but one at which he had been growing progressively more skilled. He puffed on the completed smoke—it reminded Jonathan of a joint—and looked Jonathan in the eye.

"Now, how does all this strike you?"

Jonathan put his hand on O'Bannion's shoulder. "It sounds perfect, O'Bannion. Absolutely perfect. You're right—it's brilliant. I don't know how to thank you for it."

O'Bannion clucked his tongue. "Never mind the thanking, and, yes, it is brilliant. But before you go thinking that it's all absolutely perfect, there's one troublesome little detail I've neglected to mention."

The Zouave paused, as if regretting a disclosure he felt bound to make.

"Once the exchange is done and you're back on the Johnnies' side, they'll be expecting Petrie—who'll be you by then—to go back into service. The bastards never honor the pledges of parolees, you see, and who can blame them, really, with all their casualties and desertions. They won't be bothered by your wounds, believe me. They'll consider you quite fit for the lines and probably waste little time sending you there."

Jonathan could think of nothing to say in response to this sobering news.

"Now, Miles O'Bannion is a clever factotum, as I've already made plain," the Irishman went on, "but I'll confess that my influence is a bit wanting with regard to the Confederate States Army itself. So, when it comes time for you to cut loose of the parolees—and then to steer clear of the god-awful home guards the Johnnies like to send after deserters and dodgers—well, that'll be your own chore and responsibility."

He paused and gave Jonathan a hard look in the eye. He allowed no humor in this expression, as if conveying to Jonathan the genuine dangers he would face.

"Does the plan still strike your fancy, then?"

Jonathan sighed deeply and contemplated the course his life had taken over the past several months, strange even if he didn't consider the ultimate strangeness— the fall from one century into another.

He had already consorted with Confederate spies, helped snatch a Confederate officer from a Union prison, posed as a Union officer, spent a week in a Union detention camp, escaped to fight against Confederates alongside Union troops, and ended up near death in a Union hospital. He came to the sudden realization that he had, during the whole bizarre process, become a skilled chameleon, changing his name, colors, clothing, and stories as circumstances demanded. He had, in fact, gotten rather good at it.

What O'Bannion had just proposed didn't really seem very radical at all.

"I can't wait to whistle Dixie," he said.

O'Bannion smiled widely. "You're a good man!" he replied. "A very peculiar man, 'tis true, but a sportin' crackerjack nonetheless!"

At dawn, two days later, O'Bannion and Jonathan walked past the perimeter of the hospital grounds. In the half-light, they selected a spot well away from the camp's one sleepy sentry and disappeared into the same sylvan wood in which Jonathan had grown accustomed to walking.

O'Bannion once more went over the basic plan.

"It's no more than five miles down to Chesterfield Bridge once you get to the Telegraph Road, which you should reach from this path after about an hour," he said quietly. "With all your strolling of late, I think you can manage it just fine. The prison camp is just east of the bridge itself. Once there, you're to tell the sentry that you've come to discuss Private Petrie with Lieutenant Walker. He'll take care of it from that point. Got it?"

Jonathan nodded. "And I'm to stay in uniform the whole time?"

"You'll want to remain a bluecoat at least until you get to the camp. Which reminds me, Jonathan. I've been thinking about your accent. You've a bit of the Western twang to your speech, 'tis true, but it's a far cry from the sort of mush mouth I expect somebody from Alabama to speak. You'd better try practicing while you've got the chance. I'm told these Johnnies have an uncanny ear when it comes to dialect."

"Understood."

The two soldiers—one in an elaborate arabesque costume, the other in a comparatively plain blue uniform—stared awkwardly at each other for a few moments, until O'Bannion slapped Jonathan on the arm.

"Be on your way, then! There's a lady waiting for you in Richmond Town! Take care of yourself, be on your guard at all times, and may the winds of good fortune be always at your back."

"O'Bannion, I want to..."

"You want to thank me, I know, and I've already told you it's service in trade. Just tell me one thing before you go." His dark eyes peered into Jonathan's. "There's a good deal more to your story than a bonnie lass, isn't there?"

Jonathan smiled weakly. "Yes. A good deal more."

"And it's strange-like, I'm guessing. The sort of story I wouldn't believe if you were to tell me."

"You've got amazing instincts, O'Bannion. Yes, it's just that sort of story."

"Better, then, that I not hear it. Farewell. Maybe I'll see you again, and maybe I won't."

Without another word, the Irishman headed back toward the hospital, his impossibly baggy trousers flapping gaudily in the breeze of dawn.

It took Jonathan, still limping from the shrapnel wound in his leg, nearly seven hours to make the walk to Chesterfield Bridge. On the way, he took O'Bannion's advice and practiced his accents. He repeated the phrase, "I've got a lady waiting for me in Richmond Town," over and over, despite the comical sound of the litany. His first attempts echoed O'Bannion's brogue, but after a while he began to believe that he was developing a convincing drawl. He added "y'all" to the phrase and felt that made it sound even more authentic.

While he recited, he was oblivious to the simmering heat as the sun climbed an azure sky spotted with billowy white clouds. He paid no heed to the shady groves of trees nor the farms laid out upon the rolling green land, some of them already ravaged by the Northern army for forage, others apparently unmolested.

It felt good to be away from the sickness and suffering of the hospital and energizing to be once more on the road, heading toward his objective. His heart felt lighter and more confident than it had since the morning he'd awoken alone near Culpeper, although he was aware that the next stage of his journey was sure to be like the previous stages—impossible to forecast, except for the probability of danger. He realized that he was still flying blind, with absolutely no plan for action once, and if, he made it into Richmond.

"Perhaps," he said to himself in his best Southern drawl, "the end will *illuminate* the means."

For the end—Jonathan's objective—was indeed always in sight. As he walked along the dusty road, he thought of Apollonia as he had by now grown accustomed to thinking about her. In a way, she had become a dream, a figure who grew hazier and more mythic the longer they were separated. Increasingly, he saw her as the ancient daguerreotype in which he had first glimpsed her in his other life— as something lost in the mists of time, ultimately unreachable. On the other hand, he retained amazingly vivid memories of her—the color of her eyes, her moods, her keen insight, her alternating haughtiness and warmth, the scent of her hair, the feel of her lips, all the myriad subtleties that made her who she was. He knew that he was idealizing her but did not feel it was a great overidealization.

His thoughts of her did not come without pain. He felt her absence like a heavy weight on his shoulders, a dull but omnipresent ache somewhere deep inside him. It was much easier now that he had reason to believe that she had not willingly betrayed him, and he carried her little golden locket tied to a long leather cord around his neck as a reminder of this. Still he longed for her with every fiber of his being.

He tramped for hours, clutching his staff, feeling the steadily growing pain in his leg and the shortness of breath in his chest as the sun grew ever hotter.

He was surprised to encounter no military personnel on the way. The traffic had been light, and most of the travelers seemed to be local farmers. Not one of them gave this solitary Union soldier a greeting, much less made the offer of a ride. It reminded Jonathan that he was walking through occupied territory and that the locals were none too happy about the occupation.

At last, not long after noon, he came to Chesterfield Bridge. The bridge itself was plain and ordinary, a simple wooden structure spanning a modest, mud-colored river. The land surrounding it was similarly drab. Most of the grass had been trampled into mud, as if many horses had recently been ridden here.

The setting's only notable feature was the prison camp, partially visible from the bridge. It was a large fenced area made of rough logs, as if quickly and none-too-carefully erected, not unlike the detention camp in which he had spent a week before the battle. The American flag flew above it, providing a flash of color, but it seemed a somber and sullen place.

As he approached its rude front gate, he was both saluted and challenged by a soldier standing guard, flanked by two more armed sentries.

"State your business, sir," the young man demanded.

"I've come to see Lieutenant Walker about Private Petrie."

"And your name, sir?"

Jonathan gave him a hard look. Although he knew that he would probably be forced to tell many more lies before his journey was through, he was in no mood for making up stories now.

"The lieutenant knows who I am, Sergeant, and that's all who needs to know. Now summon him for me."

The sergeant stiffened at the curt order but not in defiance. The tone of Jonathan's voice had reminded him of his place in the army. "Right away, sir!" he said, instructing a sentry to go inside.

It was not a long wait. In less than three minutes, Lieutenant Walker appeared at the gate. A short, burly man with a massive black beard, he was sweating in his knee-length coat and broad hat. He said nothing to Jonathan or the sentries, abruptly taking Jonathan by the arm and leading him inside the compound.

They walked quickly and wordlessly on a footpath leading upward to a plain log structure. Gathered around it, and stretching out for a considerable distance in all directions, were hundreds of small canvas tents—the humble living quarters of the prisoners of war. He could see only a few of them standing around, dim figures in the hazy afternoon light.

When Walker reached the log building, he held open the door. When they stepped inside, the lieutenant secured the door with a wooden plank.

Facing the door was a man about Jonathan's age and size, dressed in a ragged and filthy uniform of butternut gray. He had long brown hair and a narrow, angular face. It struck Jonathan as the sort of face—lean, hard, and wise to the ways of the frontier—that he would never see in his own time.

"Private Petrie," Walker said by way of introduction, "meet the man who's buying your freedom by taking your place. I don't know what the hell his name is, and I suppose it don't much matter."

Awkwardly, Petrie held out his hand to Jonathan who shook it, feeling its rough surface and firm grip.

"Pleased to meet you," Jonathan said. "I appreciate what you're doing."

The private's dour expression brightened a little. His accent was a languid drawl, giving Jonathan a sample of the genuine article.

"Believe me, sir, the pleasure's all mine."

Walker pulled a gold watch from the pocket of his long coat. "We're commencing the march to City Point in less than an hour, so let's get cracking, gentlemen. Petrie, take off your uniform and give it to our friendly stranger here. Put on those civilian clothes sitting on the desk."

He turned to Jonathan. "And you, whoever the hell you are, get out of those blues and prepare to become a Reb."

Jonathan waited out his hour by standing alone at the perimeter of the camp. He hoped to remain silent for as long as he could, worried about his accent and the possibility that he might say something that would give him away, as he had done not long ago with the other army.

In his new ragged tunic, trousers, and kepi—all of it filthy and redolent of both gunpowder and Private Petrie's personal essence—he had to admit that he fit right in. None of the other prisoners seemed to take the slightest notice of him.

When Lieutenant Walker loudly called them to a mob-like formation in the center of the camp, his oratory was brief but effective.

"Rebs!" he shouted. "This is your luckiest of days. You're all heading back to Richmond today, in exchange for some upright Union boys, all of them eager to miss a tour down to Andersonville, that hellhole your so-called leaders have concocted on their behalf. It'll be a good walk, more than thirty miles, so be ready for a couple of hard days marching. Once we're east of Richmond, we'll be marching near the lines of both armies, sometimes pretty much smack dab in between them, so we'll be flying a flag of truce. Let's hope your friends and mine both deign to honor it. Since you're headed for home anyway, I can see no reason why any of you punkinheads might want to escape, but be assured that my boys'll shoot any son of a bitch that tries."

The lieutenant looked at the ragtag prisoners slouching before him, many of them, like Jonathan, leaning on sticks or crutches. He had a tired, almost sad expression on his face. "Let's get you boys home, then," he said less loudly. "And pray to sweet Jesus the next time we meet will be after this damn fool war is over and done with."

At that, the Confederates managed a subdued cheer. The sound of Southern prisoners cheering, however weakly, the antiwar sentiment of a Northern officer seemed so tragically ironic to Jonathan that a chill ran along the length of his spine.

The prisoners fell into a more or less cohesive line of three or four abreast and began their long march, Jonathan shambling along with the rest. There were a few hundred of them, all enlisted men it seemed and most of them wearing the bugle insignia of the infantry. Some had been designated as color-bearers at regular intervals along the column. The flags they carried—plain white rectangles cut from old sheets—announced their noncombatant status.

They marched all through the hot afternoon, raising a lazy dust cloud as they went, and well into the evening. After his long morning walk, Jonathan's knee and chest hurt him terribly, but as the march went on, the pain was gradually replaced with an almost tolerable numbness. He leaned heavily on his makeshift staff, which helped him keep pace.

He had little discourse with his new comrades. Most of them, plagued by either fatigue or pain, said very little. A few carried on a trivial banter as they walked the Telegraph Road.

"Think old Jeff Davis will have the red carpet rolled out for us when we get back?" said one, triggering a handful of guffaws from his fellows.

"Rather doubt it," answered another. "I think old Jeff is using all of Virginia's red carpet for hisself. What he will have for us, sure enough, is an old musket and a bag of shitty powder."

"Got to have their cannon fodder, don't they?"

"Watch what you say, mister. Don't you go talking about President Davis such like, so long as I'm around to hear it."

"Oh, go to hell, you sap. You want to give your life for a lost cause, you be my guest, but don't expect me to join your ship of fools."

"Me neither. Once we get to Richmond, the hindside of me is all they're going to see and that not for very long. I plan to be true to my parole."

"Not if the home guard boys get their hands on your hide, you won't. Then you'll be kissing the trenches just like before, 'cept you'll be black and blue to boot."

The conversation ran like that for an hour sometimes and was then supplanted by prolonged silence, broken only by the sandy shuffle of the prisoners' overused shoes and boots. Occasionally, their talk would grow rancorous, but nobody seemed to have the energy or the will to actually start a fight. It was clear to Jonathan that these men were exhausted and demoralized. Many of them spoke as if the war had already been lost and that they were only going through troublesome motions with the impending prisoner exchange. Jonathan wondered if the spirits in the whole Confederate army were any higher.

It was well after sunset and nearly dark when they stopped to rest along the side of the road. They ate a meager supper of biscuits and salt pork and slept with the glow of Richmond's lights barely visible in the western distance.

The second day went much the same as the first, although the march was more sustained and the heat even greater. At eventide, they were called to a halt. They waited for half an hour in the gathering gloom before they heard orders shouted from up ahead and then began moving slowly forward. As they progressed, the prisoners came face-to-face with Union prisoners on the other side of the road, walking in the opposite direction.

The Northerners looked just as ragged and beaten as their enemies. From the hollow look of their faces, it was evident that they hadn't eaten very well. Many, if not most of them, wore bloody bandages.

"Hey, Yank," one of the Confederates said to the opposing column of soldiers.

"Hey, Reb," one of the Federals responded.

"See you in the field?"

"Reckon you will."

The actual prisoner exchange transpired almost by osmosis. By the time that Jonathan and most of the Confederates who marched with him were aware of it, the exchange had already taken place, the respective columns of prisoners back in their own commands.

As the line in which he was standing began once more to move and the Northern troops had passed into the dusk, it became apparent to them that they were no longer prisoners. Gray-clad officers who stood beside the column were barking orders, instructing those who were in reasonable physical shape to gather to the right, those whose health was questionable to limp toward the left. The soldiers obeyed, with about equal numbers heading off in different directions.

Jonathan joined the limping ones to the left.

The two groups of soldiers were gathered on opposite ends of what appeared to be a large parade ground or open field along the banks of a wide river. It was farmland here. Jonathan assumed that they were someplace near the town of City Point, but because that town was currently held by the Union, they had apparently assembled near the southern edge of Confederate lines.

No ceremony was held to commemorate the Rebels' return home, and no food was offered to sustain them after their long march. An officer who addressed them, unseen to Jonathan in the growing darkness, simply instructed them to do their best to get some sleep, as if the hard, dusty ground could simply be ignored. He also informed those wounded and lame where they might draw water from a well and where to go if they needed to use the latrine.

Finally, he told them that physicians would be on hand in the morning to assess their condition.

And if any of them were faking, he concluded, they would be very well advised to skulk to the other side of the field before sunrise. Things would go harshly, he warned, for those who sought to shirk their duties.

"Welcome home," muttered the soldier standing next to Jonathan, a balding man of at least forty years, who stared at the ground and sported a still festering musket wound on his forearm.

"Amen, brother," said another from somewhere behind.

They sounded like men who had just escaped one prison only to land in another.

And yet, despite the environment and circumstances, Jonathan was acutely aware that it was a beautiful summer night. The air was sweet with life, the breeze a soft, caressing zephyr from the west. A crescent moon came and went behind scudding silvery clouds.

He lay on his back, oblivious to the hard earth beneath him and the sounds of troubled sleep emanating from the other parolees. On such a night, he thought, the very thought of war seemed ridiculous. The idea that men—the very men who slept all around him—could be engaged in senseless slaughter and destruction, could hate and be hated to such horrific degrees, seemed as remote as the moon itself.

It was not a night to think of war but of love. He imagined himself in this meadow but without the suffering men who shared it with him. He was feeling no pain, taking in the night air and the soft fragrance of Apollonia in the same breath, feeling the soft yield of her breasts against his chest. And in this netherworld, a soft and milky place somewhere between imagination and dream, he made love to the woman he loved.

The next morning, Jonathan was among the first of the wounded to be examined.

The pain made him gasp.

The doctor held his leg firmly in one hand, while his other probed mercilessly and roughly around the wound just above the knee. The lesion was about the size of a half dollar, covered with a rust-colored scab encircled by an ominous scarlet ring.

"Where'd you get this hole?" the doctor asked Jonathan, who was lying on his back in the dust, already sweating in the early morning sun.

"Up on the Angle at Spotsylvania," he replied, hoping that the twang with which he seasoned his speech sounded genuine.

"Looks like you took a piece of cannonball, soldier. Lucky it didn't take off your whole leg. Did the Yanks pull it out for you?"

"Yes."

"Good of them. Seems it was pretty well tended, but I think it's putting on a touch of infection all the same. You having trouble walking with it?"

"I barely made it here yesterday, Doc, the pain was so bad. That lasted awhile, then the leg started getting numb about halfway down. That slowed me down."

The numbness was true enough, although the pain was considerably exaggerated. Jonathan was hoping his strained speech was at least as convincing as his attempts at a Southern dialect.

The doctor nodded. "None too surprising, none too surprising," he muttered. "And how's the chest wound feeling?"

"Starts to aching whenever I walk around a bit. It hurts, but not as bad as the leg."

The doctor rolled down Jonathan's pant leg and rose. "Well, truth to tell, there's not a great deal I can do for you, soldier. Haven't got a thing for the pain—the morphine's long gone, even the whiskey's gone. I can clean it, dress it up good, and give you a couple weeks in the sanitarium up in town. After that, I expect they'll be coming for you. I hope you're ready when they do. What's your regiment?"

"Thirteenth Alabama."

"And your name?"

"Caleb Petrie."

"Okay, Petrie. I'll have you signed into the sanitarium and let your regiment know where you are. I'll have you put on the first riverboat—should be shoving off in an hour or less. Good luck to you."

After tending to Jonathan for a few minutes, he moved on to the next walking wounded, neither awaiting nor expecting the thanks that Private Petrie gave him.

Three hours later, under a merciless sun, Jonathan entered Richmond at last.

It was not an auspicious arrival, and he was no prettier a sight than any of the other men who had just plied the River James. He was limping fearfully, thin to the point of emaciation, bearded with hair nearly to his shoulders, dressed in a torn and filthy uniform, and leaning precariously on a crooked staff of hickory—all this, yet somehow he felt like Caesar, riding in glorious triumph into the heart of Rome itself.

July

Midsummer now settles upon the stage,

The dawns come scented with heather and sage,

The noon is oppressed in a ponderous blaze

That scorches and simmers and withers the days.

Sweet nights fall like satin with crickets that sing

Of sadness that this is a passing thing.

There is nothing more resplendent than a summer night's enchantment and, alas, nothing less tragic than its passing. Such softness and gentleness in its silken shadows, such savory mystery in its perfumed air. Heaven must be more like this than the blaze of noon, I believe, and thus when the torrid morning arrives, or the chill of early autumn, we feel the slipping away of Paradise itself. And this is sadness indeed, is it not?

Yet how much greater is that sadness when one is separated from the passion of one's heart? A summer's night is a gift for lovers, for whispered endearments, for the touching of hands, and, yes—still I blush at such words!—the soft meeting of lips. But when the poor lovers are not able to touch, when they do not even know where the person they adore is, then the splendor of such a night becomes taunting torture, a merciless reminder of that which they cannot have.

I wonder if Jonathan, this very night, is aware of the nocturnal beauty and what he thinks upon as he watches the same golden moon rising, with those same crinoline clouds of silver casting their shadows across its face. Does he think of me and wonder where I am and fear for my welfare and long for my touch—all as I do of him?

I curse myself for this thought, let alone writing down the words, but does my beloved think any longer at all? I cannot help but fear, not only for his safety but for his very life. Within scant days of our abandonment of him, and within a very few miles of where we left him, two great battles have been waged. Even here, we heard the crashing of the cannons and saw the flashes of their great explosions. People gathered on the streets to listen and to watch, their eyes full of fear.

The newspapers in Richmond have been filled with reports of the places they are calling the Wilderness and Spotsylvania Court House. Untold thousands of men have died in these clashes. The wounded have been brought to the city in fearsome numbers, as have a great many Federal prisoners.

Is Jonathan somewhere among them? Was he able to avert the danger and find safe haven in some hidden place, or does he, even now on this lovely night, lie in an unmarked soldier's grave, alongside many other unfortunate ones? My ignorance is driving me mad.

Yet I must not allow despair to become my compass. I must cling to hope, as a shipwreck survivor clings to a narrow plank. I must pray for Jonathan's safety like the most devout of nuns before the statue of the Virgin. And if I am wrong to petition God in such fashion, then I will gladly accept any punishment He deems fit.

The newspapers have regarded the recent battles great victories for the South, yet I do not share their optimism. It is true that the Northern horde has yet to come roaring through the gates of Richmond, but one senses that the time is not long coming. One sees only grief and weariness and defeat on the faces in this somber city—men, women, children, white people and black alike.

The soldiers themselves, upon whose shoulders the great burden of defense rests most ponderously, seem even more dejected than the citizenry. Last week, from the window of my room, I glimpsed a column of our parolees marching toward Chimborazo. They had just been released by the enemy, and as they shuffled and limped through the streets in their rags and bare feet, they more resembled phantoms than warriors. How long can such soldiers sustain the fight?

And how much longer should they sustain it? Although my words may seem those of a traitor, if not a blasphemer, I begin to doubt the wisdom of prolonging this war. It is true that the enemy was valiantly driven back at the city's northern defenses, but at what cost and for what gain?

Grant has now massed his forces to the south of the city and is already launching even deadlier assaults from that direction. Things are no better farther to the south. General Sherman conquered Chattanooga months ago and is now making his way into Georgia. How long can Atlanta—and Savannah!—hold out against his barbarous legions? Where will my mother and father go? What will become of Bluefield and all that I hold dear?

Yet here I am in Richmond, bound to men who see such setbacks in a dramatically different light than I. To them, the predations of the Union are naught but further calls for speed, for ever more decisive action. They believe that there is still time to save it all, time yet to pluck victory and vindication from the merciless jaws of defeat.

I do not share their belief. I believe that they are mad, and yet—here is an irony that cries out to Heaven itself—I alone am the one upon whom all their dearest wishes, all their most desperate and demented hopes, shall depend.

I would be tempted to laugh at such irony, dear reader, if my heart did not long so for Jonathan, if I did not fear for my loved ones at home, if the expressions on the faces of all these war-weary people were not so ashen and bleak.

Those faces, at least, I shall leave behind on the morrow, for we shall be leaving Richmond then. It is Archer's decision that we shall now go to Charleston. He has obtained the information he needed in Richmond. He now knows the time and place for our final act, although he has yet to reveal them to me.

There yet remains safe passage by rail to Charleston. It seems strange to me that we should be heading deeper into Dixie—and so painfully close to my own home!—when we know that our ultimate destination remains so far to the north. But as I have written earlier, Archer is fearful in Richmond. I am sure he will feel safer and more comfortable in Charleston, in which, after all, he has his own considerable history.

As for me, I hardly care where we go. I have become, by my own hand, little more than a helpless piece of flotsam upon a troubled sea. I shall go where the sea directs me to go and do what it tells me to do, until, at its own pleasure, the sea decides whether I shall sink or float.

JULY

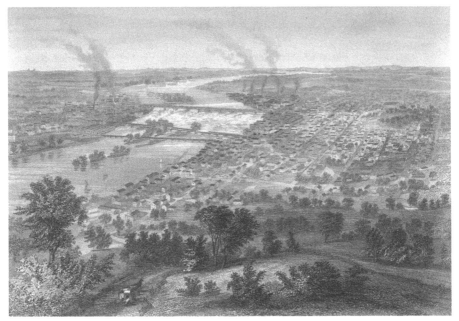

RICHMOND

RICHMOND ANNOUNCED ITS PRESENCE well before Jonathan actually saw the city.

The first sign that he was drawing near was its smell, which snaked its way down the James River as a malignant miasma, blending insidiously with the clammy midsummer air. In his nineteenth-century wanderings he had already found that cities, as a rule, smelled far worse than the cities of his own time, but Richmond took this basic reality a step or two further. Its organic reek—a mixture of rank vegetation, animal musk, and sewage—grew evident when the Confederate riverboat was still miles below the city itself.

The riverboat, flying the Stars and Bars, maneuvered through the formidable gauntlet that the Confederacy had positioned in defense of its capital. It passed, and received the salutes of, several fierce-looking gunboats, their prows facing downriver. On either side of the river, extensive fortifications were visible shortly after leaving City Point. There were at least three great earthworks in succession, stretching into the interminable distance toward the northeast and northwest, with plentiful sentries and riflemen in position. Behind the works, on man-made mounds or natural hills, were dozens of artillery batteries, their large-wheeled field pieces aligned in precise and vigilant rows.

At the moment, the lines were silent but watchful. Jonathan wasn't sure whether their air of suspenseful expectation was impatience for action or dread in anticipation of the invasion that was sure to come. He had no idea how tightly Richmond had been fenced in by Union forces, but the appearance of the defenses certainly seemed to suggest a city that if not already under siege would very likely soon be.

Once past the naval and military lines, the boat reached the city's outskirts before noon. On its southeastern edges, after the mudflats that extended beyond the riverbanks, were loose gatherings of ramshackle shanties and pens, variously occupied by white and black residents alike and an assortment of livestock. Except for the occasional fishermen, who wandered out onto the banks to drop their lines into the river, few of them seemed occupied with anything more demanding than sitting down and watching the flow of the muddy water. Once or twice in the distance, Jonathan heard faint strains of harmonica and banjo.

The replacement of shacks with more permanent structures indicated that the boat at last had entered the city itself. Jonathan watched eagerly as the buildings grew closer to one another, with small frame houses gradually giving way to larger stone and brick dwellings. He could see from the boat that the streets were paved and the pedestrian and equestrian traffic heavier and busier.

As the boat drew toward the bank, approaching what appeared to be a commercial street, he saw in the distance, high atop a promontory that rose above most of the city, the still-beating heart of the rebellion.

For that one moment, Jonathan was able to sense the glory of Richmond. The capitol of the Confederate States of America, a neoclassic marble building reminiscent of the Parthenon, seemed almost mystically suspended over Richmond in the humid haze. From the river, it looked powerful and stately, munificent and beneficent, but Jonathan knew—with a strange hindsight that only he possessed—that these were illusions. For he knew that in less than a year, that capitol and the city it surmounted would fall, that Abraham Lincoln himself would walk these streets in triumph, pace the halls of that vanquished seat of government, and place his presidential bootheels on the very desk of Jefferson Davis.

He sensed that these eventualities were already feared in Richmond but not yet known, and his exclusive knowledge gave him a strangely sad feeling. It was like visiting Atlantis, he thought, when only he knew that the cataclysm was imminent.

Most of the other wounded men aboard the boat slept during the short journey, no doubt exhausted from their long march from the Union prison camp. They began to stir only when the cries of the crewmen to men on the bank signaled the impending disembarkation.

When the order was given, they began to shuffle clumsily off the bobbing boat, gathering in a disorderly group upon a landing only a few blocks from the city's commercial center. The civilians on the adjacent street—men in businesslike suits and jaunty hats, women with elaborate dresses of satin and silk—paid little heed to the unkempt veterans in their tattered grays and butternuts, their unshaven faces and unshod feet. It seemed to Jonathan, who stood in their midst, that such assemblies of paroled prisoners must have been a common sight in downtown Richmond, one not worth even noticing much less marking in any sort of ceremonial or laudatory way.

The Confederacy, he concluded, must be well past such sentimental responses to war. It had already been raging, often within earshot of the capital itself, for four brutal years and had been harvesting the sons of the South with a predictable and greedy efficiency that seemed to have reduced the citizenry to a numb, unheeding despair.

For that matter, Jonathan thought, gazing at his fellow parolees, the soldiers themselves—members of the rebellion's once proud and fearless legion—seemed no less detached from the war, and from reality itself, than those who wore no uniforms.

A mounted captain told the men that one last march lay ahead of them, eliciting groans from the injured and fatigued.

"Now settle down, boys," he said in a soft Virginia lilt. "It's no more than two miles, and once done you'll have your chance at rest and recovery."

He told them to follow his lead, and so the long, sad procession of wasted soldiers began a weary trek behind the hoofbeats of the captain's horse, echoing on Richmond's cobblestones. They walked up hills and down them again, looking neither at each other nor at the civilized trappings surrounding them. With their agonized gait and blank expressions, they reminded Jonathan of a hundred Christs taking one last trudge up the Via Dolorosa.

Only one civilian among the hundreds they encountered made any approach. She was a middle-aged woman, portly and dignified, dressed conservatively in gray flannel. She clutched a large armful of fragrant white blossoms that might have been magnolias.

As the ragged squads walked past, she would occasionally place one of the flowers into a soldier's hand. One of those she selected was Jonathan. She gave him a blossom and spoke so low her voice was a near whisper.

"God bless you, son," she said, "for what you do."

As he looked into her melancholy eyes, a thought occurred to Jonathan. This woman was a mother, and her son had died in the war. It was the way she had spoken the word "son" that somehow told him that. He felt a lump rising in his throat.

And then he had another thought. He was looking into the wild eyes of the soldier he had killed at Spotsylvania. He was once again thrusting his bayonet into the man's abdomen, feeling the fragile life evaporate from his body.

He put the two together, of course—the kind-sounding, sad-looking woman and the wild-eyed soldier, this mother and that son—and the lump became a teardrop.

He put the flower gently back into the woman's hand.

"I don't deserve this," he said.

Sweating, even more exhausted than before, they arrived at their destination when the torrid sun was still high in the afternoon sky. The place was called Chimborazo, and it stood above the river on the city's heights.

They called it a hospital, but to Jonathan it looked more like a city unto itself. Dozens of large wooden buildings had been neatly constructed on the spacious grounds, and hundreds of tents of varying sizes and shapes had been placed in long, orderly rows in the center of the campus. Soldiers, doctors, and nurses walked purposefully on makeshift pathways between the buildings and tents. It had a sense of military order and cleanliness and a feeling of permanence that contrasted sharply with the makeshift compounds he had come to know with the other army.

In its immensity, it bore mute and overwhelming witness—even more than the sight of hundreds of Confederate corpses in the Wilderness—to the staggering toll of the war.

The wounded parolees were led in small groups by orderlies to various locations. Jonathan's group was taken to a white building near the eastern edge of the complex. Here, they lined up in a long queue as a handful of doctors did rapid triage on each soldier.

Jonathan was asked his name and unit and the nature of his injuries. When he had answered, a doctor raised his shirt to examine the chest wound and then his pant leg to regard the knee. He scrawled a few lines on a tablet he was holding. Jonathan saw that one of the words was "ambulatory."

"Tent 157," he said flatly. "Doctor Barlow will be checking in with you periodically. Chow's at six o'clock, big building next to the parade ground."

Jonathan proceeded, zombielike, to the tent, following wooden markers that showed the way. It was a large canvas structure, not unlike his former residence near Spotsylvania, and there were about fifteen men within it, lying or sitting on cots. He located an empty one and collapsed upon it.

Sleep took possession of him the moment he closed his eyes.

When he awoke, it was deep night. The air had cooled a little since the afternoon, and the tent was silent, except for the snores and breathing of the patients.

The only light came from the glow of a tiny candle, a few feet away, next to the bed that was adjacent to his. In the tenebrous flicker, a short, thin man sat on that bunk and stared directly at Jonathan. He was dressed in a presentable uniform, complete to the cap, and had a youthful face. A delicate mustache arched over his lip and drooped in long, narrow strands beyond his jaw. He bore the same expression of untamed toughness that Jonathan had seen in the real Private Petrie.

"Missed your supper," he said quietly and threw something in Jonathan's direction.

"Just hardtack, but better than nothing," he added. "I thought about waking you at chow time but figured you probably needed the rest. You a parolee?"

"Just got paroled yesterday," Jonathan said, taking a grateful bite from the cracker-like biscuit. "Thanks."

"Sorry to hear that," the man muttered. "You'd 'a' been better off up North."

Something in the man's tone caught Jonathan's attention.

"It wasn't my choice," he replied.

"Nah. It's never our choice. Where's your wound?"

"Bullet in the chest and shrapnel in the knee."

The man whistled. "Cold Harbor?"

"Spotsylvania."

"Now that was a shithole, wasn't it? I got mine at Cold Harbor, bayonet right under the arm. Son of a bitch speared me like a catfish in shallow water. How long you figuring on staying?"

"I don't know. What do you think?"

"Hell, you might get a month out of those. Me? I been here a month already. The guards are already taking to calling me a malingerer. I expect to be sent back before the end of the week."

"Where's back?"

"Twelfth Georgia, presently bivouacked at the works south of town."

"You from Georgia?"

"Yup," the man said, lying back on his bunk. "And mighty desirous of getting back there. You?"

"Alabama. What part of Georgia you come from?"

"Down Savannah way. Why you asking?"

The sound of that city's name quickened his heart. "I know some folks from Savannah. You know the Foleys?"

"You mean the *rich* Foleys?"

"They grow indigo."

"Sure, I know 'em. Or at least know *of* 'em. Folks of my stripe, meaning sharecroppers and such like, don't usually consort with folks such as them, but I heard about 'em, sometimes saw 'em in town, usually in a fancy cabriolet, if memory serves."

"How about their daughter, Apollonia. You know her?"

"Think I've seen her once or twice. Pretty thing, as I recollect, but haughty and uppity, like all the planters' daughters. Why? You her beau or something?" He flashed a mocking smile.

The simple fact that Jonathan was talking to another human being who had actually seen Apollonia—who could confirm that she was real and not a mirage arising from his fevered brain—reassured him. It brought her back into focus.

"Well, I'd like to be," he replied, "but the war seems to be getting in the way."

The man chuckled quietly. "Wars do have a way of doing that, don't they? Speaking of war, let me ask you a question, just between you and me."

"Go ahead."

"How eager are you to get back out there?"

Jonathan paused before answering. He had a feeling the conversation might take such a turn.

"Not eager at all, to tell the truth."

"Get the feeling that you've already made a big enough contribution to the cause, do you?"

"Yes."

"So do I, as it happens. Listen, you seem like a trustworthy sort, so I'm going to tell you something, make you an offer."

"I'm listening."

"I've been planning to slip out of Chimborazo for weeks, but I don't want to go it alone. I think the chances would be much better if two were to make the break. I've been waiting for someone to come along, someone who shares my philosophy on the subject, someone who can run a piece."

He leaned closer to Jonathan, looking directly into his eyes.

"Might you be that person?"

"I might be," Jonathan said, staring directly back, "providing my knee holds out."

"That's good to hear. You sleep on that tonight. Come morning, if you're game, we'll figure on taking leave tomorrow night. It'll be a good time to go—dark of the moon. How's that?"

"Sounds good."

The soldier extended his hand to Jonathan.

"Edward Calhoun, by the by."

"Caleb Petrie," Jonathan lied, grasping the hand.

"I am sincerely pleased to make your acquaintance, Mr. Petrie," he said and blew out his candle.

The following night was indeed a dark one, so dark that at first Calhoun and Jonathan had a difficult time seeing anything at all. As their eyes adjusted to the pitch, they slowly made their way through the endless phalanxes of tents stretched over a wide field in the middle of the hospital complex.

No one else stirred. It was near midnight, and the patients all seemed asleep, but Calhoun was taking no chances. He whispered that guards were likely about and instructed Jonathan to follow his lead and crouch low as they made their way.

Earlier in the evening, he had told Jonathan that Chimborazo had long been considered a prime opportunity for Confederate soldiers eager to escape the army. Over the last two years, hundreds had managed to clear its walls and guards, but more recently things had tightened up considerably. Now, escaping from Chimborazo was much easier said than done, and while some were still managing to break free, many more had been captured in the attempt. Some of them had been killed by the hardened soldiers assigned to prevent their desertion.

Stalking like alley cats, making as little sound as possible, they finally reached the area made up of permanent structures. They darted from building to building, holding their breath in shadows three times as sentries walked their posts, and finally, after what seemed like hours of agonizing suspense, they reached the wall separating hospital from city. They selected a spot that was darker than most and waited patiently for the sentry to make a full round. By a silent count, it took this one some four minutes, which seemed plenty of time for them to make the attempt.

The brick wall was tall but not dauntingly so. It was perhaps seven feet high, with no obstructions along its top to make it more difficult to cross. They calculated that they could grasp the top edge with a modest vertical jump and then rely on their upper body strength to pull themselves over.

They waited two minutes after the sentry last passed their position and then made their move. They jumped at the same time, both managing to grasp the brick sill on the first leap. It was a hard and painful climb for Jonathan, but he finally pulled himself into a sitting position on top. He was ready to jump over when he saw that Calhoun, grimacing from pain, was finding the climb more difficult.

Straddling the wall, Jonathan reached over and grabbed Calhoun's hands. It was a hard pull, with Calhoun's boots desperately trying to gain a foothold between the bricks, but at last the ascent was made. They tumbled over together, landing hard on a cobblestone street, directly before a row of dark and silent stores.

"Good work," Calhoun whispered through his labored breathing. "Now we've got to get the hell out of here. This street is patrolled."

They ran across the street, down half a block, and disappeared into a narrow alley between two buildings, without hearing a call of alarm.

But in the darkness of the alley, they discovered that they weren't alone.

Standing before them, with only his profile visible, was a man. His silhouette revealed a tall figure and the unmistakable outlines of a uniform. Some unseen source of light glinted on what looked like the long barrel of a pistol. It was pointed in their direction.

"Going somewhere, boys?" the man asked quietly, a note of cruel humor in his voice.

Jonathan and Calhoun froze, merely panting in response.

"I don't think y'all are going anywhere," the man said, "except back yonder, where y'all came from. And when the doctors see that you're well enough to climb that wall and dash down this street like that, why I'm a-wagerin' they'll figure y'all are fine to head back out to the lines. Now turn your tails around, boys, and let's all head back there, real peacefully. Right now."

Jonathan felt Calhoun tense beside him.

"Like hell we will," Calhoun said between clenched teeth.

The dark man took a step back. "If you're thinking I won't shoot you dead, you're one mistaken son of a bitch," he said. "Now do as I say, or—"

What happened next was a blur. Calhoun lunged forward, a shadow in the dark, followed by the sound of soft impact and a cry. Then, less than a second later, the man's pistol fired, its report deafening in the echo chamber of the alley and blinding in its momentary flash.

Calhoun retreated from the soldier, who kept his feet for the briefest of moments before collapsing on the stones.

"Shit!" Calhoun said, still whispering. "We've got to go, Petrie! Grab his gun!"

Jonathan moved slowly as he reached down to the prone body. When he did, he saw a knife protruding from the man's chest.

"Take the gun, man!" Calhoun hissed. "Come on!"

Jonathan took the weapon at last and chased after Calhoun, who was running, noisily now, through the narrow passageway. Behind him, in the direction of the hospital, he heard men's voices and the clatter of shoes on the street.

The fugitives reached the end of the alley, finding themselves on another street that was edged in blackness. They raced for the shadows, not realizing until they stepped into air that this was the crest of a steep hill. They tumbled, and their momentum sent them into a long roll over small bushes and rocks. They came to a halt a few yards from each other amid thick foliage.

Jonathan's chest and knee flared in pain, and he already felt the cuts and bruises from the unexpected plunge, but he was on his feet in a moment. He looked around him—all was darkness, except for the luminescent winking of fireflies—and stumbled toward Calhoun, reaching for his hand.

"Let's go," Jonathan said. "They heard the shot. They're coming."

But the other man's hand did not respond to his grasp. It felt cold.

"Ah damn," Calhoun whispered. "I don't think I'm going with you, Petrie. Seems like I'm not the only one to do killing tonight. That bastard put one in me, right in the belly."

Jonathan stepped closer and peered at him, still holding his hand. Calhoun's shirt and pants were soaked with a large black stain. He knew what it was.

"Oh Jesus, Calhoun."

Calhoun gave up the whisper. His voice was weak and raspy. "Yeah, it's a bad one, all right. I ain't walking away from this one, no sir. How about that? Got killed by one of our own, just like Stonewall did." He managed a half-hearted sardonic laugh.

"Can you walk? Do you want to try?"

"You're crazy, Petrie," Calhoun replied, his hand slipping from Jonathan's. "But *you* can walk—you can run—so go on, get the hell out of here. One of us ought to make it. I'm not going anywhere."

Jonathan knew that he was right, but he was reluctant to leave. He had known Calhoun for no more than two days, but they had escaped together. It felt like years of friendship had been forged in the last few minutes.

"I'm telling you to go," Calhoun rasped, blood now starting to trickle from the corner of his mouth. "I'll give you five minutes to run, and then I'll call out. They'll come my way, I'll tell them that I was alone—they won't know you're out."

"They can fix you up at the hospital, Calhoun. They won't let you..."

"I wouldn't bet the farm on that. I just killed one of their guards, remember? Now go, get away, and take this."

Shakily, he untied a leather bag from his belt and strained to pass it to Jonathan. It felt heavy.

"Took it off a dead Yank up around Mechanicsville. Have no idea how he got his grimy hands on it. Now it's been taken off two dead men. May it bring better fortune to you than it did us. Now go! Be gone!"

Jonathan gave Calhoun's hand one final grasp and then headed downhill. His progress was slow as the descent was steep, but the dark night and dense foliage worked together to provide excellent cover. When he looked behind him, he saw the light of torches at the top of the hill. They seemed very close.

Soon, he heard Calhoun's labored shouting. "Over here!" he cried. "Over here! I'm shot!"

Jonathan wondered whether these would be his last words.

They did not pursue him.

From his hiding place, Jonathan watched the torches descend the hillside and gather where Calhoun was lying. They lingered there, colossal fireflies suspended in place and not bobbing in his direction.

He slowly picked his way to the bottom of the hill and came to a small creek surrounded by dense bushes. He followed its course toward the southwest, where he remembered the main part of the city to be.

As he went, he thought about Calhoun and what the hospital guards might have in store for him, assuming he survived the gunshot he'd already taken. He also thought about the sort of desperation that would drive a man to kill in cold blood, as Calhoun had done, simply to avoid serving in an army. How bad must things be in the Confederate ranks, Jonathan wondered, for a man to act with such violence?

But he realized that he already knew the answer, for he himself had been no less desperate than Calhoun. He had already put his own life on the line repeatedly, including this very night, and he had already taken another man's life in the pursuit of his own goal. That goal might be very different from Calhoun's, but they were both willing to use whatever means were necessary to achieve their ends.

In his own case, that would have to change, Jonathan thought, slowing his pace as the creek drew near to the dooryards of silent dwellings. He knew that it was only through dumb luck that he had managed to survive his ordeals so far. He had been acting in some strange instinctual mode, reacting to circumstances as they occurred rather than taking control of the situation.

From now on, he would tilt the balance in his favor, relying on whatever inherent intelligence and skills he had at his disposal. He would anticipate events rather than be controlled by them—he would plan, and he would plot, and move only when his footing was sure.

And that would begin tonight.

He stopped walking, as the long and narrow belt of bushes lining the little creek had come to an end. Before him lay the very streets of the city, the creek having apparently been diverted to some subterranean man-made course. He was in a district of ordinary houses, and its dark and deserted streets in these wee hours did not feel safe.

Yet how much more perilous would they be in daylight? The Confederates' home guards were known far and wide for their hard efficiency, so notorious that it had been a Northern soldier who first told Jonathan about them. He looked at himself in the gloom. He was still wearing Caleb Petrie's pathetic uniform. The rest of his appearance—his long hair and unkempt beard, his limping gait, his unwashed condition—all shouted "Rebel deserter" in a loud, clear voice. If he tried to navigate the city in this condition, it would be a matter of hours at best before he was rounded up and sent back into service.

After Spotsylvania, he had absolutely no intention of letting that happen again, regardless of which army he happened to fall into. He regarded his days as a soldier officially behind him.

So instead, he became a thief in the night.

He crept into the backyard of a nearby house, where several articles of men's clothing had been left hanging on the line. He stole a shirt and trousers, both approximate fits, and stalked back to the creek. He stripped off his uniform, rolled it up and tucked it beneath a bush. As he did, he retrieved the army pistol he'd taken from the guard in the alley and Calhoun's heavy leather bag. He bounced its heft in his hand and then laid it methodically aside.

He slowly lowered his filthy body into the muddy, waist-high water. He scrubbed himself with his hands, doused his hair by submerging his head, and felt the creek's wonderful coolness wash away the weeks of grime he had accumulated. He emerged nearly newborn. When he had sat naked long enough for the night breeze to dry his skin, he put on the clean, workingman's clothes and ran his fingers through his sodden locks until they lay in reasonable order. He felt stronger, clearer of head, and marvelously refreshed in his new condition, and although nobody would ever mistake him for a gentleman, at least they might not immediately regard him as a deserter.

At last, he opened Calhoun's bag.

He did not cry out when its contents spilled out before him, but it did take his breath away. Fifty pieces of gold—twenty-dollar coins of U.S. mintage—rolled this way and that as Jonathan counted them. A thousand dollars. Serious money in this time and place.

He realized at once how considerably this changed things and how dramatically to his advantage. Until this moment, he had been stumbling through this century from hand-to-mouth. The gold would give him the luxury of buying his survival, rather than fighting or fleeing for it. It might do the same for his quest.

Jonathan had never been a greedy man, but the feel of the coins brought him a different kind of happiness. He could sense new options and previously unconsidered choices unfolding before him.

He assessed his overall position. He had made it behind enemy lines, into the very heart of the capital, and he was still alive and a free man—and now he had the wherewithal to make use of those advantages. In the blink of an eye, all the toil and trouble, all the fear and uncertainty of the last two months, seemed worth it, seemed like necessary and ultimately successful preludes to his arrival at this moment in time.

Jonathan rose and placed the pistol in his left pocket. He tied the cord of the leather bag to a belt loop and tucked the bag itself into his pants. It made an unsightly bulge, but the pilfered trousers were baggy, which helped.

And then he strode out of the brush into the sleeping streets of Richmond, walking with deliberate quietude but with a strong and steady gait only faintly interrupted by his limp. The double eagles clinked softly, barely perceptible, with each step.

"Thank you, Edward Calhoun," he whispered. "Wherever you are."

Jonathan spent the entire next day in a calculated process of self-reconstruction.

He satisfied his hunger at a small eatery, watching the hot sun rise over the city as he breakfasted on country eggs, ham, and grits. The coffee was ersatz—it tasted something like chicory—but it was strong and hot and seemed to strengthen him.

His meal consumed, he walked two blocks to a spotless barbershop. He bathed in a tub filled with hot water and strong soap and washed the remaining dirt out of his hair with scented shampoo. He instructed the barber to trim it to just above his shoulders and to lightly shape his beard and mustache. When all was complete, the barber finished the job with a generous splash of bay rum. When he left the shop, he looked perfectly like a man of the time—perhaps better groomed than most—but not at all out of place in the capital city.

Next came the tailor. He selected one of the more prestigious-looking shops in the central business district. He threw his entire stolen wardrobe into the store's waste bin and allowed the tailor to select a new ensemble for him. Despite the tailor's complaints that the Union blockades had made it "virtually impossible to receive the finer goods from Europe," he managed to come up with something very apropos, a gentleman's suit of lightweight cotton. It featured a frock coat of navy blue with white pinstripes that reached below his knees, narrow trousers with a pinstripe design in reverse colors, and a dove gray waistcoat. He chose three white shirts to go with it, three red neckties of the curious form that was in fashion, and a low crown top hat of gray felt, similar to the one he'd purchased up North and that had been battered, and ultimately abandoned, on his long journey south.

He kept his abused shoes only long enough to walk another block to a store that sold men's dry goods. Here, he acquired a fine new pair of black shoes that laced up to his ankles and a small leather valise into which he deposited his new belongings (and his bag of gold, as soon as the clerk's attention was diverted). Before leaving the shop, he added an ebony walking stick crowned with a silver knob and a pair of small round spectacles with gold rims and dark blue lenses, like the ones he'd seen well-dressed men wearing on the street.

When he stepped out into the blazing daylight, it was already afternoon, and Jonathan had become a new man, entirely transformed from the desperate and filthy soldier he had resembled only yesterday. In that tramp's place now stood an elegant, even dashing gentleman, a man with obvious means, entitled to respect. When a distinguished Confederate major nearly bumped into him, the officer bowed and said politely, "I do beg your pardon, sir!"—which let Jonathan know that he had achieved precisely the look, and the illusion, he wanted.

The entire inventory of his day's purchases used up less than two of his gold pieces. No trace of suspicion that he might have been a deserter had been evident on the faces of the waiter, the barber, the tailor, or the clerk, which eased his original fears and lessened the need to keep watch over his shoulder. They also all seemed to take his feigned drawl as perfectly natural, and none of them raised an eyebrow when he paid for his goods with U.S. gold and silver. The use of the enemy's currency was obviously a routine practice in the city. The fact that he was spending money at all, and often on items on the luxurious side, seemed to make the tradesmen especially solicitous. Each was clearly overjoyed at his sale, and each commented how bad business was becoming as Grant—they spoke the name with unconcealed spite—slowly tightened his noose around Richmond.

As Jonathan walked through downtown, the pain in his knee felt somewhat diminished, his gait stronger and steadier than it had been in weeks. He tipped his hat at ladies and nodded at men, drawing their admiring glances in return and looking very much like he fully belonged. To a stranger, Jonathan would have appeared carefree and lighthearted, but his mind was working hard.

He stopped in the city's central library, asked for and was shown a Richmond directory, and borrowed stationery and the librarian's pen to write down several names and addresses.

He entered a bookstore and purchased a map, placing it and the piece of paper carefully inside the valise that carried the sum total of his earthly goods.

And, finally, as the industrious sun approached the horizon, a sinking disk of fiery orange, he checked himself into the Hotel Central. In an ornate lobby redolent of lemon oil and old wood, he signed the register as "Jonathan Chase, Savannah," and the clerk made no comment and asked no questions as he took two silver dollars—enough for a week's stay—from his hand.

His room was spacious and fashionable, in the elaborate, elegant, and over-stuffed mode of the day. Jonathan removed his new garments, arranging them carefully on the back of a mahogany chair, and stretched his tired body upon the cool softness of the bedsheets and pillow. He planned to have his first night of genuine rest in a very long time and fully expected to need the respite.

Come tomorrow, he would have much work to do.

In fact, his next tasks would take several days.

He was patient and methodical in his assimilation into Richmond, assuming the pose and the air of a gentleman of relative leisure and, from all appearances, being assessed as such. He wasted little time making the acquaintance of the merchants near the hotel—the man who sold newspapers, the restaurateurs who served him eggs and chicory each morning, the ancient black man, apparently a freed slave, who gratefully took a daily nickel in exchange for a quick shine of Jonathan's fine black shoes—and from them he learned much about the city and the government that called it home.

He confirmed, for one thing, that he had chosen his hotel's location well. Situated at the northwest corner of Ninth and Grace streets, it stood directly across the wide and graceful expanse of Capitol Square, the very nerve center of the Confederacy that was housed in the old Virginia capitol building designed mere decades ago by Thomas Jefferson himself.

Much more relevant to his own purpose, he also learned that if he walked along the square from Ninth on Bank Street, he would come to a row of utilitarian-looking buildings that contained the primary divisions of the Confederate government, including the War Department.

He took regular strolls through this eminent district, admiring the large and fussy homes of the city's gentry, in far better repair and with much more gracious landscaping than the generally shabby appearance of the rest of Richmond. He acknowledged the ladies and gentlemen who promenaded here regularly, taking note of the many army officers whose gold-bedecked gray tunics betokened high rank. He sensed that had he been an expert in such things, he might have recognized many of their faces from history books—men who had led great armies and fought great battles on behalf of the rebellion.

Likewise, many of the civilians to whom he tipped his hat carried an air of busyness and prestige about them, as if they were senators or ministers of government branches. One afternoon, he saw a tall, thin man with gray hair and a wispy beard who looked familiar. Escorted by four armed guards, he was walking quickly across the central plaza, followed by a small gaggle of other important-looking types and an assortment of shabbier men with pencils and notebooks. When Jonathan noticed the grave, almost tragic expression in the man's pale blue eyes, he wondered if he'd just crossed paths with President Jefferson Davis.

Occasionally, as he leaned against a lamppost with his newspaper or sat upon a wrought iron bench in the square, he would exchange a few words with passersby. They were invariably polite, soft-spoken, and articulate, and all of them seemed melancholy. They knew that the enemy was at their gates—it was common to hear the boom of cannons or gunfire in the field, especially at night. Aside from banal comments on the muggy weather, they seemed to speak of little else. Jonathan didn't detect much hope in their observations, but the Southerners' great defiance was nonetheless apparent in everything from their speech to the way they carried themselves.

At last, on a still Friday morning when the sky had grown cloudy and the simmering humidity even greater than usual, Jonathan decided that the time had come. He dressed with special care and noticed how several days of steady meals had filled out his physique.

As he approached the large brick building housing the War Department, he sauntered with particular confidence. When he spoke to the armed sentries who stood before barred gates at the main entrance, his drawl was aristocratic and authoritative.

"Jonathan Chase of Savannah," he announced to the sentry on the left. "I have business inside with the Secret Service."

The guard, a burly man with a thin goatee, almost smiled.

"Secret Service?" he said with an expression that resembled a sneer. "Now what on earth might you be talking about, sir?"

Jonathan noticed that both guards had tightened their grips on their muskets.

"I mean the Secret Service of the Confederate States Army," he replied.

The sentry's face lost its smile. "Ain't no Secret Service located on these premises, sir," he said flatly. "And no entry will be granted to any man who asks for such. My suggestion to you is to take your leave."

Jonathan stepped closer to the man, ignoring the manner in which he placed his weapon diagonally across his chest in an obviously defensive move.

"I have information that is certain to be of grave import to officers located within this building," he said softly. "And should such officers discover—as I will make sure they will—that they obtained such information in an untimely manner because of an ignorant fool of a sentry, I suspect that they might not be terribly happy with that sentry. Does that make sense to you, soldier?"

The man's resolute expression softened a little at this threat. He did not move his body an inch, but his stance grew somewhat less aggressive.

"Just who is it you wish to see, sir?" he asked in a tone that might have carried a tiny note of respect.

"I have neither names nor titles to provide, but it is absolutely vital that I speak with an officer who represents the Secret Service or whatever department it is that handles such matters."

The soldier nodded slowly, rang a bell almost reluctantly, and then whispered something to another soldier inside the iron gates. In a few minutes, a silver-haired officer approached, walked outside, and took a good hard look at Jonathan.

"You are Jonathan Chase?" he half-asked, half-stated.

"I am indeed, sir," Jonathan replied to the meticulously attired officer, whose hair contrasted sharply with a thin mustache of jet black.

"And what sort of business is it you wish to discuss, Mr. Chase?"

"I do not believe that my business is the sort that ought to be discussed in the street, sir."

The cockiness of Jonathan's response seemed to take the authoritative officer by surprise.

"Indeed? Well, Mr. Chase, I can spare you a few minutes, provided you understand that I brook no patience for fools or impostors. Should you waste my time or raise my suspicions in any way, know that I have no compunctions against putting you in irons."

"I appreciate your candor, sir."

"Very well," the officer replied. "You will be thoroughly searched before you enter the building. And then you will have five minutes to state your case, whatever it happens to be."

They walked through a series of long, dimly lit corridors lined with offices serving a plethora of various military departments and agencies. After several twists and turns, they passed an armed sentry and entered an office marked "Signal Bureau." Once inside, the businesslike officer directed Jonathan to a small inner chamber and sat down at a desk—apparently his own—instructing Jonathan to take the chair before it.

"First of all," the man said, putting his boots on the clean surface of the desk and lighting a narrow cigar, "I think we had better stop playing games, Mr. Chase—if that is indeed your name."

"What do you mean?"

"To begin with, it's plain to me that you're no more from Savannah—or from anywhere else in the South—than I am from Damascus. Where are you really from?"

Jonathan took a good look at the man. The crossed flag insignia of the Signal Corps was on the sleeve of his tunic, and his collar was marked with the three stars of a colonel. He was clearly no fool. His eyes were hard and focused, his expression firmly set. Jonathan saw that he wasn't a man to trifle with, but he also seemed the sort who might respect a man who didn't automatically retreat at the first sign of intimidation.

"You already know my name, sir—I assure you it is genuine—but perhaps you might grant me the courtesy of giving me yours."

"I don't give a damn for courtesy, and I see absolutely no reason to give you my name."

"Perhaps I'm talking to the wrong man. I see that you belong to the Signal Corps, yet I asked the guards for the Secret Service."

"You have reached the right man, rest assured, but he happens to be impatient and overworked at the moment. I haven't all day to banter. You may state your business honestly, sir, or I shall consider alternatives."

"I am from Colorado Territory."

The officer's eyebrows raised just a little.

"That's Union."

"Yes."

"You are either brave or quite foolish, Mr. Chase, to admit to being a Union man within these walls."

"I did not admit to being a Union man."

The officer took his feet off the desk and leaned forward, as if to get a better look at this stranger.

"Then what the hell are you?"

"I come from Union territory, as you say, but I am neither a soldier in the Union army nor engaged in any sort of work for the Union government, including spying, if that's what you're thinking. I am here strictly on my own behalf."

"Pray continue."

"I am searching for a young woman—a Miss Apollonia Foley, who comes from Savannah. The last time I saw her was in late spring, close by the Culpeper Court House. I have reason to believe she was in Richmond shortly after that and may still be here today."

The officer sighed, giving no sign that he might have recognized the name Jonathan had offered. "Perhaps you have confused us with the police. I cannot see how this constitutes a military matter."

"This might serve to clarify. When I last saw Miss Foley, she was in the company of two men. Their names, at least as I know them, are Archer Blaine and Malcolm Jasper."

The officer gave a start despite his calculated composure. His narrowed eyes opened widely, his entire frame seemed to assume a seated version of attention.

"Archer Blaine? You've seen him? In Virginia?"

"As I said, near Culpeper. In May."

The officer took a long drag on his cigar. Jonathan had clearly caught his attention.

"But Blaine is supposed to be—," the officer caught himself before saying more.

"Imprisoned on Mackinac Island? I already know that. In fact, I helped him escape, with the assistance of Jasper and Miss Foley."

The colonel once again leaned closer to Jonathan, staring intensely into his eyes. He was clearly looking for some telltale sign to reveal whether Jonathan was trustworthy or a liar, and he seemed the sort of man who could be a pretty good judge.

"Mr. Chase, I have no sure way of gauging your honesty or your intentions, yet I will confess that you are telling me something of considerable interest and seem to have at least some knowledge that might interest the government. I will discuss this matter with you, to the degree that I can, so I am going to give you an extension on your five minutes. I would like you to tell me the whole story of how you came to be in Blaine's company and that of his companions."

For the next hour, Jonathan did precisely that. Although he left out the untouchable account of his time travel—and deftly avoided his bloody episode as a Union infantryman at Spotsylvania—he told the officer just about everything else. He spoke of his presence in Saginaw, his attraction for Apollonia, her plea for him to join the plot to free Blaine, the trip to and from Mackinac, the prolonged rail and stage journey into Virginia. It was refreshing to speak the truth for a change.

"And you have no doubt that the party was headed toward Richmond in early May?" the colonel asked when Jonathan finished his account.

"Reaching Richmond was the sole objective of the trip. That was said repeatedly."

A troubled look crossed the officer's face.

"What do you know of their reasons for wanting to come here?"

"Nothing. That wasn't revealed to me. Neither Blaine nor Jasper trusted me to that degree. I assume that's why they abandoned me and why I'm here today. I'm hoping that you might be able to shed some light on why he needed to get here, what his business was."

The officer snuffed his cigar. "You are a stranger and a Northerner, Mr. Chase. If I knew what Blaine was up to, I wouldn't breathe a word of it to you. I could be shot for that."

The officer's eyes had regained their narrow hardness. It wasn't really surprising that this would be his response, Jonathan thought. In fact, it was a ridiculous notion to come here to begin with, as reckless and foolhardy as joining up with an infantry battalion on the eve of battle. He would consider himself lucky if this man of stone didn't arrest him on the spot.

"I do understand that, Colonel, yet I thought it worth a try. Clearly, I was mistaken. Excuse me for wasting your time."

As Jonathan rose to leave, the officer rose as well. "Sit down, Mr. Chase. We are not finished yet."

They both resumed their seats.

"If you listened closely, you heard me say '*if* I knew what Blaine was up to.' The fact is, I have no idea. In my mind, that changes the regular rules. It allows me to speak a little more freely than is ordinarily my custom. I will tell you directly: I fear that Blaine may have become a renegade."

"I'm listening," Jonathan said.

"I already have several men on the lookout for him, but, as I am sure you can understand, these people are constantly involved with other matters, sometimes very dangerous ones. An additional set of eyes—especially eyes that are looking for Blaine in a very specific and directed manner—might prove helpful to me."

"Go on."

"First, I want to establish an understanding between us, Mr. Chase. Allow me a question or two. I am assuming that your presence in Richmond has only to do with following Blaine, in the hope that you might find this woman from Savannah. Is that correct?"

"That is entirely correct."

"On your word of honor, sir, you have no other objective? No political or military reasons for being in Richmond?"

"Absolutely none."

"And judging from your, shall we say, bold decision to come directly here and inquire about Blaine, I sense that you are very determined indeed to track him down."

"I am."

"Exactly how determined are you?"

"I will do whatever is necessary, sir."

The officer, apparently satisfied at this answer, seemed to relax. He lit himself another cigar and resumed his feet-on-the-desk posture.

"Very well, then. Understand that I cannot give you any specific information that will help you to find the man. We are both seeking him, after all, and if I had leads, I would surely be using them myself. However, I can offer you a little information, so long as you know that it will have to be an exchange. I am working from the premise that you might actually catch up to Blaine. The possibility is remote at best, but it remains possible, hence worthwhile to me. If you should manage to find him—whether in Richmond or any other place—I want you to let me know immediately where he is. If you're willing to do that—if you're willing to swear and give me your word as a man of honor that you will do precisely that—I will do two things for you. First, I won't have you thrown in irons here and now. Second, I will tell you what I know of Blaine."

Jonathan paused before replying. He had already tasted military life on the field of battle and found it bitter indeed. He was no more eager to enter the world of military espionage. It had a murky, underhanded feel to it. Who knew what trouble it might cause him if he gave his word of honor to this Confederate?

But he was at a loss for other options. It seemed a fairly straightforward proposition—information in exchange for a promise. It might not be as perilous as it felt, but he still had questions.

"I am concerned, Colonel, how such information might be used. I worry, for example, whether it will prove harmful to Miss Foley or whether it might constitute an act of treason against the United States."

"Good points, Mr. Chase. First, I will tell you up front that the information might well prove harmful to Blaine and probably to Jasper as well. If I were to locate them, my first act would be to arrest and interrogate them. What would happen to them thereafter would depend on what they had to say. We know of no reason to arrest this Miss Foley, although it would obviously be prudent to question her. I may as well tell you now that we have no idea who she is or what her connection to Blaine might be. So far as I know—and I know just about everything here—she has had no connection to this department. Short of a promise, I can provide you with a guarantee that every effort will be made to ensure her safety, should we encounter her.

"As to treason, I am in no position to answer that question. You know where you are and with whom you are dealing. You are a citizen of the North and must realize that the very act of walking into this office could be considered treasonous. If you proceed with me, you do so on your own account. I cannot speak for what your government might think or do."

It was a straightforward answer, and Jonathan respected the man's directness. He decided that he would go along, at least for now. If the time should come for making an actual decision on the matter, he would then weigh "word of honor" against "treason" on his own scale.

He took a deep breath. "I understand your terms. You may consider this my word. Should I discover Archer Blaine's whereabouts, I will inform you of his location."

"Then we have a gentlemen's agreement, Mr. Chase. If you should locate him in friendly territory, you can wire me easily here. Should you locate him in enemy territory, you may wire the pertinent information to a man in New York—I will give you his name—and he will see to it that the message makes its way to me. You would need do nothing more."

"Understood."

"And now," the colonel said, exhaling the last puff on his cigar, "I suppose you want to know about Blaine. I find this office stifling, don't you agree? Let us take a stroll in the open air, Mr. Chase, and I will tell you what I know."

⁂

They slowly walked the periphery of Capitol Square in the humid, gray afternoon. The nameless officer recognized many whom they encountered, mostly officers and politicians it seemed. He smiled at each and touched the brim of his slouch hat as they passed, giving a smooth impression of casual routine. He spoke softly to Jonathan between these encounters.

"I know very little of Archer Blaine's background, by which I mean his family and their means and the circumstances of his youth. He has told me himself—and I have not verified this—that he hails from Savannah, as does your lost lady, Mr. Chase. That suggests an obvious clue as to their connection, which is neither here nor there as far as I'm concerned. I also know that he was a cavalryman in the beginning, joining up with a Georgia regiment shortly after Sumter. He participated in several skirmishes but didn't see real action until Sharpsburg in the fall of '62. It turned out to be his first and last battle. He was captured and sent north, where he spent several months until his lucky number came up for an exchange. He ended up in Richmond last spring, somehow freed from his obligations to his old regiment and boasting a new colonel's commission. He was also bearing high-placed orders—I cannot divulge the name or rank of the officer who signed them—appointing him to the 'Signal Bureau,' which is my department. My assumption was that he had, shall we say, opportune connections."

The colonel nodded and touched his brim as a top-hatted elderly gentleman passed by. He lit a new cigar.

"I was not, at first, adverse to Blaine joining us. We needed smart men with the freedom to engage in covert activities and the personal resources to defray at least some of the expenses—and Blaine had both. We tested him on a couple of simple missions in the Maryland peninsula. He performed well, and we felt confident that he was ready for something more important than smuggling quinine."

The colonel paused and gave Jonathan a hard look.

"Listen to me now, Mr. Chase, for I am going to tell you something that is very sensitive. You would be wise to keep everything I am going to tell you safely under your hat. You must believe me when I tell you that you could find yourself just as easily upon a Northern as a Southern gallows simply for knowing it.

"Late last year, in November, we sent Blaine to a Northern city to assist one of our chief agents in a mission of the utmost complexity and importance. As this mission may yet remain active, I will tell you nothing of that operation or its location. The important thing, for your purposes, is that Blaine was involved for less than two weeks. As it turned out, Blaine proved himself argumentative, at times virtually insubordinate, in his relations with the mission's commander. He disagreed not only with the tactics but the very strategy of the operation and argued so strenuously that it appeared he might be seeking to take over by mutiny. The man in charge informed us by cipher that he was preparing to expel Blaine from the operation entirely and order his return to Richmond, but he did not have time to do that.

"Under circumstances that remain unclear to us, Blaine was captured by Union authorities in his apartment. We do not know how the enemy discovered him nor why they seemed unaware of the other operatives in the city. None of them was molested, or even approached, after Blaine's arrest. They all remain in place. We know only that before he was transferred to Mackinac, he was questioned at length. What he revealed we do not know."

The colonel nodded at yet another acquaintance and paused beneath a streetlamp.

"Jasper is another of our men, or at least he was. He disappeared from Richmond a year or so ago, leaving no trace as to where he went or why. We assumed he was merely a deserter, but your information makes it plain that he and Blaine are working on something together.

"Obviously, the capture of Blaine and the disappearance of Jasper raise disturbing questions for us. Blaine at least was intimately aware of the mission up North, an operation, I will repeat, that we still consider of the utmost importance. We have no way of knowing whether Blaine revealed nothing or everything to the enemy. It has also occurred to us, as I'm sure it has already occurred to you, that Blaine might be a double agent, that is to say, working for both sides at the same time, in which case his capture might turn out to be a feint, designed to throw us off track. On the other hand, if what you have told me of springing him from the fort is true, it suggests just the opposite—that he was indeed being kept as a prisoner of war. We simply do not know."

The officer puffed at his cigar, gazing thoughtfully at the noble equestrian statue of Washington that dominated the square. He appeared to be weighing the decision to speak further and finally decided.

"So you see the dilemma. The question, regardless of whether Blaine is one of us or one of them, is this: Do we proceed with the operation, one in which we have invested considerable money and time, on the assumption that Blaine kept his mouth shut? Or do we scotch the whole thing, waste all of our considerable effort, on the assumption that Blaine told everything and the Union authorities are only waiting for us to make our first move before they throw their net?"

"And you think that if you get your hands on Blaine, you'll get your answer," Jonathan broke in.

"That would be the hope, Mr. Chase. That possibility, however slim it may be, is precisely why I have taken the considerable risk of telling you as much as I have and why I am letting you loose to seek him. It is worth the risk to me that you might actually find him and might actually keep your promise to inform me. If a man's madness for a woman is to be the means by which I find my rogue, so be it."

Jonathan shook the colonel's hand. "So be it, then."

The officer turned to go but halted.

"One more thing," he said. "I have given you information you are not supposed to have. Should you choose to use that information in any way against the CSA, and if you and I should ever meet again, rest assured that my vengeance will be hard indeed."

"I have no doubt of that."

The colonel handed Jonathan a small piece of folded paper. He assumed it was the name of the Confederate contact in New York.

"This is to be our only meeting, Mr. Chase. If I hear from you again, it must only be by telegraph or cipher, informing me of Blaine's location. Other than that, our paths must never again cross."

"Never shall the twain meet," Jonathan replied, eliciting the barest ghost of a smile on the Confederate officer's face.

They left without farewell in separate directions, both feeling the first corpulent drops of a summer storm just about to break.

That night, as Jonathan watched the relentless summer rain descend upon Richmond, he realized how little he had really learned. He gazed from the heights of his hotel window as umbrella-shrouded pedestrians scurried across the square, their long shadows meeting the watery reflections of the gaslight.

Even the Confederate Secret Service, or "Signal Bureau" as they had apparently taken to calling themselves, seemed to know very little about Archer Blaine. That Blaine came from Savannah did not, in itself, seem especially important or surprising. That he had served in a line command also was not surprising and was of little real interest. That he had briefly participated in an unknown plot in some unknown Northern city, and was then captured under enigmatic circumstances, was all information of little or no practical value. None of it gave the least hint as to which direction Blaine might have gone once he reached Richmond, assuming that he did reach the city.

The ironic fact that the Rebel army was doing exactly the same thing as Jonathan—seeking clues as to Blaine's whereabouts—and had even tried to enlist his aid in that search would have been laughable had it not been so utterly frustrating.

Jonathan considered his options. He thought about making the trip to Savannah to seek Apollonia's parents. That was certainly feasible, but what guarantees were there? By now, the Foleys had likely heard of their daughter's disappearance from her uncle's home in Michigan, but had they heard any more than that? He considered it unlikely, considering Blaine's tight-lipped methods, not to mention Apollonia's own secretive nature. What if he were to make the lengthy trip and somehow manage to evade Sherman's already notorious onslaught in the direction of Georgia, only to hear that the Foleys knew absolutely nothing?

He decided to stay in Richmond, at least for the present. It remained possible, after all, that Blaine and his companions had stayed here. It was also probable that Blaine had come to Richmond for a specific purpose, and that purpose would likely have involved meeting somebody. Blaine may have needed orders or information or funds—and somebody in the city knew about it.

The upshot of his deliberations on this rainy night was that Jonathan became an amateur detective. He spent subsequent days scouring the city. He was well received by just about everyone, his accent and attire conferring an aura of respectability that seemed to preclude suspicion. He walked boldly into police precincts, giving names and descriptions of a party of two men and one woman who had supposedly arrived in the city in recent weeks. He went into dozens of hotels and boardinghouses and countless saloons posing the same questions. He bought each of Richmond's newspapers daily and searched the personal advertisements for some mysterious message that might shed a glimmer of light.

But after a week of this mind-numbing work, Jonathan had seen so many shaking heads and heard so many lips utter the word no that he felt himself once more sinking into despair. He didn't meet a single soul who had heard the names Apollonia Foley, Archer Blaine, or Malcolm Jasper, nor one person who had seen a trio matching their description. He realized that his exhaustive search for a needle in the haystack had brought him nothing but straw.

He arrived at that bleak conclusion one sultry Richmond evening after a long day's search. It was dusk, with burnt orange and deep purple clouds in the west, and Jonathan found himself a few blocks from the city's center. It was not a long way back to Capitol Square, and the weather was fine. He forsook the streetcars for his own feet and walked.

He thought about Apollonia and experienced the sensation he always felt when she came to mind—a strange emotion that hovered somewhere between pain and pleasure. He reached in his pocket for her tiny locket and held it between his fingers until the gold grew warm. He remembered her message within it, and its words began to push away the depression that was settling over him. His eyes took in the weather-beaten warehouses and stables that dominated this district and the workingmen and slaves who were busy closing for the day, but his mind saw only her.

And then he heard his name.

"Massa Chase!"

He stopped in his tracks and turned. To his left stood a three-story brick building, topped with a sloping roof and backed up by a narrow creek. The side facing him had a small yard, covered by a high wooden fence, the top stories similarly barricaded with planks, all obviously designed to make egress difficult, if not impossible. The structure had a penitentiary air.

A yellow wooden sign, with elongated horizontal letters in black, proclaimed: "Robert Lumpkin: Dealer in Slaves."

That voice echoed once more in the gloaming.

"Massa Chase! Over here!"

The voice—could it really be *his* voice?—surely came from one of the windows on the ground floor, securely barred like all of the others. Jonathan approached the building, his heart suddenly and painfully racing.

"Oh, thank the Lord Almighty!" came the now unmistakable voice, clearly overjoyed. "It's Massa Chase, and he's done heard old Jeremiah a-callin' out to him!"

August

It's sultry and lazy as summer grows old.

Sunbeams are slanted and tinted with gold.

Cicadas drone ceaselessly into the night,

Distant mirages play tricks on the sight.

Something is different, yet not quite there,

Something is coming, it's in the air.

Yes, something surely comes—something lurks on the none-too-distant horizon, though I fear it is not that which I so desperately desire. I do not sense the approach of Jonathan, in spite of my longing for him. My hope remains that he still lives, yet it is like a candle in the wind, flickering and under constant threat of being extinguished.

What does loom, I sense, shall not bring glad tidings. I shall rob from the good Mr. Shakespeare, who foretold that "something wicked this way comes." Yet I shall not dwell upon this, for what purpose would my dark speculations serve, what useful tool could I draw from them, when I am so powerless to avert the approaching "deed without a name"?

I am in Charleston now, scarcely a hundred miles from my own home. It is the languid late summer here, just as it is at home, and the sounds and the smells are painfully reminiscent. When I have the opportunity, I look to the south and think of Savannah, of mother and father, of blessed Bluefield—and tears never fail to come into my eyes.

It is perhaps because of my proximity to home that Archer has grown more distrustful of me. He fears the temptation to flee might be too great for me to resist, hence I am confined—a virtual prisoner—in this somber and plain house he has rented in Charleston. When Archer is gone, he makes sure to leave Jasper here to watch my movements and vice versa when Jasper has business elsewhere.

They are such fools. They have already won the match yet do not know it. Do they not realize that there is no escape for me? Do they yet not understand the sheer perfection of the trap they have set?

The house they have taken lies in a wretched district of the city. I am not sure of its exact location, but I know it is near to the slave market, for I can hear the callers, even behind their private walls, at their auctions for hours each day. When the breeze is right, I can clearly hear them describing their merchandise—male or female; young, middle-aged, or old; best suited for field or house labor—and sometimes I have heard the cries of that merchandise.

It is not, alas, a new sound to my ears. There was a time, when I was just a child, that I accompanied my father to the heart of Savannah. He had business with one of his shippers, and we were walking to the railroad depot when we passed by Wright Square.

Here, on a pleasant summer day, they were auctioning children—a boy and a girl, both of them just about my own age. The auctioneer was describing their fine health and rare strength, and the bidding was lively from the crowd. My father paused, curious perhaps as to what would be the winning offer, and we listened as the price rapidly climbed.

At last the purchase price was reached, the sale was complete, and the children were led from the auctioneer's platform into the custody of the winner. As they descended the steps, I heard a mournful wail off to the side. It was high-pitched and awful, full of pain and tears, and it sounded madly hysterical to my youthful ears. It frightened me awfully and made me begin to cry myself. My father saw this and quickly led me away from the crowd, away from the platform and that unbearable howl.

It was later, perhaps even years later, that I realized who the one weeping must have been. I realized that she was the mother of those two little children, and she was seeing them for the last time, with no chance to kiss their faces or stroke their hair or even give them a final good-bye. The sound of her cry, painful beyond the mind's power to grasp, has never left me. It gives me a shudder even now to think of it.

And this is not all. I have heard other "merchandise" cry—the pained weeping of a strong and good man, my own dear Jeremiah, when he had been whipped at my own father's hand.

Afterward, I crept back to his quarters to see to his welfare. Poor Jeremiah was crying, his back crossed with the hideous gashes left by the merciless whip, and when he saw me, his tears only intensified, I believe, in shame and humiliation. I tried to comfort him. I spoke soothingly to him and put medicine on his wounds, and he confessed to me that his whipping came about because my father suspected that he had stolen food.

I am astonished to admit this: I understood the poor man's pain and pitied him for it. Yet I also understood that his punishment was just and proper. I did not question my father's right to deliver such chastisement for such an offense. In my mind, Jeremiah's punishment was horrible but right.

You see that I am trying to understand myself. I am trying to understand how a person such as I—one who truly believes in compassion and mercy—could also be so unfeeling and so cold. Was I a monster to harbor such a paradox within my own soul?

And why am I asking such questions today?

I have long considered myself a Southern patriot, a term which I realize must equate with a champion of slavery. I have always believed it our God-given right to own Negroes and to use them for our own purposes. I did not question this institution any more than I questioned the God spoken of so adoringly by our minister, any more than I questioned the rightness of the sun's rising every day. It was part of our quotidian existence, like the air or the trees. And when it became, at last, the subject of fierce debate, when it began to be described as barbarous and evil by its opponents, even then I did not question it.

I have understood from the beginning that this horrible war is about slavery. And I understand that my present activities further its preservation.

Yet now—at long last—I question.

Now, when I hear the cries of the unfortunate souls in the Charleston slave market—so like the piteous wail I heard when I was a child—something stirs in my soul. Something forces me to wonder how I would have felt had it been my own child who was led away—a new purchase—from that wretched platform. Something makes me feel the sting of my father's whip on my bare back, as Jeremiah has more than once.

I have tried—for I have always been stubborn, as if my very head were carved of hickory—but find I cannot banish these thoughts from my mind.

I remember when Jonathan and I had our sole conversation on the subject of slavery. He told me directly that he stood firmly in opposition to it, but he did not pass personal judgment on me. He did not look at me as did those others in Michigan, as if I were an ogre just for being Southern. There was something in Jonathan's face that was above such contempt. There was a wisdom, a certain elusive knowledge, in his words. He spoke as some superior being, an angel or a wizard perhaps. He simply *knew* that it was wrong to own human beings, and he wished—I could see it in his eyes—that I could be as wise and as knowing as he.

Thus has Jonathan made me question myself, as has, I believe, the painful irony of my present circumstance, for Archer too has forced me to look ever deeper into this question. The manner in which he conducts himself, the objective toward which he strives, the painful and shocking news he has revealed to me—all these have planted seeds of doubt in my heart.

Now I fear I see the damned spots and that our hands will never be clean. I can never return to where I was, nor can I ever look upon Jeremiah, or that poor mother or any of the thousands of others I see around me every day, in the same light as once I did. For then I was an ignorant child, and now . . . well now I fear I am becoming something else.

It is nearly evening. The sun is ready to set, and the insects are singing madly in the hot air. I hear what I believe must be the last auction of the day. A man is calling out the fresh merchandise, and a tear is forming in my eye.

August

LUMPKIN'S JAIL

TWO HANDS—one black and one white—grasped one another through the rusty iron bars of Mr. Lumpkin's place of business.

As Jonathan squinted into the pervasive gloom that permeated the slave pen, he could barely make out the face of Jeremiah. The failing light from the outside world illuminated only the sweat on his face, providing a glistening cobalt outline of his forehead and cheekbones, but from this Jonathan was able to discern that the slave was smiling widely. Behind him, he saw the faint shine on other faces within the darkness and the barely visible whites of curious eyes.

"Good Lord Almighty!" the slave exclaimed, his grip desperately firm as if fearful that Jonathan might let go and disappear. "My, but you are a sight for sore eyes, Massa Chase!"

"Jeremiah," Jonathan replied, feeling a wave of affection he did not know he had. "I can't believe this. What in God's name are you doing here?"

"Oh, my goodness," the slave said breathlessly, "that's such a long, long tale I hardly know where to begin it. You see, I done been sold, Massa Chase. Old Jeremiah finds himself on the market for the first time in his life."

"Sold? What are you—"

Jonathan stopped when he felt a strong hand on his shoulder. He turned to face a short rotund man with bushy side-whiskers. A broad-brimmed straw hat cast a shadow over his face. When he spoke, it was with the guttural, slurring dialect that Jonathan had heard others, disparagingly, call "white trash."

"Y'all window-shopping for niggahs?" the man asked, slowly taking his hand from Jonathan's shoulders. "I might suggest coming over by daylight. Getting kind of dark to be shopping for darkies!" He let go a crude guffaw.

"I wasn't shopping," Jonathan replied, releasing Jeremiah's hand with difficulty and turning to face the man, "but I have found somebody I know."

The Southerner looked surprised, as if such words were very seldom, if ever, heard from a white man in reference to a black one. He peered into the window of the pen. Jonathan saw how the dim faces within retreated at his approach and realized that, instinctively, he found himself sharing their repulsion.

"That old niggah there?" he said. "That the one you was talkin' to?"

Jonathan nodded.

"That's Jeremiah. Been in the shop nearly three months now. Hard to move his kind these days. What you want with him?"

"We know each other."

"Uh-huh," the fat man replied, again flashing that puzzled expression. "Well, I guess I don't mind you talkin' with one of my niggahs, mister, at least for a little while, but I'm a businessman, you see, and business ain't been so good lately."

He moved a little closer to Jonathan and spoke in a near whisper, his bourbon-soured breath making Jonathan wince. "What I'm saying is, should you be in the market for actually buying something, I'm the man y'all want to see. I got anything you might need—I mean *anything*, mister—and the best prices in Richmond."

He stepped back and held out his plump hand. "Robert Lumpkin, at your service."

Jonathan shook the man's hand, hiding a shudder, and gave his own name.

"Now, if you'll excuse me, Mr. Chase," Lumpkin said, moving closer to the barred window, "I'm just about to close up shop."

He swung shut an outer window, made of wooden planks with no opening, completely blocking the waning sun from those inside. Before the hatch was closed, Jonathan caught a glimpse of Jeremiah. The impression of joy he had just seen was replaced with wide disappointment.

Lumpkin secured a ponderous padlock between the window's hasp and a ring on the sash. He marched deliberately down the length of the building, methodically closing each window in an identical manner. Jonathan walked alongside during the somber ritual.

"Got to close 'em up come sundown," the merchant said. "Otherwise, the local niggahs will be smugglin' things inside—things I don't want 'em to have, such as booze and tobacco. Don't want a house full of drunk niggahs, no, suh, and niggahs just love to puff that leaf, you know. The last thing I need is to see my stock in trade go up in smoke. Couldn't afford something like that, no, suh."

At the end of the building, Lumpkin turned to Jonathan. "Y'all is following me like a cat after a fish cart," he said, "so I assume there's something y'all want to talk about."

"There is."

Jonathan surprised himself at the readiness of his own reply. The thought had occurred to him almost subconsciously.

"Then let's walk up to the office and talk up a little business, Mr. Chase."

He followed Lumpkin back down the considerable length of the slave pen. Within, in what Jonathan could only assume was stifling darkness, he could hear the deep voices of the men singing a lonely song about Jesus. The harmonies, even through the shut windows, were rich and pure.

Lumpkin's office was at the front of the building. It was an unassuming room, lit by a sputtering kerosene lamp and filled with binders and notebooks containing documents. His desk was a disordered mess of papers and litter, with a half-full bottle of whiskey serving as a paperweight. He motioned Jonathan to a cane chair and took his own behind the clutter.

"Y'all know Jeremiah, do you? How'd that come to be, Mr. Chase?"

"I am acquainted with his owner. Until a few weeks ago, I was traveling with her."

Lumpkin poured himself a glass of whiskey. He motioned toward Jonathan with the bottle and grunted when his visitor shook his head no.

"I recollect now, yes, I do. Society lady, wasn't she, from somewhere down in Georgia?"

"Yes. Miss Apollonia Foley."

"Indeed so. She seemed an unhappy one, yes, she did, none too eager to sell her niggah, but that husband of hers—can't think of his name—now he was ripe for selling, sure enough."

"Her husband?" Jonathan tried not to sound shocked—or jealous.

"Yeah, the tall fellow with the long mustache."

"He identified himself as her husband?"

"Well, I'm assuming that's what he was. He was acting like it, the way he was giving the little lady orders and such. But he hardly said anything direct to me. Whispered everything to his woman there, like he was calling all the shots. She was frownin' something fierce, even shedding a tear or two."

Lumpkin belched and scratched his belly. "I been in this business for nearly forty years, Mr. Chase, and I've never been able to understand how some white folks can get worked up about niggahs in such a fashion. Especially the women folk. Damn near makes me sick every time I see it."

Jonathan pushed aside the mental image of Apollonia and Blaine and refocused on the task at hand. "Do you mind my asking when it was they came to you?"

"Hell, I don't mind t'all. Must've been sometime in May. Right around the time Lee was doing all that fighting up North, toward Chancellorsville. They come in just out of the blue, offering the niggah for sale. Didn't talk him up too much and didn't seem too particular about the price. I told 'em times were tough, niggahs weren't selling like they was a year ago, especially the old ones, so I couldn't afford a lot. They didn't seem to mind that, at least the fella didn't. When I made my offer, he whispered into the lady's ear, and she says, yes, all right, but she got all worked up, shedding one of those crocodile tears of hers. They signed the papers right quick, and that was it, save for the pathetic little scene when she had to part with the old coon."

Lumpkin spat toward a spittoon in the corner of his office, missed, and directed his gaze back to Jonathan.

"Now it's getting a bit late here, Mr. Chase, and I'm on the tired side. If you're some kind of detective, well, I've told everything I know about the transaction. If you're thinking of business, well, then, let's talk about it right now."

It was a decision that Jonathan in his wildest dreams never thought he would have to make. Was he about to become the legal owner of another human being? He had liked Jeremiah from the first and empathized with his situation the way only a man from the future could, but at this moment he had to admit the selfish truth that none of that seemed to matter. He was painfully aware that Jeremiah might prove an invaluable link to his search. Jeremiah had been with Apollonia after Jonathan was left behind. He had accompanied them all into Richmond. As much as Jonathan detested the hard reality of his motive, he knew that he had no choice.

"How much do you want for him?"

Lumpkin smiled and sipped his bourbon. "You still talkin' about the old niggah? Well, I'm sure we can reach a deal on him, Mr. Chase, but my expertise tells me that he's getting a little long in the tooth. Not too much work left in that one. Now, I've got me some fine young bucks in there—field niggahs with some hard experience in them and strong meat on their bones. Got me some fine young wenches, too—sweet and ripe as Georgia peaches. Y'all want to take a look?"

Jonathan shook his head. "It's Jeremiah I'm interested in."

Lumpkin's grin turned into a frown. "What y'all gonna use him for?"

Jonathan's ever-improving liar's instincts kicked in immediately. "For the present, he'll be a traveling companion. After that, I'll probably put him back in the house where he belongs."

The merchant nodded, reluctantly. "Well, who the hell am I to second-guess a customer? Y'all want the old niggah, that's exactly what you'll get. I suppose there's some light work in him yet. I think I'll be requiring two fifty for that one. And if you've been shopping around Richmond for old house niggahs, you'll know it's a steal at that price."

Not only did Jonathan sense the man's utter lack of ethics, he had been reading the Richmond papers regularly. He knew a great deal about the current prices for slaves. In the last year or so, prices had dropped precipitously, especially here in Virginia, where much of the Northern army was concentrated. The idea of bartering for a human life was revolting, but less so than letting this flesh merchant reap a windfall.

"I'll give you one twenty-five."

Lumpkin belched and guffawed. "Now that's a bullshit offer if I ever heard one, Mr. Chase, and pardon my French, if you please. I won't let him go for under two hundred."

Jonathan reached into his leather valise. He spoke as he pulled forth coins and placed them in a neat stack on Lumpkin's desk—six gold disks and five of silver. He looked the merchant directly in the eye, strengthened not only by his future knowledge but also what he had learned from living in this time and place.

"We both know, Mr. Lumpkin, that Richmond will probably be a Union town in a matter of months and that Confederate territory is shrinking by the day. You'll be a lucky man to be in business at all by the end of the year. I'm doing you a favor by taking him off your hands, and you know it."

Lumpkin stared at the little stack of gleaming metal. The classical face of Liberty on the top coin stared impassively back at him, but her powers of temptation were plain to see.

His deliberation lasted less than a minute. He carefully lifted the money and slipped it into his waistcoat pocket. He rose from the desk, procured a folder from a shelf, and selected a legal document from it. He spread the paper atop the layers of others on his desk, produced a fountain pen from its resting place behind his ear, and began to write.

"You're a hard-bargaining son of a bitch, Mr. Chase, but I must admit that I respect the hell out of that," he said with a defeated grin. "Y'all just bought yourself a niggah."

For the next hour, Jonathan and Lumpkin engaged themselves in the extensive paperwork involved in the legal transfer of ownership of one human being to another. It was, in its formality and attention to detail, both dreadful and fascinating. Jonathan marveled to witness the banal legalities of an institution that, by his own time, was almost universally perceived not only as an illegal and outdated but utterly barbaric practice.

In the process of signing papers, he glimpsed the document that had bound Jeremiah's body and soul to Lumpkin's business. Although he did not see the amount for which the slave had been sold, he did recognize the fine hand of Apollonia's signature at the bottom of the form.

When he inquired, Lumpkin told him that she had been obligated to offer her own proof of ownership of the slave, a detail she satisfied with an affidavit in her name bearing the seal of a notary public. As Jonathan gazed at the graceful contours of her signature, particularly the elaborate, sweeping script in which she penned the letter "A," he wondered about the state of mind in which she had relinquished Jeremiah into the hands of a stranger.

At last, Lumpkin held up a formal-looking certificate with a satisfied smile. Old English letters at the top proclaimed it to be a "Deed of Title," jarringly reminding Jonathan of such papers for automobiles that were commonplace in his own time. Beneath the allegorical figure of a seated woman, classically robed and holding in one hand a sickle and in the other a quill—symbols whose significance were totally lost on Jonathan—the document recorded the sale of Jeremiah, described as "one domestic male Negro, age approx. 55 yrs," from Robert Lumpkin, Proprietor, to Jonathan Chase, Esq.

"Sign that and he's yours," Lumpkin said with finality. "And you will take him tonight, if you please. One less breakfast come morning."

The paper was handed over, and hands were shaken. The deal was complete.

Lumpkin then led Jonathan deeper into his building, toward the massive pens in the back, holding a lit candlestick as they went. They eventually arrived at a room dominated by a large door made of metal bars. As they approached, two men serving as guards, who seemed to have been sleeping, rose to their feet, surprised to see their boss at this hour.

"Get me the old niggah, Jeremiah, and be quick about it," he barked to his men.

One of them shouted into the malodorous darkness beyond the bars. "Bring up Jeremiah!"

Jonathan heard hushed voices and the soft sound of bare feet on stone floors as Jeremiah was ushered forward. He reached the door, which was opened by one of the guards with a large copper key, and stood blinking in the unexpected light. He was dressed in a filthy white shirt, its sleeves rolled up to his elbows, and trousers that went no lower than his knees. He wore no shoes, and Jonathan saw the fear on the old man's face.

"Y'all belong to Mr. Chase here now, boy" Lumpkin said, grabbing Jeremiah by the shoulder and leading him toward Jonathan, much as a man might hand over a sheep or dog to someone who had just paid for it.

Only then, when he gazed into the face of his new owner, did the slave's wide-eyed look of apprehension give way to an all-encompassing smile. Jonathan returned the smile and firmly shook Jeremiah's hand, gestures that plainly astonished the three other white men in the room.

Lumpkin grunted and shook his head. "Well, that's done with," he said. "Let's get the hell out of here."

By the time the white man and the black man stepped outside, it was already late, and the bustling urban noises of Richmond were subdued. The dominant sound was the lazy undulating drone of summer insects. Gas streetlights, impressionistic in the hazy humidity, faintly illuminated the street before them, and for once the city was fragrant, the air bearing the sweet scent of some late summer flower.

They walked only a few steps before Jeremiah fell to his knees. He grabbed each of Jonathan's hands and looked up at him, tears streaking his face. "Massa Chase," he said with effort, "I can't hardly think of the words to say what I want to say."

"You don't have to...," Jonathan began.

"No, sir! I must have my say! I feel like the good Lord done delivered poor old Jeremiah tonight, yes, sir, he did. Sweet Jesus done delivered me smack dab into the hands of an angel, an angel named Massa Chase. I wouldn't be none too surprised to see that you was a-hidin' wings behind that dandy coat you're wearing, and what I'm trying to say is that whatever it is you want, wherever it is you want to go, then old Jeremiah's a-willin' to do it, no matter what..."

With his hands, Jonathan raised Jeremiah to a standing position. He looked directly into the teary eyes of the white-haired man before him. "I won't be giving you many orders, Jeremiah, but I'm going to give you one right now."

"Yes, sir, Massa Chase," he replied eagerly.

"From this moment forward, you are never again to call me 'sir' nor are you to use the title 'master' when addressing me."

Jeremiah looked confused, as if something fundamental and permanent in his life had just been shifted off its axis.

"Well, Mass—," he quickly cut off the word. "Well, then, what is old Jeremiah to call you?"

"My name is Jonathan."

They walked the short distance to the hotel in the sultry night, attracting little notice from those who were still up and about in spite of the late hour. It struck Jonathan that it was not at all uncommon here for a gentleman to be accompanied by his slave on a crosstown jaunt or errand. It made him uncomfortable that Jeremiah, almost instinctively it seemed, was heedful to take a position slightly behind Jonathan, but he thought it might be wise not to challenge this particular local custom.

They conversed very little on the way. Both men agreed that it would be better for them to share their news in relative privacy, not on the street. Over the past several weeks, Jonathan had learned how unusual it would be for a white man to hold a lengthy, not to mention enthusiastic, conversation with a slave in Richmond. For the most part, dialogue between white and black people in this city was limited to curt commands and appropriately respectful responses.

When they reached the Central, Jonathan again practiced protocol, instructing Jeremiah to wait for him while he went inside. Knowing already that the hotel was well prepared to accommodate the slaves of tenants—"and at a very reasonable price," the clerk assured him—he told the clerk that he now would be in need of quarters for his "boy." The clerk congratulated Jonathan on his new acquisition and gave him instructions. These were quite simple.

"Our slave quarters are in the rear, across the alley," the heavily cologned clerk informed him. "And since the Central is a prestigious institution, sir, these quarters reflect the quality of our accommodations in all reasonable respects."

The quarters were, in fact, a renovated stable with two floors. The upstairs room to which Jeremiah was assigned was reserved for male slaves, while the ground floor was used for females. When Jonathan accompanied Jeremiah upstairs, it reminded him of a barracks. Faintly lit by a single kerosene lamp, it was one wide room, with a neat line of metal-framed bunks arranged in a row. Two or three of the beds were occupied by sleeping men; the rest were unused. Although the nature of the room was unadorned and strictly spartan, it was kept neat and clean, with a washstand located at one end. Jonathan knew it could have been far worse.

"Not the nicest bedroom in Dixie," he began.

"Never you mind, sir...I mean, Jonathan," Jeremiah whispered, so as not to awaken the sleepers. "Compared to where I just come from, Massa Lumpkin's Devil's Half Acre, why this looks mighty fine to my eyes."

"We need to talk, Jeremiah," Jonathan rejoined, matching his whisper. "I think we'll be all right if we slip out to the back of the building and talk low. Are you up for it?"

"Yes, sir, I'm most surely up for a little talkin'," Jeremiah replied, this time apparently oblivious to his habitual salutation.

They crept down the back stairs into the near blackness of the August night and sat on the ground. Jonathan rolled a cigarette and offered it to Jeremiah, who took it with thanks, and rolled another for himself. The aroma of burning tobacco rose in the still air.

"I guess we need to start with the night at Culpeper," Jonathan began, "when the four of you left me behind. Tell me what happened."

"Well, Massa Chase—gosh I'm sorry to keep sayin' it over and over like that, I'm trying to learn, but, well, it's a hard thing..."

"Never mind, Jeremiah. Just talk to me."

"Well, I didn't know that Massa Blaine and Massa Jasper was a-plannin' to give you the slip, no, sir, I promise you that. I didn't know that till that morning come. Truth to tell, it wasn't even morning yet. It was nigh dawn time, and those two men rose up early, and Massa Blaine whispered to Massa Jasper to get Miss Appy to wake up. They took her aside and whispered more to her, and I could tell she was all upset at what they was a-sayin'. She was a-shakin' her head and whisperin' 'No!' over and over again, but then I heard Massa Blaine say something that made her go real quiet."

Jonathan waited while Jeremiah looked at the cloudy sky, trying to recollect the exact words. When he spoke Blaine's lines, he managed a fair imitation of

Blaine's white Southern accent, which sounded strange, and almost funny, coming from this black man's lips.

"He says to her, 'Now, Appy, I'm tired of puttin' up with this fellow here,' meaning you, Massa Chase, and then he says, 'And I'm tellin' you that if we don't leave him behind us, I'm a-goin' to kill him outright, and if you don't like neither one of those things, well, then, that's just too bad for you, Appy. Now you either come with us right now, and real quietly, or I'll shoot that son of a bitch'—I'm sorry to use such words, Massa Chase, I mean Jonathan, but that's exactly what he said—'I'm a-gonna shoot that son of a bitch right now, and you're still gonna be goin' with us all the same.'"

Jeremiah put his hands over his eyes, as if the memory still pained him. He shook his head twice and continued.

"And then Miss Appy, she says to him: 'And what if I choose not to go, Archer?' And Massa Blaine, he speaks real low, but I can still hear him 'cause it's such a quiet night by then, and he says: 'You know the deal, Appy. If'n you choose not to go along, you know what will happen. Not only will your Yankee sweetheart over there be dead as a doornail, you know what news I'll be takin' down to Savannah with me.'

"And that made Miss Appy start to cryin' and sobbin' something terrible, which made me want to get up and do something about all this nonsense, 'cause by now, I was gettin' a bit angry at such talk. So I fix to get up, but then I hear the voice of Massa Jasper. He's now a-standin' right by where I was a-layin', and I saw he had a gun in his hand. He whispers to me that I'd better be a smart nigger or I'd be a dead one right quick. So I laid myself back down."

He paused again, took a deep draw on the makeshift cigarette, and continued.

"All this time, Jonathan, you was a-sleepin' just as sound as a baby. And they told me to get up and stay quiet. Everybody starts packing up their bedrolls, real quiet and still, and they loaded everything up in the carriage, and then Massa Jasper he tells me to hitch the carriage, so I do, and then he leads the horse nice and quiet to the road. Then all of us, we leave with you unawares of it all. We was like thieves in the night, Massa Chase, just like thieves in the night."

All of this corresponded with how Jonathan had imagined that dawn departure, but one question had been on his mind since Jeremiah started speaking.

"Did Apollonia give me something before she left?"

"Yes, sir, I believe she did. She did it real quiet like, you know, sort of crept up to where you was a-sleepin' when Massa Blaine and Massa Jasper were busy with their things. Seemed like she slipped something into your coat."

"She did."

Jonathan showed Jeremiah the oval locket and opened it to reveal her portrait. Jeremiah smiled when he glimpsed the tiny simulacrum of her face.

"So then you headed for Richmond?"

"Yes, sir, for Richmond straightaway, and we moved real fast, 'cause the roads was starting to fill up with all sorts of soldiers, looking like they were a-fixin' to have themselves a big fight. We made it to the Southern lines in just about a day, and them Southern soldiers, they stopped us cold, their guns all drawn. Massa Blaine, he got us through the lines by talkin' to some of the officers who was there. They weren't gonna let us in at first, but he talked 'em into it somehow, and sure enough we was safe behind the lines in Richmond Town."

"And then Blaine sold you?"

"Yes, sir, he done sold me, just a few days after we got here. I feared it was comin', 'cause the day before I heard him talkin' to Massa Jasper, saying something about how that 'nigger has got to go—he's just gonna be in our way.'

"And same as she did with you, Jonathan, why Miss Appy, she tried everything she could to keep him from doin' it, but he said something to her again, something bad, I reckon, and she went along with what he wanted. Went ahead and signed the papers down to Lumpkin's place, and my, oh my, did she cry, Massa Chase, she cried, and she told me she was so, so sorry..."

Jeremiah stopped and wiped a solitary tear that had begun a slow descent down his cheek. When he spoke again, his voice was choked with emotion.

"And I do believe she meant it, Jonathan, I do believe she hated to see me go, seein's how I've been with her since her little girl days and how I'm nigh part of the Foley family and all, and Lordy, you know I was mighty sad to see her go myself."

As more tears streaked down his cheeks, Jonathan gave Jeremiah a little time, although he was impatient to go on. While he waited, he provided the slave a summarized version of his own adventures, including Spotsylvania, the Union hospital, the prisoner exchange, Chimborazo, and his most recent escape.

Jeremiah's eyes grew wide at the tale, and he whistled when Jonathan brought it up to date. "Lordy, you've had yourself a busy, busy summer, Massa... Jonathan," he said. "And death done stalked you the whole way, though it seems the old reaper wasn't fast enough on his feet for you."

"Maybe not," Jonathan said, "and maybe I've just had some amazingly good luck."

"Luck only goes so far," Jeremiah replied, "but I'm a-wonderin' about one thing."

"Ask me."

"Why'd you go through all that trouble just to find us?"

"I'll bet you already know the answer to that question."

"'Cause of Miss Appy?"

Jonathan nodded.

"I figured that was it. I saw how sweet you was on her all the way back to when I was in Michigan. Can I tell you something else?"

"Shoot."

"I reckon she grew pretty sweet on you, too. I know that girl, remember, and I never saw that look in her eyes before she met up with you. And when we left you up at Culpeper? Why she hardly spoke to anyone after that. Hardly made a sound at all, except for cryin'. She did it so many times that Massa Blaine, he told her to shut it up and dry it out. Real unkindly thing to say to a lady who was a-grievin' so.'"

"She's why I came to Richmond," Jonathan said, "and I'm going to be honest with you, Jeremiah. She's also the main reason why I bought you tonight. It might be damn selfish of me, but I want you to help me find her."

Jeremiah replied to this in a tone Jonathan had never heard before. His voice was lower, and most of the singsong lilt of his accent was gone.

"Then we want the same thing," he said, looking him directly in the eye.

For the first time since Jonathan met him, Jeremiah was speaking man to man, not slave to master.

Both exhausted, they let matters rest for the night. Jeremiah headed for his spartan quarters in the old stable, Jonathan to his overstuffed room in the hotel.

Early the next morning, Jonathan wasted little time joining up with the man whom he now legally owned. In their respective lodgings, both had breakfasted on much the same food—fried eggs, grits, and biscuits covered with gravy. The Central was a good hotel, even luxurious in some ways, but the absence of any kind of meat was a further indicator that times were getting increasingly tough in Richmond.

They walked off the heavy meal, traversing streets and avenues in a relatively aimless stroll under a gray, featureless sky. Jeremiah once more kept his respectful distance behind and to the side of his master, and few passersby gave them more than a cursory glance.

The black man was talkative, at least when no white strangers were within earshot. When Jonathan had first approached Jeremiah for information about the Foley family, shortly after they met in Michigan, the slave had been tight-lipped, reluctant to air family laundry before a relative stranger. Now, seven months later, he evinced no such hesitation. Jonathan wondered whether his willingness to talk was based on the traumatic experiences both had recently undergone or the fact that Jonathan was officially his new master. He decided that it didn't matter, so long as Jeremiah was talking.

This time, Jonathan wanted history. He asked Jeremiah how long Apollonia had known Blaine and what the nature of their relationship was. He was aware of his own trepidation when he asked this, realizing that the answers might be things he'd prefer not to hear.

But Jeremiah, as it turned out, did not know a great deal more about the mysterious colonel than Jonathan himself had been able to learn. Jeremiah's first sight of Blaine had been a little more than a year ago, when Apollonia was still in Savannah. Wearing the uniform of a Confederate officer, he had approached the Foley plantation and asked for an audience with her. Jeremiah believed the two had never met prior to this.

The slave had believed, as apparently did the rest of the household, that Blaine was a gentleman caller, interested in courting Apollonia. He made several more visits to the home during the following spring and always made sure to spend most of his time alone with her, walking beneath the extensive arbor that extended from the rear of the house or sitting in the shade of the ancient oak that graced its front lawn. In his later visits, Blaine took Apollonia into Savannah in a borrowed carriage. Jeremiah had no idea of their precise destination when they left the plantation on these excursions.

Her parents, Jeremiah said, were apparently impressed with the man and grateful that a "respectable gentleman" and an "honorable Confederate" was paying attention to their daughter.

It was a painful question, but Jonathan had to ask it.

"Do you think they were lovers?"

The slave hesitated before replying.

"It was the strangest thing, Jonathan," he said at last. "It sure seemed like they was, leastways some of the time, but I'm hard-pressed to be sure. Miss Appy never seemed too happy with him. She didn't do no smilin' when she was a-talkin' to him, I can tell you that, and once, maybe twice, I saw her cryin' after he'd paid one of his calls. I asked her what was the matter—it wasn't my place to do that, I know, but Miss Appy, she allowed me certain liberties the other colored folks didn't have—but this time she told me never to mind.

"And Massa Blaine, I didn't much cotton to him from the start. He held hisself and wore his uniform like some cavalier in a painting or somethin,' and when he spoke to Massa and Missus Foley, why, sugar would melt in his mouth, he spoke so sweet. But when he was all by hisself or just a-sittin' with Miss Appy, he was a different man. He was a-frownin' most of the time, sometimes lookin' right mean, and whenever he took a look at one of us colored folks, why, it was like lookin' into the eyes of the devil hisself, he seemed to hate us so much. The colored folks down at the plantation took to callin' him names behind his back, such as Ol' Catfish, on account of that mustache of his, or General Lee, 'cause he seemed like such a dyed-in-the-wool Rebel."

Blaine's visits to Apollonia did not last more than a few weeks, Jeremiah added, and by the early summer of 1863, Blaine had left Savannah, telling the family that he had been ordered back to the lines. Jeremiah was convinced that Apollonia was sincerely relieved at his absence, although she said nothing of the kind. The slaves at the plantation, for their part, were all happy to see him go.

Jeremiah didn't lay eyes on Blaine again until four months ago, after Jonathan and Jasper had hoodwinked the Union army into freeing him from confinement on Mackinac Island.

With Blaine's history out of the way, Jonathan then steered the conversation in Apollonia's direction.

The Foleys never spoke of Apollonia's reasons for wanting to leave Savannah to stay with her relatives in Saginaw, Jeremiah said, at least not in front of the slaves, nor did Apollonia ever volunteer any information on the subject. He surmised, however, as did most of the other slaves at Bluefield, that her parents were fearful that the war would soon be coming too close for comfort and felt that their daughter would be much safer up in the remote north woods, distant from the strife and violence.

Whatever her reasons, Apollonia left Savannah in September of the previous year, with apparently little time for preparation. When Jeremiah was ordered to accompany her on the trip, he was terrified at the prospect of traveling so great a distance, fearful of the North in general but grateful that he was given responsibility for her protection. The two of them traveled by rail all the way into a secluded section of Kentucky where, in a little town whose name he could not remember, they were joined by Malcolm Jasper. It was the first time either of them had met Blaine's sidekick.

In his retelling, Jeremiah made only a halfhearted attempt to conceal his contempt for Jasper and the way he seemed to assume authority over Apollonia, as if she had no choice but to follow his orders. Still, he spoke with respect for the man's resourcefulness, which Jonathan had himself witnessed. Jasper, Jeremiah explained, then expertly smuggled the party through a heavily wooded area to the banks of the Ohio River, where he had already arranged for a clandestine ferry to take them across.

Once inside Indiana, it was an easy matter for them to use the railroads to get to Michigan. They arrived in Saginaw in early October, "just when them northern trees was a-gettin' as pretty as pictures."

"I was allowed to stay in the workers' cabin at Massa Foley's place at Riverdale," he elaborated, "and I didn't see Massa Jasper around no more, 'cept for three times. Two times I seen him come up in the woods around Riverdale late at night, to have some kind of meetin' with Miss Appy. She slipped out to talk to him, like she knew he was a-comin'. That's how I knew he was still stayin' around somewhere, not too far away. The third time was when you was already there, the night we all began that long ride through the woods."

The nature of Apollonia's meetings, and the fact that they were handled so secretly, was an utter mystery to Jeremiah. It would only be several months later, when Jonathan was already involved, that the mission to spring Blaine from Mackinac would answer at least some of the questions.

"But raise just as many new ones," Jonathan said, trying, with little success, to make sense of the whole thing.

"There's a whole barrelful of questions, that's the truth," Jeremiah replied, shaking his head. "I wish to the Lord Almighty that I could answer more of them."

"You've already been a great help, Jeremiah. You've given me the pieces to the puzzle, at least some of them. Now we've just got to try to put them all together."

They had reached the foot of the long wooden bridge that spanned the waters of the James River. There was a lot of traffic on the bridge—carriages, wagons, men on horseback and some on foot. A good many of them were soldiers, no doubt busy with the increasingly urgent task of defending the capital city.

"One more question," Jonathan said.

"You just ask away," Jeremiah replied.

"Why did Blaine come to Richmond?"

Jeremiah looked at the dusty ground. It was another question to which he had no answer.

"Can't tell you, 'cause I don't know," he said. "All I know is that it must have been mighty important to him. That wasn't hard to see."

Jonathan looked at the restless traffic on the bridge and felt his heart once again begin to plummet. He was sensing the imminent arrival of yet another dead end.

"But there is one thing I can tell you, Jonathan," Jeremiah added, breaking the somber moment.

When Jonathan looked up, he saw that Jeremiah was smiling.

"I can tell you who he went to see once he got here."

In the nearly two months Jonathan had spent in Richmond, he had learned a great deal about the city's, and the Confederacy's, powerful and influential men, but he had never before heard the name of Silas Demby.

Nor had Jeremiah, who still had no idea who the man was, but he had seen the name neatly printed on the mailbox that stood before the "mighty gracious house" in which Demby lived. Earlier this summer, he had accompanied Blaine and Jasper to this house on the third day after their arrival in Richmond.

Jeremiah described Blaine as being anxious and nervous when they paid their visit. He had a particularly clear memory of that visit, Jeremiah said, because it took place the day before he was sold to the slave merchant Lumpkin.

"I stayed outside and waited for 'em," he said of Blaine and Jasper, "and they were inside the house for nigh an hour. When they came out, they was both a-smilin' wide, like they just got awful good news from that man Demby."

Jonathan felt like kissing the old man's weathered face. Excited by the prospect of a lead at last, he immediately asked for details.

Jeremiah couldn't remember exactly where the house was but thought that he might be able to trace the route if they started from the Hotel Richmond, where Blaine, Jasper, and Apollonia had stayed. Jonathan and Jeremiah walked quickly back to the center of town, with Jonathan stopping by the Central to collect a few things, and then made the short trip to the Hotel Richmond.

From there, Jonathan followed as Jeremiah slowly and methodically embarked on a zigzag yet deliberate route north of downtown. The distance was not great—less than ten blocks north and three or four west. When they arrived on a leafy street lined with opulent homes, framed by spacious lawns and elaborate wrought iron fences, Jeremiah was sure they had reached the right location. He stood before a rambling, three-story Queen Anne made of gray stone and announced that this was the place.

Indeed, the iron mailbox that stood by the sidewalk read, in bold letters, "Silas Demby," and Jonathan felt his heart race as he opened the gate and traversed the shady walk to the front door.

It was answered by a black man of about Jeremiah's age, but who looked far more elegant. He wore perfectly tailored black tails and a snowy white shirt, and his hair, even whiter than Jeremiah's, was expertly cut.

"May I help you, sir," the slave-butler said to Jonathan in a deep voice, his eyes taking in the sight of Jeremiah, who waited by the front gate. Jonathan was amazed how cultured the man sounded, how distinguished and white his accent was.

"Jonathan Chase to see Mr. Demby," Jonathan replied in his most aristocratic Southern patois.

"Is Master Demby expecting you, sir?"

"No, I'm unannounced, but here on a matter of great urgency."

"One moment, please."

The butler retreated back into the house, closing the oaken door quietly behind him. He returned in less than a minute.

"The master begs your pardon, sir, but he is engaged at the moment. If you have business with him, he suggests you state that business in a letter and post it with a return address. He will do his best to respond."

Jonathan smiled at the elegant slave and then gently pushed him aside as he walked into the house. He felt a strange tightening in his stomach that he did not yet recognize as anger.

"I'm very sorry, sir, but you are not...," the butler began helplessly, unsure how to conduct himself with a white man who acted in open defiance of his master's instructions.

"Demby!" Jonathan shouted into the hollow expanse of the tall, paneled foyer. "Demby, I must see you immediately!"

A thin, nasal voice came from the top of a curved stairway that led upstairs from the front hall. The voice spoke in a strangely arrogant accent, not unlike that of the butler, which made Jonathan think of a strange mélange of British and Southern gentry.

"Who is that?" the voice demanded imperiously. "Who is barging into my—"

"Jonathan Chase!" Jonathan shouted. "On important business."

At last, Silas Demby appeared at the top of the stairs. He was painfully thin and not a young man, perhaps well over fifty. Limp strands of mouse gray hair draped down to his shoulders; some of it had been combed over what appeared to be a bald pate. He was dressed in a severe black frock coat with a scarlet vest, across which a heavy gold watch chain dangled. Thin gold spectacles perched on the tip of his pointed nose, accenting the already sharp profile of his face.

Something about the man's appearance revolted Jonathan. It seemed to urge on that tentative spark of anger smoldering somewhere deep within him, an emotion that he now could name.

"I have given you instructions already," Demby said to the stranger, "and so I will be grateful for your immediate departure from—"

"I will see you now, sir!" Jonathan commanded. "And you will receive me now!"

The man's vulpine face hardened at these words. He addressed his next statement to the butler, who stood nervously and impotently by Jonathan's side.

"Arthur, you will hasten immediately to the police box on the next street but one, and you will sound the alarm. This man is an intruder. Go quickly!"

The slave wasted no time. He turned on his heels and rushed out the front door. Jonathan paid him no heed and bounded up the stairs, taking two at a time. He barely noticed the plush floral carpet beneath his feet or the splendid landscapes in ornate gilt frames that fairly covered the staircase wall.

Demby retreated at Jonathan's advance, backing into a book-lined office. He continued walking backward until he crumpled into a leather chair against the wall. Jonathan pulled another chair to within a few inches of Demby's, noticing with considerable satisfaction the look of dread that had spread across the man's face. He sensed the kindled rage within him, still igniting, but felt fully in control of it. He would use it to his advantage.

"Who are you?" Demby said shakily.

"I've already told you," Jonathan replied, "but it doesn't matter."

"Why have you barged into my house like this?"

"I have questions to ask."

"You have no right—"

"I need no right, sir. I am here, and I demand answers."

Demby's expression grew even more fearful, his voice even shakier, as he asked what those questions were.

"They concern an individual by the name of Archer Blaine, who visited you in this house some two months ago. I want to know the nature of his business with you."

Demby shook his head, looking anxiously toward the stairs in obvious hopes that Arthur would shortly be returning with a constable in tow.

"I know of no man by that name," he replied.

"I have a witness who accompanied him to this house in May. Blaine and another man, Jasper, spent nearly an hour in conversation with you."

Demby shook his head and stared at the ceiling, as if trying to remember. "I have no recollection of that occasion," he said. His voice was beginning to regain its imperious air.

Jonathan reached into the inner pocket of his coat. He felt the wooden handle of the ponderous pistol he had taken from a dead man in an alley, not very long ago and not very far from where he was now. He felt no reluctance in pulling it out and pointing its blue steel barrel at Demby's face, nor in slowly pulling back its hammer.

A quiet, high-pitched sound came from somewhere deep in Demby's throat.

"Perhaps this will assist you in your recollections," Jonathan said steadily.

"I...I...I cannot recall," he replied, glancing once more toward the stairs. He was clearly delaying, hoping for help.

"Mr. Demby," Jonathan said quietly, nudging his hat back from his forehead, "please believe that I won't hesitate to put a bullet through your head and that I'll have no more regrets about it than killing a rabid dog."

That strange little sound again and then this: "All right, then. All right. I'll tell you, but for God's sake take that pistol away from my face."

Jonathan complied, lowering the barrel so that it pointed instead at Demby's scarlet, gold-crossed vest.

Demby carefully took a silken handkerchief from a pocket and wiped away the sweat that had formed on his receding hairline. When he spoke, his voice had lost its authoritative elegance. It sounded raspy and forced.

"Blaine was here in May, it's true."

"Do you know him?"

"I knew that he had been involved with an army department they prefer to call the 'Signal Bureau.' He worked in," Demby trembled slightly as he searched for the right words, "in various sensitive matters."

"And why would he come to you? Are you with the Secret Service as well?"

The man made a pathetic attempt at a smile. "Lord, no," he rasped. "I work for the State Department, in diplomatic matters, but only unofficially, as a sort of go-between."

"Between whom?"

He hesitated, having apparently arrived at a point in the conversation where sensitive information would have to surface. Jonathan began slowly raising the pistol for encouragement.

"I handle certain communications between Richmond and London," he said quietly, looking furtively around as if there might be an invisible eavesdropper about. "I facilitate messages between the Confederacy and the Crown, messages that are not sent through the usual channels."

"You mean the embassy?"

"Yes, and the political sphere as well."

"Because you cannot trust the usual channels?"

"That's correct."

"And Blaine was interested in these communications?"

Again, he hesitated, and Jonathan again began to raise the pistol.

"In one communication specifically. He wanted to know only one thing—the time and place of an emissary's arrival."

"Which emissary?"

"A special representative of Queen Victoria. A man who works exclusively in clandestine affairs between the Confederacy and Great Britain, not unlike myself."

"What sort of affairs?"

"Trade, for the most part. Cotton from us; arms, steel, and medicine from them. How to pay for it. How to get it through the blockades."

Jonathan was beginning to get the uncomfortable feeling that he was stumbling perilously close to a hornet's nest.

"Who is this emissary?"

The strained expression on Demby's face conveyed that he was thinking of clamming up at this point. He thought better of it.

"His name is Lord Covington."

"And his arrival here?"

"Oh no, not here. He never comes here, nor would he dare operate in the United States. He works only in neutral territory—Canada. He travels there every so often and meets our representatives there. That's what Blaine wanted to know. The date and place of his next trip to Canada."

"And you told him?"

"Yes."

"Isn't that secret information?"

"Of course it's secret. I am one of the very few individuals informed as to Covington's whereabouts and availability. My job is to inform only those who absolutely need to know—President Davis, our man in Canada, a few others."

"So why did you tell Blaine?"

A look of extreme discomfort again crossed Demby's brow. He took another swipe at his forehead with the handkerchief.

"I had no choice in the matter. Blaine knew things. His work in intelligence, no doubt, opened doors to him. And if these things were to become known to the wrong persons in Richmond, my life would be forfeit."

Demby's defiant arrogance returned for a fleeting moment. "What he did was blackmail, pure and simple, not terribly unlike what you're doing right now with that damned pistol."

The rebuke did not cause Jonathan to reposition the weapon. Demby continued, this time voluntarily.

"Nor was Blaine's visit in May his first. He also came last December—that time alone—wanting to know precisely the same information: when would Covington next arrive and where. On that occasion, I told him that the emissary would be in Toronto the following month, which was January of this year."

"Did he tell you why he was so determined to see Covington?"

Demby suddenly became conversational, as if the release of one secret rendered all the rest academic.

"No, and I didn't ask him on either occasion. Listen to me. I don't know if Blaine is still working for the Secret Service or whether he's become a renegade, as some of his superiors seem to believe. But you can bet that he's working for *somebody*, and whoever that happens to be is likely to be powerful. You must realize that these are uncertain days in Richmond. One hardly knows who's working for whom anymore. There are too many subterranean activities to keep track of. Nobody knows who to trust. The whole thing is unraveling, falling apart at the seams. Different branches of the army have their own projects that they keep secret from everyone else, as does the Secret Service, the navy, the State Department, and God knows who else. Not to mention the Union itself. It has men everywhere, most of them posing as Confederates. For all I know, Blaine could be in league with any of them."

He peered through his spectacles directly into Jonathan's eyes. "And now you barge in. I wonder who *you're* working for."

"Strictly for myself. My interest in Blaine is entirely personal."

Demby nodded, his disbelief obvious.

"I haven't told anyone of Blaine's visits, to preclude your next question. Nor will I mention yours. It would only invite suspicion, or worse, to do so. I have enough problems as it is."

Jonathan wanted to ask Demby whether everything he'd said was true—so much would hinge on the accuracy of his statements—but then realized the ridiculousness of such a query. Demby had testified at the barrel of a gun. Jonathan had no choice but to believe him.

Demby cleared his throat. "Now, have I answered everything you want to know?"

"Everything except the time and place."

He paused for a moment before speaking.

"Covington is expected in Halifax in late September or early October. He'll be there for about a week."

"Where will he stay?"

"He'll be aboard a Royal Navy vessel in the harbor—I'm not sure of its name. Only authorized visitors will be allowed to see him, and they will be thoroughly searched before boarding. Covington is an extremely careful man. In his position, he has no choice."

Jonathan rose to his feet. "Then you and I are finished, sir," he said, uncocking the pistol and returning it to his pocket. He thought about apologizing to Demby for the intrusion and the threats but reconsidered when he realized how utterly foolish that would sound.

He settled for "Thank you, Mr. Demby," as he hastily left the study and headed for the stairs. Behind him, Demby released a deep sigh of relief and once more brought forth his handkerchief.

When Jonathan reached the sidewalk, he was amazed to see that Jeremiah had taken it upon himself to become an active player in the encounter. Arthur, Demby's elegant butler, was cowering, his back to a tree, while Jeremiah stood a few inches away, his arms folded in a posture that looked very determined and quite fierce.

The next day, Jonathan took a break from his mission. He allowed himself to sleep in late and had another long walk through the streets of Richmond.

He left Jeremiah to his own devices, sensing that he might appreciate being alone after months in the unbearably close quarters of the slave pens. He was right—Jeremiah was nervous but thrilled, not only at the promise of privacy but the prospect of having an entire day to spend in whatever manner he chose or at least to the extent that the Confederate capital would allow.

For his own part, Jonathan figured that it was unwise to wander too far from the city itself, since it was impossible to know when one might stray too close to the equally dangerous enemy or friendly lines that formed a shifting, unpredictable, crazy-quilt ring around much of Richmond.

But Jonathan needed to be alone, in a place that was quiet, so he walked as far as he felt safe. He strolled for more than hour toward the southwest, past the stately mansions of the well-to-do, the tattered shantytowns of the poor whites, and the rickety sheds that housed the black people, both freemen and slaves. As the warm afternoon began to wane, he found himself well beyond the populated sections of the city, in a semirural zone of widely dispersed houses with small, well-maintained farms. The dirt road on which he walked was free of traffic, and the woods and fields bore no trace of military activity. He had discovered an area some distance from both the front lines and Richmond's general citizenry.

It was a profound relief to be away from Richmond, even if only at this modest removal, and Jonathan realized that he would not miss the place once he was gone. With each day, it seemed to take on more of the character of a doomed city. Some of this was obvious. The streets were frequently clogged with ragged bands of wounded Confederates, much like the column in which he had himself recently marched. At other times, the traffic consisted of Union prisoners herded like starving cattle by impatient horsemen. They looked even more bedraggled and dispirited than the Southerners.

Richmond had also become the temporary haven for thousands of displaced blacks. Most of these were slaves who had fled Union advances, frequently without their masters and mistresses who had scattered in different directions. Now without homes or owners, they congregated like gypsies in makeshift camps, their shelters loosely constructed out of whatever materials they were able to scrounge from alleys and trash heaps. Jonathan wondered how these refugees were able to locate enough food to stay alive and what they would do once winter arrived.

Other manifestations of Richmond's peril were not so plain to see but were impossible not to sense. Nobody seemed to smile in this city. People still walked about, apparently engaged in personal or professional business, but in what appeared to be an aimless, reluctant manner. Their tread seemed heavy, their mouths set in tight-lipped frowns. They seldom made eye contact with passersby, keeping their gaze glued to the dusty streets. Even the saloons were somber, if not sober, places.

There was an eerie sense that Richmond knew its day of reckoning loomed just over the horizon. The feelings that the citizens projected were uniformly gloomy—grief at the staggering human losses their cause was demanding, fear of imminent Northern retribution and destruction, bitterness and anger that the Southern cause was faltering so badly, dread of a future in which former slaves would be as free as whites—perhaps even, here and there, hints of guilt over the institution of slavery itself.

To Jonathan, the city looked more like a necropolis than a metropolis, a capital of death instead of the seat of rebellion. Sometimes he could almost smell its charnel reek on himself.

And he would very soon leave it all behind. He was excited that the information he had forced from the lips of Silas Demby had given him, at long last, a place to go, but he couldn't escape the fact that even these tidings came with a disconcerting edge.

The words of both Jeremiah and Demby had made it very clear to him that Apollonia was somehow a prisoner herself, being forced to accompany her jailers. Jonathan was convinced that Blaine was holding something over her, something powerful enough to make her act against her own will. She had not wanted to abandon Jonathan, nor had she wanted to sell Jeremiah. This was good news in one way but bad in another. It suggested strongly that she was under Blaine's coercion, and Jonathan had no doubt that Blaine would use his unknown power over Apollonia—and probably even worse—to get what he wanted.

That piece of the puzzle—what Blaine wanted—remained as unclear as virtually everything else about the man. It obviously had something to do with the shadowy envoy, but what? And what was Apollonia's role in that business? Why did Blaine need her? Why was it necessary for her to be involved in the ruse that freed him from the Federal prison at Mackinac? And why had she gone to Michigan to start with?

It seemed that with every bit of information Jonathan was able to collect, more tentacles of mystery sprang forth, and all the strands, he knew, hinged on the primary one—the unspoken connection between Blaine and Apollonia. Only the potential of danger befalling her worried Jonathan more than this question. It gnawed at his very entrails.

But not enough to deter him. As he walked past cornfields going dry in the late summer sun, he was already analyzing the practical dimensions of the situation.

Apollonia, Blaine, and Jasper had probably left Richmond weeks ago, which gave them a formidable head start. Jonathan felt reasonably confident that they had headed for Halifax, and may well have already arrived there, but he still had to get there himself and had yet to come up with a plan to go about doing that.

Time was precious. It seemed clear that Blaine's purpose in heading to Canada was to meet Lord Covington. If Demby was telling the truth, the envoy would arrive there in a month or less. Jonathan was no expert in geography, but he knew that Halifax was a very long way from where he now stood. He also knew that traveling into or out of this part of Virginia was itself a daunting challenge, with Union troops striving to complete their stranglehold on the city and gunboats eager to challenge anyone brash enough to make a break for the sea.

These formed an impressive list of obstacles, Jonathan realized, but he was not cowed by them. He reflected on the last few months and felt confident that he could face whatever lay ahead. He was not afraid for himself, only for her.

Jonathan stopped in his tracks at this thought. The August sun was taking its time approaching the horizon, and as it languidly descended, its rays cast a warm golden glow and threw long, angular shadows. It illuminated the black-eyed Susans that clustered along the side of the road and intensified their already brilliant yellow hue. The still air of the countryside was laced with dry heather and alfalfa, the softly piquant scents of a summer that was growing old and tired.

It was at just about this time of year that his beloved wife from another era had left him. On a golden August afternoon much like this one, far, far into the future, Rachel had taken her leave and left Jonathan a shell of a man. He had become detritus then, as lost and empty as the human flotsam and jetsam of war that filled the condemned city behind him.

He touched the oval locket that lay hidden in his pocket, sensing Apollonia's presence within it, and promised himself that this would never happen to him again. Nor would he leave Apollonia's fate to whatever Archer Blaine had in mind.

There was a great deal to do.

Their last two days in Richmond were spent in a frenzied effort to find a way out.

Jonathan considered returning to the unnamed officer from the "Signal Bureau" but quickly abandoned the idea. The colonel had told him clearly that Jonathan should contact him only if he had located Blaine. Though he had, in fact, done just that, Jonathan could think of no way to ask for safe passage without telling the colonel where he was going and why. He didn't want to alert Confederate authorities to the possibility that Blaine was in Canada, at least not yet. He figured that the military could travel much faster and feared that Blaine—and very possibly Apollonia—might be detained and spirited away long before he got there himself. It would be far wiser, Jonathan thought, if only he and Jeremiah knew their destination.

But there were other options. In his weeks in Richmond, Jonathan had made acquaintances of many sorts. He was on good terms with any number of people who spent their lives near the edges of Confederate power and whose proximity to that power allowed them certain access to it. The barber who trimmed his hair and beard boasted of first-name familiarity with both Jefferson Davis and Robert E. Lee. The merchant who dealt in tobacco handled special cigar orders for half a dozen cabinet ministers and generals.

Some of these people were well connected in more sublime ways. The clerk at the Hotel Central, for example, was a virtuoso black marketeer. There were many commodities that were virtually impossible to obtain in Richmond at this stage of the war—certain liquors, fine jewelry, exotic fabrics, high-quality coffees—but Reginald was able to provide them all, given a little time and the proper tribute of silver. Among his clients, he had told Jonathan, were some of Richmond's most influential and powerful figures, although he was scrupulous to provide no names. He had suggested more than once that if there happened to be any "special provisions" Jonathan might be needing, Reginald would be happy to accommodate. He had also hinted, more obliquely, that the source of his eclectic stock had direct links with the CSA-sanctioned blockade-runners.

Jonathan approached him on the evening after his long walk. The elegant lobby was quiet, and Reginald seemed glad to be distracted from the ledger work he was doing.

Jonathan was direct. "I need passage to Halifax, as quickly as possible," is all he said.

Reginald nodded, as if there were nothing at all extraordinary about the request, and then paused. Jonathan discreetly placed a golden half eagle into his palm, and the clerk smiled gently.

"How quickly?"

"I need to be there by the middle of September, at the absolute latest."

The clerk nodded again. "That might not be impossible."

He peered to his left and right, assuring himself that nobody was within earshot. "I can set you up with people who, for the right price, could get you through the Union lines northeast of town and then get you across the river into Maryland, probably to Port Tobacco. They're fairly reliable people, but it's a risky business all the same and getting riskier all the time. A lot of things can go wrong out there—you could be captured and suspected of spying; you could be shot by either side, just because you startled a sentry in a lonely spot. No, if you've only got a couple of weeks, I'd say the overland route might not be the best choice."

He moistened the tip of his pen with his tongue and wrote a name and address on a sheet of the hotel's ornate stationery, folded it, and handed it to Jonathan.

"Getting out by sea is the better option and probably faster, too, although it obviously carries its own risks," he said quietly, not quite in a whisper. "At the moment, you can still travel safely to Wilmington on the Richmond and Danville line. Lee's boys are protecting it so far, though it's hard to say how long that will last. Once you get to Wilmington, contact the man whose name I've written down. He keeps an office on Water Street, just by the docks. Tell him that Reginald in Richmond sent you. He'll get you to Halifax all right, if anyone can, provided you can pay the toll. I assume you realize it won't be cheap."

"I do. Who is he?"

"George Wilkins, the best blockade-runner out of Wilmington, at least in my judgment, and I know a good many of them. Likes to anchor in the northeast branch of Cape Fear and prefers to exit around Frying Pan Shoals. He has some pretty novel means of slipping through the net. He's made at least two dozen successful runs since the blockade was set—a perfect record."

"And he goes to Halifax?"

"Specializes in it. He's probably kept half a dozen cotton mills in business in merry old England all by himself. Turns it all over to the British merchant fleet up there. I can't give you an exact date when he'll be making his next run, but I know he's in port now and that he doesn't like to sit still for very long. If I were you, I wouldn't hesitate."

Jonathan did not hesitate, but there were a few details he had to address before he took his leave of Richmond.

On the morning after his conversation with Reginald, he made three stops. The first was to a men's clothier, where he purchased several dollars' worth of presentable traveling clothes in sizes that he estimated would fit Jeremiah. He did this before he was absolutely sure that Jeremiah would be willing, or able, to accompany him.

He then spent an hour in the Henrico County Courthouse, watching carefully as a clerk transcribed lines onto a document and curious onlookers cast him expressions ranging from amazed puzzlement to unconcealed hostility.

Finally, he stopped by the Danville railroad depot, located where Fourteenth Street terminated at the toll bridge, and purchased two tickets for Wilmington, North Carolina.

The train was scheduled to depart in the late afternoon. By half past four, Jonathan and Jeremiah had signed out of their hotel and were standing on the platform, two new suitcases neatly placed beside them. Jeremiah, attired in a new gray suit and matching derby, somehow managed to look uncomfortable and distinguished at the same time.

The slave spoke quietly to Jonathan, so as not to be overheard by the other passengers who were congregating.

"Mind, I don't wish to seem disrespectful, Jonathan," he said, "but I'm a-gettin' a bit curious as to where we might be a-goin' on this here railroad."

"We're going to Wilmington, Jeremiah. At least I am. Whether or not you go along with me depends on you."

"Why, what would you mean? You're my..."

"I'm your owner, I know, but the choice is still yours. I've already told you that you won't be getting many orders from me."

Jeremiah looked at him as if regarding a raving lunatic. "Why of course I'm a-goin' with you! You're gonna need me to help find Miss Appy, Jonathan. How could you think of—"

"I knew you'd come, but all the same, it has to be your choice, not mine. And I have to tell you, Wilmington won't be the end of the trip. It'll be just the beginning. We'll be going a lot farther, mostly by sea."

A momentary expression of concern crossed Jeremiah's face, but it was soon pushed aside by one of determination. "I ain't afraid of no ocean, Jonathan. You know I done made that trip on the big lake up in Michigan, that stormy, stormy night. Why, I'd walk right on through Lucifer's fiery gates if that's where you was a-headed."

"I know that, and God bless you for it, Jeremiah, because I'm sure I'm going to need your help."

"You're gonna have it!"

Jonathan smiled at the man, realizing that he no longer thought of him as Apollonia's slave nor as a mere source of important information. Jeremiah had become a friend—the only real friend he had in this tumultuous time.

He decided that now was the moment to bring up something important.

"I find it amazing, Jeremiah," he said, looking him in the eyes, "that you're able to read."

Jeremiah started, as if someone had just caught him stealing. The expression on his face was one of pure guilt.

"You didn't think I knew that, did you?" Jonathan continued. "Want to know how I figured it out? You knew Silas Demby's name. You read the nameplate on his mailbox."

Jeremiah sighed deeply. He took out one of his new handkerchiefs and ran it over his forehead.

"Lord Almighty," he almost whispered. "I should've known you'd be smart enough to figure that out."

"You act like it's a crime."

Jeremiah took a step closer and lowered his voice. "Where I come from, Jonathan, it just about *is* a crime. Us colored folks ain't supposed to be doin' no readin'. That's called uppity down here, and that's bad, bad stuff. I've known men who was hung from trees for knowin' how to read."

"Who taught you?"

He hesitated and then relented.

"Miss Appy did."

"Apollonia?"

"She started to teachin' me the letters when she just barely knew 'em herself. Out in Massa Foley's barn, in the evenings. She kept it secret from her momma and daddy, God bless her sweet soul, and she put up with poor old stupid Jeremiah for years, Jonathan—for *years*—until I could read nigh as well as she."

"Why?"

"I've wondered about that myself, yes, I have, plenty of times. But I don't know why. I just knows that she did."

Jonathan put a hand on Jeremiah's shoulder and led him to an empty corner of the platform. He took a folded document from the inner pocket of his coat.

"So, since you're a literate man, Jeremiah, why don't you read this?"

The slave looked nervously at the paper and then back at Jonathan. Finally, he unfolded it and examined it, taking in the county clerk's beautiful penmanship in deep blue ink. He started with the oversized writing at the top, reading slowly but articulating the words carefully.

"Certificate of Manumission," he read and then stopped. "That's a word I don't know, Jonathan."

"Keep reading."

"State of Virginia, Henrico County, thirtieth day of August in the Year of Our Lord, 1864. This is to certify, to whom it may concern, that I, Jonathan Chase, temporarily a resident of the City of Richmond in the State of Virginia, do manumit and set free my Negro, Jeremiah, who is of the approximate age of . . ."

He stopped reading and stared wide-eyed at the script, his hand beginning to tremble.

"Do manumit and set free . . . ," he repeated and then looked up at Jonathan. Tears were forming in his eyes.

"Jonathan?"

"Yes?"

"This means . . . why, this means . . ."

"It means that as of this morning, Jeremiah, you are a freeman. This makes it binding and legal—signed by me, sealed by the justice of the peace, and witnessed by two citizens of Virginia. You're not a slave anymore, not here, not anywhere."

Jeremiah shakily clasped the document to his chest and closed his eyes. Jonathan couldn't tell whether his posture was one of joy or of agony. The tears that rolled down his cheeks might have signified either.

He held that static stance for a long time. Finally, after Jonathan noticed that people were beginning to stare, he tapped Jeremiah on the shoulder.

"Yes, Jonathan?"

"Are you all right?"

Jeremiah opened his eyes at last. His set expression softened into a subtle smile.

"Why, I think I'm just fine, Jonathan," he said, faintly at first, his voice rising as he spoke.

"I think...why, I think the sweet Lord Jesus just answered the prayer I've been sayin' since I was a little boy. I want to shout hallelujah just as loud as I can, I want to dance like a wild man right here on these bricks, I want to get down on my knees and thank the Lord till he's done sick and tired of hearin' old Jeremiah pray!"

People began once more to stare at him, and then the subtle smile left Jeremiah's face. What took its place was a look of bewilderment—the awestruck gaze of a man realizing that his life has suddenly taken a very dramatic and irreversible turn.

"And at the same time," he said, taking hold of Jonathan's arm as if seeking support, "why, I'm just plum terrified all the way down to my poor old bones."

September

The time that arrives is like burgundy wine,

Mellow and tart and sharply defined.

The sun is gold copper seeking a rest,

Twilight falls hazily on the harvest.

Cool winds and warm softly blend in the sky,

Rustling the trees and making them sigh.

Today, I sigh like those sloughing trees, dear reader, and lament the coming of the autumn. Its early stages are so bittersweet to me. It is so sweet and so sad all at once, like one of those ancient Irish songs about lost love and tragic death.

Of late, I have been thinking a great deal about death. I have contemplated my own death in a macabre way, which is to say that when I picture it, I do not dread or fear it. I see myself, rather, as welcoming it, as longing for the release from trouble and grief I believe it must grant. This is not healthful or wholesome—my stars, I can almost hear my mother saying those very words!—yet I no longer care. In this forsaken house in this doomed city, in this cursed silence and gloom, I see myself as one of those tragic wives whose sailor husbands have been lost at sea. Like them, I peer into the indeterminate distance from my lonely perch upon the lofty widow's walk, searching in vain for a lover who will never return.

For I have come to believe that Jonathan will never return to me. I believe that he has died in one way or another. Either he has perished at the barrel of some soldier's gun or he has abandoned me, ceased to have faith in my love for him, in which case he is dead to me and I to him. He is not coming, either because he cannot or will not. I know this, and still I wait and watch for him, still I remain a Nantucket widow on her vain and lonely vigil.

Enough of such pathos! Are not the sufferings of thousands worth a thousand times my own? The news arrived today that Atlanta has fallen to Sherman.

The dispatches say that it has been a terrible time for them. The Confederates, in their retreat, sought to destroy their own munitions by setting them afire, but the untended fires have grown out of control, and now the entire city may be in peril of the blaze. Thousands of people are said to have been displaced from their homes or are fleeing in terror or worse even than that.

Here in Charleston, one can almost hear this city's own shock and dread. One can almost feel a mighty tremble in its very streets as it contemplates the fate of great Atlanta. Can Charleston be far behind?

And how far behind is Savannah?

Of course, I have had no communication with my parents and can only imagine the fears they must be suffering to know that the enemy has drawn so close. It is widely accepted, here and elsewhere, that Sherman's next target will be Savannah by the sea. There are few forces left to resist him, and I cannot help but envision the sight of Bluefield as torches are thrown through the windows of its fair house, as mounted troops destroy and defile its fertile fields. Nor can I help but think of Mother and Papa as they flee in panic in their carriage, the sounds of battle roaring all around them.

Yet what can I do to help them? How can I spare them such a fate, when I am trapped in my present circumstance? And how can I live with the awful irony of knowing that this very circumstance has been brought about, more than anything else, by my desire to protect them? It is maddening beyond words!

One by one, our cities fall. One by one, our tragedies unfold. What I am seeing—what all those who are willing to confront the truth are seeing—is the collapse of a dream.

It is a spectacle to rend the heart, yet I must face a solemn truth. I have come to doubt the dream itself. I find I no longer fear for the South, nor do my tears fall for its inevitable demise. Yes, I fear for my parents and for my home, yet I find that the patriotism that once stirred within my heart, the Southern spirit which once I voiced as loudly and proudly as everyone else, no longer burns within me.

I question why the South is fighting with such stubborn ferocity.

Is it for honor? I do not diminish honor. I think honor is a fine thing, but at what price? When thousands upon thousands of boys have already died, when many thousands more are bound to die so long as this war continues—and when defeat looms larger and more certain with each passing day—is honor a sufficient justification? When does honor become foolishness? When does it become madness?

Or is this war strictly for the sake of slavery? If this is the heart and soul of the Southern cause, then I can no longer lend my voice to the chorus. I have questioned slavery once, as I have written before, and have discovered that, once questioned, the debate is already over. These past days, listening to the sounds of the slave market nearby, I have sought to justify it in my own heart. I have striven to find that ethic or moral or belief which would somehow make it right and good—but find that I cannot. I cannot picture a God who would bless such a practice, and if I am wrong—if He does—then I want no part of such a God.

In the end, it is this: Jonathan is right. And although enough stubborn chauvinism still remains in my Southern soul to wince when I say it, I must say it: Lincoln himself is right. U.S. Grant—even the dreadful Sherman—is right. Slavery is wrong. It is a crime and a sin. It must end. The sooner the better.

How can I endorse that which forced me to do what I did to Jeremiah? How can I favor that institution which produced such a demon as Archer Blaine?

I can no longer favor it, and will not, yet for all my noble words, I cannot escape the dreadful hypocrisy of my own position. In the end, my newfound opposition to slavery is as worthless as the Confederate money that flows like water from Richmond. If I continue on the path I tread today—and there remains naught to deter me or save me from it—I shall become the greatest heroine that slavery has ever known.

SEPTEMBER

WILMINGTON

IT WAS A JOURNEY OF SMOKE.

The small but determined locomotive that pulled the five-car passenger train over the Richmond and Danville's erratic and choppy roadbed was a wood burner. At every point of acceleration or climb, great billows of acrid smoke plumed from its wide stack, engulfing and shrouding the train behind it. Before long, the passengers smelled as if they had spent the night next to a campfire.

More smoke invaded from outside, where the lowland farmers were burning what remained of their recently harvested corn crops. Here and there—beyond a woods or rise—were the dirty bluish smudges that Jonathan suspected marked military engagements—brief and violent cavalry skirmishes, perhaps, or the opening salvos of something more substantial.

Military activity was omnipresent around the railroad. Patrols rode back and forth along the frontage roads that paralleled it, and all of the depot platforms bore a contingent of armed troops, whether in transit or serving as security it was impossible to tell. At least half of the passengers on the train's rickety cars were soldiers. Despite their obvious fatigue, they all seemed to carry an air of edgy tension, as if the enemy could be expected to emerge without warning from any copse of trees along the way. Their unease communicated to the other travelers, most of whom kept silent, their noses buried in newspapers or books.

Filtered through the smoky haze, the harvest moon that rose full over the eastern twilight was abnormally corpulent and tinted a ruddy burnt orange that seemed unnatural to Jonathan.

It was only about two hundred miles from Richmond to Wilmington, but because of the condition of the roadbed, the train was doing little better than ten miles an hour on many stretches. It had been a long, hot journey, and Jonathan was eager to reach their destination.

The presence of Jeremiah beside him obviously made several of their fellow passengers uncomfortable. Jonathan had been able to procure a seat for Jeremiah only after showing his manumission papers. It was far from customary for black people, even free ones, to ride in the same cars as whites, and it was possible now only because Jonathan had bribed the station agent with a hefty tip.

"And you're on your own once you're aboard the train," the agent had warned. "I guarantee you the folks won't much care for it."

But aside from a few hushed mutterings, in which the word "nigger" was audible, and the fact that they were surrounded by several empty seats, the others in the car seemed too somber or preoccupied to pay Jeremiah much mind. Jonathan got the impression that the Virginians and Carolinians, and perhaps all Southerners, were already becoming accustomed to the inevitable disintegration of their culture's system of racial castes, even though the war was not yet lost.

Jonathan and Jeremiah spoke quietly as the light dimmed. Soon it was dark outside, and a conductor lit a single weak gas lamp near the front of the car.

"Does it bother you when people call you names like that?" Jonathan half-whispered.

"Why should it bother me? It's what I been hearin' my whole life, Jonathan. It's just the way things are."

"I don't believe that. It must hurt."

Jeremiah turned and looked closely at Jonathan. In his gray suit and derby, he appeared dignified, like a retired doctor or somebody's kindly grandfather. He looked his age, not that of an overgrown boy, which is how most slaves appeared, no doubt a result of the regard in which they were collectively held and the lack of respect they were shown. And it was more than the clothes. The manumission itself—the hard fact of his newfound freedom—seemed to have straightened Jeremiah's back, quickened his step, and sharpened his eye. He was even beginning to speak differently. The timber of his voice was growing deeper and more sonorous than it had been, and his speech was already losing some of its slavish tone and syntax. He was taking apparent care to enunciate his words and eliminate some of the most obvious mannerisms associated with slaves. It had been two days since he'd mistakenly called Jonathan "sir" or "massa."

"It hurts, Jonathan," he replied at last. "Sure it hurts. Do you think a man who is a slave has no self-respect, no pride? Do you think he is born without those things or loses them by the way he is raised as a little child?"

"I didn't...," Jonathan began.

"I don't mean nothin' about you, Jonathan, Lord forbid. But there's no way you can understand the way such words hurt a man. Only a slave can understand what I'm talking about. A man or a woman gets used to it, sure enough. You hear it so many times, it's almost like you can't hear it at all, but never so's you become deaf to it. You always hear it, and it always hurts."

"What about the other kind of hurt? The whips, the beatings..."

"Thank Jesus, Jonathan, I never had too much of that. Massa...I mean, Mr. Foley, he was a pretty fair boss, most of the time. But nigh all us men got it, one time or another, and sometimes the women, too. There was two or three times, when I was younger, Mr. Foley took the whip to my back. Still got the scars to show for it."

"What was it for?"

"Stealin' apples one time, forgettin' to slop the pigs another."

Jonathan winced.

"How did Apollonia feel about that?"

"Miss Appy, why, she was a little girl, just about nine, the last time I was put on the post. Bless her sweet child's soul, she came out to the quarters that very night, put Cloverine salve on old Jeremiah's back. She has a heart of pure gold, that one, not like her daddy at all."

"But did she think it was right for her father to have that done to you?"

Jeremiah gave Jonathan another direct look. There was a spark of defiance in his eyes that Jonathan hadn't seen before.

"Why you want to know such things about the woman you got a fancy for?"

"It's important for me to know, Jeremiah, that's all."

He sighed. "Okay. Little Miss Appy, she understood that whippin's was just the natural course of things, not only out to our plantation but everywhere. White men get mad about somethin', black men get the whip. It's just the way it is. I recall she told me I was wrong to do whatever I did and that I had to get punished for it, and she hoped I didn't mind it too much. But even as she was speakin' to me, she put that salve on my back, easin' the worst of that pain, Jonathan, and it's acts that count to a man—acts, not words. Far as I'm concerned, Miss Appy's just about the same thing as an angel."

The train crawled past a depot. At least a dozen infantrymen in gray uniforms lounged on the platform, smoking and joking with each other.

"And how do you feel about that?" Jonathan asked, pointing to the soldiers.

"You mean the war?"

"Yes. You say that getting whipped is just the way it is, but that won't be true any longer when—I mean, if—the North wins," Jonathan attempted to correct himself, though he was sure most of his contemporaries likely saw the writing on the wall.

Jeremiah replied indirectly. "What's that word, Jonathan, for somebody who always thinks everything's gonna work out all right?"

"An optimist?"

"That's it. That's what you are, an optimist. You think all this is gonna be over once the Rebels are driven down. Well, some of it will be, true enough. I reckon some things will get easier, in time, but these white folks ain't gonna stop hatin' us just because Abe Lincoln says they oughta. They're gonna be hatin' us for many years to come and probably whippin' and killin' us, too. You can slay an army with a better army, but the only way you get rid of hate is to wait for those a-carryin' it to crawl off and die."

Jonathan knew that Jeremiah was right. He knew how prophetic his words were. From his bizarre vantage point, he already knew what horrors loomed ahead for Southern blacks with Reconstruction, Jim Crow, and the imminent rise of the Ku Klux Klan. He knew what Billie Holiday was referring to when she sang about the "strange fruit" hanging from Dixie's trees and had early memories of a minister named King who would take a white man's bullet on a Memphis balcony, but he could speak of none of these things to Jeremiah. He silently wondered what life had in store for the remainder of Jeremiah's years.

"You're probably right" is all he could come up with. "It's going to be a rough ride."

"Yes, 'tis, Jonathan, but that don't mean it ain't worth it. The North is right to fight this war, and sweet Jesus bless ol' Abe Lincoln for wagin' it. I know that's so, because a very wise man, and a very good man, by the name of Frederick Douglass wrote it down in words that oughta be carved into every man's heart."

He straightened himself in his seat, adjusted his string tie, and began speaking, loud and clear, his accent authoritative and stentorian but still unmistakably black.

"Those who profess to favor freedom and yet deprecate agitation are men who want crops without plowing up the ground, they want rain without thunder and lightning. They want the ocean without the awful roar of its mighty waters. This struggle may be a moral one, or it may be a physical one, and it may be both moral and physical, but it must be a struggle. Power concedes nothing without a demand. It never did and it never will."

There was none of Jeremiah's customary bashfulness or self-abasement after he spoke. He glanced briefly at an amazed Jonathan and then steadily met the eyes, one by one, of the passengers who had lifted their faces from their reading to stare at this eloquent black man who spoke such words. The condescending contempt with which they'd first regarded him was gone. In its place was something that might have been surprise or fear or even respect.

Nearly a day later, the long-awaited announcement came from the conductor's lips, delivered in a prolonged, booming baritone: "Wilmington, North Carolina!"

It was a profound relief to disembark the train, to smell the cool salt air of the tidewater, to take breaths that did not have smoke as a major component. Jonathan and Jeremiah could see, even at the outskirts, that Wilmington was in much better shape than Richmond. There were no visible shantytowns for refugees, no columns of the walking wounded. Although there were plentiful soldiers about—and sailors, too, Jonathan noted—the military didn't seem nearly as omnipresent. The city had a cleaner, more functional appearance, a sense that although the war remained perilously near, it could still be ignored, at least for some of the time.

But Jonathan and Jeremiah, weary and sore, spent little time sightseeing. They arrived in the early afternoon and immediately took accommodations close by the depot. Jonathan procured a room in the hotel itself, and Jeremiah, in spite of his status as a freeman, was once again relegated to a separate structure out back where all black guests were obliged to stay. He assured Jonathan that he didn't mind.

They bathed, napped, and, by prior agreement, met in front of the hotel at five o'clock. In the refreshing air, they walked the relatively short distance to Water Street, downhill all the way to the banks of the Cape Fear River. They found the address Reginald had given Jonathan back in Richmond and were glad to see a lamp glowing in its window.

There was but one occupant in the tiny storefront, the window of which bore the name of an egg merchant, apparently a departed tenant. The man now present was corpulent and attired in a dark maritime uniform, the double row of brass buttons on his long coat conspicuously tracing the dramatic contour of his considerable belly. His black hair was long and curly, and his face seemed jovial, framed by plump cheeks adorned with luxuriously bushy sideburns.

"Help you?" he asked, not looking up from the logbook in which he was busily writing.

"We're interested in passage to Halifax," Jonathan announced.

The mariner didn't look up. "How many?"

"Two."

"When you planning on leaving?"

"Next ship out, if possible."

"It's possible. Tomorrow night too early for you?"

Jonathan felt a wave of relief. They were just in time.

"Not at all."

"And is two hundred bucks too much for you?" the man asked, still scribbling in his book with a long quill.

Jonathan paused only briefly. The sum was considerable, a full third of the money he had left, but he was determined to get to Halifax as soon as he could.

"Sounds fair."

"All right, then," the man said, surrendering his pen at last and wheeling his chair back to get a better look at his visitors. He held out a fleshy hand to Jonathan, introducing himself as George Wilkins, and then extended a hand for Jeremiah to shake. This was a surprise. Jonathan had been worried all the way to Wilmington that Captain Wilkins might have a problem with a black passenger. He was hoping desperately that the manumission papers would allow him to board, convinced that any captain who would try to smuggle a slave out of the CSA would be nothing less than foolhardy.

"He's a freeman," Jonathan volunteered, as Jeremiah pulled the document out of his coat pocket.

"Don't give a tinker's damn either way," Wilkins replied in a deep drawl, his hands now clasped across the girth of his abdomen. "Nor do I care about your political views."

"I thought that..."

"You thought that as a Confederate naval officer I wouldn't carry a slave, I know, and you'd be dead wrong. I've taken a good half dozen bona fide slaves out of here this summer alone. After all, I'm a runner. Contraband is my stock-in-trade. I don't care if you're free or slave, black or white, a tightfisted Scotchman or hard-drinking Dutchman, cracker Rebel or goddamned Yankee, so long as you've got the fare. Speaking of which, where's the money?"

Jonathan began counting out the proper number of gold coins. Wilkins watched carefully as they clinked into place.

"You understand there's no guarantees on this trip," he said. "There's a slew of Union gunboats out there, and they'll be doing their goddamned best to blow us out of the water. We'll have to get by the lookouts first, who will notify the armed blockaders at the mouth of the harbor that we're coming. If we manage to outrun the blockaders, we still might have to deal with the deepwater cruisers even farther out—they're fast and deadly, all of 'em under good skippers. Assuming we slip past those sons of bitches, and we're lucky afterwards, then we just might have clear passage up to Nova Scotia."

The captain paused, carefully scooped up Jonathan's gold, and methodically deposited it into an inner pocket of his coat.

"Just so you know, about one in four runners out of Wilmington is either captured or sunk," he continued, smiling as he spoke. "Should either of those things happen, it's your own responsibility. You don't get your money back if you have to make a swim for it, and you don't get your life back if you die trying."

He snickered at his own gallows wit.

"I understand the risks," Jonathan replied, "but I'm a little confused."

"Why might that be?"

"You're running blockades for the Confederacy. Your profession is the virtual lifeline of the South, and yet you're willing to help slaves escape? I don't understand."

Wilkins smiled and stroked his whiskers. He looked at Jonathan with an expression of patient pity, as if he were addressing a simpleton.

"It's not complicated, friend. I honor the laws I agree with, defy those with which I do not agree, which, to my way of seeing, is the finest expression of true American spirit. You're making the same mistake that lots of folks do, Northerners and Southerners alike, and that is the notion that this war is about slavery. I tell you, sir, that is not the case. It's about one region imposing its will on another, one way of life seeking to obliterate another. Personally, I think slavery is despicable. I wouldn't own a slave if I were the richest man in the South, nor would I blame any black man for wanting to escape it, but I'll be damned if I'll let a bunch of abolitionist do-gooders from up North dictate how things should be run down here. It's about rights, sir, rights and honor. I see no contradiction at all."

"And that's why you risk your life running blockades—to defend the South's honor?"

"Yes, sir, that's right, but there are other advantages. There's the money for one thing, a nice percentage of which goes to me." He jingled the recently procured gold in his pocket and smiled the wide smile of an adventurer.

"That and the fact that it's one hell of a lot of fun."

Even at a dead stop, securely roped to the Wilmington pier, the *Mirage* looked fast. She was a long, sleek coal burner, shallow of draft and narrow of deck with a large, businesslike sidewheel, upon the wooden cover of which her name was painted in carnival letters. A Confederate navy jack flew from her stern.

It was dusk on the following night, and Jonathan and Jeremiah stood gazing at her two smokestacks, tilted toward the stern to offer less wind resistance and present a lower profile. The engines whose smoke went through those stacks were only part of her propulsion. The *Mirage* was also fitted with two tall masts, one fore and one aft, canvas at the ready. That she was built for speed—and her extremely low profile a means of avoiding cannon shot—was obvious even to a layman like Jonathan.

He had already learned that the ship, as usual, was hauling a substantial load of recently harvested Mississippi cotton within its slender but surprisingly commodious hull.

"Perfect night for a run," came the voice of Wilkins behind them. "New moon and not a cloud in the sky. It'll be blacker than the ace of spades out there."

He paused and turned to Jeremiah. "No offense to you intended at all, sir," he said with a grin and a short bow that immediately earned a bemused smile in return.

"Follow me, mates, we're going to Halifax."

They boarded behind the obviously energized and enthused Wilkins. An armed sailor guarding the gangplank saluted the captain and nodded at the passengers. Like all the crew, he was dressed in civilian nautical garb. Only Wilkins wore an actual naval uniform.

Jeremiah, perhaps remembering the nightmarish trip on Lake Huron in the spring, immediately headed for the tiny passenger cabin to which he and Jonathan had been assigned. His fear of the sea and the ships that sailed it hadn't changed a whit since then, and he begged Jonathan's pardon as soon as they got on board. Jonathan told Jeremiah that he would join him when the ship was safely out to sea, provided it achieved that objective, and Wilkins allowed Jonathan to accompany him to the wheelhouse, "just so long as you realize that the bridge is the favored target of the Yanks."

There was a half-hour delay as the crew made ready. The acrid but sweet smell of coal smoke pervaded the night air as the fires were stoked high in preparation for the run. Both Wilkins and the helmsman, the only two men besides Jonathan in the low but spacious wheelhouse, were itching to make way.

"Ordinarily, I try to join up with a pack of runners out of Wilmington," the captain explained as they waited. "Going out with others raises the odds of making a clean break. Unfortunately for us, no other ship is ready tonight, so we'll have to make a go of it alone. Still, I'm convinced tonight is the right night. The Yanks will be on their toes, I'm sure, but my hunch is that the stars are lined up just right for us."

At half past eight, in near total darkness, the *Mirage* was ready to go. The helmsman gently steered the ship away from the pier and nosed her downriver into the Cape Fear's strong current. The lights of Wilmington slowly passed by as the captain gave his helmsman occasional reminders about sandbars and shallows.

The first leg of the trip was uneventful. The ship slipped into inky shadows at the edge of town and made steady progress toward the sea. Less than an hour after starting out, Wilkins ordered a reduction in speed. A large light loomed dead ahead.

"That's Smith Island," Wilkins announced to Jonathan. "There's a signal station there that will let us know whether it's best to try the New Inlet or the Western Bar, the two forks that lead to open water. It depends on which one the Yanks are concentrating on most tonight."

He shouted out the porthole to his boatswain. "Give 'em our name and request directions!" he boomed. In a minute, the crewman was using a covered lantern to send his message to the island. In short order, a flashing light began blinking back. Wilkins read the reply himself.

"Western Bar it is, then," he said, nudging the helmsman.

In the darkness, it was difficult for Jonathan to determine even the direction in which the *Mirage* was being steered, but the captain and his quartermaster seemed unconcerned with such blind piloting. They showed no signs of nervousness, yet a certain quiet intensity in their manner suggested that the ship was nearing a moment of truth.

At one point, the captain pointed into the gloom. "Anchored right about there, just off the island, is the CSS *North Carolina,* one of our ironclads. She doesn't do much but sit around and wait, her guns loaded and ready, just in case one of the Yanks tries to poke around upriver. Too bad it's so dark—she's a sight to see. Speaking of which..."

Wilkins popped his head out of the wheelhouse porthole and shouted another order to the boatswain. "Light's out!" he commanded. "Time to go dark!"

Almost immediately, the half dozen lanterns and mast lights aboard the *Mirage* were extinguished. The crew also grew quiet, speaking to one another only in low, hushed tones. The groans and creaks of the *Mirage's* timbers soon became the only regular sound. That and the darkness contributed to an atmosphere of tense suspense as the ship prowled forward, a black smudge on an even blacker canvas.

They proceeded in this manner for nearly an hour, during which Jonathan eventually began distinguishing shapes. He could barely make out the bulky profile of Smith Island, now mostly behind them, and he thought he could see a murky shape to their front. It looked like a small ship.

"Is that...," he whispered to Wilkins.

"Yes, that's one of the lookouts," he replied quietly. "She doesn't see us yet, because we've got the shoreline behind us, but she will in short order. She won't engage us directly but will signal the big boys, the blockaders, a little farther out. I'm hoping there's only one or two of those out there."

Wilkins spent the next few minutes keeping a careful eye on the dim profile of the lookout and occasionally glancing at his pocket watch. Jonathan wondered how he was able to see the hands.

He finally snapped the watch's lid shut for the last time. "It's time. She's spotted us by now," he announced and once again stuck his head out the porthole. When he spoke, he made no attempt to keep his voice quiet.

"Rocket up!" he ordered. "Indicate due southeast."

The unseen crewman on deck had hardly replied "Aye, aye," when a deafening whooshing sound filled the ship, along with the painfully brilliant white light of what appeared to be a phosphorus flare. It streaked up from the deck of the *Mirage,* achieving a remarkable altitude very quickly, and arced directly toward the southeast.

A few moments later, the indistinct outline of the Union lookout vessel sent up its own rocket. It was identical in color and intensity, but it had been aimed eastward, an indication of the *Mirage's* true course. The vivid trails of both rockets were plainly visible in the sky, their conflicting directions seeming to cross at one point.

"What timing, by God!" Wilkins boomed.

"What is this all about?" a fascinated Jonathan asked.

"It's all misdirection, Mr. Chase, good old-fashioned misdirection. You see, as soon as they spot us, the lookouts reveal our presence to the blockaders with a rocket. The direction in which the rocket is fired tells the blockaders what our course is, which gives them a head start in heading us off. However, since there were two rockets fired tonight, I've forced the blockaders to choose. Which rocket should they believe? Well, my thinking is that they're more likely to trust the first one up—which happened to be ours, by Lucifer!—and that will send them dashing off in the direction of the Caribbean or thereabouts. Oh, they'll realize their mistake soon enough, but believe me, minutes count in this business. All the *Mirage* needs is a neat little head start, and the most they'll taste of us is a whiff of smoke."

"That's absolutely ingenious!" Jonathan exclaimed.

"Why thank you, sir," the captain said, turning to smile at his excited guest. "Such methods are precisely why the sons of bitches have yet to take me down."

But the chase was not yet over. Although Wilkins ordered full speed ahead and sails up as soon as the rocket was fired, his own watchman—armed with telescopes high in the ship's main mast—soon reported trouble.

"Man-of-war off the starboard in full sail!" the watchman shouted down. "She's coming about now, changing her mind—got a fix on us for sure. She's a big one! Looks like twelve guns!"

The captain, with Jonathan close behind, had gone out on the starboard deck for a better look. Above them, a reeking cloud of the ship's black smoke belched from the pounding engine, forming a plume that had to be obvious to any pursuer, even under these dark conditions.

"How's her canvas look?" the captain shouted back up.

"Hard to see," the lookout replied, "but it looks like she's picking up some breeze. She's making headway!"

The captain extended his own telescope to assess the situation. "We're lucky we diverted them as long as we did. There's not much wind, but that son of a bitch will be close," he conceded, offering the telescope to Jonathan.

With his eyes now fully accustomed to the blackness and aided by the scope's magnification, Jonathan could make out the shadowy blockader surprisingly well. It was an impressive vessel, tall and proud, its huge sails bulging forward, prow rising and falling with the waves. Despite its deadly intent, the ship was beautiful. It seemed to Jonathan a gallant and ghostly image from a Stevenson story or Wyeth illustration, even though he knew perfectly well that there was nothing fictional about it.

The pursuit was heated and lasted more than an hour. As Wilkins directed the *Mirage* on a more northeasterly course, putting the pursuer more or less directly behind them, the Union warship pressed on. It was clearly gaining on the runner at first, drawing so near at one point that it could be seen in the starlight with the naked eye.

But as the wind slackened, the sailing vessel began to lose pace to the steamer. As if sensing the change and growing desperate, the warship fired two shots.

Jonathan saw the orange flashes of its forward guns, heard their echoed booms and then, a few seconds later, faint splashes as the balls fell impotently into the water far behind them. The crewmen of the runner cheered at the sound.

It was the blockader's final and futile attempt to take the *Mirage*. Realizing that its prey was already out of range and steadily gaining distance, the Union commander called off the chase. Standing at the stern rail, peering through the lens of Wilkins's telescope, Jonathan watched it disappear into the night.

"It's gone," he said to the captain. "You've lost them."

"Yes, I have," the smiling captain replied, his pudgy hands intertwined across the straining buttons of his coat. "And the United States Navy may once again kiss Captain George Wilkins's fat Southern ass."

The first hurdle had been overcome, but the crew of the *Mirage* remained tense and vigilant throughout the night. They worried that the ship might still be spotted and assailed by one of the oceangoing cruisers, the formidable third line of the Union blockade. The cruisers were bigger, faster, and considerably better armed than the blockaders, and no runner desired a showdown with them, Wilkins assured Jonathan.

But no cruisers materialized. The *Mirage*, running steadily on steam, passed the rest of the first night unmolested. When the sun rose the next morning, no land was visible to the west, no sails appeared on any horizon, not a cloud marred a perfect azure sky.

Wilkins finally turned the bridge over to his first mate. He paused on the deck to speak with Jonathan, offering the encouraging thought that once the ship was in deep water, the chances of running into a Union warship diminished dramatically.

"Sons of bitches are all busy close by the coast," he explained. "No time to go wandering the Atlantic looking for a lost needle in a haystack."

The captain paused. "Might not be so easy once we get to Halifax, though. Union navy's all in a tizzy over the *Tallahassee* incident a few weeks back. She's a raider out of our own home port, Wilmington. Had a great couple of weeks hitting Union merchants along the seaboard—gave them absolute hell. Well, she had the Yanks on her tail all the way up to Halifax, and two of them, the *Nansemond* and the *Huron*, decided to drop anchor and wait outside the main channel of the harbor. The *Tallahassee* had to fuel up, you see, and the Brits only let us belligerents stick around for forty-eight hours, so the Yanks figured they'd blow her out of the water just as soon as she nosed out of the harbor. But they didn't give enough respect to my good buddy John Taylor Wood, the skipper—grandson of old Zachary Taylor, no less, and the nephew of Jeff Davis to boot. He slipped his big boat out by night, squeaking her through the Eastern Passage on the far side of McNabs Island. I guess he could've spit to shore—that's how tight that inlet is—but somehow the *Tallahassee* found the draft. By the time the Yanks knew what was up, John was halfway to Cape Cod."

Wilkins took in a deep breath of the fresh air and laughed with full satisfaction. "Now that's what I call a sailor, by God!" he thundered, slapping Jonathan on the back.

His mirth expelled, the mariner yawned. "Time for forty winks, mate. I suggest you do the same." He headed for his cabin.

But Jonathan was not yet ready for sleep. He leaned against the rail near the prow, taking in the cool sea air, feeling the salty breeze toss his long hair behind him. He realized that the anxiety of the previous night was not the reason for his restlessness. He was anticipating Halifax and what—and whom—he might encounter there.

Silas Demby's revelations about Blaine, as limited as they were, nonetheless pointed in an unmistakable direction. The man was involved in, or seeking to become involved in, something important. It involved no less than Great Britain's secret envoy to the Confederacy. Jonathan could only wonder at the nature of the business these two men might have together and what role Apollonia could possibly play in it. He also wondered about the stakes of his intervention in that business, not only to Apollonia and himself, which were obvious to him, but to the war itself. He sensed in his bones that Blaine was stirring something big, seeking to do something that might tilt the heavily lopsided balance of power in the South's favor.

Only then did the thought strike him: What about history itself?

He was astonished that he hadn't thought of it before. He had been a resident of 1864 for more than eight months, and it had never crossed his mind that all along he had been in a position of awesome power. He had been so preoccupied with the strangeness of his presence here, and so obsessed with Apollonia, that he hadn't even considered the titanic implications of that presence.

From his perspective as a man of the future, he knew precisely how the Civil War would end and what would follow in its bloody wake. He knew that the Confederacy had only eight months left before Grant and Sherman finally squeezed it to death. He knew that much of Richmond—the city he had so recently departed—would burn to ashes and that the legendary man who led the Union would, also in eight months, die when an assassin's bullet crashed into his skull.

But these things had yet to happen.

What if Archer Blaine's mysterious campaign in Halifax was somehow transformed by the involvement of a time-traveling intruder, and what if that altered a crucial detail in that nebulous concept the science fiction writers call the time line? What if it changed the way things were by changing things that were yet to be?

And it didn't end there, not by a long shot. What if Jonathan were to travel to Washington sometime between now and next April and seek out an actor by the name of John Wilkes Booth? What if he were to murder this man before he could murder Lincoln or warn Lincoln not to attend the theater on a certain fateful night?

For that matter, what would happen, in twenty-five years or so, if he were to travel to a little town in Austria and locate the boy who would one day grow up to become Adolf Hitler? What if Jonathan was able to strangle that innocent little boy? Would the lives of millions be spared? Would the chaotic violence of the next century—the tortured agonies of his own time—be averted if this one man, this one unexplained interloper, were to take these or any of a thousand other actions?

"My God," Jonathan muttered into the sea breeze. The realization pressed his brain like a vise clamping his skull.

From the fiction he had read and the *Twilight Zone* reruns he'd watched, he knew all the proverbial warnings. He knew that those who speculate on such matters seem to agree that a time traveler who seeks to change the course of history is embarking on a doomed mission, that history will have its way regardless, no matter how strenuous the effort.

While that idea might be dismissed as fanciful, Jonathan did know this: That even if an attempt at alteration were to succeed, there was no way to predict what course history might *then* take, no way to forecast what new, as yet unseen, horrors might unfold as a result of averting others. There was no guarantee that removing one human source of evil would result in peace or goodness, no guarantee that the traumas of an altered time line would be any less than those of the original.

Jonathan realized with a violent start that he held in his hands a terrible, godlike power, and at virtually the same moment, he knew that he could not, would not, use it. He would never seek out that Austrian boy, never pay a visit to Mr. Lincoln or Mr. Booth in Washington, never do any of the myriad other things that he could easily imagine. Such power was lightning itself, and an instinct from somewhere deep in his heart warned him against seeking to control such forces.

Except for one.

He would not surrender his pursuit of Apollonia.

He felt sure that the purpose of his presence in this century, and perhaps the reason for his survival once he got here, was her. They had been drawn together across the mighty currents of time itself. He had no idea whether there was a mystical purpose to this, or even any sort of logical reason, but he was sure that they were meant to be together. That overflowing conviction was the only sure thing, the only absolute reality, he had known since that frigid morning when he awoke in a Michigan snowbank.

That power, Jonathan knew, he would not—and could not—surrender. And if his efforts to regain her, and to save her from whatever perils she faced, were somehow to shift the awesome pillars of time itself, then so be it.

On the second day of the voyage, the *Mirage* crossed from the pale ultramarine of the open ocean into the deep cerulean of the Gulf Stream. With the strong current beneath her, the ship immediately picked up speed, and the stream's winds soon had her sails cracking smartly. The weather remained fair.

At Jonathan's insistent urging, Jeremiah finally emerged from the claustrophobic confines of the small passenger cabin, located below the forecastle. He had spent the first two days of the trip in what appeared to be a virtual state of stasis, eating nothing, drinking very little, his body curled into a fetal position on his bunk. Jonathan assured him that he'd feel better if he joined him on deck for a while.

They stood at the port rail as Jonathan pointed out the various sea creatures— dolphins, rays, even a few sharks—that were sharing the current with the *Mirage*. After a little while, Jeremiah began to appreciate the fresh breeze and endless vistas of water, although he kept a tight grip on the rail, as if not believing that this man- made structure was really capable of withstanding the powers of the sea.

"You ever been to Canada before?" he asked Jonathan, his eyes squinting against the sun.

"This will be my first time."

"Me neither. Never dreamt I'd be goin' there someday. I hears the name 'Halifax,' and it sounds like something on the other side of the world."

"Not that far," Jonathan assured him. "Only about a thousand miles from where we started."

"A thousand miles sounds like the other side of the world, too. You know, I was born at the Foleys' place down to Savannah, and ne'er once did I travel more than five or ten miles from it, not till Miss Appy and Jasper set off on that fool's errand up Michigan way last year. I'm thinking about how I've done more travelin' these past few months than my whole life before that."

"How are you liking it?"

Jeremiah gave Jonathan a bemused look. "Well, aside from survivin' some- how in that bone-chillin' northern winter, darn near takin' a bullet from Jasper one time, gettin' sold to that slave trader another time, gettin' bought by you, then gettin' freed by you, only to go to sea—which is scarier to ol' Jeremiah than any sort of spook or hoodoo you might find down in the Georgia swamps—why, I'd have to say I'm havin' the time of my life!"

They laughed together, realizing how frenzied and aimless and perilous their lives would look to any observer, including themselves.

"But I hope you don't mind me askin' you a question, Jonathan."

Jeremiah suddenly sounded earnest.

"You told me we're headed for Halifax, but you never told me why we're going there."

"That's where I think we'll find Apollonia."

"What makes you think so?"

"It was Silas Demby in Richmond, the man whose house you remembered. This comes from him. He told me that Blaine had gone to see him for only one reason—to determine when a British envoy named Covington would next be in Canada. Demby told Blaine that Covington would be in Halifax by late this month or early next. It only makes sense that Blaine is there, too, probably with Apollonia."

Jeremiah looked at Jonathan with a puzzled expression.

"Did you say the name Covington, Jonathan?"

"Yes. Why?"

"That wouldn't be a *Lord* Covington, would it?"

"It is Lord Covington, as a matter of fact."

"An Englishman?"

"Yes, a special envoy for Queen Victoria. He handles secret negotiations with the Confederacy, working from Canada. Why are you asking these questions?"

Jeremiah whistled long and low. His eyes held Jonathan's.

"I know who this man is, Jonathan. And Miss Appy, she knows him, too."

Jonathan stepped closer and put his hand on Jeremiah's shoulder, as if to steady himself. He felt his chest muscles tighten.

"Tell me what you know," he said quietly.

"It's been, oh, a few years now—maybe three years—since I saw him last. *Lord* Covington—that's what we had to call him—was workin' for some shipping company down to the Savannah River, if memory serves. Did a lot of business with the cotton and indigo men down there. He's an older sort of fellow, maybe thirty years older than Miss Appy, which is why I thought it a mite strange when he went a-courtin' her."

"Courting her!"

Jonathan practically shouted the words, attracting the stares of several sailors working nearby.

"Yes, and a-courtin' mighty persistent at that. He was one smitten fool, if ol' Jeremiah is any judge t'all. He was chums with her daddy, you see, did a lot of trade with him, shippin' his indigo back to England and such. This was before the blockades was set, maybe even before the war got started proper. Anyway, Lord Covington, he took to comin' around for all the dinners and parties the Foleys was so fond of havin', and it didn't take too long for poor Miss Appy to catch his eye. Once he got his mind set on her, he bought her nice things—diamonds, Jonathan, real fine diamonds that sparkled just like fire—to win her over. He did all sorts of favors for Miss Appy's daddy, helpin' him with good deals and such, all to win Miss Appy's hand."

Jeremiah paused and gazed at a streaking dorsal fin in the water below. Jonathan realized that he had the true raconteur's talent for timing and suspense.

"But he never did get that hand, no, sir," he continued at last. "Miss Appy, why she turned old Lord Covington down, cold and flat. She never took to him t'all, you see, even though her parents did their best to talk her into it. They kept tellin' her what a great thing it would be for the family if she was to go and marry him. But Miss Appy, she called Lord Covington a cold fish. Told me she'd sooner marry Abe Lincoln than that old snob—that was just the word she used."

Jonathan was able to speak a littler quieter now, his initial shock giving way to fascination. The murky outlines of a pattern were beginning to materialize.

"What happened to Covington?" he asked.

"Why, not long after Miss Appy told him no that last time—he asked her three times in all, you see—he took off. Left Savannah for good. I can't tell you where he went, but I guess it would be back to England."

"Can we be sure it's the same man?"

"No way to be sure about that, Jonathan, but I'd say it's likely he is, considerin' the sort of work he's doin' now and what he used to do down to Savannah."

Jonathan realized that Jeremiah was right. It had to be the same man.

"And how do you think Archer Blaine fits into all this?"

"Can't tell you that neither," Jeremiah replied. "Never saw those two together. I'm guessin' it was something like two years after Lord Covington left that Blaine showed up at the Foleys' place."

Jonathan secured his hat against the stiffening breeze and looked at the far blue horizon.

"So Blaine is headed for Halifax to meet with Covington or is already there, waiting for him to arrive. And Apollonia is with him. What does that tell us?"

Jeremiah finally let go of the rail and turned to Jonathan.

"It tells us there's a damn sight more to this situation than meets the eye."

On the sixth day of her voyage, the *Mirage* passed close by the mouth of the Bay of Fundy. It had grown a few degrees cooler with each day they traveled northward, reminding the passengers and crew that September really had arrived and that the summer waned with each fleeting mile. By the time they approached Nova Scotia, the air was nearly cold, and when it met the warm waters of the Gulf Stream, a great bank of fog enveloped the ship and the entire sea around it. They navigated on a distinctly northeasterly course now, steaming through an endless gauzy cloud that made one feel wet after standing on the deck for mere minutes.

Captain Wilkins, noticing how his two passengers shivered whenever they ventured from their cabin, made a present to them of musty, but blessedly warm, pea jackets. Jeremiah and Jonathan were wearing them, collars up, and standing near the wheelhouse when Wilkins beckoned them inside.

"Don't care much for this soup," he said as they entered. "We're still well away from the coast, which is my intent, for the rocks are horrendous closer in. Following the coast is perilous enough on clear days, but in this weather, it amounts to suicide. Won't add but six or seven hours to the trip. As it is, we should make Halifax before tomorrow's nightfall."

He turned to his guests. "I'll bet you boys are anxious to set your feet on solid land again."

"That will be a true comfort, sir," said Jeremiah, who in less than a week's time had taken a liking to the Confederate captain and spoke comfortably in his presence. "The sea just ain't my kind of place."

The captain chuckled. "And I can't imagine life without the sea. Take me away from the sea and it would be like clipping the wings of a bird."

"Will you stay long in Halifax?" Jonathan asked.

"Two days at most. That's all Queen Vicky will allow. My return load is already waiting on the dock—rifles and gunpowder. We'll load her up quick, then it's southbound once more and a return to blessed sunshine, by God! I love the sea, mates, but I don't know how these people can stand this clammy weather."

Their conversation continued in this comfortably mundane tone until it was time for supper. Jonathan and Jeremiah then returned to their cabin. Both of them read by soft candlelight until their fatigue—inspired mostly by boredom and the dreariness of the weather—eased them into sleep.

The next day was as foggy as the last, and it passed in much the same way, with the exception that they began to hear the faint cries of the foghorns, a sure sign that Wilkins's course was bringing the ship ever closer toward the harbor. Their mournful tones grew gradually louder, and by early evening the crew announced that they were seeing the first murky illumination of the coastal beacons.

As they drew near to the port, Wilkins ordered the Confederate colors stricken and the French tricolor raised in its place. It was a precautionary ruse, he told Jonathan, just in case Union warships were watching the harbor. Jonathan was fascinated with the contents of the case from which Wilkins withdrew the flag. In addition to France, there were at least half a dozen nations represented—Russia, Britain, Spain, even a homemade Jolly Roger.

"We're not very heavily armed," Wilkins explained a bit sheepishly, "but we've been known to play the part of privateer on occasion. The Roger adds a rather dramatic flair, don't you think?"

As the eventide became night, the harbor lights grew manifest at last. The captain's fears that the approaches to the harbor might be watched by enemy prowlers proved unfounded. None was visible. The *Mirage* steamed into Halifax, alone and unchallenged.

The fog was so thick that even the plentiful ships in port looked faint and ghostly. Of the city itself, Jonathan could see nothing more than the yellowish glow of windows in buildings; the structures themselves were invisible. Even the sounds of the shore—the occasional shouts of men, the barking of dogs, the bells of ships—came through soft and indistinct.

Jonathan watched as the crew prepared to throw the moorings and drop the anchor. He beheld the nearby street with its obscure shapes—men walking, casks, carts, large coils of rope—and shivered. He did not feel comfortable here. He was convinced that Apollonia was likely in the city, and felt confident of his chances of finding her, but felt none of the anticipatory joy he remembered from the first time he saw her. He still longed for her—ached for her—but he sensed hardship and danger. Regaining her would not be an easy task. He felt it in his stomach, along with a foreboding as deep and indefinable as the fog itself.

He heard the loud call of a man on the waterfront. The voice's owner wore a captain's cap and long leather coat and cupped his hands around his mouth as he shouted.

"Ahoy! Is that the ship of George Wilkins of Wilmington?"

Wilkins stepped out of the wheelhouse and peered at the hailer. He turned to Jonathan with a smile. "Jim Buskins, out of Charleston," he said.

"Wilkins it is!" he shouted back. "And how the hell are you, Buskins, you gunrunnin' son of a bitch?"

"Fit as a fiddle myself," the other captain shouted back. "And my ship's fine, too, but we've bad news from home!"

Jonathan heard Wilkins groan softly.

"What?" he yelled back.

"Atlanta fell to Sherman a week ago!" Buskins called out.

Jonathan looked at Wilkins as he received this news. The captain suddenly looked tired, somehow older. He ran his hand over his bushy hair and sighed. When he spoke, his voice had none of its customary jocular irreverence.

"Ah well, so it goes" he said quietly, watching his crew secure the ship. "Son of a bitch will turn east now, for sure. Savannah will be next."

The mention of Apollonia's hometown did not go unnoticed by Jonathan. He wondered if she had heard the news.

The farewells between passengers and crew were friendly but brief. Wilkins paused from giving orders to shake their hands—both Jonathan and Jeremiah— and looked grave as he said good-bye.

"I have no idea what sort of business brings you two to Halifax, and I know that it's none of my business at all," he said. "Just allow me to advise you that if it has anything to do with the rebellion, you had better do it quickly. Now that Atlanta has been taken, the dominoes will start to fall. This might even be my last trip up here. By next month, who knows? There might not be a Confederate port to dock in."

He made a weak effort to smile and slapped them on the back. "Good luck to you boys."

As they walked onto land, Jonathan and Jeremiah attracted little notice with bags in hand and peacoats on their backs. This was a bustling seaport. The masts of ships in the massive harbor were too many to count, and their flags heralded nations from all over the globe. Many of them Jonathan did not even recognize. Sailors and strangers were nothing unusual here.

Nor did the color of Jeremiah's skin seem to garner any special attention. The Canadians seemed as accustomed to black men as they were to mariners.

Jonathan checked them into a modest hotel named the Acadian two streets from the water, paying for separate rooms. He was pleasantly surprised when the clerk made no comment about Jeremiah's race and seemed totally oblivious to the fact. This hotel had no "colored quarters," and Jeremiah was treated with a level of respect he'd very seldom, if ever, encountered from white men. The clerk even said, "Thank you, sir," as he handed him the key to his room. Jeremiah beamed as they made their way upstairs.

"We'll rest tonight," Jonathan told him as he unlocked his door. "Tomorrow, we'll go to work."

"No argument from me," Jeremiah replied. "I'm looking forward to sleepin' in a bed that don't sway like my mama rockin' the cradle."

They laughed and said good night.

Jonathan took off his hat, coat, and shoes. He stretched out on the bed, clumsily rolled himself a cigarette, and lit it with a candle. He did not feel tired after the long journey nor relieved to be here. He was tense and anxious, keenly aware of his instincts growing taut and alert.

He retrieved the oval locket and snapped it open. The tiny image of Apollonia's face stared back at him, her enigmatic and melancholy expression as alluring as ever.

Jonathan wondered what expression might be on her face at this moment, perhaps very close to where he was now. He thought this and similar thoughts all through the long night, until the dawn finally awakened the foggy city by the sea.

For most of a week, Jonathan and Jeremiah walked the streets, covering so much ground that the city grew painfully familiar to them.

Halifax was too bustling and too utilitarian a place to be really pretty or graceful, but it did have a dusky sort of charm. Jonathan began thinking of it as "London West" for its distinctly English character, which went well beyond the dank maritime climate. The way the plaintive foghorns resounded through the hilly cobbled streets and dark Victorian architecture, the way the gaslight looked warm and inviting against the chilly fogs and mists were reminiscent to him of the London that Dickens and Doyle wrote about and that Jack the Ripper stalked.

Jonathan and Jeremiah operated separately, working out their respective assignments and routes each morning. Both knew all three of their targets—Apollonia, Blaine, and Jasper—and it was their faces that they sought. Since Jonathan felt confident that Blaine would not have been so sanguine as to register in a hotel or public house under their real names, he concluded that simple surveillance was the only realistic strategy.

The fact that both of their appearances had altered considerably—Jeremiah's by virtue of his dapper attire and Jonathan's by virtue of his long hair, beard, and dark spectacles—gave them an advantage. Jonathan hoped they would spot their prey and not be recognized in return, entertaining little doubt that such a covert approach would ultimately prove necessary.

They spent hours in public places—hotel lobbies, restaurants, railroad depots, taverns, stores, parks, the market, busy streets—hopeful that sooner or later a familiar face would appear. Jonathan was deliberate in not asking questions about those they were seeking. He suspected that Blaine and Jasper, both experienced in undercover work, possessed the skills to detect a tail careless enough to make open inquiries.

When Jonathan violated this rule, it was not by his own action, and despite his apprehension, it turned out to be fortuitous. He was spending the midafternoon in the plush lobby of the Halifax Hotel, reading a newspaper, surreptitiously glancing at each person who entered or left. It was his third visit to the hotel, one of the city's most popular, in as many days.

But it was quiet in the lobby that afternoon, and he was preparing to leave, planning to try his luck elsewhere. He didn't notice that the doorman had quietly approached him from behind the velvet sofa on which he was sitting.

The uniformed man spoke in a whisper directly into his ear.

"I might be able to help you find whom you're looking for," he said.

Jonathan started. "What do you mean? I'm not..."

The doorman held a finger to his lips. "Never mind that. I've seen you eyeing the guests for three days now. It's obvious what you're doing, and it's all the same to me."

Interested, Jonathan turned to face the man.

The doorman smiled and asked: "You American?"

Jonathan nodded.

"The city's crawling with Americans, Northern and Southern alike. You're a busy lot."

"That's true enough," Jonathan agreed.

He detected a pause in the doorman's manner and realized what he was waiting for. Jonathan discreetly placed a silver coin into his hand before continuing.

"I'm looking for three people," he whispered. "Two men, both in their thirties, and a woman, somewhat younger, who's traveling with them. They're all Southerners."

He elaborated on the physical descriptions of Blaine and Jasper and showed the doorman the portrait of Apollonia in the locket.

When he saw her, the doorman smiled.

"Oh, I've seen her all right," he said immediately. "No offense intended, but that's hardly a forgettable face, is it?"

"Well?"

The doorman paused again, significantly. Another coin was tendered.

"It happens to be your lucky day. They're here, all of them. Adjoining rooms on the top floor. Been here at least two weeks. Very quiet people. I've seen one of the men perhaps half a dozen times, the woman only once or twice. I see the other man—the short, dark one you described—every day. He goes out to the market for food and brings it back every afternoon."

Jonathan's heart raced. She was likely in the same building where he was sitting this moment, a few floors away. It was all he could do not to dash up the stairs and knock on her door—he imagined the look of surprise on her face as she opened it—but he kept a calm demeanor.

"When can I expect him to make his afternoon trip to market?" he asked.

The doorman looked at his watch. "He should be by in less than an hour, I would guess. Anything else I can help you with?"

Jonathan did not hesitate.

"Yes. I'd like a key."

The doorman stood erect, his half-smug expression suddenly serious.

"That's a pretty tall request."

"I promise that no harm will come to anyone. I'd just like to do a little... looking."

The doorman still hesitated, his indecision obvious.

Jonathan helped him out. The next coin he slipped into the doorman's palm was gold.

The man nodded and without another word reached into his waistcoat pocket. He shook Jonathan's hand, and in the grasp Jonathan felt the cold metal and unmistakable shape of a skeleton key.

"It's a master for the whole house," the doorman whispered. "You'll be wanting 405, the short man's room; 406, the tall man's room; and 407, the lady's room. I would appreciate your throwing the key into the harbor once you're finished with it."

"I will. Thank you," Jonathan said, rising to his feet.

The doorman returned to his post by the front entrance and held the door for Jonathan as he left. No further words passed between them.

Twenty minutes later, as he leaned against a lamppost across the street, Jonathan watched Malcolm Jasper walk through the same door. He was instantly familiar—the jutting cigar, the jaunty tilt of the derby, the swaggering hoodlum gait. He didn't so much as glance in Jonathan's direction as he passed.

Jonathan and Jeremiah continued their teamwork espionage but now with a specific target. Jonathan watched the Halifax Hotel by day, from dawn to dusk, and Jeremiah took over the vigil during the nocturnal hours. They did their best to remain inconspicuous during their watch, alternating between a loitering stance, leisurely strolls, and businesslike walks, keeping all the while within visible range of the main entrance, flanked by twin wooden columns and covered with a narrow porte cochère.

After several days and nights, Jonathan grew nervous and impatient. Some of the regulars who worked in the vicinity of the hotel seemed to have grown aware of their persistent presence, one of them the helmeted, stick-wielding constable who habitually spent his late afternoons near the entrance. Jonathan was grateful that so far neither the policeman nor anyone else had approached them, but he sensed it was only a matter of time before questions were asked.

Jasper left the hotel each afternoon like clockwork, departing between three and four o'clock. He spent an hour, apparently at the nearby market, and invariably returned with his arms full of some sort of victuals wrapped in brown paper. Jonathan never saw him speak to anyone, and from the way he kept his hat low over his forehead, it was apparent that Jasper was also being fastidious about keeping a low profile. Although he couldn't be sure of it, it seemed to Jonathan as if Jasper had remained consistently oblivious to Jonathan's presence.

There had been no sightings of Blaine whatsoever. Jonathan surmised he was staying hidden deep within the hotel, patiently awaiting the right moment to make his move, whatever that might be.

There was, however, a glimpse of Apollonia, and it almost broke Jonathan's heart.

It was just as he'd begun his shift, in the chill early dawn when the sky was still dark. He saw the sudden flare of gaslight in the room she occupied. She had risen very early.

The shades were drawn in the room, but her silhouette was sharply visible in black against the backlighting. He watched her as she walked past the room's two small windows, dressed in what he assumed to be a robe with her hair still in disarray. As she paced back and forth across her room, he could discern the gentle angle of her cheekbones and nose, the outline of her closed lips, the nape of her neck. He could only guess at what expression might have been animating her features at that moment.

It was maddening. The silhouette was her, and yet it wasn't. It was teasingly near yet revealed no more than an outline of the person it represented. Yet when he saw it, Jonathan realized how much he had missed her. He felt in his chest a tugging so strong that it seemed she was trying to wrest his very heart away from him. He shook his head to ward off the feeling and failed.

A strange blend of emotions—passion, loneliness, sadness, anger—filled him as he approached the entrance with a firm step, determined at last to see her, to hold her once more in his arms.

But he stopped when he was halfway across the deserted street. With a pain almost physical, he took in a deep breath and slowly walked back to the lamppost where he'd spent the last idle hour watching. He knew he could not force his hand in this way, that it would ruin everything, that Jasper and Blaine would intervene, probably violently. He had to wait. He could not make a definitive move until he had a reasonable chance to succeed.

And that chance came his way later that very day.

It was nearly dusk, foggy as it almost always was, and growing dim. He was across the street, walking slowly, when he saw the couple emerge. The light was far from bright, but there could be no mistake that it was she.

She was dressed as if for a formal affair, in a red silken gown that revealed her pale shoulders. The dress was elaborate and showy, with graceful drapes and swirls, and was extended very wide at the hem by a hoop. Her hair matched the outfit, carefully styled in a complex yet flattering arrangement of curls and ringlets.

She was beautiful—stunning—yet her expression was cool and aloof. Her lips were set firmly and evenly, neither smiling nor frowning. It was too dark to see her eyes.

Beside her, his arm intertwined with hers, was Archer Blaine. With his ubiquitous tan, dark eyes, and erect bearing, he cut a dashing figure. He, too, was dressed as if for a night out, in a spotless white shirt and elegant black tails. Completing his ensemble was a silken opera hat that, when combined with the way he stroked his pendant mustache, made Jonathan think of every stage villain to have ever haunted a melodrama. In marked contrast to Apollonia, he was smiling widely.

Jonathan nearly jumped out of his coat when he felt a hand tap his back. He turned, expecting the malignant sneer of Jasper, and heaved a sigh of relief when he saw Jeremiah instead. He had arrived right on schedule to relieve Jonathan at the watch.

From the look on his face, it was obvious that Jeremiah had also seen the couple at the doorway.

"That's them," he whispered. "Oh, sweet Lordy Jesus, that's surely them."

Jonathan's mind raced. "Yes, it is, my friend. Follow them. Find out where they're going."

"Okay," he whispered back. "What you goin' to do?"

"I'm going inside to have a look at their rooms."

There was no time for further discussion. They watched as Blaine hailed a hansom cab and helped Apollonia inside. Jeremiah responded at once. He immediately hailed his own cab that, in a moment, headed off in the same direction as Blaine's.

Jonathan walked toward the hotel doorway, his confident stride revealing nothing of the reluctance he felt. He was reasonably sure that Jasper was still in the hotel—he'd seen him return that afternoon—but realized that he could not squander the chance. Jasper stayed in a separate room. If Jonathan was quiet, things might go smoothly. In case things didn't go quite so smoothly, he felt considerable reassurance from the loaded Colt revolver that rested in his inner coat pocket. If it came to it, he had little doubt that he would use it on Jasper.

He nodded to the doorman as he entered—the same doorman who'd sold him the master key—and made his way quietly up the plush carpeted stairs to the fourth floor. Once there, he looked carefully down the corridors. Not a soul stirred.

He decided to have a look at Apollonia's room first. The key opened the door to 407 effortlessly and quietly. It was dimly lit inside—she had left the gas burning on a low flame. The room was neat and tidy and smelled faintly of lemon verbena, the scent he knew to be her favorite. Her luggage had been emptied and stowed beneath the bed, revealing the intention of an extended stay. The closet contained a meager collection of dresses, coats, shawls, and hats; the dresser several satin and silken undergarments.

In the nightstand drawer, he discovered something more intriguing. It was a quarto book of brown morocco leather, upon which the word "Diary" had been tooled in fancy script. It was held closed by a small brass latch.

Jonathan picked it up, his finger on the clasp. He speculated on how much she might have written within it, how honest and intimate she might be willing to be with the silent and invisible confidante that diaries tend to become. He felt the temptation sorely—all the answers might be there, he realized, perhaps everything he still didn't know about Blaine and his intentions and about how she and Blaine had managed to circle the same strange orbit. He bit his lip as he contemplated what, if anything, she also might have written about him within those closed pages and stood for minutes grasping the book, debating with himself.

In the end, he knew that he could not bring himself to violate her privacy. He put his lips to the diary's cover and returned it to the drawer, unopened by his hands. The room had nothing else of interest.

After a cautionary glance into the dim hallway, he exited her room and unlocked the door to Room 406—Blaine's room—with extreme caution, realizing that Jasper was likely in the room immediately adjacent. The chamber was pitch dark and smelled of tobacco and cologne. Jonathan fumbled around the wall until he located a gas jet. Striking a match as quietly as possible, he lit it, keeping the flame low.

This was a larger space than Apollonia's, with a table dominating a small parlor set off from the bedroom. Jonathan began a methodical search, going carefully through the drawers and the closet, searching under the bed and its mattress, even inspecting the toiletries in the medicine cabinet. These searches were fruitless, revealing only the banal sort of articles any traveler might carry.

At last he came to the table, upon which lay a collection of Blaine's day-to-day possessions—a half-empty bottle of whiskey, a pouch of tobacco, a long-barreled revolver, a map of Halifax, several railroad timetables, a comb and hand mirror, a thin bundle of letters held together by string.

This he found interesting.

He picked up the bundle and began to untie the knot that bound it. And then he heard voices—men's voices—in the corridor and the heavy sound of approaching footsteps.

His heart beating wildly, Jonathan put the letters back on the table, rushed to lock the door as quietly as possible and extinguish the gas jet's flame, and dashed for the coat closet. He had just squatted within its narrow confines and closed the door as the handle on the outer door turned.

Jonathan heard their entrance—two people, by the sound of it—and then he heard one of them strike a match to light the gas. A yellow glow appeared through the keyhole of the closet door.

Then came their voices, both male with Southern accents.

Blaine was the first to speak. It appeared that he was continuing a conversation that had been under way as they approached the room.

"Well, Carson, I must admit, it was quite a surprise, and a trifle unsettling, to see you waiting for me in the lobby like that."

"I expect it was," came the other voice, which sounded strangely familiar to Jonathan.

"You're a damn good tracker."

"So they say."

"How did you find me, if you don't mind my asking?"

Jonathan heard them pulling up chairs and sitting down. The sound of a bottle clinking against glass suggested that liquor was being poured.

The other man cleared his throat. "Had the help of a Northern man. Fellow who gave the name of Jonathan Chase."

Jonathan started but kept quiet.

"The hell you say!" Blaine replied loudly, his voice laced with amazement. "Chase! Well, I'll be damned."

"So you do know him."

"So to speak. He insinuated himself into my circle in Michigan. Did a fine job springing me from Mackinac, I will say that, but I found him odd, suspicious. I never figured out what his game was, nor did I ever trust the man. That's why I dumped him before we got to Richmond. How the hell did you find him?"

"He found me, actually. Came to my office in Richmond, pretty as you please, asking what I knew about you."

At these words, Jonathan silently removed his hat and painfully lowered his head to bring his eye level with the keyhole, which provided a fair view of the parlor. Two men sat at the table, glasses before them. One of them—his back to Jonathan—was Blaine, still dressed in his black finery. The other man—who faced the keyhole—was familiar, too. Jonathan recognized him as the gray-haired Confederate officer he'd contacted at the Secret Service office in Richmond, the one who made him promise to notify him of Blaine's whereabouts—a promise he had totally forgotten, he suddenly realized. The officer was now wearing ordinary civilian clothes instead of a uniform.

"I trust you didn't tell him anything," Blaine said.

"Only what I wanted him to know. I didn't trust him either, of course, although I doubt that he's a Union spy. They wouldn't dare be so bold as he was nor so foolish. All the same, I could tell he was very determined to find you—or at least the woman you have been traveling with. I let him go, figuring why not let him do some of our work for us."

"You tailed him?"

"Of course. It took him a little while, but somehow—I believe it was with the help of a slave he bought at Lumpkin's place—Chase ended up at Silas Demby's doorstep. You can probably guess the rest."

Jonathan heard a long, low whistle.

"Demby, that old fool—Goddamn him!—the one and only man in Richmond who knew where I was going. He must have told Chase everything."

"He did, Blaine, the same way he told you everything you wanted to know and then did the same for us. That's how I knew you would be in Halifax."

Jonathan heard the sound of Blaine swallowing whiskey.

"Which means that Chase is probably here, too."

"I would call that a sound assumption, although I haven't seen him. As far as I'm concerned, Chase is no longer important. He served his purpose. What matters now is the business between you and me."

"And what might that business be, Carson?"

Blaine's voice had lost its forced friendliness. His cold tone was immediately familiar to Jonathan.

"There are several disturbing matters between us, Blaine. First, our superiors in Richmond remain puzzled as to what took place in Chicago."

"What is there to be puzzled about?" Blaine rejoined. "I was captured by the city police, turned over to military authorities, interrogated at length—revealing nothing about the plot, to anticipate your question to that effect—and finally sent in chains to the island."

"Didn't you find it strange that you were the only Confederate taken in Chicago? We had five men there in addition to yourself."

"I did find it strange, Carson. I found it very strange indeed. If you want my opinion, it was Chesterton who turned me in. He managed to do it in a way that did not compromise himself or the operation."

"Chesterton? That's absurd. He was in command of the whole thing."

"So he was, but you may have heard from him that he and I did not get along. The fact is, we detested each other. The truth is, he was an utter fool, totally incapable of carrying out the mission. I knew it was doomed to failure from the start. Imagine Chesterton commandeering a ship on Lake Erie, managing to overcome the Union gunboat *Michigan*, and then using it to force the surrender of the garrison at Johnson's Island, thus freeing the Confederate prisoners. I'll wager that even you, Carson, cannot bring yourself to imagine all of that."

"You had your orders, Blaine. You were under Chesterton's command."

Jonathan heard Blaine slap his hand down hard against the table.

"And I would have followed his orders, damn it! I simply felt it wise to argue with him, to point out the weak points in his plan, and for that—for merely arguing with the cowardly fool—he betrayed me to the Chicago police. Betraying one's own comrade to the enemy, that's the sort of man Chesterton is. And don't play sanctimonious with me, Carson. You know as well as I do that it was a delusion that he could ever succeed. In the end, Richmond pulled him off the mission, did they not?"

"He was removed, yes, for precisely the reasons you mentioned. We turned the whole thing over to Thompson in Toronto. He put John Yates Beall, who was exchanged by the North last spring, in charge."

Blaine laughed long and full.

"Yes, and then came the almighty Johnny Beall! I read all about him in the newspaper just last week. I laughed, Carson, believe me, I laughed. Even under Beall—a man whom I once respected—the operation was a fiasco. Sure, he scuttled two insignificant Union ships, but he didn't dare move against the *Michigan*, and as for the poor prisoners on Johnson's Island, why they're still rotting there, aren't they? I suppose Beall is running for his life as we speak, his vaunted Rebel tail tucked neatly between his legs."

Carson's tone was now low and chagrined. "We think he's somewhere near Buffalo, probably in hiding."

Once again, Blaine nearly shouted.

"In hiding! That phrase, sir, could well serve as the very theme, the sum total, of your so-called Secret Service. All of you are men who think small, who act as fools, whose imaginations are so frightfully limited it's amazing the Yankees haven't captured the whole damn lot of you."

Now it was Carson's turn to raise his voice.

"And I suppose you could have done so much better than Chesterton or Beall? You were always disgustingly fond of yourself, Blaine. How manly is it to criticize the actions of others when you do nothing yourself? You are a quick one to condemn others more courageous than yourself but not so quick to act on your own."

Blaine's reply came calmly.

"Not so quick, am I? Not manly enough for you? If I were not a man of action—a man of daring and decisive action—then why did you take the trouble to follow me all the way to this damp sewer of a city, Carson? If you truly believed that I was nothing more than a man of words, I doubt you would have gone to such lengths to be sitting before me now."

Carson cleared his throat.

"Richmond is concerned, Blaine, about your intentions regarding Lord Covington."

Blaine's voice conveyed the sneer his face must have displayed.

"Richmond is concerned, are they? Well, let me tell you, Carson, Richmond *should* be concerned. They should be concerned that they finally have a patriot whose head is properly screwed on, who is not afraid to strike a blow that will make a difference at last."

"What are your intentions?"

Blaine replied in a tone that was instantly kinder, even pleading, as if he felt it possible to persuade his listener of his logic.

"Listen to me, Carson. For God's sake, just hear me out and tell me if the plan doesn't make sense to you. It's complicated, and I admit that it's been a rocky road carrying it out, but I've never lost confidence in the idea. I've been working on it for more than a year, since when I came to Richmond to work for you.

"It was in Richmond, in fact, in our own offices, that I first learned of Covington and the work he's been doing between London and our southern capital. I learned that he serves as the queen's personal envoy to the Confederacy and that his work is so important and so sensitive that only one man in Richmond knows when Covington makes his trips to Canada. That man, of course, is Demby, and when I first visited him last December, I was able to learn that Covington would be in Toronto in January.

"Your orders sending me to Chicago came just a week later, Carson. That was my first complication. I had to alter my original intent. I decided to meet up with Chesterton in Chicago and then beg leave of him a few weeks later, pleading crucial business in Michigan. If he had refused, I would have deserted him. The plan was to go to Michigan in early January, meet up with my contacts who were already in place in Saginaw—I will tell you of them later, they are crucial to the plan—and then quickly make the trip into Toronto to connect with Covington.

"But Chesterton's betrayal of me ruined everything. The police arrested me while I was sleeping in my hotel room—I had no time to notify anyone of anything. The army questioned me for days, and as I've said, I told them nothing of Chesterton's activities. They got nothing out of me, and so they simply packed me off to Mackinac in short order. By January, I was locked up, incommunicado. Covington came and went from Toronto, and there was nothing I could do about it."

Carson interrupted Blaine's monologue. "So your contacts—the people in Michigan—arranged to spring you from Mackinac?"

"Yes. I was able to smuggle a few letters out of the fort. I informed them, first of all, of the arrest itself and then gave them instructions for how to secure my release. By early April, the roads were thawed enough for them to travel. And they performed their assignment with brilliance."

"We already know that Malcolm Jasper was one of them. He deserted his post in Richmond last year. We assume it was to help you with your plan."

"Jasper has been invaluable to me. There should be a medal for him when this is all over. There was also an Indian with them, a man I had never seen or heard of, and another stranger—this Chase character, who somehow joined up with the others in Saginaw. Finally, with her slave in tow, there was Apollonia Foley—the keystone of the entire plan."

"Miss Foley of Savannah, if I'm not mistaken," Carson said. "Why is she important?"

Blaine's voice suddenly grew excited.

"Listen to me, Carson. She is not only important, she is everything. She is the ticket to our success. Without her, I could never hope to succeed. Ensuring her participation was my first priority. Once I managed that, I had Jasper accompany her to Saginaw—she has relations there—months before I went to Chicago and before I even knew the details of Covington's visit. It was necessary that she would be close to Canada, ready to travel on short notice when it was time to make the move. In other words, if she was not able to quickly accompany me to Canada and willing to cooperate with everything, there was no point to anything else.

"Covington loves her, you see—that was my discovery. Before the war and in its early days, he was in business in Savannah. He lost his head over her while he was there. He went so far as to ask for her hand—more than once. She refused his proposals for her own reasons, but the point is that she still holds considerable power over him. It is precisely that power that I propose to use to our advantage. I do not exaggerate when I say that Covington would grovel at her feet if he thought there was the tiniest possibility that she might reconsider."

"But if she doesn't love the man, how have you convinced her to cooperate? Why does she help you?"

Jonathan again heard the clink of the bottle against glass.

"Let us simply say that I can be an extremely persuasive man, Carson, when circumstances demand."

Blaine's words were enigmatic, suggesting both threat and suasion. They troubled Jonathan and gave him doubts he didn't want to have.

"So your associates managed to free you in April, but by then you were lacking a crucial piece of information," he said to Blaine. "You had no choice but to return to Richmond to pay yet another visit to Silas Demby. Otherwise, you would never learn the details of Covington's next visit to Canada."

"That is so. We traveled there as quickly as possible, since I had no idea when or where Covington's next visit would take place. It was by no means a simple journey, I assure you, with the railroads all discombobulated and military activity all over Virginia, but we made it at last. I got rid of Chase in the country before we got to Richmond and ordered Miss Foley to sell her nigger after we arrived. Neither of them was necessary to the plan, and I wanted to travel light. But first I went again to Demby and once more ascertained the timing of Covington's stop here."

"Which is just about now," Carson said.

"He arrived the day before yesterday, as a matter of fact. I had Miss Foley send a message to him the following morning. He wasted no time in his reply, I assure you. In fact, when you approached me this evening in the lobby, I was just returning from the harbor. She is spending the evening with him as we speak, no doubt expressing her desire to reconsider his proposal. I would imagine that Lord Covington is a very happy man tonight."

"It's all very neat and elaborate," Carson said. "I must congratulate you, Blaine. There are flashes of brilliance in your plan, but tell me this: Why did you have to go through all these motions? Why use the woman as a go-between? Why not approach Covington directly yourself? If you cleared it through our man in Canada, I'm sure that Covington would have agreed to see you."

"It's not nearly so simple as that. I could not go through any Confederate authorities, overt or covert, as you shall see. Nor, for that matter, could I approach Covington directly. In fact, it is vitally important that I do neither of those things. In order for the plan to work, all indications of my association with it and my very presence in Halifax must remain absolutely unknown to everyone involved—to our own government in Richmond, to the United States government, and to the British government."

"Then I must ask you why."

"Because," said Blaine in a lowered voice, leaning closer to Carson across the table, "in just about twenty-four hours, on Friday night, under my direction, Miss Apollonia Foley will murder Lord Covington."

Through his keyhole vantage, Jonathan saw a look of shock and astonishment cross Carson's face. His eyes, open wide, stared directly into Blaine's, his drink frozen in midair halfway between the table and his mouth.

"You're mad!" Carson cried.

Blaine's low laugh gave Jonathan another chill.

"I had a feeling you would react this way, Carson. It makes me glad that I trusted my initial instincts and decided against discussing the idea with anyone in Richmond, including you."

Carson slammed his glass back to the table.

"What in the world would you hope to gain by murdering Covington, for God's sake? He is our ally! Do you have any idea how his death would affect our supply of arms, of currency? Can you imagine the reaction in London?"

"I certainly can imagine all of those things but not in the same way that you are imagining them, Carson, for in my scenario—and according to my plan—the British will have no choice but to pin Covington's murder squarely on the Union. We will have no blame to endure."

"But..."

"Again, I plead with you: Hear me out. And trust me. The evidence I plan to leave behind, aboard Covington's ship, will be irrefutable. It is the most authentic of documentation, sure to survive the most careful scrutiny of the British authorities.

They will conclude that the Union has murdered their envoy, and we both know the likely result of that conclusion."

Carson's voice suggested that he was beginning to regain his composure.

"You are assuming that this will serve as the final straw—the act that will force Britain to recognize the Confederacy and take our side in the war?"

"Of course. When they believe that the Union has murdered the queen's handpicked envoy to the CSA, the pro-Confederate forces in London will be strengthened, inspired by the thirst for vengeance. The House of Lords is already solidly on our side, as I am sure you know; such an act might even sway the House of Commons our way. And the long-standing feud over our recognition will be settled at last, with the entire cabinet pulled along in our favor."

"Such an outcome is far from guaranteed, Blaine. Britain had the perfect chance to enter the war three years ago, when the Union seized their envoys aboard the *Trent*. They backed away then, just as they have backed away from every opportunity since. Britain has neither the stomach nor the heart to join our cause. That ought to be plain by now."

Blaine shouted his reply. "It is far from plain to me, Carson! They need cotton for their mills—great heaping shiploads of it, at low prices and of a quality that far exceeds the pitiful twine they are importing from India. They need Southern cotton, by God, unimpeded by the Yankee blockade and kept very cheap by our unique supply of slave labor. In their heart of hearts, Carson, the British are the greediest bastards in the world, and for all their pious condemnations of slavery, they drool at the prospect of Southern cotton once more flooding their mills and covering the backs of their people. When I have Covington killed, I will have done nothing more than hand them the excuse to go after that which they so desperately want."

Jonathan saw Carson shaking his head, an amazed look still dominating his features.

"You really are mad, Blaine," he said quietly.

Blaine poured himself another glass. It seemed to Jonathan as if he was trying to calm himself before responding.

"Is it mad, Carson, to hope that Atlanta could be the last Southern city to be raped and plundered by the enemy? Is it mad to contemplate that Sherman's advance will be frozen in its tracks once the Union learns that a British army is crossing the Atlantic to oppose them? Is it mad to envision the look on Grant's face when he realizes that the mighty British fleet will soon scatter his blockaders like so many marbles?"

"It is noble, not mad, to envision such things, Blaine," Carson replied, "but it is indeed mad to believe that any of them will actually occur. Not only are the British reluctant to engage the North in open conflict, there are too many ways for your plan to go wrong. The Union will not admit to murdering Covington—you must realize that. They will do everything in their power to discredit the notion.

How can you be sure that your tracks are perfectly covered? How do you know that you haven't left your own evidence behind? How can you be certain that this woman of yours—who must already know everything of your plot—will not confess to everything? And what then? What if the British learn that their envoy was murdered at the instructions of a Confederate officer?"

Blaine laughed lowly again.

"That will never happen, rest assured. I have left no tracks behind me—not a single one. And as for Miss Foley, well, she will indeed serve as my agent of destruction, so to speak, but I can promise you that she will never breathe a word of the plot to anyone who matters. In fact, her life will last but a few hours more than Covington's. I would not be so foolish as to leave such a secret in a woman's hands."

Jonathan's reaction was immediate. Without thinking, his hand reached inside his coat to the pistol. He began to draw it out, fully intending to barge into the room and put a bullet directly into Blaine's head. The threat against Apollonia enraged him to the point of blindness, but something held him back. He realized that the circumstances at the moment—with Blaine and Carson in this room and Jasper in the next—were far from ideal. He quietly took in several deep breaths and slowly returned the pistol to its place.

Through the keyhole, he saw Blaine's tall figure rise from the table. The Southerner slapped his thighs, as if to signal that the conference was about to conclude.

"I have told you everything, Carson" he said. "You know it all, from beginning to end, and so I ask once more for your backing. I plead for you to allow me to proceed."

Carson also rose from the table. Jonathan saw that his head was shaking.

"I cannot allow it, Blaine," he said evenly, "nor would any authority in Richmond—intelligence, military, or political—approve such a scheme. The risks are simply too great, and the act itself—the cold-blooded murder of a trusted ally—is so far below the threshold of honor I am shocked that you would even consider such a thing. As your superior officer, I have no choice but to forbid such an action. I order you to desist from this."

Jonathan saw the side profile of Blaine's face and was surprised that he was smiling. He walked to the hallway door and held it open for Carson.

"I am afraid I cannot do that, my friend," he said quietly.

Carson looked him directly in the eye as he stood in the doorway. "Then you know what I must do. I will inform the Halifax police of your intentions."

"You will do what you must do," Blaine echoed, placing his hand gently on Carson's shoulder as he walked out the door.

The rest happened much too quickly for Jonathan to react. He saw Blaine's other hand reach beneath the tails of his coat and retrieve a dagger—a gleaming weapon with an arabesque handle and long, narrow blade—and plunge it forcefully between Carson's shoulder blades. It sank to the hilt.

As Carson gasped and reached behind him, Blaine pulled him roughly back into the room and closed the door. He stared at Carson, whose pale face was twisted with pain and surprise, and smiled.

"And I have done what I must do," Blaine said quietly, as Carson slowly sank to the floor.

Murders, of course, are invariably followed by their aftermath. From his voyeur's lookout within the closet, a half-horrified, half-fascinated Jonathan watched as the rest of the scene unfolded.

Carson lay facedown on the floor, not moving. Blaine, slowly and methodically, looked about the room. He first strode toward the closet, causing Jonathan to once more reach for the handle of his pistol, but then Blaine seemed to see something to the side. He went to the sofa and removed from its back cushion a large covering cloth of dark material. He spread this out on the floor next to Carson. He tugged at the decorated handle of the dagger protruding from the body and, finding its retrieval difficult, placed his foot on the dead man's back and pulled it out with both hands. He took a handkerchief from his pocket, carefully wiped blood from the blade, and placed the wadded cloth into one of Carson's coat pockets.

Blaine then rolled the body into the cloth until it was completely covered. No sign of blood appeared on the carpeted floor.

Blaine left the room. Jonathan heard a quiet knock in the corridor, a few words whispered, and the footfalls of two men returning.

With a sleepy-looking Jasper behind him, Blaine reentered and closed the door.

Jasper stared at the wrapped shape on the floor with something more than his usual impassivity.

"Did you say it was Carson?" he muttered to Blaine.

"Yes. He's been on our trail for weeks."

"But, Archer, he's one of us, I mean—"

"Shut up, Jasper. I'll explain everything later. There was no choice—that's all you need to know for now. I'm leaving it to you to get rid of this." He touched the body with his shoe.

"Put it in the maid's linen cart, take it down the back stairs to the alley—quickly and quietly, Jasper. It's not far to the waterfront, and if you're careful, no one should take notice. Make sure everything is out of his pockets, first of all, and bring all of that back to me. Then tie his body up in something secure—perhaps some of that oiled hemp down by the docks. Weigh it down with something heavy before you put it in the water. If he floats, he must be impossible to recognize. Do you have all that?"

Jasper didn't sound convinced.

"But what if somebody stops me? What if that cop is out there and asks me what's in the cart?"

"Then shoot him or anybody else who gets in your way."

"Aren't you going to help me? He's a pretty big man."

"And you're a pretty strong one. No, I cannot go with you."

Blaine reached into his vest and produced his watch. "I'm already late for Appy. I have to pick her up from Covington's ship. There's no time to waste."

Jonathan heard Jasper grunt as he heaved the body across his back and shoulders. Blaine checked the hallway and motioned for Jasper to go ahead. Finally, with another furtive glance, Blaine extinguished the gas lamps and left the room, closing the door behind him.

Jonathan waited for five minutes before exiting the closet. When he rose to his feet, the numbing cramps in his thighs blossomed into open pain, almost causing him to fall. The room was once more pitch dark, and Jonathan had to feel his way as he headed for the door, limping painfully on his long-dormant legs.

He thought about taking the letters he'd seen earlier but decided to leave them. Blaine's long conversation, and the act of sudden violence with which he concluded it, had already told him everything he needed to know.

That knowledge was vast and dire, and even before Jonathan made his unobtrusive departure from the Halifax Hotel, he was trying to determine what to do with it.

October

Then like a lamp the moon glows in the night,

Daytime is brilliant with emerald light,

Topaz and ruby and sapphire above.

All is in splendor, the world seems in love,

Yet under the beauty, the mountains of leaves,

Spectres are haunting the chilly eves.

I suspect that somewhere out there, somewhere beneath this infinite fog, such a fall, such a spectrum of gems, really exists. It is October, after all, the season of the harvest queen. Should there not be such glorious color, such bewitching moons? Yet all I see is smothering gray.

Once again, it is the dreamer who reigns supreme in my poetry. I write of an exquisite autumn, one bathed in the pleasant tints and scents of nostalgia and memory, not of the present moment, when what there is of the season is cloaked in this chill and blanketing mist, this soft and mysterious child of the sea. When the horns sound in the harbor, which is often indeed, it is almost as if the mist itself has found its voice, such a lonely and forlorn cry it makes. I shudder when I hear its banshee wail. It makes me think once more of those poor widows who pace their roofs, forever searching for their beloved mariners. It makes me think once more of Jonathan, lost and unseen, alone and heartbroken, or much worse even than that.

Charleston is far behind us now, with all of its worry and woe, with all its sorrowful voices. We have journeyed far by the sea, a furtive voyage, but uneventful and drab in the end despite its stealth and danger. We have been here for a number of weeks—in honesty, I have lost count of the days—but I am assured that we shall not be here much longer.

"Here," in my inconsiderate words, is Halifax, a city to which I have never been, in a province which I have also never known. Nor do I wish ever to set foot upon these northern shores again. In truth, I am not so troubled by its fog and its chill, nor even by the foreign, yet strangely familiar, manners of its people.

It is because I know that here shall come the end to my wretched journey, here shall be my final encounter with fate. When I am done with Halifax, and it with me, I shall have committed the gravest of sins against God and man. My soul shall be stained with crimson, and I fear that I shall not have a long wait in accounting for it. I have thought much about Archer and his plans for me after the deed is done. I realize now that he cannot suffer me to live once his will has been satisfied. I was foolish to imagine otherwise. Yet I shall struggle on—a "good soldier" in Archer's sardonic words—in the faint hope that he shall be true to his own promise and spare those I love from the dark secret he and I together hold.

Again, the bulk of my days are spent in the comfortable prison of a hotel room. There is precious little to distract me here as I wait. There is a handful of old books on a shelf, and I have perused them with the hungry interest of one who has no other diversions. One of them, a very slim volume, is Longfellow's *Evangeline*. At first I thought this to be a remarkable coincidence, since her story begins in this very place, a great many years ago when Nova Scotia was called Acadia and it was a land not of the English but of the French.

It is such a sad tale. When I was finished, I placed my head upon my arm and wept deeply for poor Evangeline, destined never to find the love of her heart until the moment of his death, many miles and many years away.

Now I realize that it was no coincidence that I should read her tragedy. It was a reminder, cruel and ironic, of the turns my own life has taken. Like her, I have been displaced from my home, cast on a long and perilous sojourn through foreign and hostile lands—doomed forever to search for, but never to find, the love of my heart.

I have already told you that I am superstitious. When I discovered in the poem that Evangeline had journeyed to the distant shores of the Saginaw River— just as I did!—I knew that the poem was meant for me. I think of her now as my sister, as one with whom I am intertwined.

I imagine how she must have cursed the times in which she lived, for I curse mine in the same way. It was none of her fault that her life should be cast asunder, her heart broken, her home taken away—just as none of these things is my fault. These unfortunate truths are the progeny of nations at war, of minds consumed with power and control, conquest and victory. They are the wretched offspring of ignorance and brutality, of jealousy and rage, meanness and spite. They are the work of those who know nothing of love or those who choose to hide what they know.

My own times are no less woeful, no less cruel, than Evangeline's. In all the places to which I have traveled, and on all the roads and railroads between them, I have seen the same things, the same reminders of hatred and woe. I no longer care what color the soldiers' uniforms happen to be nor which flags they fight beneath.

Nor do I even care whether they are soldiers. Those in the capitols who make the laws and give the orders, those in the streets of the cities who make speeches, those in the offices of the newspapers who write articles—all these are no less guilty, and no less benighted, than those who wield the bayonets with their own hands.

In the midst of such shadowy and barbarous days, I dream of a time in which darkness no longer thrives. I dream of a time when love rules over all hearts, when compassion, not war, is the force upon which honor and praise are bestowed. I know not whether it will take years or centuries or millennia for this day to arrive, but I swear that it shall come.

And if, dear reader, you are now smiling and thinking me childish or naïve, perhaps you will pause before passing your final judgment upon my dream. Perhaps you will at least consider the possibility that it could be. It takes nothing more than hope to make the dream possible and nothing more than love to realize it. I believe this with all my heart.

I am sure that Jonathan would never make mockery of such a dream. I believe that he has had the very same vision, in his heart if not with his eyes, and if you care to know why my soul shall forever be joined with his, there is your answer.

How I long for him! How I wish he were by my side—my beloved ally—at this, my greatest hour of need. He would know what to do. He would know how to spare me the act of wickedness I must commit.

That act will come on the morrow. If I live to see another day beyond that, I shall beg the Lord's forgiveness and hope that Jonathan still lives, so that I—like Evangeline—can go in search of him. And if I must die, then—God forgive me!—I hope that Jonathan too has perished, so that we may be together in death, in a place where my dream is no longer a dream.

OCTOBER

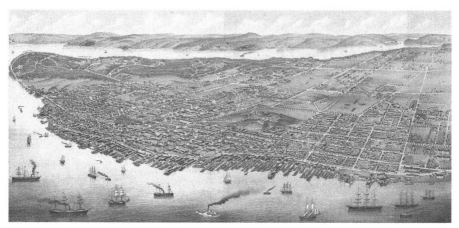

HALIFAX

JONATHAN FOUGHT IT with all his might, but the poison of Archer Blaine's words seeped into his mind.

He leaned on the railing of a pier in the Halifax harbor, his coat wrapped tight against the chill of the night, and watched through the mist the gentle undulations of the ships at anchor. He heard their occasional bells, breathed in the cool saltiness of the air, but felt no warmth from the glow of lamps within their cabins.

He considered much.

Blaine, in explaining himself to the doomed Carson, had said that he was a very persuasive man. Did he mean that he possessed the leverage to coerce Apollonia into doing something she would otherwise have refused to do? Or did he mean that she was under the spell of his influence, that she loved him, perhaps, and would do his bidding with the unquestioning faithfulness of a true lover?

As desperately as he wanted to believe that Blaine's powers were those of a blackmailer, he could not divorce from his mind the latter possibility. Even back in Mackinac, he had sensed a powerful current between them, a connection that was as impossible to deny as it was to define.

Blaine had also used the word "murder" in telling Carson what Apollonia would do to Covington once she regained his trust and intimacy. Would she do such a thing? Was she really capable, in cold blood, of taking the life of a lonely old man besotted with her? Could Jonathan possibly have read her so utterly wrong?

He had kept in his heart a cherished image of Apollonia. It had given him untold strength and hope through all his ordeals of the spring and summer—it may even have been the one thing that kept him alive. Within that image, he saw both her strengths and vulnerabilities, her basic goodness and her confusion. She had always been a figure of enigma to him—that was surely a major part of his attraction for her—but beneath the aura of mystery that surrounded her, he had taken for granted her basic goodness of heart. When she had whispered that his feelings for her were returned—on a resplendent spring day so strikingly different from this bleak autumn night—he wouldn't have dreamed of doubting her.

Yet now he doubted. With every fiber of his being, he fought such feelings, but he could not stop gnawing at himself like a desperate animal caught in a trap.

Could everything he believed about her—could the sheer joy that the simple thought of her brought to him—all be nothing more than a perfidious illusion woven by a determined and ruthless Rebel spy?

Jonathan cursed and slapped his hand against the wooden railing.

He knew himself well enough to realize that he would keep gnawing at himself until the bitter end, whatever and whenever that might turn out to be. But he also knew that he would not desert her. Even if every bad thought about her turned out to be true—even if she turned out to be worse than his worst fears—he would not desert her.

She might well succeed in becoming a murderess tomorrow night, but Jonathan would not allow her to be murdered. Blaine had told Carson very clearly of his intentions to do away with her shortly after Covington's death and then, as if to prove his own cold and murderous heart, had buried a knife in Carson's back. Jonathan had no doubt that he would do the same to Apollonia, regardless of whatever relationship existed between them.

That would never happen, he vowed.

Nor—if he was able to prevent it—would he allow Apollonia to kill Covington. He had not forgotten his own stricture against interfering in the troubled currents of the time in which he found himself, nor had he ceased to believe in the dangers such interference might present, but history—*his* history—told him that this deadly act was not meant to take place. He knew with a sense that approached clairvoyance that it would spell only ruin, not only for Covington and Apollonia, but perhaps for the very world that all of them, Jonathan included, would come to know.

He pulled up his collar against the fog and began the short walk back to the Acadian. He could feel a tiny place in his heart already hardening against her. He hated his awareness of it but faced it with a stony resolution that surprised him.

Perhaps, he thought grimly, the true reason he was here was not to love Apollonia but to stop her.

Back in the dim quiet of their hotel, Jonathan and Jeremiah compared their notes of the evening.

Jonathan related everything that had happened in Blaine's room, including a detailed retelling of the revelatory conversation between Blaine and Carson. Jeremiah took it all calmly, with only the occasional shaking of his head to reveal any sense of shock or surprise at what Blaine and Apollonia were up to. When told of Carson's murder, a grimace was his only visible reaction.

Jeremiah's story was much easier to tell. Tailing them in a cab, he had followed Blaine and Apollonia to a remote section of the harbor where a small British warship was anchored. The anchorage was heavily protected by what he estimated to be at least twenty Royal Marines, all of them armed and vigilant.

Apollonia left Blaine's cab well before arriving at the docking point and approached the officer of the guard alone. She spoke to him for a few moments and was then courteously escorted onto the ship. Jeremiah caught no further sight of her until nearly two hours later, when Blaine returned in his cab. Again, he parked it out of sight of the guards, and Apollonia approached it on foot. With no more ceremony than that, the couple returned to the Halifax Hotel. Jeremiah followed them all the way back.

Their information updated, Jonathan and Jeremiah went to work assembling facts, hunches, and theories like pieces of a puzzle. They went over a great deal, covering Apollonia's sudden decision to travel north to Michigan, her clandestine meetings with Jasper in the remote farmhouse, the wilderness trek to Mackinac, the liberation of Blaine, and their frenzied return to Richmond. They discussed Jonathan's meeting with Carson in Richmond and the confrontation with Demby.

Virtually all of the parts fit neatly together. Only a few significant gaps—most notably Apollonia's reasons for helping Blaine—remained unknown.

"So the question is," Jeremiah said at last with a sigh, "what we're gonna do about this whole business."

Jonathan looked his friend directly in the eye. He saw undeniable signs of concern and fear there, but he also glimpsed determination.

"What would *you* do, Jeremiah?"

Jeremiah returned Jonathan's hard stare.

"You got precious few choices," he said after a moment. "First, you can go up to the Halifax police station and tell them everything. You tell them about how Carson died and what you heard Blaine say about Covington. You tell them that they're Rebel spies up to no good."

Jeremiah paused significantly.

"And?" Jonathan prodded.

"You sing that song, and I reckon those Canadian police would lock Blaine up right quick, at least so long as it takes to learn the whole story themselves or to fish Carson out of the water. But we got to think about things, Jonathan. They arrest Blaine on your word, why wouldn't they arrest Apollonia, too? Ain't she part of it? Once they do that—once they think she's a Rebel spy—it'd be no easy chore to get her free again."

"You're right."

"And who's to say that if you was to go to the police as a snitch, they might not put you in irons, too? Why should they think you're no spy yourself, maybe working for the other side? I hear tell these Canadian folks don't tolerate *any* spies if they can help it, no matter which side they're workin' for."

Jonathan nodded. Jeremiah was thinking far more clearly than he was.

"So much for the first option," Jonathan said. "What are the others?"

"Only one more, Jonathan, and I reckon you know what that is."

Jonathan did indeed know.

"I go to Blaine myself. Deal with him directly."

"That's right."

"And do what? Talk him out of it? Carson already tried that."

"Man like Blaine, there's no talkin' him out of anything. You already know how far he's willin' to go. No, if you want to stop Blaine and get Miss Appy out of this mess, you know full well what you're gonna have to do."

Jonathan felt the patient pressure of the revolver inside his coat.

"I'm going to have to kill him."

"No other way to do it, my friend. No other way. And we best be quick about it."

He had indeed made his decision quickly—maybe too quickly, it seemed to Jonathan now, as he walked alone through the deserted predawn streets of Halifax. Through the ubiquitous fog—how he had grown to detest it!—his quiet footsteps attracted the notice only of the nocturnal creatures, cats and rodents, who lurked in the shadowy places.

He was now, like the cats, a nighttime predator, an assassin on the prowl. It was a new and not very welcome role to a man who had played a great many roles of late. The responsibility was forced upon him by circumstance, he realized, but this did nothing to alleviate the repulsion it held for him. He knew he had no choice but to confront Archer Blaine with grim violence. To retreat from this task was to surrender Apollonia to the cruel fate that awaited her and to put in Blaine's hand the key to God only knew what sort of future his plan of murder might spawn.

He also knew that Jeremiah was right. Blaine would never negotiate with him, never listen to any measure of reason. He was a dogged provocateur, ready to betray whoever stood in his way or resisted his will, and clearly not afraid to kill, if that should prove necessary. Carson's fate was plentiful evidence of that.

Jonathan recognized that the imminent confrontation was virtually certain to end in death—whether Blaine's or his own only time would tell. He had decided that he would invoke no ceremony in executing the act—offer no words of explanation or recrimination, make no effort to parley. He would perform the act as efficiently and mercilessly as any assassin: gain entry to Blaine's suite, rush to his bedside, and coldly put a bullet into his sleeping or just-awakened body. Then another bullet. And then he would stand in the shadows, await Jasper's inevitable hurried entrance, and kill him, too, just as neatly as he had dispatched Blaine.

Finally, he would go to Apollonia.

He refused to ponder what reaction he might receive in her chamber after the bloodletting. Whether she would flee with him, grateful for his intervention, or spit in his face, hating him for what he had just done—these he would have to handle as best he could. He would, at least, know that he had saved her. In the end, that might be the only consolation he could ever hope for.

In just the same spirit, he was acutely aware of his own mortality. He did not underestimate his foes nor their capacity to defend themselves. If Blaine or Jasper was quicker or cleverer than he was, then he would have to die, that's all. He was no more afraid of death tonight than he had been at Spotsylvania. At least he would die in the knowledge that he had done his best to prevent disaster. What more was there to do?

He did not regret that Jeremiah was not walking at his side nor that he had lied to him. Jonathan had told him two hours before that he would engage Blaine and Jasper on the following day. Jeremiah believed Jonathan fully, of course, and, exhausted, had soon fallen into a deep sleep.

Jonathan could not bring himself to expose Jeremiah to this. The man had spent his entire life in the chains of slavery. He deserved to live his last few years in freedom, not in a Canadian prison. Nor should he die as a result of Jonathan's obsession or Blaine's delusion. And if he and Jeremiah should turn out to be the successful party, Jonathan would not allow the mark of Cain to be scrawled on that good man's head. He would not wish that on any man. Jonathan still saw, virtually every night, the agonized face of the soldier he had slain at the Bloody Angle.

So now, alone and purposeful, he was about to repeat the very same deed. Despite his determination, the idea was anathema to him. To kill was wrong, he was convinced, no matter how justified, no matter how necessary. A man who deliberately takes another life, whether soldier, constable, criminal, or executioner, is condemned to carry the savagery of the act in his soul, to relive it in all its horror untold times. Jonathan could not even imagine that any person might anticipate murder with savor or sleep peacefully and guiltlessly ever after.

He walked out of the fog into the sleeping lobby of the Halifax Hotel. There was no doorman or tenants in that dark space, not even a clerk. The desk bore only a small brass bell and a sign instructing late-night arrivals to ring. The only sound was the subdued ticking of a grandfather clock, whose face revealed half past three.

The midnight of the soul, Jonathan thought, dimly recalling a literary passage. The perfect time for death.

He ascended the carpeted staircase, keeping his footsteps light. On the second and third floors, he saw empty hallways, faintly illuminated by soft gaslight.

On the fourth, an identical stillness prevailed. Jonathan stalked toward 406 and paused before the closed door. No light came from beneath it. He put his ear to the wood and heard no sounds within. He gently turned the doorknob and found it locked.

He drew the pistol from his coat and quickly checked its chamber. He took the master key from his pocket—he had never thrown it away—and gently inserted it into the keyhole. When he turned the key, the lock made a quiet clicking noise. He pushed the door open slowly and entered the dark apartment, heading straight for where he knew the bedroom to be. When he reached its threshold, he leveled his gun at the obscure horizontal shape of the bed.

And saw, even in the dim light from the window, that it was empty.

There was no human form upon it; the bed was neatly made.

He was suddenly fearful that Blaine might be lurking somewhere, ready now to spring. He turned frantically, gripping the gun with both hands, and saw that nobody else was in the room.

He stepped into the small parlor and found it, like the bedroom, neat and orderly. There were no personal articles, no pieces of clothing, no luggage anywhere to be seen.

The room was deserted, recently cleaned by the maid, silently awaiting its next visitor.

Jonathan put his ear to the wall the suite shared with 405, where Jasper stayed. No sound came forth. He crossed the room and did the same to assess whether Apollonia remained in 407. It was also silent.

He had to be sure. He made similar intrusions into both rooms, quietly unlocking them and creeping inside. They were as neat and empty as Blaine's.

He carefully closed all of the doors and stood at the head of the staircase. He released a long-held breath and allowed his tensed muscles to relax. He put the pistol back inside his coat.

They were gone.

The indisputable fact of it—coupled with its jagged contrast of what he had fully expected to happen—stunned him. He couldn't yet calculate the meaning of it nor grasp its implications. He felt a raw déjà vu of the morning near Culpeper, when he had awakened to find himself utterly deserted.

Jonathan shook his head and retraced his steps back to the lobby, just as deadly still as it had been when he had crossed it in the opposite direction. When he stepped into the street, he realized that the day must be breaking somewhere above the bank of fog that rested on the city. The indistinct shapes of streets and buildings were beginning to appear out of the mist as the feeble false dawn rose.

It was when he was halfway back to his own hotel that he understood what must have happened. It had been Carson who, in the last conversation of his life, had told Blaine that Jonathan was in Halifax. Blaine must have taken serious note of the news, even though he said little of it at the time. It was only logical that he would change locations immediately after he discovered that there was another pursuer on his trail. He couldn't take the chance that Jonathan might try something desperate—like he had just been prepared to do—before Apollonia's fateful meeting with Covington.

But Jonathan knew that he still held an advantage. Blaine had no way of knowing that Jonathan had heard his entire conversation with Carson, including his plans for Friday night, now only a half a day away. It remained possible that Blaine had decided not to deviate from those plans. With luck, Jonathan could still hope to intervene just as the drama unfolded in its moment of truth.

He reached his own hotel, as eerily quiet as the one he had just left, and realized that he really had no other choice.

He walked down the narrow corridor, dimly lit, that led to the rooms in which he and Jeremiah were staying. He hoped that Jeremiah was still asleep, oblivious to Jonathan's solitary errand, murderous in intent and vain in execution. If he remained unaware, then Jonathan would never have to explain why he had left him behind. He knew that Jeremiah's dignity, so long latent and neglected, so long abused by the circumstances of his life, had become very important to him. Jonathan respected Jeremiah. He did not want to hurt him.

The brown derby on the floor in front of Jeremiah's room was the first sign.

It lay there before the closed door, brim up—conspicuous and foreboding in its incongruity. Jonathan picked up the felt hat and examined its lining. It bore the emblem of a milliner in Atlanta and was of a relatively small size. It looked familiar.

The name of its owner shot into his mind with lightning speed: Malcolm Jasper.

Jonathan caught his breath. In one motion, he retrieved the pistol from his pocket and put his ear to his door, hearing nothing. He gently turned the knob and found it unlocked. He pushed the door inward.

By now, the gray light of the dawn was evident in the room. He saw the bed and what he took to be Jeremiah's form beneath its blankets. He was also able to make out the shape of the dresser, the washstand, and the room's solitary chair.

Jasper was sitting in it.

Jonathan jumped but immediately brought the pistol to the level of the man's eyes.

"Don't move," he said evenly.

The figure on the chair did not move, nor did it speak. Its stillness was absolute.

Jonathan took a step closer. In the murky light, he could see Jasper's face. The hair, usually slick with pomade and perfectly groomed, was in wild disarray. The eyes were wide open—shockingly so—and the expression on his face was one of extreme fear or pain, perhaps of both.

Despite his seated position and the almost natural way in which his hands clasped the arms of the chair, it was immediately clear that the man was stone dead.

Jonathan lit a kerosene lamp on the nearby table. As he raised the flame, he took in the awful portrait of death before him. It took him only a moment to see the bluish bruises on Jasper's neck—horizontal stripes that matched perfectly the outline of a man's fingers. He had been throttled.

Grasping the lamp, Jonathan turned toward the bed. As he did so, his shoe struck something hard on the floor. He held up the lamp and discovered a small derringer.

He directed the light toward Jeremiah, who lay on his back beneath a quilt, head on the pillow, eyes closed.

"Jeremiah," he said softly, aware that his voice was choked.

Jeremiah did not open his eyes, but his lips moved, and a raspy whisper issued from them.

"That you, Massa Chase?"

"It's me. Are you—"

"Not all right, Jonathan. No, not all right t'all," Jeremiah interrupted feebly. "The fool in that chair over yonder done murdered old Jeremiah, 'cept I ain't quite dead yet."

Jonathan set down his gun and lifted the blanket. A large red stain had spread over the chest of Jeremiah's nightshirt.

"Oh God, Jeremiah," Jonathan said. "Oh Jesus..."

"Now you listen, 'cause time is precious. He was fixin' to do you in first, Jonathan. Slipped into your room. I heard him in there and opened my door just as he was leavin'. He put one of his bullets in me, Jonathan—Lordy, it hurt so bad at first—but I took him by the neck and dragged him in here. He dropped his gun, and I squeezed him. 'Let go of me, you damn nigger,' he said, and all I did was smile. Smile and squeeze, tighter and tighter, till he was deader'n a doornail, Jonathan. He's one dead Rebel now, and Lord forgive me, but it sure felt good to watch him die."

Jeremiah made a pathetic attempt at a laugh that soon became a painful fit of coughing. A spray of tiny droplets of blood came with each spasm.

"I've got to get help, Jeremiah. I've got to get a doctor."

"No need for that. I'm nigh finished."

Jonathan felt a tear course down his cheek. He took hold of Jeremiah's hand and was surprised at the strength with which his grip was returned.

"Now don't you go a-cryin' on my account," Jeremiah rasped, opening his eyes at last. "I'm older than sin itself...figure I was a-goin' to die pretty soon anyhow. At least I'm dyin' a freeman, Jonathan. Got you to thank for that, you and the sweet Lord Jesus. My papa and my mama would be so proud to know that their baby Jeremiah died a freeman, in a free land, with a good man, his true friend, standin' by his side like you're doin' right now."

Jeremiah closed his eyes again, and Jonathan felt his grasp weaken.

He made another effort to speak, each word a little fainter than the one before.

"Now you listen, 'cause here's one freeman talkin' to another. You bury me up here, Jonathan. You just put up a little cross for old Jeremiah up here in Nova Scotia, on freeman's land. And you take care of Miss Appy, you hear? You're on your own now, and you got to make sure no harm comes to that...sweet... little...girl..."

His final breath was a sigh.

The sound that Jonathan made was a thin roar, the wail of a gravely wounded beast, and he cried it out with no heed of the perilous alarm it might raise, no care for the great gash it tore into the fabric of his heart.

It subsided into a sob and then many more, as he clasped his hands to the sides of his head and rocked to and fro, as if these motions of grief could ease the pain or somehow mitigate the guilt he already felt at having left Jeremiah alone, unprepared for the deadly malice of the man who sat in a chair not four feet away, a corpse himself now, his sightless eyes seeming to take in the whole mournful scene.

And when the sobs ebbed at last, what was left to Jonathan was a motionless silence, a static state he could only wish offered numbness as part of its matrix. He did not notice, nor did he care, that Jasper's earlier gunfire had somehow not aroused attention in the sleeping hotel. He stared at the colorful gingham quilt placed on the bed on which Jeremiah's body lay, oblivious to the fact that the day had come, even that the sun had risen clear and free, the first time since their arrival that the morning had come without the sea's gauzy pall. Nor did he pay heed to the shadows that changed with the course of the sun or the maddeningly fresh breeze that blew in through the open window.

Those shadows had grown long and the breeze chilly by the time Jonathan came back to himself. He rose and removed the watch from his pocket. It told him that five o'clock had come and gone. He took another look at Jeremiah's lifeless form and enshrouded it with the colorful quilt. He gazed into Jasper's eyes and, despite the sudden surge of hate that rose in his throat like bile, gently closed them with two fingers. He placed Jasper's hat and derringer neatly on the table beside the chair.

These details would have to be dealt with later, he knew. And his mourning would have to be postponed.

He saw Jeremiah's half-empty bottle of cheap brandy and uncorked it. He swallowed a considerable draught, feeling its fire work its way to his empty stomach. He splashed cold water on his face from the basin, ran a comb through his hair, and covered it with his hat. He retrieved his revolver from the bed and checked the chamber for rounds, making sure that there were more bullets in his coat pocket. He left the room, closing the door quietly as he passed through.

Jeremiah had told him where Covington's ship had its berth, and he walked straight in that direction. The bracing air revived him; the clear sight of the amber sunset beyond the deep gray line of the sea helped him focus.

It did not take him long to find the vessel. A long and slender, yet obviously formidable, frigate, it was anchored at the far end of one of the harbor's more distant piers. A Union Jack flew from its stern, barely visible in the failing light. Jonathan knelt down between three barrels at the base of the dock and began his vigil. He remained there for more than an hour, watching as guards lit a lantern at the landing, then stood patiently at parade rest.

The cab arrived at seven o'clock sharp, just as full night had settled. It stopped at the end of the pier, not more than five feet from where Jonathan crouched. He heard words whispered in both a man's and a woman's voice and then saw her alight from the carriage. His heart raced when he saw her, dressed in something very dark, her face pale and drawn.

Apollonia walked unescorted toward the ship as the carriage slipped quietly away, disappearing somewhere in the darkness behind Jonathan. As she reached the two guards, Jonathan saw them bow politely. One of them took her by the arm and helped her navigate the gangplank. She disappeared into the bowels of the warship.

Jonathan had not arrived with any sort of plan, knowing only that he would have to act when the time came. The time had now come.

He walked directly up the dock toward the sentries' lantern. When he stood before them, he was met with a considerably colder reception than Apollonia had received. The guards abandoned their military stance and drew their rifles in Jonathan's direction, their bayonets mere inches from his body.

"Who goes there?" one of them demanded, his clipped British accent jarring.

They were Royal Marines, smartly dressed in scarlet coats, spotless white breeches, and tall black shakos, brims pulled nearly to the eyes.

"My name is Jonathan Chase," he replied, trying to keep the shakiness out of his voice.

"State your business."

"Business of great urgency."

"What sort of urgency, then?"

Jonathan was at a loss for words. He wanted to tell them that Lord Covington's life was at stake—that the act of murder might in fact be under way even as they spoke—but he could not bring himself to utter the warning. He was not yet prepared to put Apollonia into a position from which she could not retreat—a position, indeed, that might well lead to a gallows.

"I can explain it only to Lord Covington himself, and time is extremely important. Please let me speak to him, for only a moment. I assure you the matter is dire."

The mention of Covington's name clearly affected the guard, as if he did not expect his charge's name to be known to a stranger.

"Lieutenant!" he cried out, pronouncing the word "leftenant" and keeping his eyes on Jonathan.

In a moment, another marine emerged from the ship, his superior rank denoted by the gold epaulets on his shoulders. He was a thin, handsome man whose accent bore considerably more refinement than that of the sentry.

"This bloke says he has to see his lordship," the sentry explained, summing up Jonathan's brief plea.

"He does, does he?" the lieutenant replied in an imperious tone. He took a good look at Jonathan, from head to foot, his nose raised as if a slightly unpleasant scent was troubling him.

The officer asked several more questions of Jonathan, who continued to refuse to offer details. He fully realized how ridiculous he sounded and found himself wishing fervently that he had spent the day devising an intelligent plan for gaining access to Covington.

"Well, sir," the lieutenant purred at last, "I'd like you to consider the situation as you have presented it to me. You wish me to allow you to see Lord Covington, without any sort of invitation whatsoever and without any explanation for your visit beyond the vague allusion that the matter is, how did you put it, dire."

He pronounced the last word in one drawn-out syllable, sarcastically.

Jonathan felt his impatience rising in direct proportion to his impotence at convincing these men. He fought the urge to tell this arrogant jackanapes that he may have just allowed a murderess to enter his master's chamber.

"You will have cause to regret your stubbornness if you don't let me pass," he told the lieutenant, his voice taking on a surly tone. "It *is* dire, damn it!"

The officer's face lost its mask of aloof refinement and took on a gray shade of anger. Jonathan thought he could see a current of cruelty in his eyes.

"Don't you dare speak thus to me, sir!" he barked. "Unless you fancy spending the night and more in irons! I warn you not to test me."

He took a deep breath, as if his sudden burst of anger had winded him.

"I will do this for you and nothing more," he said in a calmer tone. "Tell me where his lordship may contact you, and I will deliver your message at the next opportunity. And that will put an end to this business."

Jonathan took his own deep breath, his mind now made up.

"The name is Chase. He can reach me at the Acadian Hotel," he said quietly, his own voice now composed. "Thank you for your attention, Lieutenant, and please accept my apologies for my abruptness. Good evening to you."

He turned on his heel without another word and strode purposefully down the long dock. He heard the guards muttering something behind him, an epithet that included the terms "daft" and "Yank," but did not so much as tilt his head in their direction.

He approached the end of the dock with caution, his hand on the pistol in his pocket, fully expecting to see Archer Blaine emerge from some shadow, but he found himself alone when he reached the shore, with no sign of Blaine or his carriage in sight. He took another glance at the landing, where the guards had resumed their defensive stance. The lieutenant was nowhere to be seen.

Just beyond the casks where he had originally hidden, Jonathan again crouched. He untied the laces of his shoes and removed them. He took off his hat, vest, and coat, with the pistol still in its pocket, and laid them beside the shoes.

Finally, he sat on the rough log that marked the water's edge and allowed himself to fall into the harbor.

It was a short fall, maybe four or five feet, and Jonathan made only a small splash as he entered the water. It was icy, immediately sending painful stabs into his chest and groin, but Jonathan broke immediately into a vigorous swim, hoping that the exertion would defend his body against the effects of the cold. It was perhaps a hundred yards to the ship—a manageable stretch for a strong swimmer like Jonathan—but the cold water was a powerful deterrent and the distance seemed like a mile. He swam parallel to the pier, his muscles quickly tightening, already threatening to cramp. His initial strength waned rapidly.

As he drew near the long vessel, he switched from a front crawl to a breaststroke to make less noise. To his left, the guards held their positions, giving no indication that they had heard anything out of the ordinary. When he reached the slippery wooden hull of the ship itself, Jonathan was thankful that he was now fully out of their sight.

He used the anchor chain to climb aboard the warship. Its links were barely large enough to allow a foothold, and the iron was frigid and slimy. It took him two shivering and painful minutes to make the fifteen feet from the water to the rail of the main deck.

Jonathan peered over the railing just in time to see a marine finishing his round on that side. The guard walked slowly down the deck, his rifle on his shoulder, and rounded the stern, beginning what Jonathan hoped would be a long and leisurely stroll along the opposite side. At last, he clambered clumsily but silently aboard, his hands and feet fully numb by now, the cold air penetrating his soaked clothing.

He conducted a reconnaissance, peeking into every porthole and window along the way. The first two were dark; the third revealed four uniformed sailors playing a game of cards; the fourth an unoccupied galley.

Beyond the fifth porthole, in the aft section of the ship, he found what he was looking for.

He saw her in the light of a kerosene lamp. She was standing, her back to Jonathan, talking to a man across the cabin. Jonathan could see him clearly—a tall and well-built man of perhaps sixty years, his hair long and white, his attire elegant and conservative, his face intelligent and sharp. He held a glass of red wine in his hand and was listening intently to what she was saying. The expression on his face seemed one of considerable concern or worry. Through the glass, Jonathan heard the low murmur of her voice but could make out nothing of what she was saying.

He was, however, perfectly able to see what Apollonia was clutching in her left hand, behind her back and out of Covington's view. It was a small vial of cobalt blue glass. Embossed on the side of the bottle was the unmistakable symbol of the skull and crossbones.

Covington raised the glass to his lips and took a deep drink.

Jonathan hesitated no longer. Off the deck, there was a door leading to the cabin, and he seized its knob, gratified beyond words to find it unlocked. He yanked it open and rushed inside, dripping saltwater onto the fine rug beneath his frozen feet.

Apollonia also did not hesitate. With the reflexive speed of a cat, she turned at the first sound of his entry and faced him. He had never seen her face bear such an expression as it held now—eyes narrowed to slits in furious malice, jaw set in a twisted, angry rictus. She cried "No!" in a voice as cold and sinister as her expression.

In the same mad instant, he felt the cold touch of the pistol she was holding in her right hand, its barrel now firmly pressed beneath his chin, and heard the metallic sound of its cocking.

They faced one another as if suspended in time, like predator and prey in the moment just before the hunter sinks teeth and claw into the hunted.

Jonathan, who had confronted untold dangers in the past year with a lack of fear that still amazed him, could not deny his terror at this moment, although there was something about it that fascinated him as well. Here he stood, freezing and soaked, before the woman he loved with all his heart—a woman whom he dared hope might love him in return—and she was holding a cocked pistol to his throat, a shaky finger on its trigger.

What a pure, unsullied moment of absolute truth, he thought, to have his entire existence dependent on this single, static instant, on nothing more than the finger of this fragile yet majestic woman.

The look in her eyes was deadly. She was thin, paler than he remembered her, and her plain dress of pure black accentuated the severity of her appearance.

He fought to find words, even a single word, to say, but his mind refused to focus. He was caught in the surreal scene, torn between her sudden spring to violence and the great wave of love he felt to be gazing once more into her eyes.

It was those eyes—flashing the cold fire of blue topaz—that first signaled a change.

They began to widen slowly, losing their ferocity, and soon they opened fully. Their anger was gradually displaced by something new—shock or amazement, Jonathan thought—and then recognition. With that, they grew moist, and tears began to form tentatively at the corner of each. For the first time, he saw the sweet little girl who had so recently filled the last memory of a dying man.

"Jonathan?" she said in a very small, very frightened voice that barely rose above a whisper.

Still wordless, he managed only to nod.

"Jonathan?" she asked again.

The gun dropped from her grasp and landed with a thud on Lord Covington's thick rug. The tiny blue vial in her other hand immediately followed. She fell toward Jonathan, almost in a swoon, and he caught her against his chest. She buried her head beneath his chin, and Jonathan smelled the sweet scent of lemon verbena rise from her hair.

She lifted her head to meet his eyes again, and the tiniest hint of a smile came to her lips. They stared at one another, pupil to pupil. Each had an infinity to say to the other—untold tales and coveted explanations, expressions of pain and joy and grief—and these were communicated but without words. The language they spoke was that of sheer happiness—the simple and profound glory of finding themselves once more in each other's arms.

Tears ran down their cheeks, the saltwater mingling as their faces drew closer. Their looks of astonishment became children's smiles.

And then Jonathan felt the point of a bayonet directly in the small of his back.

"Make a move and be impaled," came the unmistakable voice of the insolent lieutenant. Jonathan heard the sound of several men, marines, no doubt, crowd into the cabin behind the officer.

At last, the voice of Lord Covington, deep and sonorous, took control of the room.

"Withdraw the weapon, Lieutenant," he said in a firm but quiet tone. He was clearly a man accustomed to giving orders and of seeing them promptly obeyed. The precise point of pain in Jonathan's back immediately withdrew.

"And stand your men down. This man means no harm."

"But Your Lordship," the officer protested, his voice just behind Jonathan's ear, "this man entered your quarters by force, he—"

"Unless I am very much mistaken, this man is Jonathan Chase, and I suspect his real purpose in being here was to save my life."

Covington looked over the top of Apollonia's head into Jonathan's eyes.

"Am I correct, sir?"

Jonathan nodded.

"With respect, Lordship, to save your life from what?" the lieutenant persisted.

"From a danger that thankfully never really existed, Lieutenant, which is all I'm prepared to share at the moment. As I said, stand your men down and leave us alone. We've a few matters to discuss."

Jonathan glanced over his shoulder to glimpse the confused face of the officer. He was unable to resist the temptation to smile. The lieutenant merely blinked at the gesture, raised his hand to the brim of his hat, and followed his men out the door.

In an authoritative manner, Covington directed Jonathan to help Apollonia to a small couch that faced a blazing iron stove.

"You appear to have had a brisk dip in the harbor, Chase, and I think a bit of drying off is in order. As for Miss Foley, I think the excitement of the evening has just about put her into a faint. Sit down, for heaven's sake."

He took his own chair beside the stove and poured two snifters of brandy. He handed one to Jonathan, who was grateful to feel its warmth blend with that of the fire. Apollonia sat very close beside him, not yet raising her face. He felt her heart against his chest. It seemed to be beating very fast.

With effort, Jonathan was finally able to find his voice.

"I apologize for my intrusion, Lord Covington," he began, "and I thank you—"

"Apologize, for God's sake!" Covington thundered. "Don't be a fool, Chase. I'm perfectly aware that you wanted to warn me against *her*."

He pointed to Apollonia, attached to Jonathan as if they were bound together.

"I don't know how you were able to determine Blaine's plan, but you did it, by God. You knew what she was supposed to do."

Covington rose from his chair and retrieved the tiny blue bottle from the carpet. He held it up to the light and shook its contents.

"Tincture of deadly nightshade," he said, "better known as belladonna, an Italian word meaning 'beautiful woman,' which is quite apt, considering who intended to use it tonight." He threw a meaningful glance in Apollonia's direction, but she was looking dejectedly at the floor as he spoke.

"I daresay a generous portion of this elixir in my claret would have done the job quite well. I expect I would have fallen asleep peacefully enough, well before Miss Foley, unsuspected, had left the ship, thus allowing her to escape. Mine would have been an eternal slumber, of course."

"I'm totally confused," Jonathan admitted.

Covington grinned. "Miss Foley told me all about you, of course, and it was abundantly clear that you were on her side, her 'only ally,' as she put it. When she didn't put a bullet through your neck just now, and when she whispered your name, I knew it was you. If it had been Archer Blaine in your place, I have no doubt he would be a very dead man by now."

Apollonia finally raised her head. She looked into Jonathan's eyes and smiled. Her voice still sounded shaky.

"When you came through the door, I was sure it was Archer, come to finish the job I was unable to carry out. Oh, my God, I'm so sorry, Jonathan! Can you ever forgive me? To think that I drew a weapon against *you*!"

In response, he kissed her forehead and held her tighter.

She smiled and put her head back against his chest.

Covington sipped his brandy and regarded the couple with an expression that was hard to read.

"You were fully justified in your fears for me, Chase, for Miss Foley did indeed come here with lethal intentions. She changed her mind about that, thank God. I expected nothing more than a pleasant social call this evening—what old fool like me would not look forward to a visit from a woman like her?—but instead I received the most amazing of confessions. I will not go into the details of it. That's for Miss Foley to tell or to conceal as she sees fit. Sufficient to say, she filled me in on Archer Blaine and his plans for me, and a very interesting tale it was."

Covington's perceptive face took on a more serious cast. "I must confess it was an amazingly clever plan, very detailed and elaborate. And I cannot say that it would not have succeeded. I shudder to think of the reaction in London had Miss Foley opted to go through with it."

He took a large envelope from the table beside him and held it up. "This packet illustrates the lengths to which that blackguard was prepared to go. It is a collection of official documents and correspondence, all of it forged but very expertly so. It was supposed to have been found here, along with my corpse, as if the assassin had forgotten or dropped it. It would have pointed unerringly to Washington, Chase—to a Union plot to have me murdered in cold blood. It would have implicated Lincoln himself and a host of his closest aides and confidantes, and I have little doubt that it would have convinced the warmongers in London that the time for war with the United States had finally arrived. Armed with such intelligence as this, the interventionists might well have been able to turn the tide in their direction."

Covington motioned to Apollonia. "This young woman prevented all of that, Chase. She may have saved your nation and mine from an escalation of this bloody, senseless war and spared who knows how many thousands of lives. Were all this business not of the utmost secrecy—and I emphasize to you, Chase, that it is indeed—I would submit her name for Britain's highest honors. She is a true heroine in my eyes."

Apollonia lifted her head again. "I am no heroine, Lord Covington. Far from it. I am just a very confused person who knew wrong from right in the end. And before you laud me to the heavens, I beg to remind you that I was not sure, until the very moment I entered your cabin, that I would *not* go through with it."

When she said this, Jonathan sensed a sadness in her voice and eyes that troubled him. He realized that the two of them would have a great deal to discuss when they could get a moment alone together.

"It's results that count, not might-have-beens, Miss Foley," Covington countered. "I'll have none of your modesty."

He turned back to Jonathan and raised his glass. "And permit me to drink a toast to you, Chase. I have no idea how you managed to make your way here nor how you discovered what you needed to know, but you obviously succeeded. I salute you as well."

Jonathan raised his own glass in response.

"Much of what I needed to know I learned from Blaine's own lips," he offered.

Both Apollonia and Covington looked at him with close attention.

"I was in his hotel room, concealed, just last night. I overheard him share the entire plan with another Confederate agent, a man named Carson. You should know, Lord Covington, that Blaine murdered Carson while I was there. I witnessed the whole thing without Blaine being aware that I was present."

Apollonia gasped quietly.

"And he intended to murder you, too," he said softly to her. "After you were finished here tonight, he told Carson that you would be next. That's when I knew that I had no choice but to come, not only to prevent you from killing Lord Covington, but to keep Blaine from killing you."

Apollonia's eyes began to fill once more with tears, but this time she was able to check them. "Thank you," she whispered.

Though he knew that there was much more to his story, he said nothing of Jeremiah and Jasper. He decided it was not the right moment to break this grim news.

"When Blaine discovers that Miss Foley has forsaken his plan, I suspect he'll waste little time getting out of Halifax," Covington said. "I will inform the governor of the situation tonight. With any luck, the police might have him before he's able to leave."

Covington sighed. "Meanwhile, both of you must consider yourselves to be in grave danger. Blaine will be eager to abscond, it is true, but he might well seek to exact vengeance before he does so. I would happily accommodate you here, aboard ship, but we leave for London first thing in the morning. I'll see to it that you are escorted back to town and are provided with government quarters, well protected, of course, until you determine your next destination. After what both of you have done for the Crown, it's the least I can do."

They all rose. Apollonia retreated into the washroom, while Covington stepped out to the deck to give instructions to the lieutenant. When he returned to the cabin, he and Jonathan had a few moments alone. Covington spoke quietly as they waited for Apollonia.

"I sense a certain discomfort between us, Chase. I suspect it has something to do with your knowledge about Miss Foley and me."

"I heard Blaine say that you were once her suitor."

"Indeed I was, several years ago, during the time I was in Savannah. I fear it was nothing more than an old man's infatuation for a beautiful younger woman, not terribly unusual, I suppose, and not very realistic, it is true, but passionate while it lasted, at least on my part. I'm well over all that by now. Mind you, I still find the sight of her intoxicating—and her loveliness is only enhanced by the strength and courage I witnessed here tonight—but I have thankfully gained enough wisdom to realize that greener pastures for a man at my stage of life do not really lie in a young woman's embrace."

Jonathan could only offer a wan smile in response.

"Besides, I am forced to be honest. Her heart would never have belonged to me. When she discussed you with me tonight, she made it very clear how she feels. For months, she feared that you were dead. She believed that some grave calamity had befallen you, after you were left behind in Virginia. She told me that her heart would be forever broken, that it would never again know joy. You should know this, Chase. The woman is madly in love with you."

There then came, in the wake of all that had taken place, a bittersweet time— bitter for the mourning that had to be done, sweet for the love that was allowed a chance at rebirth. The emotions reflected the newly arrived weather in this salty northern town—fitful and uncertain, with brilliant sun ruling for a while then giving way to somber clouds that spoke of gloom.

It was also a busy time, so frantic that it kept Jonathan and Apollonia from opening some subjects he desperately wanted to broach as well as others he thought better to avoid.

The governor, following Covington's instructions, had accommodated them in separate quarters within a massive military installation known as the Citadel, a star-shaped fort that occupied a hill near the center of the city.

The lodgings were clean and reasonably comfortable, but their rooms were far apart and the Citadel far from intimate. It was full of British soldiers, marines, and sailors who, apparently having little else to do, spent much of their day drilling back and forth across the large parade ground in the center of the fortification. The brisk air was filled, from dawn to dusk, with the shouted commands of officers, the beating of drums, and the mournful wail of bagpipes.

In their hurried meetings in the evenings—all that was allowed them during these hectic days—Jonathan and Apollonia would weave between the ranks to find each other. They would then head to one of the tall ramparts to watch as the powder blue dusk descended on the cluttered harbor spread out before them.

In their first such meeting, on the evening after the happenings aboard Covington's ship, there was no hiding the joy they felt. They acted like the reunited lovers they were. Jonathan took from around his neck the gold locket she had placed in his pocket in Virginia. He opened it and held it up beside her face.

She smiled and closed it, returned it to his palm, and then surrounded his closed hand with her own.

They embraced and smiled and laughed and looked deeply into each other's eyes, but they did not yet kiss, perhaps sensing that they had a distance to go before such familiarity could be restored. Nor yet did they put their feelings into words.

They talked instead of other matters until the last light of the day had gone, until they had lingered on the ramparts for too long and had to be told by the officer of the watch to leave. Jonathan described everything that had happened over the last few months, which was a great deal, and Apollonia asked him countless questions in return.

Through it all, he realized that she was saying very little about herself. When he put questions directly to her, she would cleverly sidestep them or adroitly manage to steer the conversation back to his own experiences. He knew that much was left unsaid between them and that much of what he did not know was important, perhaps vital, to the love that held the promise of blooming once more.

But with the irrational stubbornness unique to lovers, he refused to press the most critical of these questions. He decided not to ask her why she had allowed herself to progress so far with Blaine's plans or what lay at the heart of the relationship between them. He would wait until she was ready to speak of such things.

Regardless, her silence deterred him no more than it did when all she was to him was a plaintive face on a faded photograph. Of his own feelings, he was certain. Seeing her again had only poured fresh fuel onto a fire that had fallen into embers but had never been extinguished.

Yet despite the warmth of her embraces and the way she matched his gaze, he could not completely shake off the cloud that hovered over her. At times, he had no doubt of her love or that she had loved him from the start. He saw the spark in her eyes and the joy in her smile, felt them almost like an electrical current, and these signs spoke only of passion.

At other times, when she grew taciturn or looked at the Atlantic horizon with a lost, forlorn expression that evoked the little girl Jeremiah remembered, his doubts returned. He dreaded the shadow that trailed them, felt it like the cold of the oncoming night, feared that its darkness might prove more than he was able to overcome.

This was indeed bitter to ponder, but there was much more bitterness than this. There was the fate of Jeremiah, which Jonathan revealed to her at the end of their first evening together.

Jonathan told her everything that had transpired between Jeremiah and him—their reunion in Richmond, his granting of manumission, their escape by sea from Wilmington, the tense watchful days in Halifax—up to his sudden and violent death at Jasper's hand. He told her that they had become fast friends and that the last words from Jeremiah's lips were of her.

She sobbed as if her own father had died and submerged herself into a deep gloom that lasted days. It surprised Jonathan at first to witness the depth of her reaction, and he would later feel guilty for that surprise. He had assumed that as the daughter of a slave owner she would have held the attitude he'd always assumed such Southerners to have—that blacks were chattel, not fully human, and thus not really deserving of the emotions that would have been devoted to whites. He was puzzled how anyone could actually *own* a human being, and use them guiltlessly as a servant for years, yet feel such emotion—such obvious love—for them at the same time.

"You have no way of understanding something like that," she had explained when he hinted at his feelings. "You would have had to be a Southerner your entire life, and the owner of slaves, to begin to know how I feel about Jeremiah. Even for me, it's difficult to understand."

Her gloom did not subside until the burial.

In the midst of everything else, Jonathan, having secured the governor's permission, arranged that he and Apollonia would accompany Jeremiah's body by train more than a hundred miles from Halifax to an inconspicuous place called Birchtown. He had learned that a small community of blacks lived there, descendants of slaves who had fled north during the American Revolution. They still called themselves "Loyalists" with considerable pride and were gracious in allowing Jeremiah to be buried in their humble cemetery, where his last wish—a simple wooden cross—was fulfilled.

Jonathan and Apollonia were the only white people at the funeral, the only two mourners who had known him in life, but not the only mourners. Several men and women had gathered around the fresh grave and the angular wooden casket that waited beside it. Jonathan could see that they were crying, dabbing their eyes with handkerchiefs. It puzzled him and reminded him of the paid mourners he had heard about in France—*pleurants*, he thought they were called. But while those mourners were professionals, strangers paid to add drama to the funeral of a lonely deceased, these were strangers with no apparent motivation. He wondered what gave them such sympathy, such a sense of unquestioning brotherhood.

The preacher spoke of how fortunate Jeremiah had been to have "a sweet taste of freedom in this vale of tears," no matter how small the taste, before he achieved the ultimate freedom of death. The preacher was an eloquent orator with a deep baritone voice, and he made Jonathan think of the words of Frederick Douglass that Jeremiah had recited with such pride.

On the trip back to Halifax, Apollonia slowly began to brighten up. She told childhood stories of Jeremiah: how he taught her to fish when she was four or five, how she was sometimes allowed to accompany him to town on errands, and how many slaves, including Jeremiah, believed that evil spirits would take to the winds on certain nights and that it was better for everyone—especially little girls—to remain safely indoors when they took flight. Jonathan related how Jeremiah had spoken warmly of Apollonia's compassion after one of his whippings, that he had never forgotten how she had put salve on his lacerated back. The memory brought tears back to her eyes.

Parting from Jeremiah was painful, but this was not the extent of their ordeals. More difficult, in its way, was the daunting task of tidying the disordered aftermath of the chaos Archer Blaine had brought to Halifax.

The police had found no sign of Blaine in the city. On the night of Jonathan's meeting with Apollonia and Covington, Blaine had rapidly deserted the last hotel where he and his companions had stayed. Nobody matching his description was seen leaving the city by rail, and after several days of inquiries, the police theorized that Blaine might have managed to board an outgoing Confederate blockade-runner.

For their part, Apollonia and Jonathan faced a grueling series of interrogations. A serious detective with a walrus mustache and heavy Scottish brogue spent hours with Jonathan, wanting to know the intricate details of what Jonathan had overheard while hiding in Blaine's room and the murder he had witnessed there. The detective made him describe repeatedly his final meeting with Jeremiah and the discovery of Jasper's body in the Acadian Hotel.

Of Apollonia, they asked even more, but of this Jonathan knew nothing. She had, in her inflexible way, insisted upon being interviewed alone, without Jonathan or anyone besides the detective present. He had no idea what they asked her but assumed that they wanted to probe the details of her involvement in Blaine's plot and what she knew of his personal background and connections in Richmond.

Later, she refused to discuss any particulars with Jonathan, pleading with him to be understanding and patient. He did not press her.

The official investigation took nearly two weeks to run its course, and even then the authorities were hesitant to grant Jonathan and Apollonia permission to go where they pleased. The official motives were only partly based on Covington's order to protect them. The detective assigned to Jonathan divulged that the city's chief prosecutor desperately wanted to press charges against Apollonia. He felt that she had, after all, been an integral part of an international plot in Halifax, a serious crime in this strictly neutral territory, and should be held accountable for it. The only thing that kept him from acting on his convictions, it seemed, was the firm directive that Lord Covington had issued before departing for England. He had, according to the detective, described both Apollonia and Jonathan as "heroes in the eyes of the Crown" and ordered that under no circumstances should they be detained unnecessarily or charged with any offense, no matter what the police investigation might uncover.

In the end, Jonathan was very gratified that Covington's influence apparently held considerable sway. The prosecutor complied with the shadowy envoy's wishes and at last sent Jonathan and Apollonia the welcome news that the inquiry had gone as far as it could go and that they were free from scrutiny.

That evening, they stood on the Citadel's ramparts and watched the lights of a gun-laden brig of the Royal Navy as it approached the harbor. Red-coated soldiers retired to their barracks, already accustomed to the presence of this strange American couple.

The scent of the sea and the cries of the gulls made Jonathan think he would miss this place, regardless of the violence he had witnessed here and the somberness of his stay. This was where she was returned to him.

He asked her where she wished to go.

Apollonia drew close. Her eyes searched his, and her lip trembled before she spoke, but when she did her reply was direct.

"Home," she said quietly. "It's the only place I have to go. And I want you to take me there."

The city and the lovers soon parted ways.

Jonathan and Apollonia chose an arduous overland route because the most direct means of traveling from Halifax to Savannah—aboard a blockade-runner—was becoming steadily more difficult. From Jonathan's queries of seamen at the harbor, he had learned that Southern runners were growing few and far between. As the Northern armies pressed ever farther into Southern territory, their naval blockades tightened around Wilmington, Charleston, and Savannah. Many expected these ports to be bottled up entirely within weeks.

Daunted by the escalating risks and unwilling to await the next runner, they opted to journey by land. Jonathan hoped that the dwindling gold that remained in his valise would be enough to see them to Savannah.

Their sojourn began with a ferry across the fog-shrouded Bay of Fundy and continued, via railroad, through New Brunswick and the towering pine forests of Maine, where the blue-green boughs of the countless trees contrasted with an even gray sky. The scene reminded Jonathan of their northward trek through Michigan, seemingly an infinity ago but in reality only two seasons. In the springtime there, awakening from winter rather than returning to it, he had felt the same primal response to the shifting seasons that he felt here in the fall—a powerful restlessness composed strangely of joy and sadness alike.

Maine's gloomy woods surrendered to dazzling sun and azure skies in New England, where the farms were surrounded by trees that blazed in hues of yellow, gold, red, and orange. Apollonia was enchanted by this autumnal display, and during a brief stop in a spotless small town, she rushed to the thickets alongside the tracks to collect acorns and fallen leaves. The vivid leaves were carefully pressed between pages of her diary in the hope, she told him, that time would not diminish their brilliance. With a girlish laugh, she presented the acorns to Jonathan as a gift. It encouraged him to hear her laugh again.

It was a long journey through the North—by rail, stage, or ferry, depending on the location—but not a terribly difficult one. Jonathan was able to provide them with fare, sustenance, and lodging, and they did not travel at a frantic pace. There were plentiful milestones along the way, some of them literal, others of a more personal nature.

In Providence, they sat in a shower of falling leaves amid the leaning tombstones of a colonial Anglican churchyard, eating fresh apples for dinner and watching the sun set fiery gold behind the steeples and spires of the old city. They drew close to each other as the twilight air grew crisp and finally allowed their lips to meet. They held their embrace and their kiss for a long time, oblivious to whatever sacrilege their intimacy might constitute on such hallowed ground.

In New York, Apollonia was intimidated by the urban tumult and commotion and spent the entirety of their one night in Manhattan in the shelter of her hotel room. Jonathan, however, wandered the streets for a while, fascinated with all the bustle and activity. He visited a couple of taverns, where he overheard the angry talk of men unhappy with the progress of the war and even more unhappy with Lincoln's draft. He knew that he was hearing the early rumblings of the terrible riots that would wrack the city in less than a month's time and was glad that they would soon be moving on.

There was a bucolic reprieve as they passed through the rich cornucopia of the Pennsylvania and Maryland countryside, now well into the final stage of the harvest. The fields were as golden as the sun, and farmers were busily bundling their fodder corn into endless rows of tall shocks that stood like sentinels on the rolling hills. Ripe pumpkins and squash lent vibrant colors to the tawny fields, and the scent of burning leaves was the piquant incense of the towns.

As they drew farther south, the picture grew slowly but unmistakably dimmer, and Apollonia's mood seemed likewise to retreat into shade. She still smiled, but her laughter was less bright. She still embraced Jonathan at every opportunity and stayed close to him, but he sometimes saw a change come over her face when she thought he wasn't looking. She would darken, almost visibly, and her eyes would remain fixed on an invisible point on the horizon. It did not escape his notice that she always faced southward at these moments, and he began to wonder whether she was truly eager to be going home. She was torn, it seemed, between her happiness at her reunion with him and some unspoken dread.

As the miles rolled past, Jonathan sensed that his role was neither to press her for information nor to interject himself into her private thoughts. His purpose, rather, was to remain close, to let her know that he loved her and would not leave her alone. It was a responsibility he accepted readily, even as he realized its limitations.

In Washington, Jonathan's uneasy prescience was even more disturbing than in New York. Here, the physical evidence of war was much more evident than it had been elsewhere in the North. The district was surrounded by military tent cities, both camps and hospitals. The streets were filled with soldiers, many of them sporting bandages or walking on crutches, as well as throngs of blacks, probably refugees from the violence farther to the south.

During their two-day stopover in Washington, they passed the U.S. Capitol with its incomplete dome, a jarring sight to Jonathan, who had vastly different memories of this seat of federal power. Both he and Apollonia also looked in vain for a glimpse of the towering, spectral figure of Lincoln, and Jonathan, haunted by his foreshadows, privately searched the streets for the soon-to-be assassin. He scanned passersby for handsome men with dark hair and mustaches and wondered which of these strangers leaning on lampposts or sounding their bootheels on wooden sidewalks might be the actor of imminent infamy. Here, he felt stronger than ever the urge to seek out the man and be done with him, historical consequences be damned. He succeeded in restraining himself but hated himself for doing so.

He was relieved to leave the capital behind after two days and suspected that Apollonia felt very much the same, but they quickly realized that the easy stage of their journey had come to an end.

They could no longer follow the coast along its southern course, for Richmond was due south of Washington and the region between the two capitals remained the worst of the war's bleeding sores. Jonathan had no desire to revisit any of that.

He asked an artillery officer he met in Washington for the best overland route to Savannah. The man, who did not seem at all surprised by the question, advised Jonathan to travel well west of Washington and then resume their southerly journey through the relative isolation of the mountains.

"Less chance of being waylaid by raiders up there," he said, adding that he had no idea how far regular rail service might extend through the region. He recommended that they make Chattanooga their first destination.

"Once you get there," the officer said, "it won't be hard to find your way. Just follow the trail left by Sherman's boys—that shouldn't be hard to spot—then straight down to Atlanta and out to Savannah. The only question is whether Sherman will get there before you do."

The officer's prediction about Savannah made Apollonia wince, yet his was the advice they chose to follow.

They managed fairly well at first, making interrupted but steady progress via a combination of rail and less formal stage routes, sometimes even wagon rides. They had no idea when they actually passed from Union into Confederate territory or even whether there still existed any sort of recognized boundary between the two. They assumed that at some point the changeover would become known to them.

It was apparent that the steadily climbing land that lay before the Blue Ridge Mountains had already seen a share of war, but the signs of it were infrequent and irregular. Some farms had been burned, while others nearby left untouched. As they gained elevation into the wooded hills, leaving the farmland behind, virtually all physical reminders of the conflict disappeared.

In fact, when they entered this remote Appalachian wilderness, most indications of human activity disappeared altogether. There were progressively fewer towns and fewer travelers along the dusty roads. Their last hired ride, with an itinerant potter driving a rickety wagon, took them only so far as a tiny town by the name of Cloverdale, nestled against the breast of the tree-clad hills.

Jonathan spent an entire afternoon seeking someone willing to take them farther, but there was not a soul in Cloverdale interested in making a southward journey, even if they were to be paid for it. The best he could do was to purchase two reasonably healthy mares from the town's blacksmith, surrendering to the reality that the time had finally come for the travelers to be on their own. The horses, along with the necessary tackle, took nearly half the money he had left to his name.

By the time the transaction was completed, the afternoon had almost given way to evening, and the dark profile of a storm front loomed in the north. It was coming in on a cold wind.

"Blue norther blowin' down," the blacksmith said to Jonathan, studying the darkening sky as he finished the shoes on Apollonia's mare. "Just like Sherman himself—nasty, cold, northern, and blue."

The burly man laughed at his own wit and then grew suddenly serious.

"Y'all better find yourself some shelter before nightfall."

There was a small hotel in Cloverdale, but the proprietor wasted little time telling the sojourners that there were no available rooms. Jonathan didn't believe him—something in the man's eyes betrayed both fear and distrust—but there was nothing he could do about it.

They took their mares southward on the road to Chattanooga, the flat orange disk of the setting sun to their right and the arching menace of the storm to their backs. Apollonia rode her mount as Jonathan had seen her do up North, unconcerned with whether any strangers might find it unladylike. The north wind was cold, and she wrapped herself in the somber cloak she had worn on the frigid night they had abandoned Riverdale.

Their progress was slow. The road was steep, bordered by trees that cast them in shadows darker than the twilight itself. The horses, unaccustomed to their new riders and sensing the storm's approach, were hesitant and skittish.

The weather caught up with them in an hour. The winds came first, wild advance scouts of what was to follow. They roared down out of the storm's towering throat and crashed into the fallen leaves that covered the ground, sending them flying in circular patterns that reminded Jonathan of whirling dervishes. The wind smelled of rain and ozone, and lightning began to illuminate the dark road in lurid flashes.

It was during one of these flashes that Jonathan spotted what he thought was the gable of a house. A vegetation-strewn pathway led in its direction, and Jonathan motioned for Apollonia to follow him. They rode low on their horses' backs, so that the overhanging branches would not whip their faces, and soon entered a clearing.

The house was strangely out of place. It was set well back from the road behind a heavy barrier of ancient trees, as if those who had built it had desired privacy above all else, yet it was not the sort of house one would expect to find in such an isolated setting. It more resembled a city house, large with two stories and four peaked gables facing each direction. It was built in an elaborate style that resembled Carpenter Gothic, with nicely turned posts on the wraparound porch and delicate wrought iron trim crowning each gable.

It appeared to be abandoned.

As they drew nearer, feeling the first fat drops of rain fall onto their backs, they saw no light emanating from the house or any other sign of habitation. Though the glass remained intact in the windows, all of them seemed to be open. The tattered remnants of lace curtains flapped crazily in the wind.

"Hello!" Jonathan shouted above the rolling thunder that echoed through the hills.

He repeated his call two more times. The rain now began to fall in earnest.

"There's no one here, Jonathan!" Apollonia shouted to him.

"Then it's ours for the night!" he replied.

They tied their horses to hitching posts beneath a long breezeway on the north side of the structure, where they would get relative protection from the storm. Jonathan and Apollonia then entered by the covered porch, not surprised to find the front door unlocked.

It was dark as pitch within the house, and it smelled faintly of must and charred wood. Jonathan lit a match and saw that the front parlor was empty. They explored the rest of the house, shutting windows against the lashing rain as they went, and found identical emptiness.

They also discovered why the house had been deserted. Much of the rear portion of the dwelling, including the kitchen and pantry, had been devastated by fire. The flames had eaten away the entire rear outer wall, exposing this section of the house to the elements. The trespassers returned to the parlor, shutting doors behind them to ward off the rain and chill.

Before long, they found themselves in relative comfort as the storm raged. The stone fireplace was aglow with a blaze Jonathan had constructed of un-burnt pieces of the kitchen wainscoting. They ate a spare but satisfying meal of fire-roasted corn, pilfered from a field they had passed earlier in the day. Later, warm and dry, they sat before the fire upon a makeshift mattress fashioned from an assortment of horse blankets and their own garments.

Outside, all was madness as the thunder roared, the lightning flashed, and the winds howled.

"You hear them, don't you, Jonathan?" Apollonia said quietly, the firelight dancing on her face. She was smiling.

"Hear what?"

"The witches."

"Witches?"

"Yes. These mountains are full of them, you know. The hill folk from these parts must have a million tales about witches and conjuring wives. Jeremiah knew some and used to tell them to me."

"I don't believe in witches."

"Oh, don't you? That must be because you have never seen one. Do you know why? It is because they only come out on two nights of the year."

"One of which, I suppose, happens to be—"

"Tonight. All Hallows' Eve."

"It's Halloween?"

"My stars, of course it is, Jonathan. I may have my failings but losing track of the date is not among them."

Jonathan realized that losing time certainly *was* among his. He hadn't given a thought to the date in how long? Weeks? Months? It seemed that once he had broken the seals of Chronos himself such things as calendars no longer mattered. But Apollonia's words jolted him. He realized that winter was lurking just out of sight. He had been here—in the past—for nearly a year already. He was a year older, even though he had skipped from one treadmill of time onto another. Time was undeniably passing, even as it no longer seemed to have any meaning.

She sensed his pensive mood and drew closer to him.

"You are thinking sad thoughts," she said softly.

"Just thinking," he said, looking into the depth of her eyes. Flames danced within them.

"Are you thinking of home? Of where you come from?"

He nodded, saying nothing.

"I have been thinking of my home as well. And it makes me sad, too."

He ran a finger along the graceful curve of her chin and gently brought her face closer to his. Their lips barely touched, a teasing hint of a kiss.

"Perhaps," she whispered, "we should forget about our homes and our woes. Just for one night."

They held each other for a long time, watching the fire recede into embers, and then tentatively, like strangers only now discovering each other, removed each other's clothes and allowed their naked bodies to mingle and share warmth and then heat.

Jonathan had not made love to a woman since well before Rachel had left, and he did not know—nor would he ever know—whether his fair lover on this stormy night had ever known a man in the way she would know him now. Nor did any of that matter. As they surrendered themselves to each other, as Jonathan finally released Apollonia's bound hair, allowing its golden glory to cascade down her back and all around her face, they were aware only of each other.

They defied the tempest that surrounded them with a storm of their own and somehow, in a way they did not understand and were not even aware of, merged their storm with that of nature, allowing their passions to harmonize with the elemental forces outside.

They joined as souls, for that is what they were. Together, they took wing into a space in which neither had ever before really been, basking in the freedom and the ecstasy and the transcendence of complete spiritual union. They soared through the fresh air of that place, knowing that if it were not heaven, it was close and akin to it, and wordlessly thanked God for allowing them this glimpse.

And they joined as creatures of the flesh, for that is also what they were. Jonathan caressed the curves and tapers of her form, teased and explored the sweetness of her breasts, tasted the ancient sea and feminine spice of her essence. Apollonia loved him as if she were playing a musical instrument, withholding the wholeness of her body when she sensed that their symphony called for softness and subtlety, then allowing them both deep immersion into each other, and finally relinquishing herself to his full demands when the music cried for release.

They reached that crescendo together, grasping each other in a beautifully painful and desperate embrace from which neither would ever be released.

In the wanton depth of their sex, they removed not only their clothing but the cloaks of their outer selves. Jonathan, the quiet, reserved man, the lost wanderer from a distant time, and Apollonia, the melancholy belle of a formal and aristocratic world—these disguises disappeared from each other's view. In their place were brave and strong lovers determined to join, true and vital beings for whom love no longer held any hint of fear.

And when it was over, when they lay spent and exhausted, they allowed the chill air of the forsaken house to cool and dry the sweat upon their bodies. When it became too cold, they drew the blankets over themselves and gently fell back into each other's arms.

"I love you, my ally," Apollonia whispered in his ear just before she slept.

Jonathan lay awake for a little while, listening to the violent tattoo of the rain on the roof and the angry rumble of the thunder. He suddenly felt very small, as if both of them were infinitesimally tiny before the vastness of their own love, beneath the elemental force of this October gale, under the awful shadow of the human storm that still raged close-by.

There was so much that was greater and more powerful than they were, so much that threatened to sweep them and their love into oblivion. He listened to the restless wind, the shrieks of Apollonia's witches, and felt very blessed to be no longer alone.

November

In a cloak of deep gray arching over the north,
The howl of the wind comes moaning forth.
The land has gone brown, the trees grown bare,
A powerful spirit is riding the air.
Its terrible beauty is wicked and old,
Its soul is the essence of winter's cold.

Today, the dreamer within me is not the poet. Today, the poet writes of precisely that which she sees and feels here in this remote and wild land as it solemnly awaits the onset of winter. I find myself at a place that not long ago was a scene of awful death and suffering, yet is almost holy in its peacefulness now. The pale sun approaches the horizon, clearly visible across an open field, and is so muted with the soft mist of the season that one can look full upon it without hurting one's eyes. I scrawl these few words as I await my companion and contemplate the tale I hope to tell this night.

It seems a lifetime ago that I last took up my diarist's pen, not just the single cycle of a moon's passage. It was a different reality I faced then, with prospects for a future that mercifully never came to pass. I feel almost foolish in reading my last entry, so very little did I know, yet is not the future ever a curving road around whose bends and turns it is impossible to see?

Such events have unfolded! Events to heal a broken heart, events to break a heart once more in two, events to allow one to look in a mirror and not detest the visage glimpsed there.

I begin with that which grieves me. My poor, beloved Jeremiah is dead. He has died at the hand of a brute, the cretin of whom I have earlier written. He died bravely, I am told, and in a state of honor that had only recently been granted him—his freedom. He died in the midst of that which he had spent so much of his life doing, which was to serve me and see to my welfare. He had gone to Halifax because he was loyal and true and brave—all on my behalf.

I weep for him in the knowledge that I was ever undeserving of his devotion and his sacrifices. Did I not support my father's persecution of him, even as I sought to ease his pain? Did I not sell him away like a sack of flour and leave him alone and bereft, subject to the cruelties which our society has so expertly fashioned for his people? Was not the vast kindness of restoring his freedom the work of another, so much greater than myself, while I never once entertained the thought of emancipating Jeremiah from his bonds?

I am honored to have had the loyalty of such a soul, no matter how undeserving I may have been. The shame I feel for my treatment of him is a painful cross I shall bear for the rest of my days and which I will bear gladly if it only helps to balance the scale a single ounce.

How to reconcile such pain with greater joy than can be imagined?

This has been my challenge, for Jonathan has come to me at last.

He lives—thank God, he lives!—and he has come back to me. Never did he lose faith in me, never did he lose his strength or courage. Through all the travails and perils he was forced to endure, never did he waver from his path.

I am as undeserving of such love as I was of Jeremiah's faithfulness, yet I shall not turn it away for that. Now that he has been returned to me, I am fiercely selfish with my Jonathan. I shall never leave him, nor let him leave me, again. The light he has brought into my heart has made me stop wishing for death. The warmth he has brought into my soul has allowed me to cherish life again, no matter the obstacles or tragedies which stand in my way. He has made me a whole person once more and a complete woman in ways I cannot describe. He has taken a wretched and detestable thing and transformed her into a beautiful angel, inspired her to take flight in ways she only once imagined but now knows to be real and vastly more wonderful than even the best of daydreams.

My stars, I sound like my dear, girlish cousin! Yet I shall not apologize to you, my dear reader. No, for I am in love, and there can be no embarrassment, no shame, to love. To have known such love for one day, even for one moment, is to have lived a life not in vain. Am I foolish in my wish to cling to such bliss for as long as time and fate will allow?

I admit this: Whether you answer yes or no to my question matters not. I may well be a fool, but at least I have discovered that I am no longer a coward. Nor am I a murderess, something I fully expected to be a few short weeks ago.

I came hideously close, this I must confess. I faced my intended victim with a practiced smile on my face and false words of love on my lips, just as Archer had trained his puppet to do. I saw how my cruel lies brought happiness and hope to my poor victim's innocent face and, like an actress in an opera, held hidden in my hand the instrument of his death.

For one moment—a single moment in which all the agonies of hell itself were plainly visible to me—I fully believed that I would commit the act. I foresaw my secretive motion to place the deadly poison into his wine. I saw in my mind's eye, and nearly felt on my lips, the smile I would seek to hold as he drifted slowly into sleep and soon into the cold arms of Death. It was only a moment, of this I am sure, but it was an infinity to me. It was a moment in which I saw the entire course of my life up until that second and in which all the terrible consequences of my act were made manifest to me. I beheld, in that frozen splinter of time, the awesome and awful power that lay in my hands.

I stepped back from that precipice. I cannot now tell you why or explain how it was that I made this choice. It was an act that sprang forth from some hidden place, whether from the mind or the heart I have no way of knowing.

Instead of watching my victim die, I confessed our conspiracy to him and pleaded for his forgiveness. Instead of slaying him, I have slain a future that had no right to exist and which would have brought only pain and darkness in its wake. Instead of opening that terrible doorway, I slammed it shut.

I thank God for this, yet I place no victor's laurels upon my head. I realize that the right I have done in no way compensates for the many wrongs I have committed. I realize it is but a beginning.

I also know that my decision will come at a fearful price. I know that my woes, in spite of all the pain and joy that have passed my way in recent days, are far from over.

For Archer, my nemesis, has now been betrayed. He has been thwarted in his most ardent ambition, denied his most precious dream. I can only imagine the rage that swells in his heart, the dark lust for vengeance that drives him on, in whatever hidden corner he presently happens to occupy.

With Jonathan at my side—my ally!—I am racing home, for this is where the spiteful dagger of my nemesis shall surely strike. As we hasten to Savannah, I know that Archer flies before us and that a far greater foe even than he, the dreaded Northern general, hurries there, too, with his fearsome army marching behind. What we shall find when we arrive I tremble to contemplate.

Yet I will not cease to hope.

NOVEMBER

ATLANTA

THEY PASSED THROUGH the dark mountains over dreary roads, riding almost soundlessly beneath autumn clouds that hung oppressively low in the heavens. Had anyone been watching, their profiles would have been discernible against the shadowy canvas—he in his sailor's coat and she in her cloak, both on horseback, slowly but steadily ascending and then descending the steep tracks. Toward the end of their long days, they slumped in their saddles, tired and with spirits, for all their new lightness, sometimes flagged.

Jonathan and Apollonia now found themselves infinitely closer in heart than they had been just a few days before, although they displayed few outward signs of this new intimacy. All their energies were spent on a journey that only grew harder the deeper they traveled into the slowly dying South.

As they rode, first through the Blue Ridge and then crossing over to the Great Smoky range, they were careful to choose isolated routes where they were unlikely to encounter heavy traffic or military activity. They had met only a handful of fellow travelers on the roads, and in the valleys there were few farmers out in the fields. With their harvests gathered and the weather steadily growing darker and colder, the agrarians seemed content to huddle in their little clapboard houses, wisps of smoke curling from their chimneys.

Only in the towns did they come across conspicuous numbers of people, who generally displayed little congeniality to the wayfarers. The times were tense, and the locals were mistrustful of faces they did not recognize. Jonathan and Apollonia crossed country through which opposing armies had only recently marched, often not benignly, and strangers were, as a rule, not welcome. Although they were usually able to procure rooms and board, they still spent several nights sleeping under stars or clouds, eating food heated over sputtering campfires, huddled closely together to ward off the late autumn chill.

They were right to anticipate danger. On the fifth day of their journey, well into Tennessee, their fears of highwaymen were realized. As they passed through a narrow ravine, from out of nowhere, it seemed, they found themselves surrounded by a dozen men on horseback. The riders were armed with pistols and rifles and dressed in little more than tattered rags beneath the bandoleers that crossed their chests. It was only by their accents and the weathered remains of a Confederate officer's tunic worn by the leader that Jonathan was able to judge that they were probably Rebel raiders. Whether they were under any formal command or control, it was impossible to say.

The leader was the only one who addressed them. Like his cadre, his face was concealed behind a heavy beard, and his eyes held the cautious, gaunt look that Jonathan had seen in other fighting Southerners.

The man demanded to know their names, where they came from, and what business they had being where they were. Jonathan fielded the questions honestly, explaining that he was escorting Apollonia home to Savannah. He included the fact that he was a Westerner.

"Sounds like a damn Yank to me," he heard one of the raiders mutter softly.

"Let's hang the sumbitch and take his woman out for a ride in the woods," grunted another, eliciting chuckles from several others.

Apollonia herself then entered the conversation.

"You men have been hardened by the war, it's plain to see," she said in a voice that was convincingly maternal, stern but kind at the same time. "Still, I suspect you are all decent young men at heart, God-fearing and loyal to the cause, in spite of the hardships you must have endured. I am sure your mothers are proud of you, proud that their brave sons are still serving their country when so many others are running away. I am just as sure that they would be ashamed and dishonored if they were to know what some of you are thinking at this moment."

Her words silenced the laughs at once and forced the men to lower their gaze. She had struck a note.

"Good, brave Southern gentlemen that you are," she continued, "I know you will let us pass, that you will not stop this honorable man from his duty to return a Southern lady to her rightful home."

The leader of the group stroked his beard. When he finally spoke, he almost sounded apologetic.

"I reckon you're right, ma'am. Can't see the harm in letting you go." He took his soiled and misshapen slouch hat and tipped it in her direction, ordering his men to clear the road.

The raiders galloped a few yards north and then, with the perfect, instinctive symmetry of a flock of birds in flight, veered off the road and into the woods beyond, disappearing as quickly as they had come.

Jonathan put a hand on Apollonia's shoulder and smiled.

"That was a beautiful piece of oratory," he said in genuine appreciation. "You tamed the wild beasts."

She flashed him a look that he hadn't seen in quite a while—haughty, arrogant, clearly angry. She regarded the little dust cloud the raiders had left behind.

"Ignorant white trash," she hissed between her teeth, urging her mare onward.

It took them ten days of travel over rough alpine roads to reach Chattanooga. As they carefully navigated the steep descent from Lookout Mountain, the road and countryside were littered with the rueful detritus of what had obviously been a large and fierce battle, waged not very long ago. They had already learned that the city had fallen to the North during the summer and were thus not surprised to find it filled with battalions of occupation troops.

They were not prepared, however, for the blanket of sadness and resignation that seemed to have settled over Chattanooga like a funeral pall. Along streets decorated with Union flags and sharing the sidewalks with soldiers of the victorious army, the Tennesseans wandered listlessly, their expressions blank and gray. All of them—the women, the children, and the old men—appeared hopeless and exhausted. Jonathan had expected to see anger, perhaps even defiance, on their faces, but these emotions seemed to have retreated from the city along with the Confederate forces who had striven in vain to slow Sherman's advance.

The name Sherman was heard everywhere here, spoken more often than that of Lincoln or Grant, even than Davis or Lee. Local newspapers carried headlines with his name, telling and retelling the story of his relentless and bloody campaign from Tennessee all the way to Atlanta, where his army was now headquartered. They wrote of Johnston and Hood, the Rebel generals who had opposed him at a series of battlefields along the way, only to see their armies flanked and pushed violently aside time and again. Union soldiers spoke loudly and proudly of Sherman in conversations with each other, and civilians spoke of him, too, but in much quieter tones and far less laudatory terms.

Jonathan silently grappled with the idea that Sherman was still a living man, still in command of his men. He was, in fact, only about a hundred miles from Chattanooga at this moment, fighting off Rebel maneuvers to divide and weaken him and no doubt planning his next move, but he was already being spun into myth. He was no longer just another commander in a war full of them. He was becoming Alexander, Khan, and Napoleon, all rolled into one terrible and awe-inspiring figure—a national hero or an arch-assassin, an archangel or Lucifer himself, depending on which side of his sword one happened to be.

Depressed by the vanquished city's gloom, Jonathan and Apollonia left Chattanooga after only two nights of rest, but they were unable to put Sherman out of their minds. On the roads to Atlanta, signs of his work were unavoidable. Every day they passed wrecked wagons, shattered cannon and caissons, skeletal carcasses of horses and mules, spent shells, and discarded pieces of uniforms, all of it offering mute testimony to a summer's worth of steady warfare. The frequent troops who shared these roads with them, and whose impatient pace regularly pushed the travelers aside, apparently had more pressing things to do than clean up the mess of earlier fights.

They found a similar scene near the sleepy town of Adairsville, about a third of the way to Atlanta, where they stopped late one afternoon and where, once again, they found the local innkeepers unable, or unwilling, to take them in. Since the evening was dry and relatively warm, they chose to make camp on the outskirts of town. They made their fire and laid out their blankets beneath two tall trees, not caring that only a few yards away lay yet another field on which Hood had vainly sought to temper Sherman's advance.

They ate a meager supper, after which Apollonia washed their few dishes in a small stream and Jonathan stoked the fire with pieces of broken ammunition boxes he had collected from the battlefield. When they were done with these chores, they leaned back against one of the trees, holding hands and resting their heads together. They looked to the west, where the sunset ranged from pale yellow to somber auburn, and listened to the first calls of the crickets.

As the insect orchestra tuned their bows, Jonathan asked Apollonia if she was feeling all right. All that day she had looked pale and thin, her hair falling unnoticed in her face and her words few. When he spoke, he felt her hand tighten in his.

"You are a keen observer," she said. "I am troubled."

"Can you tell me about it?"

She hesitated and sighed before she answered.

"I am so burdened, Jonathan, and so weary of carrying my burden. I am struggling under the weight of my secrets and ashamed that I am keeping them from you, from the one I love."

Jonathan put his arm around her shoulders, drawing her closer, but said nothing.

She turned to him, gave him a brief, soft kiss, and managed a forced smile.

"Will you listen to my story?"

It was mild as the eventide slowly and luxuriously faded into twilight, the stillness disrupted only by the songs of insects and a flock of colorful pheasants that landed near them and wandered among the broken relics of the abandoned battleground.

Apollonia gazed at the sunset and the birds, into Jonathan's eyes, and then back to the lonely landscape. When she had finally fortified herself, she began.

"Truly, I cannot imagine the thoughts that must haunt your mind, Jonathan," she said evenly. "I beg your forgiveness for my secrecy about everything in Halifax and even more so about Archer Blaine, who is at the center of it all. I shudder to think—as I have shuddered many times over these past few months—that you imagined Archer and I to be lovers."

Jonathan winced in guilt at her words, knowing that he had indeed suspected, more than once, that very thing—knowing, in fact, that deep within his jealous heart, he still suspected it.

He had no way to prepare himself for what she was to say.

"I can understand your suspicions, my love, and even sympathize with you for them, since I am fully to blame for them all. Was it not I who held my secrets with such fierce obsession? Was it not I who stayed by his side all that time, from Mackinac to Richmond and then to Halifax? Was it not I who agreed to be his accomplice in murder, for the love of God?"

She grasped his hand with desperate strength and locked the pupils of her eyes into his.

"Archer Blaine was never my lover, Jonathan. Nor could he have been, for he is my brother."

Jonathan's face remained blank as he stared at her, in the same way that a part of the body does not immediately register the pain that follows a grievous injury. But it was not pain he felt when the import of her words finally completed its synapse loop through his mind. Nor was it pleasure or relief or even surprise. It was total shock.

"I didn't...," he began in confusion.

"You did not assume that I had a brother," she said softly. "You assumed that I was an only child. This is what everybody else believes. This is what I believed myself, until just over a year ago when Archer corrected me on those points."

"My God," he said. "I had no idea. It never even occurred to me."

"Nor had it ever occurred to me, Jonathan. Until the spring of last year, I was passing merrily and stupidly through life, believing myself to be a sophisticated and well-bred lady with none but bright prospects. I had few worries, at least no worries that amounted to anything. I suppose I fretted over growing too old for marriage, but tell me what unmarried woman of twenty-three has no such thoughts? I worried about the war, of course, which is only reasonable. But I had no *real* worries, Jonathan, no worries of my own, until the cursed Sunday afternoon when Archer first appeared at our plantation. From that moment on, continuing to this very hour, the course of my life has been out of my own hands."

She kissed him again and rested her head upon his chest. "If it weren't for you, Jonathan, if it weren't for the day when I heard you play that strange, sad song on poor Jeremiah's guitar—the very first day I saw you at Riverdale, which was the same day I think I fell in love with you—I know I would have gone mad. If you hadn't been there on that awful journey, and if just the memory of you hadn't been with me during all those bleak months when we were apart, I would be dead today, either by my own hand or by Archer's, or I would be a vile creature, living with the stain of murder on my soul."

She bit her lip, fighting tears, as Jonathan held her tightly and then raised her head and continued.

"But all this tells you nothing. To understand it, I must tell you of things that happened before my own birth and far beyond my knowledge—things I did not know until Archer told me of them."

As the twilight deepened, the pheasants took flight into the western sky. The air began to take on a chill, and Jonathan wrapped Apollonia's cloak around her.

"When my family first had contact with him, Archer was a Confederate officer, attached to a Georgia cavalry regiment. He had met my father in town, telling him that he was on some sort of leave from his regiment and staying for a brief time in Savannah. He followed protocol perfectly, asking my father beforehand for permission to pay me a visit, describing his call as a social one, perhaps the initiation of a courtship. My father is a gracious man and a patriot. He did not refuse his permission to this man whom he took to be a gallant cavalier and encouraged me to accept his invitation. Mostly because I did not wish to displease my father, I did so—would that I had not!

"But Archer's was no social call, Jonathan. When we had walked a distance from the house and stopped to rest beneath the arbor, Archer's smooth and charming demeanor changed in an instant. He became brutal in his language and fierce in his eye. His smile became a crooked sneer. Looking back on that day now, it is clear to me that he took great delight in sharing his awful news with me.

"And I believe in my heart that his cruelty was even greater than this, for he knew that I would have to confirm his ill tidings with my mother, for much of what he had to say concerned her. I was forced to do this because it was crucial for me to know that he was speaking the truth and not merely spreading spiteful slander, as I will explain to you later. And I did this. That very night, I confronted my own dear mother with everything he told me that day and everything that I will tell you now, and she confirmed its terrible truth to me, Jonathan. She told me many other things that even Archer does not know. I watched as the heart of that good woman—as true and honorable and loving a mother as ever lived—was broken in two. I performed this act of cruelty, compelled by Archer's cunning and malicious hand, and I held her and cried with her until the wee hours of that dreadful morning and promised her that her secrets would be forever safe with me, that I would never allow the mistakes of her past to return and ruin her life."

Apollonia's piercing gaze returned to his, and a pleading look was in her eyes.

"I am taking you into my confidence tonight, Jonathan, because I know you to be an honorable and trustworthy man with a kind and loving heart. Besides my mother and me—and Archer himself—you are the only living soul to know these things. I tell them to you because I trust you and love you."

"Thank you," he said quietly.

"So now you must hear it. Archer's story began when he told me that he is my half-brother. At first, I laughed at him and called him a liar and a fool, but he persisted."

She paused and sighed deeply.

"As he went on, he told me a great many things about my mother—the woman he claims as his own mother—and so, Jonathan, I must first tell you about her. Her name is Sophia. She is of the Carney family, one of Savannah's oldest and most prominent houses. Unlike my father, who was an immigrant from England as a young man, my mother descends from a family that has re-sided in Savannah since well before the Revolution. The Carneys had, and still have, great wealth and, much more important than this, a reputation in the city that is above any reproach.

"My mother was raised in the city, for the family is in shipping, not agricul-ture. They have, of course, always kept household slaves..."

She paused and looked into the gloaming distance, her breath suddenly com-ing fast. "I am sorry, Jonathan. It is a difficult story to tell. When I first heard it, I thought it was sordid and awful and shameful, but now... now it only seems sad to me. Terribly, terribly sad."

The mournful cry of a whip-poor-will broke the silence.

"I want you to try to imagine the time and place of these events. Imagine that it is 1837, for that is the year when these things took place, and that you are a young woman who resides in Savannah. Try to imagine, if you can, the reaction of the city's society if they were to learn the news that an eighteen-year-old white woman, the daughter of one of the city's most respectable men, had fallen in love with one of her father's black slaves and he with her."

"Your mother...," Jonathan began.

"And try to imagine that the love between this young white woman and this young black man had grown so passionate and so careless that their clandestine relationship was allowed to become intimate. And that out of this fatal intimacy, Jonathan, the young woman discovered herself to be carrying the child of her secret lover."

"My God," he muttered.

"This was exactly the unhappy circumstance of my mother, but despite her carelessness and her passion, she was no fool. She knew full well the sort of disaster that she had visited upon her house, and she also knew that she could not keep her secret for long. As she approached her third month, before she began to show the first outward signs of her condition, she told her parents the truth. I can only imagine how horribly frightful that must have been for her and how terribly courageous she must have been to do it.

"But this was only the beginning of her woes. Her father, my grandfather, was enraged and hurt, of course, but not to the degree that he would allow these dark feelings to cloud his judgment. He was a willful and practical man, not about to let this development ruin the family, for he knew that this could be the only result. The disgrace this would have brought down upon the Carney name would have been complete and devastating. Not only would they have lost their social standing, they would have also lost, as a result, virtually all of their business. Without that, the family fortune was doomed to stagnate, if not diminish entirely, and Isaiah Carney was not about to allow any of that to happen.

"The first thing my grandfather did was to deal with Simon, the slave who was responsible. He did this in the time-honored fashion of our kind, by personally horsewhipping the boy—he was only nineteen—to within an inch of his life. And when he was finished with this, Isaiah Carney sold Simon to a trader from Barbados, a place as distant and remote as he could think of.

"Only then did he deal with his wayward daughter. He did not beat her, to his credit, but he was far from compassionate. He demanded that she immediately have the baby removed in a medical procedure. This was, of course, the most efficient way of eliminating the problem. After all, Southern women, both white and black, had been solving such problems in this way for a very long time. But my grandfather underestimated Sophia. She defied him—my heart still swells to think of the bravery this must have taken—and she absolutely refused to abort her child. When he pressed her even harder, she promised her father that if he demanded the death of her infant, then he would guarantee his own daughter's death as well. She told him that she would cast herself into the Savannah River or stand before a locomotive before she would allow such an act to be performed.

"In the end, he gave in to her, but only on that point. My grandfather quickly spirited her away, leaving her to the care of trusted friends—discreet people who owed him favors and who owned a plantation near Charleston. There, in secrecy and hiding, my mother spent the last six months of her pregnancy, and there her child—a son—was born. She was allowed no more than five minutes with her infant before he was taken from her embrace, Jonathan. Five minutes!"

Apollonia broke into deep sobs that disturbed the stillness of the night. She held Jonathan tightly as she allowed her grief and anger to pass.

"My mother's story is not very complicated after that," she said at last, wiping the tears from her eyes. "She must be considered very fortunate, if one considers the things that might have happened to her. When she returned to Savannah, she was obliged to face no rumors or malicious gossip, let alone prosecution as a criminal, for her act of consorting with a black man was, and still remains, a crime. My grandfather had told all of their relations and acquaintances that Sophia had been to visit distant relatives in Virginia. Not a soul suspected otherwise, including Zachariah Foley, my father, who met my mother in the following year and married her the next. I was born the year after that—an only child, so far as the rest of the world was ever to know."

"And the other child," Jonathan said, "the one born in a blanket of secrecy?"

"He is my half-brother, known to the world, at least today, as Archer Blaine."

"But I'm missing something, Apollonia. Blaine is obviously a white man. Not only is he white, but a Confederate officer, and not only a Confederate, but a fanatic and a dyed-in-the-wool racist."

"Racist?" she asked, puzzled.

Jonathan realized that he had slipped again, using a modern word that would have no reference and carry no relevance for anybody in this time.

"A word I learned out West," he offered. "It means someone who supports the idea that one race is inferior to another."

She looked at him oddly. "Never mind. You say that Archer is a white man, but you are wrong, Jonathan. He is a mulatto, make no mistake, although one of those few who inherited Caucasian characteristics strongly dominant over the Negro—in his case, so dominant that he evinces scarcely a single black trait. His hair is fair and straight, his eyes green, his features almost Nordic. Only the deep shade of his skin, which most would attribute to nothing more than abundant sun, gives any hint.

"As to his feelings about the Confederacy and the beliefs you call 'racist,' there lies the paradox of the man, Jonathan, and perhaps the madness of him."

"Madness?"

"I believe him to be so, Jonathan. I believe him to be so confused, so torn about who and what he is and how he came to be and how he was raised, that he has gone to terrible extremes to erase his own past. He told me in no uncertain terms of the profound shame he feels for having a black father and for having spent his youthful life as a slave. It stoked a horrible rage within his heart . . . and a certain madness. His blind hatred of black people, of everything connected with them, is but a transfer of his hatred for himself and the circumstances of his birth."

Her words made perfect sense to Jonathan and impressed him with their insight and perception. He reminded himself that this was 1864, well before a man named Freud would put such revolutionary psychological ideas into context and perspective. Apollonia continued to surprise him.

"Do not misunderstand me," she went on. "I detest the man. I loathe the very air he breathes, the ground upon which he walks, and I will never forgive him for the pain he has caused my mother and me. And yet . . . ," she looked into the pale yellow light of a crescent moon rising above a distant grove of trees. "Yet I cannot help but pity him as well, for I cannot imagine a life more tragic than his."

She huddled against Jonathan for warmth and continued.

"According to the laws of the state of South Carolina, for that is where he was born, Archer was no slave. Had his mother been black and a slave, then he would have been the legal property of the man who owned his mother, for it is the mother's status of bondage or freedom which dictates the status of the child. Archer's mother—*my* mother—is a free white woman, of course, so although he would have been considered a mulatto, shunned and kept apart from white society, he should have been free from birth.

"But he was told none of this. The family on whose plantation he was born had made a pact with my grandfather that the child would be kept by them and raised as a slave. When he was old enough to ask, Archer was told that his mother was a slave, owned by the family, who died shortly after his birth. To make the lie more believable, Archer was also told that his father was a white man whose identity had never been known. He was assured that he was indeed a slave, and it is Archer's belief now that papers were altered in order to provide a legal provenance to support the deception."

"That is cruel beyond belief," Jonathan muttered.

"It is the inevitable result," Apollonia said evenly, "of a society which allows one human being to own another and which is, to use your Western term, 'racist' down to its roots. It is unimaginably cruel, as you say, Jonathan, but it was considered the only reasonable response to the wretched situation that was created through my mother's carelessness.

"Be that as it may, Archer proved abnormally intelligent as a boy. He did various household chores in his early childhood, chores which often put him in close proximity to the family's other children who were educated at home by tutors, as is often the custom in the country. He told me that he made a habit of listening in on their lessons—their arithmetic, their reading and spelling, their phonics—and that he had become as literate as the white children of the household by the time he was seven years of age. Thereafter, he saw to his own education, borrowing books from the master's library and secreting them away in the cabin where he lived with other slaves, reading scraps of newspapers and discarded almanacs when he could find them, practicing his numbers with the aid of a pilfered textbook and an old abacus.

"It was a breach not only of the family's rules but of the law itself for a slave to learn in this way, and when Archer's studies were discovered—as they were when he was fourteen years old—he fully expected a merciless lashing or worse. But he was fortunate. The master of the house saw Archer's knowledge not as a breach but as an opportunity. He needed someone who could handle his extensive books and correspondence. He immediately realized that Archer's skills at words and numbers would serve him well and that his Caucasian appearance made him eminently suitable for the position. Thus, he was entrusted with matters of business, a far preferable option to what would have awaited him in the cotton fields.

"He told me that in the course of his work, he dealt with white men on a daily basis and did so very professionally. He handled all matters relating to tradesmen and merchants. He corresponded with businessmen, attorneys, and physicians. In time—as he told me—he began not only to speak like educated white men speak but to act like they act, to make gestures and expressions in their fashion, to look white men in the eye and speak to them with assurance and command.

"And in time he began to think like they think. He began to sympathize with their worries and concerns, including their fears that the North was intent on abolition. Along with that, in time, there came to him genuine empathy for the white man's feelings about the Negro, for their belief in their superiority to them and their right to own and exploit them. And by the time, at last, that cries of rebellion were in the air, Archer—a half-breed born of a slave father—became as ardent, as defiant, and as eager for war as any man in the South."

"But how could that be?" Jonathan interjected. "How could a young man, forced to labor for whites his entire life, turn into something like that? It's hard to believe."

"It will never make sense to people like you and me, Jonathan, people who have tasted only freedom, who have never given a thought to what it means to be another's *property*. Do not forget that I used the word madness. I am sure that at some point in his life, Archer lost touch with what can rightfully be called sanity.

"I am guessing about this, I admit, but I believe this madness had a point of origin. You see, it was during the decade that Archer performed clerical duties for his master that he discovered the truth about himself. He came across papers hidden somewhere deep in the family's files—I don't know whether they were documents or letters—but they told him, clearly and completely, the story of his own nativity. He realized, first of all, that he had never been a slave, that he had been lied to and deceived from the beginning. And he was also able to discover that his mother was a white woman from Savannah, by then going by the name of Sophia Foley, living a life that had nothing to do with him.

"The discovery must have shocked him greatly. I believe it may have unhinged the man, but he was no fool. Archer did not take his case to the courts, seeking to establish his freedom through legal means. He had no illusions about how little credence his claims would be given or how spare his chances at receiving a fair hearing would be. Instead, he escaped from the plantation near Charleston, knowing full well that his appearance, coupled with his skills and education, would allow his easy assimilation into white society. He was skillful at records and law, remember, and he simply reinvented himself. He fled to Atlanta, took a new name, contrived a fictional history, and somehow came into money, apparently a significant sum of it, although I have no idea how or where he acquired it. The little mulatto boy born out of wedlock, hidden away under falsehood and shame, became a white man at last.

"By the time war broke out, Archer Blaine was a Confederate officer, full of hatred for the black man, eager and willing to die—and to kill—for a cause that had become much more than sacred to him."

Of Blaine's early period in the Southern army, Apollonia knew very little. She was aware only that he had fought with a Georgia regiment and that he had been captured at Sharpsburg, spending several months in a Union prison up north before returning to the South in a prisoner exchange.

When Blaine eventually showed up at her family's Savannah plantation, he divulged his story and plans to her in stages, over several visits. After he had shocked her with the news of being her half-brother, he provided his own biography, in much the same order that Apollonia had shared the story with Jonathan.

Finally, during an outing in which they strolled through one of the city's ancient cemeteries—and after Apollonia had gone through the painful process of confirming his tidings with her mother—Blaine presented his ultimatum.

He told her that he had been observing Apollonia's family in Savannah for some time and that her relationship with Lord Covington, which by then was well over, was fully known to him. Blaine also informed her that he had learned that Covington had become a key player in relations between Great Britain and the Confederacy and that it was his intention to take advantage of this relationship. He told her, without hesitation, of his intention to murder Covington in Canada with the idea of pinning blame for the crime on the North, thus providing Britain with justification for siding with the South in the American war.

"It had already become a grotesque obsession with him by then," Apollonia said. "He felt absolutely sure that it would succeed, that it was the last great act—that is exactly what he called it—that would save the Confederacy from ruin. I told him that he was a madman, that it was an evil plan doomed to failure, but he merely laughed at me."

"And then he blackmailed you," Jonathan said, beginning to see the long-mysterious pieces of Apollonia's puzzle finally come together.

"He said that he needed me for his plan to succeed. My role was to act as bait, Jonathan—again I use his word. He knew that Lord Covington, who once loved me dearly, would agree to see me. Archer himself could not have met with Covington, for that would have provided a trail of evidence that he could ill afford. If anyone knew that Blaine had met with Lord Covington before his murder, the entire plot would have been pointless. It would have been suspected, if not known for sure, that his murder had been at Confederate, not Union, hands. On the other hand, I was a person entirely unknown to the British, with the exception of Lord Covington himself. And as you discovered, Jonathan, Archer's intention was to kill me afterward, which would have forever silenced me and obscured any connections I had to him.

"Archer told me that unless I complied with his orders, he would publicly reveal the secret of his birth, that he would destroy my mother's name and our family's position. He put the entire fate of my family into my hands, knowing even before our first meeting that I would have no choice but to obey. He knows a great deal about the Southern sense of honor and estimated my character shrewdly. He was sure that I would go to great lengths—perhaps even so far as death—to preserve my mother's good name and my family's honor."

She took Jonathan's hand in hers, warming it, perhaps reassuring herself. "And he was right, Jonathan. Even before we left the cemetery that day, I told him that I would go along. I gave him my word that I would do as he said—even to the point of murder—and he gave me his word that my mother's secret would lie hidden forever after. I had no choice but to believe him or at least to hope that he was being honest."

Apollonia sighed deeply and looked at the stars that were appearing in the black sky above them. "It was a devil's bargain."

Blaine's demands were straightforward, she said. Apollonia would travel to Michigan, ostensibly to stay with her uncle's family near Saginaw, but in reality because of Michigan's proximity to Canadian territory. She would be escorted by Jasper and, once there, was to await further word from Blaine. His summons would come when he was able to ascertain the time and place of Lord Covington's next junket to Canada. When he knew that, he would come for her, and together they would travel to the location of their prey.

"It was in late June, just before Gettysburg, when we began our journey up North. I never told my mother the actual goal and circumstances of the trip—I knew it would devastate her to know—but I am sure she suspected the hand of Archer behind it all. My father, thankfully, knew nothing of Archer's true identity or purpose and believed me when I told him that I had grown weary of the war and of Savannah and hoped that a stay of several months at my Uncle Timothy's, so far from the strife and suffering, would be healthful for me. But my father would not permit me to travel alone, nor could he be made aware of my villainous escort and Archer's plan. After much pleading, Archer allowed me to bring Jeremiah along—although he detested him and hated the idea. We were led by Jasper, that wretched man. It was a difficult journey, even perilous at times, but we made it to Saginaw just as the fall was setting in.

"At Riverdale, I waited. There was nothing more for me to do. I played my Aunt Alexandra's harpsichord for hours upon hours, I conversed endlessly with my cousin Emily, I advised Phineas on the watch business he hoped to establish, I listened to Uncle Timothy's endless tales of the whispering pines and the men who cut them down. I hate myself for saying so, Jonathan, but I nearly died of boredom at Riverdale—and of dread, for hanging over me at every second, like the blade of a guillotine, was the thought of Archer and the summons I knew he would soon issue.

"Jasper, as you know, stayed in Saginaw, living in that little house in the township and posing as a photographer in town. He hired the Chippewa, the man we called Cloud, as his helper. As I had promised Archer earlier, I spoke with Jasper at regular intervals, meeting him in the woods or riding to the farmhouse, to hear if any news from Archer had arrived.

"But we learned very quickly that Archer's original plans had been interrupted. It had been his intention to come to Saginaw directly from Richmond when the time was opportune, but his affiliation with the Secret Service forced him to alter those plans. Shortly after we arrived in Michigan, Archer was ordered to Chicago to assist in an operation that had something to do with shipping on the Great Lakes. He adapted to the new situation, going to Chicago with the intention of deserting the operation when the time came, traveling to Saginaw to collect me and the others, and then making the short trip to Canada with the intent of murder.

"Before he left for Chicago, Archer had learned that Lord Covington was expected in Toronto in late December. He informed Jasper that he would be in Saginaw no later than the fifteenth of that month and instructed him to tell me to be ready to travel.

"But the fifteenth of December came and went with no word from Archer. When news of his fate finally did arrive, it was nearly Christmas, and although the news was greatly troublesome to Jasper, I confess that it gave me at least a moment of hope. I still do not know how or why it happened, but Archer was arrested in Chicago, taken as a spy by the police, and then turned over to the army. They sent him to the fort at Mackinac as a prisoner of war, and from there—no doubt using his guile and grace at furtive matters—he was able to smuggle out a letter to Jasper.

"I was joyful at first, Jonathan, hoping that his arrest would prove the death-blow to his plot against Lord Covington, but I underestimated Archer. In his letter, he described how he had already devised a plan for his own escape—the very plan in which you participated—and ordered Jasper and me to execute it when the spring thaw made swift travel possible.

"Nor had he given up his intentions regarding Lord Covington. He had no choice but to miss Lord Covington's visit to Toronto in December, of course, but he was determined to learn of the next one. That presented yet a new problem. The only way to ascertain the critical knowledge was to return to Richmond and whatever source he had there and then make the trip all the way back to Canada. All the while, I was to follow him like an obedient dog, waiting for her master's final order to attack, which I did, detesting myself at every step along the way."

"It explains the gloom that hovered over you the whole time," Jonathan said quietly.

Apollonia smiled and squeezed his hand.

"It also explains why I was so desperate to have you along, Jonathan. I knew you were meant to be my ally from the beginning. Perhaps someday I will be able to understand how I knew that, and then I will explain it to you. For now, it must suffice that I simply knew it. I knew I could not have survived the ordeal if it had not been for you.

"And Archer sensed that, too. He had agreed to allow you to accompany us to Richmond only because I finally stood up to him and demanded it. I told him that I would desert the entire plan, no matter the consequences, if he did not permit you to come. He relented at last but, as you know all too well, only for so long. As we neared Richmond, his suspicions of you grew greater than ever. I still do not know if he feared you more as a spy or as my defender—I believe he may have suspected both—but he stiffened in the end. That night near Culpeper, he gave me two choices. Either we leave you behind, asleep in the woods, or he would kill you outright. I had no doubt of his seriousness. You know which choice I made."

"And when you got to Richmond," Jonathan interjected, "Blaine wasted little time eliminating your last remaining friend."

In the starlight, Jonathan saw the pools of tears that formed around her eyes. He heard the sob she fought as she tried to speak.

"He broke my heart when we abandoned you, Jonathan. I had only a moment to slip my locket and a pitiful note into your pocket. And then he broke my heart again when he took poor Jeremiah to that trader in Richmond. He forced me to sign the papers of sale, with Jeremiah standing there to see it all! It was the last time I saw him alive, Jonathan, standing in a filthy slaver's office, signing away the life of the man who had protected me and confided in me and helped me and taught me since I was a baby. I have never done anything so terrible and wicked in my entire life. And now he's dead—murdered!—with no way to ever forgive me for what I did to him."

Jonathan pulled her closer. "It was not wicked, and Jeremiah knew that," he whispered. "He knew that you were forced to do what you did. He knew it wasn't your choice. I told you that his last words were of you. He told me to protect you from harm. You have to believe me when I tell you that he never thought for a moment that you had done anything that required his forgiveness."

When she was able to speak again, in a weak and broken voice, she thanked him for his words and for what he had done for Jeremiah. Jonathan had given him a few weeks of dignity and freedom and friendship—gifts, she said, that were so profound they defied description. She told him that what he had done in freeing Jeremiah was an atonement for the sin she had committed in selling him away and proved that she was right in knowing that Jonathan was destined to be her ally.

For that, she thanked him with a kiss.

"And yet," Jonathan said after their lips had parted, "your ally proved to be a few minutes late when the moment of truth arrived in Halifax—for Jeremiah and for you. Your hero did not appear in the nick of time."

"But you came, Jonathan! You came back to me! I cannot imagine the torment you endured to get there—the battle, the wounds, the escapes, the miles upon miles you traveled. When I saw you standing there, looking so confused, soaking wet and freezing, my gun to your throat, for the love of God—but gloriously, wondrously, beautifully alive—you gave *me* life, Jonathan. I have never had a happier moment, and I can only hope that in the years ahead I can repay you for it."

He began to speak, but she put a finger to his lips, hushing him.

"Now listen to me carefully, my love, and understand what I am about to say. You stormed into Lord Covington's cabin at the right time, not the wrong time. Had you come earlier and found me still wavering, with that dreadful bottle of poison hidden in my dress and the possibility of murder still lurking in my mind, I would never have known the truth of my own heart. I would have been condemned to live the rest of my life without knowing whether I would have made the good choice or the evil one. You spared me that torture, Jonathan, just by being a few precious minutes late."

"You made the right choice, Apollonia."

"I made the only choice I could, Jonathan."

"And that choice may come at a great cost."

"I fear it will bear an awful cost."

"Tell me why you acted as you did."

She smiled and pulled her cloak tighter.

"I have told you so many things tonight, Jonathan—happy things and tragic things—and I am weary of so much talk. We have a long road ahead of us, with plenty of time. You are tired, too. Kiss me good night."

He did kiss her, then draped a blanket over both of their forms as they huddled closely. And despite the many things they had confessed and learned, and all the unknown implications of this fresh knowledge, they slept like children beneath the diamond stars of the Georgia night.

They smelled and tasted Atlanta's doom before they ever saw it.

They realized that this once proud flagship of the Confederacy, this once critical crossroads of logistics for the Rebel army, was in dire straits long before they witnessed it with their own eyes. In the two hard days it took them to ride from Adairsville, they had seen plentiful evidence.

Not only was there ever more of the military wreckage that marked Sherman's final push to take the city late in the summer, there was human wreckage as well. Hundreds of people—both black and white—had settled along the sides of the road. Some of them were camped on open ground; others took meager shelter in shanties thrown together from scrap lumber and tin, most of them without roofs. They cooked what little food they had on struggling little fires and huddled in dirty coats and dresses as they watched the strangers travel southward.

From one of them, a thin and fidgety woman valiantly trying to keep track of her ample brood of children, they learned that these roadside castaways were former residents of Atlanta. They, along with the entire population of the city, had been ordered by Sherman to evacuate when Atlanta had fallen to Union hands. The Northern commander had shown no mercy, even evicting the old and sick, including patients in hospitals. The lucky ones had relatives or friends in the country, hence a safe haven from their newfound homelessness. The unlucky ones, such as those along this battered highway, had been simply turned out and left to their own devices.

"Y'all be finding the same thing on each and every road out of Atlanta," the thin woman said. "General Sherman, curse his name and soul, said he was a-gonna make Georgia howl, and I guess he's doin' it now. This place is howlin' like an old hound dog on a full moon's night."

Nor was the emptying of the city the end of the warrior's work.

On Jonathan and Apollonia's first night after leaving Adairsville, spent in the open near a squatter's shanty, they saw a mellow orange glow to the south. The next morning, still a day out of Atlanta, they began to smell it, at first no more than a furtive and occasional scent of bitter woodsmoke, wafting like a spirit on the cool breeze. By noon, it had become constant and pungent. By late afternoon, it stung the eyes, transformed the sun into a surreal umber sphere, and cast an appalling, dreamy haze over the bleak November landscape.

By the time they reached the outskirts of Atlanta, night had fallen, and the flames themselves were easy to see.

A lone traveler told them how Sherman's men had put the entire city to the torch, just before he steered his army toward the sea and left Atlanta behind.

"It's not enough that our own boys set the town on fire back in September, trying to destroy the munitions," lamented the stranger, a middle-aged man who limped and walked with a stick. "Now the Yanks have got to burn the whole damn thing down."

He looked behind him at the burning city, the yellow-orange glow of the flames reflecting in the shine on his face. "She was young and fair, Atlanta was," he said quietly. "And now the Lord has forsaken her."

He walked northward, tapping his stick on the hardpan road, speaking low to himself.

As they rode into the city at last, the only sound either of them made was the whispered "My God" from Apollonia.

There were no guards or sentries at the northern approach, nor did they see a single soldier, Northern or Southern, anywhere. They knew that the Northern juggernaut had already embarked on its journey to the southeast and had no idea what had become of the Southern army. Jonathan and Apollonia had the road essentially to themselves, save for an occasional figure darting here and there in the ever-shifting shadows that danced between the flames.

The flames were everywhere. In the semirural suburbs, virtually every house and barn was burning or had already been reduced to ashes. As they entered the town proper, they saw entire blocks of homes and stores charred to blackened ruins, others still engulfed in the full and furious thrall of the blaze. Here, the inferno roared, and the travelers found it useless to speak. They were reluctant, in any case, to open their mouths for fear of inhaling the heavy soot that was already settling on their heads and shoulders. Their horses, bravely fighting an instinct to panic, did their best to pick their way through the smoking debris that littered every street. The nocturnal horizon was an unassailable wall of fire, raging behind the black silhouettes of structures yet to fall.

It was all strangely familiar to Jonathan, yet horribly different at the same time.

He had seen Atlanta burn before, of course, in his own distant time, sitting before a television set that showed *Gone with the Wind*. He recalled the dramatic scene as Scarlett, Melanie, Prissy, and Rhett raced frantically before the flames and beheld the genuine scene before him now. The film had captured no more than a tiny fraction of the intensity of the reality, he realized, yet some things were uncannily familiar. He gazed at Apollonia riding beside him, her beautiful face revealing only resignation and blank shock, and seemed to remember an identical expression crossing the beautiful face of Vivien Leigh in her cinematic reflection. The feeling this gave him only enhanced the apocalyptic strangeness of the moment.

He also thought of a young man named Johnny Shawnessy, dimly remembered from a book that told a similar tale but from a drastically different point of view. Did not this youthful Johnny, from his mythical Raintree County far to the north, stand in his blue uniform at the Atlanta railroad station and watch his comrades obey their general's command to set everything afire? Did he not marvel at the grand symbolic drama that played out before his fictional eyes, much as Jonathan now marveled himself?

Yet Jonathan could not evade this: Apollonia was no Scarlett and Jonathan no Johnny, and their prosaic burning Atlantas were no match for this one. For all the skill and artistry of their authors, those stories told of a drama that was but a pale simulacrum. There was genuine drama here and now—towering, majestic, awesome, and terrible—but it was drama without aesthetic design or artistic purpose. It was the chaotic, roaring, burning, smoking, choking, earth-grinding, deathly drama of a troubled world in the act of rebirth.

And it was familiar to Jonathan in other ways.

As they traversed the city, finding routes that led away from the worst of the conflagration, they finally came upon people who were trying to stand in the way of the disaster. Perhaps half a dozen firemen encircled a single enflamed house. They had a horse-drawn tanker and pumper on the street and two men furiously trying to maintain its pressure, but the water that flowed from their hose was thin and weak.

Why did they bother, Jonathan wondered to himself. While their entire city burned, why did one frail engine company attempt, with few men and dwindling water, to save a single house? Was it because this one struggle, this solitary victory, might grant them a moment's salvation from the ultimate destruction that engulfed them?

Perhaps recognizing the futility of their efforts at last, one of the firefighters walked away from the rest and approached the street. As Jonathan and Apollonia passed, he gazed at them, saying nothing. He wore a leather fireman's helmet and a dark canvas coat that reached to his shins. His face was black from soot, and the jarring contrast of his pale blue eyes made Jonathan think of a comic in blackface, but the expression in those eyes was anything but humorous.

It spoke of something far beyond anger or sadness. It spoke of a fatigue that reached past the body and mind and had already entered the inner sanctum of the soul.

And this, too, Jonathan had seen before.

He had seen the same expression in his own time, on the faces of firemen whose helmets and coats and boots looked remarkably similar. It was the September morning that witnessed the fall of two great towers and their dissolution into dust—a day, much like this night, when the Reaper himself rode triumphantly on eddies of smoke and ash.

Jonathan looked at the curtains of fire embracing the once young, once fair Atlanta and realized how very little had changed.

It was well past midnight by the time they had picked and dodged their way to the eastern outskirts of the city. There were fires here as well, but they were spread farther apart and seemed more random, as if the Northern men with their torches had begun to grow weary of their arsonist duties.

Very few people were about as they rode through an area of humble frame houses, separated from each other by small plots of tilled land, although their livestock—horses, cows, chickens, and goats—roamed the dirt roads at will, casting leery glances at the scattered outbreaks of flame.

Jonathan glanced at Apollonia riding beside him. Her face was dusted with a layer of black ash, as his must have been. Tears from her smoke-filled eyes had left tracks down her cheeks. Her hair hung low in her face and her eyes were closed, as if she were asleep. Her posture on the horse seemed precarious.

He stopped and halted her mare by taking its reins. "We have to rest," he said, causing her eyes to shoot open. She was obviously disoriented.

"No, Jonathan," she said softly. "We have to ride on. We have to get home…"

He smiled at her smudged face. "I think you're dreaming, love. It's still over two hundred miles to Savannah. There are houses here and nobody around. Nobody will care if we homestead for a night or two."

She nodded wearily and drew her hand across her forehead, removing a swatch of soot.

They settled that night—and for the next several days and nights—in an un-burnt little saltbox house, set tidily between two young oaks. They slept deeply and undisturbed and emerged in the smoky morning to their own filthy bodies and the sight of a city reduced to smoldering rubble. Apollonia made a fire in the little stove, and Jonathan hauled buckets of water from a nearby well. They heated the water, bathed in it together, washing the ash from each other's bodies, and then washed their clothes. Later, they made coffee and breakfast, helping themselves to the modest pantry like burglars.

For several days—Jonathan lost count of their exact number—they rested, ate, talked about what they had seen in Atlanta, and watched a slow procession of residents begin to return to their homes or to smoking piles that had once been their homes—a somber exodus in reverse. During this homecoming of refugees, they heard cries and curses—and the somehow more awful silence—and Jonathan realized that they were witnessing the painful birth of a profound Southern ha-tred, stubborn vestiges of which would still linger in his own time.

At last, on a cold morning when the smell of smoke seemed to have finally grown faint, the owners of the saltbox house—a man, his wife, and two small children—returned. Jonathan and Apollonia greeted the strangers from their own porch. Jonathan apologized to the man, explained their situation, expressed his thanks, and pressed five dollars into his hand. In less than ten minutes, they were packed and mounted, nudging their horses toward the road to Savannah.

"Homestretch," Jonathan said as they headed out.

She gave him a ghost of a smile. "I didn't know you were a gambler, Jonathan. When did you spend time at the racecourse? When you were a sailor on the lakes, or when you were panning for gold in Colorado?"

The tone of her question made him uneasy. There was something disturb-ingly intuitive about it. "I don't remember" was all he offered.

She halted before the smoking skeleton of what had recently been a sizable farmhouse. Pathetic debris lay beneath their horses' hooves—the burnt remnants of books, kitchen utensils, the wooden head of a doll.

"It doesn't matter, Jonathan," she said. "I am just having fun with you, but I do want to say something serious, and I want to say it before we go out there."

She pointed a gloved hand toward the southeast, toward Savannah, in the direction of a terrible army that approached the city as a wolf approaches a wounded deer.

She brought her horse flank to flank with his and looked Jonathan in the eye.

"I have told you a great many things about myself," she said. "They have been awful, terrible things, Jonathan. It has not been easy for me to do this, but I have done it because I love you and desperately want you to have trust in me."

"I do trust you."

"Do you, my love? I have trusted you with my darkest, most terrible secrets. Why do you not trust me with yours?"

He began to blurt an automatic response of denial. It had become a necessary reflex in this time, a means of preventing the discovery of something that was far better left unknown and unsuspected. He knew that he had already given this rehearsed reply—this dishonesty—to Apollonia more than once, and now, after everything that had befallen them both, he no longer wanted to continue the charade.

And yet he stopped himself from starting his confession. He feared its consequences in spite of everything.

"You are different, Jonathan," she said, ignoring his silence. "Your speech is different, the music you play is different, the way you look at *everything* is different. And yet you are the same. I love you, but I do not understand you. You are a mystery to me. You say that you come from the West, and perhaps that is true, but I know that you come from somewhere else as well. You come from a place that nobody here has been to. You have seen things that nobody here has seen. Why do you hide it from me?"

She reached over and took his hand in hers. When she spoke, he saw the beginning of a tear form at the corner of her eye.

"Do you remember how I once told you that I dreamt of you, Jonathan, even before I met you?"

"Yes."

"I dreamt that I was in a strange place, a place I did not know. It was night and cold, and the smell of rain was in the air. It was in a room, very dark, and I dreamt that I had somehow entered the room and that my presence awakened you. And another time, I saw you in an ordinary house. I stood on a staircase and looked down on you—I *know* it was you."

Jonathan felt a chill run up his spine. He remembered his own dreams, in a dark hotel room on a cold and rainy night, in which a furtive female figure had lurked in the shadows, and after suddenly awakening in his house in Saginaw.

"In the first dream, you rose from your bed," she continued, "and came toward me. You asked me who I was, and the sound of your voice, the profile of your face frightened me. I do not know why, but it frightened me greatly, and I withdrew from you."

"You withdrew into a corner," he said softly, "and whispered no."

She gasped. "How do you know that?" The tear swelled and then released itself, collapsing under its own weight.

"I had the same dreams, Apollonia. And later, when I saw you in person, I knew it had been you who visited me."

A sob escaped from her—he could not tell if it signaled sadness or joy—and another tear followed the first.

"In my fear, I stepped back from you, Jonathan, and when I did, I retreated into darkness and then awoke. I was trembling. It was much more than a nightmare. It was too real to have been a nightmare, too real to have been just a dream."

"I think so, too."

"What does it mean?"

He shook his head and tried to smile. He felt his own tear beginning to form and wiped it away.

"I think it means that we are supposed to be together," he said, "that it was our destiny to find each other. I think it means that all of this was supposed to happen."

Jonathan gestured widely with his arms, encompassing not only the charred city around them but much beyond that. She nodded, as if she understood.

"I was in my bed at Riverdale when I had my dream. Where were you when you had yours, Jonathan?"

He hesitated. "I was far from you. A great distance away."

"Why can't you tell me, for God's sake?"

Jonathan wasn't quick enough to wipe his second tear away. It escaped and ran down his cheek, in plain view of Apollonia, whose own face was now streaked with them, and somehow this exposure, this nakedness, helped him cross a threshold from which he knew he could never step back.

"It's not easy," he said at last. "It's not an easy thing to talk about, but you're right. I am hiding something, but it's not because I don't trust you. I have hidden my past from you for the same reason that you have revealed yours to me—I don't want to lose you. I don't want to scare you away. I couldn't live with that."

"Is it something so terrible? Have you done something so very wicked?"

"My only wickedness is that I love you," he said, kissing her hand, "my only goodness the same."

This brought a tentative smile back to her lips. "Once more, you speak to me in a poet's words. How it makes me love you and want to kiss you and hold you to hear such things! But you shall not evade me, Jonathan Chase. We are to be together, are we not? We are not going to part?"

"I pray to God that we will be together."

"Then we must be true with each other—both of us. We will have no secrets in our hearts. You needn't fear that I will desert you if you tell me yours—I promise you that I will not, no matter what it is—and you must have enough trust in me to believe that."

"I do believe it."

"I shall not press you. You will tell me when you are ready, Jonathan, but please, please, do not ignore my plea. You are the man I love—the only man I have ever loved, the only man I hope ever to love. I want to share my life with you and for you to share yours with me. You must take me back to where you have been..."

She hesitated and gave him a look he had only rarely seen on her face, a strong and determined expression of will and courage.

"Or I shall follow you there."

He drew her closer and kissed her.

"You won't have to follow me," he said. "I promise that I'll tell you every-thing, as soon as our journey is complete and you're safely back home."

She smiled and nodded, putting her blessing on a deal well made.

Facing the sun, they set out across the even land of the piedmont, both of them quiet now, contemplating the road ahead and its destination.

DIARY OF
APOLLONIA
FOLEY

December

The snowy white heavens are frozen and clean,
Scented with woodsmoke and evergreen.
All living things sadly cover their heads,
Saving their warmth within winter beds.
The days have grown short, denying the sun—
Its passage completed, the year is done.

I hope that my humble song of winter is not too sad or solemn, for I do not intend it so. I do not grieve in this dark season, despite its frost and its temporary death, for I understand and value its place in the order of things. Without it, none of the other seasons could exist, just as winter could not exist without them. If I have learned anything in this tumultuous year that is about to end, it is that everything that passes bears a purpose, that all of its passions—the glory, the tragedy, the agony, and the joy—weave themselves into a mysterious tapestry we call "reality" and that somewhere within this mystery of mysteries truth resides.

Faith, I realize now, is merely the recognition of this fact, not any sort of arrogant or foolish claim to actually understand that which we idealize as truth. I do not believe this to be possible in our benighted human state. All we can do is *strive* to understand truth and to remain loyal to what we believe to be its ideals. To believe in the existence of a greater good, and to seek to attain it, is the best we can do.

Yet this is no easy task. In this vast conflict which engulfs our nation, I see manifest this very difficulty. I now believe with all my heart that the cause of the North is just and good, for how could the liberation of an entire people be anything but good? Yet in the past days, I have seen much of the means by which the North has worked to achieve this end. I have seen an entire city in flames and miles upon miles of misery. I have seen people forced from their homes—white and black people alike—and cast helplessly adrift.

I have seen a noble cause furthered in evil ways. I confess that this perplexes me. I admit that this truth is beyond my comprehension.

The currents of my own life are no easier to grasp. I strove to do good in Halifax—I remain convinced that I did—yet I know that my act will bring a woeful harvest. I feel this now more painfully than ever, for my home is desperately close to me as I write. I am filled with joy and dread at the same moment—joy at the thought of once more embracing my mother and father, at returning to the land from which I sprang, and dread at the thought of how my decision may have affected them. I am not sure whether they will be overjoyed to see their lost and wandering daughter or blinded with rage to see the one who has brought such shame and ruin upon their house.

This perplexes me no less.

Yet in spite of my apprehensions, I shall not be deterred in my homeward journey. I go steadily there, as the needle of a compass points without fail to the north, as a migratory bird flies unerringly to the south when the seasons change. For where else but home can we go when all else fails us?

It is well into December now. The blessed Yuletide draws near. I do not believe it is possible to be alive in this season without thinking of home. As I write, I smell the sweet scent of Georgia pines, the smoke of wood fires, and the great sea that grows closer by the hour. I feel the tiny flakes of snow that are falling upon my face. The whisper of home seems to resonate with my every breath.

Home—the word itself is safe and warm. I want to weep with the joy and the sadness of it, for I know that the home I once knew, and which I still blindly seek, can no longer exist. The ravages of the war, the fruits of my own choice—these will assure that neither my family nor Savannah will ever be the same for me again. I can never return to that cherished place and time, except in memory.

Just a short while ago, the knowledge of this would have broken my heart. Yet it does not do so now, for I have also come to know this: Home is not something that can be explained or measured on a map or a calendar.

Home is neither a place nor a time but a state of the soul—a vital piece of that mystery we call truth. It is the helping hand and the kind voice that reach across the greatest of distances, the courage that challenges and overcomes the most dire of perils, the light that shines through the darkest of nights.

And it is no wonder I write of home now. Jonathan and I are soon to embark upon the last stage of our journey. We propose to cross the boundary between two armies at war. I understand the dangers of such an undertaking yet feel no fear. He will be beside me as I go. I need know no more than this.

He has promised me that once we arrive he will tell me all of his secrets—all of the unseen paradoxes and riddles that have troubled me since I met him. I am grateful for his earnestness to share this with me and look eagerly forward to hearing him tell his story, yet I no longer expect to be surprised.

For I believe that I have finally come to understand Jonathan Chase, this man who was once a perplexing stranger to me. More than this, I believe I may have already divined the nature of his secret. I know it to be a strange and staggering thing to believe, and it astonishes me that I accept it without hesitation.

Yet even this does not trouble me, for I know that in him I have already come home—the true immortal home of the soul—and there can be no troubles here.

DECEMBER

SAVANNAH

THE BEACON by which they traveled on the terminal leg of their journey was the tragic and turbulent wake of Sherman's march to the sea.

The Union army was not very far before them, and the peculiar procession that clung to the tail of that army was even closer, sometimes close enough that Jonathan and Apollonia found themselves within sight of it. This caravan, like the army, was massive but, unlike the army, had no component of order or discipline to it. It was composed of thousands of black people—men, women, and children in roughly equal number—some of whom were slaves who had only recently been freed by the invaders, others newly escaped, having taken advantage of the moment's opportunity to flee.

Even from a distance of miles, their throng could be seen, a conglomeration of African faces in random shades of brown. The garments they wore were an eclectic mix of tattered rags and field clothes, elegant evening attire apparently pilfered from white closets, and outrageously colorful bandannas, shirts, and coats whose origins could only be surmised.

They were a vagabond population of American gypsies, homeless and no doubt hungry and cold much of the time, for they seemed to carry no provisions or means of shelter. Yet for all their hardships, they seemed far from disconsolate. Their songs belied any notions of misery. These could be heard by day and night alike and took several forms. Sometimes they were enthusiastic call-and-response choruses that drifted through and around the walking throng like hallelujahs in a Baptist church. Sometimes, especially at night, they were soaring gospel melodies that sounded both mournful and joyful at once. Sometimes the songs they sang eerily echoed the blues music that Jonathan remembered from his own time.

But the words to all the songs, regardless of their form, focused on an identical theme. They were invariably about freedom, with the singers often comparing themselves to the ancient Hebrews who wandered through the Sinai and arrived at the promised land. The words "free at last" were heard in many of their melodies, which made Jonathan better understand why a twentieth-century minister would choose those very words to articulate a later phase of the very same struggle.

These people were indeed free at last, a fact that triggered both the realization of an old and cherished dream and the birth of new and unknown prospects. And for the moment, the sheer fact of that freedom seemed enough to sustain them— seemed enough, at this early stage, to constitute that promised land of which they'd so long dreamed. There would be plenty of time for hunger and fatigue and worry and fear tomorrow. For now, it seemed enough for them to blindly follow this army of strangers from the distant North—the agents of their salvation—and to sing songs of jubilation and gratitude for their severance from bondage.

The sight and sound of them was the most potent proof Jonathan had yet seen that the great American struggle was finally drawing to its ragged and violent coda. The slaves' joyful and disorderly displacement, even more than the flames of Atlanta, bore loud witness to the tectonic shifting of history.

But there were plentiful additional signs for the travelers to glimpse, for in front of the black exodus marched the blue legion, the taste of victory already in its mouth but the final day not yet seized.

Jonathan knew something of the history of this march—how it destroyed virtually everything in the wide swath it cleaved through the Georgian piedmont and forests, effectively snapping the Southern spine. But as he rode with Apollonia at his side, seeing its physical devastation at every turn, Jonathan realized that his history books had barely skimmed the surface.

It was like following the path of a tornado.

The army was feeding itself off the land. Whatever late crops had been left in the ground had been scoured by its foragers, leaving little but husks and stubble behind. Barns and silos had been emptied of their harvest bounties, thousands of livestock slaughtered on the spot, even the pantries of farmhouse kitchens raided.

What they did not take with them, they burned, and what they did not need but thought the enemy might somehow profit from, they also burned. Jonathan lost count of the number of torched houses and barns they were able to see from the pummeled roads on which they traveled. Whole fields were likewise put to the torch, especially corn drying in shocks. The army seemed determined that even the animals that had somehow escaped would have nothing to eat come winter. The bitter reek of charred corn brought home to him the full meaning of scorched earth.

Bridges were blown asunder after the army crossed the rivers they spanned. Railroad tracks were methodically and thoroughly torn up, the ties burned in great bonfires, the rails laboriously twisted around trees until they looked like grotesque pretzels that the Yankees, with callous gallows humor, coined Sherman's neckties.

Some of the destruction was apparently wanton, with no tactical motive. While some small towns were almost leveled by troops as they passed through, others survived virtually unscathed, only to fall prey a day or two later to wandering bands of renegade soldiers called "bummers," whose apparent freedom from command only sharpened their appetite for atrocity. More than once, when Jonathan or Apollonia conversed with slaves straggling behind the army, they were warned to steer clear of these unpredictable and often intoxicated vandals.

It was wearying to the travelers, not only to avoid the bummers but to pass through the valley of the shadow that Sherman was casting behind him. Although Jonathan recognized the reasons for such devastation and understood how the cause to which it was dedicated was a noble and necessary one, he was still overwhelmed by the mind-boggling savagery of it all.

In his heart, he knew that he supported the cause of the North and the force that furthered that cause, but he could not help but detest the soldiers for the obvious pleasure they took in tearing the heart out of this land. He had no sympathy for slaveholders or those who fought to defend them, but he could not help but sympathize with the poor farmers and townsfolk unlucky enough to find themselves in this brutal path. He shared the joy of the newly freed slaves but worried about where they would turn when the struggle was over in a few months' time and pitied them for the bleakness of their near future.

He knew that Sherman himself, commanding his troops only a few miles away from where Jonathan and Apollonia now rode, would one day say that war is hell. As Jonathan looked at the man's work from close up, he realized that in addition to his skills as a warrior, the general had a gift for understatement. To what they were seeing, hell didn't do proper justice.

By day they rode, making only modest progress over the trampled roads. More than once they were forced to take long detours because the bridges along the way had been blasted.

By night they slept, huddling in forsaken houses and barns after ensuring that no bummers had already claimed them as their own. There had been two close calls, when Jonathan's furtive reconnaissance led to the discovery of renegade soldiers, but in neither case was his own presence detected. Food was scarce. They subsisted on what little they found in the trees and fields, occasionally getting lucky enough to find something the army and former slaves had left behind.

One night, they shared a corncrib with six women, two of them with infants, stragglers from the convoy of slaves. At first, the women were suspicious of these nomadic whites—and perhaps quietly resentful of their presence—but they grew gradually more comfortable as the night went on. Jonathan attributed this entirely to Apollonia, who, without being asked, joined their chorus of "Swing Low, Sweet Chariot," sung as a lullaby for the babies.

Apollonia's voice was pure and soft, far from strong, yet its fragility blended beautifully with the robust and rich voices of the others. She sang with a conviction that could only come from the heart, and the women who were no longer slaves were immediately sensitive to it and responded with a guarded respect.

It gave him a pleasing chill to hear her, not only because it was the first time he'd heard her sing. It was also the way she knew the song and expertly found her part in the harmony. It said something about how familiar she was with slaves and their culture and highlighted the ironic relationship that the white people of her time and place had with the black people.

It also saddened him to hear her, because he could feel the lament in her voice. On the road, she was quiet for much of the time, lost in her own thoughts, and seldom initiated conversations. When he spoke to her, he saw how she forced her smiles. He knew that she was thinking of her family and home, with the enemy army bearing down upon them, and worrying about who else might arrive there before they would. By now, Jonathan knew her well enough to realize the futility of trying to draw out her feelings. She would discuss them when she was ready to do so, not before.

But that night in a lopsided corncrib, barely lit by the flame of a solitary candle, he heard those feelings in her voice. When she sang "comin' for to carry me home," with half a dozen beautiful voices singing along, Jonathan knew exactly what she was singing about.

They parted with the women the following morning and soon came across a large crowd of the former slaves, gathered by the banks of a wide river. A soft-spoken adolescent boy told them that the army had speedily crossed the waterway and then quickly withdrew their pontoons behind them.

"Some of duh colored folks drowned in the river," the boy said, "'cos they was already tryin' to cross over when they pulled the pontoons. Duh Yankee army done leavin' us behind, so wot we all goin' to do now?"

Jonathan had no answer for him. He and Apollonia had no idea what all these displaced people were to do or where they should go. They were the inevitable human flotsam of war, the pushed aside and cast away. Their fate was much more in history's hands than their own.

Powerless to help, Jonathan and Apollonia turned from the bewildered crowd and headed south, finally coming to an undamaged bridge that spanned the river.

It cost them an entire day to head back north on the right bank and regain the Savannah road.

And in this way, weary but determined, they continued to traverse the vanquished state of Georgia, wayfarers in a broken and bleeding land.

On their seventh day out of Atlanta, Jonathan rose before dawn. He left the barn in which they'd slept and made himself a cigarette as the eastern sky turned from powder blue to gold. Well down the road ahead of him, he saw the silhouette of an abandoned church against the brightening sky. The cross atop its narrow steeple stirred something in him, a vague but moving feeling about God and Jerusalem, even though the feeling wasn't entirely a religious one. It spoke more to him of hope than it did of faith—the sort of hope that Jesus must have clung to as he dragged his crossbeam up the long climb to Calvary, the hope once beautifully expressed in the belief that the darkest hour comes just before the dawn. It called to mind something he already knew but of which he still needed to be reminded—the fact that despite the death and devastation and bitterness all around them, this too would pass. This terrible war would soon be over. Peace would be restored. Wounds would slowly begin to heal. Even some hatreds would fade or die altogether. Only Jonathan could understand that this had happened already, even as it had yet to begin.

He wished the same peace for Apollonia, whose fate even his future vision did not allow him to know. She was still waging her own personal war, still dreading its outcome, much as the people here were still dreading the outcome of their great collective struggle. He hoped and feared by her side, and by theirs, and no longer felt apart from any of it. Their struggles had become his—they had always been his—and he knew this now.

The black cross against the golden sky inspired Jonathan to do something he had not done for a very long time. He prayed. He prayed for the people of this time—all of them—and for Apollonia. And he prayed for the people of his own time—those still unborn, although in Jonathan's past. They too faced dire struggles and uncertainties, no less fearful than those before him now. Their need for peace was no less urgent, and Jonathan suddenly felt quite sure that the same could be said for the people of any place and any time.

Georgia changed as they neared its eastern edge.

The open landscape with its checkerboard farms began to give way to forests of pine, thin at first but steadily deepening as they progressed. They were nearing the coast, and Jonathan could tell by Apollonia's wistful smile when she breathed in the fragrant spice of the trees that she was drawing close to her home.

The weather was changing, too. Since before Atlanta, the climate had been unseasonably warm and clear. Now, pale gray clouds clustered above them, and the temperature was taking a slow but definite descent. Coats and gloves came out of saddlebags and once again covered their bodies. Apollonia said she could smell snow on the air, as well as the salt of the sea.

Strangely, the foreboding ashen skies and deep pine corridors of Apollonia's homeland reminded him of his own. It seemed like an eternity since he'd been in Michigan, and he wondered whether he'd ever see it again.

When at last they came within view of the army, the plumes of their breath and those of their horses were clearly visible in the cold morning air. It wasn't quite snowing, but they felt on their faces the sting of tiny ice crystals that occasionally fell from the iron gray sky.

They knew that they were close. The army was no longer moving but settling in. Tents and rapidly assembled wooden structures were already being erected in the rear. There was no sign of the once joyful procession of slaves, nor was there any evidence of the bummers. Once the main body had arrived at the coast, the renegades had somehow assimilated themselves back into the army or simply disappeared into the woods.

As Jonathan and Apollonia continued eastward, they met a local farmer, fleeing westward, who told him that Savannah still held a defensive force, at least for the moment, but that the Confederates, woefully outnumbered by Sherman's army, were not expected to make a stand. He believed that the Federals, having surrounded the city, were in the process of overtaking Fort McAllister to the south. The hurrying man said it was only a matter of time—and not very much time—before the city fell.

They discussed their options, none of which looked very encouraging. The southern approach to the city was already the scene of heavy fighting. The northern approach was apparently still open but would likely soon see combat as the Rebels in Savannah tried to make their escape.

"So we go straight in," Jonathan said, regarding the busy military activity less than a mile ahead of them. "We ride in from here, straight through the Union lines."

He glanced at Apollonia, who was taking in the same tableau unfolding before them. She said nothing of the difficulties inherent in his plan—the strong possibility that they would be arrested as spies, the chances they would take at catching a bullet or considerably worse, should the front erupt in battle, the uncertainty of what they might find in the city when, and if, they were able to reach it.

Instead she merely gave him a nod and an expression that momentarily replaced her melancholy gaze. In it, there was determination and courage but also a level of fatigue and resignation that rendered fear irrelevant. Without a word, she urged her horse toward the encampment.

It was a surreal ride.

At first, the troops in the rear—mostly engineers and other support soldiers— seemed largely uninterested in the strangers' entry into their camp. Apollonia and Jonathan were issued no challenge and heard no order to halt, although the soldiers were certainly aware of them. Many of them stood in circles around campfires, clutching tin cups of coffee, speaking quietly. They turned as the interlopers rode by, stared at them briefly, and then returned to their soldierly conversations.

Clad in their blue overcoats with short overhanging capes, the soldiers seemed relaxed, suspended in waiting mode. Some of them played music. Jonathan heard a harmonica, a guitar, and somewhere in the distance a fiddle scratching a lively melody. He finally recognized the tune "When Johnny Comes Marching Home" and realized that these thousands of soldiers all around them were probably thinking of little else at this moment.

As he and Apollonia penetrated deeper into the lines, the nature of the troops began to change. They passed by artillery units, their heavy equipment and horses arranged in orderly rows at the periphery of their encampments. Later came the cavalry units, their mounts and wagons organized in similar regimentation, and finally those who travel the lightest of all—the infantry. These men—seemingly the most numerous—had little but their packs and canvas tents to look after. Their camp smelled of tobacco in corncob pipes, woodsmoke, and frying meat.

And at last, after nearly an hour of picking their way through the clusters of men, the two civilians received their challenge.

The man who stopped them was a young officer, his face bristly behind several days of growth, his eyes obscured by gold-rimmed spectacles. He spoke in a thick German accent.

"Who the devil are you?" he asked, raising his hand in a command to halt.

Jonathan tipped his hat politely and gave him their names.

"And what do you think you are doing here?"

"I am escorting this lady to her home," Jonathan answered clearly. "She lives close to here, on the western edge of the city."

"Where in the hell are you coming from?" the officer persisted. The way he said "hell" suggested that he was practicing his profanities, probably to give his speech a more authentic American flavor.

"We have been traveling for a very long time, sir," Apollonia said, accompanying her explanation with an elegant smile.

The officer was at a loss for words. He scratched his head as if trying to find something authoritative to say. His inertia was relieved when a superior officer, drawn by the commotion, approached them. Jonathan saw the major's insignia on his shoulders, a pair of binoculars in one hand, a Colt pistol in the other.

The man with the German accent informed him of the situation.

The major, a tall, strong-looking man with bushy sideburns, rubbed his cheek with the barrel of the pistol and looked at the strangers as if they were lunatics.

"I don't know whether you realize it, and I don't know how you did it," he said, addressing them both, "but you've arrived at the front. Just a few yards that way," he pointed eastward, "is about a quarter mile of open ground. That's all that lies between us and the Rebs."

"We would appreciate it very much, Major," Jonathan said, "if you would grant us permission to cross."

"Cross? Are you out of your mind?" the major said with a laugh. "The Rebs would take you out before you were twenty yards beyond our lines. That's if one of our own boys doesn't get jumpy and do it first."

"Perhaps not, sir, if you were to inform your men of our intent and if we were to carry a flag of truce," Jonathan offered.

"And why should I allow any of that?" the major replied, a note of belligerence entering his voice. "How do I know the two of you aren't spies?"

"If we were spies," Apollonia rejoined, her voice as smooth as silk, "would we be here, in the middle of your lines, a man and a woman, both civilians, making no attempt to hide or disguise ourselves? And if we were spies, sir, would we want to enter a city that is sure to fall into your hands in the next few days? You will take Savannah before Christmas, whether or not its defenders choose to fight. You know it as well as we do."

Before the major could respond, Jonathan stepped in.

"This woman has traveled for hundreds of miles, Major, all the way from Michigan, where her uncle lives. She has passed through a great many difficulties and wants nothing more than to rejoin her parents. She fears for them and wishes to be at their side during the difficult days ahead."

The major looked at them and shook his head, with an expression that might have carried a hint of admiration. When he holstered his pistol, Jonathan knew that he had been persuaded.

"Who am I to stand in the way of fools?" he said at last. "If you're bent on dying today, it's none of my business. I'll inform my men that you'll be going over. Hopefully, they'll hold their fire. Can't speak for the Rebs, of course. Best pray for good luck. My guess is they're nervous as cats right about now."

He turned to the inferior officer at his side. "Hans, find an old bedsheet for these folks." The major then told them to wait where they were and left to see to his duties.

They waited. Jonathan paced restlessly, while Apollonia sat on the ground and leaned against a tree. She produced from somewhere a quill and small ink bottle and, with her diary positioned carefully in her lap, began busily writing. Jonathan was amazed at her perseverance and curious as to what thoughts, and perhaps dreams, she felt compelled to record. And suddenly, a disturbing thought occurred to him: Had she decided to write now because of some foreboding of what was to come? Was she like these soldiers, with their habit of writing letters to loved ones on the eve of battle?

It took the officer nearly half an hour to return with a large white sheet attached to a straight branch.

"The major says it's all right for you to cross now," he informed them. "He says you should ride slowly and hold this high."

Jonathan thanked the man and took the flag. They approached the line. It was marked by a low wall of earth, behind which soldiers in prone position were stationed every few yards. The long line of their rifles, pointed uniformly at the enemy, stretched away into the cold distance.

"What's Savannah like?" one youthful voice asked them as their horses stepped gingerly over the low barrier.

"It is beautiful," Apollonia replied to the unseen questioner.

From somewhere behind them, they heard the voice of the major.

"Let's hope it stays that way," he said.

Jonathan grasped the white flag with his right hand and held it high as they cantered slowly into the large clearing, a frosty no-man's-land bereft of trees.

He looked at Apollonia by his side, her face flushed from the icy air, her breath steaming out before her. Her blue topaz eyes caught his, and she smiled widely—the first genuine smile he'd seen on her face in days.

"You are as foolish and as mad as I am, Jonathan Chase," she said, "and I love you with all my heart."

He returned her smile. "And I love you with all of mine, Apollonia Foley, you mad and foolish woman."

They laughed together, a deep and liberating laughter that both ignored and defied the fact that they were riding exposed—easy and tempting targets—in the quiescent limbo between two hostile armies poised for battle.

Jonathan could remember no happier moment in all the days of his life.

Slowly but confidently, they directed their horses toward the row of bare trees that marked the Confederate line, their banner of peace fluttering gently between them. The distance was not great, as the major had told them, but their walking gait and the suspense made the journey seem to pass in slow motion. Jonathan felt as if they were suspended, here and now, in both space and time. There was a powerful current of portent in the winter air—whether of doom or survival he could not tell—and it seemed to increase with each step their horses took.

At last, they were able to see the brown lines of the Confederate works and the gray uniforms of the soldiers behind them.

A lone gunshot, fired well above their heads, brought them to a sudden stop.

"Halt!" came a Southern-accented voice, shouting in the distance.

Jonathan raised the flag a little higher.

"Identify yourselves!" came another shout.

"Civilians!" Jonathan shouted back. "Under flag of truce. I am bringing my companion home."

There was a pregnant pause before they heard another yell.

"You may advance. Very slowly."

They did as they were told, moving forward until they were close enough to see the expressions on the faces of the soldiers huddled low against the raised bank. Most of them seemed young, and they did indeed appear nervous.

Finally, one of them stood. He was an officer, clad in a slouch hat and long, gray duster. He pointed a pistol in their direction.

"Dismount!" he ordered. "Drop the flag and approach with your hands over your heads."

They obeyed, and the officer motioned them forward with his gun-free hand.

When they reached the earthworks, at least five feet high, the officer helped Apollonia climb over. Jonathan scaled the mound on his own. The officer then ordered a soldier to secure their horses and lead them over as well.

Oblivious to the amazed stares of the infantrymen, they followed the officer to a position several yards to the rear. Jonathan noticed how he kept his pistol at the ready. Somewhere in the distance an unseen fiddle played out "Dixie."

"You must be mad as hatters to pull such a stunt," the officer began, his voice now quiet but just as commanding as it had been at a shout. "Explain yourselves."

Apollonia ignored the question. She touched Jonathan's arm and said quietly, "This is Mulberry Grove Plantation—a very old, very storied place, Jonathan. It's been here since before the Revolution. Long ago, they grew mulberry trees here, to make silk, and this is where Eli Whitney is said to have designed his cotton gin. I know this place. I have been to picnics on this very spot." She looked around her, obviously pleased to find herself in familiar surroundings and gratified to notice that the questioning officer had overheard her history lesson—it made it quite evident that she was a local and knew the environs well.

"This is Miss Apollonia Foley," Jonathan volunteered in response. "She is from here. I'm Jonathan Chase."

"We are very close now, Jonathan," Apollonia continued, oblivious to the officer. "Just a few miles to go."

"This woman is from Savannah?" the officer asked Jonathan, as if Apollonia were incapable of communication.

"Yes. I'm bringing her home. We came directly through the lines, since there seemed to be no other way."

"How did you get through the Union positions?" The officer's tone was incredulous.

"They let us pass," Jonathan replied. "A major said it was not his business to stand in the way of fools."

"I have to second that," the officer said, a trace of a smile on his face.

"My father is Zachariah Foley," Apollonia said, finally acknowledging the officer's questions. Her tone was impatient, as if this were no time for small talk. "Our plantation is Bluefield, just west of town, near Telfair Junction. I assume we can safely reach it from here?"

The officer clearly desired to be in control of the situation. Like the Union major, he had suspicions about these wayward strangers and wanted to interrogate them, but Apollonia had somehow taken command. The timbre of her voice, perhaps the way she looked at him, implied a sort of aristocratic dominion, a Southern class awareness of which Jonathan was only vaguely cognizant but which was obviously much more apparent to the two Southerners before him.

"Why, yes, I believe you can," the officer replied, his tone subtly more courteous and accommodating. "You're a few miles northwest of town. If you pass through the center of the city, you might still be able to go west on Louisville Road. Our lines are several miles out at that point. At least they were a few hours ago."

"Then we should waste little time," Apollonia said to Jonathan and then turned to the officer. "Would your men be so kind as to feed and water our horses? They have toiled so hard and had so little to eat out there." She pointed toward the west.

The man followed the direction in which she gestured. It was plain that he was still puzzled about the hazardous route they had taken to get here, but he asked no further questions. He merely nodded to her request and instructed two soldiers to take care of the task.

Apollonia stepped a few feet away and procured a hairbrush from somewhere deep in her cloak. Without a mirror, she began expertly arranging stray strands of hair. Both Jonathan and the officer stared in amazement at the sight of a beautiful woman grooming herself in such a bleak and perilous place—vivid proof of the resilience of vanity. When the men looked at each other, a strangely bashful smile passed between them.

The officer took Jonathan's arm and led him a few feet farther away.

"What's it like on the other side?" he asked quietly.

"They're getting ready to move," Jonathan said. "Hard to say exactly when, but it won't be long."

"A whole lot of them?"

"It took us an hour to ride through their lines."

The officer whistled long and low and took in the sight of his men holding their positions. Jonathan saw that the spaces between them were considerably wider than those on the Union side and that only a handful of them wore coats of any kind.

"Then I reckon we'll be pulling out," the officer said. "This'll be a Yankee town in a few days. If there's any town remaining."

They left the shivering soldiers of both armies, invaders and defenders alike, behind them. Together, they quietly approached the besieged city on a lonely track that eventually led to a better road. As they progressed, the air grew noticeably warmer. The sleety rain gave way to a mist that began to gather into a dense blanket of ground fog, eventually concealing the earth and the hooves of their horses. The air had a salty tang that could be tasted on the tongue.

Their path eventually led them past ever-increasing numbers of houses, until it became plain that they had reached the edge of the city at last. The road eventually acquired paving stones and a name—Bay—indicating that it had become a street. Before long, there were no spaces between the dwellings.

The city was unsettlingly quiet. Although the streetlamps were lit, apparently in deference to the mist, and many of the buildings bore illumined windows, scarcely a soul was visible on the streets. What few horses they saw were tethered to posts.

"They are waiting to be taken," Apollonia said softly, as if to herself. "They know it is finished."

The stark words caught Jonathan by surprise. He had expected sadness from her at the plight of her hometown, perhaps even grief, but certainly not stony realism. He turned to her, but she did not return his gaze. She kept her eyes focused on the street directly before them, her expression impossible to read.

They rode on, the clatter of their horses' hooves the only sound to surround them, and when they reached Abercorn Street, Apollonia directed a right turn. They passed shops by the dozens—apothecaries, mercantiles, emporiums, dry goods stores, eateries, and taverns—the lot of them as spectrally still as the rest of Savannah.

Apollonia was taking everything in, her eyes alert, her head turning from side to side as she glimpsed familiar sights. A sojourner come home, she recited from memory the names of the cross streets as they approached them: Broughton. State. York. Oglethorpe. Hull.

She indicated another turn when they reached a westbound street, and they rode by more shops. In time, the businesses surrendered to the prevalence of private homes. In places, these were grand and imposing affairs with sweeping porches, towering columns, and curved drives, often clustered around picturesque squares. They were contained by ornate wrought iron fences and sheltered by huge oaks, whose branches, heavily draped in Spanish moss, looked ghostly in the mist.

The sight was eerily beautiful to Jonathan, who could only imagine how it made Apollonia feel. On either side of them stood the full artistic grace and opulent beauty of the Old South, still intact in all its aristocratic glory. It gave him a strange feeling to realize that he was seeing it in its very last moments, the tranquil and shrouded interlude before an entire civilization would forever expire. Many of the structures themselves would stand long after this, he knew, but their context would be gone. From now on, they would forever be monuments to the past, antebellum tombstones to the wealth and grace, and utter savagery, that had built them.

Jonathan saw how some of the old sidewalks here were paved of a material that, at least partially, was composed of white shells taken from the sea. When they passed them at just the right angle, they glinted with a soft sparkle that was almost opalescent, as if some lost life-light of the shells' former occupants still lingered.

What a strange and quaint custom, he mused. It struck him as very old-fashioned, and then he remembered that even in his own time, more than a century hence, Savannah had been known as a city that clung to the past like a lover, a city that placed inordinate value on anachronism for its own sake.

He wondered about those whose boots and shoes had trodden these faintly luminescent sidewalks over the years. He pictured sailors, of merchant, naval, and piratical fleets alike, singing drunken chanteys in the salty air, perhaps accompanied by equally salty ladies of the night. He pictured soldiers, the scarlet battalions of Englishmen who strove to hold the port against the Colonials hiding in the surrounding woods and, as they witnessed just today, the uneasy Confederates, walled between the Union fleet at sea and Sherman's relentless army inland.

He saw Savannah's society ladies—beautiful, dignified, and haughty—their silken dresses caressing those sidewalks as they seemed to glide beneath the gaslight. He even pictured Apollonia among them, her delicate chin held high, her piercing eyes cloaking an infinity of mysteries.

But he also heard the soft sound of bare feet upon them, the feet of many slaves, doing errands for their masters or being led from the market where their bodies had just been sold, their fates forever sealed.

Perhaps, he mused, it is the accumulation of so much boisterousness, so much war, so much elegance, and so much pain that makes these shells seem to glow softly in the gloom. Perhaps the centuries have simply sunk too much passion into them, and they must release it in this mystically silent way.

As they once again headed toward the west, the buildings grew fewer, the otherworldly pines more numerous, and the air—farther from the sea—regained its bitter chill. The afternoon waned, and they passed a railroad junction and a grove of tall oaks and then came upon a wide expanse of open ground, sloping gently toward the north. It was clearly farmland or at least had once been. What remained of its furrows was still visible, but only barely, and the ground boasted no uniformity of crops. In their place was an anarchic host of gnarled and frost-bent weeds, the size of which testified to the fact that it had been months since the land had last been tended.

Apollonia stopped suddenly and raised a gloved hand for Jonathan to follow suit. She pointed a shaky arm toward a large white house—with a curved drive, pillars, and towering oaks—that stood in the mist at the top of a rise.

She said nothing, but the plumes before her mouth revealed that her breath was coming faster. Jonathan looked at her and saw a tear flow from her eye.

"I am home," she said quietly, staring at the house in the distance.

She took Jonathan's hand and squeezed it. "My God, Jonathan. I'm really home!"

She sobbed, but smiled widely at the same time. She leaned perilously from her mount and took Jonathan clumsily in her arms. She hugged him tightly and whispered "Thank you" in his ear.

They rode up the drive slowly, almost as if in a ceremonial procession, and the house grew larger in their view. It was impressive but not massive in size, formal in a plain and dignified way, but Jonathan did not find it cold or unwelcoming. It had a homey quality, hard to pinpoint but unmistakable, and he found it easy to picture the vision of Apollonia as a little girl playing on its wide lawn on a sunnier and happier day than this.

It seemed very quiet.

No light came from any of its mullion-crossed windows, nor was there any sign of a human being about.

They dismounted when they reached the house, tied their horses, and approached the door. Apollonia had a radiant smile as she raised the brass knocker and prepared to strike the wood.

"We will surprise them," she whispered playfully. The sound of the knocker reverberated through the house.

There was no reply. She knocked again.

Still no reply. Apollonia's smile began to fade.

"That is strange," she said, knocking once more.

Once again, only the echoes of knocking reached their ears.

Now Apollonia's smile was gone. In its place was a worried frown. She grasped the handle and pushed—the door opened effortlessly, squeaking slightly on its hinges. It was dark inside the house, and a breath of cold air greeted them, as if there had been no fire in the hearths for some time.

"Hello?" There was an edge of fear in her voice as she stepped inside. Jonathan followed her in. They stood in a foyer, greeted only by a coatrack with no coats and a towering grandfather clock whose lifeless pendulum no longer measured the time.

"Mother!" she called.

"Father!"

Her own echo was the only reply.

"Where are they, Jonathan?" she asked, turning to him, her voice now laced with panic.

"I'm sure...," he began, hoping to provide an encouraging word, but another man's voice cut him off, startling them both.

"He doesn't know where they are, Appy," came the voice, deep and strong, eloquent in its Southern enunciation. "But I do."

Apollonia drew in her breath sharply as a figure emerged out of the shadow of the massive clock.

As he stepped into the dim light from the open door, Archer Blaine greeted them with a gracious bow and a dashing smile.

He was costumed this time not as a villain but as a warrior.

The gray of his uniform was so spotless and free of imperfections that it seemed almost pearlescent, the braid so rich and luminous that it appeared to be spun of pure gold. He wore a broad-brimmed officer's hat with a "CSA" emblem prominent on its crown, a heavy saber on one side of his belt, and a long-barreled pistol on the other.

Blaine smiled at the shocked silence with which Apollonia and Jonathan received him.

"Your parents," he said, turning to look directly at Apollonia, "by which term I include reference to *our* mother, are prudent and cautious people. From what I gather, they abandoned Bluefield a full week ago and took each and every slave— and no doubt a good portion of their valuables—along with them. The man who keeps the farm close-by informs me that they have taken refuge at the home of friends, cotton planters who live near Charleston. I can't help but wonder whether it's the same plantation where I spent so many warm and fruitful years."

"What are you doing here?" Apollonia hissed at him. There was cold fire in her eyes.

"I can hardly blame the Foleys for taking their leave," he said, ignoring her question. "It is well known that the Yankees take special pleasure in putting houses such as this to the torch—after thoroughly pillaging them, of course. I can understand why they wouldn't want to witness all of that."

"Why are you here, Archer?" Apollonia repeated, her tone even more piercing, even fiercer, than it was before.

"Such impudence from a lady of supposedly fine breeding," he shot back at her, shaking his head in mock indignation. "If you can't surmise it yourself, Appy, I came to Savannah to present myself formally to your parents. I had momentous news for them, as you well know, and I was eager to share it, especially with your father. I was so looking forward to seeing his face as all those years of blissful ignorance evaporated before my eyes. Unfortunately, the runner on which I was a passenger had, shall we say, a very difficult time slipping through the blockade. I arrived only three days ago, too late to meet them. But there's still plenty of time to deliver my message, dear sister."

"You are a despicable beast!" she replied, her hands curled into tight fists.

He shot her another mocking smile, clearly enjoying the sight of her rage.

"I am no such thing, Appy. What I am is a man of my word. When I make a promise—unlike you—I keep it."

Blaine's eyes lost their false charm, his voice grew loud and hard.

"Have you heard today's news, Appy? Have you heard that McAllister has fallen, leaving nothing, absolutely nothing, between Savannah and Sherman? What's left of our line of defense is going to withdraw in a matter of hours, scurrying like rats across the river so they can go hiding someplace in Carolina, perchance—and only perchance—so they might fight another day."

He took a step closer to them.

"Savannah will surrender soon. And Sherman will have a nice Christmas gift to offer Lincoln, won't he?"

Blaine breathed deeply, trying to keep himself in check.

"This town is about to be overrun, Appy. This plantation—your own home—will be under their boots. And do you want to know why all of this is happening? Do you want to know why the entire Confederacy is teetering on the edge of destruction? It's because of you! It's because you betrayed me, you stupid, spoiled little bitch!"

Jonathan took a step toward him at these words, his hand disappearing into the folds of his coat.

Blaine was quicker. He had his pistol out of his holster and in his hand before Jonathan even felt the stock of his own weapon.

"Take another step, Chase, and I'll put one right through you, so help me God."

Jonathan complied, taking a step back.

"Now open your coat and take the gun out, carefully and slowly, and set it down on that table."

Jonathan did as he was told, gently placing the Colt on the small letter table by Blaine's side.

"What are you going to do, Archer?" Apollonia asked, her voice losing some of its belligerence.

Blaine smiled again, but his sea green eyes remained cold. The hand holding the pistol was shaking slightly, as if he was losing the struggle to stay in control of his growing anger.

His answer was oblique.

"When I found the place abandoned, Appy, I decided to stick around for a few days. Somehow I just knew that you'd be showing up sooner or later and probably in the company of that bastard who's standing beside you right now. After all, where else could you go?"

"That is right, Archer," she said evenly. "Where else could I go?"

Blaine looked through the still open doorway at the inclement weather outside. "I suppose there is a sort of justice in the fact that your arrival so neatly coincides with the fall of Savannah, Appy—you couldn't have possibly timed it more precisely. I find it fitting that you should be here to witness the burning of Bluefield, the destruction of everything that your father worked so hard for, as well as the rape of your hometown. I want you to see the flames of it, Appy! You are like Nero, my hesitant little sister—Nero, whose mad arrogance wrought such destruction, yet who was condemned to witness the fiery fruits of his perfidy."

His words brought the flame back to Apollonia's eyes. She took a step closer to him, ignoring his weapon, and her voice carried an angry passion Jonathan had never before heard.

"You accuse *me* of madness and arrogance!" she shouted. "You dare to charge *me* with perfidy! You accuse me of some unforgivable, unspeakable crime, yet this was precisely what you ordered me to commit—what you *blackmailed* me to do! You compelled me to commit cold-blooded murder, the murder of a purely innocent man, all to fulfill a dream of victory that was as doomed to failure as it was lunatic."

Blaine's hand grew in its shaking. He opened his lips in an attempt to reply, but Apollonia was not finished.

"No, Archer, the arrogance is all yours, as is the madness. But I leave out your evil, for such a plot can be called nothing else. What else but evil could compel a human being to so direct another? And what do you say about Jeremiah? You directed your miserable companion to murder the sweetest, wisest man I have ever known. If you wished to wound me to the soul, you have gotten your wish. You drove a dagger straight through my heart, and I will forever feel the pain of it."

Tears now flowed freely from her eyes and her voice choked, but Apollonia's anger was still the greater force.

"So your act of murder and vengeance was successful. Take your pleasure from it, if you will, but do not speak to me of arrogance or madness or perfidy, Archer, for these are your traits, not mine."

As he listened to her tirade, the handsome features of Blaine's face began to change. A sarcastic sneer twisted itself into an expression of pure hatred. Suddenly, he appeared a very ugly man.

"What has happened to you?" he asked, his voice an enraged, raspy whisper. "You were a daughter of the South! You were once proud to be a Southerner, proud that your father fulfilled his birthright to own and command slaves, proud that your country rose in rebellion against the blind monsters of the North. And I gave you a golden opportunity to be a patriot among patriots, Appy. With one act, you could have changed the course of history, you could have brought salvation to your people. And—my God!—you squandered the opportunity! You walked away, leaving the Englishman alive, abandoning your country to a cruel fate."

Blaine turned his hateful gaze toward Jonathan. The direction of the gun followed.

"Was it because of *him*?" he asked while staring at Jonathan. "Did this man—whoever the hell he is and whatever his purposes are—weaken your resolve? Did he cause you to doubt yourself?"

Apollonia's response this time was steady and calm, all the more piercing for its even tone.

"No, Archer, it was not Jonathan who turned me away from you, although he has shown me an example of courage and goodness that gave me, in the end, the strength I needed to resist you. The truth is that I was never *with* you. You ask whether my resolve was weakened, whether I came to doubt myself. Have you forgotten that you coerced me, that none of this was of my own free will or by my own design? You say that I could have been a great Southern heroine, a wonderful patriot, but have you forgotten that you intended to kill me, just as soon as I had done the same to Lord Covington? There is no need to deny it—Jonathan heard you speak the words."

Blaine had nothing to say.

"It was *you*, Archer, who caused me to doubt—not myself, but my country and everything it has come to represent. It was *you* who caused the scales to fall from my eyes. I see what your vaunted Confederacy, your blessed Dixie, has done to you—what it has made of you. Look at yourself! Look at what you have become!"

"What are you saying?" Blaine said, his voice unable to conceal his contempt.

"You stand there in the uniform of the Confederacy, as if you were Stonewall Jackson himself. But the whole idea is ridiculous, Archer! It is absurd! You are the son of a black man and a white woman, for God's sake!"

Jonathan saw that Blaine's finger was beginning to put pressure on the trigger. He saw his face twist deeper in its rancor.

"Go no further with this!" he shouted. "I warn you!"

She ignored him.

"Your father and your mother—*our* mother, Archer, as you say—committed no crime beyond that of two human beings who fell in love with each other. They did nothing wrong! Yet their act of love, an act that should have been beautiful and blessed and smiled upon by God, was condemned and sullied by this great country of which you speak, this country whose uniform you wear with such pride.

"They hid you away like a shameful thing. They made of you an abomination whose existence must never be known. They raised you to be a slave, to use you the way a farmer uses his beasts of burden. Can you not see how wrong it all is, how horribly, tragically wrong? Can you not sympathize with *all* of the slaves—the Negroes, the mulattos, the quadroons, the octoroons, and those for whom they did not even bother to invent such detestable names? Could you not sympathize with Jeremiah?"

Blaine's finger now visibly trembled, as did his voice when he spoke.

"I have erased all of that, Appy. I have risen above it. I chose to be a white man, regardless of who my parents may have been, because I came to understand the world. I came to understand that the world is made of masters and slaves, just as it is made of predators and prey. It is simply the way it was all designed, the way it has always been and shall always be. The notion that this can somehow be changed is nothing more than a dangerous illusion—this is the great folly of the North, the very reason for this war. Listen to me, my sister, and heed my words. There are some people, such as Jeremiah, who have no choice as to which role they are to play—I pity them, I truly do—but there are others, such as myself, who are lucky enough to have been given that choice. And I made my choice long ago. I chose to be a master and a predator, a lion instead of a deer, a king instead of a pawn. You cannot condemn me for that."

"And yet I do condemn you, Archer," she said softly. "I condemn you for drawing the wrong lesson from the well of your experience, for choosing domination over compassion. I condemn you for imitating your oppressor rather than opposing him, just as I condemn myself for blindly accepting this oppression for so many years."

She paused and looked directly into her brother's eyes.

"But I thank you as well. I thank you for opening my eyes to the truth. When you told me the story of your life, I began to understand. I began to understand what this society, this wicked way of life, had done to my mother. I saw the cruelty of what they did to your father and every man, woman, and child ever to stand upon an auction block. And I began to understand how its wickedness crept into your mind and twisted you and filled you with hatred and put murder into your heart. And when I saw that, my poor brother, I knew that I could never again support it in any way, let alone serve as your puppet."

Apollonia glanced at the cold gray twilight outside the open door. Her eyes were steely in the gloaming. The mist had turned into delicate snow, and tiny flakes were flying into the house.

"If this house is to fall, that is as it must be," she said flatly, once again meeting Blaine's stare. "And if Savannah is to burn, so be it. The sight of its flames will only warm my heart."

A smile instantly crossed Blaine's face, erasing all signs of rage and hate. Somehow, Jonathan knew that Apollonia's defiant words had brought him to resolution, had settled a tiny doubt that must have still lingered somewhere in his confused and angry mind.

"Not if your heart is cold by then," he muttered, pulling the trigger.

It felt like slow motion to Jonathan as he lunged toward Blaine, like a maddening nightmare he'd once had as a child, in which he tried to crawl across a roadway, agonizingly aware of a rapidly approaching car yet unable to move beyond a snail's pace.

He heard the deafening report of Blaine's pistol and Apollonia's instantaneous gasp, just as his body collided with Blaine's. The force of the collision threw both men to the floor, beneath the looming clock, and they wrestled for only a few moments before Blaine's finger once again found the trigger.

Jonathan felt the bullet tear into his abdomen, somehow realizing in that mad and frenzied moment that he recognized the sensation of its violence—he had met it before in Spotsylvania. He discovered that its pain was not at all lessened by its familiarity. It was, in fact, an agony beyond adequate description, and it sent waves of shock through every fiber of his body. He instantly felt very dizzy, and his vision began to blur.

And yet his hatred proved stronger even than this. He had never before in his life hated another human being—not in the true and pure sense of the word—but he hated Archer Blaine now. He hated him for everything he had done since the beginning and for what he had done a moment ago. He hated every molecule and atom of the man. He hated him with a blind animal hunger that could only be satiated by his destruction.

This Jonathan proceeded to do.

Despite his pain and fading vision, a hidden source of strength opened itself to him, potent and deadly, and with it he was able to throw Blaine off balance and turn him on his back. As Blaine struggled to once again raise his pistol, Jonathan pinned both of his arms to the floor with his knees. The gun slid harmlessly from his grasp. Blaine squirmed and struggled mightily, but with each increase of his exertion, Jonathan's force of resistance grew in matching proportion.

"Goddamn you!" Blaine spat, when he finally realized his helplessness.

"We will see very soon who God chooses to damn," Jonathan replied through his teeth.

They were the last words Blaine ever heard.

Jonathan wrapped his free hands around Blaine's neck and looked him in the eye, pupil to pupil, as he adjusted and firmed his grip.

And then he killed him.

It was a violent killing, terrible and hideous in its execution, but Jonathan was only vaguely aware of the act itself. His surging rage, the pain that screamed through his body, the dimming of his vision—and, even more than these, his dread of what he would learn when it was all over—all these blinded him to the slaying that his hands so mercilessly committed.

Only when it was finished did he release his death grip. He rose to one knee, took one last look at Blaine, his pale green eyes open but sightless, and tried to stand. He took two steps, stumbled, and fell back to the floor. He crawled, a trail of blood marking his path upon the elegant tiles of the foyer, until he had passed through the door and into the chilled air of the porch.

She was on the lawn, the force of the shot having propelled her far from the door. She was lying on her back, her arms spread wide like angels' wings, her eyes open, looking into the cold sky of early night. Through her open cloak, Jonathan saw a crimson stain spreading over her white cotton blouse.

When he had managed to crawl to her side, he put his arm around her and drew himself close. He felt the soft rhythm of her heartbeat, faint within her breast, and the weak ebb and flow of her breath. There were tiny snowflakes on her eyelashes.

They knew. They whispered each other's names. They each said "I love you" but nothing more, and then they began to fade. In time, Jonathan managed to steady his vision and look at her. Her eyes were closed—their blue topaz concealed from him now—and no plumes of breath rose from her lips. She appeared peaceful, a child asleep.

A tear came from his eye and made its way slowly down his cheek. He thought it strange that he could so acutely feel its course, even as the rest of his body seemed to have grown numb.

He had a final thought, as he slipped into a dark place that he remembered well, and it gave him a small measure of peace. Jonathan knew that he would rather be here, now, dying by Apollonia's side, than forced to live without her.

POSTLUDE

HE AWOKE TO THE SOUND OF BELLS, clear and close, resonant as if their tones were echoing off unyielding surfaces. Something soft and comforting brushed gently against his cheek, and in the slowly lifting fog of his slumber, he believed it to be his lover's touch.

It was warm and easy where he was, but he felt a nameless urgency swelling within him, a distant but desperate call for his attention, for his help, for... what?

Jonathan opened his eyes and looked at what surrounded him, all cast in gray half-light. What he saw was familiar, but only vaguely and opaquely so. He gazed at the ceiling, the walls, the wooden trim of the door and window, and felt not the jolt of déjà vu but its jarring opposite, *jamais vu*, a much rarer sensation in which the familiar seems strange and unknown.

The bells rang again, and he discerned another sound beneath that, coming from somewhere outside, like the bells but seemingly drifting past wherever he was. It was a song. For a moment, the music seemed jarring and discordant, almost violent in its need, but as he absorbed its melody and components, he recognized the banshee wail of Bono's voice and the gothic thunder of The Edge's guitar. It was U2, he realized, and he knew, although he could not quite hear, that the singer was now whispering: "All this can be yours."

He felt once more the soft caress, and he looked down to its source, his eyes meeting the citrine gaze of a beautiful black cat, snuggled beside him in the blankets on the bed in which he was lying. The cat was prodding him with a soft paw, purring softly, and Jonathan knew his name.

"Pluto," he said quietly, and the cat's purring intensified.

Jonathan rose slowly and clumsily approached the room's sole window. He parted the curtains and looked outside. Another name immediately came to his mind: Throop Street. It appeared to be dawn, under a numb gray sky. It was snowing and had been for some time. The ground was covered in a thick white blanket, and the street itself revealed no trace of pavement. A car came slowly down the street, its wheels throwing sprays of snow to either side.

The sight of an automobile did not jar him at first, for Jonathan had yet to put together the broken strands of his consciousness, but it helped to crack the shell of his confusion. As he watched the car's red taillights fade into the swirling snow, he began to remember. He remembered a place where there were no automobiles, where electric music did not exist, where there was no black cat named Pluto.

He remembered that place—that time—and once he had crossed that threshold, he remembered details, a virtual infinity of them, that came rushing into his mind, vivid and beautiful and terrible in their clarity.

And he remembered more than that. He remembered a face—a soul—who had once lived then.

"No!" he cried, turning away from the window, his situation and his helplessness suddenly dawning on him. He looked around and realized that he was standing in his own bedroom. He looked at himself, at his wrinkled sweatshirt and jeans, and clearly remembered putting them on the night before, a year before, an eternity before... or was it an eternity after?

At that moment, although none of it made the least sense to him, Jonathan recognized exactly where he was. And when.

"This can't be," he said aloud.

His eyes fell upon something on the floor beside the bed, where it had fallen during the night. It was oval in shape, a picture frame, and it was lying face down. He knelt to the floor, picked it up, and looked at the face it enclosed, its fair lines now crossed by a thread of cracked glass.

His breaths came fast as he looked at her, the sepia tint and hazy daguerreotype focus obscuring, but not concealing, her awesome and melancholy beauty. Her pale eyes—he knew they were blue—stared at him, conveying longing and sadness and something else, something mysterious that he couldn't identify. Her lips were closed and turned slightly down, as if she had thought of something unhappy when the photograph was taken.

And as he gazed at the one-dimensional surface of Apollonia's portrait, Jonathan's mind saw her face in a cascade of images—walking down a staircase in a dress of deepest blue, kissing him in the hold of a tempest-tossed ship, embracing him in a forsaken house as a storm raged, smiling and laughing as they crossed enemy armies, a white flag of peace waving above their heads, and dying—a trickle of blood running down her lip—as the silent Savannah snow fell like feathers on her face.

"Oh, my love," he whispered.

He did not cry in the usual way. No deep sobs wracked his chest, no sound of soul-searing anguish came from his lips. Something deep inside him was far too numb for such demonstrative grief, but even this could not stop his tears. They fell unbidden from his eyes in a steady, soundless rain and pooled on the splintered glass he held in his hand.

Outside somebody cried "Merry Christmas!" to somebody else, and the bells rang once more, their golden, joyous tones sounding to Jonathan like peals of madness.

Only then, when the strands of his logic began to make a sincere attempt to connect to the chaotic helices of his recent reality, did the sense of déjà vu finally arrive.

For he recognized what he now felt, here in his lonely Saginaw house, here in the time from which he originally sprang. He remembered clearly falling asleep—last night?—and awakening more than a century before, in a frigid, snow-covered field, a place that he now realized was most probably the very land on which this house stood—the same place but in a distant and alien time.

The shock of displacement, the overwhelming sense of unreality, the terrifying disorientation of it all—these feelings now returned in all their disquieting and overwhelming power.

He rose from his kneeling position by the bed, laying her photograph gently on the nightstand, and returned to the window. Another car passed by—a Ford Taurus. He recognized its lines and profile instantly and knew its name, even though the sight of it seemed bizarre.

He watched as a handful of people walked on sidewalks yet to be cleared of snow, perhaps on their way to Christmas services. They very much resembled those he remembered from that other time, but the resemblance was by no means complete. The cut and color of their coats, perhaps even the way they strode, differed in slight but noticeable ways. These were people of *now*, he knew, and not of *then*. They bore the same unmistakable marks of their own time, on their person and in their bearing, the same maddeningly indefinable yet obvious signs of otherness that he had seen in the people, the trees, and the skies of that earlier, now vanished, time.

His logical instincts, of course, quickly began to resist the entire idea. It began to seek solid evidence of what his mind was telling him to be true.

He raised his sweatshirt and looked at his body beneath. There were no signs of bullet wounds, no sensations of pain or discomfort as he ran his hands over his chest and stomach. There should have been a scar near his heart, courtesy of Spotsylvania, and a hole in his belly, the work of Archer Blaine. There was no trace of either. He rubbed his knee—the locale of another battlefield souvenir—and felt nothing.

It was not madness, he felt sure of that. He dismissed the notion out of hand, refused even to consider it. He did not care whether it was ego or denial or confident self-assurance that told him he was sane—he simply accepted it as fact.

A dream, then? Could that be?

At first, the rational side of his mind insisted on it. It was the only reasonable explanation. He examined the evidence that surrounded him and simultaneously took note of the lack of evidence. He demanded of himself to admit that all of it—every single painful, heartbreaking, glorious, and wonderful moment of it—had been nothing more than the arabesque embroidery of a single night's dream.

He had been overwrought, he had been obsessed with the old photograph, he had been so terribly, painfully alone—and his troubled mind had responded with a fantastic creation of its own. It had woven the patterns of his thoughts and fantasies together into a marvelously intricate subconscious phantasmagoria, a nepenthean vapor that the helpless dreamer had no choice but to accept as real.

What he thought had happened to him could never have happened, he told himself. It did *not* happen. It was mad to even consider its possibility. It had been nothing more than a dream—the dream of a lifetime, to be sure—but nothing more than that in the end.

And yet...

The jarring ring of his telephone made him jump. He turned away from the window, not remembering at first where the phone was, and finally spied it atop the dresser. He picked it up hesitantly and uttered an uncomfortable hello.

"Jon?" It was his cousin's voice. That too he recognized immediately.

"Yes," he said. "Good morning, Tess."

"Well, good morning and Merry Christmas to you." She sounded light and happy.

He returned her salutation, but his tone must have seemed considerably darker than hers.

"Is everything okay?" she asked.

He paused before replying. "To be honest, I'm feeling a little under the weather."

That was bad news to Tess. She had been counting on Jonathan to come to Christmas dinner. He vaguely remembered the invitation, but the idea of making merry after waking up the way he did was more than he could contemplate.

He apologized, said he feared he might be contagious, and declined the offer as politely as he could.

Tess accepted with her usual grace, but her characteristic intuition sensed that something was wrong. She pressed him on the issue, genuine concern apparent in her voice.

"It's okay, Tess, really," he told her. "I'm sure I'll be fine in a day or two, and I hope you'll still have a few leftovers by then."

She forced a laugh and hung up reluctantly. Jonathan knew she didn't believe him.

He returned to the bed and stroked Pluto's elegant black fur. "Just a dream, old buddy," he said to the purring cat. "Just a crazy, crazy dream. You were here with me all night—you must have heard me say some strange things."

Pluto's contented purr was his only reply.

Jonathan picked up the photograph and took another long look at Apollonia, and as their eyes met—his in living, breathing life, hers on faded, ancient paper—he suddenly stopped believing in his dream theory. He no longer thought that everything he had gone through with her, everything he had felt about her, could have been conjured by his subconscious. It was too much, too deep, too... everything for that. He could still hear her voice, for God's sake, smell her hair, taste her lips, feel the swell of her breasts against his chest. If she were nothing more than a dream, then his whole life, then he himself, was nothing more than a dream.

And yet...

He shook his head, fending off another tear that was forming in the corner of his eye. This *was* madness. So the emotions were real, the feelings powerful; the memories nonetheless remained false, self-conjured illusions. The events he remembered could never have happened. If he continued this way, he would never emerge from the trap he had built for himself. He would never be free of his obsession. He would be no better off than he had been when he went to sleep in this bed with her photograph in his hand the night before.

Or was it a year ago?

He shook his head again and laughed—an uneasy, mirthless laugh—and set the portrait back on the nightstand. This time, out of sheer necessity, he placed it face down.

Jonathan made the attempt to fall gracefully back into reality or at least into the state he now had no choice but to accept as such. On the day of his awakening, he shaved, showered, and dressed. He turned on the television and watched until its frantic, in-your-face clamor finally forced him to switch it back off. He watched, and still marveled, as more automobiles scudded through the snow outside his window.

On the next day, almost as if nothing had happened, he dutifully opened the The Red Raven, swept its floors, dusted its shelves, and saw to the satisfaction of the handful of customers who came in for purchases. He went to Tess and Dave's house that evening, partook of holiday leftovers, and managed to convince them that everything with him was indeed fine.

Which of course it was not.

His circumstances forced him into a state of middling ambivalence, alternating between acceptance of the idea that his foray into the past was nothing more than a dream and the diametric opposite of that—the conviction that all of it, against all logic and proof, had transpired.

The only constant between these pendulum swings of disavowal and acceptance was his pain, and this was overwhelming in its depth. He played over in his mind each memory of her a thousand times, especially that of her death. When the memory invaded him in the moments that he believed in it all, it seemed to compress his consciousness, as if unseen hands were gripping his very brain with brutal strength and focusing his every feeling and thought into an intense laser point of pain. And when the memories came to him while he was in denial, the results were identical.

Even in this agony, it amazed him that the power of his memories was utterly unaffected by whether he believed in them or not. Ultimately, it seemed not to matter whether Apollonia had been real—a breathing, flesh-and-blood creature— or whether she had been nothing more than a mental projection he had hijacked from an antique image. His pain cared nothing for such distinctions. Either way, he missed her like a flower misses the sun.

He sought to distract himself, dimly but accurately aware that distraction was potent medicine for one who grieves.

He applied himself with vigor to the business of the bookshop, arranging signings for local authors, setting up special sales, rearranging shelf categories, encouraging his scouts to increase and improve their yields of salvaged books.

And he sought the truth. It may have been ironic that Jonathan tried to distract himself from his grief by seeking to establish whether his memories were genuine, but it seemed to help.

That idea first occurred to him on a bitterly cold night—at a moment when he was striving strongly to deny the reality of it all. He decided to remove Apollonia's photograph from the nightstand, where its very proximity haunted him, and return it to its old home—the aged family album from which he had first taken it. He located the old book and leafed through its pages, seeking the empty place that belonged to her.

He caught his breath when he glimpsed some of the faces. There was Timothy Foley, with that stern yet tragic expression; there was Alexandra, Timothy's wife, her face revealing maternal gentleness and pioneer strength all at once; there was Emily, darkly beautiful and coquettish; there was Phineas, cross-eyed, awkward, and friendly—just as Jonathan remembered them all.

How could such memories be dreams? How could he remember working for them, talking and laughing with them, sitting at their table—all from a dream?

He found Apollonia's place, gently returned its portrait, and looked through the rest of the album. He stopped at the last page.

"My God," he said aloud, staring at the image before him. He remembered it both from his first look through the album and from another time. He remembered the moment when the photograph had been taken.

It was an exterior shot of three people standing before a brick wall. Two of them he recognized immediately—a smiling, radiant Apollonia and a pugnacious, defiant man he knew instantly as Malcolm Jasper.

It was the sight of the third man that took Jonathan's breath away. That figure was blurred, as if he had moved at the instant of the exposure, and his face was indistinct. But the hat on his head—a felt top hat with a low crown—was in much better focus.

It was more than familiar. Jonathan knew it was his own. He had won it in a raucous contest from a clothier by the name of Seligman.

And he remembered the moment as if it had happened yesterday. It was a brisk morning at Riverdale, and Jasper, in his guise as a commercial photographer, had come to the house to warn Jonathan to stay away. Apollonia had interrupted them just as they were about to come to blows and ordered Jasper to take the photograph so that her aunt and uncle would not be suspicious of his presence.

Jonathan was sure that he was looking at a photograph of himself. And the embossed date—"March 7, 1864"—and penciled inscription—"Riverdale"—told him exactly when and where it had been taken.

Jonathan could be a fiercely stubborn man. His rational side still fought the idea, reasoning that he could not be sure that the man in the photograph was really himself. The face was indistinct at best. If his subconscious could take so much inspiration from a photograph album, why couldn't it concoct a story surrounding this single image? He hadn't actually been there when the photograph was taken, this argument went. He had simply manufactured a memory based on the picture.

But such reasoning was beginning to lose the tug-of-war. After seeing the photograph, the idea that all of it was a dream began steadily to lose its hold. He remembered that morning, that house, and the two people with whom he posed far too clearly to seriously doubt it. The ascending and strengthening conviction continuously repeated itself to him: He *had* been there, he *had* done those things— all of them—and this was his proof.

Yet what to do about it?

He took the only course open to him—he sought more evidence.

Several visits to the dusty archives within a beautiful old library on the East Side uncovered a few interesting clues—photographs of Timothy Foley and his family, woodcuts and photographs of Riverdale and the nearby booming grounds, and a large folder of various official documents relating to Foley's business interests. Unfortunately, that paper cache contained no ledgers with entries that Jonathan remembered making himself.

He wasn't sure why he hadn't thought of this before, exploring forgotten records like an academic historian, but things had happened much too quickly when his obsession began, and too intensely, for him to have pursued anything so rational as research. It wouldn't have mattered anyway. The library failed to give Jonathan information that he didn't already know.

The internet now occurred to him as well, an idea that perhaps had been too high-tech during his strangely retrogressive state when he had made his first attempts to learn about Apollonia.

Now, however, he spent numerous evenings roaming through search engines, typing in any keyword that sounded as though it might lead somewhere.

Some of the leads were fascinating but provided no smoking guns. He found, for example, various references to Timothy Foley and Riverdale on Michigan historical sites. He was an almost legendary figure in Saginaw history, admired for his pluck and courage in becoming one of the city's most successful lumbermen when pine was king, respected for his leadership and philanthropy in later years.

Cyberspace also confirmed that there really had been a slave dealer by the name of Lumpkin in Richmond in 1864—a man whose legacy was more of infamy than of fame—but Jonathan found no photograph of the man or any online list of "merchandise" bought or sold by his business.

Other discoveries had more value because they confirmed things he "remembered" from his experiences in 1864 but which he was sure he had never heard of in his own day and age. He was able to line up any number of details with things he recalled from his year in the past.

Not once had he ever read a detailed account of the Battle of Spotsylvania, for example, yet his memories of the event—from the rainy dawn on which it began, to the piles of bodies before the Rebel works at the Bloody Angle, to the bullet-riddled church at the field's periphery—were remarkably accurate. Of the multitude of photographs of the battle and its aftermath that were available online—including one fascinating view of an unidentified field hospital—many looked eerily familiar.

Time and time again, he found perfect synchronicity between his memories and historical accounts—the names of buildings, streets, towns, hotels, railroads, even the weather in certain places on certain days.

He was able to find online anecdotes about the adventures and exploits of a Rebel gunrunner out of Wilmington by the name of Wilkins, who made regular runs to Nova Scotia. He also located a brief biography of an Englishman called Covington, whose life span—1814 to 1880—roughly corresponded with the man he knew. The account noted that Lord Covington had made his name in international trade and foreign service, and spent much of his life in Canada and the United States, but carried no reference to any sort of clandestine diplomacy with the Confederacy. There was no photograph with which to compare the historical person and the one from Jonathan's memories, but if this biography was referring to the same man—and Jonathan grew convinced that it did—then Covington's professional secrets had been successfully preserved for a century and a half.

Perhaps most intriguing of all, Jonathan was able to confirm that Zachariah Foley had indeed once owned an indigo plantation near Savannah and that his plantation had gone by the name of Bluefield. The article noted that the plantation house had been one of very few properties in the Savannah area to be destroyed by Union forces in December 1864. The house and outbuildings had apparently all been reduced to ashes, and Foley sold off the property shortly thereafter. After that year, his name ceased to appear in any Savannah registries or directories.

There was absolutely no mention, however, of the discovery of any dead bodies at Bluefield—male or female—nor did the website make any reference to Zachariah Foley's family.

When Jonathan finally instructed his search engine to track Apollonia Foley, he was able to locate only one scrap of information, the only needle in the vast haystack of the internet to confirm that she had ever walked upon the earth. It was a record of her birth, from an online database of vital statistics from Chatham County, Georgia.

She came into the world, according to the graceful script on her birth certificate, "on the 7th day of April, 1840, the daughter of Zachariah and Sophia Foley."

Her place of birth was listed merely as "at home"—the very place of her death, Jonathan realized with a shudder.

Only he seemed aware of that fact, however. The archive had no further record of her, including any reference to her death.

He found even less when he searched for Archer Blaine and Malcolm Jasper. Those quests led to absolute dead ends. Both men seemed to have vanished from existence without leaving behind a single trace, masters of espionage in death as they had been in life.

Ultimately, the same dead end is where all of Jonathan's digital wandering led him. While the bits of information he had been able to gather were maddeningly intriguing, and tended to validate different aspects of his own experiences, he knew that none of them proved a thing.

Jonathan remained dissatisfied and restless—a man seeking to confirm what he believed to be true—and his need for the anesthetic balm of distraction had grown no less.

He eventually abandoned the internet for more tangible evidence, beginning by returning to the ruins of Riverdale, the somber site that he had inspected an indeterminate time ago. Was it just a few weeks or an entire year—or well over a century—since he'd last visited?

It was a day very similar to that first one—foggy and cold. He chose an early Sunday morning to minimize the chances of being seen and as before parked his car a reasonable distance away from what remained of the derelict estate.

He climbed the rusted iron gate and landed once again amid a prickly tangle of underbrush. He forged through this, clearing the way with his gloved hands, until he was able to see the house once more. When it loomed before him, he was immediately struck by two parallel but strikingly different tracks of recollection.

The first was of his visit here in this time, when it looked exactly as it did now—desolate, ruinous, depressing.

The second was when he arrived in her time, when the grounds of the estate were lush and cared for, far more spacious than the cramped, overgrown corner it now occupied, when the house itself was white and new and inviting. Riverdale was a living thing then—the nerve center of Timothy Foley's family and burgeoning business—and Apollonia was living within it. It was then a bold outpost of civilization at the very edge of a vast wilderness; today it was a decrepit relic from a distant and forgotten time.

He walked to the rear of the structure, passing by the remnants of the old trellis before which he, Jasper, and Apollonia had had their photograph taken, and looked in vain for the long, narrow building in which he and Jeremiah had once had their bunks. There was no sign of it. The very ground on which it had stood had been carved away from the plot, paved over with the concrete of Midland Road.

He regarded the once imposing house and remembered his long-ago visits to it, including the timeless evening on which he'd first set eyes on Apollonia. He also remembered entering it late one night, secretly and quietly, and following her through the sleeping house all the way to the little cupola on top. That was the night on which she had asked him—begged him—to accompany her to Mackinac. That was the moment when everything really began.

When he stepped back from the house, he saw that the cupola still occupied its place at the apex of the structure. There was no longer any glass in its arched windows, but the frame looked sturdy and straight.

He tried the door and found it locked, so he tugged on it until its brittle latch gave way. He went in through the little pantry at the back and passed into the forsaken remains of what had once been the Foleys' elegant dining room, its walls now crumbling plaster, its once beautiful floor now filthy and marred by perilous holes. He approached the staircase, which leaned precariously and was missing several steps, and saw in his mind's eye the sight of Apollonia as she descended it that first night. She was wearing a dark dress with amber beads, he recalled, and the sight of her blue eyes and golden hair was almost enough to make him swoon.

He remembered the way to the cupola exactly, once more confirming the accuracy of his memory. He walked through a large dusty room at the front of the house—formerly Foley's study—and opened the creaky door of a small closet. The metal spiral staircase was still there. It groaned and undulated slightly as he carefully ascended, but it managed to hold his weight. At its terminus, an old trapdoor still guarded the vault's entrance. At first, it resisted Jonathan's pushes, then it finally surrendered. He raised himself into the dusty, narrow space and took in the view of four directions from its empty window frames.

The panorama was no longer very inspiring, not nearly as striking as that long-distant night when the northern moon bathed the wild winter landscape in a magical glow. Now it gazed upon empty streets and the bridge spanning the frozen Tittabawassee. He could see the curved profiles of the old tombstones in the cemetery across State Street—which still clung to its little plot of land there—but virtually every other inch had been filled with the trappings of subsequent centuries: streets and roads, neat rows of beige brick ranch houses, fast-food restaurants, gas stations, and traffic lights.

He sat on the floor of the cupola and played back in his mind the conversation he and Apollonia had had that night. She had told him that Jasper was intent on killing him and that her plan for dealing with this was to have Jonathan join their party. She needed an ally, she told him, and she trusted him. He remembered the excited hush in which she'd spoken.

He had been infatuated, perhaps even obsessed, with her before that moment, but he realized now that his love for her had begun that night, in this very spot.

And it hadn't yet ended. Here he was, back in his own time, back in this wreck of a house, and despite everything that had happened between them—or at least everything he *believed* had happened—he still loved her madly, and she was once more an infinity away.

Jonathan's heart broke all over again, but this time no tear formed in his eye. Perhaps, he thought, they are all spent.

He made a careful descent down the wobbly staircase and crossed the dust-blanketed floor of the study. On the way, he found the marble statue's head that long ago crowned the winged body of a graceful angel who guarded the front door of Riverdale. He remembered it from still another time, when he had found it by accident in the yard, since detached from its original body, and had angrily tossed it through one of the windows. He had been angry because the deathly house had painfully reminded him of the mad futility of his love for Apollonia.

That love was no less mad and no less futile now, even after it had reached what Jonathan believed to be its full realization and consummation, even after its cruel destruction. But he suddenly recognized that he was no longer angry and that he no longer required any proof or explanation. The physical truth or falsity of his experiences was no longer an issue of significant moment to him.

Whatever had happened had been meant to happen, he decided. It didn't matter whether he understood the means or the purpose. He had done what he was supposed to do, as had Apollonia, and if he was ever to find peace, it would have to be in that knowledge.

He supposed that he would never stop loving her and concluded that this too was as it must be. He picked up the angel's head, brushed the dust from its classical face, and placed it carefully beneath his arm. It would be a souvenir of his mystery and of his lost love.

On his drive back into the city, Jonathan made one final quest, somehow knowing that it would be the last time he would seek out a physical legacy connected to Apollonia.

His last attempt to find the little house—the enigmatic gray house of his childhood memories and the secretive white house of his nineteenth-century recollections—had ended in failure. He had scoured the general area in which he was convinced he would find it but had come up with nothing. He had half-concluded that the house had either been torn down in the interim or that his youthful memories had been a chimera, perhaps a strange echo effect from one time line to another.

But he found it this time and with barely an effort.

It was in the same area that he had explored earlier and on the very street he had covered most thoroughly. It struck him immediately that the house must have been hiding from him then and wanted him to see it now—for what reason, he couldn't begin to fathom.

It was no longer isolated out in the country, as it had been when Jonathan peered through its window on a cold winter night and heard the first words of Apollonia's furtive plans—the same night he felt the muzzle of Cloud's pistol against his neck. And it was no longer gray or white but a satisfying shade of deep royal blue.

It was tiny, wedged between two considerably larger and obviously newer dwellings. The house was neat as a pin, its long front walk lined with round stones painted white and a steady line of flowerpots made of old buckets that, in spring-time, would bring considerable color to the scene. There were fine lace curtains in its windows and a welcome mat on its tiny porch.

He looked at the house from his parked car. It was a totally different picture from the previous aspects from which he'd viewed it. It looked to him now like the warm house of some beloved grandmother—but there was no mistaking it. It was the same house, with the same clean Midwestern lines, the same practical sloped roof and sensible gable.

The little house had been real after all, Jonathan thought, and it was still standing today, still very much alive. The thought allowed him to smile for the first time in what seemed like a very long while.

As the long Michigan winter began to wane at last, entering its cold but de-creasingly dark old age, Jonathan went on with his life.

There were times—when it was lonely and silent in the bookshop or late at night in his house and the ticking of clocks was the only sound to be heard—when he thought it wasn't much of a life. His social existence was virtually nil, save for his weekly dinners with Tess and Dave.

But loneliness wasn't the worst of it. There were also times when the pain of her loss still haunted him or—not satisfied with mere memories—seemed to tear painfully and reproachfully at his very soul. He was learning how to resist these attacks, not through denying that any of it had happened, but by countering the grief with memories of opposite emotions. He had many of these and replayed them often in his mind.

The result was not necessarily pleasure but a blessed, if temporary, cessation of pain. And while the resulting emptiness could never be equated with joy, it was easily preferable to existential agony. He hoped that with time the memories would gradually retreat, the painful alongside the pleasant ones, and that he would be allowed to return to a state of normality. He wasn't sure he remembered what that felt like.

Yet even as he sought such normalcy, another part of him struggled against release from her persistent ghost.

On a windy and unsettled day in March, he felt a powerful temptation to pay a visit to a certain ancient woman by the name of Violet Hunter, who lived in a care facility on the other side of the river. Jonathan desperately wanted to tell her everything he had learned about Apollonia Foley—the mysterious cousin of her grandmother whom Mrs. Hunter had never seen but had often wondered about and even cried over. He wanted to tell her what a warm and loving person Apollonia had really been and to destroy the image of a deceitful and nefarious spy into which family legend had wrongfully cast her. He wanted to tell her of Apollonia's terrible struggle and the act of courage and sacrifice with which she finally faced it.

In the end, Jonathan resisted this impulse. Mrs. Hunter would think him insane before he finished his first sentence, and if, by some miracle, she were actually to believe what he said, what affect would such news have on a woman well over a century old and as fragile as a dragonfly's wings? Better to let her keep her illusions, perfectly preserved in what she lovingly called "the amber of memory," than to disturb her with wild stories of raging war and desperate love across the centuries.

More than this, he realized that his motive in wanting to tell her these things was, in the end, a selfish one. He *wanted* to speak to someone of Apollonia, desperately needed to share his memories with another human being.

But this, he knew, would only keep the memories alive, only make his struggle longer and more difficult to free himself from. He had to resist the urge to keep stirring those embers in the vain and foolish hope of seeing them burst once more into a blaze.

Such were the struggles of a man who, on the outside, seemed nothing more complex than a friendly and attentive, if often somber, merchant of books.

It was undeniable that he was growing adept at the bibliographic trade. Under Jonathan's management, The Red Raven attracted a slowly but steadily growing clientele and retained an increasing number of regular readers and collectors.

They were drawn not only to the books themselves but to the warm ambiance that he had worked to create for the shop—the becalming presence of Pluto, the glow of lamplight, the comfortable easy chairs, the prominent display of rare antiquarian volumes, even the old marble angel's head that, after being cleaned and polished, had been given a new home on the counter, next to the cash register. It was becoming the kind of place where people felt comfortable lingering, whiling away their lunch hours or Saturday afternoons in light conversation with Jonathan or leafing through some title that had caught their eye.

A perfect day for such affable pursuits came in early April, a Saturday when the promise of spring flew on a gentle breeze from the west. The soft air carried the first scents of thawing earth and awakening flora, and the birds were out in force, a different song flowing from every beak. For the first time since fall, Jonathan left the door open so the breeze could freshen the shop, and a steady flow of customers passed in and out through the day. Most of them carried newly bought books when they left, and Jonathan noticed that many were novels of a romantic character.

His favorite two book scouts also dropped in, a welcome sight to Jonathan since he had seen neither of them in weeks. Phil arrived midmorning and laboriously hauled in no less than eight well-packed boxes. As usual, Phil's eye had been keen. He had a plentiful supply of recent bestsellers—four nice copies of *The Da Vinci Code*, always a reliable mover—and a remarkable haul of early twentieth-century novels for young readers. Jonathan knew any number of collectors who coveted anything having to do with *The Land of Oz* or *Betsy-Tacy* and who were willing to pay significant sums to add them to their libraries.

Phil was happy with the considerable cash Jonathan paid for the books and, like the customers, lingered awhile to chat. He had a new romance under way, he informed Jonathan, and the glorious spring day had added the perfect glow to his amorous pursuits. He was buoyant, obviously giddy with infatuation, and just looking at him made Jonathan jealous.

"And just what will *you* be doing on this wonderful Saturday night, my bookish friend?" Phil asked Jonathan as he prepared to leave.

"Staying at home," Jonathan said matter-of-factly. "And probably reading."

"Dearest Jonathan," Phil rejoined, adopting his best exaggerated queer tone and putting a concerned hand on his shoulder. "I love you, I really, really do, but you've just *got* to get yourself a life."

How painfully true, Jonathan thought as Phil walked out into the late afternoon, his air of rapture following him like a gaudy peacock's tail.

Diana showed up late, just as Jonathan was preparing to close the shop. She was dressed in her customary black sweater and jeans, her cute beret, and omnipresent sunglasses, although it was already growing dark. Her shadowy appearance seemed perfectly natural: To Jonathan, Diana had always been a nocturnal creature.

"Not too many books this time, Jonathan," she said in her mysterious Eastern accent, an exotic blend of Zsa Zsa Gabor and Bela Lugosi. She placed two Kroger bags on the counter and prepared to unload their contents.

She stopped when she saw the angel's head.

Diana stared at the marble face as if transfixed and eventually brought her hand to its cheek, stroking its smooth surface.

"Is everything okay?" he asked her.

She started as if he had awakened her from a dream.

"Oh!" she exclaimed. "I'm sorry, Jonathan, but this bust of yours, this head, it intrigues me. You must tell me how it came to you."

"It's from an old statue. I found it in an abandoned house."

"What house?"

Jonathan looked at her strangely. Her tone was insistent, almost urgent.

"An old place out on State Street, just about ready to fall down. They used to call it Riverdale."

"Riverdale," she said quietly, redirecting her gaze from the angel's face to Jonathan's. "Yes, I know the place. What in the world were you doing there?"

"I was...," he began, then hesitated because he knew that he could not divulge his true reasons. "Just exploring. A hobby of mine."

"Ah, just exploring," Diana said, a faint smile beginning to cross her lips. "Just a little hobby of yours?"

"That's all. Why is this so interesting?"

"It's interesting to me because I think you are not telling me the whole story, Jonathan."

"Excuse me?"

"I think you went to Riverdale not to explore, not to find pieces of old statues, but for another reason. You went there because you had memories...because of something that happened to you there."

She really is a witch, Jonathan thought. She's reading my thoughts.

Diana stepped closer to him. Jonathan could feel her eyes boring into his, even through her dark glasses.

"Forgive me, Jonathan," she said softly. "I don't mean to be impolite. I don't mean to pry into your life, but I must ask you. It's important for me to know. I *must* know. When you went to Riverdale, was it because of your memories?"

Something in the way she asked—something about *her*—made Jonathan lose his reserve. He was no doubt helped by his overpowering desire to talk, his need to share his experiences, or it might have been the strange fatigue that comes from holding a secret for far too long. Whatever compelled him, he suddenly didn't care if this woman heard everything, and he didn't care at all whether she might think him a raving madman.

"Yes, it was," he said at last.

"And were those memories of a woman?"

He paused briefly, bewildered by her uncanny insight.

"Yes, they were."

"A woman whom you loved?"

"Yes, very much."

"And did you travel a very great distance to be with her?"

Jonathan felt a chill traverse his spine.

"Greater than you could ever imagine."

Her subtle grin now became an open smile.

"Perhaps, Jonathan Chase, you should not underestimate my imagination. I will ask only one more question of you. What was her name?"

He hadn't spoken that name out loud for what seemed like years, but the word came out easily now and felt good—felt *natural*—passing through his lips.

"Apollonia," he said without hesitation, smiling slightly at Diana as he spoke.

"Ah," she said with a sigh, placing her hand atop Jonathan's. "I thought so."

He remembered in the instant their hands touched. It came back to him, the completion of a circle. He remembered one of Diana's visits last fall, the visit on which she had brought her latest harvest of secondhand books, and among them had been an antique photograph album—*the* album. It had been before he had gone to wherever he had gone, before everything had started. It had been the solitary stone that initiated the landslide that became his life.

"It was *you*," he said, looking into her eyes and seeing only his own reflection in the dark glass of her shades.

She grasped his hand tighter.

"It *is* me, Jonathan," she whispered, with no trace of Carpathian accent.

She took the beret from her head and placed it gently on the counter. Then, with both hands, she slowly removed a wig that he had always assumed to be her real hair. The short, jet black bob came away, releasing that which had been hidden beneath it—tresses, full and long, of a rich golden hue that reminded him of summer wheat.

The sunglasses were last, and only when these were removed—and eyes of fiery blue topaz looked into his—was he sure.

He began to speak her name, but she put a finger to his lips to silence him. She drew closer and put her lips to his, and in that kiss—in which they tasted their own and each other's tears—the dying embers did indeed erupt once more into living flame.

An infinity of mysteries awaited them.

In the wake of their initial passion, and the long seasons of deeper love that succeeded it, they shared these mysteries with each other and marveled over them, although they would always be their own exclusive secrets that were never shared with another soul.

Jonathan told Apollonia about how it started—the spectral glimpses he had of her, the breath-stealing moment when he first saw her photograph. He told her how he had first gone to her, how his sojourn through time had come without warning or explanation, and how—after everything had happened—he had returned to the place from which he started and was haunted with doubt that any of it had been real, even her. He described how he had struggled between doubt and belief in his own memories and how deeply he had grieved for her in the belief that she had perished.

She told him how she had awakened in much the same way—like him, without a wound upon her body—in a place and time that was unfamiliar, and at first very frightening. She told him how she had learned where, and when, she was—suburban Savannah, nearly a century and a half from her own time—and how challenging it had been for her to witness, let alone accept, the astonishing changes the world had undergone in what, to her, seemed like a single night's slumber. She told him that she understood how he must have felt on his own first awakening—in *her* time—so far removed and so utterly different from his own.

She had been convinced from the beginning that he had somehow survived the ordeal at Bluefield, no less than she, and that the purpose of her journey was to rejoin him. She explained how she had contrived to travel far to the north, to Saginaw, on conveyances that made the trip seem almost effortless, and that this journey had been made in the conviction that she would find him, that she was *meant* to find him, in the place and the time from which he began. This was so, she said, because she had already divined his secret, despite the fact that he never had the chance to reveal it to her, and that since he was meant to travel far to be with her, she was obliged to do the same to be with him.

Unfortunately, she had arrived too early; whatever mystical means had transported her to now somehow made a slight miscalculation. Although she was eventually able to locate him in his quiet little bookshop, she had already learned something about the mind-boggling paradoxes of traveling through time. She could not reveal herself to him, because she had learned that he had not yet *gone* himself, that none of that which *she* remembered had yet to happen, and so she was forced to wait.

But she would not stay away from him altogether and so became, in disguise, the shadowy figure of Diana. In that guise, she was able at least to see him and spend a few moments in his presence, until, at last, she was able to ascertain that he *had* made his own trip—that he knew what she knew and felt what she felt—and only then could they begin to regain what they once had.

He asked her if she had known that her own photograph was in the album and whether she brought it to him in the hopes that the sight of her image would inspire him and set the whole process in motion. But she did not. She'd had no idea and had given virtually no thought to acquiring or selling it.

This astonished them most of all, of course, because it suggested that amid all the conundra surrounding their experiences, perhaps there was some deliberate intent, some overarching *design*, to everything that had happened.

They would never learn what that intent might have been or from whence it might have come, nor did they solve most of the other mysteries with which they were confronted. They would never know, for example, why bullets did not end their physical lives or even leave a single scar upon their bodies. Nor would they even begin to understand how all of it had happened, how they defied and overcame seemingly immutable laws of universe and nature. Over the years, they would often speculate on whether it had been some sort of cosmic accident—some fissure in the fluid walls of time through which they both somehow managed to fall—or whether it had all been directed and controlled, perchance by destiny's iron hand or perhaps the will of God.

Eventually, they were forced to simply accept these things, even if they never understood them, even if some uncertainties and some doubts would forever haunt them.

But Jonathan and Apollonia would never doubt, nor even speculate upon, *why* it happened. On this they suffered no doubt, for the love that filled their days and guided their lives was its own vindication and explanation, and they came to know how sweet a sanctuary and bright a light—and how blessed a home—it truly was.

The End

A NOTE ON FACT AND FICTION

When a writer sets a fictional tale upon a historical stage, the lines between fact and fantasy can sometimes grow a bit foggy, hence this note of clarification.

While virtually all the primary and secondary characters who wander through *Apollonia* were woven of purely imaginative thread, as were the circumstances of their story, there are nonetheless several crossroads where history and fiction intersect. The author's general rule on such occasions has been to portray a historical individual, place, or occurrence as accurately and credibly as possible, given the availability of historical evidence, while, however, keeping in mind the overarching context that the book is, after all, a novel and does not aspire to serve as any sort of historical chronicle.

In this book, a handful of characters were taken from the pages of history and made what might be called cameo appearances here.

There really was, for example, a Jake Seligman who owned a clothing store in East Saginaw, Michigan, around the time of the Civil War. Known variously as the "King Clothier" and "Little Jake," he was indeed fond of throwing garments from his tower to a crowd of lumberjacks below, rewarding the man who caught the garment with a complete suit free of charge. Seligman, however, did not open his store until the early 1870s, several years after he is portrayed in the novel. I simply couldn't resist dragging Jonathan Chase into this colorful scene, so in this case I plead guilty to the charge of deliberate employment of literary license.

There also was a Confederate blockade-runner who operated out of Wilmington by the name of John Wilkinson. As depicted in the story in the character of George Wilkins, Wilkinson was a stocky fellow with bountiful sideburns—and he was an acknowledged master at using rockets to confuse Union blockaders—but I admit that considerable liberty was taken in describing his attitudes about the War between the States, slavery, and states' rights.

Another figure who really existed is Robert Lumpkin, the Richmond slave trader in whose prison Jeremiah is confined and from which he is later liberated. The site of Lumpkin's notorious jail, coined the "Devil's Half Acre" by historians, is currently the focus of an archaeological dig in the former Rebel capital.

An additional dash of literary license was used in the prisoner exchange in which Jonathan transforms himself into a Rebel soldier by the name of Caleb Petrie. The fictional exchange takes place in August 1864, while astute Civil War historians are no doubt aware that U. S. Grant put an official end to such exchanges in April of that year. However, while it's unlikely that an exchange took place that August, it's not impossible, since several historical sources indicate that a number of such exchanges did occur that summer and fall, albeit on a much smaller scale than previously.

Aside from such historically documented places as hotels, public buildings, and the Chimborazo military hospital in Richmond, most of the specific physical locations described in the book are fictional.

A notable exception is the house referred to as "Riverdale" in Saginaw Township. That house did indeed stand, at the precise location mentioned in the book, and although it was originally built by a man named Parker, it was occupied later by a family whose name was Foley.

I remember the place well from my childhood, when I lived just a few miles away, and years later when I returned to Saginaw to visit loved ones. Its grandly imposing and spectrally fading presence played no small role in helping me develop and illustrate that part of the story.

Sadly, the structure was unceremoniously torn down by developers in the summer of 2009, triggering considerable anger among heritage-minded residents in the city. Since most of what needed to be said about Riverdale had been written before the demolition, the news of the house's demise seemed strangely prescient, as Jonathan had envisioned that very thing.

I mention it not just as an anecdotal sidebar to the novel, but as an example of how fact and fantasy can sometimes walk hand-in-hand down the same path— and sometimes, it seems to me, quite harmoniously.

ACKNOWLEDGMENTS

The author wishes to express heartfelt thanks to the individuals who read this book in manuscript form and offered their encouragement, advice, and constructive criticism as the story evolved into what it ultimately became.

Turning this tale into a novel has been a delightful, collaborative process with friends and loved ones — a journey that has been both rewarding and illuminating.

Profound gratitude is owed to my wife, Lisa, who not only believed in this story from the beginning but also did masterful work on the book's graphics, typography, and overall design.

My brother, Roland Leppek, is owed thanks for designing the striking cover of this edition of Apollonia.

My dear friend, talented photographer Shari Valenta, took the author's photograph during a visit to Colorado's beautiful (and quite ominous) Stanley Hotel.

Thanks also go out to my sister-in-law, artist Vicki McDonald Leppek, who painted the beautiful portrait of Apollonia Foley, pictured below, which served as the cover for the first edition of the novel. She used as her model an original daguerreotype from the Civil War period that provided me with visual inspiration for the character.

Finally, the author is more than grateful to Dr. Leigh E. Rich of Monte Ceceri for publishing this novel under her visionary imprint. Leigh's sterling work as editor has been invaluable, as is our sustained friendship.

ABOUT THE AUTHOR

Christopher Leppek has been a storyteller and wordsmith since he was knee-high to Edgar Allan Poe. As a kid, he spun many tales for his long-suffering siblings—scaring them with spooky stories, stoking their imaginations with fantastical yarns, and occasionally making them cry with sad ones. He began writing fiction at the age of ten or eleven with a series of short stories that were shameless (though not necessarily clueless) knockoffs of a certain timeless consulting detective.

Never far from "ink," he wrote for his elementary school newspaper, edited his high school paper, edited a magazine and penned a bunch of stories for the U.S. Navy, and has made his living as a professional journalist. He has long been associated with Denver's *Intermountain Jewish News* as a reporter and editor, and his freelance work has appeared in *The New York Times*, the *Rocky Mountain News*, the *Navy Times*, *The Pueblo Chieftain*, and many other publications. He is the recipient of numerous awards for news, feature, investigative, business, and historical journalism.

Leppek is also the author of the mystery novel *The Surrogate Assassin* (Write Way Publishing, 1998), a Sherlock Holmes pastiche, and the coauthor, with Emanuel Isler, of the horror novels *Chaosicon* (Write Way Publishing, 2001) and *Abattoir* (Dark Moon Books, 2012). The latter was adapted into the feature film *The Charnel House* (2016) starring Callum Blue and Nadine Velazquez.

A native of Saginaw, Michigan, Leppek lives in Denver with his wife, Lisa, and sons, Noah and Adam.

List of Images

Images listed by month in which they appear in the novel:

Frontispiece: Map modified from "BlankMap-USA-states-Canada-provinces. svg" by Lokal_Profil, licensed under the Creative Commons Attribution-Share Alike 2.5 Generic license.

January: A. Ruger, *Saginaw City [Michigan 1867]* (Chicago: Chicago Lithographing Co., 1867). Library of Congress, Geography and Map Division, Ruger map collection, no. 100, https://www.loc.gov/item/73693445/.

February: A. Ruger, *East Saginaw, Michigan, 1867* (Chicago: Chicago Lithographing Co., 1867). Library of Congress, Geography and Map Division, Ruger map collection, no. 81.5, https://www.loc.gov/item/80691360/.

March: Illustration of "Fort Mackinack" in Benson John Lossing, *The Pictorial Field-Book of the War of 1812* (New York: Harper and Brothers, 1868), 269.

April: George Harlow White, *Georgian Bay, Lake Huron, near Meaford (Ontario)* (1874). Courtesy of the Toronto Public Library, Baldwin Collection of Canadiana, PICTURES-R-481, https://digitalarchive.tpl.ca/objects/348368/ georgian-bay-lake-huron-near-meaford-ontario.

May: Thure de Thulstrup, Battle of Spottsylvania [i.e. Spotsylvania]: *"The bloody angle"* (1887). The New York Public Library, The Miriam and Ira D. Wallach Division of Art, Prints and Photographs: Picture Collection, NYPL catalog ID: b17168683, https://digitalcollections.nypl.org/ items/510d47e0-fb04-a3d9-e040-e00a18064a99.

June: Robert Knox Sneden, *Map of Richmond, Virginia...1863* (1861–1865). Library of Congress, Geography and Map Division, Virginia Historical Society, https://www.loc.gov/item/gvhs01.vhs00051/.

July: J. Wells, Robert Hinshelwood, and Virtue Yorston & Co., *Richmond, Va. and its vicinity* (n.p.: Virtue Yorston & Co, 1863). Library of Congress, Geography and Map Division, https://www.loc.gov/item/74693212/.

August: Illustration of "Lumpkin's Jail" in Charles H. Corey, *A History of the Richmond Theological Seminary, with Reminiscences of Thirty Years' Work Among the Colored People of the South* (Richmond: J. W. Randolph Company, 1895), 47.

September: William Brotherhead, *North Carolina: city of Wilmington* (Philadelphia: H. J. Toudy & Co., ca. 1875), priJLC_VIEW_000562. Jay T. Last

Collection of Graphic Arts and Social History, The Huntington Library, San Marino, California, https://hdl.huntington.org/digital/collection/p16003coll4/id/1299/rec/3.

October: A. Ruger, *Panoramic view of the city of Halifax, Nova Scotia 1879* (n.p., 1879). World Digital Library and Library of Congress, Geography and Map Division, https://www.loc.gov/item/73693337/.

November: "Destruction of the Depots, Public Buildings, and Manufactories at Atlanta, Georgia, November 15, 1864," *Harper's Weekly*, January 7, 1865, 4. Detail of engraving, Joseph Williams and John Osborne, Archives and Special Collections, Dickinson College, https://hd.housedivided.dickinson.edu/node/43479.

December: William Brotherhead, *Georgia: city of Savannah* (Philadelphia: H. J. Toudy & Co., ca. 1875), priJLC_VIEW_000545. Jay T. Last Collection of Graphic Arts and Social History, The Huntington Library, San Marino, California, https://hdl.huntington.org/digital/collection/p16003coll4/id/1282/rec/13.

monte ceceri

In the early 1500s, it was from the heights of Monte Ceceri—otherwise known as "Swan Mountain"—in Fiesole, Italy, that inventor and artist Leonardo da Vinci let soar one of his experimental flying machines.

Envisioning a future where such fantastical creations would one day become reality, Leonardo desired to fill the world with awe-inspiring inventions and ideas.

Like its namesake's Renaissance roots, Monte Ceceri Publishers, LLC, supports avant-garde writers whose works challenge current perspectives, inspire new paths, and speak to a modern-day humanism.

Based in Savannah, Georgia, Monte Ceceri is an independent publisher of books that raise issues of social, cultural, and philosophical interest, cross disciplinary boundaries, and facilitate cross-cultural dialogue through effective and engaging writing.

We welcome you to contact us.

Imprints

- **Monte Ceceri Publishers** (Nonfiction and Academic)
- **SwanHorse Press** (Fiction, Poetry, and Plays)
- **Pescaton Press** (Science and Nature)
- **Bucket Goat Books** (Art and Illustration)

monte ceceri

SwanHorse Press is an imprint of
Monte Ceceri Publishers, LLC

9 781949 512090